THE ESSENTIAL KAFKA

THE ESSENTIAL KAFKA

The Trial, The Castle, Metamorphosis, Letter to My Father *and other stories*

Translated, with an introduction, by John Williams

COLLECTOR'S EDITIONS

Dedicated to
LOGAN and OLIVIA BARBROOK
May your lives be filled with wonderful stories,
great adventures and happily-ever-afters,
Love Mummy

Readers who are interested in other titles from
Wordsworth Editions are invited to visit our website at
www.wordsworth-editions.com

This edition published 2024 by **Wordsworth Editions Limited**
PO Box 13147, Stansted CM21 1BT

ISBN 978 1 84022 843 4

© Wordsworth Editions Limited 2024

Wordsworth® is a registered trademark of
Wordsworth Editions Limited

Wordsworth Editions
is the company founded in 1987 by
MICHAEL & HELEN TRAYLER (RANSON)

All rights reserved. This publication may not be
reproduced, stored in a retrieval system or
transmitted, in any form or by any means, electronic,
mechanical, photocopying, recording or otherwise,
without the prior permission of the publishers.

Typeset by RefineCatch Limited, Bungay, Suffolk
Printed and bound by Clays Ltd, Elcograf S.p.A.

Contents

TRANSLATOR'S NOTE	9
SUGGESTIONS FOR FURTHER READING	12

THE TRIAL

CHAPTER ONE: *Arrest – Conversation with Frau Grubach – then Fräulein Bürstner*	15
CHAPTER TWO: *First Investigation*	47
CHAPTER THREE: *In the Empty Hall – the Student – the Court Chambers*	66
CHAPTER FOUR: *Fräulein Bürstner's Friend*	93
CHAPTER FIVE: *The Flogging*	102
CHAPTER SIX: *The Uncle – Leni*	110
CHAPTER SEVEN: *The Advocate – the Manufacturer – the Painter*	133
CHAPTER EIGHT: *The Corn Merchant – Dismissal of the Advocate*	190
CHAPTER NINE: *In the Cathedral*	224
CHAPTER TEN: *End*	251

CONTENTS

THE CASTLE

CHAPTER 1	*Arrival*	259
CHAPTER 2	*Barnabas*	279
CHAPTER 3	*Frieda*	300
CHAPTER 4	*First Conversation with the Landlady*	311
CHAPTER 5	*The Mayor*	326
CHAPTER 6	*Second Conversation with the Landlady*	348
CHAPTER 7	*The Schoolteacher*	364
CHAPTER 8	*Waiting for Klamm*	376
CHAPTER 9	*Resistance to Interrogation*	387
CHAPTER 10	*On the Street*	399
CHAPTER 11	*At the School*	406
CHAPTER 12	*The Assistants*	420
CHAPTER 13	*Hans*	428
CHAPTER 14	*Frieda's Rebuke*	441
CHAPTER 15	*At Amalia's*	454
CHAPTER 16		465
CHAPTER 17	*Amalia's Secret*	484
CHAPTER 18	*Amalia's Punishment*	503
CHAPTER 19	*Petitions*	515
CHAPTER 20	*Olga's Plans*	524
CHAPTER 21		544
CHAPTER 22		555
CHAPTER 23		568
CHAPTER 24		588
CHAPTER 25		608

CONTENTS

METAMORPHOSIS AND OTHER STORIES

Metamorphosis: the Transformation of Gregor Samsa	645
In the Penal Colony	711
The Judgement	747
Letter to my Father	763
A Hybrid	833
A Message from the Emperor	835
On Metaphors	837
A Commentary	839
A Little Fable	841

Translator's Note

The Trial

It has been said by a distinguished translator that Kafka poses few problems for the translator. This is true only up to a point: his stories, however alienated from everyday experience, are written in a precise and matter-of-fact language that belies (or perhaps emphasises) the bizarre dislocations of the narrative. Nevertheless, there are certain problems, semantic and syntactical. There are complex passages of reported speech – more easily identified in German by the use of the subjunctive, but less straightforward in English; there are also some shifts in perspective between an occasionally 'omniscient' narrator and Josef K.'s subjective perceptions.

The title of the novel is universally known as *The Trial*; but *Prozeß* in German also suggests a process, an interminable searching and seeking. Fortuitously, the English word 'trial' also has an ambiguity; it can denote a court case, or more widely an emotional, psychic or spiritual ordeal, and as such is entirely appropriate as an overall title. Within the narrative, however, *Prozeß* is often better understood as Josef K.'s *case*. After all, K. is never formally tried before a court; he only appears at a chaotic and inconclusive preliminary hearing before an examining magistrate (*Untersuchungsrichter*) – the burlesque and grotesque equivalent of a French *juge d'instruction*. In German, *Richter* means a judge; but I have distinguished in the translation between the inaccessible 'higher' or senior judges (whom K. never encounters except by hearsay) and the lower 'magistrates', who appear without exception to be venal, slovenly, and lecherous.

Certain characteristically German (or Austrian) formal modes of address cannot be literally translated into English: '*[der]Herr Prokurist*' denotes K.'s senior position at the bank, but '*Herr K.*' seems a more appropriate rendering for English-speaking readers. Kafka's paragraphs frequently run to several pages, and his lengthy sentences are often structured by strings of commas. In order to make the text more reader-friendly, and risking the disapproval of specialist colleagues for interrupting the 'authentic' flow of Kafka's prose, I have broken up the text into shorter paragraphs and used semicolons more frequently than Kafka does.

The Castle

The translation is based on Franz Kafka, *Das Schloß*, ed. Malcolm Pasley, Fischer Taschenbuch Verlag, Frankfurt am Main, 2008. I have retained the original forms of German proper names (Artur, Jeremias, Henriette, etc.). Formal or professional terms of address ('*Herr Landvermesser*', '*Frau Wirtin*') go uneasily into English, and have been rendered, for example, as 'Herr K.', 'sir', or 'madam'. The term 'mayor' for *Gemeindevorsteher* is not an exact equivalent, given the differences between continental and British local government systems, and is a *pis-aller*. *Schloß* in German means not only a castle, but a lock; this can hardly be conveyed in translation, should the pun be considered deliberate, unless something like 'fortress' is used. Pepi's story in Chapter 25 changes tenses and grammatical idioms bewilderingly; I have endeavoured to reproduce the tenses as closely as possible to the original, except of course where the past and pluperfect of indirect speech is signalled in German respectively by the present and the perfect of the subjunctive. As in my translation of *The Trial*, I have modified Kafka's punctuation and split the text into more frequent paragraphs than the original in order to make it more reader-friendly (*pace* Sir Malcolm Pasley).

JOHN R. WILLIAMS
St Andrews

Suggestions for Further Reading

Samuel Beckett, *Waiting for Godot*
Albert Camus, *The Outsider*
Elias Canetti, *Kafka's Other Trial*
Charles Dickens, *Bleak House*
Fyodor Dostoevsky, *Notes From Underground*
Nikolai Gogol, *The Nose*
Nadine Gordimer, *Letter from his Father*
Hermann Hesse, *Steppenwolf*
Gustav Meyrink, *The Golem*
George Orwell, *Nineteen Eighty-Four*
Harold Pinter, *The Birthday Party*
Jean-Paul Sartre, *Nausea*

THE TRIAL

CHAPTER ONE

Arrest – Conversation with Frau Grubach – then Fräulein Bürstner

Someone must have been spreading slander about Josef K., for one morning he was arrested, though he had done nothing wrong. The cook who worked for his landlady Frau Grubach, and who brought his breakfast towards eight in the morning, did not arrive. That had never happened before. K. waited a while, and from his pillow saw the old lady who lived opposite watching him with a curiosity quite unusual for her; but then, disconcerted and hungry, he rang the bell. At once there was a knock at the door, and a man he had never seen in this house came in. He was slim but powerfully built, and wore a close-fitting black suit which, like a travelling coat, was fitted with various pleats, pockets, buckles, buttons and a belt, and seemed extremely practical, although one could not quite say what purpose it was supposed to serve.

'Who are you?' asked K., sitting up in bed. But the man ignored the question, as if his appearance ought to be taken for granted, and simply replied: 'Did you ring?' 'Tell Anna to bring me my breakfast,' said K., then without a word studied the man carefully, trying to establish just who he was. But the man did not submit to his scrutiny for very long; he turned to the door, opened it a little, and said to someone who was evidently standing close behind it: 'He wants Anna to bring his breakfast.' This was followed by a short laugh in the next room; it was not clear from the sound whether more than one person was involved. Although the stranger could not have learned from this anything that he had not known before, he now told K., as if he were making a report: 'That is impossible.' 'I've never heard such a thing,' said K., jumping out of bed and quickly pulling on his trousers. 'I'm going to find out who those people are in the next room, and see how Frau Grubach will explain this disturbance.' At once it occurred to him that he should not have said this aloud, and that by doing so he had somehow acknowledged the stranger's right to supervise him; but for the moment it seemed unimportant. Even so, that is how the stranger took it, for he said: 'Hadn't you better stay here?' 'I do not wish to stay here, nor do I wish to be addressed by you until you have introduced yourself.' 'I was only trying to help,' said the stranger, and opened the door without demur.

K. entered the next room more slowly than he intended to; at first sight it looked almost exactly as it had the previous evening. It was Frau Grubach's sitting-room, crammed with furniture, rugs, porcelain and photographs. Perhaps today there was a little more space in the room; but this was not immediately obvious, especially since the main difference was the presence of a man who sat at the open window with a book, from which he now looked up. 'You should have stayed in your room! Did Franz not tell you to?' 'What are you doing here?' said K., turning from this new acquaintance to the one called Franz, who was still standing in the doorway, and back again. Through the open window he again caught sight of the old lady, who with all the inquisitiveness of old age had moved to the window directly opposite in order not to miss anything. 'I'm going to see Frau Grubach . . .' said K., and made as if to tear himself away from the two men and leave, although they were standing some distance from him. 'No,' said the man at the window. He threw the book onto a small table and stood up. 'You may not leave; you see, you are under arrest.' 'So it seems,' said K. Then he asked: 'And why is that?' 'We have not been authorised to tell you that. Go and wait in your room. Proceedings are under way, and you will know everything in good time. I am exceeding my instructions by speaking to you in such a friendly way. But I hope no one hears it except Franz, and he is also in breach of regulations by being friendly to you. If you continue to be as lucky in the choice of your guards as you have been, you won't have to worry.'

K. wanted to sit down, but now he saw that there was no other seat in the room except the chair by the window. 'You will realise the truth of all this,' said Franz, as they both came towards him. The other man, in particular, was much taller than K., and frequently tapped him on the shoulder. Both of them examined K.'s nightshirt, and said he would now have to wear a shirt of far inferior quality, but that they would keep this one along with the rest of his linen; if his case should end favourably, it would be returned to him. 'It's better you should give us your things than let the depot have them,' they said, 'because there's a lot of pilfering in the depot, and besides they sell everything after a certain period of time, whether the relevant proceedings have been completed or not. And you don't know how long these cases can last, especially recently!

Of course, you'd get the money from the depot in the end, but in the first place it doesn't amount to much, because what matters when things are sold is not the price offered but the size of the bribe, and besides we know from experience that the sum gets smaller as it passes through various hands from year to year.' K. scarcely paid attention to these words; he did not attach much importance to his right to dispose of his things, if he still possessed such a right. It was much more important to him to clarify his position; but in the presence of these people he could not even think. Time and again the belly of the second guard – they could only be guards – pushed against him in a perfectly friendly way, but when he looked up he caught sight of a face that did not go with this fat body at all, an impassive, bony face with a large bent nose, exchanging meaningful looks with the other guard above his head. What sort of people were they? What were they talking about? What authority did they represent? After all, K. lived in a properly constituted state where things were peaceful and the laws were upheld; who dared to ambush him in his own home? He always tended to take everything as calmly as possible, to believe the worst only when the worst happened, and not to worry about the future even when everything looked threatening. But that did not seem to apply here; of course, one could regard the whole thing as a hoax, a crude joke played on him for some unknown reason by his colleagues at the bank, perhaps because today was his thirtieth birthday; that was of course possible, perhaps he only needed somehow to laugh in the guards' faces and they would join in, perhaps they were porters off the street – they looked rather like it. All the same, on this occasion, ever since he had set eyes on the guard Franz, he was quite determined not to lose the slightest advantage he might have over these people. K. was aware of a very slight risk that he might later be accused of not being able to take a joke, but he remembered – though it had not been usual for him to learn from experience – some incidents, insignificant in themselves, where unlike his friends he had deliberately and without the slightest regard for the consequences, behaved rashly and had paid for it as a result. That must not happen again, at least not this time; if it was an act, he would play along with it.

He was still free. 'Excuse me,' he said, and quickly passed between the guards into his room. 'It looks as if he's being sensible,' he heard one of them say behind him. In his room, he hurriedly pulled open the drawers of his desk; everything was in perfect order, but in his agitation he could not at first find the official papers he was looking for. Finally he found his bicycle licence, intending to show it to the guards, but then he thought this certificate too trivial, and searched further until he found his birth certificate. As he went back into the next room, the door opposite opened and Frau Grubach made to come in. He only caught a glimpse of her, for as soon as she recognised K. she clearly became embarrassed, excused herself and disappeared, shutting the door with the utmost care. 'Do come in' was all K. had been able to say; but now he stood with his papers in the middle of the room still looking at the door, which was not opened again, and he was only roused by a call from the guards, who were sitting at the small table by the open window and, as he now realised, were eating his breakfast. 'Why did she not come in?' he asked. 'She is not allowed to,' said the tall guard. 'You're under arrest, you see.' 'But how can I be under arrest? How can you arrest me like this?' 'Don't start that all over again,' said the guard, dipping a piece of bread and butter into the jar of honey. 'We don't answer questions like that.' 'You will have to answer them,' said K. 'Here are my identity papers, now show me yours, especially the warrant for my arrest.' 'Good heavens,' said the guard. 'If you'd only accept your situation. You seem intent on annoying us needlessly, when we are now probably closer to you than anyone else!' 'That's true, believe me,' said Franz. He was holding a cup of coffee in his hand, but he did not raise it to his lips; instead, he gave K. a long, probably meaningful but inscrutable look. Without wishing to, K. exchanged glances with Franz; but then he tapped his papers and said: 'Here are my official papers.' 'What have those got to do with us?' cried the tall guard. 'You're behaving worse than a child. What do you want? Do you think you'll get this damned case of yours over quickly by discussing your official papers and your arrest warrant with us, your guards? We are minor employees who can hardly understand official papers, and we have nothing to do with your case except to stand guard on you for ten hours a day. That's what we're paid for, that's all we are; but even so, we can still understand that the higher authorities we serve under don't proceed with such an arrest until they are very clearly informed about the reasons for the arrest and the character of the suspect. There is no mistake here. Our authorities, as far as I know them, and I only know the lowest grades, don't go looking for guilt among the population; they are, as the law puts it, drawn towards guilt and have to send us guards out. That's the law. How could there be any mistake?' 'I don't know this law,' said K. 'All the worse for you,' said the guard. 'I dare say it only exists in your heads,' said K., in an attempt somehow to infiltrate the guards' thoughts, to turn them to his advantage or establish himself in their minds. But the guard only said dismissively: 'You'll soon know about it.' Franz joined in and said: 'You see, Willem, he admits he doesn't know the law, and at the same time claims he's innocent.' 'You're quite right, but you can't make him understand anything,' said the other. K. made no further reply; why should I, he thought, let myself get even more confused by the babble of these underlings, which is what they admit they are? Besides, they are talking about things they do not understand. They are so certain only because they are so stupid. A few words with someone of my own standing will make everything incomparably clearer than any amount of talking to them. He walked up and down a few times in the free space of the room; opposite he saw the old woman, who had dragged an even older man to the window and was holding him in her arms. K. had to put an end to this performance. 'Take me to your superior,' he said. 'When he wants to see you, not before,' said the guard called Willem. 'And now I advise you,' he added, 'to go back to your room, keep calm and wait to see what will be done about you. We advise you not to be distracted by futile thoughts, but to compose yourself; great demands will be made on you. You have not treated us in the manner our helpfulness might have deserved. You have forgotten that whoever we may be, we are at least for the moment free men compared to you, and that is no small advantage. However, we are still prepared, if you have any money, to fetch you some breakfast from the café across the road.'

Without making any reply to this offer, K. stood there for a while. Perhaps if he opened the door to the next room, or even the door into the hall, the two men would not dare to stop him, perhaps it would be the simplest way to resolve the whole matter by bringing things to a head. But perhaps they would seize him after all, and if they did overpower him he would lose any superiority he still, in a certain sense, had over them. And so, to be on the safe side, he preferred to solve things by letting them take their course, and went back into his room without a word having been uttered by him or by the guards.

He threw himself on his bed and took a single apple from the washstand, which he had chosen the previous evening for his breakfast. Now it was all the breakfast he had; but, as he assured himself with the first bite he took, it was still far better than the breakfast he might have had from the filthy all-night café through the charity of the guards. He felt well and confident; he was absent from his work at the bank this morning, but that would be readily excused given the relatively senior position he held there. Should he report the real reason? He thought he would. If they did not believe him, which was understandable in this case, he could call on Frau Grubach as a witness, or even the two old people from across the road, who were no doubt now on their way towards the window opposite. K. was surprised, at least it surprised him from the guards' point of view, that they had driven him back into his room and left him here alone, where he had a dozen means of killing himself. And yet at the same time he asked himself, this time from his own point of view, what reason he could have to do so. Perhaps because the two of them were sitting next door and had helped themselves to his breakfast? It would have been so senseless to kill himself that even if he had wished to do so, the senselessness of it would have made him unable to do it. If the limited intelligence of the guards had not been so obvious, one might have assumed that they too, for the same reason, had seen no danger in leaving him alone. They were welcome to watch him as he went to a small cupboard in which he kept a good quality schnapps, swallowed one glass instead of his breakfast, then poured another to give himself courage – the latter only as a precaution, in the unlikely event that he might need it.

Then a shout from the next room startled him so much that he hit the glass against his teeth: 'The chief wants to see you!' It was only the shout that startled him, this curt, abrupt military bark that he would not have believed the guard Franz capable of. The order itself was most welcome to him. 'At last!' he called back, locked the cupboard and went at once into the next room. The two guards, who were standing there, drove him back into his room as if it were a matter of course. 'What are you thinking of?' they shouted. 'You think you're going to appear before the chief in your shirt? He'll have you thrashed, and us too.' 'Leave me alone, damn you!' cried K., who had already been forced back towards his wardrobe. 'If you pounce on me when I'm in bed, you can't expect me to be in my best suit.' 'That won't help,' said the guards who, whenever K. shouted, became very calm, indeed almost solemn, which confused him or to some extent brought him to his senses. 'Ridiculous formalities!' he grumbled; but he was already taking a jacket from the chair, and held it up for a while with both hands, as if presenting it for the guards' approval. They shook their heads. 'It must be a dark jacket,' they said. At this, K. threw the jacket on the floor and said – he did not know himself in what sense he meant it – 'But it's not the main hearing yet.' The guards smiled, but insisted: 'It must be a dark jacket.' 'If it speeds things up, I don't mind,' said K. He opened his wardrobe, and spent some time looking through his many clothes. He chose his best dark suit with a well-cut jacket that had made quite an impression on his acquaintances, then took out another shirt and began to dress carefully. Privately he thought to himself that he had managed to expedite matters because the guards had forgotten to make him take a bath. He watched them to see whether they might still remember to do so; but of course it did not occur to them, though Willem did not forget to send Franz to the supervisor with the message that K. was getting dressed.

When he was fully dressed, he had to go, with Willem close behind him, through the empty room next door into the far room, whose double doors stood open. This room, as K. knew very well, had recently been taken by a Fräulein Bürstner, a typist who left for work very early and came back late, with whom K. had hardly exchanged more than a brief greeting. Now her bedside table had been moved into the middle of the room as an interrogator's desk, and the supervisor was sitting behind it. He had crossed his legs and draped one arm over the back of the chair.

In a corner of the room stood three young people looking at Fräulein Bürstner's photographs, which were pinned to a mat hanging on the wall. A white blouse hung from the latch of the open window. The two old people had returned to the window across the street, but now they had more company, for behind them, towering over them, stood a man wearing a shirt open at the neck, who stroked and twisted his reddish pointed beard with his fingers. 'Josef K.?' asked the supervisor, perhaps only in order to direct K.'s distracted gaze towards him. K. nodded. 'I suppose you are very surprised by this morning's events?' asked the supervisor, while with both hands he rearranged the few objects on the bedside table, the candle, a box of matches, a book and a pincushion, as if they were things he required for the interview. 'Of course,' said K., with a flood of relief that he was at last faced with a rational person with whom he could discuss his situation. 'Of course I am surprised, but I am by no means very surprised.' 'Not very surprised?' asked the supervisor, placing the candle in the middle of the table and arranging the other things around it. 'Perhaps you misunderstand me,' K. hastened to add. 'I mean' – at this point K. broke off and looked round for a chair. 'I suppose I may sit down?' he asked. 'It is not customary,' the supervisor replied. 'I mean,' continued K., 'I am certainly very surprised, but when one has lived for thirty years and has had to make one's own way in the world, as I have, one becomes inured to surprises and doesn't take them too seriously. Especially not this one.' 'Why especially not this one?' 'I am not saying I regard the whole thing as a joke; the arrangements that have been made seem to me to be too elaborate for that. All the people in the boarding-house would have to be involved, and all of you too; that would go beyond the limits of a joke. So I would not call it a joke.' 'Quite right,' said the supervisor, and inspected the matchbox to see how many matches it contained. 'On the other hand, however,' K. continued, turning to all of them – and he would have liked to turn to the three who were looking at the photographs – 'on the other hand, the matter cannot be of great importance. I assume this from the fact that I have been accused, but I cannot think of the slightest offence of which I could be accused. But that too is beside the point; the main question is, by whom am I accused? What authority is conducting these proceedings? Are you officials? None of you has a uniform, unless your clothes' – here he addressed Franz – 'can be called a uniform; but they look more like travelling clothes. I demand a clear explanation of these matters, and I am convinced that once they have been explained, we shall be able to part on the most cordial terms.' The supervisor banged the matchbox down on the table. 'You are greatly mistaken,' he said. 'These gentlemen here and I are of no importance whatever in your case, indeed we know hardly anything about it. We could be wearing the most official uniforms, and you would be in no worse a position. And I am quite unable to tell you that you are accused of any offence, or rather, I do not know whether you are. You are under arrest, that is correct, but more than that I do not know. If the guards have told you something different, that was just idle chatter. But even if I can't answer your questions, I can still advise you not to think so much about us, but about what is going to happen to you – you would do better to think about yourself.

And don't make such a fuss about feeling innocent; it spoils the otherwise not unfavourable impression you are making. You should be altogether more careful in what you say; almost everything you have said so far, even if it was only a few words, could have been inferred from your behaviour, and besides, none of it is particularly favourable to your case.'

K. stared at the supervisor. Was he being taught lessons like a schoolboy by a man perhaps younger than himself? Was he being reprimanded for his frankness? And was he being told nothing of the reason for his arrest or who had authorised it? In a state of some agitation, he walked up and down, which no one tried to prevent, pulled back his cuffs, fingered his chest, smoothed his hair, and as he passed the three young men said: 'But it is senseless,' at which the three looked at him sympathetically but earnestly. He finally stopped again at the supervisor's desk. 'The State Attorney Hasterer is a good friend of mine,' he said. 'Can I call him?' 'Certainly,' said the supervisor, 'but I don't see the sense of that, unless you have some private matter to discuss with him.' 'You don't see the sense of it?' K. cried, more in dismay than in anger. 'Who are you, then? You look for sense and behave in the most senseless way possible? It's heartbreaking. First I'm ambushed by these gentlemen, and now they are sitting or standing around while you put me through my paces. You don't see the sense of telephoning a lawyer when I am apparently under arrest? Right, I won't call him.' 'No, go on,' said the supervisor, pointing to the hallway where the telephone was, 'please do.' 'No, I don't want to any more,' said K., and went over to the window. Across the road they were still gathered at the window, and only now, as K. appeared, did their calm attention seem to waver a little. The old couple made to get up, but the man behind reassured them. 'There are spectators over there, too!' K. cried in a loud voice to the supervisor, pointing out of the window. 'Get away from there!' he shouted across. And indeed the three at once retreated a few steps; the old couple even hid behind the man, who shielded them with his broad frame and, to judge from the movements of his lips, said something that could not be heard from that distance. They did not disappear altogether, though, but seemed to be waiting for the moment when they could once again approach the window unnoticed.

'Inquisitive, impertinent people!' said K., turning back into the room. From a sidelong glance he gave to the supervisor, it seemed to K. that he might agree with him. But it was equally possible that he had not listened at all, for he had pressed one hand firmly onto the table and seemed to be comparing the length of his fingers. The two guards sat on a chest draped with an embroidered cloth, rubbing their knees. The three young people had put their hands on their hips and were looking around aimlessly. It was as quiet as in some deserted office. 'Now, gentlemen,' cried K. – it seemed to him for a moment as if he were shouldering the responsibility for all of them – 'from the way things look, it seems my case is finished. I think it would be best not to dwell on the rights and wrongs of your behaviour and to conclude the matter amicably with a mutual handshake. If you are also of this opinion, then please' – he approached the supervisor's desk and held out his hand. The supervisor looked up, chewed his lips and looked at K.'s outstretched hand; K. still believed the supervisor would accept it. But he stood up, took a hard, round hat that lay on Fräulein Bürstner's bed, and placed it carefully with both hands on his head, as one does when trying on a new hat. 'How simple everything seems to you!' he said to K. meanwhile; 'you thought we should conclude the matter amicably? No, no, that is simply not possible. On the other hand, I'm certainly not suggesting you should despair. No, why should you? You are only under arrest, that's all. It was my job to inform you of it; I have done that, and I have also seen how you have received it. That is enough for today, and we can say goodbye to each other – though only for the time being. I suppose you will want to go to the bank now?'

'To the bank?' asked K., 'I thought I was under arrest.' K. said this with a certain defiance, for although his handshake had not been accepted, he felt, especially since the supervisor had stood up, more and more independent of all these people. He was playing with them. If they should leave, he intended to follow them to the front door and invite them to arrest him. And so he said again: 'But how can I go to the bank when I'm under arrest?' 'Ah,' said the supervisor, who had already reached the door, 'you have misunderstood me. You are under arrest, certainly, but that does not prevent you from doing your job. Your normal way of life will not be affected.' 'Then being under arrest is not so bad,' said K., going up to the supervisor. 'I never intended to suggest otherwise,' he replied. 'In that case it seems it was not even particularly necessary to inform me of my arrest,' said K., stepping even closer. The others had also approached; they were now all gathered into a small space near the door. 'It was my duty,' said the supervisor. 'A stupid duty,' said K. implacably. 'Perhaps,' answered the supervisor, 'but we won't waste time with such talk. I had assumed that you wanted to go to the bank. Since you pay attention to everything that is said, I would add: I am not forcing you to go to the bank, I had only assumed you wanted to. In order to make that easier for you, and to make your arrival at the bank as unobtrusive as possible, I have placed these three gentlemen, your colleagues, at your disposal.' 'What?' cried K., and stared at the three in amazement. These insipid young men, so unremarkable, whom he had noticed only as a group around the photographs, were indeed officials from his bank – not colleagues, that was saying too much, and it indicated a flaw in the omniscience of the supervisor; but they were certainly junior clerks. How could K. not have noticed them? He must have been so preoccupied with the supervisor and the guards that he did not recognise these three! Rabensteiner, who held himself stiffly and flapped his hands, Kullich, fair-haired, with deep-set eyes, and Kaminer with his insufferable smile that was caused by a chronic muscular spasm. 'Good morning,' said K. after a pause, and offered his hand to the gentlemen as they bowed politely. 'I did not recognise you. So, let us go to our work now, shall we?' The men nodded eagerly and smiled, as if that was what they had been waiting for all the time; but when K. realised he had left his hat in his room, all three ran to fetch it, which still suggested a certain embarrassment on their part. K. stood there and watched them through the two open doors. The diffident Rabensteiner, who had merely broken into an elegant trot, was of course the last; Kaminer handed him his hat, and K. was forced to remind himself, as he had often had to at the bank, that Kaminer's smile was involuntary, indeed that he was incapable of smiling intentionally.

In the hallway Frau Grubach, who seemed to have no feelings of guilt, opened the door of the apartment for the whole company, and K. looked down, as he often did, at her apron-string, which was tied so unnecessarily tight it cut deeply into her ample body. Downstairs K., his watch in his hand, decided to take a cab to avoid any unnecessary delay; for they were already half an hour late. Kaminer ran to the corner to fetch the cab, and the other two were making obvious efforts to distract K., when Kullich suddenly pointed to the front door of the house opposite, in which the tall man with the ginger beard had just appeared. Initially somewhat embarrassed that he could now be seen at his full height, he stepped back to the wall and leaned against it. The old couple were probably still on the staircase. K. was annoyed with Kullich for drawing his attention to the man; he had already seen him, indeed, he had even expected him. 'Don't look over there!' he snapped, without realising how odd it was to speak to a grown man like that. But there was no need to explain himself, for at that moment the car arrived, they got in and drove off. Then K. remembered that he had not seen the supervisor and the guards leave; the supervisor had distracted his attention from the three clerks, and then they had distracted him from the supervisor. That did not show very much presence of mind, and K. resolved to be more observant in these matters. But he still turned round in spite of himself, and leaned over the back of the car to see if he could catch sight of the supervisor and the guards. But he turned round again at once, and leaned back comfortably in the corner of the car without even having made the effort of looking for anyone. Although he did not appear to invite it, at this point he would have welcomed some conversation. But the gentlemen seemed tired now, Rabensteiner looked out of the car to the right, Kullich to the left, and only Kaminer with his grin was available; unfortunately, K.'s better feelings did not allow him to remark on it.

That spring K. usually spent his evenings taking a short walk alone or with some colleagues after work – if he could, for more often than not he stayed in the office until nine o'clock – and then went to a small tavern, where he would sit at a reserved table with a circle of mostly older gentlemen, usually until eleven o'clock. But there were exceptions to this routine, when K. for instance was invited by the bank manager, who valued his diligence and reliability highly, for a drive in his car or to supper at his villa. Once a week K. also paid a visit to a girl called Elsa who worked through the night in a wine bar, and only received visitors from her bed during the daytime.

On this evening, however – the day had passed quickly with hard work and many flattering and friendly good wishes for his birthday – K. wanted to go straight home. He had thought about it during all the short breaks in the day's work; without knowing exactly what he meant to do, it seemed to him that the events of that morning had disrupted the whole of Frau Grubach's household, and he was the only person who could restore order. Once this had been done, all traces of those events would be removed and everything would return to normal. In particular, he had nothing to fear from the three clerks; they had been absorbed into the vast bureaucracy of the bank, and he noticed no change in their behaviour. Several times K. had called them into his office, individually and together, with no other purpose than to observe them, and each time he was able to let them go without any cause for concern on his part.

When he came home at half-past nine that evening, he met a young lad at the door who was standing in his way and smoking a pipe. 'Who are you?' asked K. abruptly, peering closely at the young man; he could not see very clearly in the gloom of the hallway. 'I am the caretaker's son, Sir,' answered the young man, taking the pipe out of his mouth and standing aside. 'The caretaker's son?' asked K., tapping his stick impatiently on the floor. 'Is there anything you need, Sir? Shall I fetch my father?' 'No, no,' said K., with a note of reassurance in his voice, as if the lad had done something wrong for which he forgave him. 'It's all right,' he said, and walked on; but before going up the stairs he turned round again.

He could have gone straight to his room, but since he wanted to talk to Frau Grubach, he went to her door and knocked. She was sitting darning a stocking; on the table in front of her lay a pile of old stockings. Embarrassed, K. excused himself for calling at such a late hour, but Frau Grubach was very friendly and brushed his apology aside. She always had time for him; he was, as he well knew, her best, her favourite lodger. K. looked around the room; everything had been put back in its place as it had been before, the breakfast things that had earlier stood on the small table by the window had also been cleared away.

'Women's hands do a lot of work unseen,' he thought; he would perhaps have smashed the crockery on the spot, and he would certainly not have been able to clear it away. He looked at Frau Grubach with some gratitude. 'Why are you working so late?' he asked. They were now both sitting at the table; now and again K. buried a hand in the stockings. 'There's a lot of work to do,' she said, 'during the day I am here for the lodgers; if I want to tidy up my own things, I only have the evenings to do it.' 'I suppose I have made an extraordinary amount of work for you today.' 'How is that?' she asked, becoming rather more agitated, and letting her work rest in her lap. 'I mean the men who were here this morning.' 'Oh,' she said, recovering her composure, 'that didn't give me much work.' K. looked on silently as she resumed her darning. She seems surprised that I mentioned it, he thought, she seems to think it's not right for me to speak about it. Then it's all the more important that I should; I can only talk about it to an older woman. 'I'm quite sure it made work for you,' he replied, 'but it will not happen again.' 'No, it can't happen again,' she said reassuringly, and smiled almost sadly at K. 'Do you really think so?' asked K. 'Yes,' she said more softly, 'but above all you mustn't take it too badly. All sorts of things happen in this world! Since you have confided in me, Herr K., I can admit I listened at the door for a while, and the two guards told me a few things as well. It's a question of your happiness, and I really have that at heart, more perhaps than I ought to, for I am only the landlady. Well now, I heard some things, but I can't say they were particularly bad. No, you are under arrest, but not like a thief is under arrest. If you are arrested like a thief, that's serious, but this arrest – it's too difficult for me, excuse me if I'm being stupid, it's something above my head that I don't understand – but then I don't have to understand it either.'

'What you have said, Frau Grubach, is not at all stupid, indeed I partly share your view; but I judge the whole thing more critically than you, and I don't think it's above your head. I think it is totally insignificant. I was taken by surprise, that's all. If I had got up as soon as I was awake, without being put out by Anna's absence, if I had gone to you and ignored anyone who stood in my way, if I had just this once had my breakfast in the kitchen and asked you to bring me my clothes from my room, if I had acted sensibly, then nothing would have happened, all these things would have been avoided. But one is so unprepared. In the bank, for example, I am prepared for everything, something like that could not possibly happen there; I have my own attendant, the public telephone and the internal telephone are on my desk in front of me, people are always coming and going, customers and colleagues, but most of all I am constantly involved in my work, so I have my wits about me. It would give me real pleasure to be faced with such a situation there. Well, it's all over now, and in fact I don't want to talk about it any further; but I just wanted to hear how you, as a sensible woman, judged the matter, and I am very glad that we agree about it. Now you must give me your hand; such an agreement must be confirmed with a handshake.'

Will she shake my hand? The supervisor did not offer me his hand, he thought, and looked at the woman in a different way, with a more searching look. She stood up because he had also risen, she was a little embarrassed because she had not understood everything K. had said. And because she was embarrassed she said something she did not mean to say, something quite inappropriate: 'Don't take it so much to heart, Herr K.,' she said tearfully, and of course forgot the handshake. 'I didn't know I was taking it to heart,' said K. He suddenly felt tired, and realised how worthless all this woman's reassurances were.

At the door he asked: 'Is Fräulein Bürstner home?' 'No,' said Frau Grubach laconically, then gave him a smile of belated but sincere sympathy. 'She is at the theatre. Do you want to see her about something? Shall I give her a message?' 'Oh, I only wanted to have a few words with her.' 'I'm afraid I don't know when she will be back; when she goes to the theatre she usually gets back late.' 'It doesn't matter,' said K.; with his head bowed he turned towards the door to leave. 'I only wanted to apologise for having taken over her room today.' 'There is no need for that, Herr K., you are too considerate, the young lady knows nothing about it, she has not been in since early this morning. Everything has been put back in order, as you can see.' She opened the door to Fräulein Bürstner's room. 'Thank you, I believe you,' said K., but all the same he went to the open door. The moon shone softly into the dark room. As far as could be seen everything was indeed in its proper place, even the blouse was no longer hanging from the window-latch. The pillows on the bed lay partly in moonlight; they seemed to be piled up remarkably high. 'The young lady often gets back late,' said K., looking at Frau Grubach as if she were responsible. 'That's how young people are!' said Frau Grubach apologetically. 'Of course, of course,' said K., 'but it can go too far.' 'It can indeed,' said Frau Grubach, 'how right you are, Herr K. That might well be the case here. I certainly don't want to speak ill of Fräulein Bürstner, she is a good girl, a nice girl, friendly, neat and tidy, hard-working too. I admire all that very much, but one thing is for sure: she should have more pride, she should not be so forward. I've seen her twice this month already in out-of-the-way streets, and each time with a different gentleman. I find it very embarrassing, I'm only telling this to you, Herr K., upon my word, but there's no way round it, I shall have to talk to Fräulein Bürstner about it. And that's not the only thing about her that makes me suspicious.' 'You are quite mistaken,' said K., scarcely able to hide his anger, 'and what's more, you have obviously misunderstood what I said about the young lady; that is not what I meant. I warn you expressly not to say anything to Fräulein Bürstner, you are completely mistaken, I know her very well, all you have said is quite untrue. But perhaps I'm going too far, I don't wish to stop you, tell her what you like. Good night.' 'Herr K.,' Frau Grubach implored him, and hurried after K. as far as his door, which he had already opened, 'I don't want to speak to the young lady yet, of course I want to keep an eye on her a little longer before I do, you're the only one I've told what I know. After all, it must be in every lodger's interest if I try to keep the boarding-house respectable, and that is all I'm trying to do.' 'Respectable!' cried K. through the partly closed door, 'if you want to keep these lodgings respectable, you'll have to give me notice first.' Then he slammed the door shut, and paid no further attention to a faint knocking on the other side.

Nevertheless, since he had no wish to sleep, he decided to stay up and take this opportunity to find out when Fräulein

Bürstner would get back. It would perhaps even be possible, however unsuitable it might be, to have a few words with her. As he lay by the window and closed his weary eyes, he even thought for a moment of punishing Frau Grubach by persuading Fräulein Bürstner to give in her notice at the same time as he did. But this immediately struck him as a gross over-reaction, and he even suspected himself of wishing to move out of his apartment because of the events of that morning. Nothing would have been more senseless, above all nothing would have been more pointless and contemptible.

When he had tired of looking out at the empty street, he lay down on the sofa, having first opened the door to the hallway a little so that he could see anyone who entered the apartment. Until about eleven o'clock he lay quietly on the sofa, smoking a cigar. But then he felt he could not lie there any longer, and went a little way out into the hall, as if by doing so he could hasten Fräulein Bürstner's return. He had no particular desire for her, he could not even remember exactly what she looked like; but he did want to speak to her, and it irritated him that by coming back so late she had brought disruption and disorder to the end of that day too. It was also her fault that he had not eaten that evening, and that he had put off his planned visit to Elsa. To be sure, he could still make up for that by going to the wine bar where Elsa worked; he would do this later after his talk with Fräulein Bürstner.

It was gone half-past eleven when he heard someone on the stairs. K., who was pacing up and down in the hallway lost in thought as if he were in his own room, quickly retreated behind his door. Fräulein Bürstner had arrived. Shivering, she drew a silk shawl around her narrow shoulders as she locked the door. In a moment she would go into her room, which K. certainly could not enter at midnight, so he had to speak to her now. Unfortunately he had not switched on the light in his room, and if he emerged from the unlit room she might think she was being attacked; at the very least it would give her a great shock. Feeling helpless, and because there was no time to lose, he whispered through the door: 'Fräulein Bürstner.' It sounded more like a plea than a summons. 'Is someone there?' asked Fräulein Bürstner, looking round anxiously. 'It's only me,' said K. as he stepped forward. 'Oh, Herr K.!' said Fräulein Bürstner with a smile. 'Good evening.' She held out her hand. 'I wanted to have a few words with you just now, would you mind?' 'Now?' asked Fräulein Bürstner. 'Does it have to be now? Isn't that a little odd?' 'I have been waiting for you since nine o'clock.' 'Well, I was at the theatre. I had no idea you were waiting.' 'The reason I wanted to talk to you is something that only happened today.' 'I see; well, I have no real objection, except that I'm so tired I'm ready to drop. Come into my room for a few minutes, then. We can't possibly talk out here, we would wake everyone up, and that would be even worse for us than for them. Wait here until I've switched the light on in my room, and then turn this one off.'

K. did so, but then waited until Fräulein Bürstner from her own room quietly asked him once again to come in. 'Do sit down,' she said, pointing to the ottoman. She remained standing by the bedpost, in spite of the fatigue she had mentioned; she did not even remove her hat, which, though small, was decorated with a mass of flowers. 'Well, what is it?

I'm really curious to know.' She crossed her legs casually. 'Perhaps you will say,' began K., 'that the matter is not so urgent that it must be discussed now, but . . .' 'I never pay any attention to preambles,' said Fräulein Bürstner. 'That makes my task easier,' said K. 'In a sense, it was my fault that this morning your room was thrown into some disorder, it was done by strangers and against my will, but as I say, through my fault; I wanted to apologise for it.' 'My room?' asked Fräulein Bürstner, looking enquiringly at K., not at the room. 'Yes,' said K., and now for the first time they looked into each other's eyes. 'Just how it happened is not worth discussing.' 'But surely that is the whole point,' said Fräulein Bürstner. 'No,' said K. 'Well,' said Fräulein Bürstner, 'I don't wish to pry into secrets; if you insist that it's unimportant, I have no objection. I gladly accept your apology, especially since I can see no sign of disorder.'

With her hands laid flat on her hips, she made a tour of the room. She stopped at the screen with the photographs. 'Yes, look!' she cried, 'my photographs are all mixed up. But that's horrible. So someone has been in my room, someone who has no right to be here.' K. nodded, and silently cursed the clerk Kaminer, who could never control his silly, pointless fidgeting. 'It's strange,' said Fräulein Bürstner, 'that I have to forbid you to do something you should not have permitted yourself to do, namely, to enter my room in my absence.' 'But I have explained, Fräulein Bürstner,' said K., also going over to the photographs, 'that I didn't interfere with your photographs; since you don't believe me, I must tell you that the investigating commission brought the bank clerks with them, one of whom probably handled the photographs. I shall have him dismissed from the bank at the earliest opportunity. Yes, there was an investigating commission here,' added K., for the young lady was looking at him quizzically. 'To investigate you?' she asked. 'Yes,' replied K. 'No!' she cried, and laughed. 'Oh yes,' said K., 'do you think I'm innocent, then?' 'Well, innocent . . .' she said, 'I don't want to make a snap judgement on what might be a serious matter, and I don't know you; but it must be a serious crime if they sent an investigating commission after you. But since you are clearly at liberty – and I assume, since you are so calm, that you haven't escaped from prison – you cannot have committed such a crime.' 'Yes,' said K., 'but the commission might have realised that I am innocent, or at least not as guilty as they had assumed.' 'That's certainly possible,' said Fräulein Bürstner, paying close attention. 'You see,' said K., 'you don't have much experience in legal matters.' 'No, I don't,' said Fräulein Bürstner, 'and I've often regretted it, for I would like to know about everything, and I'm particularly interested in legal matters. The law has a peculiar attraction, doesn't it? But I shall certainly be able to learn a great deal about it, because next month I am joining the staff of a legal firm.' 'That's very good,' said K., 'then you will be able to give me some help with my case.' 'Perhaps I will,' said Fräulein Bürstner, 'why not? I like to make good use of my knowledge.' 'I mean it seriously,' said K., 'or at least half-seriously, as you do. The matter is too trivial to engage a lawyer, but I could do with an adviser.' 'Yes, but if I am to advise you, I ought to know what it is about,' said Fräulein Bürstner. 'That's just the snag,' said K., 'I don't know what it is myself.' 'Then you have been making fun of me,' said

Fräulein Bürstner, extremely disappointed, 'it was quite unnecessary to come and tell me so late at night.' And she moved away from the photographs where they had been standing together for so long. 'But Fräulein Bürstner,' said K., 'I wasn't joking. I do wish you would believe me. I have already told you what I know about it, in fact more than I know; it was not an investigating commission, that's what I said because I didn't know what else to call it. There was no investigation. I was simply arrested, but I was arrested by a commission.'

Fräulein Bürstner sat down on the ottoman and laughed again. 'What was it like, then?' she asked. 'Dreadful,' said K.; but now he was not thinking about that at all. Instead, he was wholly engrossed in the figure of Fräulein Bürstner, who was lying with one hand under her chin, her elbow resting on the cushion of the ottoman, while her other hand slowly caressed her hip. 'That's too vague,' she said. 'What is too vague?' asked K. Then he recovered himself and asked: 'Shall I show you what happened?' He wanted to move, but he did not want to leave. 'I'm so tired,' said Fräulein Bürstner. 'You came back so late,' said K. 'So now I'm getting the blame, and that's quite right, because I shouldn't have asked you in; and there was no need to, as it turns out.' 'Oh, yes, there was, you'll see,' said K. 'May I move the bedside table away from your bed?' 'What are you thinking of?' said Fräulein Bürstner, 'of course you may not!' 'Then I can't show you what happened,' said K. with agitation, as if this caused him profound distress. 'All right, go on, move the table then, if you need to in order to show me what happened,' said Fräulein Bürstner; and after a pause she added wearily: 'I am so tired that I'm letting you do more than

I ought to.' K. placed the table in the middle of the room and sat behind it. 'You must imagine just where people were in the room, it's most important. I am the supervisor, the two guards are sitting on the chest there, three young people are standing by the photographs. Oh, and by the way, a white blouse is hanging on the window-latch. Now I can begin. But I was forgetting: the most important person, that is myself, is standing here in front of the table. The supervisor is sitting very comfortably, his legs crossed, his arm draped over the back of the chair here, a slovenly oaf. Now we can begin. The supervisor shouts as if he wants to wake me up, he really yells at me. I'm afraid I shall have to shout too, to show you just how it was; but it's only my name that he yells like that.' Fräulein Bürstner, who was listening and laughing, put a finger to her lips to stop K. shouting, but it was too late. K. was too involved in the part he was playing, and called slowly: 'Josef K.!' – not as loudly as he had threatened, but still in such a way that the sudden burst of sound only seemed to spread gradually through the room.

Then there was a knocking on the door of the next room, a short series of loud, regular knocks. Fräulein Bürstner went pale and put her hand on her heart. K. was particularly startled, because for a while he was quite incapable of thinking of anything other than the events of that morning and of the young woman to whom he was demonstrating them. No sooner had he pulled himself together than he rushed over to Fräulein Bürstner and took her by the hand. 'Don't be afraid,' he whispered, 'I'll see to everything. But who can it be? Next door there's only the sittingroom, and no one sleeps there.' 'Oh yes,' whispered Fräulein Bürstner into K.'s ear, 'since yesterday Frau

Grubach's nephew, a captain, has been sleeping there. There's no other room at the moment. I forgot about it. Why did you have to shout like that? It really upset me.' 'There's no need for that,' said K., and as she sank back onto the cushion, he kissed her on the forehead. 'No, no,' she said, getting hurriedly to her feet, 'go away, go away, what are you thinking of, he's listening at the door, he can hear everything. Stop tormenting me!' 'I'm not going,' said K., 'until you have calmed down a little. Come over to the far corner of the room, he can't hear us there.' She let him lead her there. 'You don't realise,' he said, 'although this is embarrassing for you, you are not in any trouble. You know how Frau Grubach worships me and believes implicitly everything I say; she has the last word in this matter, especially as the captain is her nephew. Besides, she is under an obligation to me because she borrowed a large sum of money from me. I will support anything you suggest that might help to explain why we are here together, and I guarantee that I will persuade Frau Grubach to believe it, and not just for the sake of appearances, but truly and sincerely. You must have no consideration for me. If you wish to make it known that I have assaulted you, then Frau Grubach will be informed of it, and she will believe it without losing any of her faith in me, she is so devoted to me.'

Fräulein Bürstner, drained and motionless, hung her head. 'Why should Frau Grubach not believe I have assaulted you?' continued K. He looked at her hair, her auburn hair, parted, gathered at the back and firmly fastened. He thought she would turn to look at him, but she remained as she was and said: 'I'm sorry, I was so startled by that sudden knocking, not so much by the presence of the captain or what that might lead to. It was so quiet after you had called out, and then there was the knocking; that's why I was so startled, I was sitting near the door, it was very close to me. I'm grateful for your suggestions, but I won't accept them. I can take responsibility for everything that happens in my room, I can answer to anyone. I am surprised that you don't realise what a slur your suggestions cast on me, though of course I recognise that they are well meant. But now go, leave me alone, I need to be alone now even more than I did earlier. The few minutes you asked for have turned into half an hour or more.' K. grasped her by the hand, and then by the wrist. 'You are not angry with me, though?' he said. She removed his hand and replied: 'No, no, I never get angry with anyone.' He took her by the wrist again; this time she let him take it and so led him to the door. He was firmly resolved to leave. But as they reached the door, he hesitated as if he had not expected to find a door there, and Fräulein Bürstner took advantage of this moment to free herself, open the door, and slip out into the hallway. From there she spoke quietly to K.: 'Now, come, please. Look,' – she pointed to the captain's door, under which a strip of light could be seen – 'he has put his light on and is laughing at us.' 'I'm coming,' said K., quickly following her. He put his arms round her and kissed her on the mouth, then all over her face, like a thirsty animal greedily lapping the water of a pool it has at last discovered. Finally he kissed her throat, letting his lips linger there. A noise from the captain's room made him look up. 'Now I am going,' he said. He wanted to call Fräulein Bürstner by her first name, but he did not know it. She nodded wearily, and offered him her hand to kiss, already half turning away as if she were unaware of it, and with her head bowed went back into her room. Soon afterwards K. lay in his own bed. He fell asleep quickly, but before he did he thought for a while about his behaviour. He was satisfied with it, but surprised that he was not even more satisfied; because of the captain he was seriously concerned for Fräulein Bürstner's sake.

CHAPTER TWO

First Investigation

K. had been informed by telephone that a brief investigation into his case would be held the following Sunday. He was told that these investigations would take place regularly; not every week, perhaps, but at frequent intervals. On the one hand it was in everyone's interest to finish the case quickly, but on the other hand the investigations had to be thorough in every respect; yet because of the strain involved they must not be allowed to last too long. For this reason the authorities had resorted to this series of short but frequent interviews. Sunday had been chosen in order not to interfere with K.'s work. It was assumed that he agreed to this; but if he should prefer a different time, they would try to meet his wishes as far as possible. It would, for example, be possible to hold the interviews at night; but no doubt K. would then be too tired. And so, provided he had no objection, they would settle on Sunday. It was understood that he must appear without fail – they were sure he did not need to be reminded of this. He was given the number of the house to which he should report; it was a house in the remote suburbs, in a street K. had never been to before.

When he had heard this message, K. hung up the receiver without replying. He had made up his mind at once to go there that Sunday, he must certainly do that, his case was getting under way and he had to fight it; this first interview was also going to be the last. He was still standing by the telephone deep in thought, when behind him he heard the voice of the deputy manager who was wanting to use the telephone, but found K. in his way. 'Bad news?' asked the deputy manager casually, not because he wanted to know, but in order to get K. away from the telephone. 'No, no,' said K., who moved to one side but did not go away. The deputy manager took the phone, and while he was waiting to be put through lowered the receiver and said: 'Just one question, Herr K. Would you give me the pleasure of joining a group of us on my yacht on Sunday morning? It will be quite a large party, and there are sure to be some people you know among them. The State Attorney Hasterer, among others. Won't you come along? Please do!' K. tried to pay attention to what the deputy manager was saying. It was not unimportant to him, for this invitation from the deputy manager, with whom he had never got on very well, signified an attempt at reconciliation on his part; it showed how important K. had become in the bank and how much its second most senior official valued his friendship, or at least his neutrality. It was also chastening for the deputy manager to issue this invitation, even if it had been made casually while he was waiting for an answer on the telephone. But K. had to chasten him even further. 'Thank you, but no,' he said. 'I'm afraid I have no time on Sunday. I already have an engagement.' 'A pity,' said the deputy manager, and having just been put through, turned to speak into the telephone. It was a brief conversation, but K., preoccupied, stood by the instrument all the while. Only when the deputy manager rang off, he started, and by way of excuse for his unnecessary presence, said: 'I have just been told by telephone to report somewhere, but they forget to tell me what time I should be there.' 'Why don't you ring back and ask?' said the deputy manager. 'It's not that important,' said K., although this weakened his earlier excuse, which had already been unconvincing enough. Before he left, the deputy manager talked of other things. K. forced himself to answer, but above all else he was thinking that it would be best to get there at nine o'clock on Sunday morning, since all the courts began work at this time on weekdays.

The weather on Sunday was dull. K. was very tired. There had been a celebration at his regular table at the inn; he had stayed late into the night, and almost overslept. Hurriedly, having no time to collect his thoughts or to think over the various plans he had devised in the course of the week, he dressed and without taking any breakfast rushed off to the designated suburb. Strangely, although he had little time to look around, he came across the three clerks involved in his case, Rabensteiner, Kullick, and Kaminer. The first two were in a tram that crossed K.'s path; Kaminer was sitting on a café terrace, and just as K. went by he leaned with some curiosity over the balcony. No doubt they all stared after him, surprised to see their senior colleague rushing along. A certain sense of defiance had prevented K. taking any form of transport. He hated the idea of having the slightest help from anyone else in his case; he did not wish to call on anyone and thus make them even remotely privy to his affairs; and finally, he did not have the slightest wish to demean himself before the investigating commission by being too punctual. Even so, he was now hurrying in order to get there at nine o'clock, although he had not even been given a specific time.

He had thought he would recognise the house long before he reached it by some sign that he had not clearly imagined or some sort of activity around the entrance. He paused for a moment at the end of the Juliusstrasse, where he was to be interviewed; but on both sides stood almost uniform tall grey tenements where poor people lived. This Sunday morning most of the windows were occupied, men leaned out in their shirtsleeves, some smoking, others holding small children cautiously and tenderly on the window ledges. In other windows bed-linen was piled high for airing, above which the tousled head of a woman would appear momentarily. They were calling to each other across the way, and one such shout provoked a great burst of laughter just above K.'s head. At regular intervals along the street were small shops, a few steps below street level, selling various kinds of food. Women were going in and out or chatting on the steps. A fruit-seller who was hawking his wares to the windows above, and paying as little attention to where he was going as K. was, almost knocked him over with his barrow. Just then a gramophone that had done long service in a better area of the town began to play with a murderous noise.

K. ventured further down the narrow street, slowly, as if he now had time to spare, or as if the examining magistrate could see him out of one of the windows and so knew that K. had arrived. It was shortly after nine. The house was some distance away, it was more extensive that the rest; in particular, the main entrance was high and wide. It was obviously designed for the waggons belonging to the various warehouses, now closed, that surrounded the broad courtyard and displayed the names of firms, some of which K. knew from his work at the bank. Taking in all these external features more closely that he would normally do, he stood for a while at the entrance to the yard. Nearby a man sat barefoot on a crate reading a newspaper. Two boys were playing seesaw on a handcart. A frail young girl was standing at a pump in her nightgown, staring at K. while the water poured into her bucket. In the corner of the yard a line was stretched between two windows, on which laundry was already being hung out to dry. A man was standing underneath directing the work with occasional shouts.

K. turned towards the staircase to get to the interview room, but then stopped, for as well as these stairs he could see three other staircases in the yard, and at the far end a narrow passage also seemed to lead to a second courtyard. He felt annoyed that he had not been given the location of the room more accurately; he really was being treated in a most casual and offhand way, a point he intended to make loud and clear. In the end he climbed the first set of stairs, reflecting on the words of the guard Willem that the court was drawn towards guilt, from which it followed that the interview room must be on the staircase that K. happened to choose.

As he climbed the stairs he disturbed a large group of children playing there, who scowled at him as he brushed past them. 'If I have to come here again,' he said to himself, 'I must bring some sweets with me to make friends with them, or else a stick to beat them with.' Just before he reached the first floor he even had to wait a while until a marble had stopped rolling.

Two small boys with villainous adult faces held on to his trousers; he could have hurt them if he had shaken them off, and he was afraid they might scream.

On the first floor his search began in earnest. He could scarcely ask where to find the investigating commission, so he invented a joiner called Lanz – the name occurred to him because that was the name of Frau Grubach's nephew, the captain – and he intended to ask at all the apartments whether Lanz the joiner lived there, so that he would have an opportunity to look into all the rooms. But it turned out that he could do this anyway, for nearly all the doors stood open, and children were running in and out. By and large they were small rooms with a single window, in which meals were being cooked. Some of the women held babies on one arm and worked at the stove with their free hand. Teenage girls, apparently dressed only in an apron, were busiest of all, rushing to and fro. In all the rooms the beds were still occupied by invalids or people sleeping or lying there fully dressed. K. knocked at the apartments whose doors were closed and asked whether a joiner called Lanz lived there. Usually it was a woman who opened the door, listened to his question and turned to someone who was getting out of bed. 'The gentleman wants to know whether Lanz the joiner lives here.' 'Lanz the joiner?' asked the man from the bed. 'Yes,' said K., although it was clear the investigating commission was not here, so he had no more business there. Many people thought it must be very important for K. to find Lanz the joiner; they thought it over for some time, mentioned a joiner, but not one called Lanz, or a name that sounded vaguely like Lanz, or they asked their neighbours, or led K. to a door some way away, where they thought such a person might be living as a lodger, or where someone lived who might be able to give him better information than they could. In the end K. hardly needed to repeat his question; in this way he was dragged through every floor. He regretted the plan that had seemed so practical to him at first. Before he reached the fifth floor he decided to give up the search, said goodbye to a friendly young workman who wanted to take him further up, and went down the stairs. But then he felt annoyed again at the pointlessness of the whole business; he went back and knocked on the first door of the fifth floor. The first thing he saw in the small room was a large wall-clock that already pointed to ten. 'Does Lanz the joiner live here?' he asked. 'Please come in,' said a young woman with bright dark eyes, who was washing children's clothes in a tub, pointing with a wet hand towards the open door of the next room.

To K. it was as if he had entered a large gathering. A crowd of all kinds of people – no one took any notice of the newcomer – crammed into a medium-sized room with two windows, around which ran a gallery just below the ceiling which was also packed with people who could not stand upright and crouched with their heads and backs pressed against the ceiling. K. found the air too stuffy; he went back out and said to the young woman, who seemed to have misunderstood him: 'I was looking for a joiner, a man called Lanz.' 'Yes,' said the woman, 'please go in.' K. would perhaps not have done as she said if she had not gone up to him, taken hold of the door handle and said: 'I must lock the door after you; no one else may go in.' 'Very sensible,' said K., 'it's far too full already.' But then he went in again after all.

Between two men who were talking just by the door – the one was holding his hands out in front of him as if he were counting out money, while the other looked him closely in the eye – a hand reached out to K. It was a small rosy-cheeked boy. 'Come on, come on,' he said. K. let the boy lead him; it turned out that there was after all a narrow way through the teeming crush of people, possibly marking the dividing line between two factions – an impression that was confirmed by the fact that in the first rows on either side K. scarcely saw a single face turned towards him, but only the backs of people who addressed their words and gestures to those on their side. Most were dressed in black, in old, long tailcoats that hung loosely on them. These clothes were the only thing that confused K.; but for them he would have taken the whole assembly for a local political meeting.

At the other end of the hall, towards which K. was being led, a small table was set at an angle across a very low, also overcrowded platform. Behind the table near the edge of the platform sat a small, stout man who wheezed as he talked amid much laughter to a man standing behind him, who had crossed his legs and was leaning against the back of the chair. Now and again he threw his arm into the air as if he were mimicking someone. The boy who was leading K. had some difficulty in delivering his message; twice already, standing on tiptoe, he had tried to say something, without being noticed by the man above. Only when one of the people on the platform drew his attention to the boy did the man turn to him and bend down to hear as he whispered to him. Then he drew out his watch and glanced quickly at K. 'You should have appeared an hour and five minutes ago,' he said. K. was about to answer; but he had no time, for the man had scarcely finished speaking when a general murmur of disapproval rose from the right-hand side of the hall. 'You should have appeared an hour and five minutes ago,' the man repeated, raising his voice and glancing down quickly into the hall. Immediately the muttering grew louder, but as the man said nothing further, it died down gradually. It was now much quieter in the hall than when K. had come in. Only the people in the gallery continued to make comments. As far as it was possible to make out anything in the hazy, dusty half-light up there, they seemed to be more poorly dressed than those below. Some had brought cushions with them to put between their heads and the ceiling to protect them from injury.

K. had made up his mind to observe things rather than to speak, so he made no excuses for his alleged lateness and simply said: 'I may have arrived late, but I am here now.' A burst of applause, again from the right-hand side of the hall, greeted these words. These people are easily swayed, thought K.; he was put out only by the silence from the left-hand side directly behind him, from which only sporadic clapping could be heard. He thought about what he could say to win them all over at the same time, or, if that was not possible, to win over the others for the time being at least.

'Yes,' said the man, 'but I am no longer obliged to examine you now' – again the muttering started, but this time its meaning was unclear, for the man waved it aside and continued: 'Exceptionally, however, I will do so today. But such unpunctuality must not occur again. Now, step forward!'

Someone jumped down from the platform to make room for K., who climbed up to take his place. He stood pressed up against the table; the crush behind him was so great that he had to resist it to avoid pushing the examining magistrate's table, and even the magistrate himself, off the platform.

The magistrate, however, was unconcerned; he sat quite comfortably in his chair, and after exchanging a final word with the man behind him, picked up a small notebook, which was the only object on his table. It was like an old school exercise-book, worn out of shape from constant thumbing. 'So,' said the magistrate. He leafed through the notebook and addressed K., as if establishing a fact: 'You are a house-painter.' 'No,' said K., 'I am a senior official in a large bank.' This answer was greeted by such hearty laughter from the right-hand section below that K. could not resist joining in. People doubled up with their hands on their knees, shaking as if from a severe fit of coughing. Even one or two in the gallery laughed. The examining magistrate, who probably had no authority over the people in the hall below, instead turned in fury to the gallery; he jumped to his feet, and as he threatened those in the gallery his eyebrows, inconspicuous until now, bristled dark and menacing above his eyes.

The left-hand side of the hall, however, was still quiet; the people there stood in rows, they had turned to face the platform and were listening to the exchanges above them just as calmly as they had to the noise from the other section. They even allowed some from their own ranks to mingle here and there with the other side. Those on the left, who were less numerous, might well in fact have been just as insignificant as the faction on the right, but their composure made them seem more important. As K. now began to speak, he was convinced that what he said reflected their views.

'You asked, Sir, whether I was a house-painter – or rather, you did not ask me at all, but told me so to my face; this is typical of the whole way this investigation is being conducted. You may object that it is not an investigation at all; you are quite right, for it is only an investigation if I recognise it as such. So for the time being I do recognise it, on sufferance as it were. If one is going to take it at all seriously, one can only take it on sufferance. I am not saying these proceedings are slovenly; but I would put it to you in these terms for your own consideration.'

K. paused and looked down into the hall. He had spoken sharply, more so than he had intended; but he was right. He might have deserved some applause, but all was quiet; they were clearly waiting expectantly for what was to follow, perhaps out of that silence a great burst of applause would put an end to everything once and for all. But then came a distraction; the door at the back of the hall opened, and the young washerwoman, who had no doubt finished her work, came in and in spite of her caution attracted several glances. Only the examining magistrate's reaction gave K. unqualified satisfaction, for the words seemed to have an immediate effect on him. Until then he had been listening while standing up, for K.'s speech had taken him unawares as he stood up to address the gallery. Now, during the pause, he sat down slowly, as if he wanted no one to notice. No doubt in order to compose himself, he again picked up the notebook.

'There is no more to be said,' K. continued. 'Your own notebook, Sir, bears me out.' K. heard his own calm words in this unfamiliar assembly with satisfaction; he even dared without further ado to take the notebook from the magistrate and hold it up fastidiously between his fingertips by one of the middle pages, so that the closely-written, stained, yellowing pages hung down on either side. 'These are the examining magistrate's records,' he said, dropping the notebook on the table. 'Just carry on reading them, Sir; I assure you I am not afraid of these records, although they are inaccessible to me since I can only pick them up between two fingers and would never handle them.' It could only be a sign of deep humiliation, or at least it could only be perceived as such, that the magistrate picked up the book as it lay there on the table where it had fallen, tried to put it into some kind of order, and began to read it again.

The faces of the people in the front row were fixed on K. so expectantly that he gazed down at them for a while. They were all elderly men, some with white beards. Were they perhaps the ones who made decisions and could influence the whole assembly, which could not be roused from the apathy into which it had sunk since K's speech, even by the humiliation of the examining magistrate?

'What has happened to me,' K. continued, rather more quietly than before, all the while scrutinising the faces in the front row, which made his words sound somewhat distracted, 'what has happened to me is only an individual case, and as such not very important because I do not let it affect me; but it is typical of the proceedings taken against many people. It is these I represent here, not myself.'

He had raised his voice without realising it. In the hall someone clapped, his hands held above his head, and shouted: 'Bravo! Why not? Bravo! And bravo again!' Those in the front row tugged at their beards, but none of them turned round at this outburst. Nor did K. attach any importance to it, though it did encourage him. He no longer thought it necessary that everyone should applaud; it was enough for him if the majority began to think about his case, and if just an occasional one was won over by persuasion.

'I do not seek success as an orator,' said K., following this train of thought. 'That may be beyond my abilities. The examining magistrate no doubt speaks much better than I do, that is his profession after all. All I ask for is the public discussion of a public outrage. Hear what I have to say. About ten days ago I was arrested; I find that fact itself risible, but that is neither here nor there. I was seized in bed early in the morning. Perhaps the order had been given – it is quite possible, given what the examining magistrate said – to arrest some house-painter who is just as innocent as I am; but they chose me. The next room was occupied by two boorish guards. If I were a dangerous criminal they could not have taken better precautions. These guards, moreover, were unprincipled riff-raff; they talked all kind of nonsense, they solicited bribes, they tried to take my clothes and linen by false pretences, they asked for money, supposedly to bring me some breakfast after they had shamelessly eaten my own breakfast in front of my eyes. And that was not all. I was taken into a third room to appear before their supervisor. The room belongs to a lady for whom I have the greatest respect, and I had to look on as this room, through no fault of mine and yet on my account, was as it were polluted by the presence of the guards and their supervisor. It was not easy for me to remain calm. I managed to do so, however, and asked the supervisor perfectly calmly – if he were here, he would have to agree – why I was under arrest. And what did this supervisor reply? – I can still see him sitting there in front of me, in that lady's chair, the very image of ignorant arrogance. Essentially, gentlemen, he did not answer me at all. Perhaps he really knew nothing; he had arrested me and was content with that. As if that were not enough, he had brought three minor officials from my bank to that lady's room, who spent their time handling photographs, which were that lady's property, and disarranging them. The presence of these employees, of course, had a further purpose; they were, like my landlady and her maid, to spread the news of my arrest, to damage my public reputation and, quite particularly, to jeopardise my position at the bank. Now, they have not succeeded, not in the slightest, in any of these things; even my landlady, who is quite an ordinary person – I mention her name here with all due respect, she is called Frau Grubach – even Frau Grubach was intelligent enough to see that such an arrest had no more significance than being attacked in the street by some unruly youths. I repeat: the whole affair merely caused me some embarrassment and annoyance for a while, but could it not also have had more serious consequences?'

Here K. broke off and looked over at the silent magistrate; as he did so, he thought he saw him glance at someone in the crowd, as if giving a signal. K. smiled and said: 'I see the examining magistrate here has just given one of you a secret sign. So there are some among you who take instructions from above. I do not know whether this sign was meant to provoke disapproval or applause; by exposing this ruse in good time, I quite deliberately forgo the opportunity of knowing what it might mean. I could not care less about it, and I publicly authorise the magistrate to give his instructions to his hirelings down there out loud instead of by secret signals, by telling them either "Hiss now!", or else "Clap now!" '

Whether with embarrassment or impatience, the magistrate shifted about on his chair. The man behind him, to whom he had spoken earlier, bent over him again, perhaps to give him some specific piece of advice or simply to encourage him. Down below the audience talked in hushed but animated voices. The two factions, who had earlier seemed to have such opposing views, mingled with each other; some individuals pointed at K., others at the magistrate. The thick haze in the hall was most oppressive; it even made it impossible to make out the people at the back. It must have been particularly annoying for those in the gallery, who were forced, albeit with nervous and furtive glances at the magistrate, to whisper questions to members of the assembly in order to find out what was going on. The answers were given just as quietly behind raised hands.

'I have almost finished,' said K., and since there was no bell available, he banged his fist on the table. Startled, the magistrate and his adviser immediately looked up from their huddle. 'I am quite detached from the whole matter, so I can judge it calmly; and if you attach any importance at all to this so-called court, you would do well to listen to me. I beg you to put off discussing my submission among yourselves until later, for I am short of time and I am going to leave soon.'

Such was K.'s hold over the audience that there was immediate silence. People no longer shouted across each other as at the beginning, they did not even applaud any more; they seemed already convinced, or very nearly so.

'There can be no doubt,' said K. very quietly, for he was pleased with the expectant attention of the whole assembly; in that silence arose a murmur that was more stimulating than the wildest applause. 'There can be no doubt that all the activities of this court, and therefore my own arrest and today's investigation, are backed by a large organisation. An organisation that not only employs corrupt guards, foolish supervisors, and examining magistrates who are at best minor officials, but which also supports a high-ranking judiciary with its inevitable vast retinue of attendants, clerks, police, and other auxiliaries, perhaps even – I am not afraid to use the word – executioners. And what is the purpose of this organisation, gentlemen? It is to arrest innocent individuals and to institute meaningless and for the most part – as in my case – fruitless proceedings against them. If the whole system is as senseless as this, how could the whole body of officials avoid being grossly corrupt? It would not be possible, even the highest judge could not preserve his own integrity. That is why the guards attempt to steal the clothing off the backs of those they arrest, that is why supervisors break into other people's homes, that is why innocent people, instead of being interrogated, are humiliated in front of large assemblies. The guards talked of depots where the property of those under arrest is kept; I would like to see these depots in which their hard-earned possessions are left to rot, if they are not stolen by thieving officials.'

K. was interrupted by shrieks from the back of the hall. He shielded his eyes to see what was going on, for the dim daylight made the hazy atmosphere white and dazzling. It was the washerwoman who, as K. had noticed, had caused a considerable disturbance when she had come in. It was not possible to tell whether this time she was to blame or not; he only saw how a man had pulled her into a corner by the door, and was hugging her closely. But it was not the woman who was shrieking; it was the man. His mouth was wide open and he was looking up at the ceiling. A small circle had gathered round them; the people in the gallery nearby seemed delighted that the solemn note K. had introduced into the proceedings had been interrupted in this way. K.'s first impulse was to rush over to them. He thought it would be in everyone's interest that order should be restored and that the pair of them should, at the very least, be expelled from the hall; but the nearest rows in front of him stayed put, no one moved, and no one let K. through. On the contrary, they obstructed him, old men held out their arms, and someone's hand – he did not have time to turn round – held him from behind by the collar.

K. was no longer thinking about the couple; it seemed to him that his freedom was being restricted, as if he were really under arrest, and throwing caution to the winds he leapt down from the platform. Now he was face to face with the crowd. Had he judged these people correctly? Had he overestimated the effect of his speech? Had they concealed their reactions while he was speaking, and had they had enough of this pretence once he had concluded his argument? What faces surrounded him! Their small dark eyes darted to and fro, their cheeks drooped like those of drunkards, their long thin beards stiffened, and when they pulled at them, it was as if they were clawing at them rather than stroking them. But underneath the beards – and this was a real revelation to K. – badges of various sizes and colours gleamed on their lapels. As far as he could see, they all wore these badges. These factions, apparently divided into right and left, all belonged together; and when he suddenly looked round, he saw the same badges on the lapel of the examining magistrate, who was looking on calmly with his hands folded in his lap. 'Ah, I see!' cried K., throwing up his hands to emphasise his sudden discovery, 'you are all officials, you are the corrupt gang my speech was aimed at, you have packed this hall as spectators and eavesdroppers, you pretended to form factions, and one of them applauded to test me, you wanted learn how to lead innocent people astray! Well, I hope you haven't wasted your time here. Either you have derived some amusement from listening to someone who expected you to defend innocence, or – leave me alone, or I'll hit you!' K. shouted at a trembling old man who had come particularly close to him – 'or else you really have learnt something. And so I wish you good luck in your trade.'

He grabbed his hat, which was lying on the corner of the table, and amid general silence, or at any rate amid the silence of stunned surprise, pushed his way towards the exit. But the examining magistrate appeared to have moved even more quickly than K., for he was waiting for him at the door. 'One moment,' he said. K. was not looking at the magistrate, but at the door; his hand was already on the handle. 'I simply wanted to let you know,' said the magistrate, 'that, although you may not have realised it, you have deprived yourself of the advantage that an examination invariably gives to someone who is under arrest.' Still turning towards the door, K. laughed. 'You scoundrels,' he cried, 'you can keep all your examinations!' He opened the door and hurried down the stairs. Behind him rose the hubbub of the assembly, which had come to life again and was probably starting to discuss the morning's events like a class of students.

CHAPTER THREE

In the Empty Hall – the Student – the Court Chambers

During the next week K. waited daily for a further communication; he could not believe that his refusal to be questioned had been taken literally, and when the expected notification had not arrived by Saturday evening, he assumed that he was tacitly summoned to the same house at the same time. And so on the Sunday he again made his way there, this time going straight up stairs and along passages; some people, who remembered him, greeted him from their doorways, but he did not need to ask the way and soon arrived at the right door. He knocked, and it was opened at once; without bothering to turn to the same woman as the week before, who was standing by the door, he made straight for the next room. 'There is no meeting today,' said the woman. 'Why is there no meeting?' asked K., who could not believe her. But the woman convinced him by opening the door into the next room. It was indeed empty, and its emptiness made it look even more dismal than the previous Sunday. On the table, which stood on the platform as before, lay a few books. 'Can I take a look at these books?' asked K., not because he was particularly curious, but because he did not wish his visit to be completely wasted. 'No,' said the woman, shutting the door again, 'that is not allowed.

The books belong to the examining magistrate.' 'I see,' said K., nodding. 'I suppose these books are legal texts, and it is in the nature of this legal system to condemn people who are not only innocent but also ignorant of the charges against them.' 'That will be it,' said the woman, who had not understood him properly. 'Well then, I shall be off,' said K. 'Shall I give the examining magistrate a message?' said the woman. 'Do you know him?' asked K. 'Of course,' said the woman, 'my husband is a court attendant.'

Only then did K. notice that the room, which the previous week had contained nothing but a wash-tub, was now a fullyfurnished living-room. The woman noticed his surprise and said: 'Yes, we live here rent-free, but we must clear out the room on days when there is a sitting. My husband's position has some disadvantages.' 'I'm not so surprised by the room,' said K., giving her a stern look, 'but rather that you are married.' 'Perhaps you are referring to what happened at the last meeting, when I interrupted your speech,' said the woman. 'Of course,' said K. 'That's all in the past now and I had almost forgotten about it, but at the time I was really furious. And now you tell me you are a married woman.' 'It was in your own interests that your speech was interrupted,' said the woman. 'They judged you very unfavourably afterwards.' 'That may be so,' said K. dismissively, 'but it doesn't excuse your behaviour.' 'Everyone who knows me will excuse it,' said the woman. 'The man who threw his arms around me has been pursuing me for a long time. I may not be attractive to everybody, but I am to him. No one can protect me, and my husband has come to terms with it; he has to put up with it if he wants to keep his job, for that man is a student and is expected to reach a position of some power. He is always after me; he left just now before you came.' 'It fits in with everything else,' said K., 'it doesn't surprise me.' 'I suppose you want to improve some things here?' asked the woman slowly, watching K. as if she were saying something dangerous both to herself and to him. 'I gathered that from your speech, which personally I liked very much. Of course, I only heard part of it; I missed the beginning, and for the end of it I was lying on the floor with the student.'

After a pause she took K.'s hand and said: 'Oh, it's so dreadful here. Do you think you will be able to improve things?' K. smiled, rubbing her soft hands lightly with his fingers. 'It's not really my place,' he said, 'to improve things here, as you put it, and if you said that to the examining magistrate, for instance, you would be laughed at or punished. It's true that I would never have interfered with things here of my own accord, and I would never have lost any sleep over the need to improve this judicial system. But because I was allegedly arrested – you see, I am under arrest – I have been forced to intervene here strictly in my own interests. However, if I can also help you in any way while I am about it, I shall be very glad to do so – not simply out of human kindness, but also because you can help me too.' 'But how could I do that?' asked the woman. 'By showing me those books on the table, for example.' 'Of course', cried the woman, dragging him quickly after her. They were old, tattered books; one of the covers was almost split down the middle, held together only by threads. 'How dirty everything is here,' said K., shaking his head, and before he could reach out for the books the woman wiped off at least some of the dust with her apron.

K. opened the first book and found an indecent picture. A man and a woman were sitting naked on a sofa; the lewd intention of the illustrator was quite clear, but it was done so clumsily that all that could be seen was a man and a woman who stood out all too boldly in the flesh, sitting stiffly upright. Because of the poor perspective, they seemed to have some difficulty turning towards each other. K. did not peruse the book further, but simply opened the second book at the title page. It was a novel entitled 'The Sufferings of Grete at the Hands of her Husband Hans'. 'So these are the law books they study here,' said K. 'I am to be judged by people like this.' 'I will help you,' said the woman. 'Do you want me to?' 'Could you really do that without putting yourself at risk? Didn't you tell me just now that your husband was entirely dependent on his superiors?' 'I want to help you all the same,' said the woman, 'come with me, we must talk it over. Don't say any more about the risks to me, I'm only afraid of risks if I want to be. Come over here.'

She pointed to the platform and invited him to sit on one of the steps with her. 'You have lovely dark eyes,' she said, sitting down and looking into K.'s face. 'They tell me I have beautiful eyes too, but yours are much nicer. I noticed them as soon as you came in here the first time. That was why I came into the hall later, something I normally never do, in fact in a sense I am not allowed to.' So that's it, thought K. – she's offering herself to me, she's corrupt like all of them round here, she's had enough of the court officials, which is understandable, so she welcomes every stranger who comes along with a compliment about his eyes. He stood up without a word, as if he had spoken his thoughts out loud and had thus made his attitude clear to the woman. 'I don't think you can help me,' he said. 'To give me any real help, you would have to be in touch with senior officials. But I'm sure you only know the minor officials who swarm around here. I dare say you know them very well, and no doubt they could do quite a lot for you; but even the best they could do would not have the slightest effect on the outcome of my case, and in the process you would only lose some of your friends. I don't want that. Just continue your relationship with these people, because it seems important to you. I say this with some regret, for if I may return your compliment, I find you very attractive, especially when you look at me so sadly like that, although you have no reason at all to do so. You belong to the organisation I have to fight against, and you are quite comfortable with it; you even have the student – or, if you don't love him, then at least you prefer him to your husband. That was easy to tell from what you said.' 'No!' she cried. She would not get up, and seized K.'s hand, which he did not withdraw quickly enough. 'You can't go now, you can't go away with a false impression of me. Could you really bring yourself to leave now? Am I really so worthless that you won't even do me the favour of staying here for just a little while?'

'Don't misunderstand me,' said K., sitting down. 'If it really means so much to you, I'll be glad to stay here, after all I have plenty of time; I came here expecting that a hearing would be held today. What I said just now was only to ask you not to do anything to help me with my case. But there's no need to be offended, because the outcome of the case is of no concern to me at all, and I should only laugh if I were convicted. If, that is, the case ever comes to a proper conclusion, which I very much doubt. I think it more likely that the proceedings have already been suspended, or very soon will be, because of laziness, forgetfulness, or perhaps even fear on the part of the officials. Of course, it's also possible that they will pretend to continue with the case in the hope of some fat bribe; but I can tell them now it's a waste of time, because I never give bribes. Still, you could do me a good turn by informing the examining magistrate, or anyone who likes spreading important news, that I shall never be induced to pay a bribe, not by any of the tricks I'm sure these gentlemen have up their sleeves. It would be quite pointless to try, you can tell them straight. Besides, they may already have noticed this themselves, and even if they haven't, it doesn't bother me if they are told now. It would only save these gentlemen trouble, and indeed it would save me some unpleasantness – though I'd be glad to cope with that as long as I know I'm striking a blow for others at the same time. And I'll make sure that is what I shall be doing. By the way: do you know the examining magistrate?'

'Of course,' said the woman, 'he was the first one I thought of when I offered to help you. I didn't know he was only a minor official, but if you say so, it's probably true. Even so, I think the reports he submits to the authorities still have some influence. And he writes so many reports. You say the officials are lazy, but I'm sure not all of them are, especially not the examining magistrate, he writes a lot. Last Sunday, for instance, the session went on into the evening. They all left, but the magistrate stayed in the hall, I had to bring him a lamp. I only had a small kitchen lamp, but he was quite happy with that and started writing straight away. My husband, who happened to have that Sunday off, arrived in the meantime; we fetched our furniture and arranged the room, and then some neighbours came round. We talked by candlelight, forgot about the magistrate and went to bed. Suddenly – it must have been the middle of the night – I woke up and found the magistrate standing by the bed, shielding the lamp with his hand so that the light didn't fall on my husband; it was an unnecessary precaution, my husband sleeps so soundly that even the light wouldn't have wakened him. I was so startled I almost screamed, but the magistrate was very friendly and told me not to stir. In a whisper he told me that he had been writing until now, that he was returning the lamp, and that he would never forget the sight when he found me asleep. I'm only telling you all this to show that the examining magistrate really does write a lot of reports, especially about you, because your interrogation was definitely one of the main items in Sunday's session. And I'm sure these long reports can't be completely insignificant. Besides, you can see from this incident that the examining magistrate has taken a fancy to me, and at this early stage – he can't have noticed me until then – I can have a lot of influence with him. Since then, too, there have been other signs that I mean a lot to him. Yesterday he sent me silk stockings as a present, delivered by the student who works with him and is trusted by him; they were supposedly in return for tidying the assembly hall, but that is only a pretext, that's my job after all, and my husband is paid for it. They're beautiful stockings, look' – she stretched out her legs, drew her skirt up to her knees and looked at the stockings herself – 'they're beautiful stockings, but they're really too good for me.'

Suddenly she broke off, put her hand on K.'s as if to calm him, and whispered: 'Hush, Berthold is watching us.' K. looked up slowly. In the door of the hall stood a young man; he was small, his legs were not quite straight, and he sought to lend himself some dignity by means of a short, sparse, reddish beard which he fingered constantly. K. looked at him with interest, for this was the first time he had met personally, as it were, a student of this alien legal system, a man who would very probably rise to a high official position one day. For his part, the student appeared to ignore K. completely; he simply beckoned to the woman with a finger, which he removed from his beard for a moment, and went to the window. The woman leaned over to K. and whispered: 'Don't be angry with me, please, don't think badly of me. I must go with him now, with this dreadful person – just look at his bandy legs. But I'll be back right away, and then I'll go with you, if you will take me with you. I'll go wherever you want, you can do what you like with me, I'll be happy to get away from here for as long as possible, preferably for ever, in fact.'

She fondled K.'s hand once more, then jumped up and ran to the window. Automatically, K. reached out for her hand, but she was gone. He was strongly attracted to the woman, and despite all his reservations could find no good reason why he should not give in to this temptation. He quickly dismissed the momentary suspicion that she might be working for the court and leading him into a trap. How could she entrap him? Was he not still free enough that he could, at least as far as his case was concerned, destroy the whole court in a moment? Surely he had enough confidence in himself? Her plea for help sounded honest; it might perhaps be of some value to him – and there was probably no better way of taking revenge on the examining magistrate and his hangers-on than to take this woman from them and have her for himself. It might even happen some time that the magistrate, after slaving over his lying reports on K., would come to her bed late at night and find it empty. Empty because she belonged to K., because this woman at the window, this voluptuous, lithe, warm body clothed in a dark dress made of coarse, heavy material, belonged to him alone.

After ridding himself of his suspicions about the woman in this way, he began to feel that the whispered conversation at the window had lasted long enough; he rapped his knuckles on the platform, then banged it with his fist. The student glanced briefly over the woman's shoulder in K.'s direction, but carried on undisturbed, in fact he moved closer to the woman and embraced her. She bent down towards him as if she were listening attentively, and as she bent down he gave her a loud kiss on her neck without any great interruption to what he was saying. K. saw this as a confirmation of the tyranny which, according to the woman's complaints, the student exercised over her. He stood up and walked around the room, glancing sideways at the student from time to time, deliberating how to get rid of him as soon as possible. So he was glad when the student, clearly annoyed by K.'s walking up and down, which by now had developed into a steady tramp, remarked: 'If you are so impatient, you can go. You could have left earlier, no one would have missed you. In fact, you ought to have left as soon as I arrived, and you should have been quick about it too.' While this outburst might have been one of intense fury, it also had all the arrogance of a future court official addressing a defendant he disliked. K. went to stand very close to him and said with a smile: 'I am impatient, that's true, but the easiest way to cure it is for you to leave us. If you have perhaps come here to study – I have heard you are a student – I will gladly make room for you and leave with this woman. What's more, you have a lot of studying to do before you become a magistrate. Although I don't know your legal system very well, I assume it requires a great deal more than just making offensive remarks – which you certainly seem able to do shamelessly well already.'

'They shouldn't have let him run around so freely,' said the student, as if trying to explain K.'s insulting remarks. 'It was a mistake. I said so to the examining magistrate. They should at least have kept him in his room between interrogations. Sometimes I don't understand the examining magistrate.' 'All this talk is pointless,' said K., holding out his hand to the woman, 'come with me.' 'I see,' said the student, 'no, no, you're not having her.' And with a strength one would not have thought him capable of, he lifted her with one arm and, bent under her weight, ran to the door, gazing tenderly up at her. He could not disguise a certain fear of K., but he still dared to provoke him by fondling and squeezing the woman's arm with his free hand. K. ran a few paces alongside him, prepared to get hold of him and, if necessary, to throttle him, but the woman said: 'It's no use, the examining magistrate has sent for me, I can't go with you; this little horror' – as she said this, she stroked the student's face with her hand – 'this little horror won't let me.' 'And you don't want to be rescued!' cried K., grasping the student by the shoulder. The student snapped at K.'s hand with his teeth. 'No!' cried the woman, pushing K. away with both hands, 'no, you mustn't do that, what do you think you're doing? That would ruin me. Leave him alone, please leave him. He is only carrying out the examining magistrate's orders and taking me to him.' 'Let him go then, and as for you, I never want to see you again,' said K., furious with disappointment, and gave the student a push in the back which made him stumble for a moment; but then, so pleased was he not to have fallen, he hoisted his burden even higher. K. walked slowly after them; he realised that this was the first unmistakable defeat he had suffered at the hands of these people. Of course, that was no cause for concern; he had been defeated only because he had set out to fight them. If he stayed at home and carried on with his normal life he would be infinitely superior to every one of them, and could kick any of them out of his way. And he imagined to himself the most ridiculous scene if this wretched student, for example, this arrogant child, this bandylegged bearded creature, were to kneel by Elsa's bed, clasp his hands together and beg for mercy. K. was so pleased with this idea that he decided, should the opportunity ever arise, to take the student to meet Elsa.

Out of curiosity, K. hurried to the door to see where the woman was being taken; the student would scarcely carry her through the streets in his arms. Just across from the flat was a narrow wooden staircase, probably leading to a garret; it had a bend in it, so it was not possible to see where it ended. The student carried the woman up this staircase; by now he was climbing very slowly and gasping for breath, for his previous exertions had exhausted him. The woman looked down and waved to K. in an attempt to suggest that she was not to blame for her abduction; but the gesture did not convey very much regret. K. watched her blankly as if she were a stranger; he did not wish to show his disappointment, but neither did he wish to suggest that he could easily get over it.

The two soon disappeared, but K. still stood in the doorway. He was forced to conclude that the woman had not only betrayed him, but had also lied to him when she had told him she was being taken to the examining magistrate. The magistrate would surely not sit and wait in a garret. The wooden staircase gave him no clue, however long he looked at it. Then K. saw a small notice at the foot of the stairs. He went over to it and read it. In an immature childish hand was written: 'Entrance to the Court Chambers'. So the court chambers were here, in the attic of this tenement? It was not an establishment to inspire much respect, and it was reassuring for a defendant to think how impoverished this court must be if its chambers were housed in a part of the building where the tenants, who were themselves from the poorest classes, threw their useless junk. Of course, it was not impossible that the court had enough money, and that the officials seized it before it could be used for legal purposes. To judge from K.'s previous experiences, this was indeed very probable; and yet, although such a corrupt court might seem to demean the defendant, it was still more reassuring than an impoverished court would be. K. now understood why at the first hearing they had been ashamed to summon the accused to their attic, and why they preferred to plague him in his apartment. What a superior position he was in compared to the magistrate, who sat in a garret, while at the bank he had a large office with a waiting-room and a view of the busy main square through a huge window! Of course, he could not supplement his income with bribes or embezzlement, nor could he have a woman brought to his office in the arms of a servant; but he was willing to forgo all that, in this life at least.

K. was still standing in front of the notice when a man came up the stairs, looked through the open door into the living-room, from which the courtroom could also be seen, and finally asked K. whether he had seen a woman here just now. 'You are the court attendant, aren't you?' asked K. 'Yes,' said the man. 'Ah, you're the defendant K. Now I recognise you. Welcome.' And to K.'s surprise he held out his hand. 'But the court is not sitting today,' continued the attendant when K. did not reply. 'I know,' said K., examining the attendant's everyday jacket; the only indication of his official position was the two gilt buttons which stood out from the other ordinary buttons, and which seemed to have been taken from an old officer's uniform. 'I was speaking to your wife a while ago. She is no longer here; the student has carried her up to the examining magistrate.' 'You see,' said the attendant, 'they're always taking her from me. It's Sunday today, and I'm not on duty, but just to get me out of the way they send me off with a quite unnecessary message. They don't send me far, either, so that if I really hurry I can hope to get back in good time. So I run as fast as I can, and shout my message through the half-open door of the office I've been sent to, but I'm so out of breath they won't have understood half of it. Then I run back, but the student is even quicker; of course, he doesn't have so far to go as I did, he only has to run down the stairs from the attic. If I weren't so dependent on them I would have smashed the student against this wall long ago. Just here, by this notice; I dream about it all the time. Here, a little bit off the floor, he's squashed tight, his arms spread out, his fingers splayed, his bandy legs bent into a circle, and splashes of blood all round. But so far it's only a dream.'

'Is there no other way?' asked K., smiling. 'Not that I know of,' said the attendant. 'And it's getting worse, until now he's only taken her for himself, now he takes her to the magistrate as well. But then, I've been expecting that for a long time.' 'But don't you blame your wife for all this?' asked K. He had to control himself as he said it, for even now he felt fiercely jealous. 'Of course,' said the attendant, 'she's to blame most of all. She's thrown herself at him. As for him, he chases all the women. In this block alone he's been thrown out of five apartments he's sneaked into. The fact is, my wife is the best-looking woman in the whole place, and I'm the only one who can't fight back.' 'If that's the way it is, then I'm sure nothing can be done,' said K. 'Why ever not?' asked the attendant. 'That student is a coward. Somebody ought to give him such a thrashing when he tries to touch my wife that he'll never dare to do it again. But I can't do it, and no one else will do it for me because they're all afraid of the power he has. Only a man like you could do it.' 'But why could I do it?' asked K., astonished.

'Because you're a defendant,' said the man. 'Yes,' said K., 'but that means I have all the more reason to fear that, even if he might not be able to influence the outcome of my trial, he could probably have some influence on the preliminary hearings.' 'Yes, certainly,' said the attendant, as if K.'s view were just as valid as his own. 'But as a rule the trials here are not hopeless cases.' 'I don't agree with you,' said K., 'but that won't stop me teaching the student a lesson some time.' 'I would be most grateful to you,' said the attendant somewhat formally; he did not seem to believe his fondest wish could be granted.

'Perhaps,' continued K., 'some of your other officials, perhaps even all of them, deserve the same.' 'Yes indeed,' said the attendant, as if there were no question about it. Then he gave K. a confiding glance, which for all his friendliness he had not done before, and added: 'There's always something to protest about.' But the conversation seemed to have made him uneasy, for he broke off, saying: 'Now I must report to the chambers. Do you want to come with me?' 'There's nothing for me to do there,' said K. 'You can have a look at the chambers. No one will bother about you.' 'Is there anything worth seeing?' asked K. uncertainly, though he very much wanted to go with him. 'Well,' said the attendant, 'I thought you would be interested.' 'All right,' said K. finally, 'I'll come with you.' And he ran up the stairs faster than the attendant.

As he went in he almost fell, for there was another step behind the door. 'They don't have much consideration for the public,' he said. 'They don't have any at all,' said the attendant, 'just look at the waiting-room.' It was a long corridor with a series of crudely constructed doors, each leading to a compartment in the attic. Although there was no direct light source, it was not completely dark, for some of the compartments were boarded off from the corridor not by solid walls, but by wooden grilles, and though the grilles reached to the ceiling some light shone through them. Behind them individual officials could be seen writing at their desks or standing at the grilles and watching the people in the corridor through the gaps. Probably because it was Sunday, there were few people in the corridor; they made a very modest impression, sitting at almost regular intervals on two rows of long wooden benches either side of the corridor. They were all shabbily dressed, though most of them, to judge by their expression, their bearing, the cut of their beards, and many other scarcely definable small details, belonged to the better classes. Since there were no hat-stands, they had placed their hats under the benches – no doubt following each other's example.

When those sitting nearest to the door caught sight of K. and the attendant, they stood up by way of greeting; when the others saw this they felt they ought to do the same, so that everyone stood as the two went by. None of them stood fully upright; their backs and knees were bent, and they stood like street beggars. K. waited for the attendant, who was walking just behind him, and said: 'How humiliated they must be.' 'Yes,' said the attendant, 'they are all defendants, all these people here are defendants.' 'Really?' said K. 'Then they are my colleagues.' And he turned to the nearest one, a tall, slim man with almost completely grey hair. 'What are you waiting here for?' asked K. politely. But the man became confused at being addressed so unexpectedly, and looked all the more embarrassed because he was clearly a man of the world who in any other situation would surely know how to keep his selfcontrol, and would be reluctant to give up the superiority he enjoyed over many others. Here, however, he did not know how to answer such a simple question, and looked at the others as if they were duty bound to help him, and as if he could not be expected to answer unless such help were forthcoming. Then the attendant went up to him and said, by way of reassurance and encouragement: 'This gentleman is only asking what you are waiting for. Why don't you answer him?' The no doubt familiar voice of the attendant had a better effect: 'I'm waiting . . .' he began, then hesitated. He had obviously chosen to begin like this in order to answer the question with complete accuracy, but now he did not know how to continue. Some of the people waiting had approached and gathered round; the attendant told them: 'Get back, get back, keep the corridor free.' They moved back a little, but did not return to their places.

Meanwhile the man who had been questioned had composed himself and even smiled faintly as he replied: 'A month ago I submitted some evidence in my case, and I am waiting for the result.' 'You seem to be going to a lot of trouble,' said K. 'Yes,' said the man, 'it's to do with my case, after all.' 'Not everyone thinks as you do,' said K., 'I, for instance, have also been accused, but I give you my solemn word that I have not submitted any evidence or anything of the kind. Do you think it is necessary, then?' 'I don't know exactly,' said the man, once again totally uncertain of himself. He clearly thought K. was joking, and he would probably have preferred, for fear of making another mistake, to repeat his earlier answer all over again; but seeing K.'s impatient expression he said only: 'For my part, I have submitted my evidence.' 'I suppose you don't believe I've been accused?' said K. 'Oh yes, of course,' said the man, moving aside; but his answer suggested not belief, but fear. 'So you don't believe me?' asked K. Unconsciously provoked by the man's servile demeanour, he seized him by the arm as if he were trying to force him to believe him. He had no wish to hurt him, and had only taken hold of him quite lightly, but in spite of this the man shrieked as if K. had grasped him not with two fingers, but with red-hot pincers. This ridiculous screaming made K. lose patience with him. If this man did not believe he was a defendant, so much the better; perhaps he even thought he was a magistrate. And before he moved on, he gripped the man even tighter and pushed him back onto the bench. 'Most of the defendants are so sensitive,' said the attendant. Behind them nearly all those who were waiting gathered round the man, who had stopped screaming by now, and seemed to be questioning him closely about the incident. A man now approached whom K. took to be a guard, mainly because he wore a sabre in a sheath which, to judge by its colour, was made of aluminium. This surprised K., and he even put out his hand to touch it. The guard, who had come to see what the screaming was about, asked what had happened. The attendant spoke a few words to reassure him, but the guard insisted he must look into it himself. He saluted and walked on with rapid but very short steps, probably the result of gout.

K. did not concern himself for very long with the guard or the people gathered in the corridor, especially since he saw that on the right about half-way along the corridor he could turn off through an opening that had no door. He asked the attendant whether this was the right way to go; the attendant nodded, and K. turned off to the right. It annoyed him that he always had to walk a step or two ahead of the attendant, because it might appear, at least in this place, that he was being escorted under arrest. So he often stopped to wait for the attendant, but the man immediately held back. Finally, to put an end to his unease, K. said: 'Now I've seen what it's like here, I'm going to leave.' 'But you haven't seen everything yet,' said the attendant artlessly. 'I don't want to see everything,' said K., who now felt really tired, 'I want to leave. Where is the way out?' 'Surely you haven't lost your way?' asked the attendant in surprise. 'You go to the corner here, and then turn right down the corridor straight to the door.' 'Come with me,' said K., 'and show me. I won't be able to find it, there are so many ways here.' 'It's the only way,' said the attendant, who was beginning to lose patience, 'I can't go back with you, I have to deliver my message, and I'm already very late because of you.' 'Come with me!' repeated K. more sharply, as if he had finally caught the attendant trying to deceive him. 'Don't shout so loud,' whispered the attendant, 'there are chambers everywhere here. If you don't want to go back alone, you can come along with me for a while or wait here until I've delivered my message, then I'll be glad to go back with you.' 'No, no,' said K., 'I won't wait, and you must come with me now.'

So far K. had not so much as glanced at his surroundings, and only now, when one of the many wooden doors opened, did he look up. A young woman, no doubt in response to K.'s shouting, appeared and asked: 'Can I help you, Sir?' Some way behind her in the gloom a man was also approaching. K. looked at the attendant; he had told K. that no one would bother about him, and now there were already two people here; before long every official would be alerted and would want him to explain why he was there. The only convincing and acceptable explanation was that he was a defendant who wanted to know the date of the next examination; but he was particularly reluctant to offer that explanation because it was not the truth, for he had only come here out of curiosity or – and this was even more impossible as an explanation – because he wanted to find out whether this legal organisation was just as repugnant from the inside as it was from the outside. And since it seemed that he was correct in this assumption, he had no wish to go any further into it; what he had already seen of it was quite depressing enough, and just now he was in no state of mind to deal with a senior official who might emerge from any of these doors. He wanted to leave, whether with the court attendant or, if needs be, on his own.

But he must have drawn attention to himself by standing there mutely, because the young woman and the attendant looked at him as if at any moment they expected him to undergo some great transformation which they did not want to miss. And in the doorway stood the man K. had noticed earlier some distance away; he was holding on to the lintel of the low door and standing on tiptoe like an eager spectator. But the young woman was the first to realise that K. was not feeling very well. She brought a chair and asked: 'Won't you sit down?' K. sat down at once and rested his elbows on the arms of the chair to support himself. 'You're feeling a bit dizzy, aren't you?' she asked him. Her face was now close up to him; it wore the severe look that many women have in the most beautiful phase of their youth. 'Don't worry about it,' she said, 'it's nothing out of the ordinary here, nearly everyone is affected like that the first time they come here. Is this your first time? Well then, it's quite normal. The sun heats up the rafters, and the warm wood makes the air close and heavy. That's why this place is not very suitable as office space, though it has many other advantages. When it's very busy here – that's nearly every day – the air is hardly fit to breathe. And when you think of all the washing the tenants hang out to dry – they can't ban it completely – then you can't be surprised if you don't feel very well. But in the end you get quite used to the atmosphere; the second or third time you come, you'll hardly notice how oppressive it is. Are you feeling better now?'

K. did not answer; he was too put out that his sudden faintness had put him at the mercy of these people. Besides, now that the cause of his nausea had been explained to him he felt no better, but rather worse. The young woman noticed this at once; in order to give K. some fresh air, she took a pole with a hook that was propped against the wall and pushed open a small skylight just above K.'s head to let in some air. But so much soot fell in that she had to shut the skylight at once and use her handkerchief to clean the soot off K.'s hands, for he was too tired to do this for himself. He would have been happy to sit there quietly until he felt strong enough to leave; the less they bothered him, the sooner he would recover. But now the young woman went on: 'You can't stay here, we are in the way.' K. looked at her enquiringly, as if to ask what sort of obstruction he could be causing. 'If you wish, I'll take you to the sick-room.

Help me, please,' she said to the man in the doorway, who came at once. But K. did not want to go to the sick-room, indeed he wanted to avoid being taken any further; the further he went, the more difficult it would become. So he said: 'I can walk now.' But because he had got used to sitting, he trembled as he stood up. Then he found he could not stand upright. 'I just can't manage,' he said, shaking his head, and with a sigh he sat down again. He thought of the court attendant, who could easily show him the way out in spite of everything, but it seemed that he had gone some time ago; K. looked between the young woman and the man, who were standing in front of him, but he could not see the attendant.

'I believe,' said the man, who was smartly dressed, with a particularly striking grey waistcoat which ended in two sharp points, 'that this gentleman's faintness is due to the atmosphere in here, so it would be best not to take him to the sick-room, but to get him out of the chambers altogether. I'm sure that's what he would prefer.' 'That's it,' cried K., almost interrupting the man in his delight, 'I shall feel better at once, and I'm not so weak at all, just some support under my arms is all I need, I won't give you much trouble. It's not very far, just take me to the door, then I'll sit on the steps for a while and soon get over it. I don't usually have these attacks, it's taken me by surprise. I'm an official too, you see; I'm used to an office atmosphere, but here it just seems too much for me, as you say. So if you would be so kind as to give me some help, because I feel dizzy and sick if I stand up by myself.' And he raised his shoulders so that the two of them could take him under the arms.

But the man did not do as he was asked; he calmly kept his hands in his pockets and laughed out loud. 'You see,' he said to the young woman, 'I was right. It's only in here the gentleman feels unwell, not elsewhere.' The woman smiled too, but struck the man lightly on the arm with her fingertips, as if he had gone too far in his amusement at K.'s expense. 'What is that supposed to mean?' said the man, still laughing, 'I really am going to show the gentleman the way out.' 'Very well then,' said the woman, nodding her dainty head briefly. 'Don't take his laughter too seriously,' she said to K., who was gazing dejectedly into space and did not appear to need an explanation, 'this gentleman – may I introduce you?' – the man made a gesture of assent – 'this gentleman is the information officer. He gives our waiting clients all the information they need, and since the public knows very little about our legal organisation, a great deal of information is asked for. He can answer any questions, if you wish you can try him out. But that is not his only quality; the other is his elegant clothing. We, that is the officials, decided that the information officer, who is always dealing with clients and is the first person they meet, should be smartly dressed in order to make a good first impression. I'm afraid the rest of us, as you can see from me, are very badly dressed in old-fashioned clothes; there is not much point in spending anything on our clothes, because we are nearly always in chambers, in fact we even sleep here. But as I say, we thought the information officer really ought to be well dressed. But we couldn't get any smart clothes out of our administration (they are rather odd in that respect), so we made a collection – even the clients contributed to it – and bought him this good suit, and other things as well. So we did everything to make a good impression, but then he spoils it by laughing, which alarms people.'

'That's how it is,' said the man sardonically. 'But I don't understand, Miss, why you are telling this gentleman all our secrets, indeed why you force them on him when he isn't in the least interested. Just look at him, he's sitting there obviously preoccupied with his own affairs.' K. did not even feel like contradicting him; the young woman might have meant well, perhaps she wanted to divert his attention or let him gather his thoughts; but she had not gone the right way about it. 'I had to explain to him why you were laughing,' she said, 'because it was rude.' 'I think he would excuse far worse rudeness if I were to show him the way out.' K. said nothing, he did not even look up; he let the two of them argue over him as if he were some inanimate object, in fact he preferred it. But suddenly he felt the information officer's hand on one arm and the young woman's on the other. 'Up you get then, you poor weak man,' said the information officer. 'Thank you both very much,' said K., surprised and delighted; he stood up slowly and guided the strangers' hands to where he most needed their support. 'It may look,' whispered the young woman in K.'s ear as they approached the corridor, 'as if I were particularly keen to show the information officer in a good light; but believe me, I'm just telling you the truth. He is not callous – he's not duty bound to show clients who have been taken ill the way out, but as you can see, he does it all the same. Perhaps none of us are callous, perhaps we all want to help, but as court officials we can easily appear callous and unhelpful. I feel really bad about it.'

'Wouldn't you like to sit down here for a while?' asked the information officer. By now they had reached the corridor and were standing in front of the defendant K. had spoken to earlier. K. felt almost ashamed in his presence; then he had been standing so straight when he spoke to him, now he needed two to support him. The information officer was balancing K.'s hat on his outstretched fingers, his hair was untidy and hung down over his forehead, which was drenched in sweat. But the defendant seemed to notice nothing of all this; he stood humbly in front of the information officer, who ignored him, and attempted only to excuse his presence there. 'I know,' he said, 'that my submissions cannot be dealt with today, but I came all the same. I thought I could wait here – it's Sunday after all, and I'm not bothering anyone.' 'There's no need to apologise,' said the information officer, 'your conscientiousness is very commendable. You may be taking up space here unnecessarily, but as long as you don't get in my way I haven't the slightest wish to interfere with your close attention to the progress of your case. When one has seen people who shamelessly neglect their duties, one learns to have patience with people like you. Please sit down.' 'Doesn't he know how to talk to clients?' whispered the young woman. K. nodded, but then started when the information officer again asked him: 'Won't you sit down here?' 'No,' said K., 'I don't need a rest.' He said this as decisively as he possibly could, though in fact it would have done him a lot of good to sit down. It was as if he were seasick, as if he were on a ship in heavy seas, as if the waves were crashing against the wooden walls, as if from the far end of the corridor he could hear the roaring of surf, as if the corridor were rolling from side to side and the waiting clients were rising and falling on either side.

All the more baffling, then, was the calmness of the young woman and the man beside him. He was at their mercy; if they let go of him, he would surely fall like a wooden post. They darted keen glances from their small eyes, K. could feel their steady gait, but could not keep pace with them; he was practically being carried step by step. Finally, he realised that they were talking to him, but he could not understand them; he heard only a noise that filled the whole place, through which a constant high-pitched note wailed like a siren. 'Louder,' he whispered, his head hanging; he felt embarrassed, because he knew that they had been speaking loud enough, though he had not been able to understand. Then at last, as if the wall in front of him had been torn down, a draught of fresh air came to meet him, and he heard someone beside him say: 'First he wants to leave, and then you can tell him a hundred times that this is the way out, and he doesn't move.'

K. noticed that he was standing in front of the outside door, which the young woman had opened. He felt as if he had suddenly recovered all his strength; in order to get a foretaste of freedom, he at once stepped out onto the stairs and from there took leave of his companions, who bent down over him. 'Many thanks,' he repeated, shook them both again and again by the hand, and only desisted when he thought he noticed that they, accustomed as they were to the atmosphere of the chambers, could not tolerate the relatively fresh air on the staircase. They could scarcely answer him, and the young woman might well have collapsed had K. not immediately closed the door. He then stood there for a moment, tidied his hair with the help of a pocket-mirror, picked up his hat, which was lying on the step below – the information officer must have thrown it down there – and then ran down the stairs so smartly and with such long strides that he almost felt alarmed by this sudden change in himself. His otherwise perfectly healthy constitution had never before given him such a shock. Was his body trying to rebel and present him with a new challenge because he had managed so effortlessly before now? He did not entirely reject the idea of seeing a doctor at the next opportunity; but at any rate – and in this matter he could take his own advice – he would spend all his future Sunday mornings more profitably than this one.

CHAPTER FOUR

Fräulein Bürstner's Friend

Over the following days it proved impossible for K. to exchange even a few words with Fräulein Bürstner. He tried to approach her in all manner of ways, but she always managed to avoid him. He came home straight after work, stayed in his room and sat on the sofa without switching on the light, and did nothing but watch the entrance hall. If the maid went by and closed the door of the apparently empty room, after a while he would get up and open it again. In the mornings he got up an hour earlier than usual in the hope that he might catch Fräulein Bürstner on her own as she went to work; but none of these attempts succeeded. Then he wrote her a letter, sending one copy to her office and one to her apartment, in which he again sought to justify his behaviour, offered to make amends in every way, promised to respect any restrictions she might impose on him, and asked only for one chance to speak to her, especially since he could not approach Frau Grubach until he had consulted her first. Finally, he informed her that for the whole of the following Sunday he would wait in his room for a sign from her that she might be prepared to grant his request, or at least that she would be willing to explain why she could not do so – though he had admittedly promised to defer to her in every way. The letters were not returned, but they were not answered either.

On Sunday, however, there was a sign that was quite clear enough. Very early K., looking through the key-hole, noticed an unusual degree of activity in the hallway, which was soon explained. A French teacher, a German woman called Montag, a frail, pallid young woman with a slight limp who had until then occupied a room of her own, was moving into Fräulein Bürstner's room. For hours he saw her shuffling along the hallway; there was always a piece of linen or a tablecloth or a book that had been forgotten, that had to be fetched separately and taken to the new room.

When Frau Grubach brought K.'s breakfast – since K. had been so angry with her she did not leave even the most trifling task to the maid – K. could not avoid speaking to her for the first time in five days. 'Why is there so much noise in the hallway today?' he asked as he poured his coffee. 'Can nothing be done about it? Must the house be cleaned on a Sunday?' Although K. did not look up at Frau Grubach, he still noticed that she breathed a deep sigh of relief. She took even K.'s abrupt questions as a sign of forgiveness, or as the beginning of a reconciliation. 'It's not being cleaned, Herr K.,' she said. 'Fräulein Montag is just moving into Fräulein Bürstner's room and taking her things in there.' She said no more, but waited to see how K. would react and whether he would let her continue. But K. did not help her; he stirred his coffee thoughtfully and said nothing. Then he looked up at her and said: 'Have you given up your suspicions about Fräulein Bürstner?' 'Herr K.,' cried Frau Grubach, who had only been waiting for this question. She clasped her hands and held them out to him. 'Recently you took a casual remark of mine so seriously. I never had the slightest thought of offending you or anyone else. You've known me long enough, Herr K., to be sure of that. You have no idea how I've suffered these last few days! That I should slander my lodgers! And you, Herr K., believed that! You said I should give you notice! Give you notice!' This last cry was stifled by her tears; she lifted her apron to her face and sobbed aloud.

'Please don't cry, Frau Grubach,' said K., looking out of the window; he was thinking only of Fräulein Bürstner, and how she had taken a stranger into her room. 'Please don't cry,' he repeated as he turned back into the room to see that Frau Grubach was still crying. 'I didn't really mean to upset you the other day; it was just a misunderstanding. That happens sometimes, even among old friends.' Frau Grubach removed her apron from her eyes in order to see whether K. really meant it. 'That's all it was,' said K. And since he gathered from Frau Grubach's attitude that the captain had not told her anything, he ventured to add: 'Do you really think I would fall out with you over a young woman I don't know?' 'That's just it, Herr K.,' said Frau Grubach – it was an unfortunate failing of hers that as soon as she felt less anxious, she immediately said something tactless – 'I kept asking myself: why should Herr K. be so concerned about Fräulein Bürstner? Why should he fall out with me over her, when he knows I lose sleep over every cross word from him? After all, I didn't say anything about the young lady that I hadn't seen with my own eyes.' K. said nothing; if he had, his first impulse would have been to drive her out of the room, and he did not want to do that. He contented himself with drinking his coffee and letting Frau Grubach feel she was not wanted.

Outside they heard Fräulein Montag again as she shuffled the length of the hallway. 'Can you hear it?' asked K., pointing to the door. 'Yes,' said Frau Grubach with a sigh. 'I wanted to help her, I wanted the maid to help too, but she is stubborn, she wanted to move everything herself. I'm surprised at Fräulein Bürstner. I often regret having Fräulein Montag as a lodger, but now Fräulein Bürstner has taken her into her own room.' 'You mustn't let that bother you,' said K., crushing the remains of the sugar in his cup. 'But will it cause you any loss of income?' 'No,' said Frau Grubach, 'actually it's quite welcome, it gives me a free room, and I can put up my nephew the captain there. I've been afraid for some time that he might have disturbed you over the last few days while I had to let him live in the sitting-room next door. He is not very considerate.' 'What are you thinking!' said K., standing up. 'Nothing of the sort. You seem to think I'm over-sensitive because I can't stand Fräulein Montag's comings and goings – there she is again.' Frau Grubach felt quite helpless. 'Herr K., shall I tell her to put off the rest of her move? If you wish, I'll do it at once.' 'But she has to move in with Fräulein Bürstner!' said K. 'Yes,' said Frau Grubach; she did not fully understand what K. meant. 'Well then,' said K., 'she's got to move her things in there.' Frau Grubach simply nodded. This dumb helplessness, which outwardly just looked like defiance, irritated K. even more. He began to walk up and down between the window and the door, and thus prevented Frau Grubach from leaving, which otherwise she probably would have done.

Just as K. reached the door again, there was a knock. It was the maid, who said Fräulein Montag would like a few words with Herr K., and that she had asked him to come into the diningroom, where she was waiting for him. K. listened carefully to the maid, then he turned and glanced almost scornfully at Frau Grubach, who looked startled. This glance seemed to suggest that K. had long since expected Fräulein Montag's invitation, and that it was all part and parcel of the harassment he had to put up with from Frau Grubach's tenants that morning. He sent the maid back with the reply that he would come straight away, then he went to the wardrobe to change his coat; he had nothing to say to Frau Grubach, who was muttering under her breath about this tiresome person, except to ask her to clear the breakfast table. 'But you've hardly touched anything!' said Frau Grubach. 'Oh, just take it away!' cried K.; he felt that Fräulein Montag was somehow involved in everything and was making things difficult for him.

As he went through the hallway he glanced at the door to Fräulein Bürstner's room, which was closed. But he was not invited in there, so he flung the door of the dining-room open without even knocking. It was a very long narrow room with one window. There was just enough space for two cupboards to be placed at an angle on either side of the door, while the rest of the room was fully occupied by the long dining-table that stretched from near the door right up to the large window, which as a result was almost inaccessible. The table was already laid with places for several people, for on Sundays almost all the lodgers took their midday meal here.

As K. entered, Fräulein Montag moved away from the window and came towards him along one side of the table. They greeted each other silently. Then Fräulein Montag, who as always held her head unusually high, said: 'I don't know whether you know me.' K. frowned at her. 'Of course,' he said, 'after all, you have been staying with Frau Grubach for a long time.' 'But I rather think you don't take much notice of things in the boarding house.' 'No,' said K. 'Won't you sit down?' said Fräulein Montag. Without a word, they each pulled out a chair at the far end of the table and sat down opposite one another. But Fräulein Montag immediately stood up again, for she had left her handbag on the window-sill and went to fetch it, shuffling the whole length of the room. When she returned, swinging the handbag gently, she said: 'I would just like to say a few words to you on behalf of my friend. She would have come herself, but she feels rather unwell today. She asks you to excuse her and listen to me instead. She would have had no more to say to you than what I shall say. On the contrary, I even think I can say more than she can because I am relatively uninvolved. Don't you agree?'

'What is there to be said, then?' replied K., who was growing tired of seeing Fräulein Montag's eyes constantly fixed on his lips; it was an attempt on her part to control what he had to say before he said it. 'Fräulein Bürstner is clearly unwilling to speak to me personally, as I asked her to.' 'That is so,' said Fräulein Montag, 'or rather, that is not the case at all; you express yourself in a strangely forthright way. After all, it is not usual to require consent to talk to someone, nor to refuse it. But it can be thought unnecessary to talk to someone, and that is exactly the case here. Now, after your remarks I can speak frankly. You have asked my friend to communicate with you, in writing or by word of mouth. But my friend knows – at least, this is what I must assume – what you wish to discuss with her, and she is convinced, for reasons unknown to me, that such a discussion would benefit no one. Besides, she only mentioned it to me yesterday, quite incidentally, and said you cannot attach much importance to it anyway, because the idea had only occurred to you by chance, and that you would, even without any specific explanation, very quickly realise how pointless the whole thing was – if not now, then before very long. I replied that she might well be right, but that I thought it would help to clear the whole matter up if she were to give you a definite answer. I offered to do this myself, and after some hesitation my friend agreed. But I hope I have also acted in your interests; for even the slightest uncertainty in the most trivial matter is always cause for concern, and when it can easily be cleared up, as it can in this case, then the sooner it is done the better.'

'Thank you,' said K. at once. He stood up slowly, looked at Fräulein Montag, then across the table out of the window – the house opposite lay in sunshine – and went to the door. Fräulein Montag followed a few steps behind him, as if she did not quite trust him. But at the door both of them had to step back, for the door opened and Captain Lanz came in. It was the first time K. had seen him close at hand. He was a tall man of about forty with a plump tanned face. He made a slight bow, which also included K., then he went up to Fräulein Montag and respectfully kissed her hand. He was very poised in his movements. His courtesy towards Fräulein Montag was in striking contrast to the manner in which K. had treated her. In spite of this, Fräulein Montag did not seem angry with K., for she was actually about to introduce him to the captain, or so K. imagined. But K. did not want to be introduced, he would not have been capable of being at all civil to either the captain or Fräulein Montag; that gesture of kissing her hand, he felt, had made them party to a plan that was designed, under the guise of the utmost innocence and consideration, to keep him away from Fräulein Bürstner. But that was not all K. suspected. He also realised that Fräulein Montag had chosen a clever, if two-edged stratagem; she was exaggerating the significance of his relationship with Fräulein Bürstner, and especially the significance of the interview he had requested, and at the same time she was trying to convey the impression that it was K. who was exaggerating everything. Let her fool herself; K. did not wish to exaggerate anything, he knew that Fräulein Bürstner was just a little typist who could not resist him for long. In this he deliberately ignored what Frau Grubach had told him about Fräulein Bürstner.

He was thinking about all this as he left the room with scarcely a gesture of farewell. He intended to go straight to his room; but when he heard Fräulein Montag's quiet laugh from the diningroom behind him, it occurred to him that he could surprise them both, the captain and Fräulein Montag. He looked round and listened in case there might be any interruption from one of the surrounding rooms, but all was quiet; he could hear only the conversation in the dining-room and, from the corridor leading to the kitchen, the voice of Frau Grubach. It seemed an opportune moment; K. went to Fräulein Bürstner's door and knocked softly. There was not a sound, so he knocked again; still no reply. Was she asleep? Was she really unwell? Or was she pretending not to be there because she knew that only K. would knock so softly? K. assumed that she was pretending and knocked louder; finally, since there was no response to his knocking, he opened the door carefully, not without feeling that he was doing something wrong and indeed futile. There was no one in the room; moreover, it was now scarcely recognisable as the room K. had known. Now there were two beds placed one behind the other against the wall, three chairs near the door were piled high with clothes and linen, and a wardrobe stood open. Fräulein Bürstner had probably left while Fräulein Montag was holding forth to K. in the dining-room. K. was not too dismayed by this; by now he hardly expected to meet Fräulein Bürstner so easily – he had made this attempt almost entirely to defy Fräulein Montag. Even so, he was all the more embarrassed when, as he shut the door behind him, he saw Fräulein Montag and the captain talking to each other at the open door of the dining-room. Perhaps they had been standing there since K. had opened the door. They avoided any impression that they might have been watching K.; they talked quietly and only followed his movements with the casual look of those who glance round during a conversation. But these glances weighed heavily on him; keeping close to the wall, he hurried along the hallway to his room.

CHAPTER FIVE

The Flogging

On one of the following evenings, as K. was passing along the corridor that led from his office to the main staircase – today he was almost the last to leave, only two bank messengers in the post room were still working by the sparse light of a single lamp – he heard groans coming from behind a door to what he had always assumed was a lumber-room, although he had never seen it himself. Astonished, he stopped and listened again to make sure he was not mistaken; for a while it was quiet, but then he heard the groans again. His first thought was to call one of the messengers in case a witness was needed; but then he was gripped by such overwhelming curiosity that he just wrenched the door open. It was, as he had correctly suspected, a lumber-room. Inside, useless out-of-date printed documents and empty earthenware inkwells lay scattered about behind the door. But in the room itself stood three men, stooping in the confined space. A candle, stuck on a shelf, provided some light. 'What's going on here?' demanded K., who could barely control his agitation, though he kept his voice down. One of the men, who was evidently in control of the other two, caught K.'s attention first; he was dressed in some sort of dark leather costume that left his neck open to his chest and his arms bare. He did not reply, but the other two cried: 'Sir! We're going to be flogged because you complained to the examining magistrate about us.'

It was only then that K. realised that they were in fact the guards Franz and Willem, and that the third man was holding a cane to beat them with. 'Why,' said K., staring at them, 'I did not complain; I only said what had happened in my room. And after all, your behaviour left something to be desired.' 'Sir,' said Willem, while behind him Franz was obviously trying to shield himself from the third man, 'if you knew how badly we were paid, you would not judge us so harshly. I have a family to feed, and Franz here was going to get married. You try to make some money as best you can, but you can't do it just by working, however hard you work. I was tempted by your fine linen; of course guards are forbidden to behave like that, it wasn't right, but it's traditional that the clothes belong to the guards, it's always been like that, believe me. It's understandable, too – what's the importance of such things to anyone who's unfortunate enough to be arrested? But then, if he mentions it publicly, punishment is bound to follow.'

'I knew nothing of all this, and I did not once demand that you should be punished; for me it was a matter of principle.' 'Franz,' said Willem to the other guard, 'didn't I tell you the gentleman didn't ask for us to be punished? He's telling us he didn't even know we were going to be punished.' 'Don't be swayed by that kind of talk,' said the third man to K., 'the punishment is as just as it is inevitable.' 'Don't listen to him,' said Willem, breaking off only to lift his hand to his mouth when it was caught by a slash of the cane, 'we are only being punished because you complained about us. Otherwise nothing would have happened to us even if they had found out what we had done. Do you call that justice? Both of us, especially me, had done good service as guards for a long time – you must admit yourself that from the authorities' point of view, we guarded you well. We had good promotion prospects, and would certainly have been made floggers like this man, who happened to be lucky enough not to be accused by anyone, for complaints like that are really very rare. And now, Sir, we've lost everything, our careers are finished, we shall have to do much more menial work than being guards, and on top of that we are now getting these dreadfully painful floggings.'

'Can the cane be so painful, then?' asked K., examining the cane which the flogger was swishing in front of him. 'We shall have to strip naked,' said Willem. 'I see,' said K., looking at the flogger; he was sunburnt like a sailor, with a fierce, healthy face. 'Is there no way these two can be spared their flogging?' he asked him. 'No,' said the flogger, smiling and shaking his head. 'Take off your clothes!' he ordered the guards. To K. he said: 'You mustn't believe all they say, they're already a bit witless because they're afraid of the flogging. What this one told you about his possible career' – he pointed to Willem – 'is just ridiculous. Look how fat he is; the first strokes will be lost in his fat. Do you know how he got so fat? He has a habit of eating the breakfast of anyone he arrests. Didn't he eat your breakfast? There you are, I told you. But a man with a belly like that can never become a flogger, it's quite out of the question.' 'There are floggers like that,' Willem insisted as he unfastened his belt. 'No,' said the flogger, striking him such a blow on the shoulder that he winced. 'Don't listen to us, just get undressed.'

'I'd pay you well if you let them go,' said K., and without looking at the flogger – these transactions are best conducted with eyes averted by both parties – he took out his wallet. 'And then I suppose you'll report me as well,' said the flogger, 'and get me flogged too. Oh no.' 'Do be reasonable,' said K., 'if I had wanted these two to be punished, I wouldn't be trying to get them off now; I could just shut this door behind me, refuse to see or hear anything further and go home. But I'm not doing that, on the contrary I'm seriously interested in freeing them; if I had had any idea they were going to be punished, or even that they could be punished, I would never have mentioned their names. Because I don't hold them guilty at all, it's the system and the higher officials that are guilty.' 'That's right!' cried the guards, who were immediately given a stroke of the cane across their bare backs. 'If you were about to flog one of the senior judges,' said K., holding down the cane just as it was about to be raised again, 'I promise you I wouldn't stop you; far from it, I would even pay you to do it more vigorously.' 'What you say sounds plausible,' said the flogger, 'but I'm not going to be bribed. I am employed to do the flogging, so that's what I do.'

The guard Franz who, perhaps hoping that K.'s intervention might work out in their favour, had so far been quite reticent, now went to the door, dressed only in his trousers, knelt down, hanging on K.'s arm, and whispered: 'If you can't manage to get a reprieve for both of us, then at least try to get me off. Willem is older than me, he's far less sensitive, and he has had a light flogging before, a few years ago. But I have never been disgraced before, and I was only led astray by Willem, who is my teacher for better or worse. Downstairs outside the bank my poor fiancée is waiting to see what happens. I'm so miserably ashamed.' He dried his face, which was streaming with tears, on K.'s coat. 'I'm not waiting any longer,' said the flogger. He seized the cane with both hands and lashed out at Franz, while Willem cowered in a corner and watched furtively without daring to turn his head. Franz uttered a scream that seemed not to be that of a human being, but to come from an ill-treated instrument. It rose in a single unwavering note and filled the whole corridor; it must have been heard through the whole building. 'Don't scream,' cried K., unable to contain himself. On tenterhooks, he looked in the direction from which the messengers must surely appear, and bumped into Franz, not violently, but hard enough to knock the dazed man to the ground, where he clawed the floor feverishly with his hands. But he could not escape the blows, and the cane reached him even as he lay on the floor; as he writhed under it, the tip swished up and down in regular strokes.

And now, some way off, a messenger did appear, with another a few paces behind him. K. had quickly slammed the door, gone over to one of the windows overlooking the courtyard and opened it. The screams had stopped completely. To prevent the messengers coming any closer, K. called: 'It's me!' 'Good evening, Sir,' came the reply. 'Is anything the matter?' 'No, no,' replied K., 'it's only a dog howling in the courtyard.' When the messengers still did not move away, he added: 'You can go back to your work.' In order to avoid having to speak to them, he leaned out of the window. After a while he looked back down the corridor again, and they had gone. But K. stayed at the window; he did not dare to go back into the lumber-room, and he did not want to go home either. He was looking down into a small square courtyard with offices all round; all the windows were now dark, only the upper ones caught the reflection of the moon.

K. strained his eyes to see into a dark corner of the courtyard where some handcarts had been stacked together. It distressed him that he had not been able to stop the flogging, but it was not his fault that he had not succeeded; if Franz had not screamed – of course, it must have hurt very much, but at crucial moments one has to control oneself – if he had not screamed, then K., in all probability at least, would have found some way of dissuading the flogger. If all the lower officials were menials, why should the flogger, who held the most inhumane post, be an exception? K. had noticed how his eyes had lit up at the sight of the banknote; clearly he had only carried on with the flogging in earnest because he wanted to increase the amount of the bribe. And K. would have increased it – he really had wanted to free the guards; since he had already embarked on a battle against this corrupt legal system, it went without saying that he should have intervened at this point. But of course that became impossible the moment Franz had started to scream. K. could not let the messengers and perhaps all kinds of other people come and interrupt him in his dealings with those creatures in the lumber-room; no one could really expect that of him. If that was what he had intended, it would almost have been easier to take his own clothes off and offer himself to the flogger in place of the guards. But in any case, the flogger would certainly not have agreed to this substitution, because he would have seriously violated his duty without any advantage to himself, and would probably have made things far worse because surely no court employee could lay a hand on K. as long as he was under investigation – though of course, special conditions might apply here too. At all events, K. had had no alternative but to slam the door, though this had by no means put him out of danger. It was regrettable that he had bumped into Franz; only his agitation could excuse that.

In the distance he heard the messengers' footsteps; he did not want them to see him, so he shut the window and went towards the main staircase. At the door of the lumber-room he stopped and listened; it was all quiet. The man could have flogged the guards to death, they were completely at his mercy. K. had already put out his hand towards the door-handle, but then withdrew it. He could not help anyone now, and the messengers might appear at any moment; but he vowed that he would bring the matter up and, as far as it lay in his power, would see that the truly guilty parties, the senior officials, not one of whom had dared to show his face, were suitably punished. As he went down the steps outside the bank he carefully observed all the passers-by, but even in the wider vicinity there was no sign of a young woman who might be waiting for someone. Franz's claim that his fiancée was waiting for him turned out to be a lie, albeit an excusable one, which was only designed to arouse greater sympathy.

The next day K. could still not get the guards out of his mind; he could not concentrate on his work, and in order to get it done he had to stay in the office rather later than the previous day. As he left, he once again passed the lumber-room, and opened the door as if by habit. He had expected nothing but darkness; but what he saw unsettled him completely. Everything was exactly as he had found it when he had opened the door the evening before: the papers and inkwells just behind the door, the flogger with his cane, the still quite naked guards, the candle on the shelf – and the guards started to lament, shouting 'Sir!' K. immediately slammed the door, and then banged it with his fist as if that would shut it more firmly. Almost in tears, he rushed to where the messengers were working quietly at their duplicating machines; they stopped, astonished. 'It's high time the lumber-room was cleared out!' he shouted. 'We're up to our ears in filth!' The messengers were willing to do it the next day. K. nodded; he had intended to tell them to do it there and then, but he could not force them to – it was too late in the evening. He sat down for a moment to keep them company for a while, and shuffled through some papers as if he were checking them, then, seeing that the messengers would not dare to leave at the same time as himself, he went home exhausted, his mind quite blank.

CHAPTER SIX
The Uncle – Leni

One afternoon, when K. was working hard to catch the post, his uncle Karl, a small landowner from the country, pushed his way into the room past two messengers who were bringing papers for him. K. was not too alarmed to see him; for some time he had been dreading the thought of a visit from his uncle. He was bound to come – K. had been quite certain of that for a month. He had already imagined how he would arrive, slightly stooped, his Panama hat crushed in his left hand, his right hand extended long before he rushed over and held it out across the desk with illconsidered haste, knocking over everything in his way. His uncle was always in a hurry, for he was haunted by the unhappy notion that every time he visited the capital – and he only ever came for the day – he had to complete all the business he had set himself. On top of this, he could not miss any opportunity of a chance conversation, a business transaction, or any form of entertainment. In all this K. was under a particular obligation to his uncle, who had been his guardian; he had to help him in every possible way, and in addition he was expected to put him up for the night. He called him 'the Spectre from the Country'.

As soon as they had exchanged greetings – K. invited him to sit in an easy chair, but he had no time for that – he asked

K. if he could speak to him privately for a moment. 'It is essential,' he said, gulping painfully, 'it is essential for my peace of mind.' K. at once sent the messengers out of the room with instructions to let no one in. 'What is this I hear, Josef?' cried his uncle when they were alone; he sat down on the desk, and to make himself more comfortable stuffed a sheaf of papers under him without looking at them. K. said nothing; he knew what was coming, but, suddenly released from the strain of his work, he surrendered for the moment to a pleasant weariness and looked out of the window to the far side of the street. From where he was sitting he could see only a small triangular section, a stretch of blank house wall between two shop windows. 'You're gazing out of the window!' cried his uncle, throwing up his arms, 'for heaven's sake, Josef, answer me! Is it true, can it be true?' 'Dear Uncle,' said K., shaking himself out of his reverie, 'I have no idea what you're driving at.' 'Josef,' said his uncle reprovingly, 'you have always told the truth, as far as I know. Should I take what you've just said as a bad sign?' 'I can imagine what you mean,' said K. obediently, 'you must have heard about my trial.' 'That's right,' replied his uncle, nodding slowly, 'I have heard about your trial.' 'Who told you, then?' asked K. 'Erna wrote to me,' said his uncle. 'She has not seen you – I'm sorry to say you don't have very much to do with her – but still she got to know about it. I had her letter today, and of course I came here right away. For no other reason, but that seems reason enough to me. I can read out what she says about you.'

He took the letter from his wallet. 'Here it is. She writes: "I have not seen Josef for a long time. Last week I went to the bank, but Josef was too busy to see me. I waited for nearly an hour, but then I had to go home because I had a piano lesson. I would have liked to talk to him, perhaps I shall have an opportunity before long. He sent me a big box of chocolates for my birthday, which was very kind and thoughtful of him. I had forgotten to write to you about it, I only just remembered when you asked. You see, chocolates disappear very quickly in the boarding school, you hardly know you've been given them before they're gone. But about Josef – there's something else I wanted to tell you. As I said, I was not allowed to see him at the bank because he was in a meeting with a gentleman. After I had waited quietly for a while, I asked one of the attendants whether the meeting would last very long. He said it might well, because it probably concerned the case being brought against Herr K. I asked him what sort of case it was, he must be mistaken; but he said he was not mistaken. Proceedings were under way, and they were serious, but he did not know any more about it. For his part, he would like to help Herr K., for he was a good and fair man; but he did not know how to go about it, and he wished that some influential people would take up his case. This, he said, would surely happen, and it would all turn out well; but for the time being things were not going well – he could tell that from Herr K.'s mood. Of course, I did not attach much importance to what he said, and tried to reassure the man; I told him not to talk to anyone else about it, and that I thought it was all just gossip. All the same, perhaps it would be as well, dear Father, if you were to look into the matter on your next visit, it will be easy for you to find out more details and, if it should be really necessary, to intervene with the help of some of your important and influential acquaintances. However, should it not be necessary, which is the most likely outcome, it will at least give your daughter the opportunity to embrace you before long, which would give her great pleasure".'

'She's a good child,' said K.'s uncle when he had finished reading, and wiped the tears from his eyes. K. nodded; because of the various upsets of the last few days he had completely forgotten about Erna. He had even forgotten her birthday, and the story about the chocolates was clearly only invented to put him in a good light with his aunt and uncle. It was very touching, and the theatre tickets he intended to send her regularly from now on would certainly not be reward enough; but at the moment he did not feel up to visiting her in her boarding school and holding conversations with a little eighteen-year-old schoolgirl. 'And what do you say to that?' asked his uncle. The letter had made him forget all his haste and agitation, and he seemed to be reading it all over again. 'Yes, Uncle,' said K., 'it is true.' 'True?' cried his uncle. 'What is true? How can it be true? What sort of a case is it? Surely not a criminal case?' 'It is a criminal case,' replied K. 'And you sit here calmly with a criminal case hanging over you?' cried his uncle, whose voice was getting louder. 'The calmer I am, the better it is for the outcome,' said K. wearily, 'there's nothing to fear.'

'That's no comfort!' cried his uncle, 'Josef, my dear Josef, think of yourself, think of your relatives, think of our good name! Until now you have been a credit to us, you cannot disgrace us.' He looked at K. reproachfully from under his eyebrows. 'I don't like your attitude. An innocent man in his right mind who has been accused of a crime doesn't behave like that. Quick, tell me about it so that I can help you. It's a bank matter, I suppose?' 'No,' said K., standing up. 'But you are speaking too loud, dear Uncle, the attendant is probably standing by the door listening to us, and that makes me uncomfortable. We'd better go somewhere else, then I will answer all your questions as far as I can. I know very well that I owe the family an explanation.' 'That's right!' shouted his uncle. 'Quite right, but hurry up, Josef, hurry up!' 'I still have to give some instructions,' said K., and summoned his assistant on the telephone, who appeared a few moments later. In his agitation, his uncle gestured to indicate that K. had called for him, though this was perfectly clear. Standing in front of his desk, K. referred to various documents and explained to him in a low voice what needed to be done in his absence. The young man listened impassively but attentively. At first K.'s uncle stood there glaring and biting his lip nervously; though he was not listening, he gave the impression that he was, which was distracting enough. But then he walked up and down the room and paused every now and then by the window or in front of a picture. Each time he stopped he made some exclamation such as: 'I find it quite incomprehensible!' or: 'Just tell me what's to become of this!' The young man listened calmly to all K.'s instructions as if he did not hear any of this, noted down a few things and left after bowing to K. and his uncle just as the latter turned away to look out of the window and stretched out his arms to clutch at the curtains.

He had scarcely shut the door when the uncle cried: 'At last that clown has gone, now we can go too. At last!' Unfortunately, they reached the entrance hall of the bank, where some officials and attendants were standing around, just as the deputy manager was crossing the hall, and K. could not stop his uncle asking questions about the case. 'So, Josef,' he began, acknowledging the bows of those around him with a casual nod, 'now tell me frankly what sort of a case this is.' K. made a few vague remarks, laughing from time to time; only when they reached the steps outside did he explain to his uncle that he had not wanted to speak openly in front of these people. 'Very well,' said his uncle, 'but talk now.' He listened with his head bowed, taking short, quick puffs at a cigar. 'The main point, Uncle,' said K., 'is that this is not a case that is being tried before an ordinary court.' 'That's bad,' said his uncle. 'Pardon?' said K., looking at him. 'I say that's bad,' repeated his uncle. They were standing on the steps leading down to the street; since the porter seemed to be listening, K. led his uncle away, and they were swallowed up in the busy traffic.

K.'s uncle, who had taken his arm, stopped asking such urgent questions about the case, and for a while they walked on in silence. Finally he asked: 'But how did it happen?' He stopped so suddenly that the people behind him, startled, had to swerve to avoid him. 'Things like that don't happen out of the blue, they take a long time to develop. There must have been some indications; why didn't you write to me? You know I'll do anything for you, in a way I'm still your guardian, and until today I was proud to be. Of course I'll still help you, but now that the trial is under way, that's very difficult. At all events, the best thing for now would be for you to take some leave and come and stay with us in the country. You've lost some weight, I can see that now. In the country you'll get your strength back, that will do you good, because you're going to have a hard time, that's for sure. Besides, that way you will be out of the court's reach to a certain extent. Here they have all sorts of powers they can use against you, which they have to do as a matter of course; but out in the country they have to delegate these powers to others, or get at you by letter or telegraph or telephone. That, of course, is less effective; it may not set you free, but it will give you a breathing space.' 'They might forbid me to leave,' said K., who was beginning to follow his uncle's train of thought. 'I don't think they will do that,' said his uncle thoughtfully, 'they wouldn't lose very much authority if you were to go away.' 'I thought,' said K., taking his uncle's arm to prevent him standing still, 'that you would attach even less importance to the whole thing than I do, and now you are taking it so seriously.' 'Josef,' cried his uncle. He tried to shake him off in order to stop, but K. would not let go. 'You have changed. You always had such a clear mind, why can't you see? Do you want to lose your case? Do you know what that means? It means you will simply be ostracised. It means the whole family will be disgraced, or at least deeply humiliated. Josef, pull yourself together. Your nonchalance is driving me out of my mind. When I look at you, I can almost believe the adage: "With a case like that, it's as good as lost".'

'Dear Uncle,' said K., 'there's no point in either of us getting worked up about it. You don't win a case that way. Give me some credit for my practical experience, just as I have always given you credit for yours, and still do, even when it surprises me. Since you tell me the family would also be made to suffer from this case – for my part, I can't possibly imagine why, but that's by the by – I shall be glad to follow your advice in everything. It's just that I think your plan for going to the country, even for the reasons you give, would be inadvisable, because it would suggest I was running away and suffered from a sense of guilt. What's more, although while I am here I can be followed more closely, I can also give the matter more of my attention.' 'That's true,' said his uncle in a voice that suggested they were at last coming to see each other's point of view, 'I only suggested it because I thought your lack of commitment would jeopardise your case if you stayed here, and I thought it would be better if I acted for you instead. But if you are willing to put all your effort into it, of course that is much better.' 'Then we are agreed,' said K. 'And now have you any suggestion as to what my first step should be?' 'Of course, I shall have to give the matter more thought,' said his uncle, 'you must remember that I've been living in the country almost continuously now for twenty years, and that blunts one's instincts in such things. Over the years I have lost touch with several important people who know more about such matters. You know quite well that I'm rather isolated in the country, but one only realises it at times like this. Your case rather took me by surprise, although strangely enough I guessed it was something of the sort after reading Erna's letter, and when I saw you today I was almost certain. But that is beside the point; the important thing now is not to lose any time.'

Even as he was speaking, he had been standing on tiptoe to hail a cab, and now, as he shouted an address to the driver, he pulled K. after him into the taxi. 'We're going to see Huld, the advocate,' he said, 'he was at school with me. You must have heard of him. No? That's astonishing. He has a huge reputation as a defence lawyer and as an advocate for the poor. But I have particular confidence in him as a person.' 'I'm quite willing to do anything you suggest,' said K., although he felt uneasy at the hasty and urgent way his uncle was treating the matter, and as a defendant he was not very happy to be taken to a poor man's lawyer. 'I didn't know,' he said, 'that one could engage an advocate in a case like this.' 'But of course,' said his uncle, 'that goes without saying. Why not? And now tell me everything that has happened so far, so that I know all about the case.' K. began to tell him. He did not withhold anything; complete candour was the only protest he could make against his uncle's view that his trial was a great disgrace. He only mentioned Fräulein Bürstner's name once quite casually; but that did not detract from his candour, because she had no connection with his case.

As he told his story, he looked out of the window and saw that they were approaching the suburb where the court chambers were situated; he drew his uncle's attention to this, but he did not find the coincidence particularly striking. The cab stopped in front of a darkened house; his uncle rang the bell at the first door on the ground floor. While they were waiting, he bared his big teeth in a smile and whispered: 'Eight o'clock – an unusual time for a client to call, but Huld won't mind.' Through a hatch in the door two large dark eyes appeared, examined the visitors for a while, and disappeared, but the door did not open. K. and his uncle agreed that they had seen the two eyes. 'A new parlour-maid who is afraid of strangers,' said his uncle, and knocked again. Again the eyes appeared; one could almost imagine they looked sad, but perhaps this was only an impression caused by the naked gas flame which burned with a loud hiss just above their heads, but shed little light. 'Open the door!' cried the uncle, banging it with his fist, 'we are friends of the advocate.' 'The advocate is ill,' whispered a voice behind them. In a doorway at the other end of the short passage stood a man in his nightgown who conveyed this information in an extremely quiet voice. The uncle, by now furious because they had had to wait so long, turned round abruptly and cried: 'Ill? He's ill, you say?' He went up to him almost threateningly, as if the man himself were the illness. 'They've opened the door now,' said the man, pointing to the advocate's door. He pulled his nightgown around him and disappeared.

And indeed, the door had been opened; a young woman – K. recognised her dark, slightly protruding eyes – stood in the hall-way in a long white apron, a candle in her hand. 'Open it a bit sooner next time!' said the uncle by way of greeting to the maid, who bobbed a small curtsey. 'Come along, Josef,' he said to K., who pushed slowly past the maid. 'Herr Huld is ill,' she said as the uncle made straight for a door. K. was still staring at the maid, who had turned to lock the front door. She had a round doll's face; not just her pale cheeks and chin, but also her temples and forehead were rounded. 'Josef,' his uncle called again, and asked the maid: 'It's his heart, isn't it?' 'I think so,' said the maid, who had had time to light their way to the door and open it. In a corner of the room where the candle shed no light, a face with a long beard rose from the pillows of a bed. 'Who is it, Leni?' asked the advocate, who was dazzled by the candlelight and did not recognise his visitors. 'It's your old friend Albert,' said K.'s uncle. 'Oh, Albert,' said the advocate, and fell back onto the pillows as if he needed to make no effort for these visitors. 'Are you really in such a bad way?' asked the uncle, sitting down on the edge of the bed. 'I don't think you are. It's a recurrence of your heart trouble, and it will pass as it has before.' 'Perhaps,' said the advocate quietly, 'but it's worse than ever. I find it hard to breathe, I can't get any sleep, and I'm getting weaker by the day.' 'I see,' said the uncle, squashing his Panama on his knee with his large hand. 'That's bad news. Are you getting the right treatment, though? It's so dark and gloomy here. It's a long time since I was here last, but it seemed more cheerful to me then. And your little Missie here doesn't seem very cheerful either, at least she doesn't look it.'

The maid was still standing by the door with the candle, looking at them vaguely; she seemed to be looking at K. rather than at his uncle, even while he was talking about her. K. leaned against a chair that he had pushed up close to her. 'When you are as ill as I am,' said the advocate, 'you need peace and quiet. I don't feel gloomy.' After a pause he added: 'And Leni looks after me well, she's a good girl.' But the uncle was not convinced. He clearly did not think the maid capable of caring for the patient; he made no reply, and followed her with severe looks as she went over to the bed, placed the candle on the bedside table, bent over the sick man and whispered to him as she rearranged his pillows. He almost forgot any consideration for the patient; he stood up and followed her to and fro, and

K. would not have been surprised if he had seized her from behind by her skirt and dragged her away from the bed. K. himself watched it all calmly, indeed the advocate's illness was not entirely unwelcome to him; he had been unable to restrain his uncle's zeal in pursuing his case, and he was now glad to see this zeal diverted without any intervention on his part. Then, perhaps only to annoy the maid, his uncle said: 'Fräulein, please leave us alone for a while, I have a personal matter to discuss with my friend.' The maid, who was bending right over the patient to smooth the bedclothes by the wall, simply turned her head and in a very calm voice, in striking contrast to the uncle who spluttered and ranted in his rage, said: 'You can see, my master is too ill to discuss any matters.'

She had probably only repeated the uncle's words unthinkingly, but even an impartial observer might have taken it as mockery; the uncle of course jumped as if he had been stung. 'Damn you!' he spluttered, somewhat indistinctly in his initial fit of rage. K. was alarmed, although he had expected something of the sort; he rushed over to his uncle with the firm intention of putting his hands over his mouth to silence him. But fortunately the invalid sat up behind the maid, the uncle grimaced as if he had swallowed something disgusting, and then said more calmly: 'Of course, we haven't taken leave of our senses yet. I'm not asking the impossible, otherwise I wouldn't ask. Now leave us, please!' The maid stood at the bed and turned to face the uncle; with one hand, K. fancied, she was stroking the advocate's hand. 'You can say anything in front of Leni,' said the patient with an urgent plea in his voice. 'It's not about me,' said the uncle, 'it's not my secret.' And he turned as if he did not intend to discuss the matter further, but was giving the other time to think it over. 'What is it about, then?' asked the advocate in a frail voice, sinking back into the pillows. 'My nephew,' said the uncle. 'I've brought him with me.' He introduced him: 'Josef K., assistant bank manager.' 'Ah,' said the invalid with more animation, holding out his hand to K., 'forgive me, I didn't notice you. Leave us, Leni,' he said to the maid, who did not protest at all; he gave her his hand as if they were parting for a long time.

'So,' he said at last to the uncle, who, now mollified, had moved closer to him, 'you haven't come to see me because I am ill, you're here on business.' The advocate looked so robust now; it was as if the idea of a visit to his sickbed had enfeebled him earlier. He supported himself all the while on his elbow, which must have been quite a strain, and kept tugging at a strand of hair from the middle of his beard. 'You look better already,' said the uncle, 'now that witch has gone.' He broke off, whispered, 'I'll bet she's listening!' and sprang to the door. But there was no one behind the door, and he returned, not disappointed (for he seemed to think that not listening was an even greater piece of villainy on her part), but certainly annoyed. 'You misjudge her,' said the advocate; but he did not say any more in her defence. Perhaps he wished to suggest that there was no need to defend her. But he continued in a much more sympathetic tone: 'Concerning this affair of your nephew's, I would be only too happy if I had enough strength for this extremely difficult task; I am afraid I may not, but I shall make every effort. If I cannot do it, we could bring in someone else. To be honest with you, I find this case too interesting to be able to resist taking some part in it. If my heart is not up to it, then at least this is a worthy cause in which it can fail completely.'

K. could not understand a word he was saying; he looked at his uncle for an explanation, but he was sitting holding the candle on the bedside table, from which a bottle of medicine had already fallen onto the floor. His uncle nodded at everything the advocate said, agreed with everything, and every now and then looked at K., inviting his agreement too. Had his uncle perhaps already told the advocate about his case? But that was impossible; everything that had happened suggested otherwise. So he said: 'I don't understand . . .' 'Have I perhaps misunderstood you, then?' asked the advocate, just as astonished and embarrassed as K. was. 'Perhaps I was too hasty. What did you want to talk to me about? I thought it was about your case.' 'Of course,' said the uncle, and asked K.: 'Isn't that what you want?' 'Yes, but how can you know anything about me or my case?' asked K. 'Ah,' said the advocate, smiling, 'you see, I am a lawyer, I move in legal circles, where various cases are discussed. And one remembers the more striking ones, especially when they involve the nephew of a friend. Surely there's nothing remarkable about that.' 'What is it you want, then?' K.'s uncle asked him again. 'You're so agitated.' 'So you move in these legal circles?' asked K. 'Yes,' said the advocate. 'You're asking questions like a child,' said his uncle. 'Who should I associate with, if not with my professional colleagues?' added the advocate. It sounded so undeniable that K. did not reply. 'But surely you work at the High Court, not that one in the attic,' was what he wanted to say, but he could not bring himself to say it. 'You must understand,' continued the advocate in a manner that suggested he was explaining, quite unnecessarily and incidentally, something that was perfectly obvious, 'you must understand that I gain considerable advantages for my clients in all sorts of ways from such contacts, though one must be discreet about all that. Of course, just now I am rather hindered by my illness; but I still have visits from good friends at the court and get to hear quite a lot. Perhaps I learn more than many of those who are in the best of health and spend all day at the court. For example, at this very moment I have a visit from a dear friend.'

He pointed to a dark corner of the room. 'Where?' asked K., almost brusquely in his surprise. He looked round him uncertainly; the light shed by the small candle did not reach anywhere near the far wall. Then something did begin to stir over in the corner. By the light of the candle, which K.'s uncle was now holding up, an elderly gentleman could be seen sitting at a small table. He could scarcely have been breathing to have remained unnoticed for so long. Now he reluctantly stood up, clearly unhappy to have their attention drawn to him. It was as if, by flapping his hands like short wings, he wished to fend off all greetings and introductions, as if he had no wish whatever to disturb the others by his presence, and was begging them to allow him to return to the darkness and forget all about him. But this was no longer possible. 'You took us by surprise, you see,' said the advocate by way of explanation, beckoning him to come nearer, which he did slowly, looking around hesitantly, yet with a certain dignity. 'This is the Head of Chambers – oh, forgive me, I have not introduced you. This is my friend Albert K., and this is his nephew Josef K., assistant bank manager – our Head of Chambers, who was kind enough to pay me a visit. The value of such a visit can only be really appreciated by those in the know, who are aware that the Head of Chambers is inundated with work. Well, he came in spite of that, and we were having a quiet talk as far as my weak condition allowed. We had not forbidden Leni to let in any visitors, for we did not expect any, but we both thought we should be left alone. Then you started banging on the door, Albert, so the Head of Chambers moved into a corner with a table and chair; but now it turns out that we might have a matter of mutual interest to discuss – that is, if it is your wish – so we would do well to sit down together.'

'Sir,' he said to the Head of Chambers, inclining his head with an obsequious smile, indicating an armchair by the bed. 'I am afraid I can only stay a few minutes.' said the Head of Chambers affably, settling himself in the armchair and looking at his watch. 'Business calls; all the same, I don't want to miss the opportunity to get to know the friend of a friend.' He gave a slight nod to K.'s uncle, who seemed very pleased with this new acquaintance, but who was by nature unable to express any feelings of obligation and responded to the Head of Chambers' words with a burst of embarrassed but loud laughter. A hideous sight! K. was able to watch all this calmly, for no one had paid any attention to him. Now that he had been given due prominence, the Head of Chambers took the lead in the conversation, as he was evidently used to doing. The advocate, whose initial weakness had perhaps only been designed to get rid of his most recent visitors, listened attentively, his hand cupped to his ear; the uncle, who was holding the candle – he was balancing it on his thigh, and the advocate made frequent anxious glances in his direction – soon got over his shyness and was simply delighted both by the Head of Chambers' conversation and by the delicate flowing gestures that accompanied his words. K., who was leaning on the bed-post, was completely ignored by the Head of Chambers, perhaps deliberately, and served only as an audience for the old gentlemen. In any case, he hardly knew what they were talking about; he was either thinking about the maid and how badly she had been treated by his uncle, or else wondering whether he had seen the Head of Chambers before, perhaps even at the meeting during his first examination. Even if he was mistaken, he would have fitted perfectly into the front row of the assembly, among the elderly gentlemen with straggling beards.

Just then a noise from the hall, as of breaking crockery, made them all stop and listen. 'I'll go and see what it is,' said K., and left the room slowly, as if he were giving the others the chance to stop him. He had scarcely reached the hall and was still holding the door handle, trying to find his bearings in the dark, when he felt a much smaller hand on his own, and the door was gently closed. It was the maid, who had been waiting there for him. 'There's nothing wrong,' she whispered, 'I only threw a plate at the wall to get you out here.' K. said shyly: 'I was thinking about you too.' 'I'm glad,' said the maid, 'come on.' In a few steps they reached a door with frosted glass, which the maid opened for K. 'Do go in,' she said. It was apparently the advocate's study; as far as he could see in the moonlight, which only shed a small patch of light on the floor, it was fitted with heavy, old-fashioned pieces of furniture. 'Over here,' said the maid, pointing to a dark brown bench with a carved wooden back. K. sat down and continued to look round the room. It was a large, high room; the advocate's poorer clients must have felt lost in it. K. imagined them shuffling up to the massive desk with short, timid steps. But then he forgot about them and had eyes only for the maid, who sat close next to him, almost pushing him against the arm of the bench.

'I thought,' said the maid, 'I wouldn't have to call you out here; I thought you would come of your own accord. It was strange; when you first came in you stared at me all the time, and then you made me wait. Call me Leni, by the way,' she added quickly and abruptly, as if she had no time to lose. 'Certainly,' said K., 'but I can easily explain why I acted so oddly. Firstly, I had to listen to those two old men chattering, and I couldn't walk out of the room for no reason; and secondly, I'm not a forward person, in fact, I'm shy, and you, Leni, didn't look as if you were to be had just like that.' 'That's not it,' said Leni, draping her arm over the back of the bench and looking at K., 'you didn't like me, and you probably still don't like me.' 'It wouldn't mean much if I only liked you,' said K. evasively. 'Oh?' she said, smiling. K.'s remark and her brief reply seemed to give her the upper hand, so K. said nothing for a while. By now he had grown used to the darkness in the room, and he could make out various details of the furnishings. He noticed in particular a large picture hanging to the right of the door, and leaned forward to see it better. It was a portrait of a man in a judge's gown, who sat enthroned on a raised gilded chair; the gold shone out of the canvas. What was unusual about the portrait was that this judge was not sitting there in a calm and dignified posture, but was pressing his left arm firmly against the back and side of the chair, while his right arm was quite free; but that hand grasped the arm of the chair, as if at any moment he would jump up with a violent and perhaps furious gesture to make some decisive judgement or even to pronounce sentence. One could picture the accused standing at the foot of the steps of which the topmost, covered with a yellow carpet, could be seen in the picture.

'Perhaps that is my judge,' said K., pointing at the picture. 'I know him,' said Leni, also looking at the portrait, 'he often comes here. It was painted when he was young, but he can never have looked anything like his portrait, because he's a tiny little man. He had himself painted very tall, he's insanely vain like all of them here. But I'm vain, too, and I'm very unhappy you don't like me.' K. did not reply to this last remark, but simply put his arm around Leni and drew her close to him. She said nothing, and laid her head on his shoulder. Returning to the previous subject, he said: 'What sort of position does he hold?' 'He's an examining magistrate,' she said; she took K.'s hand, which was round her waist, and played with his fingers. 'Just another examining magistrate,' said K. in disappointment, 'the senior officials stay out of sight. But he's sitting on a high court bench.' 'That's all for show,' said Leni, bending her face over K.'s hand, 'actually he is sitting on a kitchen chair covered with an old horse-blanket. But must you always be thinking about your trial?' she added slowly. 'No, not at all,' said K., 'I probably don't think about it enough.' 'That's not the mistake you're making,' said Leni, 'you're too stubborn, or so I've heard.' 'Who told you that?' asked K. He could feel her body against him, and looked down at her thick, tightly-plaited dark hair. 'I'd be giving too much away if I told you that,' she answered. 'Please don't ask me for names, but do try to correct your mistake. Don't be so stubborn, you can't defend yourself against this court, you have to admit your guilt. Take the first opportunity to admit it. Until you do, you'll have no chance of being cleared, none at all. But even that is not possible without help from someone else, but you mustn't worry about that, because I'll help you.'

'You know a lot about this court and the tricks you have to use,' said K. She was pressing against him too heavily, so he lifted her onto his knee. 'That's better,' she said, settling onto his knee while she smoothed her skirt and adjusted her blouse. Then she clasped both hands about his neck, leaned back and gave him a long look. 'And if I don't make an admission – can you help me then?' he asked tentatively. I'm taking on female helpers, he thought in amazement; first Fräulein Bürstner, then the court attendant's wife, and now this little sick-nurse who seems to have taken a fancy to me. She's sitting on my knee as if that were the only proper place for her! 'No,' replied Leni, 'then I couldn't help you. But you don't want my help at all, you're not interested, you are stubborn and won't be persuaded.' After a while she asked: 'Do you have a girlfriend?' 'No,' said K. 'Go on,' she said. 'Actually, yes,' said K. 'Just think – I told you I didn't, and yet I'm actually carrying her photograph on me.' At Leni's request he showed her a picture of Elsa and, crouching on his knee, she examined it. It was a snapshot which had been taken just as Elsa had finished whirling round in a dance as she often did in the wine bar; the folds of her skirt were still flying round her as she pirouetted, she had put her hands on her broad hips, and with her head thrown back was smiling as she looked to one side. It was not possible to tell from the photograph who she was smiling at.

'She's very tightly corseted,' said Leni, pointing to where she thought this was visible. I don't like her, she's clumsy and coarse. But perhaps she's gentle and kind to you, I can see that from the picture. Big hefty girls like that are often kind and gentle, they can't be anything else. But would she make sacrifices for you? ' 'No,' said K., 'she isn't kind and gentle, and she wouldn't make sacrifices for me either. In fact, I haven't even examined her picture as closely as you have.' 'So she doesn't mean very much to you at all,' said Leni. 'She isn't your girlfriend, then.' 'Yes, she is,' said K., 'I'm not going back on what I said.' 'Well, even if she is your girlfriend at the moment,' said Leni, 'you wouldn't miss her very much if you lost her, or changed her for someone else like me, for example.' 'Certainly,' said K. with a smile, 'that's possible, but she has one great advantage over you; she knows nothing about my trial, and even if she did, she wouldn't give it a thought. She wouldn't try to persuade me to give in.'

'That's no advantage,' said Leni. 'If that's the only advantage she has over me, I shan't be discouraged. Does she have a physical defect?' 'A physical defect?' asked K. 'Yes,' said Leni, 'you see, I've got a small defect, look.' She splayed the ring finger and middle finger of her right hand; the skin between them almost reached the top joint of her short fingers. In the darkness K. did not at first notice what she was trying to show him, so she guided his hand to let him feel it. 'What a freak of nature!' said K. After he had examined her hand all over, he added: 'What a pretty little claw!' Leni watched with something like pride as K. opened and closed her two fingers over and over again in amazement, until finally he kissed them lightly and let them go. 'Oh!' she cried at once, 'you kissed me!' Her mouth wide open, she clambered up quickly and kneeled in his lap. K. looked up at her, almost dismayed. Now that she was close to him she gave off a bitter, enticing smell like pepper; she drew his head towards her, bent over him, bit and kissed his neck, and even took his hair between her teeth. 'You've swapped her for me!' she cried from time to time. 'See, I've taken her place now!' Her knee slipped, and with a small cry she almost fell onto the carpet. K. held her tight to stop her falling, and was pulled down towards her. 'Now you belong to me!' she said.

'Here is the house key, come whenever you like,' were her last words, and a misdirected kiss landed on the back of his neck as he left. A light drizzle was falling when he emerged from the front door; he was about to step out into the middle of the street to see whether he could catch a glimpse of Leni at the window, when his uncle jumped out of a car waiting outside the house, which K. in his distraction had not noticed. He seized K. by the arms and pushed him against the front door as if he wanted to nail him to it. 'Wretched boy!' he cried. 'How could you do that? Your case was going well, and now you've done it terrible harm. You crawl into a corner with that dirty little creature, who in any case is obviously the advocate's mistress, and you're away for hours. You don't even look for an excuse, you don't try to hide anything; no, you're quite open about it, you run after her and spend your time with her. And meanwhile we're sitting there together, your uncle who is doing his best to help you, the advocate whose support you need, and above all the Head of Chambers, that distinguished man who is actually in charge of your case at this stage. We're trying to discuss how best to help you; I have to handle the advocate carefully, he has to do the same with the Head of Chambers, and you have every reason to support me, at least. Instead of which you stay away. In the end there was no hiding it. Well, these are polite, clever men; they don't mention it, they spare my feelings, but in the end even they can't keep up the pretence, and since they can't talk about it, they say nothing. We sit there in silence for several minutes, and listen to see whether you are finally going to come back; but no. In the end the Head of Chambers, who had stayed for longer than he had intended, stands up and takes his leave. It's clear he feels sorry for me, but can't do anything to help me; then he shows extraordinary kindness by waiting for a while at the door, then he goes. Of course I was glad he had gone; I could hardly breathe. And all this affected the advocate far more, ill as he is; the good man could hardly speak when I left. You have probably contributed to his total collapse and hastened the death of a man you depend on. And then you leave me, your uncle, frantic with worry, waiting here for hours in the rain. Just feel my coat, I'm wet through!'

CHAPTER SEVEN

The Advocate – the Manufacturer – the Painter

One winter morning – outside in the gloom snow was falling – K. was sitting in his office. Although it was still early, he was extremely tired. In order not to be disturbed, by the junior clerks at least, he had instructed his attendant to let none of them in as he was busy with important work. But instead of working he twisted and turned in his chair, slowly rearranged a few objects on his desk, then, without realising it, let his whole arm rest on the desk-top and sat motionless, his head bowed.

The thought of his trial never left him now. He had often considered whether it would be best if he were to write out a plea in his defence and submit it to the court. He would include a short account of his life; for every event of any importance he would explain why he had acted as he did, he would state whether in his present opinion that course of action was commendable or reprehensible, and would put forward reasons for his judgement. The advantages of submitting such a plea, rather than simply being defended by an advocate who was in any case not above criticism, could not be doubted. K. had no idea what the advocate was doing; not very much at any rate, because he had not sent for K. for a whole month now, and at none of his earlier interviews had K. been under the impression that this man could achieve very much for him. Especially since he had hardly asked him any questions – and there were so many questions to ask. Asking questions was the whole point. K. felt that he himself could ask all the necessary questions; the advocate, however, instead of putting questions, either talked himself or sat in silence opposite him, bending forward slightly over his desk, presumably because he was hard of hearing, pulling at a hair from the depths of his beard, and gazing at the carpet – perhaps at the very spot where K. had lain with Leni. Now and then he cautioned K. with empty words of warning, like those one gives to children, useless and tedious words for which K. resolved not to pay a penny in the final account.

When the advocate thought he had humiliated K. sufficiently, he would usually begin to encourage him a little; he would tell him that he had won, or partially won, many similar cases. Cases which, even if they were not actually as difficult as this one, had on the face of it been even more hopeless. He had a list of these cases here in a drawer – he tapped at one of the drawers of his desk – but unfortunately he could not show them to him, they were official files, and confidential. Even so, K. would of course benefit from the great experience he had accumulated from all these cases. Naturally, he had started work at once, and the first submission was almost ready; this was most important, because the first impression made by the defence often determined the whole course of the proceedings. Unfortunately, it sometimes happened – it was his duty to remind K. – that the first submissions were not read in court at all. They were simply filed away, which showed that in the first instance, questioning and observing the accused was more important than any written evidence. If the defendant insists, before the final judgement is made, and after all the evidence has been assembled, they will additionally examine all the files in their proper order, including of course the first submission. Unfortunately, however, even this was not always the case; usually the first submission would be mislaid or completely lost, and even if it was preserved until the end of the trial, it was hardly ever read, or so the advocate had heard it rumoured, at least.

This was all regrettable, but not wholly unjustified. K. should also bear in mind that the proceedings were not public; if the court thinks it necessary, they can be made public, but the law did not stipulate that they should. It followed from this that all court documents, and above all the indictment, were not available to the accused or to his defence, and so there was no means of knowing in general, or at least in particular, how the first submission should address the charges, since only by accident could it contain material bearing on the case. Only later could effective and pertinent submissions of evidence be prepared, once the separate charges, and the grounds for these charges, emerged more clearly, or could be inferred, during the examination of the defendant. Under these conditions the defence is of course in a difficult and most unfavourable position. But that, too, is intentional; for the defence is not actually sanctioned by the law, only tolerated, and there is some controversy as to whether the relevant passage in the statutes can be interpreted even as tolerating it.

So strictly speaking, there are no advocates who are recognised by the court; all those who appear before this court are basically only hole-in-the-corner advocates. This, of course, casts the whole profession in a very disreputable light, and when K. next went to the court chambers, he could visit the advocates' room to see for himself. He would probably be horrified at the people who gathered there. The low, cramped room allocated to them would be enough to show the contempt in which the court held these people. The only light comes from a small skylight, which is so high up that anyone who wants to look out of it has to find a colleague who will let him climb onto his back; he also has to put up with the smoke from a nearby chimney that gets up his nose and blackens his face. Just as another example of the conditions here, for more than a year there has been a hole in the floor of this room, not big enough to fall into, but big enough to put one's leg through. The advocates' room is in the upper attic; if anyone does put his leg through the hole, it goes through the ceiling of the corridor below, just where the clients are waiting.

The advocates call these conditions disgraceful, and that is no exaggeration. Complaints to the administration have not the slightest effect; but the advocates are strictly forbidden to make any changes to the room at their own expense. And yet there is a reason why the advocates are treated like this: to exclude the defence as far as possible – everything should be left to the defendant. Not a bad point of view in principle; but it would be quite wrong to conclude that in this court the defendant does not need an advocate. On the contrary, in no other court is an advocate as essential as in this one; the proceedings are not only kept secret from the public, but also from the defendant – only as far as this is possible, of course, but it is possible to a very great extent. For the defendant has no access to the court documents, and it is very difficult to infer from the hearings what they might contain, especially for the defendant, who is inhibited and has all sorts of worries to distract him.

This, explained the advocate, was where the defence comes in. Defence counsel are not generally allowed to attend the hearings, and so immediately after each one, if possible at the door of the courtroom, they must question the defendant closely about the hearing and extract any information helpful to the defence from these often very confused reports. But this is not the most important thing, for there is not much to be learned from this, though of course here, as everywhere else, a competent person can learn more than others. The most important thing is still the advocate's personal connections, these are the most valuable factors in the defence. Now, as K. had no doubt gathered from his own experiences, the very lowest echelons of the court are not quite perfect; corrupt officials who neglected their duties could be said to subvert the proper functioning of the court.

This was where the majority of advocates seized their chance; at this level bribery and gossip flourished, indeed, there were even cases when documents had been stolen, at least in earlier times. It could not be denied that these methods achieved, at least for a while, surprisingly good results for the defendant, and these minor advocates boasted about their success and attracted more clients; but this had no effect on the progress of the trial, and even jeopardised it. Only reputable personal connections had any real value – that is, connections with higher officials, which means, of course, with higher officials of the lower ranks. Only in this way could the progress of the trial be influenced, at first perhaps imperceptibly, but later more and more decisively. Of course, only a few advocates could do this, and in this respect K. had made a fortunate choice. Perhaps only one or two advocates could boast such good connections as Dr Huld, and they paid no attention to that crowd in the advocate's room, in fact they had nothing to do with them. But their relations with the court officials were all the closer. Dr Huld did not even have to go to court and hang about in the magistrates' waiting-rooms on the chance that they might appear and, depending on their mood, gain some no doubt illusory advantage, or perhaps not even that. No – K. had seen it for himself – the officials, some of them quite senior, came to see him themselves and willingly gave him information, either openly or at least easily inferred; they discussed the next stages of the case, indeed they were even open to persuasion in individual cases and glad to adopt someone else's view.

And yet in this respect especially they could not be trusted too far, however firmly they expressed their new judgement in favour of the defence, because they might go straight back to their chambers and draw up a court ruling for the next day which affirmed just the opposite, and which might be even more severe on the defendant than the original judgement they claimed to have abandoned completely. Of course, nothing could be done about that, for what they had said in private was only said in private and could not be used in public, even if the defence were not in any case obliged to make every effort to retain the favour of these gentlemen. On the other hand it was also true that these gentlemen did not communicate with the defence (and they communicated, of course, only with expert defence counsel) simply out of friendship or kind-heartedness, but rather because in a certain sense they were also dependent on the defence. It was this that showed up the drawbacks of a legal system that had established the secrecy of the courts from the very beginning. The officials have no contact with the public at large; they are well equipped to deal with ordinary run-of-the-mill cases, which run along well-worn lines and only require small adjustments now and again. But confronted with very simple cases as well as particularly difficult ones, they are often at a loss. Because they are forever bound up in their laws, day and night, they do not have a proper understanding of human relationships, and in such cases that is quite essential.

Then they come to an advocate for advice, with an attendant behind them carrying the files that are otherwise so secret. At this very window one could have seen many of these men, among them those one might least expect, gazing despondently out into the street while he, the advocate, studied the documents on his desk in order to give them some sound advice. It was on occasions such as these, moreover, that one could tell how uncommonly seriously these gentlemen took their profession, and how they fell into deep despair when they came across obstacles which by their very nature they could not cope with. Their position was in no way an easy one; one would do them an injustice to think it was. The ranks of the court hierarchy were endless, and even an initiate could not grasp it in its entirety. Generally, court proceedings were kept secret from minor officials, so they could hardly ever wholly follow the cases they were dealing with as they progressed; court matters came to their notice without their knowing where they came from, and continued without their knowing how or where. So any knowledge that might be gained from studying the separate stages of a trial, the final verdict and the reasons for it, was all lost to these officials. They were allowed only to deal with the particular stage of a trial that is designated for them by the law, and in most cases they know less about its further progress, that is about the results of their own work, than the defence, which as a rule stays in touch with the accused almost until the end of the case. So in this area, too, the officials can glean valuable information from the defence.

Bearing all this in mind, said the advocate, could K. be surprised that the officials were so irritable and – as everyone had experienced – sometimes treated the clients insolently? All officials were in a state of agitation, even when they appeared calm. Of course, the lesser advocates in particular had to put up with this. For example, the following story had the ring of truth: an elderly official, a kind, quiet man, had worked continuously day and night on a difficult case that had been made particularly complicated by the submissions of an advocate – these officials really are hard-working, more than anyone else. Well, towards morning, after twenty-four hours of probably not very profitable work, he went to his front door, hid behind it, and threw every advocate who tried to come in down the stairs. The advocates gathered at the foot of the staircase and discussed what they should do. On the one hand they had no actual right to be admitted, and so they could scarcely take legal action against him – as I have already mentioned, they must be careful not to antagonise the officials; on the other hand, however, every day not spent in court is a day lost for them, and it was most important that they should be let in. In the end they agreed to tire the old gentleman out. Again and again an advocate was sent running up the stairs and, while putting up all possible, albeit passive, resistance, was thrown back down again. This went on for about an hour, when the old gentleman, who was in any case already tired out by working through the night, became exhausted and went back into his chambers. Those below could not believe it at first, and sent someone up to look behind the door to see that there was really no one there. Only then did they go in, and probably did not even dare to complain.

You see, the advocates – and even the most junior ones have at least some insight into court matters – have not the slightest wish to introduce or implement any improvements, whereas it is notable that almost every defendant, even quite simple people, will start thinking up suggestions for improvements as soon as their case gets under way, and thus often waste time and energy that could have been better expended on other things. The only proper thing to do is to come to terms with things as they are. Even if it were possible to improve some details – but that is an absurd notion – then at best one would achieve something that might affect future cases; but one would do immeasurable harm to one's own case by attracting the attention of officials who are always ready for revenge. Just don't draw attention to yourself! Keep quiet, however much it goes against the grain! Try to understand that this huge legal body is, as it were, forever in a state of balance; by making changes to one's own situation, it is possible to lose one's footing and come to grief, whereas the whole system can easily compensate for such a minor disturbance by making an adjustment elsewhere and so remain unchanged, for everything is interrelated. Indeed, it is more likely that as a result the system will become more impenetrable, more vigilant, even more severe, even more cruel. So one should leave things to the advocates and not interfere.

Recriminations, the advocate went on, were not much use, especially when one could not fully explain the reasons for them; but it had to be said that K.'s behaviour towards the Head of Chambers had greatly jeopardised his case. This influential man might as well be removed from the list of those who could help K.; it was clear he was deliberately ignoring even the most casual references to K.'s case. In some matters the officials were just like children; often they could be so offended by trivialities (though unfortunately K.'s behaviour could not be classed as such) that they would stop speaking even to old friends, would turn away when they met them, and would do everything they could to obstruct them. But then, unexpectedly and for no particular reason, some small joke that one made because everything seemed hopeless would make them laugh, and they would be reconciled. It was at one and the same time difficult and easy to handle them; there were scarcely any basic principles for dealing with them, and sometimes one could not imagine that an average lifetime's experience would be enough to learn how to achieve anything.

Indeed, there were gloomy times, such as everyone experiences, when one thought nothing whatever had been achieved, when it seemed that the only successful cases were those that were destined to succeed from the start, as they would have done without any assistance, while all the others were lost in spite of all one's running about, all one's efforts, and all the apparent minor triumphs that one was so pleased with. At such times nothing seemed certain any more, and one had to admit that some cases that were in themselves going quite well were actually thrown off course by one's own intervention. Even that could give one some sense of achievement – but that was all one was left with. Advocates were especially prone to such moods – and they were of course just moods, nothing more – when a case they had been conducting satisfactorily for some time was suddenly taken out of their hands. That was probably the worst thing that could happen to an advocate. He would not be removed from the case by the accused, that would never happen; a defendant who had instructed a certain advocate was obliged to stay with him, come what may. How could a defendant who had accepted counsel possibly manage on his own? That did not happen; but sometimes it could be that the case took a turn in a direction beyond the scope of the advocate. The case, the defendant, and everything else was simply withdrawn from the advocate, and then even his best contacts with officials were of no help, because they knew nothing themselves. The case had simply reached a stage where no more help might be given, it was being dealt with by inaccessible courts, where even the advocate could not reach the defendant. Then one could come home one day and find on one's desk all the submissions one had made in the case with such labour and such high hopes; they had all been returned because they could not be transferred to the stage the case had now reached, they had become worthless scraps of paper. But the case was not necessarily lost for all that, not by any means, or at least there was no compelling reason for this assumption; it was simply that one knew nothing further about the case, nor would one be able to find out any more about it.

Fortunately however, the advocate assured him, such cases were exceptional, and even if K.'s case were one of them, it was for the time being far from reaching that stage. There was still plenty of scope for the help of an advocate, and K. could rest assured that it would be used to his advantage. As he had said, the plea had not yet been submitted, but there was time enough for that; the preliminary discussions with the relevant officials were much more important, and they had already taken place. With varying degrees of success, he had to admit quite frankly. It was much better not to reveal any details for the time being, for these could have an undesirable effect on K.; his hopes might be raised unduly, or he might become over-anxious. The advocate could only say this much: some had spoken very favourably and had expressed great willingness to help, while others had been less favourable, though they had by no means refused their support. So the result was on the whole very gratifying; but one should not draw any particular conclusions from this, since all preliminary discussions began in a similar fashion and it was during the course of further developments, and only then, that the value of these early discussions would emerge. At all events, nothing had been lost, and if in spite of everything the Head of Chambers could be won over – various steps had already been taken to achieve this – then the whole affair, as surgeons say, would be 'a clean wound', and one could await further developments with confidence.

The advocate had an inexhaustible fund of such pronouncements, which were repeated at every visit. There was always some progress, but the exact nature of this progress could never be divulged. Work continued on the first submission, but it was always unfinished; this usually turned out at the next visit to be a great advantage, because these last few days would have been a most unfavourable time to hand it in – something that could not have been foreseen. If K., drained by all this talk, occasionally remarked that even taking account of all the problems, things were progressing very slowly, the answer was that they were not going at all slowly, though certainly they would have progressed much more quickly if K. had approached the advocate at the right time. Unfortunately, however, he had not; and this omission would entail other disadvantages than simply a loss of time.

The only salutary diversion during these visits was provided by Leni, who always contrived to bring the advocate his tea while K. was there. Then she would stand behind K., pretending to watch the advocate as he poured out his tea and drank it, bending greedily over the cup, and let K. surreptitiously hold her hand. This was done in complete silence; the advocate drank, K. squeezed Leni's hand, and Leni sometimes ventured to stroke K.'s hair gently. 'Are you still there?' the advocate would ask her when he had finished. 'I was going to take the cups away,' she would say, giving K.'s hand a last squeeze; the advocate would wipe his mouth and begin to harangue K. with renewed energy.

What was the advocate trying to achieve: to reassure him, or drive him to despair? K. did not know, but he was convinced that his defence was not in good hands. All the advocate told him might well be true, even if it was clear that he was keen to present himself as a leading player as far as he could, and that he had probably never conducted a case as important as K. believed his own to be. What he found dubious was the constant emphasis on personal contacts with the officials. Were these necessarily being used to K.'s advantage? The advocate never failed to mention that they were only very minor officials in very dependent positions, whose careers would probably be furthered by steering the case in certain directions. Were they perhaps using the advocate to steer it in directions that would always be unfavourable to the defendant? Perhaps they did not do this in every case, surely that was improbable; then again, there must be cases in which they granted the advocate certain favours for his services, for they too must have an interest in preserving his good reputation. But if it was really like that, how would they intervene in K.'s case which, as the advocate had explained, was a very difficult and therefore very important one that had aroused great interest in the court from the very beginning? There could be little doubt as to what they would do; one could already read the signs. The first plea had still not been submitted, although the case had been going on for months; everything was still in the early stages, according to the advocate. All this was of course designed to dupe the defendant and keep him helpless until he was suddenly taken unawares by the verdict, or at least by the announcement that the commission of investigation had not ruled in his favour and had referred his case to the higher authorities.

It was absolutely vital for K. himself to intervene. It was especially when he was exhausted, as he was on this winter's morning when all these thoughts raced through his mind, that this conviction was overwhelming. The earlier contempt with which he had treated the case was no longer appropriate. If he had been alone in the world, he could easily have ignored it – though for sure it would then not have been brought at all. But now that his uncle had taken him to the advocate, the family had to be considered. He was no longer wholly independent of the course of his trial; he himself had been careless enough to mention it, with a certain inexplicable sense of satisfaction, to his acquaintances. Others had got to know about it, he did not know how, and his relations with Fräulein Bürstner seemed as unpredictable as his case – in short, he hardly had the choice any more whether to accept or reject his trial, he was in the middle of it and had to defend himself. It would not help him if he was so tired.

Nevertheless, for the time being there was no reason to be unduly worried. At the bank he had managed to work his way up to his present senior position in a relatively short time and to prove himself worthy of it, as everyone recognised; now he only had to apply to his case some of the abilities that had made that possible, and there could be no doubt that it would end well. Above all, in order to achieve anything, it was essential to resist from the start any notion that he might be guilty. There was no guilt. The trial was no more than an important business deal such as he had often made to the benefit of the bank, a deal in which, as was usually the case, lurked various dangers that had to be guarded against. To handle it successfully, one could not entertain notions of some kind of guilt, but do everything to concentrate on one's own interests. In this respect it was necessary to take the case out of the advocate's hands very soon, preferably that very evening. According to everything the advocate had told him, this was an outrageous thing to do, and probably a great insult; but K. could not allow his efforts in the case to be hindered by obstacles that his own advocate might put in his way. Once he had got rid of the advocate, his plea must be submitted at once, and if possible every day must be used to ensure that the court took notice of it. Of course this could not be achieved if K. were simply to sit in the corridor like the others and put his hat under the bench. He himself, or the women, or anyone else he might send must pester the officials day after day and force them to sit down at their desks and study K.'s submission, instead of peering through the grille into the corridor. These efforts must be unremitting, everything must be organised and controlled; the court would finally come across a defendant who knew how to defend his rights.

However, though K. was confident he could manage all this, the difficulties involved in drawing up his plea were overwhelming. Earlier, until about a week ago, he had felt only shame at the very thought that he might have to write such a plea himself; it had not occurred to him that it might also be difficult to write it. He remembered how one morning, just when he was inundated with work, he had suddenly pushed everything to one side and taken a notepad to sketch out the broad lines of a submission which he could hand on to his ponderous advocate. At that very moment the door to the manager's office opened and the deputy manager came in, laughing heartily. It had been very awkward for K., although the deputy manager had not, of course, been laughing at his submission, of which he knew nothing, but at a funny story he had just heard from the stock exchange. A sketch was needed to explain the joke, so the deputy manager leaned over K.'s desk, took the pencil out of his hand, and drew on the notepad intended for the plea.

Today K. no longer felt ashamed; the submission had to be written. It was most unlikely that he would have time for it in the office, so he would have to do it during the night at home. If the nights were not enough, he would have to take leave. He must not get stuck halfway – that was the most stupid thing to do, not only in business, but as a general rule. To be sure, the submission would involve an almost endless amount of work. Though he was not a worrier by nature, he could very easily come to believe that it would never be finished, not out of laziness or deviousness, which were all that prevented the advocate from completing it, but because he did not know either what he was accused of or any further charges that might arise; as a result, he would have to recall the most trivial events and actions of a whole lifetime, record them and examine them from every angle. What a dismal task! In retirement, say, it might serve to occupy a senile mind and help to fill out the long days. But now, when K. needed to concentrate on his work, when he was making his way professionally and even posing a threat to the deputy manager, when every hour passed so quickly and he wanted to enjoy the short evenings and nights as a young man should – now he was supposed to write this submission!

Once again his thoughts had turned into self-pity. Almost automatically, just to put an end to all this, he felt for the button of the electric bell that rang in the anteroom. As he pressed it, he looked at the clock. It was eleven o'clock; he had wasted two hours daydreaming, two long precious hours, and was of course feeling more listless than before. However, the time had not been wasted; he had made decisions that could prove valuable. The messengers brought in various letters and two business cards from gentlemen who had been waiting to see K. for some time. They happened to be very important customers of the bank; on no account should they have been kept waiting. Why did they come at such an inconvenient time? And why – so the gentlemen behind the closed door seemed to ask in turn – was K., a hard-working employee, using prime business hours for his private affairs? Weary from all that had gone before, and wearily awaiting what was to come, K. stood up to receive the first customer.

He was a small, cheerful man, a manufacturer K. knew well. He apologised for interrupting K. in important work, and K. for his part apologised for keeping the manufacturer waiting so long. But he expressed his apologies in such a mechanical way, almost stumbling over his words, that the manufacturer would surely have noticed it if he had not been wholly absorbed in his business. Instead, he took tables and calculations out of every pocket, spread them out in front of K., explained various points, corrected a small error in the figures that he had noticed at a glance, reminded K. of a similar agreement he had made with him about a year before, mentioned casually that this time another bank was prepared to offer the very best terms to secure his custom, and finally paused to hear K.'s opinion. At first K. had indeed followed what the manufacturer was saying, and had also been interested in this important piece of business, but unfortunately not for long; he soon stopped listening, then for a while he nodded at the manufacturer's louder remarks, but finally he even gave up even that and confined himself to gazing at the bald head bent over the papers and wondering when the manufacturer would finally realise that everything he was saying was fruitless.

When the manufacturer finally stopped talking, K. at first actually thought he had done so to give him the chance to admit that he was not capable of paying attention; but he was disappointed to see from the man's expectant look that he was obviously prepared to answer any objections, and that the business discussion would have to be continued. So he nodded as if obeying an order and began to move his pencil slowly across the papers, stopping now and again to examine a figure. The manufacturer assumed K. had reservations; perhaps the figures were not really final, he conceded, perhaps they were not the deciding factor; at any rate, he covered the papers with his hand, pulled his chair very close to K., and embarked on a general presentation of his proposal. 'It's difficult,' said K.; he pursed his lips, and since the only thing he could hold on to

– the papers – were covered up, he slumped limply against the arm of his chair.

He hardly had the strength to look up as the door to the manager's office opened and he saw the deputy manager appear, indistinctly, as if through a gauze veil. K. did not give this any further thought; he only noticed the immediate consequence, which came as a great relief to him. For the manufacturer jumped up from his chair and rushed over to the deputy manager – though K. could have wished he were ten times more agile, for he feared the deputy manager might disappear again. But there was no need; the two gentlemen met, shook hands, and came over to K.'s desk. The manufacturer complained that the bank had shown so little enthusiasm for his proposal, pointing at K., who under the deputy manager's eye had bent over the papers again. As the two of them leaned over the desk, the manufacturer began to try to win over the deputy manager; K. felt as if the two men, whom he imagined to be far taller than they were, were haggling over him above his head. Slowly and cautiously, he turned his eyes upwards to see what was going on, and without looking picked up one of the papers from the desk, laid it on the palm of his hand, stood up slowly and presented it to the two men. He was not thinking of anything in particular as he did so; he simply felt that this was what he ought to do when he had finally completed the great submission that was to free him from his burden once and for all.

The deputy manager, who was wholly engrossed in conversation, glanced briefly at he document without reading a word of it – for what was important to K. was of no importance to him – and took it, saying: 'Thank you, I know all about it,' then put it calmly back on the desk. K. looked at him resentfully, but the deputy manager either did not notice or, if he did, was only amused; he frequently burst out laughing, at one point clearly embarrassed the manufacturer with a sharp riposte, then immediately made up for it, and finally invited him into his office where they could conclude their business. 'It is a very important matter,' he said to the manufacturer, 'I can see that quite clearly. And I am sure Herr K.' – even as he said this, he was speaking only to the manufacturer – 'will be only too glad if we relieve him of it. It needs to be thought out calmly, and he seems to be overworked today; besides, there are some people outside who have been waiting to see him for hours.' K. had just enough self-control to turn away from the deputy manager and give the manufacturer a friendly but forced smile. Otherwise he said nothing; leaning forward, he supported himself with both hands on his desk like a junior clerk and watched as the two men continued their conversation, took the papers from the desk and disappeared into the manager's office. At the door the manufacturer turned to say that he would not say goodbye to Herr K. just yet, as he would of course report to him the result of the discussion; moreover, he had a further small matter to speak to him about.

At last K. was alone. He had no intention of admitting any other clients, and he realised vaguely how glad he was that the people outside believed he was still in discussion with the manufacturer, and so no one, not even the bank messenger, could come in. He went to the window, sat on the sill, holding on to the latch with one hand, and looked out into the courtyard. It was still snowing, and the light had not improved.

He sat there for a long time, not really knowing what was worrying him; but every now and then, startled, he looked back over his shoulder at the door to the anteroom, where he mistakenly thought he had heard a noise. But when no one appeared he became calmer, went over to the wash-stand, washed his face in cold water and returned to his seat at the window with a clearer head. His decision to take his case into his own hands seemed to him more momentous that he had originally assumed. As long as he had left his defence to the advocate, the case had not greatly affected him. He had observed it distantly, it had scarcely encroached directly on his life, he had been able to find out how things stood when he wanted to; but he had also been able to draw back from it whenever he wished. But now that he was going to conduct the case himself, he would be at the mercy of the court, at least for the time being; the end result would be his final and unconditional acquittal, but to achieve this he would in the meantime be exposed to far greater danger than he had been so far. If he doubted this at all, today's encounter with the deputy manager and the manufacturer would have convinced him; he had simply sat there, bewildered by his decision to conduct his own defence. What would it be like when he did? What lay in store for him? Would he find his way through all this to a successful outcome? If he were to conduct a considered defence – and anything other than that would be pointless – did that not mean he would virtually have to abandon all other activities? Was he capable of doing that? And how could he do it while he was at the bank? There was not just the matter of his plea – a spell of leave might have been sufficient for that, though to ask for leave just now would be most ill-advised; there was his whole trial to consider, and there was no saying how long it would last. What an obstacle had suddenly been put in the way of his career!

And how was he supposed to do his job at the bank? He looked at his desk. Was he supposed to see clients and discuss things with them? While his case was proceeding, while up there in the attic court officials sat examining the documents in his case, was he supposed to do the bank's business? Was this not some kind of torture sanctioned by the court that was all to do with his trial? Perhaps it was part of it? And would they make allowances at the bank for his particular situation when they assessed his work? No one would ever do that. They were not entirely unaware of his trial, even if it was not yet clear who knew about it and how much was known. He hoped the news had not reached the deputy manager; if it had, it would surely have been quite obvious, because he would have used it against K. with no regard for human feelings or consideration for him as a colleague. And the manager? He certainly thought well of K., and as soon as he heard of the case would probably have done what he could to lighten his duties; but he would surely not have been able to, because K.'s position had become weaker and he could no longer counter the influence of the deputy manager, who also took advantage of the manager's ill-health in order to bolster his own power. So what could K. hope for? Perhaps he was weakening his resistance by indulging in such thoughts; but it was also essential not to delude himself and to view everything as clearly as he possibly could at present.

For no particular reason, just to avoid having to go back to his desk, he opened the window. He had some difficulty doing this, and had to use both hands to turn the latch. Then a great cloud of smoke and fog poured through the window, and a faint smell of burning filled the room. A few snowflakes drifted in too. 'A terrible autumn,' said the voice of the manufacturer behind K.; he had entered the room from the deputy manager's office unnoticed. K. nodded and looked uneasily at the manufacturer's briefcase, expecting him to pull out his papers and tell him the result of his discussions with the deputy manager. But the manufacturer caught K.'s glance, tapped his briefcase and, without opening it, said: 'You'll want to know how it turned out; the whole thing is practically settled – it's in here. A charming man, your deputy manager; but you've got to watch your step with him.' He laughed and shook K.'s hand, trying to make him join in the laughter. But now it struck K. as suspicious that the manufacturer did not want to show him the papers, and he found nothing to laugh about in the manufacturer's words.

'Herr K.,' said the manufacturer, 'the weather must be affecting you, you look so depressed today.' 'Yes,' said K., putting his hand to his temples, 'headaches, family problems.' 'Yes indeed,' said the manufacturer, who was an impatient man, unable to listen to anyone, 'we all have our cross to bear.' Automatically, K. had made towards the door to see the manufacturer out; but he said: 'I have something else to tell you, Herr K. I'm afraid today may not be the best time to bother you with it, but I've been to see you twice recently, and each time I forgot about it. But if I put it off any longer, there will probably be no point in telling you. That would be a pity, for what I have to say may not be entirely worthless.' Before K. had time to answer, the manufacturer stepped up close to him, tapped his knuckles lightly on his chest and said quietly: 'You are on trial, aren't you?' K. stepped back and cried: 'The deputy manager told you that!' 'Oh no,' said the manufacturer, 'how could the deputy manager know?' 'And how did you find out?' asked K., more composed now. 'I hear things now and again from the court,' said the manufacturer, 'that's just what I was going to tell you.' 'So many people are in touch with the court!' said K., hanging his head. He led the manufacturer to his desk, they sat down as before, and the manufacturer said: 'I'm afraid I can't tell you very much; but in such matters one should not overlook the slightest detail. Besides, I'm keen to help you, however modest my contribution may be. We have been good business friends, have we not? Well, then.'

K. wanted to apologise for his conduct at their earlier meeting, but the manufacturer would not be interrupted. He tucked his briefcase firmly under his arm to show he was keen to leave, and continued: 'I know about your case from a man called Titorelli. He is a painter, Titorelli is his *nom d'artiste*, I've no idea what his real name is. For years he has been coming to my office now and again; he brings some small pictures for which I give him a sort of handout – he's almost a beggar. Besides, his paintings are quite pretty, moorland landscapes, that sort of thing. These purchases – we had both got into the habit – went quite smoothly. But then he started coming too frequently, and I objected; we fell into conversation, because I was interested to know how he could support himself just by painting, and to my astonishment he told me his main source of income was portrait painting. He worked for the court, he said. "For which court?" I asked. And then he told me about the court. I'm sure you can well imagine how astonished I was at this information. Since then I hear bits of news from the court every time he comes, and so I gradually get some idea of what goes on. Certainly, Titorelli is a chatterbox, and I often have to stop him, not just because I'm sure he is a liar, but above all because a businessman like myself, with my back almost breaking under my own troubles, can't bother much about other things. But that is by the way. Then I thought: perhaps Titorelli can be of some help to you; he knows many of the judges, and even if he may not have much influence himself, he can still give you some tips on how to approach various influential people. And even if his tips are not so vital in themselves, I still think it very important that you should have them. You are almost an advocate. I always say: Herr K. is almost an advocate. Oh, I have no worries about your case. Would you like to see Titorelli, then? He is sure to do everything he can on my recommendation. I really think you ought to go and see him; it needn't be today – some time, any time. But let me add that of course you are not obliged to go and see him just because I advise you to, not in the slightest. No – if you think you can do without Titorelli, it would certainly be better to do without him. Perhaps you already have a definite plan, and Titorelli could upset it; then of course you must not think of seeing him! It certainly goes against the grain to take advice from a fellow like that. Well, just as you wish. Here is my letter of introduction, and this is the address.'

Disheartened, K. took the letter and put it in his pocket. Even at best, the benefits this introduction might bring were far outweighed by the fact that the manufacturer knew about his case and that the painter was spreading news of it. He could hardly bring himself to murmur a few words of thanks to the manufacturer, who was already making for the door. 'I will go and see him,' he said as he saw the manufacturer out, 'or else write and ask him to come and see me at the office; I'm very busy at the moment.' 'Of course I knew you would find the best solution. Though I thought you might prefer to avoid inviting someone like Titorelli to the bank to discuss your case. It isn't always advisable for letters to get into the hands of people like him. But I'm sure you have thought it all over and know what you should do.' K. nodded and accompanied the manufacturer through the anteroom. But though he was outwardly calm, he was very disturbed at what he had said. He had actually only told the manufacturer that he would write to Titorelli in order to give him the impression that he appreciated his recommendation, and he was already thinking how he could meet Titorelli. If he really thought Titorelli's help would be worthwhile, he would not hesitate to write to him; but it was only when the manufacturer mentioned it that he realised how dangerous this might be. Had he really taken leave of his senses? If he was capable of writing an explicit letter to such a dubious person inviting him to the bank, where only a door separated him from the deputy manager, to ask his advice about the case, was it not possible, even very probable, that he was also overlooking other dangers – or running straight into them? He did not always have someone standing beside him to warn him. And now, just as he should be summoning up all his energy in the conduct of his case, he was having such doubts about his own alertness as he had never had before! Were the problems he was having with his work in the office now affecting his conduct of his case too? At any rate, he could no longer understand how he could possibly have intended to write to Titorelli and invite him to the bank.

He was still shaking his head over this when the messenger came up to him and drew his attention to three gentlemen sitting there on a bench in the anteroom. They had been waiting a long time to see him. They stood up when they saw the messenger talking to K., and each tried to approach K. before the others. Since the bank had been so inconsiderate as to make them waste their time waiting, they had no intention of acting considerately either. 'Herr K.,' one of them began. But K. had already asked the messenger to bring his overcoat, and as he helped him on with it, K. addressed all three of them: 'Forgive me, gentlemen, I'm afraid I cannot see you at the moment. I am very sorry, but I have some very urgent business to do, and I must leave at once. You have seen for yourselves how long I have been held up. Would you be so kind as to come back tomorrow or some other time? Perhaps you would like to discuss matters over the phone? Or could you tell me briefly here and now what your business is, and I will give you a detailed reply in writing? It would of course be best if you could come again before long.' The three men, who now saw that they had waited so long to no purpose, were so astonished that they looked at each other in silence. 'We are agreed, then?' asked K., turning to the messenger, who was now bringing him his hat. Outside, as could be seen through the open door of K.'s office, the snow was falling more heavily; K. pulled up his coat collar and buttoned it right up to his chin.

At that moment the deputy manager came out of the next room, and smiled when he saw K. discussing matters with the three men in his overcoat. 'Are you leaving just now, Herr K.?' he asked. 'Yes,' said K., pulling himself up, 'I have to go out on business.' But the deputy manager had already turned to the three men. 'And these gentlemen?' he asked, 'I believe they have been waiting some time.' 'We have come to an agreement,' said K. But now the men would not be put off; they surrounded K. and protested that they would not have waited for hours unless they too had important business that must be dealt with immediately in great detail and in private. The deputy manager listened to them for a while, then looked at K., who was holding his hat and brushing some dust off it. Then he said: 'Gentlemen, there is a very simple solution. If you are agreeable, I will be glad to take over the negotiations from my colleague. Of course your business must be seen to without delay. We are businessmen like you, and we know very well how valuable your time is. Will you come in?' And he opened the door leading to the anteroom of his office.

The deputy manager certainly knew how to take over everything that K. was forced to give up! But was K. not giving up more than was strictly necessary? While he was going to see an unknown painter with vague and, as he had to admit, very slim hopes, his prestige at the bank was being damaged irreparably. It would probably have been much better if he had taken off his overcoat and tried to make amends, at least with the two men who must still be waiting next door. And K. might still have tried to do that if he had not caught sight of the deputy manager in his room, searching for something in K.'s bookcase as if it were his own. As K. went to the door in a state of agitation, the deputy manager called: 'Ah, you haven't gone yet!' He turned towards K., his heavily-lined face appearing to suggest power rather than age, then immediately resumed his search. 'I'm looking for the copy of a contract,' he said, 'which, according to the firm's representative, should be in your room. Would you help me to find it?' K. took a step forward, but the deputy manager said: 'Thank you, I've got it,' and returned to his own room with a large bundle of papers that must have contained not only the copy of the contract, but much more besides.

'I can't cope with him just now,' said K. to himself, 'but once my personal problems are out of the way, I swear he'll be the first to know about it, and he'll be sorry, too.' This thought calmed him a little; he told the messenger, who had been waiting for some time holding the corridor door open for him, to inform the manager at the first opportunity that he was out on business and, feeling almost glad that he could now devote himself for a time entirely to his case, he left the bank.

He immediately took a cab to the painter, who lived in a suburb on the other side of the city from the court chambers. It was an even poorer area; the houses were even more dismal, and the narrow streets were choked with rubbish floating sluggishly in the slush from the melting snow. At the entrance to the painter's house, only one of the double doors was open; at the foot of the other door a hole had been hacked in the wall, through which, just as K. approached, poured a revolting yellow, steaming stream of liquid, driving some rats before it into the nearby canal. At the foot of the stairs a small child lay on its belly crying; but its cries could hardly be heard above the deafening noise from a plumber's workshop on the other side of the entrance. The door of the workshop was open, and three workmen were standing in a semicircle hammering at some piece of metalwork. A large sheet of tin hanging on the wall reflected a pallid light between two of the workmen that shone on their faces and aprons. K. gave all this only a fleeting glance; he wanted to get things done here as quickly as possible, to put a few questions to the painter and return to the bank at once. If he were to have only the slightest success here, it would help him in his day's work at the bank.

By the time he reached the third floor he was quite out of breath and had to slow down; the stairs were long, the house was surprisingly high, and the painter, he had been told, lived in a garret at the very top. The air was most oppressive, too; there was no stairwell, the narrow stairs were enclosed on both sides by walls that only had a few small windows high above him.

K. stopped for a moment, and just then some young girls ran out of one of the apartments and rushed up the stairs laughing. K. followed them slowly, overtaking one of the girls, who had tripped and fallen behind the others. 'Does a painter called Titorelli live here?' he asked her. The girl, who was scarcely thirteen and slightly hunchbacked, nudged him with her elbow and leered up at him. She was already quite depraved; neither her youth nor her deformity had been able to protect her. She did not even smile, but gazed at K. intently with a bold inviting look in her eyes. K. pretended not to notice her behaviour, and asked: 'Do you know Titorelli the painter?' She nodded, then asked: 'What do you want him for?' K. thought he should take the opportunity to learn something about Titorelli. 'I want him to paint my portrait,' he said. 'Paint your portrait?' said the girl. She gaped at him open-mouthed, gave him a gentle slap with her hand as if he had said something unexpected or inappropriate, lifted her skirt, which was already short enough, in both hands and ran as fast as she could after the other girls whose shouts were growing fainter further up the stairs. But round the next turn in the stairs K. ran into them all again; the deformed girl had obviously told them what he was doing there, and they were waiting for him. They stood on either side of the stairs, pressed against the walls so that K. could get past, smoothing their aprons with their hands. All their faces, and the way they lined up against the walls, suggested a mixture of childish innocence and wickedness. Laughing, they clustered behind K.; in front was the little hunchback, who was now leading the way. It was thanks to her that he knew where to go; he was about to continue straight up the stairs, but she indicated that he had to turn off to one side to find Titorelli. The staircase leading to his room was particularly narrow, very long and straight; it was possible to see right to the very top where it ended at Titorelli's door. The door, which in contrast to the rest of the staircase was relatively well-lit by a small skylight above it, was made of unvarnished boards on which the name Titorelli had been written in red paint with broad brushstrokes. K. and his companions were scarcely half-way up when, clearly as a result of the noise of so many feet on the stairs, the door above opened a little, and a man evidently wearing only a nightshirt could be seen through the half-open door. 'Oh!' he cried when he saw the crowd coming towards him, and disappeared. The little hunchback clapped her hands for joy, and the other girls swarmed behind K., driving him on.

They had scarcely reached the top when the painter threw the door open and with a deep bow invited K. to enter; but he turned the girls away and would not let any of them in, however much they pleaded and tried to get past, whether with his permission or not. Only the hunchback managed to slip past under his outstretched arm, but the painter ran after her, grabbed her by her skirts, swung her round and set her down in front of the door with the other girls, who had not dared to venture into the room while the painter was away from his post. K. did not know what to make of all this, for it all seemed to be done in a friendly spirit. The girls at the door craned their necks one behind the other and shouted various droll comments at the painter which K. did not understand; the painter laughed too as he threw the little hunchbacked girl into the air. Then he shut the door, bowed once more to K., put out his hand and said by way of introduction: 'I am Titorelli, the artist.'

K. pointed to the door, behind which the girls were whispering, and said: 'You seem to be very popular in this house.' 'Oh, those rascals!' said the painter, trying unsuccessfully to button up his nightshirt at the neck. Otherwise he was barefoot, and dressed only in a pair of wide yellowish linen trousers secured by a belt with a loose end that flapped about. 'They're a real pest,' he went on. He stopped fiddling with his nightshirt, the top button of which had just come off, brought a chair and made K. sit down. 'I painted one of them once – she's not even with them today – and since then they all chase after me. When I'm here they can only come in if I let them, but when I'm out there's always at least one of them here. They've had a key to my door made, and they lend it to each other. You can't imagine what a nuisance it is. For instance, if I bring home a lady I'm supposed to paint, I open the door and find that hunchback at the table over there painting her lips red with one of my brushes, while her little brothers and sisters she's supposed to be looking after are rushing around and messing up the room. Or I come back late at night, as I did just yesterday – that's why I'm in this state, and why the room is so untidy, please excuse all this – I come back late and get into bed, and something pinches me in the leg; I look under the bed and pull another of these creatures out. Why they pester me like this, I don't know; as you must have noticed just now, I don't encourage them, and of course they distract me from my work. If I didn't have this studio rent-free I'd have moved out long ago.' Just then a small voice behind the door called out gently and pleadingly: 'Titorelli, can we come in now?' 'No,' answered the painter. 'Not even just me?' the voice asked. 'Not even you,' said the painter, going to the door and locking it.

In the meantime K. had looked round the room; it would never have occurred to him to call this wretched little garret a studio. It scarcely measured more than two good paces each way. Everything, the floor, walls, and ceiling, was made of wood, and there were narrow gaps visible between the boards. Opposite K. against the wall was the bed, piled high with bedclothes of various colours. In the middle of the room was a painting on an easel, covered with a shirt, its sleeves dangling to the floor. Behind him was a window through which the snow-covered roof of the neighbouring house could be seen through the mist.

The sound of the key turning in the lock reminded K. that he had meant to leave before long. So he took the manufacturer's letter out of his pocket, handed it to the painter and said: 'This gentleman, an acquaintance of yours, told me about you and advised me to come and see you.' The painter read the letter cursorily and dropped it onto the bed. If the manufacturer had not made it perfectly clear that he knew Titorelli and that he was a pauper who depended on his charity, it would have been quite possible to believe that Titorelli did not know the manufacturer, or at least that he did not remember him. Moreover, the painter then asked: 'Do you want to buy some pictures, or have your portrait painted?' K. looked at the painter, astonished. What did the letter actually say, then? K. had assumed as a matter of course that the manufacturer had explained to the painter in his letter that K. only wanted to ask him about his trial. So he had rushed over here far too quickly without thinking! But he had to give the painter some sort of answer, so he said, looking at the easel: 'Are you working on a picture just now?' 'Yes,' said the painter, and threw the shirt hanging on the easel onto the bed with the letter. 'It's a portrait. A good piece of work, but it's not quite finished.'

This was most fortunate for K.; it gave him a clear opportunity to mention the court, for it was obviously the portrait of a judge. It was, moreover, strikingly similar to the picture in the advocate's study. It was true that this was a quite different judge, a stout man with a full black bushy beard covering his cheeks; that one was an oil-painting, while this one was done sketchily and lightly in faint pastel colours. But everything else was similar; here too the judge was grasping the arms of his chair, about to rise menacingly from his judgement seat. 'But that's a judge,' K. had been about to say; but he checked himself for the moment and went up to the picture as if he wanted to study it in detail. There was a large figure hovering over the back of the chair that he could not make out, and he asked the painter what it was. He replied that it still needed to be worked on; he fetched a pastel crayon from a small table and drew a few strokes at the edges of the figure, but this made it no clearer to K. 'It is Justice,' the painter said finally. 'Ah, now I recognise it,' said K., 'this is the blindfold, and these are the scales. But aren't those wings on her ankles, and is she not flying?' 'Yes,' said the painter. 'I was commissioned to paint it like that; actually, it's Justice and the goddess of Victory all in one.' 'That's not a very happy combination,' said K., smiling. 'Justice must be still, otherwise the scales will waver and no just verdict is possible.' 'I must do as my clients tell me,' said the painter. 'Yes, of course,' said K., who had not intended his remark to cause offence. 'You have painted the figure just as it really is on the seat of judgement.' 'No,' said the painter, 'I haven't seen either the figure or the chair, that's all imagined; but I was told what I had to paint.' 'What?' asked

K., pretending that he did not fully understand the painter. 'But it is a judge sitting there, isn't it?' 'Yes,' said the painter, 'but he's not a senior judge, and he never sat on a chair like that.' 'But he still has himself painted with such ceremony? He's sitting there like a high court judge.' 'Yes, they're vain, these gentlemen,' said the painter. 'But they have the authorities' permission to be painted like that. Everyone is given precise instructions how he may be painted. But I'm afraid it's not possible to judge the details of the costume or the chair from this particular picture; pastels are unsuitable for portraits like this.' 'Yes,' said K., 'it's odd that it's done in pastel.' 'The judge wanted it like that,' said the painter, 'it's meant for a lady.'

Looking at the picture seemed to have made him keen to set to work; he rolled up his sleeves, picked up some crayons, and K. watched as under the delicate strokes of the crayons a reddish shadow formed about the judge's head and radiated out towards the edge of the picture. Gradually the shadows began to play about the head like a halo or a sign of special distinction. The figure of Justice, however, remained set against a bright background, except for a discreet touch of colour. This brightness seemed to highlight the figure, so that it now scarcely suggested either the goddess of Justice or the goddess of Victory; it looked exactly like the goddess of Hunting. The painter's work took up more of K.'s attention than he wished; finally he began to reproach himself for staying here so long without yet having done anything to further his own interests. 'What is this judge's name?' he asked abruptly. 'I'm not allowed to say,' replied the painter. He was hunched over the picture and was clearly ignoring the guest he had received so courteously at first. K. put this down to the painter's mood and felt annoyed because he was wasting his time.

'I suppose you are on familiar terms with the court?' he asked. At once the painter put down his crayons, stood up straight, rubbed his hands together and smiled at K. 'Let's not beat about the bush,' he said. 'You want to learn something about the court – after all, that's what it says in your letter of introduction; but you began by talking about my pictures to win me over. But I don't mind; you weren't to know that's not the way to go about it. No, please!' he said sharply as K. was about to protest. Then he went on: 'Besides, you are perfectly correct, I am on familiar terms with the court.' He paused as if to give K. time to digest this. Now the girls could again be heard outside the door. They were probably crowding around the keyhole; perhaps they could also see into the room through the cracks. K. made no effort to apologise, for he did not wish to distract the painter; but neither did he wish the painter to feel so superior as to be inaccessible. So he asked: 'Is that an official appointment?' 'No,' said the painter curtly, as if the question made him unable to say anything further. But K. wanted him to go on, so he said: 'Well, these unofficial positions are often more influential than the official ones.' 'That is just the case with mine,' said the painter, and nodded, frowning. 'I spoke to the manufacturer yesterday about your case. He asked me if I would help you, and I told him: "Let the man come and see me some time"; and now I'm glad to see you here so soon. The case seems to affect you closely, which of course doesn't surprise me at all. But won't you take your coat off for now?'

Although K. only intended to stay for a short time, the painter's suggestion was most welcome. He had found the atmosphere in the room more and more oppressive, and had frequently cast puzzled glances at a small iron stove in the corner, which was clearly not working; the room was inexplicably stuffy. While he was removing his overcoat and unbuttoning his jacket, the painter said apologetically: 'I must have warmth. It's really very cosy here, isn't it? The room is very well situated in that respect.' K. did not reply. It was not so much the warmth that made him uncomfortable, but rather the stuffy atmosphere that made it difficult to breathe properly; the room had probably not been ventilated for a long time. K.'s discomfort increased when the painter asked him to sit on the bed, while he seated himself in front of the easel on the only chair. Moreover, the painter did not seem to understand why K. stayed perched on the edge of the bed; he urged him to make himself comfortable, and when K. hesitated, came over and pushed him down deep among the bedding and the pillows. Then he returned to his chair and at last put the first relevant question, a question that made K. forget everything else.

'Are you innocent?' he asked. 'Yes,' said K. It gave him real pleasure to answer this question, especially as it was addressed to him in private, and therefore involved no liability. No one so far had asked him so candidly. In order to savour this pleasure, he added: 'I am completely innocent.' 'I see,' said the painter. He bent his head as if in thought. Suddenly he raised his head and said: 'If you are innocent, then the matter is quite simple.' K.'s face fell; this man who claimed to be familiar with the court was talking like an ignorant child. 'My innocence does not make things any simpler,' he said. In spite of everything he had to smile, and shook his head slowly. 'There are many subtleties in which the court gets involved; but in the end it drags some serious form of guilt out of nowhere.' 'Yes, yes, of course,' said the painter, as if K. were interrupting his train of thought unnecessarily. 'But you are in fact innocent?' 'Why, yes,' said K. 'That is the main thing,' said the painter. He could not be persuaded otherwise; but in spite of his decisiveness it was not clear whether he was saying this out of conviction or simply out of indifference. K. wanted to establish which it was, so he said: 'I'm sure you know the court much better than I do; I don't know much more about it than what I have been told, though I have listened to various people. But they were all agreed that frivolous charges are not brought, and that if the court does bring charges it is firmly convinced of the guilt of the accused, and it is very difficult to shake this conviction.' 'Difficult?' cried the painter, flinging his arms into the air. 'The court's view can never be shaken. If I were to paint all the judges here side by side on a canvas, and if you were to defend yourself before this canvas, you would have more success than you would before the real court.' 'Yes,' said K. to himself, forgetting that he had only intended to sound out the painter.

Once again a girl outside the door started up: 'Titorelli, will he be going soon?' 'Quiet!' the painter shouted at the door. 'Can't you see I'm having a discussion with this gentleman?' But the girl would not be put off, and asked: 'Are you going to paint him?' And when the painter did not reply, she added: 'Please don't paint him, he's so ugly.' A confused babble of argument followed. The painter leapt to the door, opened it just a crack, through which the girls' hands could be seen, clasped together and stretched out imploringly, and said: 'If you don't keep quiet I'll throw you all down the stairs. Sit on the steps and behave yourselves.' Apparently they did not obey at once, so he ordered them: 'Sit down on the steps!' Only then was there silence.

'Excuse me,' said the painter as he returned to K., who had scarcely looked towards the door; he had left it entirely to the painter whether and how he wished to protect him. And even then he hardly moved as the painter bent down and whispered into his ear so that those outside could not hear: 'These girls belong to the court, too.' 'What?' asked K., turning to look at the painter, who sat down again in his chair and said, half in jest, half by way of explanation: 'Everything belongs to the court.' 'I had not noticed that before,' said K. shortly; the painter's all-embracing remark had removed any disquiet K. felt at his reference to the girls. Still, for some time K. stared at the door, behind which the girls were now sitting quietly on the stairs, except that one of them had pushed a straw through a crack in the boards and was moving it slowly up and down.

'You don't seem to have any overall picture of the court yet,' said the painter; he had spread his legs wide apart and was tapping his feet on the floor. 'But since you are innocent, you won't need to. I can get you out of this myself.' 'How are you going to do that?' asked K. 'You said yourself just now that the court is quite impervious to evidence.' 'Only to evidence that is submitted to the court,' said the painter, raising his index finger as if K. had not grasped a subtle distinction. 'But what is done outside the public courts, that is in committee rooms, in the corridors, or even here in my studio for example – that is a different matter.' What the painter was now saying no longer seemed so incredible to K., indeed it closely matched what he had also heard from others. It even gave him cause for hope. If the judges were as easily influenced by personal relationships as the advocate had suggested, then the painter's connections with these vain judges were particularly important; at all events they should not be underrated. So the painter was a valuable addition to the circle of helpers K. was gradually gathering around him. His talent for organisation had been praised in the bank; now that he was relying on his own resources, it was a good opportunity to show his talents to the full.

The painter observed the effect of his remarks on K., and continued rather anxiously: 'Has it not occurred to you that I almost talk like a lawyer? It's because I am constantly in touch with the gentlemen of the court. Of course, I profit from it greatly, though I lose much of my artistic impulse.' 'How did you first come in contact with the judges?' asked K.; he wanted to gain the painter's confidence before fully engaging his services. 'That was very simple,' said the painter, 'I inherited my connections. My father was painter to the court before me. It's one of those positions that are always inherited. They can't take on new people for it; you see, there are so many different rules, complex and above all secret rules, for the painting of the various grades of officials, that they are quite unknown except to certain families. In the drawer there, for example, I have my father's drawings, which I show to no one; but only someone who knows them is capable of painting judges. Even if I lost them, I still carry so many rules in my head that no one can challenge my position. And every judge wants to be painted just like the great judges of old were painted, and only I can do that.' 'That's enviable,' said K., thinking of his position at the bank. 'So your position is unassailable?' 'Yes, unassailable,' said the painter, drawing himself up proudly. 'That's why I can occasionally take the risk of helping some poor wretch with his case.' 'And how do you do that?' asked K., as if he were not the one the painter had just called a 'poor wretch'. But the painter went on undeterred: 'In your case, for example, since you are entirely innocent, I shall proceed as follows.' K. found the repeated references to his innocence becoming tiresome. At times such remarks suggested that the painter was only prepared to help him if the successful outcome of his trial were guaranteed – in which case, of course, his help was unnecessary. In spite of these doubts, however, K. controlled himself and did not interrupt. He was determined not to forgo the painter's help, which in any case seemed no more dubious than that of the advocate. Indeed, K. much preferred it to the latter because it was offered more candidly and openly.

The painter had drawn his chair nearer to the bed. He continued in a low voice: 'I forgot to ask you firstly what kind of acquittal you want. There are three possibilities, namely, final acquittal, apparent acquittal, and deferred judgement. Final acquittal is the best, of course; but I have not the slightest influence on this kind of result. In my opinion there is not a single person who could have any influence on final acquittal; probably only the innocence of the accused carries any weight in this instance. Since you are innocent, it would be quite possible for you to rely on your innocence alone; but in that case you do not need my help or anyone else's.'

K. was initially bewildered by this systematic exposition, but then he said in equally hushed tones: 'I think you are contradicting yourself.' 'How is that?' said the painter patiently, leaning back with a smile. His smile made K. feel that he was attempting to discover contradictions not in the painter's argument, but in the legal process itself. But he went on undeterred: 'You stated earlier that the court was impervious to evidence; later you limited that to the public courts, and now you even tell me that an innocent person needs no help before the court. That already contains a contradiction. What's more, you said earlier that the judges can be influenced personally, but now you deny that final acquittal, as you call it, can ever be achieved by personal influence. That is a further contradiction.' 'These contradictions can easily be resolved,' said the painter. 'We are talking about two different things here: what the law says, and what I have experienced personally. You must not confuse the two. The law of course says (though I haven't read it myself) on the one hand that an innocent person will be acquitted; but on the other hand it does not say that judges can be influenced. But I have experienced just the opposite. I don't know of any instance of final acquittal, but I do know of many cases where influence has been brought to bear. Of course, it is possible that in all the cases I know of, no one was innocent. But isn't that improbable? Not one innocent person in so many cases? Even as a child I listened carefully to my father at home when he talked about trials, and the judges who came to his studio talked about the court. People in our circles talk about nothing else; as soon as I had the chance to go to court myself, I always made the most of it. I've listened to countless trials at important stages, and followed them as long as they were public – and I must admit I have never seen a single instance of a final acquittal.'

'I see,' said K., as if he were addressing himself and his own hopes. 'Well, that confirms the opinion I already have of the court. So it is pointless in that respect too; a single executioner could replace the whole court.' 'You must not generalise,' said the painter in annoyance, 'I was only talking about my experiences.' 'But that's quite enough,' said K., 'or have you heard of final acquittals in earlier times?' 'Indeed, it is said that there have been such acquittals,' said the painter, 'but it is very difficult to confirm this. The final verdicts of the court are not published; they are not even available to the judges, and as a result only legends survive about earlier judgements. The majority of these legends do provide cases of final acquittal; they can be believed, but they can't be proved. Nevertheless, one should not ignore them; they are sure to contain a certain amount of truth, and they are very beautiful. I have myself painted some pictures based on these legends.' 'Mere legends do not alter my opinion,' said K. 'I don't suppose one can invoke these legends before the court?' The painter laughed. 'No, that's not possible,' he said. 'Then it is pointless to talk about them,' said K.

For the time being, K. was willing to accept the painter's views, even if he found them implausible or if they contradicted other accounts. He did not have time just now to check the truth of everything the painter said, let alone to refute it; the most he could achieve was to persuade the painter to help him in some way, even if it should turn out to lead nowhere. So he said: 'Leaving final acquittal aside, you mentioned two other possibilities.' 'Apparent acquittal and deferred judgement. These are the only options,' said the painter. 'But before we discuss that, won't you take your jacket off? I'm sure you're feeling warm.' 'Yes,' said K. So far he had given his whole attention to the painter's explanations; but now that he was reminded of the warmth of the room, his forehead streamed with sweat. 'It is almost intolerable.' The painter nodded, as if he understood K.'s discomfort very well. 'Couldn't you open the window?' asked K. 'No,' said the painter, 'it's just a fixed pane of glass, it can't be opened.' Now K. realised that all the time he had been hoping that either he or the painter would suddenly go over to the window and fling it open. He was even prepared to breathe in the fog through his open mouth. The thought that he was here completely cut off from the fresh air made him feel dizzy. He patted the bedclothes beside him feebly and said in a faint voice: 'But that's uncomfortable and unhealthy.' 'Oh no,' said the painter in defence of his window, 'although it's only a single pane, if it can't be opened the heat here is kept in better than with a double window. If I need ventilation, which isn't really necessary, because draughts get through between all the boards, I can open one of my doors, or even both.' K., somewhat reassured by this explanation, looked around for the second door. The painter noticed and said: 'It is behind you, I had to block it with the bed.'

Only now did K. see the small door in the wall. 'This is all just far too small for a studio,' said the painter, as if to forestall K.'s disapproval. 'I had to arrange it as best I could. Of course, the bed is in a very bad place in front of the door. For instance, the judge I'm painting at the moment always comes in by the door behind the bed, and I've given him the key to that door so that he can wait in the studio if I'm not here. But then he usually comes early in the morning while I'm still asleep, and so it drags me out of a deep sleep when he opens the door by the bed. You would lose all respect for the judges if you could hear how I curse him when he climbs over my bed early in the morning. I could take the key away from him, of course, but that would only make things worse; it only needs the slightest effort to break open all the doors here.'

All the time the painter was speaking, K. was thinking whether he should take off his jacket; but he eventually realised that if he did not, he would be incapable of staying here any longer. So he took it off, but kept it over his knees so that he could put it back on when the interview was over. He had hardly taken it off when one of the girls cried: 'He's taken his jacket off now!' They could all be heard as they scrambled to look through the cracks in the door to see the spectacle for themselves. 'You see,' said the painter, 'the girls think you're undressing because I'm going to paint you.' 'I see,' said K., not much amused, for he did not feel much better than before, though he was sitting there in his shirtsleeves. Almost irascibly he asked: 'What did you say the other two options were?' He had already forgotten the terms. 'Apparent acquittal and deferred judgement,' said the painter. 'It's up to you which you choose. I can help you achieve either of them, though of course it will take some effort. The difference is that apparent acquittal requires brief but intense effort, while deferred judgement requires much less but more protracted effort. First of all, apparent acquittal: if that is what you wish, I write a statement of your innocence on a sheet of paper. The text of such a statement was handed down to me by my father, and cannot be contested. With this statement I then go round all the judges I know. For instance, I shall start by submitting it this evening to the judge I am painting at the moment when he comes for a sitting. I shall show him the statement, explain to him that you are innocent and myself testify to your innocence. This testimony is not superficial, it is real and binding.'

The painter's expression seemed to suggest he was reproaching K. for burdening him with such a testimony. 'That would be very kind,' said K. 'And the judge would believe you and still not fully acquit me?' 'As I have told you,' replied the painter. 'Besides, it is by no means certain that they would all believe me; for example, some judges will demand I take you to them in person. In that case, you would just have to come along with me; still, if that happens, the case is already half won, especially since I would of course tell you beforehand exactly how to conduct yourself before that particular judge. It's much worse with the judges who turn me down from the start – that can happen, too. Although I shall not fail to make several approaches, we shall have to do without those judges; but we can afford to do that, because individual judges cannot affect the outcome. Then when I have a sufficient number of judges' signatures on this statement, I take it to the judge who is conducting your trial. It may be that I have his signature too, in which case everything will proceed rather more quickly than otherwise. Generally, there are no further obstacles after that, and this is when the confidence of the accused is at its highest. It is remarkable, but true, that during this time people are more confident than after their acquittal. Now no further effort is needed; the presiding judge has in the statement the testimony of a number of judges, he can acquit you without any trouble, which he will undoubtedly do as a favour to me and his other colleagues, though there will be various formalities to complete. And you walk from the court a free man.'

'So then I am free,' said K. uncertainly. 'Yes,' said the painter, 'but you are only apparently free, or more accurately, provisionally free. You see, the lowest judges, who are among those I know, do not have the right to pronounce a final acquittal; only the very highest court, which is inaccessible to you, to me, to all of us, has that right. What goes on there we do not know, and between you and me we don't want to know. So though our judges do not have the supreme right to free the accused from the charges against him, they do have the right to release him from those charges. That is, if you are acquitted in this way, you are released from the charges for the time being, but they remain hanging over you and can be brought against you as soon as the order comes from above. Because I am in such close contact with the court, I can also tell you the difference between final acquittal and apparent acquittal in purely procedural terms, according to the regulations issued to the court chambers. In the case of final acquittal, the files relating to the case must be struck from the record, they are completely eliminated; not only the charges, but the trial and even the acquittal, are destroyed, everything is destroyed. With an apparent acquittal it is different. The files are unchanged, except that the declaration of innocence, the acquittal, and the reasons for it, are added to the record. Moreover, they remain in the system; as the ongoing business of the court requires, they are forwarded to the highest courts, referred down to the lowest ones, and so they shuttle to and fro, sometimes rapidly and expeditiously, at other times subject to shorter or longer delays. These processes are incalculable. Seen from the outside, it can sometimes seem that everything has been long forgotten, that the files have been lost and the acquittal has been made final. No one who knows how the courts work will believe that, however. No file gets lost; the court does not forget. One day, when no one expects it, some judge will examine a file more carefully, realise that in this case the charge still stands, and will order an immediate arrest. I am assuming here that a long time has elapsed between the apparent acquittal and the second arrest; that is possible, and I know of such cases, but it is equally possible that the person acquitted comes home from the court and finds officers waiting there to re-arrest him. That of course is the end of his freedom.'

'So the trial starts all over again?' asked K. almost incredulously. 'Indeed,' said the painter, 'the trial starts all over again, but again there is the possibility, just as before, of obtaining an apparent acquittal. Again, one must summon up all one's energy and not give in.' It may be that the painter spoke these last words because he saw K. slump in dejection.

'But,' asked K., as if he wished to forestall any of the painter's revelations, 'isn't it more difficult to obtain a second apparent acquittal that the first one?' 'It is impossible to be certain,' the painter replied. 'I suppose you mean that because of the second arrest the judges might be biased against the accused? That is not the case. You see, the judges anticipated this arrest when they issued the acquittal, so that hardly affects things. However, for countless other reasons, the attitude of the judges as well as their legal judgement of the case might well have changed, and any efforts to obtain a second acquittal must be adapted to the different circumstances, and must be every bit as strenuous as for the first acquittal.' 'But then this second acquittal is not final either,' said K., shaking his head in disbelief. 'Of course not,' said the painter. 'The third arrest follows the second acquittal, the fourth arrest follows the third acquittal, and so on. That is in the nature of an apparent acquittal.'

K. was silent. 'Obviously you don't think there is any advantage in a provisional acquittal,' said the painter. 'Perhaps deferred judgement would suit you better. Shall I explain what deferment means?' K. nodded. The painter had sprawled back in his chair, his nightshirt was wide open; he had shoved a hand inside and was rubbing his chest and sides. 'Deferment,' he said, staring in front of him for a moment as if he were searching for an exact explanation, 'deferment means that the trial is permanently restricted to the initial stages. To achieve this, the accused and his adviser, but especially the adviser, must constantly keep in personal touch with the court. As I said, it is not necessary to invest so much effort in this as it is for a provisional acquittal, but it requires much closer attention. You must visit the appropriate magistrate at regular intervals and on specific occasions, and make every effort to keep him well disposed towards you. If you do not know him personally, you must try to influence him through other magistrates you know; but this should not lead you to neglect direct interviews with him. If you spare no efforts in this respect, you can be fairly certain that the trial will not progress beyond its initial stage. The trial goes on, but the accused is almost as safe from being sentenced as if he were free. Deferment has the advantage over provisional acquittal that the defendant's future is less uncertain, he is protected from the shock of sudden arrest, and he has no cause to fear that he might, perhaps when other circumstances make it least convenient for him, have to put up with the stresses and strains involved in obtaining a provisional acquittal. However, deferment does have certain disadvantages for the accused that must not be underestimated. I don't mean so much that in this instance the accused is never free, because he is not really free if he is provisionally acquitted either. There is a further disadvantage. The trial cannot be suspended unless there are at least ostensible reasons for doing so; something must be seen to be happening. So from time to time various processes have to be gone through, the accused has to be interrogated, investigations carried out, and so on. The trial must constantly move within the small circle to which it has been arbitrarily restricted. That, of course, involves certain disagreeable aspects for the accused; but you must not imagine that these are too unpleasant. It is all for form's sake; the interrogations for example are quite brief, and if you have no time or if you do not want to attend, you can make your excuses. With some magistrates you can even agree the arrangements far in advance; what it amounts to essentially is that as a defendant you must report to your magistrate from time to time.'

Before the painter had finished speaking, K. had folded his jacket over his arm and stood up. Immediately a shout came from outside the door: 'He's getting up now!' 'Are you leaving already?' asked the painter, who had also got to his feet. 'I'm sure it's the stuffiness in here that's driving you away. I'm sorry; I could tell you a lot more. I had to be brief, but I hope I made myself clear.' 'Oh yes,' said K., whose head ached from the strain of forcing himself to listen. In spite of K.'s assurance, the painter said by way of summary, as if he wanted to reassure K. as he left: 'Both methods have one thing in common – they prevent the conviction of the accused.' 'But they also prevent his actual acquittal,' said K. quietly, as if he were ashamed to have recognised this. 'You have grasped the nub of the matter,' said the painter shortly. K. picked up his overcoat, but could not even bring himself to put on his jacket; he would have preferred to bundle everything up and rush out into the fresh air. Even the girls outside could not make him put them on, although they were shouting to each other, prematurely, that he was getting dressed.

The painter was eager to gauge K.'s feelings, so he said: 'I dare say you haven't reached a decision yet about what I have told you. I think that's right. In fact, I would have advised you not to make an immediate decision. There is a very fine line between the pros and cons. You must consider everything very carefully; but you should not lose too much time either.' 'I shall come again soon,' said K. Making a sudden decisive effort, he put on his jacket, threw his overcoat over his shoulders and hurried to the door; the girls outside started to shriek. K. thought he could see them through the door. 'You must keep your word,' said the painter, who had not followed him, 'otherwise I shall come to the bank and find out for myself.' 'Won't you open the door?' said K., tugging on the handle, which he realised the girls outside were holding firmly shut. 'Do you want to be pestered by those girls?' asked the painter. 'Use this way out instead.' He pointed to the door behind the bed. K. agreed and leapt towards the bed. But instead of opening the other door, the painter crawled under the bed and asked from there: 'Just a moment; wouldn't you like to see a picture I might sell you?' K. did not wish to be impolite. The painter had really taken an interest in him and promised to help him further; moreover, because of K.'s forgetfulness no mention had been made of any payment for his help, so he could not refuse him. Though he was trembling with impatience to get out of the studio, he agreed to see the picture.

The painter pulled a pile of unframed pictures from underneath the bed, which were so thick with dust that when he tried to blow it off the top one, the dust swirled around K. for some time, making it difficult for him to breathe. 'A moorland scene,' said the painter, handing the picture to K. It showed two scrawny trees growing some distance apart in dark green grass. In the background was a colourful sunset. 'Fine,' said K., 'I'll buy it.' Inadvertently, he had spoken so curtly that he was glad when the painter, instead of taking offence, picked up another picture. 'This is a companion piece to that one,' he said. It might have been intended as a companion piece, but there was not the slightest difference to be seen between them; here were the trees, there was the grass, and there was the sunset. But it mattered little to K. 'They are very nice landscapes,' he said, 'I'll buy both of them and hang them in my office.' 'You seem to like the subject,' said the painter, picking up a third picture, 'so you're lucky I've got another similar one here.' But it was not a similar one; it was exactly the same. The painter was making the most of this opportunity to sell off his old pictures. 'I'll take that one too,' said K., 'how much do all three cost?' 'We'll discuss that another time,' said the painter. 'You're in a hurry now, and we'll keep in touch. I must say I'm glad you like the pictures. I'll give you all the ones I have down here. They're all moorland scenes. I've painted so many of them. Some people don't like them because they're too gloomy, but some people like gloomy scenes best of all, as you do.'

But just then K. had no wish to listen to the professional views of the mendicant painter. 'Pack them all up!' he cried, interrupting him. 'I will send a messenger tomorrow to collect them.' 'That won't be necessary,' said the painter, 'I hope I can find you a porter who will come with you right away.' At last he leaned over the bed and unlocked the door. 'Don't be afraid of stepping on the bed,' said the painter, 'everyone who comes in here does that.' Even without this invitation, K. would not have hesitated; he had already put one foot on the middle of the bed when he looked through the open door and drew his foot back again. 'What is this?' he asked the painter. 'What are you surprised at?' the painter asked, surprised in his turn. 'These are the court chambers. Didn't you know there are court chambers here? They are in almost every attic, why shouldn't they be here as well? In fact, my studio is part of the court chambers, but the court has let me use it.' What alarmed K. was not so much that he had discovered court chambers here too; what alarmed him most was his own ignorance of court matters. A fundamental rule for an accused person, it seemed to him, was always to be prepared, never to be caught off guard, not to look unsuspectingly the other way when a magistrate was standing next to him – and it was this rule that he constantly violated.

Before him stretched a long corridor from which wafted a thick fug compared to which the air in the studio was refreshing. Benches stood on either side of the corridor, just like the waiting-room of the chambers that were dealing with K.'s case. It seemed there were exact prescriptions for the furnishing of chambers. At the moment there were not many clients here. A man was slumped on one bench, his face buried in his arms, seemingly asleep; another man stood in the gloom at the end of the corridor. K. climbed over the bed, and the painter followed with the pictures. They soon met a court attendant – K. could now recognise all court attendants by the gold button they all wore on their everyday clothes alongside their ordinary buttons – and the painter instructed him to accompany K. with the pictures. K. staggered rather than walked, holding his handkerchief pressed to his mouth. They had almost reached the way out when the girls rushed towards them; so he had not escaped them after all. They had evidently seen that the second door to the studio had been opened, and had gone all the way round to get in this side. 'I can't come with you any further!' cried the painter, laughing among the crush of girls. 'Goodbye! And don't take too long to think about it!'

K. did not even give a backward glance. When he reached the street, he took the first cab that came along. He was keen to get rid of the attendant, whose gold button constantly caught his eye, though probably no one else noticed it. In his eagerness to be of service the attendant tried to sit next to the driver, but K. ordered him to step down. It was long past noon when he arrived back at the bank. He would rather have left the pictures in the cab, but feared he might some time have to show the painter he had kept them. So he had them taken to his office and locked them away in the bottom drawer of his desk, so that at least for the next few days they would be safe from the eyes of the deputy manager.

CHAPTER EIGHT

The Corn Merchant – Dismissal of the Advocate

K. had finally decided to take his case out of the advocate's hands. He could not entirely rid himself of doubts as to whether this was the right thing to do; but these were overridden by his conviction that it was necessary. On the day he was to go and see the advocate, this decision had distracted K. from his work, which took him so long that he had to stay late in his office, and it was past ten o'clock when he at last reached the advocate's door. Before he rang the bell he reflected whether it might not be better to dismiss the advocate over the telephone or by means of a letter; a personal interview would certainly be very embarrassing. But in the end K. did not wish to forego an interview. Dismissal by any other means would be met by silence or a few formal words, and unless Leni could find out something about it, K. would never know how the advocate had taken his dismissal, or what the consequences might be for K. in the not unimportant opinion of the advocate. But if the advocate were sitting opposite K., and if he were to be surprised at his dismissal, then even if the advocate gave little away K. would easily be able to infer everything he wanted to know from his expression and his demeanour. It was even quite possible that he could be persuaded to leave his defence in the advocate's hands and that he would withdraw his dismissal.

As usual, there was no response the first time he rang at the advocate's door. 'Leni could be a little quicker,' K. thought. But at least no other person interfered, as usually happened, whether it was the man in the nightshirt or someone else. As K. pressed the bell a second time, he looked back at the other door; but this time it remained shut. At last a pair of eyes appeared at the hatch of the advocate's door; but they were not Leni's. Someone unlocked the door but still held it shut, called back into the apartment: 'It's him!' and only then opened the door wide. K. had pushed at the door when he had heard the key turn quickly in the door of the other apartment, so when the door in front of him was finally opened, he burst straight into the hall just in time to see Leni as she ran down the corridor between the rooms in her nightdress. It was to her that the man who opened the door had shouted a warning. K. looked after her for a while and then turned to the man. He was a small, scraggy man with a beard, and was holding a candle. 'Are you employed here?' asked K. 'No,' the man replied, 'I am a visitor, the advocate is representing me. I am here on a legal matter.' 'Without a jacket?' asked K., indicating the man's state of undress. 'Oh, I'm sorry!' said the man, looking at himself by the light of the candle as if he had only just noticed the state he was in. 'Are you Leni's lover?' K. asked curtly. He stood with his legs a little apart, his hands clasped behind his back, holding his hat. Simply because he was wearing a heavy overcoat he felt very superior to this skinny little man. 'Good God, no!' said the man, raising one hand to his face in a gesture of alarm and denial, 'no, whatever are you suggesting?' 'You look like a man of your word,' said K. with a smile, 'even so – come along.' He waved him on with his hat and let him lead the way. 'So what is your name?' asked K. as they went. 'Block. I'm a corn merchant,' said the little man, turning round to introduce himself; but K. did not let him stand still. 'Is that your real name?' asked K. 'Of course,' came the answer, 'why do you doubt it?' 'I thought you might have some reason to conceal your name,' said K. He felt at ease, as one does only when speaking to one's inferiors in a foreign country, keeping one's own affairs to oneself and flattering them by taking a casual interest in them while being able to dismiss them at will.

K. stopped at the door of the advocate's study, opened it, and called to the merchant, who had obediently followed him: 'Not so fast! Bring the light over here!' K. thought Leni might have hidden in here; he made the merchant search every corner of the room, but it was empty. In front of the judge's portrait K. held the merchant back by his braces. 'Do you know him?' he asked, pointing up at it. The merchant lifted the candle, peered up at the portrait, and said: 'It's a judge.' 'A senior judge?' asked K., stepping to one side to observe the impression the portrait made on the merchant. He looked up with awe. 'He is a senior judge,' he said. 'You haven't much idea,' said K. 'Of all the junior judges, he is the lowest.' 'Now I remember,' said the merchant, lowering the candle, 'I have heard that too.' 'But of course,' cried K., 'I was forgetting, of course you must have heard.' 'But why, though, why?' asked the merchant as K. pushed him with both hands towards the door. Outside in the hall K. asked: 'Do you know where Leni is hiding?' 'Hiding?' said the merchant. 'No, she's probably in the kitchen making soup for the advocate.' 'Why didn't you tell me that straight away?' asked K. 'I was going to take you there, but you called me back,' replied the merchant. He seemed confused by these conflicting instructions. 'I suppose you think you're very clever,' said K. 'Take me there, then!'

K. had never been in the kitchen, which was surprisingly large and well-equipped. The stove alone was three times as big as a normal one; of the rest only a few details could be made out, for the kitchen was lit simply by a small lamp hanging by the entrance. Leni stood at the stove in her usual white apron, tipping eggs into a pan over a spirit burner. 'Good evening, Josef,' she said, glancing sideways at him. 'Good evening,' said K., gesturing to the merchant to sit in a chair to one side, which he did. K., however, went to stand close behind Leni, leaned over her shoulder and asked: 'Who is this man?' Leni put one arm around K., stirring the soup with her other hand, pulled him towards her and said: 'He's a pathetic creature, a poor merchant called Block. Just look at him.' They both looked round. Block was sitting in the chair as K. had indicated; he had blown out the candle that was no longer needed, and was pinching the wick between his fingers to stop it smoking. 'You were in your nightdress,' said K., taking her head in his hand and turning it back towards the stove. She said nothing. 'Is he your lover?' asked K. She tried to reach for the soup-bowl, but K. took hold of both her hands and said: 'Answer me!' 'Come into the study,' she replied, 'I will explain everything.' 'No,' said K., 'I want you to tell me here.' She clung to him and tried to kiss him, but K. pushed her away and said: 'I don't want you to kiss me now.' 'Josef,' said Leni, looking at K. pleadingly but candidly, 'you're surely not going to be jealous of Herr Block?' Then she turned to the merchant and said: 'Rudi, help me, you can see he suspects me, leave that candle alone.' One might have thought Block had not been paying attention, but he knew exactly how things stood. 'I don't know why you should be jealous,' he said humbly. 'Actually, I don't know either,' said K., smiling at the merchant. Leni burst out laughing. While K.'s attention was diverted she slipped her arm into his and whispered: 'Let him be, you can see what he's like. I've looked after him a bit because he's one of the advocate's best clients, for no other reason. What about you? Do you want to see the advocate today? He's very poorly today, but I'll tell him you're here if you like. You'll stay the night with me, for sure. You haven't been to see us for so long; even the advocate has been asking after you. Don't neglect your case! I've found out various things to tell you about, too. But first of all, take your coat off!'

She helped him off with his hat and coat, dashed into the hall to hang them up, then hurried back to keep an eye on the soup. 'Shall I announce you now, or take him his soup first?' 'Tell him I'm here,' said K. He was annoyed. He had originally intended to discuss his business closely with Leni, especially the matter of dismissing the advocate; but the presence of the merchant put him off. He now thought the whole thing was too important for this little man to be allowed to interfere, perhaps decisively, and so he called back Leni, who was already in the hallway. 'No, take him his soup first,' he said, 'it will give him some energy for the interview with me; he'll need it.' 'So you're one of the advocate's clients too,' said the merchant quietly from his corner, as if wishing to confirm this. His question was not well received. 'What business is that of yours?' said K., and Leni added: 'Will you be quiet. – I'll take him his soup first, then,' she said to K., and poured the soup into a bowl. 'The only problem is that he might fall asleep, because he often goes to sleep soon after a meal.' 'What I have to tell him will keep him awake,' said K. He wanted everything he said to convey the impression that he had important business with the advocate; he wanted Leni to ask him about it and then to seek her advice. But she simply did exactly as she was told. As she passed him with the bowl of soup, she nudged him gently and whispered: 'When he's had his soup I'll announce you straight away so that I'll get you back as soon as possible.' 'Get on,' said K., 'just get on with it.' 'Don't be so rude,' she said, turning round in the doorway with the bowl of soup.

K. looked after her; it was now finally settled that the advocate was to be dismissed. It was probably better, too, that he could not talk to Leni about it beforehand; she scarcely had sufficient knowledge of the whole matter, and would certainly have advised against it. She might even have prevented K. from dismissing him just then; he would have remained in a state of doubt and anxiety, and in the end he would still have done what he had decided, for he was quite determined. The sooner it was done, moreover, the less damage would be done. Perhaps the merchant would have something to say about it.

K. looked round; as soon as the merchant noticed him, he began to get up. 'Stay there,' said K., pulling up a chair beside him. 'Are you an old client of the advocate?' he asked. 'Yes,' said the merchant, 'a very old client.' 'How long has he been acting for you?' asked K. 'It depends what you mean,' said the merchant. 'In business affairs – I am a corn merchant – the advocate has been my lawyer since I took over the business, that's about twenty years; but in my trial, which you're presumably referring to, he has represented me from the beginning, that's more than five years. Yes, well over five years,' he added, pulling out an old pocket-book. 'I've written it all in here; I can tell you the exact dates if you like. It's hard to remember everything. My trial has probably been going on much longer – it began shortly after my wife's death, and that's more than five and a half years ago.' K. moved his chair closer. 'So the advocate also takes on ordinary cases too?' he asked. He found this relationship between the criminal court and civil legal practice oddly reassuring. 'Certainly,' said the merchant, then whispered to K.: 'He is said to be better at civil cases than at others.' But then he seemed to regret what he had said. He put a hand on K.'s shoulder and said: 'I beg of you, please don't give me away.' K. patted his leg reassuringly and said: 'No, I don't betray confidences.' 'You see, he's vindictive,' said the merchant. 'Surely he won't do anything to a faithful client like you,' said K. 'Oh yes, he will,' said the merchant, 'when he's upset he makes no allowances; in any case, I'm not really faithful to him.' 'How is that?' asked K.

'Can I trust you?' asked the merchant doubtfully. 'I think you can,' said K. 'Well,' said the merchant, 'I'll tell you part of it; but you must tell me a secret of yours, so that we stick together against the advocate.' 'You are very cautious,' said K., 'but I will tell you a secret that will reassure you completely. So how have you been unfaithful to the advocate?' 'I have,' said the merchant hesitantly, as if confessing to something dishonourable, 'I have another advocate besides him.' 'But that's nothing so terrible,' said K., a little disappointed. 'It is here,' said the merchant; since he made his confession he had been breathing heavily, but gained in confidence after K.'s remark. 'It is not allowed. And what is allowed least of all is to take on hole-in-the-corner advocates as well as an official advocate. And that's just what I have done; apart from him I have five hole-in-the-corner advocates as well.' 'Five!' cried K., astonished by the number alone. 'Five advocates besides this one?' The merchant nodded. 'I'm negotiating with a sixth one just now.' 'But why do you want so many advocates?' asked K. 'I need them all,' said the merchant. 'Will you explain why?' asked K. 'Certainly,' said the merchant. 'Above all, I don't want to lose my case, that goes without saying. And so I can't ignore anything that might help me; even if there's very little hope of any advantage in a particular instance, I can't reject it. That's why I've spent everything I have on my case. For example, I have taken all the money out of my business; my premises used to occupy almost a whole floor; now I manage with a small room at the back where I work with an apprentice. Of course, this decline is not just due to the withdrawal of the funds, but more to the fact that I had to give up my work. If you want to do something for your case, you can't devote yourself to very much else.' 'So you work at the court yourself?' asked K. 'That's just what I would like to know about.' 'I can't tell you much about that,' said the merchant. 'I did try at first, but I soon gave it up. It's too exhausting, and it doesn't get you very far. For me, at least, it proved quite impossible to work there.

It's a great effort just sitting there and waiting. You know for yourself how stuffy the atmosphere is in those chambers.'

'How do you know I've been there?' asked K. 'I was in the waiting-room when you went through.' 'What a coincidence!' cried K., so engrossed now that he had quite forgotten how ridiculous the merchant had seemed earlier. 'So you saw me! You were in the waiting-room when I walked through. Yes, I did pass through once.' 'It's not such a coincidence,' said the merchant, 'I'm there almost every day.' 'And now I shall probably have to attend more often,' said K., 'but I don't suppose I shall be received as respectfully as I was then. Everyone stood up; I expect they thought I was a magistrate.' 'No,' said the merchant, 'we were greeting the court attendant. We knew you were a defendant. News like that travels fast.' 'So you knew me even then?' said K. 'Perhaps you thought I was behaving arrogantly. Didn't anyone comment on it?' 'No,' said the merchant, 'on the contrary. But it's all nonsense.' 'What is all nonsense?' asked K. 'Why do you want to know?' said the merchant impatiently. 'You don't seem to know the people there yet; you might get the wrong impression. You must realise that in this situation many matters constantly arise that are beyond understanding, one is simply too tired and too distracted to do very much, and people fall back on superstition instead. I'm talking about the others, but I'm no better myself. One of these superstitions, for example, is that many believe you can predict the result of a case from the defendant's face, especially from the lips. So these people claimed that judging by your lips you would definitely be convicted before long. As I said, it's a ridiculous superstition, and in most cases it turns out to be quite unfounded; but when you mix with people like that it's difficult to get away from these ideas. Just imagine what an effect these superstitions can have. You spoke to one of them, didn't you? But he was scarcely able to answer you. Of course, there were plenty of reasons for his confusion, but one of them was the sight of your lips. He told us later that he believed he had seen a sign of his own sentence on your lips.'

'On my lips?' asked K., taking out a pocket mirror and looking at himself. 'I can't see anything peculiar about my lips. Can you?' 'No, I can't,' said the merchant, 'nothing at all.' 'How superstitious these people are!' cried K. 'Didn't I tell you?' said the merchant. 'So do they have so much to do with each other and discuss things among themselves?' said K. 'I've kept to myself so far.' 'As a rule they don't have much to do with each other,' said the merchant, 'that wouldn't be possible, there are so many of them. And they have very little in common. Occasionally some of them might think they have found a common interest, but it soon turns out to be a mistake. As a body they cannot act against the court. Each case is examined individually; the court is most meticulous. So nothing can be done through combined action; just occasionally an individual might achieve something covertly. But the others only get to know about it when it has been done; no one knows how it happened. So there is no common cause; people meet now and again in the waiting-rooms, but not much is discussed there. These superstitious beliefs have existed for ages and just proliferate.' 'I saw the men in that waiting-room,' said K., 'it seemed to me that they were waiting pointlessly.' 'Waiting is not pointless,' said the merchant. 'Only individual intervention is pointless. As I told you, I now have five advocates as well as this one. You might think – I thought so myself at first – that I could leave the matter entirely to them now. But that would be quite wrong; I can't leave it to them any more than I could if I only had one. You don't understand that, I suppose?' 'No,' said K. He laid his hand reassuringly on the merchant's in order to stem his all too rapid flow of talk. 'I would just ask you to speak a little more slowly; all these things are of great importance to me, and I can't quite follow you.' 'I'm glad you reminded me,' said the merchant, 'of course you are a newcomer, a beginner. Your case is six months old, isn't it? Yes, I've heard about it – your case is in its infancy! But I have already thought these things through countless times, I just take them as a matter of course.' 'I suppose you're glad your case is so far advanced?' asked K. He did not wish to ask straight out how the merchant's affairs stood, nor was he given a very clear answer. 'Yes, I've been pushing my case along for five years,' said the merchant, bowing his head. 'That's no small achievement.' Then he fell silent for a while.

K. listened to hear whether Leni was coming back. On the one hand he did not want her to come, for he still had many questions, and did not want her to find him in this confidential discussion with the merchant; but on the other hand he was annoyed that while he was here she was spending so much time with the advocate, far longer that she needed to serve his soup. 'I remember the time very clearly,' the merchant resumed; K. at once gave him his full attention. 'I remember when my case was about as far on as yours is now. Then I only had this advocate, but I wasn't very satisfied with him.' Now I shall find out everything, thought K., and nodded eagerly as if this would encourage the merchant to tell him everything that was worth knowing. 'My case,' continued the merchant, 'made no progress, although hearings were being held. I went to all of them, too; I collected evidence, handed over all my business ledgers to the court, which, as I learned later, was not even necessary. I went to see the advocate time and time again, and he submitted various pleas . . .' 'Various pleas?' asked K. 'Yes, of course,' said the merchant. 'This is most important to me,' said K. 'He is still working on my first submission. So far he has done nothing; I see now that he is neglecting me disgracefully.' 'There may be several good reasons why the submission is not ready yet,' said the merchant. 'In any case, my submissions later turned out to be quite worthless. I even read one of them myself through the good offices of a court official; it was very learned, but lacked any substance. In particular, there was a great deal of Latin, which I cannot understand, then whole pages of general appeals to the court, then flattery of certain individual officials who, although they were not named, could easily be identified by anyone in the know, then words of praise for the advocate from himself as he fawned on the court like a dog, and finally studies of ancient cases that were supposed to be similar to mine. These studies, as far as I could follow them, were certainly made with great care. All this is not meant as a criticism of the advocate's work, and the submission I read was only one of many; at all events, though, as I shall explain, I could not see that my case had made any progress at that point.'

'What sort of progress were you expecting?' asked K. 'That is a perfectly sensible question,' said the merchant with a smile. 'You only rarely see any progress in these proceedings, but I did not know that then. I am a merchant, and I was much more so then than now; I wanted to see real progress, I wanted to get the whole thing over, or at least see the case advance properly. Instead of that there were only interviews, most of which followed the same course; I had the answers ready like a litany. Several times a week messengers came from the court to my office, my apartment, or wherever they could find me. Of course, it was a nuisance – nowadays at least it's much better in that respect, a telephone call is less of a nuisance. And rumours began to spread about my case among my business colleagues, and especially among my relatives, so a great deal of harm was done all round; but there was not the slightest sign to suggest that even the first court hearing would take place in the near future. So I went to the advocate and complained. He explained things at great length, but he firmly refused to do anything I put to him; no one, he said, had any influence on when a hearing should be held – to insist on this in a submission, as I had wanted to, was unheard of and would ruin us both. I thought to myself: if this advocate won't or can't do anything, another one will and can. So I looked for another advocate, but I'll tell you this straight away, none of them ever requested a date for the main hearing, none of them ever obtained one; that is quite impossible (though there is one exception I will tell you about). So in this respect the advocate did not mislead me; but otherwise I had no reason to regret having engaged other ones. You may well have heard quite a lot from Dr Huld about hole-in-the-corner advocates; he has probably described them as beneath contempt, and in fact they are. However, when he talks about them and compares them with himself and his colleagues, he always makes a small mistake which I will point out in passing: he always draws a distinction between them and the advocates in his circle, whom he calls the "great" advocates. That is wrong; of course, anyone can call himself "great" if he likes, but only court convention decides these things. And according to this convention there are, apart from the hole-in-the-corner advocates, lesser and greater advocates. However, this advocate and his colleagues are only lesser advocates; the great advocates, of whom I have only heard and have never seen, are incomparably higher in rank than the lesser advocates – as high above them as *they* are above the despised hole-in-the-corner advocates.'

'The great advocates?' said K. 'Who are they, then? How can they be reached?' 'So you have never heard of them?' said the merchant. 'There is hardly a defendant who doesn't dream about them for some time after he has been told about them. But you should not be tempted to do that. I don't know who the great advocates are, and I don't suppose they can ever be reached. I don't know of a single case of which it could be said with certainty that they had intervened. They do defend some people, but that can't be achieved at your own request; they only defend those they wish to defend. But the cases they take on must have gone further than the lower court. Apart from that, it is better not to think about them, because if you do, you find your consultations with the other advocates, their advice and their proposals, so off-putting and useless – I've experienced it myself – that all you want to do is give it all up, take to your bed and forget all about it. But of course that would be completely stupid, because even in bed you wouldn't get any peace for very long.' 'So you didn't consider going to the great advocates at the time?' asked K. 'Not for very long,' said the merchant with another smile. 'Unfortunately you can't get them out of your mind completely, and such thoughts come to you at night especially. But at the time I wanted immediate results, so I went to these hole-in-the-corner advocates.'

'So you've got your heads together!' cried Leni, who had returned with the soup-bowl and was standing in the doorway. They were indeed sitting so close to each other that at the slightest movement they would have bumped their heads together; the merchant, who was in any case very small, was hunched up so that K. was forced to bend low in order to hear everything. 'Just a moment!' cried K., motioning to Leni with an impatient wave of his hand, which was still resting on the merchant's. 'He wanted me to tell him about my case,' the merchant said to Leni. 'Go on, then, tell him all about it,' she said. She spoke condescendingly but affectionately to him. K. was annoyed; he now recognised that the man was of some value to him, at least he had some experience and was perfectly able to pass it on. Leni had probably misjudged him. He looked on with irritation as Leni took the candle from the merchant, who had been holding on to it all this time, wiped his hand with her apron and then knelt down beside him to scrape off some wax that had dripped onto his trousers. 'You were about to tell me about the hole-in-the-corner advocates,' said K., pushing Leni's hand away without further comment. 'What are you after?' Leni asked, giving K. a gentle slap and going about her work. 'Yes, the hole-in-the-corner advocates,' said the merchant, rubbing his brow as if in thought. K. tried to prompt him: 'You wanted quick results, so you went to the hole-in-the-corner advocates.' 'Quite right,' said the merchant, but he did not continue. 'Perhaps he doesn't want to talk about it in front of Leni,' thought K. He restrained his impatience to hear any more just now, and did not press the merchant any further.

'Have you announced me?' he asked Leni. 'Of course,' she replied. 'He's waiting for you. Leave Block alone now, you can talk to Block later, he's staying here.' K. still hesitated. 'Are you going to stay here?' he asked the merchant. He wanted him to answer for himself, and did not want Leni to talk about the merchant as if he were not there. Today he was filled with suppressed anger against Leni. Again it was Leni who spoke: 'He often sleeps here.' 'He sleeps here?' cried K. He had imagined the merchant would wait here for him while he quickly concluded his interview with the advocate, and that they would then both leave and discuss everything thoroughly without being disturbed. 'Yes,' said Leni, 'it's not everyone who is allowed to see the advocate any time he likes as you are, Josef. You don't seem in the least surprised that he will see you at eleven o'clock at night in spite of his illness. You just take everything your friends do for you far too much for granted. Well, your friends do it willingly, at least I do. I just want you to be fond of me; I don't ask for any other thanks, and don't need any either.' 'To be fond of you?' was K.'s first thought; only then did he think to himself: 'Well, yes, I am fond of her.'

Nevertheless, putting all this aside, he said: 'He will see me because I am his client. If I needed anyone else's help to see him, I would be pleading with them and thanking them all the time.'

'Isn't he awful today?' Leni asked the merchant. 'Now I'm the one who is being ignored,' thought K., and almost felt angry with the merchant too when he said, falling in with Leni's rudeness: 'That's not why the advocate will see him. It's because his case is more interesting than mine. What's more, his case is still in the early stages, so it's probably not in such a muddle, so the advocate is glad to take it up. Later it will be different.' 'Get away with you,' said Leni, laughing at the merchant, 'what nonsense! You see,' she said, turning to K., 'you can't believe a word he says. He's very nice, but he chatters so much. Perhaps that's why the advocate can't stand him. At any rate, he only sees him when he's in a good mood. I've gone to a lot of trouble to alter things, but it's impossible. Just think – sometimes I announce Block, but he only sees him three days later. But if Block isn't there when he's called, he's lost his chance and I have to announce him all over again. That's why I allowed Block to sleep here; he's even rung for him in the middle of the night. So Block is ready to see him during the night, too. But then it sometimes happens that when the advocate sees Block is there, he changes his mind and won't see him.'

K. looked questioningly at the merchant, who nodded and said with the same candour as he had shown to K. earlier – perhaps his embarrassment had confused him – 'Yes, later on you come to depend on your advocate very heavily.' 'He's only making a show of complaining,' said Leni. 'He likes sleeping here, as he has often admitted to me.' She went to a small door and pushed it open. 'Do you want to see his bedroom?' she asked. K. went over and from the door looked into the low, windowless room; there was just enough space for a narrow bed, which could only be reached by climbing over the end of it. At the head of the bed was a recess in the wall in which stood, neatly arranged, a candle, a pen, an inkwell, and a bundle of papers – probably papers relating to the merchant's case. 'You sleep in the maid's room?' asked K., turning back to the merchant. 'Leni made it up for me,' he replied, 'it's very convenient.' K. took a good look at him. Perhaps his first impression of the merchant had been correct; he had a lot of experience, but he had paid dearly for it.

Suddenly K. could no longer stand the sight of the merchant. 'Put him to bed!' he cried to Leni, who did not seem to understand him. But he wanted to go to the advocate and dismiss him, thus liberating himself not only from the advocate, but from Leni and the merchant too. However, before he reached the door, the merchant addressed him in a low voice: 'Sir.' K. turned, frowning angrily. 'You have forgotten your promise,' said the merchant, holding out his arms imploringly to K. from his chair. 'You were going to tell me your secret.' 'So I was,' said K. with a glance at Leni, who was watching him attentively. 'Well, listen; it's scarcely a secret any more. I'm going to see the advocate now to dismiss him.' 'He's dismissing him!' cried the merchant. He jumped up from his chair and ran round the kitchen waving his arms in the air. 'He's dismissing the advocate!' Leni tried to rush at K., but the merchant got in her way, so she hit him with her fist. Then, her fists still clenched, she ran after K., but he was well ahead of her. He had already reached the advocate's room when she caught up with him; he had almost shut the door behind him, but Leni, holding the door open with her foot, seized his arm and tried to pull him back. But he gripped her wrist so tightly that she gasped and let him go. She did not dare to enter the room, but K. turned the key in the lock anyway.

'I have been waiting for you for a very long time,' said the advocate from his bed. He laid a document he had been reading by candlelight onto his bedside table and put on a pair of spectacles through which he looked at K. severely. Instead of apologising, K. said: 'I shall not be staying very long.' Since it was not an apology, the advocate ignored K.'s remark and said: 'I shall not admit you again at such a late hour.' 'That suits my purposes,' said K. The advocate looked at him inquiringly. 'Take a seat,' he said. 'If you wish,' said K., pulling a chair up to the bedside table and sitting down. 'It seems that you have locked the door,' said the advocate. 'Yes,' said K., 'it was because of Leni.' He did not intend to spare anyone. But the advocate asked: 'Has she been making a nuisance of herself again?' 'Making a nuisance of herself?' asked K. 'Yes,' said the advocate, laughing. He had a fit of coughing, then when he had recovered, began to laugh again. 'You have surely noticed how forward she is?' he asked, and tapped K.'s hand; in his distraction he had let his hand rest on the bedside table, but now withdrew it quickly. 'So you don't take much notice of it,' said the advocate when K. did not reply. 'All the better. Otherwise I might have had to apologise to you. It is one of Leni's peculiarities that I have long since forgiven her; I would not mention it if you had not locked the door just now. You are the last person I should have to explain this to, but since you look so dismayed, I will. It is Leni's peculiarity that she finds most defendants attractive. She becomes attached to all of them, she loves them all, and indeed all of them seem to love her. Sometimes, if I let her, she tells me about it to entertain me. It is a remarkable phenomenon, almost a law of nature. Of course, it is not as if there is any clear or definable alteration in their appearance as a result of being accused. It is not like other court cases; most of them carry on with their normal lives and are not hindered by their trial if they have a good advocate who looks after them. Nevertheless, those with experience of these things are able to pick out defendants, one by one, from any crowd, however large. How do they do this, you will ask. My answer will not convince you; it is because the accused are the most attractive ones. It cannot be their guilt that makes them attractive, since – at least, I have to say this as an advocate – they are not all guilty; nor can it be the appropriate punishment that makes them attractive at this stage, because they are not all punished. So it can only be because proceedings have been taken against them; somehow this clings to them. Some of them are especially attractive; but they are all attractive, even that miserable creature Block.'

When the advocate had finished, K. was completely calm. He had even nodded vigorously at these last words, thus confirming his previous opinion that the advocate was once again, as always, distracting him by making general observations that were quite irrelevant and deflected attention from the main question, namely, what he had actually achieved in K.'s case. The advocate evidently noticed that K. was more determined than usual, for he fell silent in order to give K. a chance to speak. Then, when K. said nothing, he asked: 'Did you come here today with a specific purpose in mind?' 'Yes,' said K., shielding his eyes from the light of the candle with his hand in order to see the advocate better. 'I wanted to tell you that as from today I am dispensing with your services.' 'Do I understand you correctly?' asked the advocate, half rising from the bed and supporting himself on the pillow. 'Presumably,' said K., who was sitting bolt upright as if on guard. 'Well, we can also discuss this plan,' said the advocate after a pause. 'It is no longer a plan,' said K. 'Perhaps,' said the advocate, 'but all the same, we don't want to be too hasty.' He used the word 'we' as if he had no intention of letting K. go, as if he intended to remain as his adviser even if he could not represent him. 'I am not being over-hasty,' said K. He stood up slowly and went to stand behind his chair. 'I have thought it over carefully, perhaps even too long. My decision is final.'

'Then allow me to say just a few more words,' said the advocate, lifting the quilt and sitting on the edge of the bed. His bare legs covered in white hairs were shivering with cold. He asked K. to pass him a blanket from the sofa. K. fetched the blanket and said: 'You are quite unnecessarily risking a chill.' 'The matter is important enough,' said the advocate, as he wrapped the quilt around himself and covered his legs with the blanket. 'Your uncle is my friend, and I have grown fond of you, too, in the course of time. I admit that freely; I do not need to be ashamed of it.'

K. found the old man's sentimental words most unwelcome, for they forced him to give a more detailed explanation, something he would rather have avoided; besides, as he had to admit to himself, they distracted him too, though of course they could never make him go back on his decision. 'I am grateful for your kindness,' he said. 'I also recognise that you have helped me in my case as far as you could, and as it seemed to you to be in my interests. However, I have recently become convinced that this is not sufficient. Of course, I shall never attempt to convert an older and so much more experienced man as you to my way of thinking. If I have at times unwittingly tried to do so, please forgive me; but the matter, as you say yourself, is important enough, and I am convinced it is necessary to pursue the case much more forcefully than hitherto.' 'I understand,' said the advocate. 'You are impatient.' 'I am not impatient,' said K. with some irritation, not choosing his words very carefully. 'You may have noticed that on my first visit to you with my uncle I was not too concerned about my case; indeed, unless I was reminded of it rather forcefully, I forgot all about it. But my uncle insisted that I should engage you, and I did it to please him. After that, one might have expected that the case would have concerned me even less than before, since one engages an advocate in order to take some of the burden of the case from one's own shoulders. But the opposite happened; I had never worried about my case so much until the moment I engaged you to represent me. When I was on my own, I did nothing about my case, I was scarcely aware of it; but now that I had someone to represent me, everything was set for something to happen. At every moment, and with ever greater expectation, I waited for you to act; but you did not. To be sure, I received from you various communications about the court, which I could not perhaps have had from anyone else. But that is insufficient now that the case, which is being conducted entirely in secret, is affecting me more and more closely.'

K. had pushed his chair away and was now standing there upright, his hands in his pockets. 'From a certain stage in the conduct of a case,' said the advocate calmly and quietly, 'nothing really happens any more. How many clients have stood before me like you at a similar stage in their case and have said something similar!' 'Then all these similar clients,' said K., 'were just as right as I am. That does not prove me wrong at all.' 'I do not wish to prove you wrong,' said the advocate, 'but I wished to add that I would have expected more judgement from you than from the others, especially as I have given you more insight into the court and into my activities than I usually do to my clients. And now I am forced to realise that in spite of everything you do not have sufficient confidence in me. You are not making it easy for me.'

How the advocate was humbling himself before K. – and without any regard for the dignity of his position, which is surely at its most sensitive on this point! And why did he do this? By all appearances he was a busy advocate, and a rich man too; neither the loss of income nor the loss of a client could in themselves mean very much to him. Moreover, he was ailing and should be taking good care to shed some of his work. But still he clung to K.! Why? Was it a personal attachment to his uncle, or did he really regard K.'s case as so extraordinary, and hope to gain prestige from it, either in K.'s eyes or – and this possibility could not be excluded – in the eyes of his friends in the court? Nothing could be gathered from his demeanour, however searchingly K. studied him. One might almost suppose that he was deliberately masking his expression in order to assess the effect of his words. But he clearly interpreted K.'s silence only too much in his own favour when he continued: 'You will have noticed that although I have a large practice, I do not employ any assistants. Once it was otherwise, there was a time when some young lawyers worked for me; but now I work alone. This is partly due to the changes in my practice, in that I restrict myself more and more to cases such as yours, and partly to the more profound experience I have of these cases. I found that I was unable to let anyone else do this work without violating my obligations to my clients and to the duties I had taken on. But the decision to do all the work myself had the natural consequence that I had to refuse almost all those who asked me to represent them, and was only able to accept those I had a personal interest in – and there are enough poor wretches, indeed some not far from here, who are glad to snap up any scraps I throw them. On top of that, I became ill from overwork; but still I did not regret my decision. Perhaps I should have refused to take on more cases than I did; but it turned out that it was absolutely necessary for me to devote myself fully to the cases I accepted, and this was justified by their successful outcomes. I once read a document that expressed very well the difference between representing a client in ordinary legal cases and cases such as these. It said that one advocate leads his client on a thread to the verdict, while another lifts his client straight onto his shoulders and carries him, without once putting him down, to the verdict and beyond. It is so. But I was not quite right when I said that I never regret this hard work. When it is so completely misunderstood, as in your case, well, then I almost regret it.'

Far from convincing K., these words only made him more impatient. He rather imagined that he could gather from the advocate's tone what he could expect if he relented: the assurances would begin all over again, references to the progress of his plea, to the improved mood of the court officials, but also to the huge difficulties to be faced – in short, everything he was all too familiar with would be trotted out in order to delude him with vague hopes and torment him with vague menaces. This had to be prevented once and for all, so he said: 'What do you intend to do in my case if your services are retained?' The advocate submitted even to this insulting question, and answered: 'I would continue to do what I have already done for you.' 'I knew it,' said K., 'anything further you have to say is superfluous.' 'I will make one more attempt,' said the advocate, as if K.'s anxieties were his rather than K.'s. 'You see, I suspect you have not only misjudged the legal support I have given you, but that you have been misled into behaving as you do because, although you are a defendant, you have been too well treated – or, to be more accurate, you have been leniently treated, or so it seems. I have good reason for suspecting this; it is often better to be in chains than to be free. But I would like to show you how other defendants are treated; perhaps you might learn a lesson from it. I will now summon Block; unlock the door and sit here by the bedside table.' 'With pleasure,' said K., doing as the advocate told him; he was always willing to learn. But to avoid any misunderstanding, he added: 'You realise that I am removing you from my case?' 'Yes,' said the advocate, 'but you still have time to reverse that decision.' He got back into bed, drew the quilt up to his chin and turned towards the wall. Then he rang the bell.

Almost immediately Leni appeared. She glanced round the room quickly, trying to gather what had been going on; she seemed reassured that K. was sitting calmly by the advocate's bed. She nodded at K., smiling, but he looked at her blankly. 'Fetch Block,' said the advocate. But instead of going to fetch him, Leni went only as far as the door and called: 'Block! The advocate wants you!' – and then, no doubt because the advocate remained facing the wall and was paying no attention, she slipped behind K.'s chair. Then she began to pester him by leaning over the back of the chair or, very gently and carefully, running her hands through his hair and stroking his cheeks. Eventually K. had to stop her by seizing one of her hands, which with some reluctance she surrendered to him.

Block had appeared as soon as he was called; but he stood outside the door and appeared unsure as to whether he should come in. He raised his eyebrows and cocked his head, as if he were listening for the advocate's summons to be repeated. K. could have encouraged him to come in, but he had made up his mind to break off all relations not only with the advocate, but with everything and everybody in this house; so he did not stir. Leni, too, said nothing. Block, noticing that at least no one was driving him away, came in on tiptoe, his face tense and his hands clasped tight behind his back. He had left the door open as a possible avenue of escape. He did not give K. a glance, looking only at the piled quilt under which the advocate, who had rolled over close to the wall, was not even visible. But then his voice was heard: 'Is Block here?' Block had by now advanced some way into the room; the question seemed to have the effect of a blow to his chest, and then another in his back. He staggered, stood bending low, and said: 'At your service.' 'What do you want?' asked the advocate, 'this is a most inconvenient time.' 'Wasn't I called?' asked Block, more to himself than to the advocate; he held up his hands to protect himself, and stood ready to run away. 'You were called,' said the advocate, 'but it is still an inconvenient time.' After a pause he added: 'You always come at an inconvenient time.'

As soon as the advocate began to speak to him, Block stopped looking towards the bed; instead he stared at a corner of the room and simply listened, as if the sight of the speaker were too dazzling to bear. But even listening was difficult for him, because the advocate talked towards the wall, and he spoke quietly and rapidly. 'Should I go away?' asked Block. 'Now you're here,' said the advocate, 'stay here!' One might have thought that the advocate, instead of granting Block's wish, had threatened him with a beating, because now Block really began to shake. 'Yesterday,' said the advocate, 'I was with my friend the third judge, and I gradually brought the conversation round to you. Do you want to know what he said?' 'Oh, yes please,' said Block. When the advocate did not reply immediately, Block repeated his plea and bent down as if he were about to fall to his knees. But K. shouted at him: 'What are you doing?' – and because Leni had tried to stop him calling out, he seized her other hand, too. It was not with a lover's touch that he held her; she sighed several times and tried to escape his grasp. But Block was made to suffer for K.'s outburst, for the advocate asked him: 'Who is your advocate?' 'You are,' said Block. 'And who else apart from me?' asked the advocate. 'No one else,' said Block. 'Then don't take advice from anyone else,' said the advocate.

Block assented wholeheartedly; he scowled angrily at K. and shook his head at him violently. These gestures, if translated into words, would have expressed coarse abuse. And this was the man K. had tried to engage in a friendly discussion of his own case! 'I won't interrupt you again,' said K., leaning back in his chair, 'you can kneel or crawl on all fours if you wish, it won't bother me.' But Block still had his self-respect, at least towards K., for he went up to him, shook his fists and shouted as loud as he dared in the advocate's presence: 'You are not to speak to me like that, it's not right. Why are you insulting me here in front of the advocate, where both of us, you and I, are tolerated only out of the goodness of his heart? You are no better than I am, you are also a defendant with a case on your hands. If you still think you're a gentleman, I'm a gentleman too just as much as you, if not more so. And I will be treated like a gentleman, especially by you. If you think you are superior because you can sit here and listen calmly while I, as you put it, crawl around on all fours, I'll remind you of the old legal maxim: movement is better for the suspect than staying still, because those who are still might be on the scales being weighed along with their sins.'

K. said nothing; he could only stare in amazement at this crazed man. What a change had come over him in the last hour! Was his case causing him such confusion that he failed to distinguish friend from foe? Could he not see that the advocate was deliberately humiliating him, and was now seeking only to impress K. with his power, and thereby perhaps to dominate him too? But if Block was not capable of realising this, or if he was so afraid of the advocate that even this realisation could not help him, how was it that he was cunning or bold enough to deceive the advocate and conceal from him that he had other advocates working for him? And how did he dare to attack K., who after all could betray his secret there and then? But he dared to do more than that; he approached the advocate's bed and began to complain about K. 'Sir,' he said, 'have you heard how this man spoke to me? His case has only been going for a few hours, and he is trying to give advice to me, someone whose case has been running for five years. He even abused me. He knows nothing and abuses me, who to the best of my poor abilities have studied closely all that decency, duty and the customs of the court demand.' 'Pay no attention to anyone,' said the advocate, 'and do what seems right to you.' 'Certainly,' said Block, as if to give himself courage, and after glancing briefly to one side kneeled down close to the bed. 'I am on my knees, your Honour,' he said. But the advocate said nothing. Block cautiously stroked the quilt with one hand.

In the ensuing silence Leni freed herself from K.'s grasp, saying: 'You are hurting me. Let me go, I want to be with Block.' She went over and sat on the edge of the bed. Block was delighted by this, and immediately begged her with silent but lively gestures to plead with the advocate on his behalf. He obviously needed the advocate's advice very urgently, but perhaps only in order to make use of it through his other lawyers. Leni evidently knew exactly how to approach the advocate; she pointed to his hand and put out her lips as if for a kiss. At once Block kissed the advocate's hand and, encouraged by Leni, did it twice more. But still the advocate said nothing. Then Leni leaned over the advocate, revealing the lovely form of her body as she stretched, and bending down close to his face she stroked his long white hair. This did force an answer from him. 'I hesitate to tell him,' said the advocate; one could see him shaking his head gently, perhaps the better to feel the touch of Leni's hand. Block listened, his eyes lowered as if by listening he was transgressing some law. 'Why do you hesitate?' asked Leni. K. had the feeling that he was listening to a well-rehearsed conversation that had often been repeated and would often be repeated in the future, one that only for Block would never lose its novelty. 'How has he behaved today?' asked the advocate instead of replying. Before Leni answered, she looked down at Block and watched for a short while as he raised his hands towards her, wringing them imploringly. At last she nodded gravely, turned to the advocate and said: 'He has been quiet and hard-working.' An elderly merchant, a man with a long beard, was pleading with a young girl for a favourable report! Whatever Block's ulterior motive might be, nothing could justify his behaviour in the eyes of a fellow human being.

K. did not understand how the advocate could have imagined that this spectacle would win him over. If K. had not dismissed him already, this performance would have made him do so; it almost degraded the onlooker. So this was the effect of the advocate's method, to which K. had fortunately not been exposed for too long: the client finally forgot the whole world and could only drag himself along this illusory path to the end of his trial. He was no longer a client; he was the advocate's dog. If the advocate had ordered Block to crawl under the bed as if into a dog kennel and bark, he would have done it willingly. K. listened intently but with detachment, as if he had been commissioned by a higher authority to take careful note and to submit an eyewitness account and full report of everything that was said here. 'What did he do all day?' asked the advocate. 'I locked him in the maid's room so he couldn't disturb me in my work,' said Leni. 'That's where he usually stays anyway. Now and again I took a look through the hatch to see what he was doing. He was kneeling on the bed all the time; he had spread out the documents you lent him on the windowsill and was reading them. That made a good impression on me, because the window only opens onto a ventilation shaft and lets in hardly any light. The fact that he was reading in spite of this showed me how obedient he is.' 'I am pleased to hear that,' said the advocate, 'but did he understand what he was reading?'

During this exchange Block was constantly moving his lips; clearly he was formulating the answers he hoped Leni would give. 'Well, of course,' said Leni, 'I can't say definitely. At any rate, I saw that he was reading very carefully; he spent the whole day on one page, and as he read he followed the words with his finger. Whenever I looked in he sighed, as if reading was a great effort. I suppose the documents you gave him are hard to understand.' 'Yes,' said the advocate, 'they certainly are. And I don't believe he understands them either. They are meant to give him some idea of what a hard struggle it is to defend him. And who is it I struggle like this for? It's almost absurd to say it – for Block. He must learn to understand what that means, too. Did he study without a break?' 'Almost without a break,' Leni answered. 'Just once he asked me for a drink of water, so I handed him a glass through the hatch. Then at eight I let him out and gave him something to eat.' Block glanced sideways at K., as if what Leni was saying was greatly to his credit and ought to impress K. Now he seemed to have high hopes, he moved more freely and shuffled to and fro on his knees.

It was all the more noticeable, then, how he froze at the advocate's next words. 'You are praising him,' said the advocate, 'but that only makes it hard for me to tell him. The fact is, the judge has not given a favourable opinion, either on Block or on his case.' 'Not favourable?' asked Leni. 'How is that possible?' Block looked at her with such a tense look on his face, as if he believed she could, even now, turn the judge's opinion, which had been given so much earlier, to his advantage. 'Not favourable,' said the advocate. 'He was even unpleasantly surprised when I started to talk about Block. "Don't talk about Block," he said. "He is my client," I replied. "He is taking advantage of you," said the judge. "I do not regard his case as hopeless," I said. "He is taking advantage of you," he repeated. "I don't think so," I said, "Block works hard on his case and follows it closely. He almost lives with me so that he can keep up with it. One does not always see such zeal. It is true he is personally unattractive, he has disgusting manners, and he is dirty; but in the conduct of his case he is exemplary." When I said exemplary, I was deliberately exaggerating. Then he said: "Block is just cunning. He has gained a lot of experience and knows how to drag out his case. But his ignorance is much greater than his cunning. What do you think he would say if he discovered his case has not started, if he were told that the bell has not even been rung to mark the beginning of his trial?" Be still, Block!' said the advocate, for Block had just begun to stand up shakily, and clearly wanted to ask for an explanation. This was the first time the advocate had addressed himself directly to Block. With weary eyes he looked vacantly down at Block, who under the advocate's gaze sank slowly back to his knees.

'This pronouncement by the judge is of no significance to you,' said the advocate. 'Do not be alarmed by every word I say. If this happens again, I won't confide in you any more. I can't open my mouth without you looking at me as if you were about to be sentenced. You should be ashamed to act like that in front of my client! And you're destroying the confidence he has in me. What more do you expect? You're still alive, you're still under my protection. Your anxiety is pointless! You have read somewhere that in some cases the final verdict comes unexpectedly, from any source at any time. With many reservations that is in fact true; but it is equally true that your anxiety repels me, and that I see it as a lack of necessary confidence. What have I said, then? I have repeated the words of a judge. You know that various opinions spring up in the course of proceedings until they become impenetrable. This judge, for example, understands the case as starting at a different point from my understanding of it. It's a difference of opinion, that's all. At a certain stage of the trial, according to an old custom, a bell is rung. In the opinion of this judge the trial begins at that point. I can't give you just now all the arguments against this view, and you wouldn't understand them; it's sufficient for you to know that there are many arguments against it.' Embarrassed, Block rang his fingers over the surface of the blanket; for the moment, his anxiety at the judge's words made him forget his own inferior position vis-à-vis the advocate; he thought only of himself and turned the words over and over in his mind. 'Block,' Leni cautioned him, pulling him up by his collar, 'leave the blanket alone and listen to the advocate.'

CHAPTER NINE

In the Cathedral

A very important Italian business associate of the bank was visiting the town for the first time, and K. had been instructed to show him some of the local monuments. It was a task that at any other time he would have considered an honour; but now that it was such a great effort to maintain his own position at the bank, it was one he accepted unwillingly. Every hour spent away from the bank caused him anxiety; although he could not take advantage of his time at the office nearly as much as he could before – he spent many hours in the feeblest pretence of doing any real work – he worried all the more when he was not there. He imagined that the deputy manager, who had always watched him closely, would come into his office now and again, sit down at his desk and look through his papers, or receive clients with whom K. had for years been almost on terms of friendship and turn them against him, or even that he might discover mistakes he had made; for K. now felt threatened on every side by mistakes made at work, mistakes he could no longer avoid. And so whenever he was instructed to go out and meet clients, or even to make a short business trip, however much of an honour this might be – and quite by chance, such assignments had recently come his way more frequently – he still had the suspicion that he was being removed from the office for a while so that his work could be checked, or at least that he was regarded as quite dispensable. He could have refused most of these assignments without difficulty, but he did not dare to do so; for if his suspicions were even remotely justified, to refuse would be to admit his fears.

For this reason he accepted the assignments with apparent calm; he even concealed a severe cold when he was asked to go on a strenuous two-day business trip, simply in order to avoid the risk of having to call it off because of the prevailing wet autumnal weather. When he returned from the journey with a raging headache, he learned that he was expected to show the Italian business associate around the next day. The temptation to refuse just this once was very strong, especially since this assignment had nothing directly to do with business, though it was no doubt important enough to fulfil this social obligation to a colleague; but it was not important to K., who knew very well that he could only maintain his position through success at work, and that if he did not achieve this it would do him no good even if, against all expectations, he were to charm the Italian. He did not wish to be absent from his work, even for a day, for his fear that he might not be allowed back was too great. He knew perfectly well that this fear was exaggerated, but still it oppressed him. In any case, on this occasion it was almost impossible to invent an acceptable excuse; his knowledge of Italian was not great, but it was adequate. More decisive was the fact that he had earlier acquired some knowledge of the history of art – an expertise that had become known at the bank, although it was a wholly exaggerated impression, because for a while K., if only for reasons to do with business, been a member of the Society for the Preservation of Ancient Monuments. Now it happened, or so rumour had it, that the Italian was an art lover, so the choice of K. as his companion was perfectly obvious.

It was a very wet and windy morning when K., extremely annoyed at the prospect of the day in front of him, arrived at the office at seven o'clock so that he could at least do some work before his visitor made him leave it all. He was very tired, for he had spent half the night studying an Italian grammar by way of preparation. The window, at which he had recently been in the habit of sitting far too often, attracted him far more than his desk, but he resisted the temptation and sat down to work. Unfortunately, at that moment the messenger appeared and told him that the manager had sent him to see whether Herr K. had arrived yet; if he had, would he kindly step over to the reception area because the gentleman from Italy was already there. 'I'm coming right away,' said K. He put a small dictionary into his pocket, picked up a folder of places of interest in the town that he had put together for the visitor, put it under his arm and went through the deputy manager's office into the reception room. He was very pleased that he had come in so early that he was available at once, which no one could seriously have expected. The deputy manager's office was of course as still and empty as if it were the middle of the night; the messenger was no doubt supposed to have summoned him to the meeting, but without success.

As K. entered the reception room the two men rose from their deep armchairs. The manager gave him a friendly smile; he was obviously very pleased that K. had arrived. He introduced K. at once; the Italian shook K.'s hand firmly and with a smile referred to someone as an early riser. K. did not at first understand what he meant; it was a strange word, the sense of which he only guessed after a while. He replied with some polite phrases that the Italian also received with a smile, frequently passing his hand nervously over his bushy grey-blue moustache. It was evidently scented; K. almost felt tempted to go up to him and smell it. When they were all seated and had exchanged a few introductory words, K. was most put out to find that he only understood fragments of what the Italian was saying. When the man spoke calmly he understood him almost perfectly, but this happened only occasionally; mostly the words came pouring out of his mouth as he shook his head with delight. But when he talked like this he regularly lapsed into some form of dialect that K. did not recognise as Italian, but which the manager not only understood but also spoke. K. could of course have anticipated this, for the visitor was from southern Italy, where the manager had also lived for some years. At all events, K. realised that there was little possibility of communicating with the Italian, whose French was also difficult to understand; moreover, his moustache concealed his lip movements, which might have helped K. to follow him.

K. began to foresee many problems; for the time being he gave up trying to understand the Italian – it would have been an unnecessary effort while the manager was there because he understood him so easily – and confined himself to watching morosely as the Italian sat back comfortably in his armchair. He tugged frequently at his short close-fitting jacket, and at one point tried, by raising his arms and flapping his wrist, to express something that K. could not grasp, although he leaned forward in order not to lose sight of these gestures. Eventually K., who had desultorily and mechanically followed the exchanges with his eyes, became overwhelmed by his earlier weariness, and to his horror only checked himself, fortunately just in time, as in his confused state of mind he been about to stand up, turn round and leave. At last the Italian looked at the clock and jumped up. When he had said goodbye to the manager he approached K., but he came up so close that K. had to push back his armchair in order to move. The manager, who could clearly read in K.'s eyes the desperate situation he found himself in with this form of Italian, joined in the conversation so tactfully and discreetly that he appeared merely to be offering scraps of advice, while in fact he was succinctly explaining to K. all that the Italian, who was constantly interrupting him, had to say.

K. learned that the Italian first had some business to see to, that he would unfortunately have only a little time, and that he had no intention whatever of rushing round all the sights, but had decided – of course, only if K. was agreeable, it was his decision alone – to visit just the cathedral; but he wished to do this thoroughly. He was exceptionally delighted, he said, to do this in the company of such a learned and amiable man – by which he meant K., who was intent on ignoring what the Italian was saying and trying to follow the manager's words. He asked K., if it was convenient to him, to meet him in the cathedral in two hours' time, say, at ten o'clock. For his part, he was confident that he could be there by then. K. said a few words in reply, the Italian shook the manager by the hand, then K., then the manager once more, and made to leave, still in full flow but only half turning towards them as they followed him to the door. K. stayed behind for a while with the manager, who looked particularly unwell today. The manager felt he ought to apologise to K., and confided to him (they were standing very close to each other) that he had initially intended to accompany the Italian himself, but then – he gave no further reason – he had decided to send K. instead. If he did not at first understand the Italian, he should not be put out, he would soon pick it up, and even if he did not understand very much at all, that was no bad thing, because it did not matter very much to the Italian whether he was understood or not. Besides, K.'s Italian was surprisingly good, and the manager was sure he would cope very well. With these words he let K. go.

K. spent the rest of the time left to him writing out from the dictionary some unfamiliar terms he would need for a tour of the cathedral. It was a most irksome task. Messengers brought in the post, clerks came in with various inquiries and, when they saw that K. was busy, stood around at the door and would not leave until he had heard what they had to say. The deputy manager did not miss this opportunity to interrupt him; he came in frequently, took the dictionary from him and flicked through the pages, clearly quite aimlessly. Even clients appeared in the gloom of the waiting room when the door was opened and bowed hesitantly, wishing to attract his attention, but uncertain whether they were visible. All this went on around K. as if he were at the hub of it, while he drew up a list of the terms he needed, then looked them up in the dictionary, wrote them out, practised pronouncing them, and finally tried to learn them by heart. But his once reliable memory seemed to have deserted him, and at times he felt so furious with the Italian who was the cause of all this effort that he buried the dictionary under a pile of papers with the firm intention of doing no more preparation; but then he realised that he could not simply walk around the cathedral with the Italian in silence, and took out the dictionary again feeling even more furious.

At half past nine, just as he was about to leave, the telephone rang. Leni wished him good morning and asked how he was. K. thanked her hastily and told her he could not possibly talk to her, as he had to go to the cathedral. 'To the cathedral?' asked Leni. 'Yes, yes, to the cathedral.' 'Why do you have to go to the cathedral?' said Leni. K. tried to explain briefly, but he had hardly begun when Leni suddenly said: 'They are hounding you.' K., who could not bear anyone feeling sorry for him unexpectedly or gratuitously, broke off abruptly with just two words; but as he hung up the receiver he said, half to himself and half to the distant woman who could no longer hear him: 'Yes, they are hounding me.'

Now it was getting late; he was in danger of not being on time. He took a cab – at the last minute he had remembered the folder; he had not had the chance of handing it over before, so he took it with him now. He held it on his knees and drummed his fingers on it nervously for the whole journey. The rain had eased, but it was damp, cool and dark; they would be able to see very little in the cathedral, and K.'s cold would undoubtedly get much worse there by standing around on the cold flagstones. The square in front of the cathedral was quite empty; K. remembered that it had always struck him even as a small child that in the houses on this narrow square almost all the window blinds were always down. Of course, this was more understandable than usual in weather like this. The cathedral too seemed deserted; clearly, no one would think of coming here today. K. walked along both side aisles, but saw only an old woman wrapped warmly in a shawl kneeling in front of an image of the Virgin and gazing at it. Some way away he also saw a sacristan with a limp disappearing through a door in the wall. K. had arrived punctually; just as he walked in it had struck ten, but the Italian was not there. He went to the main porch, stood there for a while undecided, then walked around the outside of the cathedral in the rain to see whether the Italian might be waiting at a side entrance. He was nowhere to be seen. Had the manager perhaps been mistaken about the time? How could one understand this man properly? Whatever the case, K. would have to wait half an hour for him anyway. He felt tired and wanted to sit down, so he went back into the cathedral and on a step found a small scrap of carpet-like material. With his foot he pulled it over to a nearby bench, wrapped himself more closely in his overcoat, pulled up his collar and sat down. To pass the time he opened the folder and glanced through it, but soon had to stop because it was getting so dark that when he looked up he could scarcely make out any details in the nearby aisle.

In the distance a large pyramid of candles flickered on the high altar; K. could not have said for sure whether he had noticed them before. Perhaps they had only just been lit. Sacristans go about their work stealthily, they go unnoticed. K. happened to turn round, and not far behind him also saw a candle burning, a tall, thick candle fixed to a pillar. Beautiful as it was, it was quite inadequate to light the altarpieces, most of which hung in the obscurity of the side-chapels; indeed, it only increased the gloom. The Italian's discourtesy in not coming was matched by his good sense; there would have been nothing to see, and they would have had to be content with inspecting a few pictures inch by inch by the light of K.'s pocket lamp. In order to find out what might be achieved by this, K. went to a nearby side-chapel, climbed a few steps to a low marble balustrade and, bending over it, shone his torch onto the altarpiece. The sanctuary light glowed in front of it, interrupting his view. The first thing K. saw, partly by guesswork, was a tall knight in armour at the very edge of the picture. He was leaning on his sword, which he had thrust into the bare earth in front of him; only a few blades of grass emerged here and there. He seemed to be watching attentively something that was going on in front of him. It was astonishing that he stood there like that and did not move closer. Perhaps he was meant to be standing guard. K., who had not looked at any pictures for a long time, looked at the knight for quite a while, though he constantly had to strain his eyes because of the weak greenish light of his torch. As he shone it over the rest of the picture, he found a conventional portrayal of the Burial of Christ; moreover, it was a modern painting. He put his torch away and returned to his seat.

By now it was probably pointless to wait for the Italian; it was sure to be pouring with rain outside, and since it was not as cold in the cathedral as K. had expected, he decided to stay for the time being. Nearby was the great pulpit; on its small round canopy were fixed two crosses, slanted so that their tips overlapped. The outer wall of the balcony and the area between it and the supporting pillar consisted of carved green foliage to which small angels were clinging, some in movement, some at rest. K. stepped up to the pulpit and examined it from all sides; the stone carving was most delicate, the deep shadow between and behind the foliation seemed to have been caught and held there. He put his hand into one of the gaps in the foliage and felt the stone carefully. He had not previously been aware of the existence of this pulpit. Then K. happened to notice the sacristan behind the nearest row of benches; he was standing watching him in a long black flowing gown and holding a snuff-box in his left hand. What does the man want? thought K. Does he find me suspicious? Does he want a tip? When the sacristan saw that K. had noticed him, he pointed with his right hand, in which he was still holding a pinch of snuff between two fingers, in a vague direction. His behaviour was almost incomprehensible; K. waited for a while, but the sacristan continued to indicate something with his hand, emphasising the gesture by nodding his head. 'What does he want?' muttered K. to himself; he did not dare to call out loud in here. Then he took out his wallet and pushed along the next row of benches to reach the man; but he immediately held out his hand to stop K., shrugged his shoulders and limped off. His rapid limping gait was similar to that with which K. as a child had tried to imitate a horseman. 'A silly old man,' thought K., 'with just enough wits to serve in a church. Look how he stops when I stop and peers at me to see whether I am coming.' Smiling, K. followed the old man the whole length of the aisle almost as far as the high altar. The man kept pointing at something, but K. deliberately refrained from looking round; all this pointing was only meant to stop K. following him. Finally he let him go; he did not wish to alarm him too much, nor to frighten him away completely, just in case the Italian turned up after all.

As he returned to the nave to find the seat on which he had left his folder, he noticed against a pillar very close to the choir-stalls a small, quite simple side-pulpit of pale bare stone. It was so small that from a distance it looked like an empty niche intended for the statue of a saint. A preacher could certainly not take a full step back from the balustrade. Moreover, the stone vaulting over the pulpit began unusually low down and, though it was not decorated, rose in such an abrupt curve that a man of average height could not stand upright there, but would have to lean forward over the balustrade all the time. It was as if the whole thing were designed for the discomfort of the preacher; it was incomprehensible why this pulpit was needed when the other one, which was large and so finely decorated, was available.

K. would certainly not even have noticed this small pulpit if a lamp had not been fixed over it, as is usually done shortly before a sermon. Was a sermon about to be delivered? In the empty church? K. looked towards the foot of the steps clinging to the pillar, which led up to the pulpit and were so narrow that they seemed designed not for people, but only to decorate the pillar. Then K. smiled in astonishment – the priest was in fact standing at the foot of the pulpit steps; his hand was on the rail ready to climb them, and he was looking at K. Then he gave a little nod of the head, and K. crossed himself and genuflected, something he should have done before. The priest pulled himself up by the rail and climbed to the pulpit with short, quick steps. Was a sermon really about to begin? Had the sacristan not been quite such a fool, had he meant to guide K. towards the preacher – a very necessary expedient in the empty church? And yet there was still an old woman somewhere in front of an image of the Virgin who should have been here too. And if a sermon was about to begin, why was there no organ music to introduce it? But the organ remained silent and only gleamed faintly out of the gloom high above.

K. wondered whether he should not make a hasty exit just then; if he did not go now, there would be no chance of leaving during the sermon, and then he would have to stay as long as it lasted. He was losing so much time he could have spent at the office, and he was no longer obliged to wait for the Italian. He looked at his watch; it was eleven. But could there really be a sermon now? Could he be the only one in the congregation? What if he had been a stranger who only wanted to visit the church? That was essentially the case. It was absurd to imagine a sermon was about to be delivered now, at eleven o'clock on a weekday in this appalling weather. The priest – he was undoubtedly a priest, a young man with a smooth, dark face – was obviously only going up there to extinguish the lamp that had been lit by mistake.

But this was not the case. Instead, the priest examined the lamp and turned it up a little, then he turned slowly to the balustrade and grasped the front edge with both hands. He stood like that for a while, and without moving his head looked around. K. had moved quite a long way back and leaned his elbows on the first row of benches. Somewhere he could dimly make out, without being able to identify the exact spot, the sacristan, slumped at rest as if his task had been done. What silence reigned now in the cathedral! But K. had to disturb it; he had no intention of staying here. If it was the priest's duty to preach at a particular time whatever the circumstances, let him do so; he would manage without K.'s support, just as K.'s presence would not enhance the effect. So K. slowly began to move; on tiptoe he felt his way along the bench, reached the broad central gangway and walked down it quite undisturbed, except that the stone floor rang with his lightest footstep, continuously echoing and re-echoing from the vaults in a faint but regularly repeated rhythm as he walked. He felt rather isolated as he walked alone between the empty benches; perhaps the priest was watching him, and the vastness of the cathedral seemed to him to border on the limits of what a human being could endure. When he reached his earlier seat where he had left the folder he did not stop, but just snatched it up and took it with him. He had almost reached the end of the rows of benches and was approaching the open space between them and the way out when he heard the priest's voice for the first time. It was a powerful, well-trained voice; how it rang through the expectant spaces of the cathedral! But it was not a congregation the priest was addressing. There was no mistaking it, and no escaping it; he was calling 'Josef K.!'

K. stopped and looked at the floor. He was still free for the moment; he could still go on and get away through one of the small, dark wooden doors not far from him. It would simply indicate that he had not understood, or that he had indeed understood but was paying no heed. But if he turned round, he was caught, for that would be to admit he had understood very well that he had been the one addressed, and that he would obey the summons. If the priest had called him again, K. would certainly have left; but since all remained silent while K. waited, he turned his head a little to see what the priest was doing. He was standing in the pulpit as before, but it was clear that he had seen K.'s head turn. It would have developed into a child's game of peek-a-boo if K. had not now turned round completely. As he did, the priest beckoned him with his finger. Since everything could now be done openly, K. ran – both out of curiosity and in order to cut things short – with long, raking strides towards the pulpit. When he reached the first row of benches he stopped, but the priest seemed to think he was still not close enough; he stretched out his hand and pointed his forefinger straight down towards a spot right in front of the pulpit. K. followed this instruction too, though from here he had to bend his head right back in order to see the priest.

'You are Josef K.,' said the priest, lifting one hand from the balustrade in a vague gesture. 'Yes,' said K. He thought how freely he used to give his name; for some time now it had been a burden to him. Moreover, people he met for the first time knew it; he thought how much better it was when they did not know his name until he had introduced himself. 'You have been accused,' said the priest in a particularly low voice. 'Yes,' said K., 'so I have been informed.' 'Then you are the man I am looking for,' said the priest. 'I am the prison chaplain.' 'I see,' said K. 'I have had you called here,' said the priest, 'to talk to you.' 'That is not what I understood,' said K. 'I came here to show an Italian round the cathedral.' 'That is beside the point,' said the priest. 'What are you holding in your hand? Is it a prayer book?' 'No,' replied K., 'it is a collection of places to visit in the city.' 'Put it down,' said the priest. K. threw it away so violently that it burst open and slid across the floor, its pages crumpled. 'Do you know that your case is going badly?' asked the priest. 'That is my impression too,' said K. 'I have taken a great deal of trouble, but so far without success. However, I have not yet submitted my plea.' 'How do you think it will end?' asked the priest. 'At first I thought it would end well,' said K., 'but now I sometimes have doubts. I don't know how it will end. Do you?' 'No,' said the priest, 'but I fear it will end badly. You are thought to be guilty. Your case might never get any further than a lower court. Your guilt is thought to be proven, at least provisionally.' 'But I am not guilty,' said K., 'it is a mistake. How can any human being be guilty – we are all human after all, every one of us.' 'That is correct,' said the priest, 'but all guilty men talk like that.' 'Are you biased against me too?' asked K. 'I am not,' said the priest. 'I am grateful to you,' said K., 'but all the others involved in the case are biased against me. They also influence those who are impartial. My position is becoming increasingly difficult.' 'You misinterpret the facts,' said the priest. 'The verdict is not arrived at all at once, the proceedings move gradually towards a verdict.'

'So that is how it is,' said K., bowing his head. 'What do you intend to do next in the matter?' asked the priest. 'I shall seek help,' said K., raising his head to see how the priest would react, 'there are still certain possibilities I have not explored yet.' 'You seek too much help from others,' said the priest disapprovingly, 'especially from women. Can you not see that this is not true help?' 'In some cases, indeed in many cases, I would agree with you,' said K., 'but not in every case. Women have great power. If I could persuade some women I know to work together for me, I would surely succeed – especially in this court, which consists almost entirely of womanisers. If the examining magistrate sees a woman on the other side of the room, he will trample over the bench and the defendant to get at her.' The priest bent his head over the balustrade; only now did the canopy of the pulpit seem to press down on him. K. wondered what the weather might be like outside; it was no longer a gloomy day, it was deepest night. Not all the stained glass in the great window could cast a single gleam of light to relieve the darkness – and the sacristan chose that moment to extinguish the candles on the high altar one by one. 'Are you angry with me?' K. asked the priest. 'Perhaps you do not know what sort of a court you serve.' He received no answer. 'These are only my own experiences,' said K. Still no answer came from above. 'I did not mean to offend you,' said K. At this the priest shouted at K.: 'Can you not see what is right in front of your eyes?' It was a shout of anger, but at the same time it was that of a man who sees someone falling and, because he is himself alarmed, shouts involuntarily and spontaneously.

Neither spoke for some time. The priest could certainly not see K. at all clearly in the darkness below, while K. could see the priest distinctly by the light of the small lamp. Why did the priest not come down? He had not delivered a sermon, but had only given K. some information which, if he took full account of it, would probably do more harm than good. And yet K. did not doubt the priest's good intentions; it was not impossible that if he were to come down, they would see eye to eye. It was not impossible that he could give K. some crucial and welcome advice which would, for example, show him, not perhaps how his trial could be influenced, but how he could escape from it, how it could be circumvented, how he could live beyond the reach of the court. This possibility must exist; K. had recently given it much thought. But if the priest knew of such a possibility, would he reveal it to him if he were asked to, even though he belonged to the court himself, and when K. had attacked the court, had suppressed his mild nature and had even shouted at K.?

'Won't you come down?' said K. 'You are not going to preach a sermon. Come down here to me.' 'I can come down now,' said the priest; perhaps he regretted shouting at K. As he unhooked the lamp, he said: 'I had to talk to you at first from a distance. Otherwise, I can be too easily influenced and forget my duty.'

K. waited for him at the foot of the steps. As he came down, the priest held out his hand from one of the steps above. 'Can you spare me a little time?' asked K. 'As much time as you need,' said the priest, handing him the small lamp to carry. Even when he was close to K., he still retained a certain solemnity. 'You are very kind to me,' said K. as they walked up and down the dark aisle together. 'You are an exception among all those who belong to the court; I trust you more than anyone else I have met. I can speak frankly to you.' 'Do not be deluded,' said the priest. 'How should I be deluded?' asked K. 'You are deluding yourself about the court,' said the priest. 'In the preamble to the law, this is what it says about that delusion:

'Before the law stands a doorkeeper. A man from the country comes to this doorkeeper and asks to be admitted to the law. But the doorkeeper tells him he cannot grant him admittance to the law now. The man considers this, and asks whether he can be admitted later. "It is possible," says the doorkeeper, "but not now." Since the door to the law is standing open as it always does, the man stoops to look inside through the door as the doorkeeper steps to one side. When the doorkeeper sees this he laughs and says: "If you are so keen, try to get in against my orders. But take note of this: I am powerful, and I am only the lowest doorkeeper. But in one hall after another there are more doorkeepers, each more powerful than the last. Even I cannot bear to look at the third one." The man from the country did not expect such difficulties. The law should be accessible to everyone at all times, he thinks; but now that he looks more closely at the doorkeeper in his fur coat, with his great hooked nose and long, thin, black Tartar's beard, he decides he would rather wait until he gets permission to enter. The doorkeeper gives him a stool and lets him sit down to one side of the door. He sits there for days and years. He makes many attempts to be admitted and wearies the doorkeeper with his pleas. The doorkeeper often asks him a few questions, asks him about where he comes from and all sorts of other things;

but they are casual questions, like those asked by important people, and in the end he tells him once again that he cannot admit him yet. The man, who has made great provision for his journey, gives up everything, however precious, to bribe the doorkeeper, who accepts everything; but as he does, he says: "I am only accepting it so that you don't think you have neglected anything." During these many years the man watches the doorkeeper almost continuously. He forgets about the other doorkeepers, this first one seems to him the only obstacle to his admission to the law. He curses his unhappy fate, in the first years out loud, but later, when he is old, he only mutters to himself. He becomes childish, and because after years of observing the doorkeeper he has even become familiar with the fleas in his fur collar, he appeals to the fleas to help him change the doorkeeper's mind. In the end his eyesight grows weak, and he cannot tell whether it is really getting darker around him or whether his eyes are deceiving him. But he does now notice an inextinguishable radiance that streams from the entrance to the law. By now he does not have very long to live. Before he dies, everything that he has experienced during all this time focuses in his mind into one question that he has not asked the doorkeeper before. He beckons him, for he can no longer lift his stiffening body. The doorkeeper has to bend low to hear him, for the difference in their height has increased, much to the disadvantage of the man. "What is it you want to know now?" says the doorkeeper. "You are insatiable." "Everyone aspires to the law," says the man, "so how is it that in all these years no one except me has demanded admittance?" The doorkeeper realises that the man is finished, and so that the dying man's ears can catch his words, he roars at him: "No one else could be admitted here; this door was meant only for you. Now I am going to shut it." '

'So the doorkeeper deceived the man,' said K. immediately, much taken by the story. 'Don't be over-hasty,' said the priest, 'do not accept another's opinion uncritically. I told you the story according to the letter of the text. It says nothing about deception.' 'But it's clear,' said K., 'and your initial interpretation was quite correct. The doorkeeper only spoke the words of deliverance when it was too late to help the man.' 'He had not been asked before,' said the priest. 'Remember, he was only a doorkeeper, and as such he fulfilled his duty.' 'What makes you believe he fulfilled his duty?' asked K. 'He did not. It was perhaps his duty to deter all strangers, but he ought to have admitted this man, since the door was meant for him.' 'You do not have enough respect for the text, and you are altering the story,' said the priest. 'The story contains two important statements by the doorkeeper about admittance to the law, one at the beginning, one at the end. The one is that he cannot admit him now, and the other is that this entrance was meant only for him. If there were a contradiction between these two statements, you would be right, and the doorkeeper would have deceived the man. But there is no contradiction. On the contrary, the first statement even implies the second. One could almost say the doorkeeper exceeded his duty by holding out the prospect that the man might be admitted at some time in the future. At first, it seems, it was his duty only to refuse to admit the man, and indeed many interpreters of the text express surprise that the doorkeeper hinted at such a possibility, for he seems keen to be precise and performs his official duties punctiliously. Over many years he does not leave his watch, and only shuts the door at the very end; he is very conscious of the importance of his duty, for he says: "I am powerful". He has respect for his superiors, for he says: "I am only the lowest doorkeeper". He is not talkative, for during all those years he only puts, as the text has it, "casual questions"; he is not corruptible, for he says about a gift: "I am only accepting it so that you don't think you have neglected anything". As for fulfilling his duty, he is not to be moved by pleas or entreaties, for it says of the man that "he wearies the doorkeeper with his pleas". Finally, even his appearance indicates his punctilious nature, the great hooked nose and the long, thin, black Tartar's beard. Can there be a more dutiful doorkeeper?

'The doorkeeper, however, also has other characteristics which are very favourable to anyone who seeks admittance and which help to explain why he exceeded his duty somewhat in suggesting the possibility of future admittance; for it cannot be denied that he is rather simple-minded and therefore rather conceited. Even if his statements about his own power and that of the other doorkeepers, and about their fearsome appearance which even he cannot bear – as I say, even if all these statements are correct in themselves, the manner in which he expresses them indicates that his perceptions are clouded by naïvety and conceit. The commentators say to this: "Truly to understand something and to misunderstand the same thing are not entirely mutually exclusive". Nevertheless, we must assume that such naïvety and conceit, in however trivial a form they are expressed, still impair his ability to guard the entrance; they are defects in the character of the doorkeeper. In addition to this, the doorkeeper seems to have a kind nature, he is by no means an official through and through. In the very first moments he laughs and invites the man to enter in spite of the express and strictly enforced ban on admittance; then he does not send him away, but, as the text says, gives him a stool and lets him sit down to one side of the door. The patience with which he tolerates the pleas of the man during all those years, the brief questions he asks him, his acceptance of the gifts, the courtesy with which he allows the man beside him to curse the unhappy fate that has placed the doorkeeper here – all this suggests that he feels pity for the man. Not every doorkeeper would have acted like that. And finally he bends right down when the man beckons him to give him the chance to put his last question. He expresses only faint impatience – the doorkeeper knows, after all, that it is all over with the man – in the words: "You are insatiable". Some go even further in this interpretation, and believe the words "you are insatiable" express a sort of kindly admiration, though they are not free from condescension. At all events, the figure of the doorkeeper emerges in a different light from how you see it.'

'You know the story better than I do, and you have known it for longer,' said K. They were silent for a while. Then K. said: 'So you believe the man was not deluded?' 'Don't misunderstand me,' said the priest. 'I am only giving you the opinions that have been expressed. You must not pay too much attention to opinions. The text is unalterable, and opinions are often only an expression of bewilderment. In this connection there is even a view that it is the doorkeeper who is deluded.' 'That is a far-fetched view,' said K. 'How is that justified?' 'It is based,' said the priest, 'on the naïvety of the doorkeeper. The argument is that he does not know what lies beyond the entrance to the law; he knows only the area he must patrol in front of the entrance. His notions of what is inside are held to be childish, and it is assumed that he himself is afraid of the very things he describes in order to frighten the man. Indeed, he is more afraid than the man is, for the man is still eager to be admitted even when he hears of the fearsome doorkeepers inside; the doorkeeper, on the other hand, has no wish to enter – at least, we are told nothing of this. Of course, others say he must have been inside, because he has after all been appointed as a servant of the law, and that, they say, can only have taken place inside. Against that it can be argued that he might well have been appointed as doorkeeper by a call from inside, and in any case he cannot have been very far inside, because he could not even bear the sight of the third doorkeeper. Moreover, there is no indication that during all those years he said anything about what was inside, except for his remark about the doorkeepers. He might have been forbidden to enter; but he says nothing about this. From all this, it is inferred that he knows nothing about the appearance or the significance of the interior, and is deluding himself about it. But he is also thought to be deluding himself about the man from the country, for he is inferior to this man and does not know it. That he treats the man as his inferior is clear from many details that you will no doubt remember; but according to this view it should be just as clear that he is in fact inferior to the man. Above all, a free man is superior to a man in service. Now, the man is indeed free, he can go wherever he wishes; only entrance to the law is forbidden him – and this, moreover, only by one individual, the doorkeeper. When he sits on a stool to one side of the door and stays there for the rest of his life, he does this voluntarily; the story does not mention any compulsion. The doorkeeper, on the other hand, is bound to his post by his office; he may not move away from the entrance, but apparently he may not go inside either, even if he wanted to. Moreover, although he is in the service of the law, he only serves at this entrance, so he is there only for this man, for whom alone this entrance is intended. For this reason too he is inferior to the man. We must assume that for many years, perhaps for a whole lifetime, his service has in a certain sense been fruitless, for we are told that a man arrives. The man is an adult; so the doorkeeper must have had to wait a long time in order to perform his duty, that is, as long as it suited the man, because he came voluntarily. But the length of his service is also determined by the death of the man, so he remains subordinate to him right to the end. And it is emphasised time and again that the doorkeeper knows nothing of all this. But this is seen as nothing remarkable, for in this view the doorkeeper is even more gravely deluded in the matter of his service. At the end he refers to the door and says: "I am now going to shut it"; but at the beginning the text says that the door to the law stands open as it always does.

Now, if it always stands open – always, that is, irrespective of the life-span of the man for whom it is intended – then the doorkeeper will not be able to shut it. Opinions are divided on whether the doorkeeper, when he announces that he is going to shut the door, is simply answering a question, whether he is emphasising his devotion to duty, or whether he is trying to cause the man sorrow and regret at his very last moment. But many agree that he will not be able to shut the door, they even believe that he is, at least at the end, inferior to the man also in what he knows; for the man sees the radiance streaming from the entrance to the law, while the doorkeeper, as is his duty, presumably stands with his back to the entrance and says nothing to suggest that he has noticed anything new.'

'That is well argued,' said K., who had been repeating to himself some passages from the priest's explanation under his breath. 'It is well argued, and I also now believe that the doorkeeper is deluded. But that still doesn't change my earlier opinion, for the two views coincide to some extent. The decisive factor is not whether the doorkeeper is deluded or otherwise. I said the man was deceived. If the doorkeeper sees correctly, one might doubt this; but if the doorkeeper is deluded, then his delusions must necessarily be shared by the man. In that case, the doorkeeper is not deceiving the man; but he is so naïve that he ought to be dismissed from office at once. You must take account of the fact that the delusion the doorkeeper suffers from does him no harm, whereas it harms the man enormously.' 'There is an argument against that,' said the priest. 'Many say that the story gives no one the right to judge the doorkeeper. However he may seem to us, he is a servant of the law, so he belongs to the law, hence he is beyond human judgement. In that case one cannot believe that the doorkeeper is inferior to the man. Being bound to his service, even if it is only at the entrance to the law, is incomparably better than living freely in the world outside. When the man comes to the law, the doorkeeper is already there. He is a servant appointed by the law; to doubt his status would be to doubt the law.' 'I do not agree with that,' said K., shaking his head. 'If we take that view, we must accept that everything the doorkeeper says is true. But you yourself have demonstrated in detail that this is not possible.' 'No,' said the priest, 'we must not accept everything is true, we must only accept it is necessary.' 'A dismal thought,' said K., 'it makes untruth into a universal principle.'

K. said this by way of conclusion, but it was not his final judgement. He was too tired to consider all the implications of the story; it led him into unfamiliar trains of thought, unreal notions that were more suitable for discussion by an assembly of court officials than for him. The simple story had become confused, he wanted to be rid of it, and the priest, who now showed great delicacy of feeling, accepted this and made no reply to K.'s comment, although he cannot have agreed with it.

They walked on for a time in silence. K. kept close to the priest, not knowing where they were. The lamp in his hand had long since gone out. Once the silver statue of a saint shone with a whitish gleam just in front of him, then was immediately lost in the darkness. K. did not wish to remain wholly dependent on the priest, so he asked him: 'Are we not near the main porch?' 'No,' said the priest, 'we are a long way from it. Do you want to leave?' Although it had not been in K.'s mind just then, he said immediately: 'Of course, I must go. I am a senior official in a bank, I am expected back. I only came here to show a foreign business associate round the cathedral.' 'Well,' said the priest, 'go then.' 'But I cannot find my way alone in the dark,' said K. 'Go left as far as the wall,' said the priest, 'then keep to the wall, and you will find a way out.' The priest was only a few steps away, but K. called out: 'Please wait!' 'I am waiting,' said the priest. 'Is there anything else you want from me?' asked K. 'No,' said the priest. 'You were so kind to me earlier,' said K., 'and explained everything to me. But now you dismiss me as if I meant nothing to you.' 'But you have to go,' said the priest. 'Yes, I do,' said K., 'you must understand that.' 'You must first understand who I am,' said the priest. 'You are the prison chaplain,' said K., moving closer to the priest; his immediate return to the bank was not as necessary as he had made out, he could well stay here for a while. 'So I belong to the court,' said the priest. 'Why then should I want anything from you? The court wants nothing from you. It receives you when you come, and it releases you when you go.'

CHAPTER TEN

End

On the eve of his thirty-first birthday – it was towards nine in the evening, the time when the streets fall silent – two men in frock coats came to K.'s apartment; they were pale and plump, with top hats clamped firmly on their heads. After some formalities at the front door concerning who should enter first, the same formalities were repeated more elaborately at K.'s door. Although the visit had not been announced, K. sat in a chair near the door, also dressed in black, slowly pulling on new gloves that fitted tightly over his hands, in the attitude of someone who was expecting guests. He stood up at once and looked at the men with curiosity. 'So you have come for me?' he asked. The men nodded, each pointing to the other with top hat in hand. K. admitted to himself that he had been expecting different visitors. He went to the window and looked out into the dark street. Almost all the windows on the far side were dark; in many of them the blinds were lowered. In one of the lighted windows on the block, small children were playing behind a window grille; they were still too small to move around, but reached out to each other with tiny hands. 'They are sending ageing second-rate actors for me,' K. said to himself, and looked round to confirm this impression. 'They are trying to get rid of me cheaply.' He suddenly turned to them and asked: 'Which theatre are you appearing at?' 'Theatre?' one of them turned to ask the other, the corners of his mouth twitching. The other acted like a deaf mute struggling to control an unmanageable disability. 'They are not trained to answer questions,' said K. to himself and went to fetch his hat.

On the staircase the men tried to hold K. by the arms, but he said: 'Not until we are on the street. I am not ill.' But just as they reached the door they took hold of him in a way no one had done before. They kept their shoulders close behind his, and without bending their arms held his tight along their full length, grasping his hands in an expert, practised, irresistible grip. K., held rigid, walked between them; the three of them formed such a close unit that if one of them had been knocked over, the others would have followed. It was the kind of unity that only inanimate forms can achieve.

Under the street lamps K. frequently attempted, difficult though it was when he was being held so closely, to see his companions more clearly than had been possible in the dim light of his room. 'Perhaps they are tenors,' he thought, looking at their heavy double chins. Their shiny faces nauseated him; he could easily imagine the hand reaching to wipe the corners of the eyes, rubbing the upper lip, smoothing out the folds of the chin.

When K. thought of this, he stopped. The others stopped too; they were at the edge of a deserted open space with some flowerbeds. 'Why did they have to send you!' he cried out rather than asked. The men appeared to have no answer; they waited with their free arms hanging down, like medical orderlies pausing for the invalid to take a rest. 'I am not going any further,' K. ventured. The men did not bother to answer; without slackening their grip they tried to drag him off, but he resisted. 'I shall not need my strength much longer, I shall use it all now,' he thought. He was reminded of flies that tear off their wings struggling to free themselves from a flypaper. 'These gentlemen will have to work hard.'

At that moment Fräulein Bürstner emerged into the square from a small flight of steps leading from a lane below. It was not quite certain that it was Fräulein Bürstner, but the resemblance was very close. But it did not matter to K. whether it was or not; all he was aware of just then was the futility of resistance. He would be doing nothing heroic if he resisted, if he caused trouble for these men, if by defending himself he attempted to enjoy a last glimmer of life. He set off again, and some of the pleasure this gave the men communicated itself to him too. They now allowed him to choose which way they went; he led them in the direction Fräulein Bürstner was taking, not because he wanted to catch up with her, nor because he wanted to keep her in view as long as possible, but only so that he would not forget the rebuke she represented for him. 'The only thing I can do now,' he said to himself, and the steady rhythm of his steps and those of his companions confirmed his thoughts, 'the only thing I can do now is to keep calm and marshal my thoughts rationally. I always wanted to rush headlong at things, not always for the best reasons. That was quite wrong. Am I now to show that not even a case that has lasted a whole year could teach me anything? Am I to leave the world as a man who is impervious to argument? Are people to say of me that when my case started, I wanted to finish it, and now that it is finishing I want to start it again? I don't want them to say that. I am grateful that I have been given these inarticulate, ignorant companions, and that it has been left to me to tell myself what has to be said.'

The young woman had meanwhile turned off into a sidestreet; but K. could now do without her and let his companions lead him. All three now walked with one accord across a bridge in the moonlight. The men willingly yielded to K.'s slightest movement; if he swerved slightly towards the parapet, they also wheeled round in that direction. The water, glinting and shimmering in the moonlight, flowed round a small island on which trees and shrubs crowded together in a dense mass of foliage. Underneath them, invisible now, ran gravel paths with comfortable benches where K. had stretched himself out and relaxed during many a summer. 'I didn't want to stop,' he said to his companions, embarrassed by their ready compliance. One of them seemed to reproach the other mildly behind K.'s back for this misunderstanding, then they went on.

They climbed through narrow streets in which policemen stood here and there or walked up and down, some in the distance, others very close. One, with a bushy moustache, his hand grasping the hilt of his sabre, approached this not wholly innocent-looking group, it seemed with intent. The men hesitated, and the policeman seemed about to open his mouth, but K. used all his strength to pull the men on. Several times he turned round cautiously to see whether the policeman was following them; then as soon as they turned a corner, he began to run, and the men had to keep up with him, gasping for breath.

They quickly left the town, which on this side soon gave way to open fields. A small quarry, bleak and deserted, lay near a house that looked just like a town house. Here the men paused, perhaps because this place had been their destination from the start, perhaps because they were too exhausted to go any further. Then they let K. go. He waited in silence; they removed their top hats and mopped the sweat from their brows with their handkerchiefs while they looked round the quarry. The moonlight lay over the whole scene with the natural serenity no other light has.

After an exchange of polite formalities concerning who was to perform the following task – the men seemed not to have been given separate instructions – one of them went up to K. and removed his coat, his waistcoat and finally his shirt. K. shivered involuntarily, at which the man gave him a light, reassuring pat on the back. Then he folded the clothes carefully, as if they might still be needed, though not perhaps in the immediate future. In order to give K. some exercise to protect him from the night air, which was cold enough, he took him by the arm and walked him up and down for a time, while the second searched the quarry for a suitable spot. When he had found it, he beckoned, and the first man led K. to it. It was close to the quarry face; a stone that had broken loose lay there. The men sat K. on the ground, laid him against the stone and cushioned his head on the top. In spite of all the trouble they took, and in spite of all K.'s cooperation, his posture was still most awkward and unnatural, so one of them asked the other to leave the positioning of K.'s body to him; but that made things no better. Finally they left him in a position that was not even the most comfortable of those they had already tried. Then one of the men unbuttoned his frock-coat, and from a sheath hanging from a belt around his waistcoat he took a long, thin, double-bladed butcher's knife and held it up in the moonlight to judge its sharpness. Again they started their dreadful courtesies; the one handed the knife to the other, who handed it back again. K. now knew perfectly well that it should have been his duty, as the knife was passed from hand to hand over him, to take hold of it and plunge it into himself. But he did not; instead he turned his head, which was still free, and looked about him. He could not bring himself to do it; he would not relieve the authorities of all their duties. The responsibility for this final failing lay with those who had deprived him of the remaining strength he needed.

His eyes fell on the upper storey of the house that stood near the quarry. Like a flash of light, the windows there flew open, and a man, indistinct and tenuous at that distance and elevation, suddenly leaned out and stretched out his arms still further. Who was he? A friend? A good man? Someone who cared? Someone who wanted to help? Was it one man? Was it all men? Was there still help? Were there objections that had been overlooked? Certainly there were some. Logic is unshakeable, but it cannot prevail against a man who wishes to live. Where was the judge he had never seen? Where was the high court he had never had access to? He raised his hands and spread out all his fingers.

But one of the men took K. by the throat while the other plunged the knife deep into his heart and twisted it twice. As his sight failed, K. could still see them in front of his face, leaning together cheek by cheek as they watched the final moment. 'Like a dog!' he said; it was as if the shame was to outlive him.

THE CASTLE

I

Arrival

It was late evening when K. arrived. The village lay deep in snow. Nothing could be seen of the Castle Hill, it was hidden in mist and darkness, and not even the faintest gleam of light indicated the great castle there. For a long time K. stood on the wooden bridge leading from the main road to the village, looking up into the apparent emptiness.

Then he set out to find lodgings for the night. At the inn they were still up; the landlord was taken aback and disturbed by the late arrival of a guest, but although he had no rooms free he was willing to let K. sleep on a straw mattress in the parlour, which K. found acceptable. Some peasants were still sitting over their beer, but he did not want to speak to anyone, so he fetched the mattress from the attic himself and lay down by the stove. It was warm, the peasants sat quietly, he studied them for a while through tired eyes and then fell asleep.

But shortly afterwards he was woken. A young man dressed in town clothes with an actor's face, narrow eyes and dark eyebrows, was standing beside him with the landlord. The peasants were still there too; some had turned their chairs round in order to see and hear better. The young man apologised very politely for having woken K., introduced himself as the son of the Castle Warden, then said: 'This village belongs to the Castle. Anyone who lives here or spends the night here is, as it were, staying at the Castle. No one may do this without the permission of the Count. You have no such permission, at least you have not presented it.'

K. sat up and smoothed his hair. He looked up at them and said: 'Which village have I strayed into? Is there a castle here, then?'

'Indeed there is,' said the young man slowly, while one or two of those present shook their heads at K.'s question, 'it is the castle of Count Westwest.'

'And I must have permission to stay the night?' asked K., as if trying to convince himself he had not dreamed what he had just heard.

'You must have permission,' came the reply, and with what seemed to K. a gesture of crude mockery the young man held out his arm to the landlord and his guests and asked: 'Or perhaps he doesn't need it?'

'Then I shall have to go and get permission,' said K., yawning. He threw off the blanket and made to get up.

'From whom, then?' asked the young man.

'From the Count,' said K.. 'That is all I can do.'

'You want to obtain permission from the Count now, at midnight?' cried the young man, taking a step backwards.

'Is that not possible?' asked K. calmly. 'Then why did you wake me up?'

At this the young man flew into a rage. 'You are behaving like a tramp!' he shouted. 'Show some respect for the Count's representative! I woke you in order to inform you that you must leave the Count's territory at once.'

'That's enough play-acting,' said K. quietly. He lay back and pulled the blanket over him. 'You are going a little too far, young man, and I shall come back to your behaviour tomorrow. Should I require witnesses, the landlord and these gentlemen will bear me out. Apart from that, let me inform you that I am the surveyor the Count has sent for. My assistants are arriving tomorrow in a carriage with my instruments. I took the opportunity to take a walk through the snow, but unfortunately I lost my way several times, which is why I arrived so late. I realised for myself that it was too late to report to the Castle before you chose to tell me. That is why I made do with this place for the night, where you – to put it mildly – were rude enough to disturb me. That is all I have to say by way of explanation. Good night, gentlemen.' With this, K. turned towards the stove.

'Surveyor?' he heard someone ask uncertainly behind him, then there was silence. But the young man soon recovered himself and said to the landlord, quietly enough to suggest he did not wish to disturb K.'s sleep, but loudly enough for him to hear: 'I'll phone and ask.' So there was even a telephone in this village inn? They were very well provided for. This detail took K. by surprise, though in general terms he had in fact expected that to be the case. The telephone turned out to be situated just above his head; he had been so sleepy he had not noticed it. If the young man had to use it, with the best will in the world he would have to disturb K.; it was just a matter of whether K. was going to allow him to. He decided not to object; but in that case there was no point in pretending he was asleep, so he turned over on his back again. He saw the peasants talking together in a huddle; the arrival of a surveyor was quite an event. The door to the kitchen had opened, and the bulky figure of the landlady filled the doorway; the landlord went over on tiptoe to tell her what was going on. Then the phone conversation began. The Warden of the Castle was asleep, but a deputy warden, one of the deputy wardens, Herr Fritz, was there. The young man, who gave his name as Schwarzer, explained that he had found K., a very shabby-looking man in his thirties, sleeping calmly on a straw mattress using a tiny rucksack as a pillow, with a stout stick within his reach. Naturally, he said, he had found the man suspicious, and since the landlord had obviously neglected his duty, it had been up to him, Schwarzer, to look into the matter. On being woken up and questioned, then officially threatened with expulsion from the Count's territory, he went on, K. had reacted discourteously – perhaps with some justification as it turned out, for he claimed to be a surveyor engaged by the Count. Clearly it was at the very least his official duty to verify this claim, so Schwarzer was asking Herr Fritz to enquire at central office whether a surveyor was actually expected, and to ring him back with the answer at once.

Then there was silence; Fritz made his enquiries up there, while here they waited for a reply. K. remained lying on his back, he did not even turn over, and appearing to show no curiosity stared in front of him. The combination of malice and caution in Schwarzer's account gave him an idea of the quasi-diplomatic conventions so effortlessly assumed by those in the Castle, even by minor officials like Schwarzer. They were not idle there, either; the central office worked though the night.

They obviously replied very promptly, too, for Fritz soon rang back. The answer was evidently very brief, for Schwarzer immediately slammed down the receiver in a rage. 'I knew it!' he cried. 'No trace of a surveyor. He's lying, he's a common tramp, probably worse.' For a moment K. thought they were all going to assault him, Schwarzer, the peasants, the landlord and his wife; in order to protect himself from the initial onslaught, at least, he crawled under his blanket. Then the telephone rang again – particularly loudly, it seemed to K. – and slowly he put his head out again. Although it seemed improbable that it was again about K., they all hesitated and Schwarzer returned to the phone. He listened to a lengthy explanation and then said quietly: 'So it was a mistake? That makes it very awkward for me. The Head of Department himself rang? That's very strange. But how am I going to explain that to the surveyor?'

K. listened closely. So the Castle had appointed him as surveyor. On the one hand this was unwelcome news, for it showed that they knew all about him at the Castle, that they had weighed up the strengths and weaknesses and were ready to do battle with a smile. On the other hand, however, it was also fortunate, for it showed that they underrated him and that he would enjoy more freedom than he could previously have hoped. And if they thought they could keep him in a constant state of terror with this lofty acknowledgement of his status as a surveyor, they were mistaken; he felt mildly uneasy, that was all.

K. dismissed Schwarzer, who was approaching timidly, with a wave of his hand. He declined the landlord's urgent invitation to move into his own room, accepting only a drink to help him sleep and the landlady's offer of a wash basin with soap and towels; he did not even have to ask them to leave the room, for they all hurried out, turning their faces away so that he would not recognise them the next day. The lamp was extinguished, and he was left in peace at last. He slept deeply until morning, scarcely disturbed by one or two rats that scuttled past him.

At breakfast, which the landlord assured him would be paid for by the Castle together with all his board and lodging, he intended to go out into the village at once. Remembering the landlord's behaviour the previous evening, K. had exchanged no more words with him than strictly necessary; but since the man constantly hovered around his chair with mute pleas, he invited him to sit down with him for a while.

'I don't know the Count yet,' said K. 'They say he pays well for good work, is that so? If you travel so far from your wife and children as I have, you want to take something home with you.'

'No need to worry about that, sir; no one complains about bad pay.'

'Well,' said K., 'I'm not shy, and I can speak my mind to the Count; but of course it's better to be on good terms with these people.'

The landlord sat opposite K. on the edge of the window sill – he did not venture to sit more comfortably – and all the while gazed at K. anxiously with his large brown eyes. At first he had pressed himself on K.; now, it seemed, he would rather run away. Was he afraid to be quizzed about the Count? Did he not fully trust the 'gentleman' he took K. for? K. had to divert his attention. He looked at the clock and said: 'My two assistants will be here soon; can you give them accommodation here?'

'Of course, sir,' he replied, 'but won't they be staying at the Castle with you?'

Was he so keen to lose customers, then, and K. in particular, that he insisted on assigning them to the Castle?

'That is not yet clear,' said K. 'First I must find out what sort of work they have for me. If I have to work down here, for instance, it would be more sensible to live down here. I fear life at the Castle may not suit me. I always like to be free.'

'You don't know the Castle,' said the landlord quietly.

'Of course,' said K., 'one should not jump to conclusions. For the moment, all I know about the Castle is that they know how to choose a proper surveyor. Perhaps they have other qualities up there.' And he stood up to escape from the landlord, who was biting his lip nervously. It was not easy to gain the man's confidence.

As he was about to go, K. caught sight of a sombre portrait hanging in a dark frame on the wall. He had already noticed it from where he slept, but at that distance he had not made out any details; he had thought the picture itself had been removed from the frame, leaving only the dark backing. But now he saw that it was in fact a portrait, the head and shoulders of a man of about fifty. His head was sunk so low on his chest that scarcely anything could be seen of his eyes; his heavy domed forehead and strong hooked nose seemed to weigh his head down. His full beard, pressed in at the chin by the inclination of his head, spread down over his chest. His thick head of hair rested on the splayed fingers of his left hand, which supported the head but could not raise it. 'Who is that?' asked K., 'the Count?' He was standing in front of the picture and did not turn to look at the landlord. 'No,' said the landlord, 'it's the Warden of the Castle.' 'Indeed, they have a handsome warden,' said K., 'a pity that he has such an ill-mannered son.' 'No,' said the landlord, pulling K. closer to him and whispering in his ear, 'Schwarzer was exaggerating yesterday. His father is only a deputy warden, and one of the lowest ones, too.' At this moment the landlord seemed to K. like a child. 'The scoundrel!' said K., and laughed; but the landlord did not join in his laughter, saying: 'Even *his* father is powerful.' 'Get away!' said K., 'you think everyone is powerful. Me too, I dare say?' 'You?' replied the landlord, timidly but seriously. 'I don't believe you are powerful.' 'You're very observant, I see,' said K. 'In fact, between you and me, I'm not powerful, and so I probably have no less respect than you do for those who are powerful, only I'm not as honest as you, so I won't always admit it.' And K. patted the landlord lightly on the cheek in a friendly gesture of reassurance. And indeed, this did make the landlord smile faintly. He really looked like a boy with his soft, almost beardless face; however did he come to marry his spreading wife, older than himself, who could be seen through a hatch to the kitchen next door, bustling about with her elbows held out wide? But K. did not wish to question him any further just then, in case the smile he had finally coaxed from him should fade, so he gestured towards the door; it was opened for him and he stepped out into the fine winter morning.

Now he saw above him the distinct outlines of the Castle in the clear air, even more sharply defined by the thin layer of snow that lay everywhere and picked out all its shapes. However, there seemed to be much less snow up on the hill than here in the village, where K.'s progress was no less laborious than on the road he had travelled the previous day. Here the snow piled up to the windows of the cottages and weighed down on the low roofs, but up on the hill everything towered upwards lightly and freely, or so it seemed, at least from down here.

As it appeared from this distance, the Castle was much as K. had expected. It was neither an ancient fortress nor a more recent palace, but an extensive site consisting of a few two-storey structures and a number of lower buildings packed close together; if one had not known that it was a castle, it could have been taken for a small township. K. could only see one tower, and he could not make out whether it belonged to a domestic building or a church. Swarms of crows wheeled round it.

His eyes fixed on the Castle, K. went on with nothing else in mind. But as he approached it, the Castle disappointed him. It really was just a wretched little village, a collection of mean houses, whose only distinction was that they were stone-built; but the paint had long since peeled and the stone seemed to have crumbled. K. was briefly reminded of his native town, which was scarcely inferior to this supposed castle. If he had simply come to see it, it would not have been worth the long journey; he would have done better to revisit his own home town that he had not seen for so long. In his mind he compared the church tower there with the tower that rose above him here. The former thrust boldly and vigorously upwards, tapering towards its summit, its broad roof covered with red tiles; a secular structure – what else can we build? – but with a higher aspiration than this mean huddle of houses and making a clearer statement than just dreary everyday existence. The tower up here – it was the only one visible, and as now became clear, it was the tower of a residence, perhaps of the main castle building – was a uniform round structure, mercifully part-covered in ivy, with small windows now glinting in the sun and creating a somewhat bizarre effect, and ending in a parapet topped with battlements that jutted into the blue sky, precarious, irregular, and fragile, as if drawn by the anxious or careless hand of a child. It was as if some mournful inhabitant, who should by rights have shut himself into the furthest room of the house, had burst through the roof and stood up in order to show himself to the world.

Once more K. stopped, as if by standing still he could judge the scene better. But he was interrupted. Behind the village church where he had stopped – it was actually only a chapel onto which a barn-like extension had been added to accommodate the congregation – was the school. It was a long, low building, its appearance suggesting a remarkable combination of a temporary structure and one of great age, which stood behind a fenced garden now under a blanket of snow. Children were just coming out with their teacher. They surrounded him in a dense horde, all gazing up at him and chattering incessantly on all sides, so rapidly that K. could not make out what they were saying. The teacher, a young, small, narrow-shouldered man, who nevertheless held himself very upright without appearing ridiculous, had already noticed K. some way off; in any case, apart from his own flock K. was the only person to be seen anywhere. K., as the stranger, made the first move to greet this little man who had such an air of authority. 'Good morning, sir,' he said. The children immediately stopped chattering; this sudden silence may well have pleased the teacher as a prelude to his reply. 'You are viewing the Castle?' he asked in a milder tone of voice than K. had expected, but one that suggested he did not approve of what K. was doing. 'Yes,' said K., 'I am a stranger here, I only arrived yesterday evening.' 'You don't like the Castle?' asked the teacher quickly. 'What?' replied K., nonplussed. Then he reiterated the question more calmly: 'Do I like the Castle? What makes you think I don't like it?' 'No stranger likes it,' said the teacher. K. did not wish to give offence, so he changed the subject and asked: 'I suppose you know the Count?' 'No,' said the teacher, making to turn away. But K. persisted, and again asked: 'What? You don't know the Count?' 'Why should I know him?' said the teacher softly, adding aloud in French: 'Please bear in mind there are innocent children present.' K. took this as a pretext to ask him: 'Could I call on you some time, sir? I am here for a while, and I feel somewhat isolated; I have nothing in common with the peasants, nor, I imagine, with the Castle.' 'There is no distinction between the peasants and the Castle,' said the teacher. 'That may be so,' said K., 'but it does not alter my position. May I call on you?' 'I live at the butcher's in the Schwanengasse.' It was an indication of where he lived rather than an invitation; nevertheless, K. said: 'Very well, I will call round.' The teacher nodded and moved off with his horde of children, who immediately resumed their shouting. They soon disappeared down a steeply sloping lane.

K., however, was unsettled and irritated by this exchange. For the first time since his arrival he felt really tired. Initially, his long journey to this place had not seemed to weary him at all – he had trudged steadily on, day by day, step by step – but now he felt the effect of his exertions, at an inconvenient time, too. He felt impelled to seek out new acquaintances, but each new encounter increased his weariness. If he forced himself in his present state to walk on as far as the entrance to the Castle, he would have done more than enough.

So he carried on walking, but it was a long way, for this road, which was the main street of the village, did not lead up the hill to the Castle, only towards it; then, as if by design, it turned off, and while it did not lead away from the Castle, it did not get any nearer to it either. The whole time K. thought the road must at last turn off to the Castle, and it was only that thought that made him go on; clearly, because he was so tired, he was reluctant to leave the road. Moreover, he was amazed at the extent of the village; it seemed endless, always the same little cottages and frosted window-panes and snow and no sign of life. Finally he forced himself to leave this street and turned into a narrow lane where the snow lay even deeper; his feet sank into it and it required a great effort to pull them out again. He broke out in a sweat, then suddenly he stopped; he could go no further.

He was not completely lost, though; there were cottages on either side. He made a snowball and threw it at one of the windows. The door opened at once – it was the first door that had opened during his whole walk through the village – and a frail old peasant in a brown fur jacket stood there, his head on one side, with a kindly look. 'May I come in for a while?' said K., 'I am exhausted.' He did not hear anything the old man said, but was thankful when a plank was pushed towards him, which soon helped him out of the snow. A few steps and he was standing inside.

It was a large, dimly lit room. Coming from outside, K. could at first see nothing; he stumbled against a washtub, and a woman's hand supported him. In one corner children were shouting noisily; from another corner steam billowed, turning the dim light into darkness. K. stood as if he were in the clouds. 'He's drunk,' someone said. 'Who are you?' called a commanding voice, then, presumably addressing the old man: 'Why did you let him in? Are we going to let in everyone wandering about the streets?' 'I am the Count's surveyor,' said K. in an attempt to explain himself to this unseen person. 'Oh, he's the surveyor,' said a woman's voice. There was complete silence. 'Do you know me?' asked K. 'Of course,' the same voice replied shortly. The fact that he was known did not appear to recommend him.

Eventually the clouds of steam dispersed, and K. was gradually able to find his bearings. It seemed to be a general washday. Near the door clothes were being washed, but the steam came from the left-hand corner, where two men were bathing in a wooden tub of steaming water, which was bigger than any K. had ever seen; it was as wide as two beds. But in the right-hand corner was an even more surprising sight, though it was difficult to say just what was so surprising about it: through a large window – the only one in the back wall of the room – a pale light reflected from the snow in the yard outside fell onto a woman who was slumped wearily in a high-backed armchair in the corner, making her dress shine like silk. She was holding an infant to her breast. Around her children were playing, evidently peasants' children, but she seemed not to be related to them – though of course illness and exhaustion can make even peasants seem refined.

'Sit down,' said one of the men, wheezing open-mouthed through his bushy beard and moustaches. He waved his hand – it was a comical sight – over the edge of the tub towards a bench, spraying warm water all over K.'s face. The old man who had let K. in was already sitting on the bench gazing vacantly. No one took any further notice of him. The woman at the washtub, fair-haired and in the bloom of youth, sang softly as she worked, the men in the bath stamped and rolled about, the children tried to get near but were driven back by vigorous splashings, which also reached K., the woman in the armchair lay motionless, staring upwards, paying no attention to the child at her breast.

K. must have been watching her for some time as she lay there, a still, sad, lovely sight; but then he must have fallen asleep, for when he was abruptly wakened by a loud voice, his head was lying on the shoulder of the old man next to him. The children, supervised by the fair-haired woman, were now playing in the bath vacated by the two men who stood, fully clothed, in front of K. He noticed that the bearded man with the loud voice was the less powerfully built of the two; the other, who was no taller and whose beard was less full, was a quiet, deliberate man with a burly figure and broad face who held his head bent. 'Sir,' he said, 'you cannot stay here. Please excuse our discourtesy.' 'I had no wish to stay,' said K., 'only to rest for a while. Now I have done that, and I will go.' 'You are no doubt puzzled by our lack of hospitality,' said the man, 'but hospitality is not our custom; we have no need of visitors.' Refreshed by his sleep and more alert than earlier, K. was glad to hear such candid words. He moved more freely, tapping here and there with his stick, and went over to the woman in the armchair; he also saw that he was the tallest person in the room.

'Of course,' said K., 'why should you need visitors? But occasionally you need someone like me, a surveyor.' 'I don't know about that,' said the man slowly. 'If you have been sent for, you are probably needed, I dare say that is an exception. But people like us who are not so grand, we stick to the rules, you can't blame us for that.' 'No, not at all,' said K., 'I'm just grateful to you, to you and all of you here.' And to everyone's surprise, K. quickly turned round and stood in front of the woman. She looked at him out of her tired blue eyes; a fine silk headscarf hung down over her forehead, the child slept on her breast. 'Who are you?' asked K. Dismissively – it was unclear whether her disdain applied to K. or to her own words – she answered: 'A girl from the Castle.'

This had all taken only a moment, but already K. found the two men on either side of him, and with all their strength, as if there were no other way of making him understand, they pushed him in silence towards the door. Something in all this delighted the old man, who clapped his hands. The woman bathing the children laughed too, while the children suddenly started to scream madly.

K. was soon standing in the street. The men were watching him from the doorway, snow was falling again, but still it seemed to be a little brighter. The bearded man shouted impatiently: 'Where do you want to go? The Castle is up that way, the village is down there.' K. did not answer him, but said to the other man, who though he was more imposing seemed more approachable than the other: 'Who are you? Whom do I have to thank for taking me in?' 'I am Lasemann the tanner,' he replied, 'but there's no need for thanks.' 'Good,' said K., 'perhaps we shall meet again.' 'I don't think so,' said the man. At this moment the bearded man raised his hand and shouted: 'Hello, Artur, hello Jeremias!' K. turned – so there were people on the streets of this village after all! From the direction of the Castle came two young men of medium height, both very slim, dressed in close-fitting clothes. They were very similar in the face; against their dark complexions their even darker pointed beards stood out clearly. Even in these conditions they made astonishing progress, marching in step on their slim legs. 'What are you up to?' the bearded man called. They did not slow their pace, and were walking so fast that it was only possible to communicate with them by shouting. 'Business,' they called back, laughing. 'Where?' 'At the inn.' 'I'm going there too,' cried K. louder than any of them. He felt an urgent desire to go along with them; he felt their acquaintance might not be very rewarding, but they would clearly be good, cheery companions. They heard K.'s words, but only nodded, then they were gone.

K. was still standing in the snow; he was reluctant to lift a foot out of the snow only for it to sink back in again. The tanner and his companion, happy to be rid of K. at last, went slowly back into the house through the half-open door, all the time glancing over their shoulders at K., and he was alone with the snow falling around him. 'Cause for some slight desperation,' he thought to himself, 'if I were just standing here by chance, not by design.'

Then in the cottage to his left a tiny window opened; it had looked dark blue when closed, perhaps in the light reflected from the snow, and it was so tiny that now it was open he could not see the whole of the face that was looking out, only the eyes; they were brown eyes, those of an elderly person. 'There he is,' a quavering woman's voice said. 'It's the surveyor,' said a man's voice. Then the man came to the window and asked, in a not unfriendly way, but as if it were his business that everything should be in order on the street in front of his house: 'Who are you waiting for?' 'For a sleigh to pick me up,' said K. 'No sleighs come this way,' said the man, 'there's no traffic here.' 'But this is the road that leads to the Castle,' K. protested. 'Even so, even so,' the man insisted, 'there's no traffic here.' They both fell silent. But the man was obviously thinking things over, for he was still holding the window open. Smoke poured out of it. 'It's a bad road,' said K., prompting him. But all he said was: 'It certainly is.' But then after a while he said: 'If you like, I'll take you in my sleigh.' 'Please do,' said K., delighted, 'how much would you charge?' 'Nothing,' said the man. K. was astonished. 'After all, you're the surveyor,' the man said by way of explanation, 'and you belong to the Castle. Where do you want me to take you?' 'To the Castle,' K. answered quickly. 'Then I won't take you,' said the man at once. 'But I belong to the Castle,' said K., repeating the man's own words. 'Perhaps,' he replied, equivocating. 'Take me to the inn, then,' said K. 'All right,' said the man, 'I'll bring the sleigh round right away.' The whole impression was not of any special kindness on his part, his manner suggested instead a nervous, punctilious attempt in his own interests to get rid of K. from in front of his house.

The gate to the yard opened, and a small lightweight sleigh, quite flat and with no seats, emerged, drawn by a puny little horse and followed by the man, who was not old, but frail, bent and lame; he was sniffling, and a woollen scarf wound tightly round his neck made his red, pinched face look particularly small. The man was clearly ill, and it was obviously only to get rid of K. that he had ventured out. K. made some allusion to this, but the man ignored the remark. K. learned only that he was Gerstäcker the coachman, and that he had chosen this uncomfortable sleigh because it happened to be available and it would have taken too long to bring another one out. 'Sit down,' he said, pointing to the back of the sleigh with his whip. 'I'll sit next to you,' said K. 'I shall walk,' said Gerstäcker. 'Why?' asked K. 'I shall walk,' repeated Gerstäcker. He was seized by a fit of coughing which shook him so violently that he had to brace his legs in the snow and hold on to the edge of the sleigh; gradually the coughing subsided, and they set off.

Above them the Castle, which K. had hoped to reach that day, already looked strangely dark as it receded from view. As if to bid him farewell for the time being, a bell rang out with a cheerful sound that, at least for a moment, set his pulse racing. It was also a poignant sound, as if it threatened to fulfil the obscure yearnings of his heart. But this great bell soon fell silent and was followed by a smaller one with a feeble, monotonous sound that might still have come from the Castle up there, or perhaps from the village below. Its chime was certainly better suited to his journey in the slow-moving sleigh and its pitiful but grimly determined driver.

'Tell me,' K. suddenly called out to him – since they had now almost reached the church and were no great distance from the inn, K. felt it was safe to speak out – 'I'm very surprised that you dare to drive me around at your own responsibility. Are you allowed to do that?' Gerstäcker ignored him and walked on beside the horse. 'Hey!' cried K.; he gathered some snow from the sleigh into a ball and threw it at Gerstäcker, hitting him right in the ear. This made him stop and turn round; the sleigh slid on a few feet further, which enabled K. to examine him more closely. Looking at this bent, apparently ill-treated figure, this tired, red, pinched face with cheeks that looked lop-sided – flat on one side, sunken on the other – this mouth gaping open and displaying a few stumps of teeth, K. felt he should out of pity repeat what he had just said out of malice; so he asked Gerstäcker whether he could be punished for offering K. transport. 'What do you mean?' replied Gerstäcker, mystified; but without waiting for any explanation he gave an order to the horse, and they went on.

A bend in the road told K. that they were approaching the inn; to his astonishment it was already dark. Had he been away so long? Surely only an hour or two, he reckoned. He had left in the morning, and had felt no need for food. Only a short while ago it had been broad daylight, and now it was dark. 'Short days, indeed,' he said to himself, slipped off the sleigh and went towards the inn.

He was very glad to see the landlord standing at the top of the front steps, holding a lantern for him. Briefly remembering

Gerstäcker, he stopped; somewhere in the darkness he heard coughing – he was out there. Well, he would see him again before long. Only when he got up to the landlord, who greeted him respectfully, did he notice two men at each side of the door. He took the lantern from the landlord and by its light saw that they were the men he had met earlier, who had been addressed as Artur and Jeremias. They saluted him; recalling the happy days of his military service, he laughed. 'Who are you?' he asked, looking from one to the other. 'Your assistants,' they replied. 'They are your assistants,' confirmed the landlord in a whisper. 'What?' asked K., 'you are my old assistants, the ones I am expecting, the ones I told to follow me here?' They said they were. 'Good,' said K. after a pause, 'I'm glad you came.' After a further pause, K. said: 'Even so, you have taken a long time, that's very slack of you.' 'It was a long way,' said one of them. 'A long way,' K. repeated. 'But I met you as you came from the Castle.' 'Yes,' they said without further explanation. 'Where are the instruments?' asked K. 'We don't have any,' they replied. 'The instruments I gave you,' said K. 'We don't have any,' they repeated. 'What kind of assistants are you?' said K. 'Do you know anything about surveying?' 'No,' they said. 'But if you are my old assistants you must know something about it,' said K. They said nothing. 'Come on, then,' said K., pushing them in front of him into the house.

2

Barnabas

The three of them were sitting in silence drinking beer at a small table in the parlour of the inn. K. sat in the middle, with the assistants on either side. Otherwise only one table was occupied by peasants as on the previous evening. 'It's not easy with you two,' said K., comparing their faces as he had already done many times. 'How am I going to tell you apart? The only difference between you is your names, otherwise you're like' – he broke off, then went on in spite of himself – 'you're as like each other as two snakes.' They smiled. 'Other people can tell us apart easily,' they assured him. 'I believe you,' said K., 'I saw that for myself. But I can only use my own eyes, and I can't see any difference between you. So I shall treat you as one single person and call you both Artur, that's what one of you is called, after all. Is it you, perhaps?' K. asked the one. 'No,' he said, 'I'm Jeremias.' 'Well, it doesn't matter,' said K., 'I shall call you both Artur. If I send Artur off anywhere you must both go, and if I give Artur a job to do you must both do it. That has the great advantage for me that you both carry the responsibility for all the work I give you. How you divide the work up between you I don't care, but you mustn't make excuses by blaming each other – you're both one man as far as I'm concerned.' They thought this over and said: 'We wouldn't like that at all.' 'Why should you?' said K. 'Of course you won't like it, but that's how it's going to be.'

For some time K. had noticed one of the peasants creeping round the table; he finally made up his mind, went up to one of the assistants and tried to whisper something to him. 'Excuse me,' said K., banging his hand on the table and jumping up, 'these are my assistants, and we are having a discussion. No one has the right to interrupt us.' 'Oh, sorry, sorry,' said the peasant timidly, backing off towards his companions. 'Above everything else you must take note of this,' said K., sitting down again. 'You may not speak to anyone without my permission. I am a stranger here, and if you are my old assistants, you are strangers too. So we three strangers must stick together; give me your hand on it.' All too eagerly they held out their hands to K. 'Never mind that,' he said, 'but my orders stand. I am going to get some sleep now, and I advise you to do the same. We have missed a day's work, so we must start very early tomorrow. You must order a sleigh to take us to the Castle; be ready with it at six o' clock outside the inn.' 'Very good,' said one of them, but the other interrupted: 'You say "very good", but you know that's not possible.' 'Stop!' said K. 'You're trying to act individually, aren't you?' But then the first one said: 'He's right, it's not possible. No stranger can visit the Castle without permission.' 'Where must we apply for permission?' 'I don't know, perhaps to the Warden.' 'Then we shall apply by telephone. Ring the Warden at once, both of you.' They rushed to the instrument, were put through – how eagerly they went about it, outwardly they were absurdly obedient – and asked whether K. might come to the Castle with them the next day. K. heard the answer 'No' from his table, but the reply went into more detail: 'neither tomorrow nor any other time.' 'I'll ring myself,' said K., standing up. While K. and his assistants had attracted little attention so far, apart from the earlier incident with the peasant, this last remark aroused general interest. Everyone stood up along with K., and although the landlord tried to push them back, they gathered closely round K. in a semicircle as he stood by the telephone. The majority were of the opinion that he would get no answer at all. K. had to ask them to keep quiet – he had no wish to hear their opinions.

From the receiver came a buzzing sound K. had never heard on the telephone before. It was as if the humming of countless children's voices (though even this was not a humming, but the song of voices in the very furthest distance) merged, in some quite impossible way, into one single high-pitched but powerful voice that struck the ear as if it sought to penetrate more deeply than mere hearing. K. rested his left arm on the telephone stand and simply listened without attempting to speak into the instrument.

He stood like that – how long, he did not know – until the landlord plucked at his coat and told him a messenger had arrived for him. 'Get off!' shouted K. furiously; perhaps he had shouted into the telephone, for now someone replied. 'Oswald here, who is that?' a voice called, a severe, imperious voice in which K. thought he could detect a slight speech defect that the speaker was trying to compensate for by assuming a more severe tone. K. hesitated to announce himself; he was defenceless on the telephone, the person at the other end could bawl him out or put down the receiver, and K. would have cut off what might be a quite important means of contact. His hesitation made the man impatient. 'Who is that?' he repeated, adding: 'I would appreciate it if there were less telephoning from over there; a call was made only a moment ago.' K. did not really reply to this remark; on the spur of the moment he announced: 'This is the surveyor's assistant.' 'What assistant? What surveyor?' K. remembered the previous evening's telephone conversation. 'Ask Fritz,' he said curtly. To his amazement, it helped. But what amazed him more than that was the unanimity of response on the part of the administration up there. The voice answered: 'Yes, I know. It's that surveyor yet again. Yes, yes, what else? Which assistant?' 'Josef,' said K. He was somewhat put out by the muttering of the peasants behind him, who were apparently voicing their disapproval that he had not identified himself correctly. But K. had no time to deal with them; the phone conversation demanded all his attention. 'Josef?' came the reply. 'The assistants are called' – there was a brief pause, evidently to ask someone else what the names were – 'Artur and Jeremias.' 'Those are the new assistants,' said K. 'No, they are the old ones.' 'They are the new ones. I am the old assistant, I arrived here today to join the surveyor.' 'No!' the voice shouted. 'Then who am I?' asked K., remaining calm. And after a pause the same voice with the same speech defect now replied, though it seemed like another, deeper and more authoritative voice: 'You are the old assistant.'

K. was listening so carefully to this new tone of voice that he almost missed the next question: 'What do you want?' He would have preferred to put down the receiver; he did not expect anything further from this conversation. But he felt constrained to reply: 'When may my chief come to the Castle?' 'Never,' came the reply. 'Right,' said K. and hung up the receiver.

Behind him the peasants had by now crowded quite closely round him. The assistants, with frequent sidelong glances at K., were busy holding them back. But it all seemed to be an act, and the peasants, apparently satisfied with the result of the conversation, fell back slowly. Then they moved to one side to let through a man who strode through them with swift steps, bowed to K. and handed him a letter. K. held the letter and looked at the man, who at that moment seemed to him more important. There was a close resemblance between him and the assistants. He was as slim as they were, and wore the same close-fitting clothes; he was just as supple and nimble, and yet he was quite different. How much K. would have preferred him as an assistant! He reminded him somehow of the woman with the child he had seen at the tanner's house. He was dressed almost entirely in white, and though it was scarcely silk that he was wearing – it was an ordinary winter coat – it had all the delicacy and dignified elegance of silk clothing. His face was alert and open, his eyes very large, and his smile was uncommonly cheering; he passed his hand over his face as if to efface his smile, but he could not. 'Who are you?' asked K. 'Barnabas,' he replied, 'I am a messenger.' As he spoke, his lips moved in a manly but gentle way. 'How do you like it here?' asked K., indicating the peasants, who had still not lost their interest in him and were staring at him curiously with their thick-lipped mouths hanging open and their truly tortured faces turned on him – their skulls seemed to have been beaten flat on top, and their features to have contorted with the pain of the blows; then again they were not staring at him, for at times they looked away, their gaze lingering on some insignificant object before fixing on him again. Then K. also pointed to his assistants, who stood smiling arm in arm and cheek to cheek, whether respectfully or mockingly it was impossible to tell. K. pointed to them all as if he were presenting a following forced upon him by special circumstances, and as if he expected Barnabas would be sensible enough to draw a distinction between them and him; this would indicate a bond of sympathy between the two of them, and that was what mattered to K. But Barnabas – in all innocence, that much was clear – did not take up the question; he let it pass, as a well-trained servant ignores some remark only apparently addressed to him by his master. In response, he simply looked around, raised his hand to greet some acquaintances among the peasants, and exchanged a few words with the assistants, all of which was done with an easy air of independence that preserved a certain distance between them. K., rebuffed but not embarrassed, turned his attention back to the letter he was holding and opened it. It went: 'Dear Sir, you have, as you know, been engaged in the Count's service. Your immediate superior is the mayor of the village, who will inform you of all the details of your employment and your remuneration, and to whom you are answerable. Nevertheless, I shall not lose sight of you. Barnabas, the bearer of this letter, will see you from time to time to hear your wishes and report them to me. You will always find me willing to be of service to you as far as I can. It is important to me that our workers have no cause for complaint.' The signature was illegible, but beneath it was printed: Head of X Department.

'Wait here,' said K. to Barnabas, who was bowing to him; then he called the landlord to show him to his room, where he wished to study the letter alone for a while. Then he remembered that Barnabas, for all the liking he had for him, was after all no more than a messenger, and ordered a glass of beer for him. He watched to see how Barnabas would react to his offer; he clearly accepted it gladly and drank the beer at once. Then K. went off with the landlord. The inn was so small that they had only been able to prepare a tiny room in the attic for K., and even that had caused problems, because two maids who had slept there previously had to be accommodated elsewhere. In fact, nothing had been done except to move out the maids; otherwise, it seemed, the room was unchanged, there were no sheets on the only bed, just a few pillows and a coarse blanket, everything was in the same state as it had been the night before. On the walls were a few sacred pictures and photographs of soldiers, and the room had not been aired; clearly they hoped the new guest would not stay long and they were doing nothing to help him. But K. did not mind; he wrapped himself in the blanket and began to read the letter over again by the light of a candle.

The letter was not consistent; in parts he was treated as a free man whose independence was acknowledged – the opening address, or the section dealing with his own wishes. But then there were also passages where he was explicitly or implicitly treated as a minor employee who was almost beneath the notice of the Head of Department; the authorities would make an effort 'not to lose sight of him', his superior was merely the mayor of the village – perhaps his only colleague was the village policeman. These were obvious contradictions, so obvious that they must be intentional. K. scarcely entertained the thought that they might be a sign of indecisiveness – with an authority like this, that was a ridiculous idea. Rather, he saw the letter as offering him a clear choice; it was left to him what to make of his instructions – whether he wished to be an employee of the village with a privileged but only apparent connection with the Castle, or someone who appeared to work for the village but whose conditions of employment were in fact entirely communicated to him through Barnabas. K. did not hesitate in his choice; he would have had no hesitation even without the benefit of his experiences so far. Only as a village employee, removed as far as possible from the gentlemen in the Castle, was he in a position to achieve anything in the Castle.

These village people who were still so suspicious of him would start to speak to him once he became, if not their friend, then at least a fellow-citizen; and once he was indistinguishable from Gerstäcker or Lasemann – and this must happen very soon, everything depended on it – then surely he would at a stroke have access to all those channels which, had it been left to the grace and favour of those gentlemen up there, would have remained not only blocked, but quite invisible to him. Of course, there was one danger that had been quite sufficiently stressed in the letter, indeed it had been spelt out with a certain relish, as if it were inescapable, namely, his status as an employee: worker, service, employment, remuneration, a superior to whom he was answerable – the letter was full of such terms, and even when it touched on other, more personal matters, it was all expressed in that spirit. If K. was to become a worker, he could do it, but he would do it with a grim seriousness of purpose, without looking right or left. He knew that there had been no real threat of compulsion, he had no fear of that, here least of all; but the powerful effect of such dispiriting surroundings, of becoming accustomed to disappointment, of constant imperceptible influences – these things he feared, certainly, but they were the dangers he had to struggle against. Nor had the letter omitted to suggest that should it come to a dispute, K. had been foolhardy enough to start it; this had been expressed so discreetly that only an uneasy conscience – an uneasy, not a bad, conscience – could detect it. It lay in the three words concerning his engagement in the Count's service: 'as you know'. K. had reported for service, and since then he had known, as the letter put it, that he had been engaged.

K. took down a picture from the wall and hung the letter on the nail; he would be living in this room, and that was where the letter should hang.

Then he went down to the parlour. Barnabas was sitting at a small table with the assistants. 'Ah, there you are,' said K., for no reason except that he was glad to see Barnabas, who jumped up immediately. As soon as K. entered the room, the peasants got up to approach him; it had already become their habit to follow him around. 'What do you want from me all the time?' he cried. They did not take offence, and slowly returned to their places. As they did, one of them said casually by way of explanation: 'You always hear something new.' He licked his lips as though such news were something to savour. K. made no attempt to smooth things over, he was happy to have some respect from them; but he had scarcely sat down beside Barnabas when he felt one of the peasants breathing down his neck. He said he had come to fetch the salt-cellar, but K. stamped his foot angrily and the peasant ran off without the salt-cellar. It was in fact very easy to approach K., they only had to set the peasants on him; their stubborn interest seemed to him more sinister than the secretiveness of the others. In any case, the peasants were secretive too – if he had gone over to sit at their table, they would certainly not have stayed there. Only the presence of Barnabas prevented another outburst, but he still turned to face them angrily; they, too, were facing him. But when he saw them sitting there, each at his own place, without speaking to each other, apparently with nothing in common except that they were all staring at him, it occurred to him that it was not malice that made them follow him around; perhaps they actually wanted something from him, but just could not say what. Or if it was not that, perhaps it was simply a childish naivety, a naivety that seemed to prevail here; did it not also include the landlord, who was standing there holding a glass of beer that one of his customers had ordered, staring at K. and ignoring his wife, who was calling to him through the hatch from the kitchen.

Calmer now, K. turned to Barnabas. He would have preferred to dismiss the assistants, but could think of no pretext; besides, they sat quietly gazing into their beer. 'I have read the letter,' K. began. 'Do you know what it says?' 'No,' said Barnabas; his look seemed to say more that his words. Perhaps K. was as mistaken about his goodness as he was about the malice of the peasants, but K. still found his presence comforting. 'You are also mentioned in the letter; you are to carry messages now and then between me and the Castle. That's why I thought you would know what it said.' 'I was only instructed to hand the letter to you, wait while you read it, and bring back an answer if you thought it necessary, in writing or by word of mouth.' 'Good,' said K. 'A written answer is not needed. Convey my thanks to the Head of Department – what is his name? I couldn't read the signature.' 'Klamm,' said Barnabas. 'Then convey my thanks to Herr Klamm for his welcome and for his great kindness, which, as someone who has not yet made his mark here, I much appreciate. I shall follow his wishes in everything I do. For the moment I have no particular requests.' Barnabas, who had listened carefully, asked permission to repeat the message to K. He agreed, and Barnabas repeated it word for word. Then he stood up to leave.

All this time K. had been studying his face, and now he gave him one last look. Barnabas was about as tall as K., and yet he seemed to look down on him; but this was done almost with humility, it was impossible that this man could make anyone feel uncomfortable. Of course, he was only a messenger and did not know the content of the letters he had to deliver; but his look, his smile, his walk, seemed to convey a message too, even if he was quite unaware of it. And K. held out his hand, which clearly surprised him, for he had only intended to make a bow.

As soon as he had gone – before opening the door he had stood for a while leaning against it and had surveyed the room with a look that was not directed at any single individual – K. said to the assistants: 'I am going to fetch the drawings from my room, then we shall discuss the work we have to do.' They stood up to go with him. 'Stay here!' said K. Still they made to go with him; K. had to repeat his command more sharply. Barnabas was no longer in the hallway, though he had only just left. But K. could not see him outside either – snow had started to fall again. He called: 'Barnabas!' No reply. Was he still in the house? There seemed to be no other possibility. Even so, K. shouted his name at the top of his voice; the name boomed out in the night like thunder. From the distance came a faint reply, Barnabas was already so far away. K. called him back and went to meet him; when they met, the inn could no longer be seen.

'Barnabas,' said K., scarcely able to control the tremor in his voice, 'there's something else I wanted to tell you. It occurs to me that our arrangements are most unsatisfactory; it's a matter of chance whether you happen to be here when I need something from the Castle. If I had not managed to reach you just now – you fly along, I thought you were still at the inn – who knows how long I might have had to wait for your next appearance.' 'Well,' said Barnabas, 'you can ask the Head of Department to arrange for me to come at certain times specified by you.' 'That would not be satisfactory either,' said K. 'I might not have any message for a year, while there might be something of the utmost urgency just a quarter of an hour after you had left.' 'Then should I report to the Head of Department,' replied Barnabas, 'that you should use someone other than myself to communicate with him?' 'No, no,' said K., 'not at all. I only mention it by the by; after all, I was lucky enough to catch up with you this time.' 'Should we go back to the inn?' said Barnabas, 'so that you can give me your new message?' He had already started to make for the inn. 'There's no need for that, Barnabas,' said K., 'I'll come along with you for a while.' 'Why don't you want to go to the inn?' asked Barnabas. 'The people there annoy me,' said K. 'You've seen how the peasants pester me.' 'We can go to your room,' said Barnabas. 'It's the maids' room,' said K., 'it's dirty and stuffy; it was to avoid having to stay there that I wanted to come with you for a while. Only you must help me along,' added K. in order to put an end to his resistance, 'you are more sure-footed than I am.' And K. took hold of his arm. It was quite dark, K. could only make out Barnabas indistinctly, and could not see his face at all; he had already been trying for some time to take hold of his arm.

Barnabas consented, and they turned away from the inn. K. felt that even with the greatest effort he was not capable of keeping up with Barnabas, that he was impeding him; he felt that even under normal circumstances this trivial factor could ruin everything – perhaps in those side-streets like the one where K. had been stuck in the snow that morning, from which he could only escape if Barnabas were to carry him. But he put these worries behind him, and Barnabas' silence reassured him; if they walked on in silence, it could only mean that for Barnabas, too, the purpose of their companionship was simply to walk on together.

They went on, but K. did not know where they were going, he recognised nothing, he did not even know whether they had passed the church by now. Just the effort of walking prevented him from marshalling his thoughts; instead of concentrating on his destination, they became confused. Memories of his home town constantly surged up and filled his mind. There, too, a church stood on the main square, partly surrounded by an old graveyard which was itself surrounded by a high wall. Only very few lads had climbed this wall, and K. had not yet managed to. It was not curiosity that made them try, for the graveyard held no mystery for them; they had often gone in through its small iron gate – they only wanted to scale that smooth high wall. One morning when the square was quiet and empty and flooded with light – when had K. ever seen it like that, before or after? – he managed it with surprising ease; he climbed the wall at his first attempt with a small flag gripped between his teeth. Loose stones were still rolling down beneath him when he reached the top. He rammed the flag in, it unfurled in the wind, he looked down and around and over his shoulder at the crosses half-buried in the ground; here, at this moment, no one was greater than he. Then the teacher happened to come by; his angry look had forced him to come down. As he jumped, K. had injured his knee and reached home only with some difficulty; but he had climbed the wall, and it seemed to him at the time that the sense of this triumph would give him support for the rest of his life – not such a foolish notion, for now after many years it came to his aid that snow-bound night as he grasped Barnabas' arm.

He held on more tightly, Barnabas was almost dragging him along, and their silence was unbroken; K. did not know which way they had come, he could only conclude from the state of the road that they had not yet turned off into a side-street. He vowed to himself that he would not be deterred from going on by any difficulties on his way, or even by any worries he might have about getting back; he would surely still have enough strength to be dragged along. And the journey could not be endless. By day the Castle had seemed within easy reach, and the messenger must know the shortest way.

Then Barnabas stopped. Where were they? Were they going no further? Was Barnabas going to leave him now? He would not let him; K. gripped Barnabas' arm so tightly that he almost felt the pain himself. Or had the unbelievable happened – were they already in the Castle or at its gates? But as far as K. could tell, they had not made any progress upwards. Or had Barnabas led him up a road that climbed imperceptibly? 'Where are we?' asked K. softly, addressing himself more than Barnabas. 'At home,' said Barnabas in the same voice. 'At home?' 'But take care not to slip, sir. We must go down here.' Down? 'Just a few steps,' he added, and already he was knocking at a door.

A girl opened it, and they were standing on the threshold of a large living-room which was almost in darkness, lit only by a tiny oil lamp hanging above a table at the back of the room. 'Who is that with you, Barnabas?' asked the girl. 'The surveyor,' he said. 'The surveyor,' the girl repeated in a louder voice towards the table. At this two elderly people, a man and a woman, as well as a second girl, stood up. They greeted K., and Barnabas introduced them all to K.; they were his parents and his sisters Olga and Amalia. K. hardly gave them a glance as he let them take off his wet coat and put it by the stove.

So it was only Barnabas, not K., who was at home. But why were they here? K. took Barnabas to one side and said: 'Why did you come here? Or do you live in the Castle precincts?' 'In the Castle precincts?' Barnabas repeated, as if he did not understand K. 'But Barnabas,' said K., 'you were going from the inn to the Castle.' 'No, sir,' said Barnabas, 'I was going home, I only go to the Castle early in the morning, I never sleep there.' 'I see,' said K., 'you weren't going to the Castle, just coming here.' His smile seemed to have faded, and his presence seemed less imposing. 'Why didn't you tell me?' 'You didn't ask me, sir,' said Barnabas. 'You were going to give me another message, but you didn't want to do it in the parlour or in your room at the inn, so I thought you could give me the message here at my parents' house – they will leave us alone if you wish; and if you prefer it here, you could spend the night with us. Did I not do the right thing?' K. could think of no reply; so it had been a misunderstanding, a plain, ordinary misunderstanding, and K. had succumbed to it. He had been bewitched by Barnabas' close-fitting shiny silky jacket, which he was now removing to reveal a rough greyish shirt, much darned, which covered the square muscular chest of a labourer. And everything around him confirmed, indeed heightened, this impression – the old gout-crippled father, whose groping hands helped him to move along better than his stiff, shuffling legs, and the mother, her hands folded across her breast, who was so stout she could take only the tiniest steps.

As soon as K. had arrived both of them, the father and the mother, had left their corner to approach him and had still not reached him. The two sisters, big strapping blondes who looked very much like each other and their brother, though with coarser features than Barnabas, stood next to the two new arrivals, expecting some word of greeting from K., but he could think of nothing to say. He had thought that everyone in this village was important to him, and no doubt this was the case; but he had no interest whatever in these people. If he had been capable of making his way back to the inn alone, he would have left immediately. He was not at all attracted by the possibility of going to the Castle with Barnabas in the morning. He had wanted to get into the Castle now, at night, unnoticed, led by Barnabas – but by the Barnabas he thought he had known until now, a man closer to him than anyone he had met so far, who, he had also believed, was far more intimately connected with the Castle than his apparent status warranted. But the son of this family, of which he was an integral part, with whom he was even now sitting at table, this man who, it must be remembered, was not even permitted to sleep in the Castle – to go to the Castle on this man's arm in broad daylight was out of the question, it was an absurd, hopeless undertaking.

K. sat down on a window-seat, resolved to spend the night there and to make no further demands on the family. The people in the village who had got rid of him or appeared to be afraid of him seemed to him less dangerous; they made him more self-reliant, they helped him to summon all his resources. But those who purported to help him, who by means of a silly charade introduced him to their family instead of into the Castle – they distracted him whether they wished to or not, and contrived to weaken him. He paid no attention to an invitation to join the family at the table, and stayed on the window-seat, his head bowed.

Then Olga, the gentler of the two sisters, came over to K. and asked him, not without a trace of girlish shyness, to join them at table; there was bread and bacon for him, she said, and she would fetch some beer. 'Where from?' asked K. 'From the inn,' she replied. This was very welcome news to K., who asked her not to fetch him any beer, but to go with him to the inn, as he had important work to do there. But it turned out that she was not going as far as his inn, but to another inn, the Herrenhof, which was much nearer. Even so, K. asked if he could go with her; perhaps, he thought, he would find somewhere to sleep there – whatever it might be like, he would prefer it to the best bed in this house. Olga did not answer at once, but looked back towards the table. Her brother stood up, nodded obligingly and said: 'If the gentleman wishes.' This ready agreement almost made K. withdraw his request; Barnabas could not agree to anything worthwhile. But then, once they began debating whether K. would be admitted to the inn, he insisted on going, though he did not bother to think up any very good reason for wanting to. This family had to accept him as he was, he had no inhibitions as far as they were concerned – though he was a little put out by Amalia's solemn, direct, unblinking and perhaps also rather dull-witted gaze.

During their short walk to the inn – K. had taken Olga's arm and had no choice but to be dragged along by her almost as he had been earlier by her brother – he learned that this inn was really only for gentlemen from the Castle, who would take their meals there whenever they had business in the village, and would even stay the night there sometimes. Olga spoke to K. softly and confidingly, and it was agreeable to walk along with her, almost as agreeable as with her brother; K. resisted this pleasant feeling, but it persisted.

From the outside, the inn looked very similar to the one at which K. was staying. There seemed to be no great differences in the external appearance of the buildings in the village, but some small variations were immediately noticeable. The front steps had a hand-rail, a handsome lantern hung over the door, and above them as they entered fluttered a flag in the Count's colours. In the hallway they met the landlord, who was obviously on a tour of inspection; as they passed, he gave K. a searching – or perhaps a tired – look through narrowed eyes, and said: 'The surveyor may only go into the bar.' 'Of course,' said Olga, coming to K.'s support at once, 'he's just keeping me company.' But K. showed no gratitude; he let go her arm and took the landlord on one side. Meanwhile, Olga waited patiently at the end of the corridor. 'I should like to spend the night here,' he said. 'I'm afraid that is impossible,' said the landlord, 'you don't seem to realise, but the inn is reserved exclusively for gentlemen from the Castle.' 'That may be the rule,' said K., 'but surely it must be possible to let me sleep in a corner somewhere.' 'I would be only too pleased to oblige you,' said the landlord, 'but quite apart from this very strict rule, which you talk about as a stranger would do, it is also impossible for the reason that the gentlemen are extremely sensitive; I am quite sure they cannot tolerate the sight of a stranger, at least not without some warning. So if I let you spend the night here and you were to be discovered by chance – and chance is always on the gentlemen's side – then not only would I be done for, so would you. It sounds absurd, but it is true.'

This tall, tightly buttoned man who stood with one hand braced against the wall and the other on his hip, his legs crossed, leaning towards K. and addressing him confidentially, hardly seemed to belong to the village now, although in his dark clothes he just looked like a peasant dressed in his finery. 'I believe you implicitly,' said K., 'and I do not underrate the importance of the rule at all, though I may have expressed myself clumsily. I would just draw your attention to one thing. I have important contacts in the Castle, and shall have even more in the future; these will safeguard you from any risk you might run from my staying here, and guarantee that I shall be in a position to return in full any small favour you may do me.' 'I know,' said the landlord. 'I know,' he repeated.

K. could now have put his request more forcefully, but this reply from the landlord distracted him, so he simply asked: 'Are many of the gentlemen from the Castle staying here tonight?' 'In that respect things look good,' said the landlord, as if to encourage him, 'only one gentleman is here.' Still K. was unable to insist; by now he almost had hopes of being accepted, so he simply asked the gentleman's name. 'Klamm,' said the landlord casually, turning to his wife, who came bustling along in a strangely old-fashioned, well-worn costume, overloaded with frills and pleats but of good quality. She had come to fetch the landlord, she said, because the Head of Department wanted something. Before the landlord left, he again turned to K. as if it were no longer his decision whether he could stay overnight, but K.'s. But K., dumbfounded by the news that his superior was here, could say nothing; he could not explain to himself exactly why, but he felt more inhibited towards Klamm that he had towards the Castle authorities so far. To be caught here by Klamm would not have been such cause for alarm as the landlord had suggested, but it would be awkward and embarrassing, as if he were to play a thoughtless trick on someone to whom he owed a debt of gratitude; and yet at the same time he was dismayed to realise that the very fact that he had such scruples demonstrated what he feared, namely, the position of inferiority resulting from his status as an employee, which he was in no position to combat even here, where it was so conspicuous. So he stood there biting his lip, and said nothing. Once again the landlord looked back at him before disappearing through a door, but K. simply watched him go and did not move from the spot until Olga came and pulled him away. 'What did you want with the landlord?' she asked. 'I wanted to stay the night here,' said K. 'But you are staying with us,' said Olga with surprise. 'Yes, surely,' said K., leaving her to make what she could of his words.

3
Frieda

The bar was a large room, quite empty in the middle; around the walls some peasants were sitting at seats and tables made from barrels, but they looked different from the people at K.'s inn. They were dressed more smartly and uniformly in loose jacket and close-fitting trousers of coarse yellow-grey cloth. They were small men who at first sight resembled each other closely; their faces were flat and bony, but their cheeks rounded. They all sat quietly and scarcely moved; only their eyes followed K. and Olga as they entered, but slowly and without curiosity. Even so, because there were so many of them and because it was so quiet, they made an impression on K. He took Olga's arm again to explain his presence there. In one corner a man, an acquaintance of Olga's, stood up and tried to approach her, but K. took her arm and steered her in another direction. No one but she could have noticed it, and she gave him a sidelong smile as she let him lead her.

The beer was poured out by a young girl called Frieda. She was an unremarkable fair-haired girl with a sad face and hollow cheeks, yet surprisingly she had a look of distinct superiority. As she glanced at K., he had the impression that this look had already settled certain things about him, things of which he was still quite unaware, but which were confirmed by her look.

K. continued to scrutinise Frieda from the side even while she was speaking to Olga. Frieda and Olga appeared not to be friends, for they exchanged only a few distant words. K. wanted to help the conversation on, so he broke in with: 'Do you know Herr Klamm?' Olga burst out laughing. 'Why are you laughing?' asked K. angrily. 'I'm not laughing at all,' she said, but went on laughing. 'Olga is still very childish,' said K., leaning right over the bar counter to catch Frieda's gaze again. But she kept her eyes lowered and said quietly: 'Do you want to see Herr Klamm?' K. said he did. She pointed to a door just to her left. 'There's a small peephole here you can look through.' 'What about these people?' asked K. She curled her lip and pulled K. towards the door with an unusually soft hand. Through the small aperture, which had obviously been made for the purpose of observation, he could see almost the whole of the room next door. In a comfortable armchair at a desk in the middle of the room sat Herr Klamm in the harsh light of a lamp hanging in front of him. He was a stout, ponderous man of medium height. His face was still unlined, but his sagging cheeks betrayed his age. He had a wide black moustache. His eyes were hidden behind the glint of his pince-nez, which he wore askew. If Herr Klamm had been sitting square on to his desk, K. would only have seen him in profile, but because he was sitting at an angle K. could see his whole face. Klamm was resting his left elbow on the desk, while his right hand, in which he held a cigar, rested on his knee. On the desk stood a beer-glass; because there was a raised edge around the desk, K. could not quite see whether there were any papers lying on it, but to him it looked empty. To make certain, he asked Frieda to look through the peephole and tell him whether it was, but since she had been in the room only a short while before, she was able to assure him that there were no papers on the desk. K. asked Frieda whether he should move away from the door, but she told him he could look as long as he liked.

K. was now alone with Frieda; a brief glance told him that Olga had made her way to her friend and was sitting up on a barrel swinging her legs. 'Frieda,' whispered K., 'do you know Herr Klamm very well?' 'Oh yes,' she said, 'very well.' She bent over towards K. and coquettishly adjusted her flimsy, low-cut cream blouse which K. had only just noticed, and which sat incongruously on her scrawny body. Then she said: 'Don't you remember how Olga laughed?' 'Yes, the cheeky girl,' said K. 'Well,' said Frieda in mitigation, 'she had good reason to laugh. You asked if I knew Klamm, and actually' – here she involuntarily pulled herself up slightly and again gave K. that superior look that seemed to bear no relation to what she was saying – 'actually, I'm his mistress.' 'Klamm's mistress?' said K. She nodded. 'In that case,' said K. with a smile, in order to avoid things becoming too serious between them, 'I have a lot of respect for you.' 'You're not the only one,' said Frieda in a friendly way; but she did not return his smile. K. had a weapon to combat her pride, so he used it. 'Have you ever been to the Castle?' he asked. But it failed, for she replied: 'No, but isn't it enough that I'm serving at the inn?' Her vanity was clearly outrageous, and she had chosen K., it seemed, to satisfy it. 'Of course,' said K., 'here in the taproom; you're working for the landlord.' 'That's right,' she said, 'and I started as a cow-maid at the Bridge Inn.' 'With such delicate hands,' said K. It was almost meant as a question; he did not know whether he was just flattering her, or whether he was actually attracted to her. Her hands were indeed small and delicate, but they could also be called weak and unremarkable. 'No one noticed them then,' she said, 'and even now' – K. looked at her questioningly, but she shook her head and would say no more. 'Of course,' said K., 'you have your secrets, and you don't want to tell them to someone you only met half an hour ago, who hasn't had a chance to tell you anything about himself.' But this turned out to be an ill-advised remark; it was as if he had roused Frieda from a dream in which she was well-disposed towards him. She took a small piece of wood from the leather purse hanging from her belt, blocked the peephole with it and said to K., with a visible effort to conceal any change in her attitude towards him: 'I know all about you; you're the surveyor.' Then she added: 'I must get back to work,' and went back to her place behind the bar-counter, where every now and again she refilled the customers' glasses.

K. wanted to have a quiet word with her again, so he took an empty glass from a stand and went over to her. 'Just one more thing, Fräulein Frieda,' he said. 'It takes a quite exceptional effort to work one's way up from cow-maid to barmaid; but is that all a person like you aspires to? It's a silly question. I can read in your eyes, Fräulein Frieda – please don't laugh at me – not so much your past struggle, but rather the struggle still to come. But the world puts great obstacles in one's way, the higher one aims the greater the obstacles, and it is no disgrace to enlist the help of a man whose influence may be small, but who is struggling like you. Perhaps we can have a quiet word with each other some time without so many people staring at us.' 'I don't know what you want,' she replied, in a tone of voice that seemed in spite of herself to convey, not the triumphs, but the endless disappointments of her life. 'Are you trying to take me away from Klamm, perhaps? Good heavens!' – and she clapped her hands. 'You have seen through me,' said K., as if he had had enough of this mistrust, 'that is exactly what I secretly intended. I wanted you to leave Klamm and be my mistress. And now I can go. Olga!' he called, 'we're going home.' Olga obediently slid down from her barrel, but could not get away from her circle of friends for a while. Frieda gave K. a cautious look and said in a low voice: 'When can I talk to you?' 'Can I spend the night here?' asked K. 'Yes,' said Frieda. 'Can I stay here now?' 'Go back with Olga, so I can get rid of the people here. Then after a while you can come back here.' 'Right,' said K., and waited impatiently for Olga.

But the peasants would not let her go. They had devised a dance with Olga in the middle; they danced round her in a ring, and they all whooped as one of them stepped up to her, seized her by the waist and whirled her round a few times. They danced faster and faster, their wolfish deep-throated shouts finally almost merging into one single howl; Olga, who at first had tried to break out of the circle with a smile, could now only reel from one to the other, her hair flying. 'You see the sort of people I get here,' said Frieda, biting her thin lips angrily. 'Who are they?' asked K. 'Klamm's servants,' said Frieda, 'he always brings them here with him, they get on my nerves. I can hardly remember what I've been telling you today, sir; if I was unpleasant, I'm sorry; it's because of them, they are the most despicable and repulsive people I know, and I have to fill their beer glasses for them. How many times have I begged Klamm to leave them behind; I already have to put up with the other gentlemen's servants, he could have some consideration for me, but it's no use pleading with him, an hour before he arrives they rush in here like a herd of cattle. If you weren't here, I'd fling this door open and Klamm would have to chase them out himself.' 'But can't he hear them?' asked K. 'No,' said Frieda, 'he's asleep.' 'What?' cried K., 'he's asleep? When I looked into his room he was sitting at his desk, wide awake.' 'He's still sitting there,' said Frieda. 'He was already asleep when you saw him – otherwise, I wouldn't have let you look; that's how he goes to sleep, these gentlemen sleep a lot, you can hardly credit it. Besides, if he didn't sleep so much, how could he put up with these people? But now I shall have to chase them out myself.'

She took a whip from the corner and with a single not very steady spring, rather as a young lamb jumps, leapt towards the dancers. At first they turned to her as if she had come to join the dance, and indeed for a moment it looked as if Frieda were about to drop the whip, but then she raised it again. 'In the name of Klamm,' she shouted, 'back to your shed, all of you, back to your shed.' Now they saw that she was serious, and in a panic that was incomprehensible to K. they began to crowd towards the end of the room; under the impact of the first of them a door at the back flew open, the night air rushed in, and they all disappeared, including Frieda, who was evidently driving them across the yard into the cowshed. In the sudden silence that followed K. heard footsteps from the hallway. To be safe, K. jumped behind the bar counter, which was the only place for him to hide; although the bar was not forbidden to him, he had to avoid being seen there now if he wanted to stay the night. So when the door did open he slipped under the counter. There was a risk he might be discovered there, but still he had a plausible excuse – that he had hidden there from the raucous behaviour of the peasants. It was the landlord who came in. 'Frieda!' he called, walking up and down the room. Fortunately, Frieda soon came back; she did not mention K., but only complained about the peasants. She went to look for K. behind the bar-counter, where K. could touch her foot; now he felt much safer. Since Frieda did not mention K., it was the landlord who had to. 'And where is the surveyor?' he asked. He seemed to be a courteous man, his manners had no doubt been refined as a result of his frequent and relatively free association with his superiors; but he addressed Frieda with particular respect, which was all the more striking because he was still an employer talking to a member of his staff – and a very pert one, too.

'I completely forgot about the surveyor,' said Frieda, placing her small foot on K.'s chest. 'I expect he left long ago.' 'But I didn't see him,' said the landlord, 'and I was in the hall nearly all the time.' 'Well, he's not here,' said Frieda coolly. 'Perhaps he's hiding somewhere,' said the landlord, 'from what I've seen of him, he can get up to anything.' 'I don't think he'd have the nerve,' said Frieda, pressing K. more firmly with her foot. There was something cheerful and uninhibited about her that K. had not noticed before, and that became apparent quite unexpectedly when she suddenly laughed and said: 'Perhaps he's hiding under here.' She bent down towards K., kissed him lightly, then jumped up and said sadly: 'No, he's not here.' But the landlord, too, caused K. some surprise when he said: 'It's a nuisance, not knowing whether he's gone. It's not just Herr Klamm, it's the rules. And the rules apply to you, Fräulein Frieda, just as much as to me. You see to the bar, and I'll search the rest of the house. Good night, sleep well!'

He had hardly left the room when Frieda turned off the electric light and joined K. under the counter. 'My darling! My sweet darling!' she whispered, but she did not touch K.; as if she were swooning with love, she lay on her back and spread out her arms, the ecstasy of love must have made time stand still for her, and she sighed, rather than sang, a little song. K. sat quietly, absorbed in his thoughts, then Frieda sat up abruptly and started to tug at him like a child: 'Come on, it's suffocating under here.' They embraced each other, K. felt the heat of her small body; in vain K. tried to come to his senses as they clung to each other, oblivious to everything. They rolled round and bumped against Klamm's door with a thud, then lay together in the pools of beer and other debris littering the floor. Then hours went by, hours of breathing as one, of hearts beating as one, hours in which K. could not rid himself of the feeling that he was lost, or that he had strayed into a foreign country where no one had been before him, a country where even the air was completely foreign to him, so foreign that it might suffocate him, so irrationally alluring that he could only go on and lose himself more deeply in it. So, at least initially, he felt no fear but rather a gleam of comfort when from Klamm's room a deep voice called for Frieda with a tone of impassive authority.

'Frieda,' K. spoke into her ear, repeating the summons. Acting out of an inherent sense of obedience, Frieda made to jump to her feet, but then realised where she was, stretched with a smile, and said: 'No, I won't go, I'm never going back to him.' K. wanted to object, to make her go to Klamm; he began to straighten her blouse, but he could not say anything to her, he was too blissfully happy just holding Frieda in his arms, and too fearful in his happiness, for he felt that if he lost Frieda he would lose everything he had. And as if she too drew strength from K.'s support, she clenched her fist, banged on the door and shouted: 'I'm with the surveyor! I'm with the surveyor!' That certainly silenced Klamm; but K. got up, kneeled beside Frieda and looked around him in the dim light of dawn. What had happened? Where were his hopes? What could he expect of Frieda now that everything had been revealed? Instead of proceeding with the utmost caution that the power of his enemy and the importance of his goal demanded, he had spent the night wallowing in these pools of beer, the stench of which was now overwhelming. 'What have you done?' he said to himself, 'we're both done for.' 'No,' said Frieda, 'I'm the only one who's done for, and I've got you. Keep calm. Look at those two laughing, though.' 'Who's that?' asked K., turning round. On the counter his two assistants were sitting, bleary-eyed, but with a cheerful look that suggested they were conscious of having done their duty. 'What are you doing here?' cried K., as if they were to blame for everything. He looked around for the whip Frieda had had the previous evening. 'We had to look for you,' they said, 'because you didn't come down to the parlour at the inn. Then we went to

Barnabas' house, and finally found you here. We've been sitting here all night; our job isn't easy.' 'I need your help in the daytime, not at night,' said K., 'go away!' 'But it's daytime now,' they said, and did not move. It was indeed day; the door to the courtyard opened and the peasants poured in, together with Olga, whom K. had completely forgotten. She was as lively as she had been the evening before, though her hair and clothes were disordered; as soon as she came in, she caught K.'s eye. 'Why didn't you take me home?' she said, almost in tears. 'Just for the sake of a woman like her!' she added, repeating it several times over. Frieda, who had left the room for a moment, returned with a small bundle of clothes. Olga stepped aside sadly. 'Now we can go,' said Frieda, clearly meaning that they should go to the Bridge Inn. K. went with Frieda, followed by the assistants. The peasants treated Frieda with contempt, which was understandable since she had controlled them so strictly until now; one of them even took a stick and held it as if he would not let her go unless she jumped over it – but one look from her was enough to send him packing.

Outside in the snow K. breathed more freely. He was so happy to be out in the open air that walking seemed less arduous; if he had been alone he would have made even better progress. At the inn he went straight to his room and lay on the bed; Frieda made up a place to sleep on the floor beside him. The assistants had followed them into the room; they were chased out, but came back in through the window. K. was too tired to chase them out again. The landlady herself came up to greet Frieda, who called her 'grandma', and there was an unaccountably heartfelt exchange of long hugs and kisses.

There was hardly any peace in the room. The maids in their men's boots frequently lumbered in, bringing things with them and taking other things away; if they wanted any of the various things piled on the bed, they pulled them unceremoniously from beneath K. They greeted Frieda as an equal. In spite of all these disturbances, K. stayed in bed all day and all that night. Frieda did small services for him. He finally got up, much refreshed, the following morning. He had now been in the village for four days.

4

First Conversation with the Landlady

He would have liked to speak privately to Frieda, but he was prevented from doing this simply by the intrusive presence of the assistants, with whom Frieda also laughed and joked from time to time. However, they were not too demanding; they had made themselves comfortable on the floor in the corner of the room, sitting on two old skirts. As they frequently assured Frieda, they were keen not to disturb the surveyor and to take up as little room as possible; and indeed they made various efforts to do so, albeit with much whispering and giggling. They crouched together, arms and legs intertwined, so that in the dim light all that could be seen of them was a large heap in the corner. Unfortunately, however, as K. knew from his experiences by daylight, they were most attentive observers; they were always watching him, up to what seemed to be childish tricks like using their hands as telescopes or some other silly game, or else simply peering at him while they seemed absorbed in grooming their beards, with which they took a great deal of trouble, forever comparing one with the other in length and thickness and calling on Frieda for her opinion. K. often watched the three of them fooling about, utterly indifferent.

As soon as he felt he had the energy to get up, all three rushed to help him. He was not yet strong enough to resist their services; he realised that this somehow made him dependent on them, which could have unfortunate consequences, but he had to put up with it. And it was by no means unpleasant to sit at table drinking the excellent coffee that Frieda brought him, to warm himself at the stove that Frieda had lit, and make his assistants run up and down stairs in their clumsy eagerness to fetch water, soap, a comb and a mirror, and even, because he had quietly hinted that he would like one, a small glass of rum.

Amid all this flurry of giving orders and being served, K. said, more because he felt relaxed than with any hope of success: 'Get out now, you two; I don't need anything else just now, and I want to speak to Fräulein Frieda in private.' When he saw from their faces that they were not actually showing any resistance, he added by way of compensation: 'Then we three shall go to see the mayor. Wait for me downstairs in the parlour.' Remarkably, they did as they were told, except that before leaving they said: 'We could wait here, too.' 'I know, but I don't want you to,' K. replied.

It annoyed him, though in a way he was also pleased, when as soon as the assistants had gone Frieda sat on his lap and said: 'Darling, what have you got against the assistants? We mustn't keep any secrets from them. They are loyal.' 'Loyal!' said K. 'They're forever watching me, it's futile, but I find it atrocious.' 'I think I know what you mean,' she said. She clasped her hands round his neck and was going to say more but could not, and because the chair was next to the bed they toppled over and fell onto it. They lay there, but without the abandon of the other night. She was searching for something and he was searching for something; furious and grimacing, they each buried their head in the other's breast, their embraces and their heaving bodies could not make them forget, but reminded them of their duty to search; like dogs frantically scratching at the ground each tore at the other's body and, helplessly frustrated, hungrily licked the other's face in an attempt to capture one last ecstasy. Only when they were exhausted could they lie still in mutual gratitude. Then the maids came upstairs. 'Look at them lying there,' said one, and taking pity threw a blanket over them.

Later, when K. threw off the blanket and looked around, he was not surprised to see the assistants were back in their corner. They pointed at K., urging each other to be serious, and waved to him; but besides them, the landlady was also sitting there close to the bed darning a stocking, a delicate task ill-suited to her huge figure, which almost blocked out the light in the room. 'I've been waiting a long time,' she said, looking up from her work. Her face was broad and much lined with age, but on the whole her features were regular; she might have been beautiful once. Her words sounded like a reproach, which was uncalled-for, since K. had not asked her to come. So he simply acknowledged them with a nod and sat upright; Frieda got up too, but left K. and leaned against the landlady's chair. 'Madam,' said K. absently, 'could we leave whatever you have to say until after I have been to see the mayor? I have an important meeting with him.' 'Believe me, sir, what I have to say is more important,' said the landlady. 'Your business is probably only about work, but this is about a person who is very dear to me, Frieda.' 'I see,' said K., 'of course; but I don't see why it can't be left to us.' 'Because I love her and care about her,' said the landlady, holding Frieda's head closer to her; even when she was standing, Frieda's head only reached up to the landlady's shoulder as she sat there. 'Since Frieda confides in you so much,' said K., 'I must do so too. And since Frieda said just now that my assistants were loyal, then we must all be friends. So I can tell you, madam, that I think it would be best that Frieda and I should marry, and very soon too. Most unfortunately, that will not compensate Frieda for what she has lost for my sake, namely her position at the Herrenhof and Klamm's friendship.'

Frieda raised her head. Her eyes were full of tears; they held no sign of triumph. 'Why me?' she said. 'Why choose me, of all people?' 'What?' asked K. and the landlady simultaneously. 'She is confused, poor child,' said the landlady, 'confused by so much happiness and unhappiness coming at once.' And as if to confirm her words, Frieda threw herself at K., kissed him passionately as if there were no one else in the room, then, still holding him, fell weeping to her knees in front of him. While K. stroked Frieda's hair with both hands, he asked the landlady: 'I think you agree with me?' 'You are an honest man,' said the landlady; she too spoke tearfully, and looked rather old. She breathed with difficulty, but still managed to say: 'Now we just have to think about what assurances you can give Frieda, for however much I respect you, you are after all a stranger, no one can answer for you, no one knows your private circumstances, so you will understand, sir, that assurances are required; after all, you yourself pointed out how much Frieda has to lose because of her relationship with you.' 'Of course, yes, assurances,' said K. 'It would be best to declare them to a lawyer, but perhaps some other of the Count's officials will be involved. Besides, there is something I have to settle before the marriage; I must speak to Klamm.' 'That's impossible!' said Frieda, getting up and clinging to K., 'the very idea!' 'It has to be done,' said K., 'if it's not possible for me to do it, you must do it.' 'I can't, K., I can't,' said Frieda, 'Klamm will never speak to you. How can you ever believe Klamm will speak to you?' 'And would he speak to you?' asked K. 'Not to me either,' said Frieda, 'not to you, not to me, it's just impossible.' She turned to the landlady with outstretched arms: 'Do you hear what he wants, Grandma?'

'You are an odd person, sir,' said the landlady. She looked intimidating now, as she sat there bolt upright, her legs apart and her massive knees bulging through her thin skirt. 'You are asking for the impossible.' 'Why is it impossible?' asked K. 'I will explain to you,' said the landlady in a tone of voice that suggested her explanation was not some final favour she was doing him, but rather the first punishment she was inflicting on him. 'I shall be glad to give you an explanation. I know I don't belong to the Castle, and I'm only a woman, I'm only a landlady at an inferior inn – it's not the worst, but it's not far from it – so you may not attach much importance to my explanation; but I've kept my eyes open during my life and come in contact with a lot of people, and I've taken on all the work of running the inn myself. My husband's a decent man, but he's no landlord and will never understand what responsibility means. For instance, it's only because of his negligence – I was dropping with exhaustion that evening –

that you're here in the village, that you're sitting here on this bed in peace and comfort.' 'What?' asked K., waking from a kind of reverie and roused more by curiosity than indignation. 'It's only because of his negligence,' repeated the landlady, wagging her forefinger at K. Frieda tried to soothe her. 'What else can I say?' said the landlady, swiftly turning her whole body towards Frieda. 'The surveyor asked me, and I have to give him an answer. How else is he going to understand what is obvious to us, that Herr Klamm never will speak to him – what am I saying, never *will* – that he never *can* speak to him. Listen, sir. Herr Klamm is one of the gentlemen from the Castle; that in itself means that he is of very high rank, quite apart from any other position he might have. But who are you, that we're so humbly begging you to agree to marry Frieda? You're not from the Castle, you're not from the village, you're nobody. But unfortunately you are somebody, you're a stranger who is one too many and gets in everyone's way, who is forever causing trouble, who takes up the maids' room, whose intentions are unknown. You have seduced our dear little Frieda, and now unfortunately we have to let you marry her. I'm not actually blaming you for all that; you are what you are, and I've seen too many things in my life not to be able to face this prospect as well. But just think what it is you're asking for. You want a man like Klamm to speak to you. It pained me to hear that Frieda let you look through the peephole; as soon as she did that, she had fallen for you. Tell me, how could you bear to look at Klamm? You needn't answer – I know you could quite easily. You are not capable of really seeing Klamm, and I'm not being high and mighty, because I couldn't do it myself either. You think Klamm is going to speak to you, but he doesn't even speak to people in the village, he's never spoken to anyone from the village. It was a great honour for Frieda, an honour I shall take pride in to my dying day, that he at least used to call Frieda by name, and that she could speak to him whenever she wanted to and had permission to use the peephole. But he has never spoken to her. And if he called Frieda sometimes, it doesn't necessarily mean what you might like to think, he just called out her name – who knows what his intentions were? – and if Frieda naturally went to him straight away, that was her business, and it was thanks to Klamm's kindness that she was allowed in to see him without question; but it can't be said that he ever actually called her in to see him. Now, of course, that's all over and gone for ever. Perhaps Klamm will still call out Frieda's name, that's quite possible; but she certainly won't be admitted any more, a girl who had gone off with you. And the one thing my poor head can't understand is that a girl who was said to be Klamm's mistress – which I think, by the way, is a very exaggerated description – even let you touch her.'

'That is certainly extraordinary,' said K., taking Frieda onto his lap. She complied at once, but kept her head bowed. 'But I believe it shows that in other respects the situation is not exactly as you think. I am sure you're right, for example, when you say I am a nobody compared with Klamm, and even if I still insist on speaking to Klamm and am not put off even by your arguments, that doesn't mean to say that I can bear the sight of Klamm without having a door between us, or that I might not run out of the room the moment he appeared. But such fears, however justified they may be, are no reason for me to lose my nerve. Still, if I do manage to come face to face with him, then there is no need for him to speak to me; it's quite enough for me to see the impression my words make on him, and if they make no impression or if he refuses to listen, then at least I shall benefit from having spoken freely in front of a powerful man. But you, madam, with your great experience of life and of people, and Frieda, who was until yesterday Klamm's mistress – I see no reason to avoid this word – I am sure you can easily arrange for me to speak to Klamm, even at the Herrenhof if there is no alternative; perhaps he is still there now.'

'It is impossible,' said the landlady, 'and I can see that you simply cannot understand why. But tell me: what do you want to talk to Klamm about?'

'About Frieda, of course,' said K.

'About Frieda?' asked the landlady, baffled. She turned to Frieda: 'Do you hear, Frieda? This man wants to talk to Klamm about you. To Klamm!'

'Oh,' said K., 'you are such an intelligent and admirable woman, but every small thing alarms you. Look – I want to talk to him about Frieda; there's nothing dreadful about that, it's perfectly normal. And I'm sure you are mistaken if you think Frieda has meant nothing to Klamm since I appeared on the scene. You underestimate him if you think that. I realise it's presumptuous of me to try to lecture you on this, but I have to. Nothing in Klamm's relationship with Frieda can change because of me. Either there was no real relationship between them – that's what people mean who deny Frieda the honour of being Klamm's mistress – in which case there is still no relationship; or there was one, in which case how could it be affected by me, when as you say quite rightly I am a nobody in Klamm's eyes? We may believe such things in our initial alarm, but it only needs a moment's reflection to realise we were mistaken. But in any case, let Frieda say what she thinks about it.'

With a faraway look, her cheek on K.'s breast, Frieda said: 'It's certainly right what grandma says. Klamm will have nothing to do with me any more. But that's not because you came along, darling; something like that could never upset him. But I do think it was thanks to him that we found ourselves together under the bar-counter, and I bless that moment, I don't curse it.'

'In that case,' said K. slowly, for Frieda's words were sweet to his ears, and he shut his eyes for a few seconds in order to savour them, 'in that case there is even less reason to fear an interview with Klamm.'

'Really,' said the landlady, looking down at K., 'you remind me sometimes of my husband, you are as stubborn and childish as he is. You've only been here a few days, and you think you know everything better than the people who were born here, better than an old woman like me, better than Frieda who has seen and heard so much in the Herrenhof. I don't deny that it's sometimes possible to achieve something against all the rules and customs; I've never experienced anything of the sort, but there are apparently instances of it, that may be so, but I'm sure it never happens in the way you are doing it, always saying no and sticking to your own ideas and not listening to well-meant advice. Do you think it's you I'm worried about? Did I ever bother with you as long as you were alone, even though it would have been for the best and would have avoided a lot of trouble? The only thing I said to my husband at the time was "Keep away from him". And I would have kept to that today as well if Frieda hadn't got mixed up with you. Whether you like it or not, you have her to thank for my concern, or even for taking any notice of you. And you can't just brush me off, because you are answerable to me, the only person who looks after little Frieda like a mother. Frieda may be right, perhaps everything that's happened is according to Klamm's will, but I'm not talking about Klamm now, I'll never speak to him, he's completely beyond my reach; but you sit here looking after Frieda, and – why should I not say it – being looked after by me. Yes, being looked after by me, because if I throw you out of the house, young man, just you try to find somewhere else in the village to stay – you won't even find a dog-kennel.'

'Thank you,' said K. 'You have spoken frankly, and I believe you completely. So my position is as insecure as that, and as a result, so is Frieda's.'

'No!' cried the landlady, interrupting him furiously, 'Frieda's position in this respect has nothing whatever to do with yours. Frieda belongs in my house, and no one has the right to call her position here insecure.'

'Very well, very well,' said K., 'I accept that too, especially since Frieda, for reasons unknown to me, appears to be too afraid of you to get involved. So let's just stick to my situation for the moment. My position is most insecure, you don't deny that, on the contrary, you take pains to prove it. But as with everything you say this too is largely, but not entirely, correct. For instance, I know of a very good place where I could spend the night.'

'Where? Where is that?' cried Frieda and the landlady simultaneously, so eagerly that they might have had the same reason for asking.

'At Barnabas' house,' said K.

'That rabble!' cried the landlady. 'That crafty rabble! At Barnabas' house! Do you hear' – and she turned to the assistants in the corner, but they had long since emerged from their corner and were standing arm in arm behind the landlady, who now seized one of them by the hand as if she needed support. 'Do you hear who this gentleman is associating with? Barnabas' family! Of course they'll let him stay the night, I only wish he had gone there rather than to the Herrenhof. Where were you two, then?'

'Madam,' said K. before the assistants could answer, 'they are my assistants, but you treat them as if they were your assistants, and my keepers. In all other matters I am at least prepared to discuss your views as courteously as possible; but not where my assistants are concerned, because things are perfectly clear in that respect. So I would ask you not to talk to my assistants, and if my request is not enough for you, I shall forbid them to answer you.'

'So I am not allowed to speak to you,' said the landlady, and they all three laughed, the landlady derisively, but much more mildly than K. had expected, and the assistants in their usual non-committal way, which meant much or nothing and evaded all responsibility.

'Please don't be angry,' said Frieda. 'You must understand why we are so upset. In a way, it's thanks to Barnabas that we belong to each other now. When I first saw you in the bar – you came in on Olga's arm – I already knew something about you, but on the whole you didn't mean anything to me at all. Well, not just you – I didn't care about anything, really. Even then I was unhappy about a lot of things, and I had a lot to be unhappy and angry about. For example, when one of the customers insulted me – they were always after me, you saw those creatures in there, but there were far worse than that, Klamm's servants weren't the worst – anyway, when one of them insulted me, so what? It felt as if it had happened years ago, or as if it hadn't happened to me at all, or as if I'd only been told about it or as if I'd already forgotten about it. But I can't describe, I can't even imagine it any more, everything has changed so much since Klamm left me . . .'

Frieda broke off, hung her head sadly, and folded her hands together on her lap.

'You see,' cried the landlady, as if the words were not hers, but Frieda's. She moved over to sit close to Frieda. 'You see, sir, the consequences of what you have done – and your assistants, too, though I'm not allowed to speak to them, can learn from what they see. You have deprived Frieda of the greatest happiness she has ever known, and you only managed to do that because the child felt so excessively sorry for you and could not bear to see you clinging to Olga, it seemed to her that you were in the clutches of the Barnabas family. She saved you, and sacrificed herself for it. And now that has happened, now that Frieda has given up everything she had for the happiness of sitting on your knee, you come along and cap it all by telling us that you had the choice of spending the night at Barnabas' house. I suppose that is meant to show that you're not dependent on me. Certainly, if you really had spent the night at Barnabas' house, you would be so independent of me that you would have to leave my house this instant, and very quickly too.'

'I am not aware of the faults of the Barnabas family,' said K., carefully lifting Frieda, who seemed insensible, and slowly letting her down onto the bed. 'Perhaps you are right about that, but I am quite sure I was right when I asked you to leave Frieda and me to arrange our own affairs. You said something earlier about love and caring, but I haven't noticed much of that since; there's been more in the way of hate and contempt and talk of throwing me out. If you were intending to drive us apart, it was done very cleverly, but I don't think you will succeed, and if you should – allow me to issue vague threats as well – you will be bitterly sorry. As for the accommodation you are kindly offering me – which can only refer to this miserable hovel – it is by no means certain that you are doing this of your own free will; it seems to me more likely that it is on the authorities' instructions. I shall now report to them that I have been given notice here, and if they then allocate me new lodgings, you may breathe a sigh of relief, but my relief will be even greater. And now I am going to discuss this and other matters with the mayor; please take care of Frieda, at least. You have done her enough harm with your so-called motherly advice.'

With this he turned to his assistants. 'Come along,' he said, taking Klamm's letter from its hook and making to go. The landlady had watched him in silence, and spoke only when his hand was on the door-handle: 'Sir, I will tell you something else before you go, because whatever you may say and however much you try to insult me, an old woman, you are still Frieda's future husband. I'm only telling you this because you are so dreadfully ignorant about the circumstances here; it makes my head spin when I listen to you expressing your opinions, and compare what you say with the actual situation. Your ignorance can't be cured all at once, and perhaps it can't be cured at all, but things can be made better if you only believe some of what I say, and if you always remember how little you know. Then you would judge me more fairly, for instance, and you would get some idea of what a shock I had – and I can still feel the effects of it – when I realised that my dearest child had, so to speak, left the protection of the eagle for the company of the slow-worm; but the actual situation is much worse, and I must keep trying to forget it, otherwise I could not say a single word to you with any composure. Ah, now you're getting angry again. No, don't go until you hear what I ask of you: wherever you may be, remember that you are the most ignorant person here, and be careful. Here with us, where you are protected by Frieda's presence, you can open your heart and say what you like, here you can tell us, for example, how you intend to speak to Klamm; but please, I beg of you, please don't actually do it.'

She stood up, trembling slightly in her agitation, went over to K., grasped his hand, and looked at him imploringly. 'Madam,' said K., 'I don't understand why you humble yourself to appeal to me about something like this. If it is, as you say, impossible for me to speak to Klamm, then I shall simply not be able to, however much you may beg me not to. But if it did turn out to be possible, why should I not do it, especially since your main objection would then be groundless, and any other fears you might have would also be open to question. Of course I am ignorant, that is the truth and it is most unfortunate for me; but it also has the advantage that ignorance makes us bolder, and so in the meantime I will gladly put up with my ignorance, and the unfortunate consequences it must have, as long as I still have the strength to do so. But these consequences really only affect me, so what I don't understand is why you are pleading with me. I am sure you will always look after Frieda, and if she should never see me again, to your mind that would just be a stroke of luck. So what are you afraid of? Surely you are not afraid – to the ignorant all things seem possible' – at this point K. was already opening the door – 'surely you are not afraid on Klamm's behalf?' The landlady watched in silence as he hurried down the stairs, followed by his assistants.

5
The Mayor

Almost to his surprise, K.'s interview with the mayor caused few problems. He sought to explain this by telling himself that in his experience so far, he had found making official contact with the Count's authorities very easy. This was because on the one hand, as far as his affairs were concerned, firm standing instructions had evidently been issued to give him favourable treatment, and on the other hand because of the admirable uniformity of the administration, which, he felt, was most perfectly integrated precisely where it appeared not to be. On the occasions when he thought about these matters, K. was almost inclined to feel satisfied with his position, though he always reminded himself quickly, whenever he succumbed to such complacent feelings, that it was just here that danger lay. Direct communication with officials was not too difficult, for however well organised they might be, they only ever had to defend remote and invisible interests on behalf of remote and invisible masters, while K. was fighting for something utterly vital and close to him, namely for himself; moreover he was, at least at the very beginning, doing so of his own free will, for he was the aggressor. And he was not the only one fighting on his behalf; there were clearly other forces unknown to him, but in which he could believe because of the measures taken by the authorities. But because the authorities had from the start met his wishes fully in more trivial matters – so far there had been nothing more than that – they had deprived him of the chance of enjoying these easy minor victories, thereby also denying him both the satisfaction such small victories would have given him and the resulting well-founded confidence for greater struggles to come. Instead they allowed K. to roam wherever he chose – though only, of course, within the village; in this way they pampered him and weakened him, removing any possibility of conflict and confining him to an unofficial, utterly diffuse, dismal, outlandish existence. Thus it could well happen, unless he was constantly on his guard, that one day – in spite of all the kindness of the authorities, in spite of the scrupulous fulfilment of all his absurdly undemanding official obligations – that one day, deceived by the favour apparently bestowed on him, he might behave so incautiously in his private life that he would come to grief here, and the authorities, kind and gentle as ever, seemingly against their will but under some public decree unknown to him, would be obliged to intervene and get rid of him. And what was this private life, in fact? Nowhere had K. seen private and professional life so closely intertwined as here, so closely that at times it seemed that professional duties and private life had changed places. For instance, what was the purely notional power Klamm had so far exercised over K.'s work, compared with the very real power he exercised in K.'s bedroom? So it followed that while he could allow himself a somewhat unconcerned approach, a degree of relaxation in his direct dealings with the authorities, in other respects he must proceed with the utmost caution, taking care to look round before every step he took.

K. found his perception of the local authorities fully confirmed when he met the mayor. He was a friendly, stout, clean-shaven man who was suffering from a severe attack of gout, and received K. from his bed. 'So you are our surveyor,' he said, struggling to sit up and greet K.; but he was unable to, and fell back onto the pillows, pointing to his legs by way of apology. A silent woman, an almost shadowy presence in the dim light from the small windows of the heavily-curtained room, brought K. a chair and placed it by the bed. 'Sit down, sir,' said the mayor, 'sit down and tell me your business.' K. read out Klamm's letter, adding some remarks of his own. Once again he felt how remarkably straightforward it was to deal with the authorities. They simply assumed all responsibility, one could leave everything to them, leaving oneself free and uninvolved. As if he, too, sensed this in his own way, the mayor shifted uneasily in his bed. Finally he said: 'As you will have noticed, I know all about the matter. If I myself have not taken any action so far, that is firstly on account of my illness, and also because you have been so long in coming to me; I thought you had lost interest in the matter. But since you have been so kind as to visit me, I must of course tell you the whole truth, unpleasant though it is. You have been appointed as surveyor, as you say; but unfortunately we do not need a surveyor. There is not the slightest work here for a surveyor. The borders of our small district are well marked, everything is properly recorded, property scarcely ever changes hands, and any minor disputes we settle for ourselves. Why should we need a surveyor?'

Although he had not actually thought about it before, K. was inwardly convinced that he had expected some such information. For that very reason he was able to reply immediately: 'That surprises me greatly. It throws out all my plans. I can only hope there is some misunderstanding.' 'I am afraid not,' said the mayor. 'It is as I say.' 'But how is that possible?' cried K. 'I didn't make this endless journey just to be sent back again now.' 'That is a different matter,' said the mayor, 'and one that I cannot decide; but I can certainly explain how this misunderstanding arose. In an authority as large as the Count's, it may happen that one department decides this, and another decides that; neither one knows of the other, and though the bureau of control is most scrupulous, by its very nature it intervenes too late, and so some small degree of confusion can arise. Of course, this only happens in very trivial matters such as yours, for example. I have never heard of any mistakes in serious matters, but these minor things are often annoying enough. As far as your case is concerned, I will tell you all about it quite frankly, and not hide behind official secrecy; I am not enough of an official to do that – I'm a peasant, nothing more.

'A long time ago, when I had only been mayor for a few months, an order was issued (from which department I can't remember), in the categorical way these gentlemen have, announcing that a surveyor was to be called in, and the local population was instructed to make available all the plans and drawings he needed for his work. Of course, this order cannot have referred to you because it was issued many years ago, and I wouldn't have remembered it myself if I weren't ill just now and have had ample time in bed to think about the most ridiculous things. Mizzi,' he said, abruptly interrupting his account, to the woman who was still bustling about the room engaged in some mysterious activity, 'please look in the cabinet there, you might find the order. You see,' he said to K. by way of explanation, 'it dates from my early days in office, when I still kept everything.' The woman opened the cabinet at once while K. and the mayor looked on. It was stuffed full of papers; as it was opened, two great bundles of documents rolled out, tied together like firewood. Startled, the woman leapt to one side. 'It's probably down there, underneath,' said the mayor, directing things from his bed. The woman obediently gathered up the bundles of documents in both arms and threw them out of the cabinet to get at the papers underneath. The documents already covered half the floor. 'There was a lot of work done,' said the mayor, nodding, 'and that's only a small part of it. I've kept a lot of it in the barn, and most of it has been lost in any case. Who can keep all that stuff? There's still a lot more in the barn, though.' 'Can't you find the order?' he said, turning to his wife again. 'You should look for a file with the word "Surveyor" underlined in blue.' 'It's too dark here,' said the woman, 'I'll get a candle.' She walked over the papers and out of the room. 'My wife is a great help to me,' said the mayor. 'I have to do all this official work in my spare time, and though the teacher helps me out with the written work, it's impossible to keep up with it, and there's always a lot that doesn't get done. It's all kept in that box over there.' He pointed to another cabinet. 'And now that I'm ill as well, it's too much,' he said, sinking back wearily, but with a note of pride. 'Could I not,' said K., when the woman had returned with a candle and was on her knees in front of the cabinet searching for the order, 'could I not help your wife to look for it?' The mayor smiled and shook his head. 'As I said, I'm not hiding behind official secrecy, but to let you look through the files yourself – well, that would be going too far.'

There was silence in the room now, only the rustling of papers could be heard; perhaps the mayor was even dozing lightly. A gentle knocking at the door made K. turn round; it was of course his assistants. But they did show some manners and did not barge straight into the room, but first whispered through the half-open door: 'It's too cold for us out there.' 'Who's that?' asked the startled mayor. 'It's only my assistants,' said K. 'I don't know where to tell them to wait for me; it's too cold outside, and they're a nuisance in here.' 'They won't bother me,' said the mayor amiably, 'let them come in. Besides, I know them – they're old friends.' 'But they bother me,' said K. candidly, glancing from the assistants to the mayor and back to the assistants; he found that all three had the same smile. 'Well, since you're here now,' he went on cautiously, 'you can stay and help this lady to look for a file marked "Surveyor", underlined in blue.' The mayor raised no objection; what K. could not do, his assistants were allowed to do, and they immediately threw themselves on the papers. But they did not search as much as rummage among the pile of documents, and when one of them tried to spell out the contents of a file, the other kept snatching it out of his hand. The woman, however, knelt in front of the empty box and no longer seemed to be looking for anything – at any rate, the candle stood some way away from her.

'So you find your assistants a nuisance, do you?' said the mayor with a self-satisfied smile, as if everything were being done according to his instructions but no one but himself had any idea that it was. 'But they are your own assistants.' 'No,' said K. coldly, 'they just turned up.' 'What, just turned up?' replied the mayor. 'You mean they were assigned to you?' 'All right, yes, they were assigned to me,' said K., 'but there was no reason for it, they might just as well have turned up out of the blue.' 'Nothing happens here without a reason,' said the mayor; he even forgot the pain in his foot and sat upright. 'Nothing?' said K. 'What about my appointment, then?' 'Your appointment was carefully considered, too,' said the mayor, 'but certain circumstances intervened to confuse the issue; I can prove it to you by referring to the papers.' 'But the papers can't be found,' said K. 'Can't be found?' cried the mayor. 'Mizzi, hurry up and find them! Still, I can tell you about it even without the papers. We replied to the order I mentioned with thanks, saying we didn't need a surveyor. But this reply apparently didn't reach the original department – let's call it Department A – but was mistakenly sent to another one, Department B. So Department A received no reply; but unfortunately, even Department B did not receive the whole of our reply. Whether the contents of the file stayed here, or whether they were lost on the way – they were certainly not lost in the department, I can guarantee that – at all events, only a folder arrived at Department B, on which nothing was noted except that the enclosed (but unfortunately missing) file dealt with the appointment of a surveyor. Meanwhile Department A was waiting for our reply; they had made some notes on the proposal, but as so often happens, understandably enough, even with the most meticulous procedures, the official in charge of the case was relying on us to reply so that he could then either appoint a surveyor or, if necessary, correspond with us further on the matter. As a result, he ignored the notes and the whole matter was shelved as far as he was concerned. But in Department B the folder came to the attention of an official well known for his conscientiousness, an Italian called Sordini. Even I, as an insider, cannot comprehend how a man of his abilities is kept at what is almost the lowest level. This man Sordini naturally sent the empty folder back to us for further details. But many months, if not years, had passed since the original order from Department A, which is understandable, for if, as usually happens, a file goes through the proper channels, it reaches the relevant department in a day at the most, and is dealt with the same day; but if it goes through the wrong channels – and given the efficiency of the system it takes a great deal for this to happen – then, indeed, it takes a very long time. So by the time we received Sordini's note, we could only remember the matter very vaguely. There were only two of us to do the work then, Mizzi and I; the teacher had not yet been assigned to me, and we only kept copies in the most important cases – in short, we could only reply in the most general terms that we knew nothing of such an appointment, and that we had no need of a surveyor here.

'But,' – at this point the mayor broke off as if he had been carried away by his own account and had gone on for too long, or as if it were at least possible that he had gone on too long, 'don't you find this story boring?'

'No,' said K., 'I find it entertaining.' To which the mayor replied: 'I'm not telling it to entertain you.'

'I only find it entertaining,' said K., 'because it gives me an insight into the absurd confusion that can sometimes determine a person's existence.'

'You have had no insight yet,' said the mayor gravely, 'and I can tell you more. Of course Sordini was not satisfied with our reply. I admire the man, even though he plagues me. You see, he mistrusts everyone; even if he has learnt from innumerable instances that someone is a person of the utmost reliability, he will mistrust him on the next occasion as if he did not know him at all, or more accurately as if he knew he was a scoundrel. I think that is quite right, an official must act like that; unfortunately I am unable to stick to that principle, it is against my nature. You can see how I explain everything so frankly to a stranger like yourself, I just can't help it. Sordini, on the other hand, treated our reply with suspicion from the start, and a lengthy correspondence developed. Sordini asked me why I had suddenly got the idea that no surveyor should be appointed; with the help of Mizzi's excellent memory I replied that the original suggestion had come from the Department itself (we had of course long since forgotten that it was from a different department). Sordini then asked why I only now mentioned this official notice, to which I replied that I had only just remembered it. Sordini thought this quite remarkable; I answered that it was not at all remarkable when the whole affair had been so protracted. Sordini insisted that it was remarkable, since the notice I had just remembered did not exist, to which I replied of course it didn't exist because the whole file had gone missing. Sordini said there ought to be an entry about the original notice, but there was none. At this point I hesitated, not daring either to claim or to believe that Sordini's department had made a mistake. You, sir, may be minded to blame Sordini because he should have taken my assertion more seriously, and should at least have been prompted to make enquiries in other departments. But that would have been the wrong thing to do; I do not wish you to think ill of this man in the slightest. The authorities work on the fundamental principle that no allowance whatever is made for error. This principle is justified by the excellent organisation of the whole system, and it is essential if matters are to be conducted with the utmost speed. So Sordini could not make any enquiries at all in other departments, and in any case those departments would never have answered him because they would have seen at once that it was a question of investigating a possible error.'

'Mr Mayor, may I interrupt you with a question?' said K. 'Did you not earlier mention a bureau of control? From your description of the system it is unthinkable that it should not have an overall governing body.'

'You judge very strictly,' said the mayor, 'but if you were a thousand times more strict, it would still be nothing compared with the strictness the authority exercises over itself. Only a complete stranger could ask such a question. Is there a bureau of control? There are only bureaus of control. Of course, they are not meant to detect errors in the crude sense of the word, for errors are not made, and even if one is made, as in your case for instance, who can say for certain that it is an error?'

'This is quite new to me,' cried K.

It's nothing new to me at all,' said the mayor. 'Rather like yourself, I am convinced there was an error, and it caused Sordini such despair that he fell seriously ill; the first control bureaus, which we must credit with discovering the source of the error, also recognise that an error has been made. But who can say that the next control bureaus will come to the same conclusion, and the next ones and the ones after that?'

'That may be,' said K. 'I would rather not get involved in such speculations for the moment, and in any case it's the first I have heard of these bureaus of control, and of course I don't understand them yet. I just believe we must distinguish two things here: firstly, what goes on inside the bureaus and what official conclusions may be reached one way or the other, and secondly my own position, standing as I do outside the official organisation which threatens to hamper me in such a senseless way that I cannot take their threats seriously. As to the former, what you, sir, tell me with such astonishing and uncommon insight, is no doubt true; but I would like you to tell me something about my own position too.'

'I am coming to that,' said the mayor, 'but you would not be able to understand what I tell you without some preliminary explanation. Even to mention the control bureaus just now was premature, so I will go back to my differences with Sordini. As I said, my resistance gradually weakened. But as soon as Sordini has the slightest advantage over someone, he has won, for then he concentrates his attention, sharpens his wits and redoubles his energies; to his opponent it is a frightening prospect, but a splendid one to the opponent's enemies. It is only because I have experienced him in the latter situation that I can speak about him as I do. Even so, I have never managed to see him face to face, he is too inundated with work. His room has been described to me; all the walls are covered with great bundles of files stacked one on top of the other, and these are only the files Sordini is working on at the moment, and since files are always being removed from the bundles and added to them, and all in a great hurry, these piles are always collapsing, and the constant sound of one pile after another crashing to the floor has become associated with Sordini's office. The fact is, Sordini is a worker who devotes the same care to the most trivial cases as he does to the most important ones.'

'Mr Mayor,' said K., 'you always refer to my case as one of the most trivial, and yet it has kept so many officials busy; and while it may have been quite trivial at first, through the diligence of officials like Herr Sordini it has become an important one. This is most unfortunate, and very much against my will; I do not aspire to have great stacks of files devoted to my case being piled up and come crashing down, but to work quietly as a humble surveyor at my small drawing-board.'

'No,' said the mayor, 'yours is not an important case, you have no reason to complain in that respect; it is one of the least important of all. The importance of the case does not depend on the amount of work it creates; if you think that, you are a long way from understanding the authorities. But even if it did depend on the amount of work, your case would still be one of the least important; normal cases, that is, those that do not involve any so-called errors, create much more work – though the work is then much more productive. Besides, you still know nothing of the actual work caused by your case, which I will now tell you about. At first Sordini left me out of it, but his officials came to see me; every day on-the-record hearings took place at the Herrenhof, attended by leading members of the community. Most of them supported me, only a few were suspicious; a land survey touches closely on peasants' interests, they smelt secret deals and injustices of some kind, and what's more they found a leader, and their submissions forced Sordini to conclude that if I had raised the matter at the village council not everyone would have been against the appointment of a surveyor. In this way, what was obvious – that a surveyor was not needed – was at least thrown into doubt. A man called Brunswick in particular stood out in all this; you wouldn't know him, he may not be a bad man, but he's stupid, a fantasist. He's Lasemann's brother-in-law.'

'The tanner?' asked K. He described the man with the bushy beard he had seen at Lasemann's house.

'Yes, that's him,' said the mayor.

'I know his wife, too,' K. hazarded.

'That is possible,' said the mayor, and fell silent.

'She is good-looking,' said K., 'but rather pale and sickly. I suppose she is from the Castle?' he added half-questioningly.

The mayor looked at the clock, poured some medicine into a spoon and swallowed it hastily.

'I suppose you only know the official departments at the Castle?' said K. curtly.

'Yes,' replied the mayor with an ironic but grateful smile, 'and they are the most important. As for Brunswick, if we could get rid of him nearly everyone would be happy, not least Lasemann. But at that time Brunswick had some influence; although he's not a speaker, he shouts a lot, and that's enough for some people. So it came about that I was forced to put the matter to the village council, which was Brunswick's only success, because of course the great majority of the council didn't want anything to do with a surveyor. That was years ago now; but all this time the matter hasn't been allowed to rest, partly because of Sordini's conscientiousness in trying to assess the motives of the majority and of the opposition by making the most careful enquiries, and partly because of the stupidity of Brunswick, who was forever inciting his various personal contacts among the authorities with new fantasies he had dreamed up. Certainly, Sordini didn't let Brunswick fool him – how could Brunswick fool Sordini? – but simply to ensure he wasn't fooling him, further enquiries were needed, and before they had finished Brunswick had thought up something else. He's a live wire, you see – that's part of his stupidity.

'And now I come to a particular feature of our official administration. Its precision is matched by its extreme sensitivity. When a matter has been under review for a very long time, it can happen, even before enquiries are completed, that suddenly, at a quite unexpected stage that cannot be identified afterwards, a decision is reached at lightning speed which settles the whole affair, more often than not quite properly, but still in an arbitrary way. It is as if the administrative apparatus could no longer bear the strain of years of aggravation caused by the same matter, in itself perhaps insignificant, and had taken the decision of its own accord without involving the officials. Of course, no miracle has occurred, and certainly some official will have written the decision, or else made an unwritten decision; but at all events no one – at least no one on our side here, and not even anyone from the authorities – can say which official has made the decision, and for what reasons. Only the bureaus of control establish this much later, but we aren't told, and in any case hardly anyone would be interested any longer. Now as I said, these decisions in particular are mostly perfectly sound; the only annoying thing about them is that we usually hear of them too late, and so cases that have long since been decided are still being discussed passionately in the meantime. I don't know whether such a decision was made in your case – some things suggest it was, some suggest otherwise – but if it had been, you would have been told of your appointment and would have made the long journey here, it would all have taken a great deal of time, and meanwhile Sordini would still have been working himself into a state of exhaustion on the same case, Brunswick would still have been plotting and I would have been plagued by both of them. I only mention this as a possibility, but this I know for sure: one of the control bureaus discovered in the meantime that many years ago Department A had sent the council an enquiry about a surveyor, but that so far no answer had been received. I was approached about it recently, and then of course the whole matter was settled – Department A was satisfied with my reply that a surveyor was not needed, and Sordini had to accept that he had had no responsibility for this case and had, through no fault of his own, done so much nerve-racking work to no purpose. If we had not had new work coming at us from all directions as always, and if your case had not been a very trivial one – one might almost say one of the most trivial – I dare say we would all have breathed a sigh of relief, even Sordini himself, I should think; only Brunswick grumbled, but that was just absurd. And now, sir, imagine my disappointment just now, after the whole business had been happily settled and after so much time had passed, when you suddenly appear and it looks as if it is going to start all over again. You will surely understand that I am determined to do everything I can to prevent this.'

'Certainly,' said K., 'but I understand even more that this is a dreadful abuse of my position, and perhaps even of the law. As for myself, I intend to fight it.'

'How will you do that?' asked the mayor.

'I cannot reveal how,' said K.

'I do not wish to be importunate,' said the mayor, 'but I would ask you to consider that in me you have – I would not say a friend, after all we are complete strangers – but a colleague, as it were. One thing, however, I cannot agree to is that you should be taken on as a surveyor. Otherwise you may turn to me with confidence at any time – that is, within the limits of my powers, which are not extensive.'

'You keep talking,' said K., 'about the prospect of my appointment as surveyor; but I have been appointed. Here is Klamm's letter.'

'Klamm's letter,' said the mayor, 'is valuable and deserves respect because of Klamm's signature, which appears to be genuine. As for the rest – but I don't dare to express myself independently on the matter. Mizzi!' he called, and then: 'What are you up to?'

The assistants and Mizzi, unnoticed all this time, had obviously not found the file they were looking for, so they had tried to cram everything back into the cabinet, but had been unable to because it was overflowing with untidy bundles of papers. So the assistants had evidently had the idea they were now putting into action. They had placed the cabinet on the floor, stuffed all the files into it, and now they and Mizzi were sitting on the doors of the cabinet and trying to close them inch by inch.

'So the file has not been found,' said the mayor. 'A pity, but you already know the story, and we don't actually need the file any more. In any case, it's sure to turn up sometime; it's probably still with the schoolteacher, he has a lot more files. But now come over here with the candle, Mizzi, and read this letter with me.'

Mizzi came over, looking even greyer and less personable as she sat on the edge of the bed and hugged the robust, vigorous man who held her in his arms. Only her small face stood out in the candlelight now, its sharp austere lines softened only by advancing old age. She had hardly glanced at the letter when she gently clasped her hands and said: 'From Klamm.' Then they read the letter together, occasionally whispering to each other, and finally, just as the assistants shouted 'Hooray!', having at last managed to shut the doors of the cabinet – at which Mizzi gave them a silent look of gratitude – the mayor said:

'Mizzi fully agrees with me, and so I may venture to give you my opinion. This is not an official communication at all; it is a private letter. That is quite obvious just from the way it is addressed: "Dear Sir". Besides, it contains not a word to say you have been appointed as surveyor, it speaks only in general terms about your being in the Count's service, and even that is not stated expressly; it says only that you are appointed "as you know" – that is, it is up to you to prove that you have been appointed. In the end, as far as the authorities are concerned, you are referred exclusively to me, the mayor, as your immediate superior, for any further information; and that of course has already been done for the most part. To someone who knows how to read official communications, and therefore knows even better how to read non-official letters, it is all too clear; but I'm not surprised that you, as a stranger, fail to see it. All in all the letter simply means that Klamm intends to take a personal interest in you if you should ever be employed in the service of the Count.'

'Mr Mayor,' said K, 'you interpret the letter as if it amounted to nothing but a signature on an empty sheet of paper. Can you not see that in doing so you are demeaning Klamm's name while claiming to respect it?'

'That is a misunderstanding,' said the mayor. 'I do not fail to recognise the importance of the letter, and my interpretation does not discredit it. On the contrary, a private letter from Klamm of course has more significance than an official communication; it's just that it doesn't have the significance you attach to it.'

'Do you know Schwarzer?' asked K.

'No,' said the mayor. 'Do you happen to know him, Mizzi? You don't either. No, we don't know him.'

'That is remarkable,' said K., 'he is the son of one of the deputy wardens.'

'My dear sir,' said the mayor, 'how should I know all the sons of every deputy warden?'

'Very well,' said K., 'then you must believe me when I tell you he is. On the day I arrived I had a disagreeable encounter with this Schwarzer. He then telephoned to enquire of a deputy warden named Fritz, and was told that I had been appointed as surveyor. How do you explain that, Mr Mayor?'

'Very simply,' replied the mayor. 'You have never really had any contact with our authorities. All these contacts are only apparent, but because of your ignorance of the circumstances you take them to be real. As for the telephone, look: I can tell you I have quite enough dealings with the authorities, and I have no telephone here. It may have its uses in bars and such places, rather like a machine that plays records, but it's no more use than that. Have you ever made a telephone call here? You have? Well, then perhaps you'll know what I mean. At the Castle the telephone obviously works excellently; I'm told they use it all the time up there, and of course it speeds their work up no end. In our telephones here, we hear their continuous phoning in the form of buzzing and humming sounds; you must have heard it too. Now, this buzzing and humming is the only genuine and reliable message that our telephones convey to us, everything else is misleading. There is no established telephone link with the Castle, no exchange to put our calls through; if you ring up someone in the Castle from here, all the phones ring in the lowest departments up there, or rather they would all ring if they hadn't nearly all, as I know for certain, taken their phones off the hook. But now and again an overworked official feels the need to take his mind off things, especially in the evening or at night, and puts the phone on; then we get an answer – but that's just by way of a joke. And that's quite understandable too; how can anyone think of ringing up about his own little troubles in the middle of all the frantic and highly important work going on up there? And I can't understand either how even a stranger can imagine that if he rings up Sordini, for instance, it's actually Sordini who answers him. It's more likely to be some junior clerk from a quite different department. On the other hand, it may happen just once in a while that when you ring the junior clerk, Sordini himself will answer. In that case, of course, you'd do better to run away from the phone before a word is spoken.'

'I must say that is not how I saw it,' said K. 'I couldn't know any of those details, but I didn't have much confidence in these telephone conversations, and I always realised that the only matters of real importance were what one gets to know or achieves at the Castle itself.'

'No,' said the mayor, seizing on a single word, 'these replies are of real importance, how could it be otherwise? How could information given by an official from the Castle be of no importance? As I said before with reference to Klamm's letter, none of these statements have any official significance; if you attach official significance to them you are misleading yourself. But whether they are benevolent or malevolent, privately they are of the utmost importance, far more than any official statement could be.'

'Very well,' said K., 'if that is the way things are, I must have many good friends at the Castle. It would be correct to say that when it occurred to that department all those years ago that a surveyor might be sent for, it was a benevolent act, which was followed by one after another; but then I was lured here for a malign purpose, and am now threatened with dismissal.'

'There is a degree of truth in your view,' said the mayor. 'You are right that statements from the Castle cannot be taken literally. But caution is always necessary, not just in this case, and the more important the statement in question, the more caution is needed. However, I cannot understand what you say about being lured here; if you had followed my explanation more closely, you should know that the question of your appointment here is far too difficult to be answered in the course of a brief conversation.'

'So the upshot is,' said K., 'that everything is quite unclear and insoluble, except for my dismissal.'

'Who would dare to dismiss you, sir?' said the mayor. 'It is the very lack of clarity in the preliminary arrangements that guarantees you will be treated with the utmost courtesy; but you appear to be over-sensitive. No one is keeping you here, but that is quite different from being dismissed.'

'Ah, Mr Mayor,' said K., 'now it's you who are seeing things far too clearly. I will tell you some of the things that are keeping me here: the sacrifices I made in leaving home, my long and difficult journey, the reasonable hopes I had of my appointment, my complete lack of resources, the impossibility of finding similar work at home, and last but not least my fiancée, who is from here.'

'Oh, Frieda!' said the mayor, registering no surprise. 'I know. But Frieda would follow you anywhere. As for the other matters, I agree that some things must be taken into account, and I will report on them to the Castle. If any decision is made, or if it should be necessary to interview you again beforehand, I will send for you. Is that agreeable to you?'

'No, not at all,' said K. 'I want no favours from the Castle, only my rights.'

'Mizzi,' said the mayor to his wife. She was still sitting close to him, absently playing with Klamm's letter, which she had folded into the shape of a small ship; K. took it from her in alarm. 'Mizzi, my leg is getting very painful again, we must renew the poultice.'

K. stood up. 'Then I will take my leave,' he said. 'Yes,' said Mizzi, who was already preparing an ointment, 'there's a terrible draught.' K. turned to go; the assistants, in their usual misplaced eagerness, had opened the double doors as soon as K. had spoken. In order to protect the sickroom from the rush of cold air, K. was only able to bow briefly to the mayor. Then, dragging his assistants with him, he hurried from the room and shut the door quickly behind him.

6

Second Conversation with the Landlady

Outside the inn the landlord was waiting for him. He would not have dared to speak unless spoken to, so K. asked him what he wanted. 'Have you found somewhere to stay yet?' asked the landlord, looking at the ground. 'Your wife told you to ask that,' said K. 'I suppose you're very dependent on her, aren't you?' 'No,' said the landlord, 'I'm not asking for her. But she's very upset and unhappy because of you, she can't do any work, she's lying in bed sighing and complaining all the time.' 'Shall I go and see her?' asked K. 'Please do,' said the landlord. 'I was going to fetch you from the mayor's place. I listened at the door, but you were talking; I didn't want to interrupt, and I was worried about my wife, so I hurried back here. But she wouldn't let me in, so all I could do was to wait here for you.' 'Come on, then, quickly,' said K., 'I'll soon calm her down.'

They went through the brightly-lit kitchen, where three or four maids, going about their tasks in different parts of the room, visibly froze at the sight of K. Even from the kitchen the landlady's sighs could be heard. She lay in a windowless cubby-hole separated from the kitchen by a flimsy wooden partition, which had room only for a large double bed and a wardrobe. The bed was arranged so that from it she had a view of the whole kitchen and could supervise the work there. From the kitchen, however, scarcely anything could be seen of it; it was very dark in there, only the white and red bedclothes gleamed faintly. Not until K. entered and his eyes had got used to the darkness was he able to make out any details.

'Here you are at last,' said the landlady in a feeble voice. She was lying stretched out on her back; she clearly had difficulty with her breathing and had thrown back the quilt. In bed she looked much younger than when fully dressed, but the nightcap of fine lace on her head, though it was small and perched on top of her hair, made her sunken face look pathetic. 'Why should I have come?' said K. gently. 'You didn't send for me.' 'You should not have kept me waiting so long,' said the landlady with the stubborn insistence of an invalid. 'Sit down,' she said, pointing to the edge of the bed, 'but the rest of you, go away.' Meanwhile not only the assistants but also the maids had pushed their way in. 'Should I go too, Gardena?' said the landlord. It was the first time K. had heard the woman's name. 'Of course,' she said slowly, adding absently, as if her mind were on other things, 'why ever should you stay here?' But when they had all withdrawn into the kitchen – this time even the assistants left at once, but only because they were after one of the maids – Gardena was still alert enough to realise that everything she said could be heard from the kitchen, for the cubby-hole had no door, so she ordered everyone out of the kitchen too. They went immediately.

'Sir,' Gardena began, 'just inside the wardrobe there is a shawl hanging up, please hand it over here, I want to put it round me. I have such difficulty breathing, the quilt is too heavy for me.' When K. had brought the shawl, she said: 'Look, isn't it a lovely shawl?' To K. it looked like an ordinary woollen shawl; he felt it between his fingers just to please her, but said nothing. 'Yes, it's a lovely shawl,' said Gardena, wrapping it round her. She was lying peacefully now, all suffering seemed to have been lifted from her, and she even realised that her hair was disordered from lying in bed; for a few moments she sat up and tidied it a little round her nightcap. She had a fine head of hair.

K., growing impatient, asked: 'You wanted to know, madam, whether I had found somewhere else to stay.' 'I wanted to know?' said the landlady. 'No, that's not true.' 'Your husband just asked me whether I had.' 'I can believe that,' said the landlady. 'I have fallen out with him. When I didn't want to have you here, he kept you here. Now that I'm happy for you to live here, he drives you away. He's always like that.' 'So you have changed your mind about me so much,' said K., 'in the course of an hour or two?' 'I have not changed my mind,' replied the landlady, her voice weaker again now. 'Give me your hand. There. Now promise to be perfectly honest with me, and I will be perfectly honest with you.' 'Very good,' said K., 'but who is going to begin?' 'I will,' said the landlady; she did not give the impression that she meant to confide in K., but rather that she was eager to speak first.

She took a photograph from under the pillow and handed it to him. 'Look at this picture,' she said urgently. In order to see it better, K. stepped into the kitchen, but even there it was not easy to make anything out in it, for it was faded with age and badly creased, torn and stained. 'It's not in very good condition,' he said. 'I'm afraid not,' said the landlady. 'That's what happens if you carry it around with you for years. But if you look at it closely, I'm quite sure you will make out everything. Besides, I can help you; tell me what you can see, I always love hearing about the picture. What do you see?' 'A young man,' said K. 'Right,' said the landlady. 'And what is he doing?' 'I think he's lying on a board, stretching and yawning.' The landlady laughed. 'That's quite wrong,' she said. 'But here's the board and here he is lying on it,' K. insisted. 'Look more carefully,' said the landlady impatiently. 'Is he really lying down?' Now K. said: 'No, he's not lying down; he's in the air, and I can see now – it's not a board at all, it's probably a cord, and the young man is doing the high jump.' 'There, you see,' said the landlady, delighted, 'he is jumping, that's how the official messengers do their exercises; I knew you would make it out. Can you see his face, too?' 'I can see only very little of his face,' said K. 'He is obviously making a great effort, his mouth is open, he is screwing up his eyes and his hair is flying.' 'Very good,' said the landlady appreciatively. 'No one could make out any more unless they had seen him in person. But he was a good-looking lad; I only saw him once briefly, and I'll never forget him.' 'Who was he, then?' asked K. 'He was,' replied the landlady, 'the messenger sent by Klamm the first time he summoned me to him.'

K. could not listen closely to what she was saying; he was distracted by the sound of glass rattling. He discovered the cause of the disturbance immediately: the assistants were standing outside in the courtyard in the snow, hopping from one foot to the other. They behaved as if they were pleased to see K. again, pointing him out to each other with delight and continually rapping on the kitchen window. At a threatening gesture from K. they stopped at once and tried to pull each other away, but one of them kept slipping from the other's grasp, and soon they were both back at the window. K. hurried back to the cubby-hole where they could not see him from outside, and he could avoid seeing them; but even here he was pursued for a long time by the gentle, almost pleading, tapping on the window-pane.

'It's my assistants again,' he said apologetically to the landlady, pointing outside. But she paid no attention to him; she had taken the picture from him, looked at it, smoothed it and pushed it back under the pillow. Her movements had become slower, not from weariness but under the burden of memory. She had wanted to tell K. about it, and in the telling had forgotten about him. She toyed with the fringe of her shawl. It was a while before she looked up, passed her hand over her eyes, and said: 'This shawl is from Klamm, too. And the nightcap. The picture, the shawl, and the nightcap – they are the three mementoes I have of him. I'm not young like Frieda, I'm not as ambitious as she is, and not as sensitive, she's very sensitive; in other words, I know how to adapt to life, but one thing I must admit – without these three things I wouldn't have stood it here so long, in fact I probably wouldn't have stood it for a day. They might seem trivial to you, but Frieda, you see, who was with Klamm for so long, Frieda has no mementoes at all, I've asked her, she's too high-spirited and hard to please, whereas I was only with Klamm three times – after that he didn't send for me again, I don't know why – and I took these mementoes because I had an idea I wouldn't be with him for long. Of course, you have to see to these things for yourself, Klamm doesn't offer you anything, but if you see something you fancy lying around you can ask him for it.'

K. felt uncomfortable listening to these stories, although they concerned him too. 'How long ago was all this?' he asked with a sigh.

'More than twenty years ago,' said the landlady, 'well over twenty years.'

'So people stay loyal to Klamm for as long as that,' said K. 'But do you realise, madam, that these confessions of yours make me very worried when I think of my future marriage?'

The landlady disapproved of K.'s attempt to introduce his own concerns at this point, and gave him an angry sidelong look.

'Don't be annoyed, madam,' said K., 'I'm not saying a word against Klamm, but circumstances have forced me into a certain relationship with him; even Klamm's greatest admirer cannot deny that. So whenever Klamm is mentioned I also have to think of myself, that can't be altered. Besides, madam,' – at this point K. grasped her reluctant hand – 'remember how badly our last conversation turned out. Let us part in peace this time.'

'You are right,' said the landlady, bowing her head, 'but you must spare my feelings. I am no more sensitive than other people, far from it; everyone has a sensitive spot, and this happens to be mine.'

'Unfortunately it is mine too,' said K. 'however, I shall certainly control myself. But tell me, madam – if Frieda feels as you do, how am I to put up with this terrible loyalty to Klamm when I am married to her?'

'This terrible loyalty?' repeated the landlady angrily. 'Is that loyalty? I am loyal to my husband; but Klamm – I was once Klamm's mistress, how can I ever lose that status? And you ask how you are going to put up with it in Frieda's case? Who are you, sir, that you dare to ask such a thing?'

'Madam!' warned K.

'I know,' said the landlady, calming herself, 'but my husband never asked such questions. I don't know which of us could be called unhappier, I as I was then or Frieda as she is now – Frieda who wilfully left Klamm, or I who was never sent for again. Perhaps it is Frieda after all, even if she doesn't seem to realise it fully yet. But at the time I was completely preoccupied with my unhappiness, more so than she is now, because I had to keep asking myself, and in fact even today I still haven't stopped asking myself why it happened. Three times Klamm sent for you, but not the fourth time and never again! Nothing else mattered then. I married my husband shortly afterwards; what else could I talk to him about? We had no time during the day, this inn was in a dreadful state when we took it over, and we had to get it into shape – but at night? For years during the night we talked about nothing but Klamm and the reasons why he changed his mind. And if my husband fell asleep during these conversations, I would wake him up and we would continue.'

'If I may,' said K., 'I will now ask you a very rude question.' The landlady said nothing.

'Then I may not,' said K. 'That suits me too.'

'Yes,' said the landlady, 'of course that suits you too, that suits you very well. You misinterpret everything, even silence. You just can't help it. You may ask your question.'

'If I misinterpret everything,' said K., 'perhaps I also misinterpret my question; perhaps it isn't so rude at all. I only wanted to know how you met your husband and how this inn came into your possession.'

The landlady frowned, but replied equably: 'That's a very simple story. My father was a blacksmith and Hans, who is now my husband, was a stable boy on a large farm and frequently visited my father. That was after my last meeting with Klamm; I was very unhappy, but I really shouldn't have been, because everything had been done quite properly, and it was Klamm's decision that I should not see him again, so it was quite properly done. But his reasons were not clear; I was free to think about them, but I ought not to have been unhappy, still, I was, I couldn't do any work and sat in our front garden all day. Hans saw me there and came to sit with me sometimes; I didn't complain to him about it, but he knew the situation, and being a nice lad he would weep with me. The landlord at that time was an old man who had lost his wife and had to give up his business. One day he was passing our garden and saw us sitting there. He stopped and offered us the lease on the inn there and then; because he trusted us he asked for no money in advance and gave us the lease on very cheap terms. I didn't want to be a burden on my father, nothing else mattered to me, so in view of the inn and the new job that might help me to forget things a little, I gave Hans my hand. That is the story.'

For a while neither spoke, then K. said: 'The landlord behaved generously, but rashly – or did he have particular reasons for his confidence in you both?'

'He knew Hans well,' said the landlady. 'He was his uncle.'

'That explains it,' said K. 'I suppose it meant a lot to Hans's family to be connected to you?'

'Perhaps,' said the landlady. 'I don't know; I never thought about it.'

'But it must have done,' said K., 'if the family were prepared to make such a sacrifice and hand over the inn without surety.'

'It was not rash of them, as it turned out,' said the landlady. 'I threw myself into the work, I was strong, being the blacksmith's daughter, I didn't need a maid or a servant, I was everywhere, in the bar, in the kitchen, in the stables, in the yard. I was such a good cook I even attracted customers from the Herrenhof. You haven't been in the bar at lunchtime, so you haven't seen our customers; there used to be even more then, a lot of them have stopped coming in the meantime. And the result was that we didn't just keep up with the rent, after a few years we bought up the whole place, and today we hardly owe anything on it. However, as a further result it ruined my health; I contracted heart disease, and now I'm an old woman. You may think I'm much older than Hans, but in fact he's only two or three years younger, and in any case he'll never show his age, because with the work he does – smoking his pipe, listening to the customers, then knocking out his pipe and fetching a beer occasionally – you don't get old with that sort of work.'

'What you have achieved here is remarkable,' said K., 'there's no doubting that. But we were talking about the time before you were married; and at that point it would surely have been extraordinary for Hans's family to make such a financial sacrifice, or at least to take such a risk in handing over the inn, and to insist on your marriage just in the hope that you would be a good worker, which they could not have known at the time, and that Hans would also work hard at it when they must have known that he would not.'

'Well, yes,' said the landlady wearily, 'I know what you're getting at, and I know how wide of the mark you are. Klamm had nothing to do with all this. Why should he have to look after me, or rather, how could he possibly have looked after me? He knew nothing about me any more. It showed that he had forgotten about me when he stopped sending for me. Anyone he doesn't send for, he forgets completely. I don't want to talk about it in front of Frieda. But it's not just that he forgets, it's more than that. If you forget someone, you can always get to know them again. With Klamm that's not possible. When he stops sending for someone, it doesn't just mean that he's forgotten them completely as far as the past is concerned, but absolutely for ever. If I really try, I can imagine what you are thinking; but while such ideas may make sense in the foreign parts you come from, they make none here. You might even be crazy enough to imagine that Klamm had given me someone like Hans simply so that I wouldn't have any trouble going to him if he were to send for me some time in the future. Well, you can't get crazier than that. Show me the husband who could stop me running to Klamm if Klamm gave me a sign! It's nonsense, complete nonsense, you're just fooling yourself if you indulge in such nonsense.'

'No,' said K., 'let's not fool ourselves. I had not thought things out nearly as far as you suppose, though to tell you the truth, I was thinking along those lines. Initially I was only surprised that Hans's relatives hoped for so much from the marriage, and that those hopes were in fact fulfilled, even if it was at the cost of your heart and your health. It did occur to me, it's true, that there was some connection between these things and Klamm, but I hadn't gone so far as to imagine it in such coarse terms as you put it – obviously because you want to get at me again, which you enjoy doing. Well, I hope you enjoy it! But what I was thinking was: first of all, it was clearly because of Klamm that you got married. But for Klamm you would not have been unhappy, you would not have been sitting doing nothing in your front garden, but for Klamm Hans wouldn't have seen you there; if you had not been sad, someone as shy as Hans wouldn't have dared speak to you; but for Klamm you would never have found yourself weeping with Hans; but for Klamm Hans's kind old uncle the innkeeper would never have seen the two of you sitting there quietly together; but for Klamm you would not have expected so little from life, so you would not have married Hans. Well, there's quite enough of Klamm in all that, I should have thought. But there's more to it than that. If you had not tried to forget, you would certainly not have worked without sparing yourself and made such a success of the inn. So Klamm is in that too. But quite apart from that, Klamm is also the cause of your illness, because even before your marriage your heart was worn out by your unhappy passion for him. The only question that remains is what Hans's relatives found so attractive about the marriage. You yourself once mentioned that being Klamm's mistress conferred an unassailable status; well, perhaps that appealed to them. But beside that, I believe, they hoped that the lucky star that had led you to Klamm – assuming it was a lucky star, but you insist it was – would follow you and stay with you, and would not abandon you as quickly and abruptly as Klamm did.'

'Do you mean all this seriously?' asked the landlady.

'Indeed I do,' said K. quickly, 'but I believe that Hans's relatives were neither entirely justified nor entirely mistaken in their hopes; and I also believe I can see the mistake you made. Outwardly, it all seems to be a success; Hans is well looked after, he has a fine wife, he is respected, the inn is free of debt. But in fact it's not all a success; he would certainly have been much happier with a simple girl whose first great love he had been. If, as you complain, he sometimes stands there in the bar looking lost, this is because he really does feel lost – without feeling unhappy about it, certainly, I know him well enough by now – but what is just as certain is that this good-looking, sensible lad would have been happier with another wife; and I don't just mean happier, I mean more independent, more hard-working, and more manly. And you yourself are certainly not happy; as you said, without your three mementoes you wouldn't want to go on living, and you have a weak heart. So were Hans's relatives mistaken in their hopes? I don't think so. You were blessed by your lucky star, but no one was able to make use of it.'

'What was it we failed to do, then?' asked the landlady. She was now lying at full stretch on her back, gazing at the ceiling.

'To ask Klamm,' said K.

'So now we're back to you again,' said the landlady.

'Or to you,' said K. 'Our affairs go hand in hand.'

'So what do you want from Klamm?' said the landlady. She had sat up and shaken out the pillows so that she could support herself on them, and looked K. straight in the eye. 'I have told you my story frankly; you could have learned a thing or two from it. Now tell me just as frankly what you want to ask Klamm. I had a lot of trouble persuading Frieda to go up to her room and stay there; I was afraid you would not speak frankly enough in front of her.'

'I have nothing to hide,' said K. 'But first there's something I want to point out to you. You say Klamm forgets immediately. Firstly, that strikes me as most improbable, and secondly it cannot be proved; it's clearly nothing but a myth, dreamt up in the minds of the young women who happen to be favoured by Klamm. I'm surprised that you believe such a feeble story.'

'It is not a myth,' said the landlady, 'far from it, it's based on common experience.'

'So it can also be refuted by other experience,' said K. 'And then there is another difference between your case and Frieda's. One could say that it simply wasn't the case that Klamm stopped sending for Frieda; on the contrary, he did send for her, but she didn't go to him. It is even possible that he is still waiting for her.'

The landlady said nothing, but only looked K. up and down closely. Then she said: 'I will listen calmly to everything you say. Speak frankly and don't spare my feelings. I only ask one thing: do not use Klamm's name. Say "him" or something like that, but don't mention his name.'

'By all means,' said K. 'But it is difficult to say what I want from him. First of all, I want to see him close up, then I want to hear his voice. Then I want to know his attitude towards our marriage. What I might then ask of him depends on the course of our conversation. All sorts of things might be discussed, but the most important thing for me is to come face to face with him. You see, so far I have not spoken directly to a proper official. That seems to be more difficult to achieve than I thought. But now it is my duty to talk to him as a private individual, and in my opinion this is much easier to arrange. I can only speak to him as an official in his office, which is perhaps inaccessible, in the Castle or, less probably, in the Herrenhof; but I can see him as a private individual anywhere, inside, outside in the street, or wherever I happen to meet him. I'm willing to accept that in that case I shall also be talking to him as an official, but that is not my main purpose.'

'All right,' said the landlady, pressing her face into the pillows as if she were embarrassed to say it, 'if I manage to pass on your request for an interview with Klamm through my contacts, promise me you will do nothing on your own initiative until the reply comes back.'

'I cannot promise that,' said K., 'much as I would like to grant your wish or satisfy your whim. The matter is becoming urgent, you see, especially after the unsuccessful outcome of my discussion with the mayor.'

'That is not a valid reason,' said the landlady. 'The mayor is a person of no consequence at all. Did you not notice that? He couldn't keep his position for a single day if it weren't for his wife, who runs everything.'

'Mizzi?' asked K. The landlady nodded. 'She was there,' said K.

'Did she say anything?' asked the landlady.

'No,' said K., 'but I didn't get the impression she could have, either.'

'There you are,' said the landlady, 'that's how wrongly you see everything here. In any case, whatever the mayor did on your behalf is of no significance, and I will have a word with his wife sometime. And if I also promise you that Klamm's reply will arrive within a week at the latest, you can surely have no further reason to refuse what I ask.'

'All that makes no difference,' said K. 'I stand by my decision, and I would act on it even if the reply were negative. But since this is my intention from the start, I cannot very well request an interview beforehand. Without such a request, any action I take might be foolhardy, even if it were done in good faith; but if my request were refused, it would be an act of open defiance, and that of course would be far worse.'

'Worse?' said the landlady. 'It's defiance in any case. You can do as you like. Hand me my dress.'

Ignoring K., she pulled on her dress and hurried into the kitchen. For some time there had been sounds of a disturbance from the direction of the bar. Someone had been knocking on the hatch. The assistants had opened it and shouted through that they were hungry. Then other faces had appeared. Even a few voices could be heard singing quietly.

K.'s discussion with the landlady had of course greatly delayed the cooking of the midday meal; it was not yet ready, but the customers had gathered, though no one had dared to defy the landlady's orders and set foot in the kitchen. But when those peering through the hatch reported that she was coming, the maids ran into the kitchen at once, and as K. entered the bar the surprisingly large crowd of customers moved away from the hatch where they had congregated and made for the tables to make sure of a seat. There were more than twenty of them, men and women, dressed in country fashion, but not in peasants' clothes. At one small table in a corner a couple were already sitting with a few children; the man, a kindly blue-eyed man with dishevelled grey hair and beard, was leaning towards the children and beating time with a knife to their singing, trying all the while to keep the volume down. Perhaps the singing was meant to make them forget their hunger. The landlady apologised to the guests with a few casual words, but no one complained. She looked round for her husband, who had presumably long since fled this awkward situation. Then she went slowly into the kitchen, ignoring K., who hurried back to his room to see Frieda.

7
The Schoolteacher

Upstairs K. met the schoolteacher. Frieda had been so busy, he was pleased to note, that the room was scarcely recognisable. It had been well aired, the stove was going well, the floor had been scrubbed, the bed tidied, the maids' unsightly rubbish, including their pictures, had disappeared, and the table, which had previously been such a prominent eyesore with its top encrusted with filth, had been covered by a white cloth. It was now fit to receive guests; K.'s small stock of linen, which Frieda had obviously washed early that morning and hung up by the stove to dry, made little difference to the effect. The schoolteacher and Frieda, who were sitting at the table, stood up as K. entered. Frieda greeted him with a kiss; the teacher gave a small bow. Distracted and still agitated by his conversation with the landlady, K. began to apologise that he had been unable to pay the teacher a visit before now, as if he assumed the teacher had grown impatient at K.'s failure to appear and had now called himself; but the teacher, in his deliberate way, seemed only now to recall that some sort of arrangement had been made between them. 'Of course, sir,' he said slowly, 'you are the stranger, the surveyor I spoke to in the church square a few days ago.' 'Yes,' said K. curtly; what he had then tolerated as a lonely stranger, he was not prepared to put up with in his own room. He turned to Frieda to tell her about an important visit he had to make very shortly, for which he had to dress as smartly as possible. Without questioning K. further, Frieda immediately called the assistants, who were busy examining the new tablecloth, and ordered them to take K.'s clothes and boots, which he began removing at once, down to the yard and clean them thoroughly. She herself took a shirt from the clothesline and hurried downstairs to the kitchen to iron it.

K. was left alone with the teacher, who was once more sitting silently at the table. He made him wait a little longer while he took off his shirt and started to wash in the basin. Only then, with his back to the teacher, did he ask him the reason for his visit. 'I have come here on behalf of the mayor,' said the teacher. K. was prepared to listen to what he had to say; but because K.'s splashings made his words difficult to understand, the teacher was forced to move closer and lean against the wall beside him. K. excused his hurried ablutions on the grounds of the urgency of his forth-coming appointment. The teacher ignored this and said: 'You were discourteous to the mayor, who is an elderly, distinguished, experienced and respected man.' 'I was not aware that I was discourteous,' replied K. while he dried himself, 'but it is true that I had other things to think about than good manners, because it was a matter that concerned my whole existence, which is being threatened by a disgraceful administrative system, the details of which I do not need to explain to you because you yourself are an active member of this system. Has the mayor made a complaint about me?' 'Who should the mayor have complained to?' asked the teacher. 'And even if there were someone, would he ever complain? I merely drew up a brief report of your discussion that he dictated to me, and it told me quite enough about the mayor's kindness and the nature of your answers.'

While K. was searching for his comb, which Frieda must have tidied away somewhere, he asked: 'What's that? A report? Drawn up retrospectively in my absence by someone who was not present at the discussion? That's a fine thing. And why a report? Was it an official meeting?' 'No,' said the teacher, 'a semi-official meeting, and the report is only semi-official; it was drawn up because with us everything must be done in strict order. At all events, it has been drawn up, and it is not to your credit.' K. had finally found his comb, which had slipped into the bed, and he continued more calmly: 'So it has been drawn up. Did you come here to tell me that?' 'No,' said the teacher, 'but I am not a machine, and I had to give you my opinion. My commission, however, is further evidence of the mayor's kindness; I must emphasise that such kindness is incomprehensible to me and that I am carrying out this commission solely by virtue of my position and out of respect for the mayor.'

K., now washed and combed, was sitting at the table waiting for his shirt and clothes. He was not much interested in what the teacher had to report, and he was also influenced by the landlady's poor opinion of the mayor. 'Surely it's past noon by now?' he asked, thinking of his appointment, then he corrected himself and said: 'You had a message for me from the mayor.' 'Well, yes,' said the teacher with a shrug of his shoulders as if disclaiming all responsibility, 'the mayor is afraid you might act rashly on your own initiative if you have to wait too long for a decision about your position. For my part, I don't know why he fears that, my view is that you can do what you like. We are not your guardian angels and we are not obliged to follow you around everywhere. However, the mayor thinks otherwise. Of course, he cannot expedite the decision itself, which is a matter for the Count's authorities; but within his own sphere of influence he is prepared to make a truly generous provisional decision, which is to offer you a temporary post as school caretaker.' At first K. scarcely paid attention to what he was being offered, but the fact that he was being offered something seemed to him not without significance. It indicated that the mayor believed that K. was capable of taking steps to defend himself, and that the community was justified in going to some expense to protect itself against him. It also showed how seriously they were taking the matter; the teacher had already been here for some time, and had drawn up the report before he left – the mayor must have sent him here post-haste.

Seeing that he had given K. cause for thought, the teacher continued: 'I put my objections to him. I pointed out that the school had not needed a caretaker before; the church caretaker's wife clears up from time to time and Fräulein Gisa, the schoolmistress, supervises things. I have enough trouble with the children, I don't want to be bothered with a caretaker as well. The mayor pointed out that the school was very dirty all the same. I replied that it was not so bad, which is the truth. And, I added, would it be any better if we took the man on as caretaker? It certainly wouldn't. Apart from the fact that he knows nothing about that kind of work, the school building only has two classrooms and no other space, so the caretaker and his family would have to live and sleep in one of the classrooms, perhaps even use it for cooking, which of course would not make it any cleaner. But the mayor replied that this post was a lifeline for you, and so you would make every effort to do your duties well; moreover, the mayor thought, we would also gain the services of your wife and your assistants, so not only the school but the school grounds could be kept in excellent order as well. I was easily able to refute all that; in the end the mayor could say nothing else in your favour, he simply laughed and said, well, you were a surveyor and so the flowerbeds in the school garden would be quite beautifully laid out. Well, you can't argue against jokes, so I came here with my message.' 'You need have no worries, sir,' said K., 'it wouldn't occur to me to accept the job.' 'Excellent,' said the teacher, 'excellent. You refuse absolutely.' He took his hat, bowed, and left.

Immediately afterwards Frieda came upstairs looking distraught, holding his shirt, which was still unironed; she would not answer his questions. To divert her, K. told her about the teacher and his offer; she had scarcely heard it when she threw the shirt on the bed and rushed out again. She soon returned, but with the teacher, who looked resentful and offered no greeting. Frieda begged him to be patient – she had obviously done this several times already on the way here – then she dragged K. through a side door he had never noticed before into the neighbouring loft and there, flustered and out of breath, finally told him what had happened to her. The landlady, furious that she had demeaned herself by confiding in K. and, what had annoyed her even more, by falling in with his plans for a meeting with Klamm, and having gained nothing from this but, as she put it, a cold and evasive response, was determined not to tolerate K. in her house any longer. If he had connections with the Castle, she had said, he should make use of them at once, because he was to leave the inn that day, that very minute. She would have him back only on the direct orders of the authorities; but she hoped it would not come to that, because she too had contacts with the Castle and would know how to use them. Besides, he had only got into the inn thanks to the landlord's carelessness, and he was not in any kind of need, because that very morning he had boasted that he had somewhere else to stay the night. Frieda, of course, should stay; if she were to leave with K., then she, the landlady, would be deeply upset. Just now downstairs she had collapsed in tears by the stove at the very thought of it, this poor woman with a weak heart; but what else could she do when, to her way of thinking at least, the honour of Klamm's memory was at stake? That, then, was the landlady's position. Frieda assured him that of course she would follow K. wherever he wanted to go, through snow and ice, that went without saying; but still, the situation was very bad for both of them – that was why she had been so glad to hear the mayor's offer. Even if it was not a suitable post for K., it had been made quite clear it was only a temporary one; they would gain time and would easily find other possibilities, even if the final decision went against them. 'If necessary,' cried Frieda finally, her arms around K.'s neck, 'we can leave this place, what is there in the village to keep us? But let's accept this offer meanwhile, darling, shall we? I've brought the schoolteacher back, you only have to say "I accept", and we can move into the school.'

'This is terrible,' said K., but he did not mean it too seriously; he was not particularly bothered where he lived, and he was getting very cold in his underclothes up here in the loft with no walls or windows on two sides and a chill draught blowing through it. 'You have arranged the room so nicely, and now we have to move out. I would be most unwilling to accept the post; I find it embarrassing enough at present to be humiliated in front of this little schoolteacher, and now he is to be my superior. If we could only stay here for a while, perhaps my situation will change this afternoon. If you were to stay here at least, we could give the teacher a vague answer and then wait and see. I can always find a bed for myself if I really have to, with Bar—' Frieda put her hand over his mouth. 'No, not there,' she said anxiously, 'please don't say that again. But otherwise I'll do everything you say. If you like, I'll stay here alone, however sad it would make me. If you want to, we'll refuse the offer, however wrong I think it would be. Look, if you find something else, perhaps even this afternoon, then of course we'll give up the job at the school at once, no one can stop us. As for feeling humiliated in front of the schoolteacher, I'll make sure you won't. I'll talk to him myself, you just stand there and say nothing, and afterwards it will be just the same, you'll never have to speak to him yourself if you don't want to, I'll be the only one who really takes orders from him, and I shan't even have to do that, because I know his weaknesses. So that way we have nothing to lose if we accept the job, whereas if we refuse it we have a lot to lose, especially if you don't get anything out of the Castle today; because you would never find a place for the night anywhere in the village, not even just for yourself, anywhere, that is, I should not feel ashamed of as your future wife. And if you don't find anywhere for the night, do you really expect me to sleep here in this warm room when I know you are wandering about in the cold and the dark?' K., who all this time had been attempting to warm himself by swinging his arms across his chest and beating himself on the back, said: 'Then we have no alternative but to accept. Come on!'

Back in the room he went straight to the stove, ignoring the teacher who was sitting at the table. The teacher took out his watch and said: 'It's getting late.' 'Never mind, sir, we are quite agreed,' said Frieda. 'We accept the post.' 'Good,' said the teacher, 'but the post was offered to the surveyor, and he must say so himself.' Frieda came to K.'s help. 'Of course he accepts the post,' she said, 'don't you, K.?' Thus K. could confine himself to a simple 'Yes', which was not even addressed to the teacher, but to Frieda. 'In that case,' said the teacher, 'it only remains for me to inform you of your duties, so that we are quite agreed on the matter. You, Herr K., are to clean and heat both schoolrooms daily, to undertake minor repairs around the school and to teaching or gymnastic equipment, to keep the path through the grounds free of snow, to deliver messages for myself and the schoolmistress, and to do all the garden work in the warmer season. In return you have the right to live in whichever of the schoolrooms you choose; but except when classes are being taught in both rooms at the same time, if you are occupying the room that is required for teaching you must of course move into the other room. You may not do any cooking in the school, but you and your family will be fed here at the inn at the council's expense. You must behave in a manner befitting the dignity of the school and ensure that the children, especially during lessons, are never allowed to witness any unseemly incidents in your domestic affairs; I only mention this by the by, for as an educated man you must know that. In that connection I would add that we must insist that your relations with Fräulein Frieda be regularised as soon as possible. A contract of employment will be drawn up dealing with all this and some other details, which you must sign the moment you move into the schoolhouse.'

All this seemed of no importance to K.; it was as if it did not apply to him or at any rate was not binding on him, but he was irritated by the schoolteacher's pomposity, and said casually: 'Yes, well, these are the usual conditions.' In order to gloss over this remark, Frieda asked about the wages. 'Whether any wages are paid,' said the teacher, 'will be considered only after a month's probation.' 'But that's hard on us,' said Frieda. 'We are supposed to get married on hardly any money and set up house on nothing. Sir, couldn't we apply to the council for a small advance against wages? Would you advise it?' 'No,' said the teacher, still directing his remarks to K. 'Such an application would only be met on my recommendation, and I would not support it. This post is only being offered to you as a favour, and if one is mindful of one's public obligations, favours must not be taken advantage of.' But now K. did intervene, almost in spite of himself. 'As for favours, sir,' he said, 'I believe you are mistaken. In this case the favour is perhaps more on my part.' 'No,' said the teacher with a smile – he had forced K. to speak after all – 'I am fully informed on this matter. We need a school caretaker about as urgently as we need a surveyor; caretaker or surveyor, both are a burden on us. It will cost me a great deal of further thought how I am to justify the expense to the council; the best and most honest course would be simply to submit the proposal without any attempt to justify it.' 'That is just what I mean,' said K. 'You have to take me on against your will; even though you have serious reservations, you must take me on. And when someone is forced to take a person on, and that person agrees to be taken on, he is the one doing the favour.' 'That is odd,' said the teacher. 'Why should we be forced to take you on? It is the mayor's kind heart, his too kind heart, that forces us. I can see, sir, that you will have to rid yourself of some illusions before you can become a useful caretaker. And of course such remarks are not helpful when it comes to considering a possible remuneration. I also note with regret that your behaviour will cause me a great deal of trouble; all this time you have been wrangling with me – I keep looking at you and can scarcely believe it – in your shirt and underpants.' 'Indeed!' cried K., laughing and clapping his hands, 'those dreadful assistants, what is keeping them?'

Frieda hurried to the door; the teacher, realising that he would get no more out of K., asked her when they would move into the school. 'Today,' said Frieda. 'Then I shall come along tomorrow morning to check up,' said the teacher, and waved his hand as he turned to go. He made to leave by the door, which Frieda had opened for herself, but bumped into the maids who had already arrived with their belongings to settle back into the room; they would not have made way for anyone, so he had to edge past them. Frieda followed him. 'You're in a hurry, aren't you?' said K., very pleased with them on this occasion. 'Must you move back in while we're still here?' They did not reply, only twisting their bundles in embarrassment, from which, K. noticed, the familiar dirty rags were hanging out. 'I suppose you haven't washed your things once,' he said, not with malice but with some affection. They noticed this and laughed soundlessly, simultaneously opening their hard mouths and showing their fine, strong, animal-like teeth. 'Come in then,' said K., 'and make yourselves at home, it's your room after all.' But when they still hesitated, no doubt because their room seemed too much changed to them, K. took one of them by the arm to lead her into the room. But they both gave him a look of such astonishment that he let go of her at once, whereupon after a swift glance of mutual complicity they kept their eyes fixed on K. 'Now you've looked at me long enough,' said K., suppressing a vaguely uneasy feeling. He took his clothes and boots, which Frieda, followed timidly by his assistants, had just brought in, and got dressed. As always, he once again found Frieda's patience with the assistants incomprehensible. They ought to have been cleaning his clothes in the yard, but after a lengthy search she had found them down-stairs calmly having lunch, holding the soiled clothes in a heap on their laps. Then she had had to clean everything herself, and yet, for all her ability to deal with common people, she did not scold them in the least; she just spoke of their gross negligence in front of them as if it were an amusing foible, and even patted one of them lightly, almost fondly, on the cheek. K. meant to take her to task about this presently; but now it was high time he was going. 'The assistants will stay here and help with the removal,' he said. But they were by no means agreeable to this; well-fed and content as they were, they would have welcomed a stroll. Only when Frieda said: 'Yes, of course, you stay here,' did they comply. 'Do you know where I'm going?' asked K. 'Yes,' said Frieda. 'And you don't want to hold me back any more?' asked K. 'You'll find so many obstacles in your way,' she said, 'what difference would it make what I had to say!' She kissed K. goodbye, and since he had not eaten any lunch gave him a small packet of bread and sausage that she had brought up for him, reminded him that he should not come back here afterwards but go directly to the school, and with one hand on his shoulder saw him out of the house.

8

Waiting for Klamm

At first K. was glad to have escaped the crush of maids and assistants in the warm room. It was now also freezing slightly, the snow was firmer and the going easier; but it was already getting dark and he quickened his pace.

The Castle, its outlines already becoming blurred, lay as quiet as ever. So far K. had never seen the slightest sign of life up there; perhaps it was quite impossible to make out anything at that distance, and yet his eyes still sought it out and could not accept its stillness. When he looked at the Castle, it was sometimes as if he were watching someone who was sitting there gazing out calmly, not so much sunk in thought and therefore cut off from everything, but aloof and unconcerned, as if alone and unobserved, yet someone who must be aware that he was being observed without letting it disturb his calm in the slightest; and indeed – it was impossible to tell whether this was cause or effect – the gaze of the observer could find no hold and slipped away. Today this impression was further intensified by the early onset of darkness; the longer he looked at it, the less he could distinguish, the deeper everything sank into the dusk.

Just as K. reached the still unlit Herrenhof, a window opened on the first floor and a stout clean-shaven young man in a fur coat leaned out and stayed at the window. He did not appear to acknowledge K.'s greeting with even the faintest nod. K. met no one in the hall or in the bar; the smell of stale beer in the bar was even worse than before – something he supposed would never happen at the Brückenhof. K. went straight to the door through which he had recently watched Klamm and cautiously pulled down the handle, but the door was locked; then he felt for the peephole, but the cover must have been so closely fitted that he could not locate it, so he struck a match. He was startled by a cry. In the corner by the stove, between the door and the sideboard, a young girl was crouching, staring at him as the match flared, her eyes so heavy with sleep that she could scarcely open them. She was obviously Frieda's successor. She soon recovered her composure and put on the light; her face still wore an angry look, but then she recognised K. 'Oh, the surveyor,' she said with a smile. She held out her hand and introduced herself: 'I'm Pepi.' She was small, rosy-cheeked and healthy-looking, her thick auburn hair was tied into a heavy plait, except where it grew in curls round her face; her ill-fitting dress of shiny grey material hung straight down and was gathered clumsily like a child's at the hem with a silk ribbon tied in a bow, restricting her movements. She enquired about Frieda, asking whether she would be coming back soon. The question verged on the malicious. Then she said: 'I was sent for urgently straight after Frieda left, because they can't just take on anyone here. I was a chambermaid until then, but it wasn't a good move. There's a lot of evening and night work here, it's very tiring, and I shall hardly be able to do it. I'm not surprised Frieda gave it up.' 'Frieda was very happy here,' said

K. in order to make Pepi aware once and for all of the difference between her and Frieda, which she was leaving out of account. 'Don't you believe her,' said Pepi, 'there aren't many people who can control themselves like Frieda. She won't give anything away if she doesn't want to, and you can never tell whether she has anything to give away. I've worked with her for quite a few years now, we always slept in the same bed, but we're not on close terms and I'm sure she doesn't think about me any more. Her only friend is maybe the old landlady at the Brückenhof, and that tells you quite a lot.' 'Frieda is my fiancée,' said K., all the time searching for the peephole in the door. 'I know,' said Pepi, 'that's why I'm telling you. Otherwise it wouldn't matter to you, would it?' 'I see,' said K., 'you mean I can be proud of the fact that I've won such an independent girl?' 'Yes,' she replied, and smiled happily as if she and K. had established a secret understanding about Frieda.

But it was not really what she said that drew K.'s attention and distracted him somewhat from his search, but rather her appearance and her presence in this place. It was true that she was much younger than Frieda, but she was still almost a child, and she was ridiculously dressed; she had obviously dressed according to her exaggerated ideas of the importance of a barmaid. And indeed, by her own lights she was quite right to have these ideas, since she had no doubt been given the job, to which she was quite unsuited, provisionally and without expecting it or meriting it; she had not even been entrusted with the leather pouch that Frieda had always carried on her belt. And her purported dissatisfaction with the job was nothing but conceit. And yet for all her childlike naivety she probably had contacts with the Castle; she had after all, unless she was lying, been a chambermaid, and was sleeping away her time here unaware of the knowledge she possessed. By embracing this small, plump, slightly hunchbacked body he might not be able to wrest this knowledge from her, but he might be able to tap into it and so draw courage for his difficult journey. Then perhaps it was no different with her than with Frieda? Oh yes, it was different; he only had to think of how Frieda looked at him to see that. K. would never have touched Pepi; and yet he was now looking at her so hungrily that he had to avert his eyes for a moment.

'We don't have to have the light on,' said Pepi, switching it off again. 'I only put it on because you gave me such a fright. What are you doing here? Has Frieda forgotten something?' 'Yes,' said K., pointing to the door. 'She left a tablecloth in the next room, a white embroidered tablecloth.' 'Oh yes, her tablecloth,' said Pepi, 'I remember. It's a nice piece of work, I helped her with it. But I don't think it will be in that room.' 'Frieda thought it would be. Whose room is it, then?' asked K. 'Nobody's,' said Pepi, 'it's the gentlemen's room, it's where they eat and drink, at least that's what it's meant for, but most of the gentlemen stay upstairs in their rooms.' 'If I knew,' said K., 'that there was no one in there just now, I would like to go in and look for the tablecloth. But you can't be sure; for instance, Klamm often sits in there.' 'Klamm is certainly not in there just now,' said Pepi. 'He's just leaving, the sleigh is waiting for him in the yard.'

At once, without a word of explanation, K. left the bar; when he reached the hall he did not turn towards the front door but towards the back of the inn, and in a few steps he reached the yard. How beautiful and peaceful it was here! It was a square courtyard enclosed on three sides by the house, and towards the street – a side-street K. did not know – by a high white wall with a large heavy gate that was now standing open. From this side the building seemed higher than at the front, at any rate the first floor was complete and looked bigger, for a wooden gallery ran round it, entirely closed in except for a narrow gap at eye level. To one side from where K. was standing, still in the central block but nearer the corner where the opposite wing adjoined it, was an open entrance into the building which had no door. In front of it stood an unlit closed sleigh with two horses harnessed to it. Except for the coachman, whose presence at that distance in the dusk K. assumed rather than identified, no one was to be seen.

With his hands in his pockets, looking around him cautiously, K. kept close to the wall as he walked round two sides of the yard until he reached the sleigh. The coachman, one of the peasants who had recently been in the bar, swathed in his fur coat, had watched K.'s approach as impassively as if he were following the path of a cat. Even when K. stood next to him and greeted him, and the horses became a little restive as this man emerged from the darkness, he remained quite unconcerned. This was most welcome to K. He leaned against the wall and unwrapped his food, thinking gratefully of Frieda who had provided for him so well, and peered into the interior of the building. A right-angled staircase led down from above to meet a low but apparently deep corridor running across it; everything was clean and whitewashed, with clear, sharp lines.

The wait lasted longer than K. had expected. He had long since finished his meal, he could feel the chill, dusk had turned to complete darkness, and still Klamm did not come. 'It could be a long time yet,' said a rough voice suddenly, so close to K. that he started. It was the coachman who was stretching himself, yawning loudly as if he had just woken up. 'What could be a long time?' asked K., not ungrateful for this interruption, for the constant silence and suspense had become tedious. 'Before you go away,' said the coachman. K. did not understand him, but asked no more questions; he thought this would be the best way to make this insolent man talk. A refusal to answer in this darkness was almost a challenge. And indeed after a while the coachman asked: 'Do you want some brandy?' 'Yes,' said K. spontaneously; the offer was too tempting, for he was chilled. 'Then open the sleigh,' said the coachman, 'there are some bottles in the side pocket, take one and have a drink, then hand it up to me. It's too awkward for me to get down in these furs.'

It annoyed K. to have to wait on the coachman like this, but since he had already become involved with the man he did as he was asked, even at the risk that he might be surprised by Klamm in the sleigh. He opened the wide door and could have just taken the bottle out of the pocket on the inside of the door; but now that the door was open, he felt so strongly drawn to the interior of the sleigh that he could not resist. He only wanted to sit inside for a moment; he scrambled in. The warmth in the sleigh was extraordinary, and remained so although the door, which K. did not dare to close, was wide open. He was so deep in blankets, cushions and furs he could not tell that he was sitting on a bench, he could turn and stretch any way he wished and always sank back into a soft warmth. Spreading out his arms, his head resting on the cushions that were readily available, K. looked out of the sleigh into the darkened building. Why was Klamm so long coming down? As if dazed by the warmth after standing so long in the snow, K. wished that Klamm would finally appear.

The thought that it would be better not to be seen by Klamm in his present situation occurred to him only vaguely, as a faint stirring of consciousness. This sense of amnesia was encouraged by the behaviour of the coachman, who must surely know that he was in the sleigh and was letting him stay there without even asking for the brandy. That was considerate of him, but K. still wished to oblige him. Awkwardly, without changing his position, he reached for the side pocket, not in the open door, which was too far to reach, but behind him in the closed door – it was just the same, there were bottles here too. He took one out, unscrewed the top and sniffed it. He smiled involuntarily; it smelt so sweet, so appealing, as when one hears kind words, words of praise from someone very dear and has no idea what they are for and has no wish to know, when one is simply happy in knowing who is speaking them. 'Can this be brandy?' K. asked himself doubtfully, and took a sip out of curiosity. Yes, it was brandy, strangely enough, it burned and warmed him. How it changed as he drank it, from something that was little more than a source of fragrance into a drink fit for a coachman! 'Is it possible?' K. wondered as if in self-reproach, and took another sip.

Then – he was just taking a good mouthful – everything was lit up, the electric lights blazed inside on the stairs, in the corridor, in the hall, outside above the entrance. Footsteps could be heard coming down the staircase, the bottle fell from K.'s hand and spilt brandy over one of the furs. He leapt out of the sleigh and just managed to shut the door, which slammed noisily, and shortly afterwards a man slowly emerged from the building The only relief seemed to be that it was not Klamm – or was that a matter for regret? It was the gentleman K. had already glimpsed at the first-floor window. A young man, very distinguished-looking, freshfaced, but with a stern look. K. scowled at him, but he was angry with himself. He ought to have sent his assistants instead; even they could have behaved as rashly as he had. The man facing him still did not speak, as if he had insufficient breath in his broad chest for what he had to say. 'This is dreadful,' he said, pushing his hat back from his forehead. How so? The man presumably knew nothing of K.'s occupation of the sleigh, and yet something seemed to dismay him. Was it perhaps because K. had found his way into the yard? 'How did you get here?' the man then asked more quietly, now breathing out as if accepting the inevitable. What questions! What answers! Should K. perhaps make himself perfectly clear to this man and tell him that he had set out with such hopes, and that his efforts had been in vain? Instead of answering, K. turned towards the sleigh, opened it and retrieved his hat, which he had left inside. He was disturbed to see that brandy was dripping onto the running-board.

Then he turned back to face the man. He no longer felt any misgivings about showing him that he had been in the sleigh, that was not the worst of it; if he were asked, but only then, he would reveal that the coachman himself had encouraged him to open the door of the sleigh, at least. The really unfortunate thing was that the man had taken him by surprise, that there had been no time to hide from him and let K. wait for Klamm undisturbed, or that he had not had sufficient presence of mind to stay in the sleigh, shut the door and wait for Klamm there among the furs, or at least to stay there as long as this man was in the vicinity. To be sure, he could not have known whether Klamm himself might be on his way, in which case it would of course have been much better to have met him outside the sleigh. Yes, there had been much to think about here, but now there was nothing more, for it was all over.

'Come with me,' said the man. It was not exactly a command, but the compulsion lay in the brief, deliberately casual gesture that accompanied his words. 'I am waiting here for someone,' said K., no longer in the hope of achieving anything, but simply to make a point. 'Come,' said the man again unperturbed, as if to indicate that he had never doubted that K. was waiting for someone. 'But then I shall miss the person I am waiting for,' said K. with a convulsive gesture. In spite of all that had happened he had the feeling that what he had achieved so far was something gained, and even if he only appeared to have achieved it, he should not surrender it in response to some chance command. 'You'll miss him either way, whether you go or stay,' said the man; although he expressed himself brusquely, he seemed remarkably attuned to K.'s train of thought. 'Then I would rather wait and miss him,' said K. defiantly; he was certainly not going to be driven away from here simply by a few words from this young man. At this the man put his head back with a disdainful expression and shut his eyes, as if he wished to return from K.'s foolishness to his own sound reason, ran the tip of his tongue round his half-open lips and said to the coachman: 'Unharness the horses!'

The coachman, obedient to his master but with an angry glance at K., now had to climb down in his fur coat and very reluctantly, as if expecting not that the gentleman would countermand his order but that K. would change his mind, began to back the horses with the sleigh towards the side wing, where the stables and the coach-house were evidently situated behind a large door. K. found himself left alone; to one side the sleigh was moving away, to the other the young man was walking back the way K. had come. Both, however, went very slowly, as if to indicate to K. that it was still in his power to recall them.

Perhaps it was in his power, but it would have been of no use to him; to call the sleigh back would mean he would have to leave. So he stayed where he was, the only one to stand his ground; but it was a victory that gave him no pleasure. He looked alternately after the young man and the coachman. The former had already reached the door through which K. had first entered the yard; he looked back one more time, and K. thought he saw him shaking his head over such obstinacy, then he turned with a final abrupt, decisive movement, stepped inside the hall, and quickly disappeared. The coachman stayed in the yard longer. He had a lot of work with the sleigh; he had to open the heavy stable door, back the sleigh into position, unharness the horses, and lead them to their stalls. All this he did with gravity, completely self-absorbed, having given up all hope of setting out again soon; he went about his tasks in silence, without so much as a glance at K., which seemed to represent a much harsher reproach than the behaviour of the young man. And when, after finishing his work in the stables, the coachman now crossed the yard with his slow, rolling gait, closed the great door, then walked back again, all very slowly without raising his eyes from his own tracks in the snow, then shut himself into the stables and switched off all the electric lights – for whom should they be left on? – and the only light left came from the wooden gallery above and caught the eye for a moment, it seemed to K. as if all contact with him had been broken off, as if he were now indeed freer than ever, as if he could wait here in this otherwise forbidden place as long as he wished; as if he had fought for this freedom as few others could have done, as if no one could touch him or drive him away, or even speak to him, and yet at the same time – and this conviction was at least as strong – as if there were nothing more senseless, more desolate than this freedom, this waiting, this invulnerability.

9

Resistance to Interrogation

He tore himself away and went back into the inn, this time not along the wall, but straight through the snow. In the hall he met the landlord, who greeted him in silence and pointed to the door of the bar. K. acquiesced because he was freezing and wanted company, but he was very disappointed to see, seated at a small table that must have been placed there specially, for usually they made do with barrels in the bar, the young man and standing in front of him – a dispiriting sight for K. – the landlady from the Brückenhof. Pepi, holding her head high with pride and with a fixed smile, serenely confident of her dignity, tossing her plait with her every movement, bustled to and fro. She brought beer, then pen and ink, for the gentleman had papers spread out in front of him; he was comparing information in one document with a second document at the other end of the table and was preparing to write. The landlady was looking down calmly at the gentleman and his papers, pursing her lips slightly as if she had just paused, having said all that was necessary and content that it had been properly recorded. 'At last, the surveyor,' said the gentleman, looking up briefly as K. entered, then immersed himself in his papers again. The landlady also gave K. a casual glance in which there was no hint of surprise; but Pepi only seemed to notice K. when he went to the bar and ordered a glass of brandy.

K. leaned on the counter, put his hand to his forehead, and disregarded everything. Then he took a sip of the brandy and pushed it away; it was undrinkable, he complained. 'All the gentlemen drink it,' said Pepi shortly. She poured the rest away, washed the glass and put it on the shelf. 'The gentlemen also have better brandy,' said K. 'Maybe,' said Pepi, 'but I don't,' and having dealt with K. she returned to wait on the gentleman again. He needed nothing, however, so she went on pacing to and fro behind him, making discreet efforts to catch a glimpse of the papers over his shoulder; but it was nothing but vapid curiosity and showing off on her part, at which the landlady frowned in disapproval.

Then suddenly the landlady started and stared, listening intently. K. turned round; he could not hear anything in particular, nor did the others seem to hear anything. But the landlady ran on tiptoe with long strides to the door at the back that led into the yard, peered through the keyhole, then turned to the others, her eyes wide and her face flushed; she beckoned them over, and now they took turns to look through. The landlady was the most eager, but Pepi had her turn too; the gentleman was the least interested. Pepi and he soon came back, but the landlady went on straining to look, bent double, almost kneeling, as if she were imploring the keyhole to let her through, though it was unlikely that there had been anything to see for some time. When she finally got up she ran her hands over her face, smoothed her hair, took a deep breath, and then apparently had to let her eyes adjust to the room and the people in it, which she did with some reluctance. K. said, not in order to confirm what he already knew, but to forestall an attack which in his present vulnerable state he almost feared: 'Klamm has already left, then?'

The landlady walked past him without a word, but the gentleman spoke from his table: 'Yes, of course. Since you abandoned your watch, Klamm was able to leave. But it's strange how sensitive the man is. Did you notice, madam, how he looked all round so uneasily?' The landlady appeared not to have noticed this, but the man continued: 'Well, fortunately there was nothing left for him to see, and the coachman had smoothed out the footprints in the snow.' 'The landlady noticed nothing,' said K., but he said this for no particular reason, only because he was annoyed by the man's remark, which had been intended to sound so conclusive and incontestable. 'Perhaps I wasn't watching just then,' the landlady began, as if to support the gentleman, but then she felt she should give Klamm his due and added: 'Even so, I don't believe Klamm is so very sensitive. Of course we worry about him and try to protect him, so we assume that he is extremely sensitive; that is only right, and it's certainly what Klamm wishes. But we don't know how things really are. Certainly, Klamm will never speak to anyone he doesn't want to speak to, however much trouble that person might go to and however intolerably intrusive he may be; but the fact that Klamm will never speak to him and never let him come face to face with him is surely quite enough – why should he in fact not be able to bear the sight of anyone, whoever it may be? In any case, it can't be proved, because it will never be put to the test.' The man nodded eagerly. 'That of course is essentially my opinion too,' he said. 'If I expressed myself rather differently, that was in order to make it clear to the surveyor. All the same, the truth is that when Klamm stepped outside he looked round him several times.' 'Perhaps he was looking for me,' said K. 'That is possible,' said the man, 'I hadn't thought of that.' They all laughed; Pepi, who hardly understood anything of all this, laughed loudest of all.

'Since we are all so happily gathered here,' the man then said, 'I would like to ask you, sir, to add some information to my files.' 'There's a lot written here,' said K., looking at the files from where he was standing. 'Yes, it's a bad habit,' said the man, laughing again. 'But perhaps you don't even know who I am yet. I am Momus, Klamm's village secretary.' At these words a solemn hush fell over the room; although of course the landlady and Pepi knew the man well, they still seemed awestruck by the mention of his name and status. And the man too, as if he had said too much even for himself to take in, and as if attempting to deflect any further solemnity that might be adduced from his own words, buried himself in his own files and began to write, so that the scratching of his pen was the only sound to be heard in the room. 'What is a village secretary, then?' asked K. after a while. Having introduced himself, Momus no longer thought it appropriate to have to explain such things, so the landlady answered for him: 'Herr Momus is Klamm's secretary like any of his other secretaries, but his office and, if I am not mistaken, his official duties too ...' Momus, still writing, shook his head vigorously, and the landlady corrected herself: 'Well, only his office is confined to the village, but not his official duties. Herr Momus deals with the written work relating to the village for Klamm and is the first to receive all applications addressed to Klamm from the village.'

When K., still unmoved by this information, stared blankly at the landlady, she added uncomfortably: 'That's the way it is; all the gentlemen from the Castle have their village secretaries.' Momus, who had been listening much more attentively than K., added to the landlady's account: 'Most village secretaries work only for one gentleman, but I work for two: Klamm and Vallabene.' 'Yes,' said the landlady, now remembering for her part and turning to K., 'Herr Momus works for two gentlemen, for Klamm and for Vallabene, he is a village secretary twice over.' 'Twice over, is he?' said K. to Momus who was now almost bent double, but looked up at K., who was nodding to him as if to a child whose praises had just been sung. If there was a certain contempt in this, it was either not noticed or else positively expected. To K. of all people, who was not worthy to be seen by Klamm even by chance, the merits of a man on close terms with Klamm were being described in detail with the undisguised intention of eliciting K.'s recognition and praise. But K. was in no mood for that; he, who was doing his utmost to catch Klamm's eye just once, did not value very highly the status of someone like Momus who was permitted to live in Klamm's presence. He was far from feeling admiration, let alone envy, for what he most wished to achieve was not Klamm's presence as such, but for him, K., and no other, to be able to approach Klamm with his wishes and no one else's, and to approach Klamm not just in order to reach him but to get further, past him and into the Castle.

He looked at his watch and said: 'But now I must get back home.' At once the situation shifted in Momus's favour. 'Yes, of course,' he said, 'the caretaker's duties call. But you must give me a moment. Just a few short questions.' 'I have no wish to,' said K., making for the door. Momus slammed a file on the table and stood up: 'In Klamm's name, I demand that you answer my questions.' 'In Klamm's name?' repeated K. 'Does he concern himself with my affairs, then?' 'Of that,' said Momus, 'I know nothing, and I imagine you know even less; so we can safely leave that to him. But I am ordering you by virtue of the position granted to me by Klamm to stay and answer my questions.' 'Sir,' the landlady interjected, 'I hesitate to advise you any further, for my advice to you so far, which was given with the best of intentions, has been rejected by you in the most outrageous manner. I only came here to the Secretary – I have nothing to hide – in order to give the office a proper report of your behaviour and intentions and to ensure that I never again have to offer you accommodation, that is how matters stand between us and I don't suppose they will ever be any different, and so if I express my opinion now I do it not so much to help you, but to make it a little easier for the Secretary to cope with the difficulty of dealing with a man like you. But even then, you might be able to turn my complete candour in what I say – I can only be frank with you, and even that is in spite of myself – to your advantage if you only wish to. If you do wish to, I would point out that the only way for you to reach Klamm is through the submissions of the Secretary here. But I don't wish to exaggerate; perhaps this path will not lead to Klamm, perhaps it will stop long before you reach him, that is for the Secretary to decide. At any rate, it is the only way that will at least lead you towards Klamm. And you intend to reject the only way there is, simply out of defiance?' 'Oh, madam,' said K., 'that is not the only way to Klamm, nor is it any better than the others. And you, Herr Momus, you decide whether what I might say here is allowed to reach Klamm or not?' 'Indeed,' said Momus, lowering his eyes with pride and looking right and left at nothing in particular. 'Why else should I be his secretary?' 'You see, madam,' said K., 'I don't need to find my way to Klamm, only to his secretary.' 'I wanted to help you to find that way,' said the landlady. 'Did I not offer to pass your request on to Klamm this morning? That would have been done through his secretary. But you declined, and now you still have no alternative but to do it this way. Of course, after your behaviour today, after your attempt to waylay Klamm, you have even less prospect of success. But that final, tiny, dwindling hope, which in fact is no hope at all, is all that is left.'

'How is it, madam,' said K., 'that at first you tried so hard to stop me trying to reach Klamm, while you now take my request so very seriously, and seem to think I am as good as lost because my plans failed? If before you could advise me sincerely against trying to gain access to Klamm, how is it that now, apparently just as sincerely, you are actually urging me on to seek Klamm, even if, as you admit, he is not to be reached in this way?' 'Am I urging you on, then?' said the landlady. 'Does it mean I am urging you on when I tell you your attempts are futile? It really would be extremely rash if you tried to shift the responsibility for your own actions onto me. Is it perhaps the presence of Herr Momus that makes you want to do that? No, sir, I am not urging you on to do anything. One thing I will admit – that when I first saw you, I might have overestimated you slightly. I was alarmed when you won Frieda's heart so quickly, I did not know what else you might be capable of, I wanted to prevent any further misfortune and thought the only way to do this was to put you off with pleas and threats. In the meantime I have learnt to look at the whole business more calmly. Perhaps your antics will leave deep footprints in the snow outside, but nothing more.' 'It seems to me that the contradiction has not quite been cleared up,' said K., 'but I will content myself with having pointed it out. But now, Herr Momus, would you please tell me whether the landlady's opinion is correct, that is, that the statement you wish to take down from me might result in my being allowed to appear before Klamm. If that is the case, I am prepared to answer all your questions here and now. To that end I am prepared to do anything.' 'No,' said Momus, 'that does not follow at all. I am concerned only with obtaining an exact account of this afternoon for Klamm's village records. The account is already complete, you have only to fill in two or three gaps for the sake of form, this has no other purpose, and no other purpose can be achieved.' K. looked at the landlady in silence. 'Why are you looking at me?' she asked. 'Did I tell you anything different? That's how he always is, Herr Momus, that's how he always is. He distorts the information he's been given, then he claims he was given false information. I told him time and again that he hasn't the slightest chance of being seen by Klamm, so if he has no chance, he won't get one through this statement either.

What could be clearer? What's more, I say that this statement is the only real official contact he can have with Klamm, that is clear enough and beyond all doubt. But if he doesn't believe me and goes on hoping – I don't know why or to what purpose – then the only thing that can help him, if we follow his way of thinking, is the one real official link he has with Klamm, which is this statement. That is all I have said, and whoever claims otherwise is maliciously twisting my words.'

'If that is so, madam,' said K., 'then I beg your pardon, for I have misunderstood you. You see, from what you said earlier I understood, mistakenly as it turns out, that there was still some tiny glimmer of hope for me.' 'Certainly,' said the landlady, 'that is indeed my opinion. You are twisting my words again, but now you are twisting them the other way. I believe there is some such hope for you, but it rests entirely on this statement. However, it's not a case of your simply being able to spring the question on Herr Momus: "Shall I be allowed to see Klamm if I answer these questions?" If a child asks a question like that, we laugh, if an adult does it, it is an insult to authority, which Herr Momus was gracious enough to conceal in the tactfulness of his reply. But the hope I am referring to is that the report gives you, or might give you, a sort of contact with Klamm. Isn't that hope enough? If you were asked what you had done to deserve such hope, could you suggest the slightest thing? Of course, nothing more precise can be said about this hope, and Herr Momus in particular in his official capacity will never be able to give even the slightest hint of it. For him, as he said, it is merely a matter of drawing up an account of this afternoon, for form's sake, he will not say any more than that, even if you ask him about it here and now in the light of what I have said.' 'So will Klamm read this report, Herr Momus?' asked K. 'No,' said Momus. 'Why should he? Klamm cannot read all the reports, in fact he doesn't read any at all. He always says: "Keep away from me with your reports!"'

'Herr K.,' the landlady complained, 'you are exhausting me with these questions. Is it necessary then, or even desirable, that Klamm should read this report and learn how worthless your life is with every word he reads? Should you not rather humbly ask that it should be hidden from Klamm – though that request would be quite as senseless as your previous one, for who can hide anything from Klamm? But it would show your character in a more attractive light. And is it necessary, then, for what you call your hope? Have you not yourself declared that you would be content just to have an opportunity to speak to Klamm, even if he didn't look at you or listen to you? And won't you achieve at least as much with this report, perhaps even much more?' 'Much more?' asked K. 'How?' 'If only,' cried the landlady, 'you didn't always want everything handed to you on a plate like a child. Who can answer such questions? The report will go to Klamm's village registry, as you have been told, nothing more can be said with certainty. But you still don't realise the full significance of the report, of Herr Momus, or the village registry. Do you know what it means to be interrogated by the Secretary? Perhaps, or rather probably, he doesn't even know himself. He sits here quietly and does his duty, for form's sake, as he said. But remember this: Klamm appointed him, he works on behalf of Klamm, and what he does has Klamm's approval in advance, even if it never reaches him. And how can anything have Klamm's approval unless it is done entirely in the spirit of Klamm? What I am saying is not a clumsy attempt to flatter the Secretary – far be it from me to do that, and he himself would be most put out by it; I'm not talking about Herr Momus personally, but about what he is when he has Klamm's approval as he does at the moment. Then he is Klamm's right hand, and woe betide anyone who does not obey him.'

K. had no fear of the landlady's threats, and he had grown tired of the hopes with which she was trying to entice him. Klamm was far away; the landlady had once compared Klamm to an eagle, which K. had found ridiculous, but now he no longer did. He thought of his remoteness, of his impregnable eyrie, of his silence, broken perhaps only by such cries as K. had never heard before, of his piercing downward gaze that could never be ascertained and never contradicted, of the fleetingly glimpsed circles he described above, governed by mysterious laws and unassailable from K.'s position far below – all this Klamm had in common with the eagle. But surely there was no connection between that and this report, over which Momus was just then snapping a salted pretzel he was enjoying with his beer, scattering salt and caraway seed all over his papers.

'Good night,' said K. 'I detest any kind of interrogation.' And now he actually did move towards the door. 'So he is going,' said Momus almost anxiously to the landlady. 'He won't dare,' she replied. K. heard no more; he was already in the hall. It was cold and a strong wind was blowing. The landlord emerged from a door across the way; he had evidently been keeping an eye on the hall from behind a hatch. Even here in the hallway the wind tore at his coat-tails so fiercely that he had to wrap them round him. 'Are you going already, Herr K.?' he said. 'Are you surprised?' asked K. 'Yes,' said the landlord. 'Were you not interrogated, then?' 'No,' said K., 'I refused to be interrogated.' 'Why?' asked the landlord. 'I don't see,' said K., 'why I should be interrogated, why I should fall in with some joke or pander to an official's whim. Perhaps another time I might have done it as a joke or because I felt like it, but not today.' 'Well, yes, of course,' said the landlord; but his agreement was prompted by politeness rather than conviction. 'Now I must let the servants into the bar,' he continued, 'it's well past time. I just didn't want to disturb the interrogation.' 'Do you think it's so important?' asked K. 'Oh yes,' said the landlord. 'So I shouldn't have refused?' asked K. 'No,' said the landlord, 'you shouldn't have done that.' When K. did not reply, he added, either to reassure K. or to get away more quickly: 'Ah well, I don't suppose it will bring fire and brimstone down on us.' 'No,' said K., 'the weather doesn't look that bad.' And they parted with a laugh.

10

On the Street

K. emerged onto the front steps buffeted by the wind and peered out into the darkness. Dreadful weather, dreadful. Somehow in connection with the weather it occurred to him how the landlady had done her best to make him comply with Momus's report, and how he had stood firm. Her efforts had not been straightforward, of course; secretly she had at the same time been deterring him from the report, and in the end it was impossible to say whether he had stood firm or given in. She was scheming by nature, apparently working aimlessly like the wind, following some remote and alien bidding that could never be discerned.

He had scarcely set out along the road when he saw two lights swinging to and fro in the distance; he was glad to see this sign of life and quickened his pace to meet them. The lights were also moving towards him. He did not know why he was so keenly disappointed when he recognised his assistants; after all, they were coming to meet him, probably sent by Frieda, and the lanterns that dispelled the tumultuous darkness surrounding him were probably his own. But still he was disappointed; he had expected strangers, not these old acquaintances who were a burden to him. However, it was not only the assistants; between them Barnabas emerged from the darkness. 'Barnabas,' cried K., holding out his hand to him, 'have you come to see me?' Initially, K.'s surprise at seeing him again made him forget all the trouble Barnabas had caused him before. 'Yes, to see you,' said Barnabas, friendly as ever, 'with a letter from Klamm.' 'A letter from Klamm!' said K. He looked up and snatched it out of Barnabas' hand. 'Bring the light over here!' he told his assistants, who pressed close to him on either side and raised their lanterns. In order to read it, he had to fold the large sheet of paper very small to protect it from the wind. Then he read: 'To the surveyor at the Brückenhof. The surveys you have made so far meet with my approval. The work done by the assistants is also commendable; you know how to keep them to their tasks. Continue your efforts! Bring your work to a successful conclusion! Any interruption would incur my displeasure. Meanwhile rest assured that the question of your remuneration will be settled shortly. I shall keep you in mind.'

K. did not look up from the letter until the two assistants, who read much more slowly than he did, gave three cheers and swung their lanterns to celebrate the good news. 'Calm down,' K. told them, then said to Barnabas: 'It is a misunderstanding.' Barnabas did not follow him. 'It is a misunderstanding,' K. repeated, and the weariness he had felt that afternoon returned. He still seemed a long way from the schoolhouse, behind Barnabas loomed his whole family, and the assistants still crowded him so much that he elbowed them aside. How could Frieda have sent them to meet him when he had given orders for them to stay with her! He would have found his way back alone far better than in their company. On top of this, one of them had wrapped a scarf round his neck, the loose ends of which flapped about in the wind and several times had hit K. in the face; and though the second assistant had always removed the scarf from K.'s face at once with his long, tapering fingers, this did nothing to improve matters. Both of them even seemed to enjoy the repeated ritual, just as they were delighted by the wind and the wildness of the night. 'Come along!' shouted K., 'if you came out to meet me, why didn't you bring my walking stick? I've nothing to chase you back home with.' They cowered behind Barnabas, but they were not too terrified to set their lanterns on their protector's shoulders, though he immediately shook them off. 'Barnabas,' said K., and it worried him that Barnabas clearly did not understand him, that when things were calm his coat shone beautifully, but when the situation was serious no help was forthcoming, only silent resistance, resistance that could not be broken down, for he himself was defenceless, only his smile shone, but that helped no more than the stars above against the storm raging here below.

'See what the fellow has written to me,' said K., holding the letter in front of Barnabas' face. 'He is badly informed. I'm not doing any surveying, and how much use my assistants are you can see for yourself. And of course I can't interrupt the work I'm not doing, either; I can't even incur his displeasure – how am I to earn his approval? And I can never rest assured.' 'I will deliver your message,' said Barnabas, who all this time had been ignoring the letter, which he could not have read anyway because he was holding it so close in front of his face. 'Oh yes,' said K., 'you promise me that you will deliver the message, but can I really believe you? I badly need a trustworthy messenger, now more than ever!' K. gnawed his lip with impatience. 'Sir,' said Barnabas with a gentle bow, which almost tempted K. to believe him again, 'I shall certainly deliver your message, and I shall certainly deliver the one you gave me last time.' 'What?' cried K., 'haven't you delivered that one yet? Weren't you at the Castle the next day?' 'No,' said Barnabas, 'my dear father is old, you have seen him yourself, and there was a lot of work to do just then, I had to help him, but now I shall soon be going to the Castle again.' 'But what are you thinking of? I don't understand you,' cried K., clutching his brow, 'don't Klamm's affairs come before everything else? You have an important job as messenger, and you carry out your duties so disgracefully? Who cares about your father's work? Klamm is waiting for news, and instead of falling over yourself to deliver it, you prefer to muck out the stable?'

'My father is a cobbler,' said Barnabas unmoved. 'He had work to do for Brunswick, and I am my father's assistant after all.' 'Cobbler – work – Brunswick,' snarled K., as if he were making each word unfit for use ever again. 'Who needs boots here then, in these eternally deserted streets? And what concern of mine is all this cobbling business? I gave you a message to take straight to Klamm, not for you to forget it and get it mixed up at your cobbler's bench.' At this point, K. calmed himself a little when it occurred to him that Klamm had probably been at the Herrenhof the whole time, not at the Castle, but Barnabas irritated him again as he began to recite K.'s first message to show that he had remembered it. 'That's enough, I don't want to hear it,' he said. 'Don't be angry with me, sir,' said Barnabas. He looked away from K., averting his eyes as if in unconscious rebuke; but it was doubtless dismay at K.'s shouting. 'I'm not angry with you,' said K., his agitation now turned against himself, 'not with you; but it makes things very difficult for me when I only have a messenger like you for important matters.' 'But you see,' said Barnabas – and it was as if he was saying more than he ought to in order to defend his honour as a messenger – 'Klamm is not waiting for your message, in fact he even gets annoyed when I arrive. "More messages again," he said once, and he usually gets up when he sees me coming, goes into the next room and won't see me. And it's not laid down that I have to deliver every message at once; if it were, of course I would go at once, but it's not laid down, and if I never brought one, I wouldn't be reprimanded about it. If I deliver a message, it's done voluntarily.'

'Right,' said K., looking at Barnabas and studiously ignoring his assistants, who were taking it in turns to emerge slowly as if from a trapdoor behind Barnabas' shoulders and then quickly disappear again as if alarmed at the sight of K., making a soft whistling sound to imitate the wind; this kept them amused for quite some time. 'I don't know how things are with Klamm,' he continued, 'I doubt whether you fully understand everything that goes on there, and even if you did we could do nothing to improve things. But you can deliver a message, and that's what I'm asking you to do. Just a short message. Can you deliver it first thing tomorrow and bring me the answer at once, or at least tell me how you were received? Can you do that, and will you do it? It would be of great value to me. And perhaps I shall have an opportunity to thank you accordingly, or perhaps you already know of something I can do for you?' 'Certainly I will deliver it,' said Barnabas. 'And will you make every effort to do it as well as you can, will you hand it to Klamm himself and do it all at once, tomorrow morning – will you do that?' 'I will do my best,' said Barnabas, 'but I always do that.' 'We won't argue about that any more for now,' said K. 'This is the message: the Surveyor K. requests the Director's permission to speak to him personally. He accepts in advance all conditions that may attach to such permission. He is obliged to make this request because hitherto all intermediaries have failed completely, in proof of which he cites the fact that so far he has not carried out any surveying work whatever, and that according to the information conveyed by the mayor will never do so; consequently he read the Director's most recent letter with despair and dismay, and only a personal interview with the Director can help in this matter. The Surveyor is aware how much he is asking, but he will make every effort to cause the Director the least possible inconvenience, he accepts any limitation of time as well as any limitation on the number of words it is thought necessary for him to use during the interview; he believes he will require no more than ten words. With deepest respect and with the greatest impatience he awaits the Director's decision.'

K. had forgotten himself while saying all this, as if he were standing at Klamm's door and were speaking to the doorkeeper. 'It has turned out much longer than I thought,' he said then, 'but you must still deliver it by word of mouth. I don't want to write a letter, it would only have to go through the endless process of filing.' So K. scribbled the message on a piece of paper for Barnabas, using the back of one of his assistants for support while the other held up a lantern, but he found he could write it out as Barnabas dictated it; he had remembered it all and repeated it word for word like a schoolboy, without paying any attention to the assistants' distracting interruptions. 'You have an extraordinary memory,' said K., giving Barnabas the paper. 'Now show me you are extraordinary in other ways too. But don't you have any wishes for yourself? I must admit it would rather reassure me about the fate of my message if you did.' At first Barnabas said nothing, but then he replied: 'My sisters send you their best wishes.' 'Ah, your sisters. Yes, those tall, strapping girls.' 'They both send their best wishes, but Amalia especially,' said Barnabas. 'She also brought this letter for you today from the Castle.' K. seized on this information above all else, and asked: 'Couldn't she take my message to the Castle too? Or could you both go and each try your luck?' 'Amalia is not allowed into the offices,' said Barnabas, 'otherwise I'm sure she would be glad to do it.' 'Perhaps I shall come and see you tomorrow,' said K., 'but first bring me the answer. I'll expect you at the school. Give your sisters best wishes from me too.' K.'s promise seemed to make Barnabas very happy; after a farewell handshake he also touched K. lightly on the shoulder. As if everything were once again as it had been when Barnabas had first appeared in his splendour among the peasants at the inn, K. felt this gesture, albeit with a smile, to be an honour. In a softer mood now, he let the assistants do as they pleased on the way back.

11

At the School

He arrived at the school chilled to the marrow. It was dark everywhere, the candles in the lanterns had burned low. Led by his assistants, who already knew their way around, he felt his way into one of the classrooms. 'The first commendable thing they've done,' he said, remembering Klamm's letter. From the corner Frieda, still half asleep, called: 'Let K. sleep! Don't disturb him!' – she was still thinking only of K., even if she was so overcome with sleep that she had not been able to stay up for him. Now a lamp was lit, though it could not be turned up very high because there was so little paraffin left; the new household was still deficient in various respects. Although the room had been heated, it was so large – it was also used as a gymnasium, and bits of apparatus were lying about or hanging from the ceiling – that all the available wood had been used; it had, K. was assured, been pleasantly warm, but unfortunately had cooled down again completely. There was in fact a plentiful supply of wood in a shed, but the shed was locked and the teacher had the key, and only allowed wood to be taken to heat the rooms during lessons. That would have been tolerable if they had had quilts to cover them, but there was nothing of the sort except a single straw mattress, which Frieda had neatly covered with one of her woollen shawls; but there was no feather quilt, only two coarse stiff blankets that provided little warmth. Even this inadequate straw mattress attracted greedy looks from the assistants, though of course they could never hope to be allowed to lie on it.

Frieda looked anxiously at K. At the Brückenhof she had shown that she could make even the most wretched room habitable; but here, deprived as she was of all resources, she had not been able to do more. 'Our only furniture is the gym apparatus,' she said, making an effort to smile through her tears. But as far as the worst deficiencies were concerned, the unsatisfactory sleeping arrangements and the lack of heating, she gave a firm promise that things would be put right the next day and begged K. to be patient until then. No word, no hint, no look gave any indication that she felt the slightest resentment towards K., even though, as he had to admit to himself, he had dragged her away first from the Herrenhof and now from the Brückenhof. For this reason K. endeavoured to put up with everything, which he did not find too difficult because in his thoughts he accompanied Barnabas on his journey and repeated his message word for word, not as he had given it to Barnabas, but as he thought it would sound to Klamm's ears. At the same time, however, he also looked forward eagerly to the coffee that Frieda was making for him on a spirit cooker; leaning against the cooling stove he followed her deft, practised movements as she spread the inevitable white cloth over the desk and placed on it a flower-patterned coffee cup together with bread and bacon and even a tin of sardines. Now everything was ready; Frieda had not eaten yet either, but had waited for K. There were two chairs, on which K. and Frieda sat at the desk, while the assistants sat on the rostrum at their feet; but they were never still, even while they were eating they were disruptive. Though they had been given ample portions of everything and had not nearly finished, they would get up from time to time to see whether there was enough left on the table for them to expect more. K. ignored them, and it was only Frieda's laughter that drew his attention to them. He fondly put his hand over hers on the table and asked quietly why she put up with so much from them and even tolerated their bad behaviour so cheerfully. In that way they would never be rid of them, whereas by treating them with the severity their behaviour actually called for they could either be controlled or, more probably and indeed preferably, things could be made so disagreeable for them that in the end they would leave. It did not look as if their stay in the schoolhouse was going to be a very pleasant one, he said, but it wasn't going to last very long either; however, they would hardly notice all the drawbacks if they were rid of the assistants and the two of them could be alone in the house in peace. Did she not notice, too, that the assistants were getting more impudent by the day? It was as if Frieda's presence only encouraged them and gave them hope that K. would not deal with them as firmly in front of her as he would have done otherwise. Moreover, he went on, there might be a quite simple means of getting rid of them immediately without any fuss; perhaps Frieda could think of a way, after all she was familiar with conditions here. And they would probably only be doing the assistants a favour by getting rid of them, because they were not living in any great comfort here and even the idle life they had enjoyed so far would have to come to an end, at least to some extent, because they would have to work, while Frieda had to take things easy after all the recent upsets and he, K., was going to be busy finding a way out of their present hardship. But if the assistants were to leave he would feel so relieved that he would easily be able to carry out all his duties as school caretaker as well as everything else.

Frieda, who had been listening attentively, slowly stroked his arm and said she agreed with everything he said, but perhaps he was exaggerating the assistants' bad behaviour, after all they were young lads, high-spirited and rather simple. They were in the service of a stranger for the first time, released from the strict discipline of the Castle, so they were always a little excited, everything was new for them, and in this state of course they sometimes did stupid things, and while it was quite natural to get annoyed about their behaviour, it was more sensible to laugh at it. At times she could not help laughing; all the same, she quite agreed with K. that it would be best to send them away and for the two of them to be alone together. She moved closer to him and buried her face in his shoulder, then she said, so indistinctly that K. had to bend down to hear, that she knew of no way to get rid of the assistants, and she was afraid that none of K.'s suggestions would work. After all, as far as she was aware, K. had asked for them, and now they were there and he had to keep them. It was best to treat them lightly for the fools they were, that was the best way to put up with them.

K. was not happy with her answer. She seemed to be in league with them, he said, half joking and half serious, or at least to be very fond of them; they were good-looking lads sure enough, but you could get rid of anyone if you really wanted to, as he would show her with the assistants.

Frieda said she would be most grateful to him if he could. What's more, she wouldn't laugh at them again and wouldn't speak to them any more than she had to. She didn't find them funny any more, and it really was too much to be constantly watched by two men; she had learned to see the two of them through K.'s eyes. And in fact she did flinch slightly when the assistants jumped up again, partly to see whether there was any food left over, partly to find out what the constant whispering was about.

K. took this opportunity to turn Frieda against the assistants; he drew her close to him and they finished their meal sitting side by side. Now they should have gone to bed, they were all very tired, and one of the assistants had even fallen asleep over his meal; this amused the other one greatly, and he tried to get them to look at the sleeping man's silly face, but they would not. K. and Frieda sat at the table and ignored them. The cold was becoming unbearable, which made them reluctant to go to bed; finally K. declared that the heating must be restored, or else they would not be able to sleep. He looked around for an axe; the assistants knew where there was one, they fetched it and off they went to the woodshed. The flimsy door was quickly forced open, and the delighted assistants, as if they had never had such a good time, began carrying wood into the classroom, chasing and pushing one another. Soon there was a large pile of wood, the stove was lit and they all gathered round it; the assistants were given a blanket to wrap themselves in, which was quite sufficient, for it had been arranged that one of them should stay up and look after the fire. Soon it was so warm by the stove that the blankets were no longer needed. The lamp was extinguished and K. and Frieda lay down to sleep, happy in the warmth and the silence.

During the night K. was woken by a noise, and reaching out sleepily for Frieda noticed that one of the assistants was lying in her place. No doubt because he was already in a nervous state from being woken so suddenly, it gave him the biggest shock he had had since he came to the village. He sat up with a shout and instinctively hit the assistant such a blow with his fist that he began to cry. However, the situation soon became clear. Frieda had been woken, at least so she believed, when some large animal, probably a cat, jumped onto her chest and then ran off at once. She had got up and searched the whole room for the animal with a candle. This had given one of the assistants the chance to enjoy the straw mattress for a while, and now he was paying for it dearly. Frieda, however, could find nothing, perhaps she had only imagined it; she came back to K., but as she did she comforted the cowering, whimpering assistant by stroking his hair as if she had forgotten that evening's conversation. K. made no comment, but only told the assistant to stop feeding the fire, for they had used up nearly all the wood they had brought in and it was now too warm.

Next morning none of them woke until the first schoolchildren arrived and were clustering curiously round their sleeping quarters. This was embarrassing, because the heat in the room, though it had given way towards dawn to a distinct coolness, had made them strip down to their underwear, and just as they began to dress Gisa, the schoolmistress, a tall, handsome, fair-haired, though rather prim young woman, appeared at the door. She had clearly been told about the new caretaker, and had no doubt been informed of the rules of conduct by the schoolteacher, for as soon as she crossed the threshold she said: 'This is intolerable. What a state of affairs! You might have permission to sleep in the classroom, but I am not obliged to teach in your bedroom. A caretaker's family, lounging in bed late in the morning. How disgraceful!' Well, there were a few things he could reply to this, thought K., especially about the family and the bed, as he and Frieda – his assistants were of no use in this situation, they were lying on the floor gaping at the schoolmistress and the children – quickly pulled up the bars and the vaulting-horse and threw the blankets over them, forming a small space in which they could at least get dressed out of the children's sight. However, that did not give them a moment's peace; the schoolmistress began by complaining that there was no clean water in the washbasin – it had just occurred to K. to fetch the washbasin for Frieda and himself, but he gave up the idea in order not to provoke the schoolmistress. However, this did not help, for shortly afterwards there was a great crash; unfortunately they had neglected to clear the remnants of their supper from the desk, and the schoolmistress swept everything away with her ruler, sending it all onto the floor. It was no concern of hers that the sardine oil and the remains of the coffee were spilt or that the coffee pot was smashed to pieces – the school caretaker would soon clear it up.

Still not fully dressed, K. and Frieda leaned on the bars watching the destruction of their few possessions; the assistants, who clearly had no intention of getting dressed, peered out from under the blankets to the great delight of the children. What upset Frieda most of all was of course the loss of the coffee pot; only when K., to console her, promised he would go straight to the mayor to demand a replacement, was she able to control herself sufficiently to dash out of their shelter, wearing only a blouse and underskirt, and at least retrieve the tablecloth to save it from being soiled any further. She managed to do this despite the schoolmistress, who was attempting to deter her by hammering away with her ruler on the desk, making a nerve-racking noise. When K. and Frieda were fully dressed they had to order the assistants, who seemed dazed by these events, to get dressed, pushing them about and even at times having to put them into their clothes themselves. Then when they were all ready, K. gave out the next tasks: the assistants were to fetch wood and light the stove, but first Frieda was to scrub the floor in the other classroom, where great danger still threatened, for the schoolteacher was probably already in there; K. would fetch water and clean up the rest. There was no question of having breakfast for the moment.

K. wanted to be the first to emerge from their shelter in order to get an impression of the schoolmistress's mood; the others were to follow if he called them. He made this arrangement on the one hand because he did not want to let the assistants' stupidity make the situation even worse from the start, and on the other hand because he wished to spare Frieda as far as he could, for she had ambitions while he had none, she was sensitive while he was not; she was only thinking about the present minor unpleasantness, but he was thinking about Barnabas and the future. Frieda followed all his instructions faithfully, scarcely taking her eyes off him. He had hardly emerged when the schoolmistress called out to him amid the laughter of the schoolchildren, which from now on never stopped: 'Well, have you had a good sleep?' When K. took no notice because it was not actually meant as a question, but went straight to the washstand, she asked: 'What have you done to my poor cat, then?' A large, fat old cat lay stretched out lazily on the desk, and the schoolmistress was examining its paw, which it had evidently injured slightly. So Frieda had been right after all: this cat had not actually jumped on her, it was scarcely able to jump any more, but it had crawled over her. It had been frightened by the presence of people in the usually empty building, had rushed to hide and in its unaccustomed haste had injured itself. K. tried to explain this calmly to the schoolmistress, but she was concerned only with the result and said: 'Well, you've hurt her, that's what you've done. Just look.' She called K. up to the desk, showed him the injured paw, and before he realised had dragged the cat's claws across the back of his hand. Although its claws were blunt with age, the schoolmistress had, without any thought for the cat, pressed them down so hard that the scratches bled. 'Now get back to your work,' she snapped, bending over the cat again. Frieda, who had been watching from behind the bars with the assistants, shrieked at the sight of blood. K. showed the children his hand and said: 'Look what that nasty sly cat has done to me.' He said this not for the children's benefit, of course; their shouting and laughing had already developed its own momentum, it needed no further pretext or encouragement, and no words could have any effect on it. But since the schoolmistress also responded to the insult only with a brief sidelong glance and for the rest remained occupied with the cat, it seemed that her initial fury had been stilled by the bloody punishment she had inflicted, and K. called Frieda and his assistants to begin their work.

When K. had taken the bucket of dirty water outside, fetched clean water and begun to sweep out the classroom, a boy of about twelve slipped from his desk, touched K.'s hand, and said something that it was quite impossible to hear in the uproar. Then suddenly the noise stopped completely. K. turned round. What he had feared all morning had happened. In the door stood the schoolteacher; with each hand the little man was holding one of the assistants by the collar. He had no doubt caught them as they were fetching wood, for he shouted in a powerful voice, pausing after every word: 'Who dared to break into the woodshed? Where is he, I'll break his neck!' At this, Frieda got up from the floor, which she had been trying to scrub clean at the schoolmistress's feet, looked across at K. as if to give herself courage, and said, with something of her previous authority in her look and bearing: 'I did, sir. I had no alternative. If the classrooms were to be heated early this morning, the shed had to be opened. I didn't dare to come and get the key from you in the middle of the night, my fiancé was at the Herrenhof, it was possible he was going to spend the night there, so I had to decide for myself. If I have done wrong, please excuse my inexperience; I have already been scolded soundly enough by my fiancé when he saw what I had done. He even forbade me to light the stove first thing, because he thought that by locking the shed you had indicated that you didn't want the school to be heated until you yourself arrived. So it's his fault that there's no heating, but my fault that the woodshed was broken into.' 'Who broke the door down?' the teacher asked the assistants, who were still trying vainly to squirm out of his grasp. 'He did,' they both said, pointing at K. to dispel all doubt. Frieda laughed, and her laughter sounded even more convincing than her words; then she picked up the cloth she had been using to wash the floor and began to wring it out in the bucket, as if her explanation had put an end to the matter, and what the assistants had said was just a belated joke. Then when she was on her knees again ready to resume her work, she said: 'Our assistants are children, in spite of their age they should be sitting at these desks. You see, I broke the door open myself with the axe yesterday evening, it was quite easy, I didn't need any help from the assistants, they would only have got in the way. But then when my fiancé arrived last night and went out to inspect the damage and tried to repair it, the assistants went with him, probably because they were afraid to stay here on their own. They saw my fiancé working on the broken door, and that's why they're saying now – well, they're just children.'

During Frieda's explanation the assistants had continued to shake their heads and kept pointing at K., doing their best with silent grimaces to make Frieda change her mind; but when this failed they finally gave up, taking Frieda's words as a command, and gave no reply to the teacher when he questioned them again. 'I see,' said the teacher, 'so you were lying? Or at least you made a false accusation against the caretaker?' Still they did not reply, but they were shaking and looking anxious, which seemed to suggest they felt guilty. 'Then I am going to give you a good thrashing right away,' said the teacher, and sent one of the children into the next room to fetch the cane. But just as he raised it, Frieda cried: 'The assistants were telling the truth!' In despair she threw the cloth into the bucket with a great splash and ran to hide behind the bars. 'They're a bunch of liars,' said the schoolmistress, who had just finished bandaging the cat's paw and was lifting the creature onto her lap, for which it was almost too big.

'So that leaves the caretaker,' said the teacher. He pushed the assistants away and turned to K., who all this time had been leaning on his broom and listening. 'The caretaker, who out of cowardice calmly allows others to be falsely accused of his own knavery.' 'Well,' said K., who had noted that Frieda's intervention had in fact calmed the teacher's initial uncontrolled fury, 'if the assistants had been given a bit of a thrashing, I wouldn't have minded; when they've been let off ten punishments they deserved, they can make up for it with one they didn't deserve. But apart from that, I would have been glad to avoid a direct quarrel with you, sir; perhaps you would rather have done so too. But now that Frieda has given me away to save the assistants' – here K. paused, and in the silence Frieda could be heard sobbing behind the blankets – 'the matter must of course be dealt with openly.' 'Outrageous,' said the schoolmistress. 'I agree with you entirely, Fräulein Gisa,' said the teacher. 'As caretaker you are of course dismissed immediately for this scandalous breach of duty; I have not yet decided what punishment is to be imposed, but for now you will leave the building at once and take all your things with you. It will be a great relief to us, and we can get on with our lessons at last. So hurry!' 'I am not moving from here,' said K. 'You are my superior, but you did not appoint me to the job. The mayor did that, and I will only accept my dismissal from him. I don't suppose he gave me the job so that I and my dependants could freeze here, but – as you said yourself – in order to prevent any rash or desperate measures on my part. So to dismiss me now so suddenly would be the last thing he intended; until I hear otherwise from his own mouth, I shall not believe it. Moreover, it would undoubtedly be very much in your own interests if I did not accept your thoughtless dismissal.' 'So you do not accept it?' said the teacher. K. shook his head. 'Think carefully,' said the teacher. 'Your decisions are not always for the best; think of yesterday afternoon, for example, when you refused to be questioned.' 'Why do you raise that now?' asked K. 'Because I wish to,' said the teacher, 'and now for the last time: get out!' But when this had no effect either, the teacher went to the desk and held a whispered consultation with the schoolmistress. She said something about calling the police, but the teacher demurred; finally they came to an agreement, and the teacher told the children to transfer to his class, where they would be taught together with the other children. This change delighted them all; laughing and shouting they emptied the room immediately, followed by the teacher and the schoolmistress. She carried the class register and on it the corpulent and entirely impassive cat. The teacher would rather have left the cat behind, but she firmly resisted this suggestion by pointing out K.'s cruelty, so on top of all the other irritations K. had caused the teacher, he had to put up with the cat as well. And no doubt it was this that prompted his last words to K. as he went out of the door: 'Fräulein Gisa has been forced to leave this room with the children because of your wilful refusal to accept your dismissal, and because no one can ask a young woman to give lessons surrounded by your squalid household. So you are on your own and you can settle down here just as you please, undisturbed by the disgust of decent people. But it will not be for long, I can assure you.' With that he slammed the door.

12

The Assistants

As soon as they had all gone, K. told the assistants: 'Get out!' Astonished by this unexpected order, they obeyed, but when K. locked the door behind them they tried to get back in, whimpering outside and knocking on the door. 'You are dismissed,' called K. 'I will never employ you again.' But they would have none of it and hammered on the door with their hands and feet. 'Let us back in, sir!' they cried, as if K. were on dry land and they were about to drown. But K. took no pity on them, and waited impatiently for the intolerable din to force the schoolteacher to intervene. This soon happened. 'Let your accursed assistants in!' he shouted. 'I have dismissed them,' K. shouted back; this had the unintended effect of showing the teacher what happened when someone was strong enough not just to give notice but to carry it out. Then the teacher tried to soothe the assistants, telling them in a kindly way to wait there quietly, K. would have to let them back in again for sure. Then he went away. And now things might have remained quiet if K. had not started to shout at them again that they had been dismissed once and for all and did not have the slightest hope of being re-engaged, whereupon they began to make as much uproar as before. Again the teacher appeared, but this time he did not try to persuade them but chased them, evidently with his dreaded cane, out of the schoolhouse.

They soon reappeared at the windows of the gym hall, knocking on the glass and shouting, but their words were indistinct. However, they did not stay there for long; in the deep snow they could not jump about sufficiently to express their agitation. So they rushed to the railings around the school garden and jumped onto the stone parapet, from which they had a better, if distant, view into the room; holding on to the railings they ran to and fro, then stopped and held out their clasped hands beseechingly towards K. They went on with this for a long time, regardless of the futility of their efforts; they were as if possessed, and no doubt continued even after K. drew the curtains to get them out of his sight.

In the now darkened room K. went over to the bars to find Frieda. He watched while she stood up, tidied her hair, dried her face and without a word started to make coffee. Although she knew all about it, K. formally announced that he had dismissed the assistants. She simply nodded. K. sat at one of the desks and watched her weary movements. It had always been her vivacious and confident bearing that had lent beauty to her insignificant physique, and now that beauty was gone. Living with K. for just a few days had been enough to achieve that. Her work in the bar had not been easy, but had probably suited her better. Or had she lost her attractiveness because she had left Klamm? It had been her proximity to Klamm that made her so alluring; that was what had drawn K. to her so strongly, and now she was fading in his arms.

'Frieda,' said K. She put down the coffee grinder at once and came over to him at the desk. 'Are you angry with me?' she asked. 'No,' said K., 'I don't think you can help it. You were happy at the Herrenhof; I should have left you there.' 'Yes,' said Frieda with a sad look, 'you should have left me there. I'm not good enough to live with you. If you were free of me, perhaps you would achieve everything you want. For my sake you put up with that bullying teacher, you take on this miserable job and do your utmost to get an interview with Klamm. All for my sake, but I reward you poorly.' 'No,' said K., putting his arm around her to console her, 'all those things are trivial, they don't hurt me, and it's not just for your sake that I want to see Klamm. Look how much you've done for me! Before I met you I was utterly lost here. No one accepted me, and if I forced myself on anyone, they soon got rid of me. And the only people I might have found peace with were those I ran away from – like Barnabas' family . . .' 'You ran away from them? Is that true? My darling!' Frieda broke in eagerly, only to relapse into her weariness again after a hesitant 'yes' from K.

But even he no longer had the will to explain how everything had gone better for him as a result of his association with her. He slowly withdrew his arm from her, and for a while they sat in silence until Frieda, as if K.'s arm had given her warmth she could no longer do without, said: 'I won't be able to put up with this life here. If you want me to stay with you, we must go away, anywhere, to the South of France, or Spain.' 'I can't go away,' said K. 'I came here to stay. I shall stay here.' Then, contradicting himself but making no effort whatever to explain why, he added as if he were talking to himself: 'What else could have enticed me to this desolate place but the wish to stay here?' Then he said: 'But you want to stay here too, it's your home after all. You miss Klamm, that's all, that's why you get these wild ideas.' 'I miss Klamm?' said Frieda. 'There's more than enough Klamm here, too much Klamm. It's to get away from him that I want to leave. It's not Klamm I miss, it's you. It's because of you I want to leave, because I can't get enough of you here, with everyone pawing at me. If only I could lose my looks, if only I had an ugly body so that I could live in peace with you.'

K. could only read one thing into this. 'Is Klamm still in touch with you?' he asked quickly. 'Does he send for you?' 'I know nothing about Klamm,' said Frieda. 'I'm talking about other people, the assistants for instance.' 'Oh? The assistants?' said K. with surprise. 'Are they pestering you?' 'Haven't you noticed?' asked Frieda. 'No,' said K., trying in vain to remember any details, 'they're a nuisance and they're lecherous young devils, but I haven't noticed that they dared to misbehave towards you.' 'Haven't you?' said Frieda. 'Didn't you notice how we couldn't get them out of our room at the Brückenhof, how they spied on our affair so jealously, how one of them took my place on the mattress earlier today, and how they accused you just now to get rid of you, ruin you, and be alone with me? Didn't you notice all that?' K. looked at Frieda without replying. These charges against the assistants were indeed true, but they could all be explained much more innocently as part of their whole absurd, fidgety, childish, undisciplined characters. And were these charges not at odds with the fact that they had always attempted to go everywhere with him, and not stay behind with Frieda? K. mentioned something to this effect. 'They're pretending,' she said. 'Couldn't you see through that? Why did you dismiss them, then, if it wasn't for that?' And she went to the window, drew the curtain aside, looked out, and called K. over. The assistants were still outside by the railings; tired as they obviously were by now, now and again they still summoned up all their strength and stretched out their arms, pleading, towards the school. One of them had hooked his coat onto the railings behind him to avoid having to hold on to it all the time.

'The poor lads! The poor lads!' said Frieda. 'Do you know why I dismissed them?' asked K. 'You were the direct cause of that.' 'I was?' asked Frieda, still looking out of the window. 'You treated them too kindly,' said K. 'You excused their bad behaviour, you laughed at them and stroked their hair, you constantly felt sorry for them. "The poor lads, the poor lads," you keep saying, and finally there was that scene just now, when you gave me away to save them from a thrashing.' 'But that's it,' said Frieda, 'that's what I mean, that's what makes me so unhappy, what keeps us apart when I can't imagine any greater happiness than being with you, always, the whole time, for ever, even though I dream that there's nowhere on earth where our love can be undisturbed, not in this village or anywhere else, and so I imagine a grave, deep and narrow, where we can hold each other as if we were chained together, where I can hide my face against you and you can hide yours against me, and no one will see us ever again. But here – look at the assistants! It's not you they are pleading with, it's me.' 'And it's not me who is looking at them, it's you,' said K. 'Of course it is,' said Frieda almost angrily, 'that's what I keep saying. Why else should they pester me all the time, even if they are Klamm's agents ...' 'Klamm's agents!' said K., astonished at this term, though it struck him as obvious at once. 'Yes, of course, Klamm's agents,' said Frieda, 'even if they are, they're also young fools who still need a good thrashing to teach them. What ugly, swarthy lads they are, and what a horrid contrast between their faces, which make them look grown up, almost like students, and their silly childish behaviour. Don't you think I can see that? I'm really ashamed of them. I can't keep my eyes off them. When I ought to be angry with them, I have to laugh. When they ought to be beaten, I have to stroke their hair. And when I'm lying beside you at night and can't sleep, I have to lean across you and watch them, the one rolled up in his blanket fast asleep, and the other kneeling in front of the stove putting wood on the fire, and I have to lean right across you so that I almost wake you up. And it's not the cat that scares me – I know what cats are like, and I know what it's like to be constantly woken up from working in the bar – it's not the cat that scares me, I scare myself. And it doesn't take that horrid beast of a cat, the slightest noise makes me jump. One minute I'm afraid you'll wake up and it will all be over, the next I jump up and light the candle to wake you up as soon as I can so that you can protect me.' 'I knew nothing about all that,' said K. 'It was just a vague suspicion that made me get rid of them, but now they're gone and perhaps everything will be all right.' 'Oh yes, they've gone at last,' said Frieda, but she looked distressed rather than pleased, 'but we still don't know who they are. Klamm's agents – that's how I think of them as a joke, but perhaps they really are. Their eyes, that simple but bright look in their eyes, remind me somehow of Klamm's eyes; yes, that's it – it's the look in Klamm's eyes that they turn on me sometimes, it goes through me. So I was wrong when I said I was ashamed of them. I only wish it was that. Of course, I know if anyone else behaved like that anywhere else, it would be stupid and give offence, but it's not like that with them, I admire and respect their stupid behaviour. But if they are Klamm's agents, who will rid us of them, and would it do us any good to be rid of them? In that case, shouldn't you call them back in here straight away and be glad if they are still willing to come?'

'Do you want me to let them back in?' asked K. 'No, no,' said Frieda, 'that's the last thing I want. If they came rushing back in here, I don't think I could stand the sight of them, their joy at seeing me again, the way they jump about like children and hold out their arms like grown men. But then again, when I think you might be preventing Klamm from getting in touch with you if you go on treating them so harshly, I want to do everything I can to save you from that. Then I want you to let them back. Just let them back, now. Don't think about me, what do I matter? I'll resist as long as I can, but if I give in, well, that's just too bad – at least I shall know it was all for your sake.' 'You are only confirming my opinion of them,' said K. 'As far as I'm concerned, they will never come back here. Just throwing them out shows that there are ways of controlling them, and that in turn shows that they can't really have anything to do with Klamm. Only yesterday evening I had a letter from Klamm that made it clear that he is quite wrongly informed about the assistants, from which we can only conclude that he hasn't the slightest interest in them, because if he had he could surely have got hold of accurate information about them. The fact that they remind you of Klamm proves nothing, because unfortunately you are still under the influence of the landlady and you see Klamm everywhere. You're still Klamm's mistress, you're not my wife yet by a long way. Sometimes that makes me feel quite gloomy, it's as if I had lost everything, because then I feel as if I've only just arrived in the village, but not full of hope as I actually was then, but knowing that I have only disappointments in store, and that I shall have to experience them one after the other to the bitter end. But that is only sometimes,' added K. with a smile when he saw how despondent Frieda looked at his words, 'and in the end it's all to the good, because it shows how much you mean to me. And if you now tell me to choose between you and the assistants, that means the assistants have already lost. What an idea, for me to choose between you and the assistants! But now I want to be rid of them once and for all. Besides, who knows whether this weakness that has come over us both isn't because we haven't had breakfast yet?' 'Maybe,' said Frieda with a tired smile, returning to her work. And K. took up the broom again.

13
Hans

Shortly afterwards there was a soft knock at the door. 'Barnabas!' cried K. He threw the broom aside and with a few steps reached the door. Alarmed by the name more than anything else, Frieda stared at him. K. fumbled with the old lock, which he could not open at once. 'I'm opening the door,' he said over and over again, instead of asking who was knocking. Then he flung the door open and saw not Barnabas, but the little boy who had tried to speak to him earlier. But K. had no wish to see him again. 'What do you want here?' he said. 'The lesson is being held next door.' 'That's where I came from,' said the boy and stood there, his arms held stiffly by his sides, looking calmly up at K. with his big brown eyes. 'What do you want, then? Quickly!' said K., bending down slightly, for the boy spoke softly. 'Can I help you?' asked the boy. 'He wants to help us,' said K. to Frieda, then to the boy: 'So what is your name?' 'Hans Brunswick,' said the boy, 'I'm in class four, I'm the son of Otto Brunswick, shoemaker in the Madeleinegasse.' 'Ah, so your name's Brunswick,' said K., more kindly now. It turned out that Hans had been so upset by the bloody scratches the schoolmistress had scored on K.'s hand that he had resolved there and then to stand by K. on his own initiative and at the risk of severe punishment he had slipped out of the class next door like a deserter. Perhaps it was chiefly some boyish whim that had made him do it, which was in keeping with the seriousness that informed everything he did. At first only shyness held him back, but he soon became accustomed to K. and Frieda; after he had been given some good hot coffee to drink, he became more lively and trusting, and questioned them eagerly and insistently as if he wished to find out the most important facts as quickly as possible so that he could draw his own conclusions about their situation. There was something imperious about him, but this was combined with a childish innocence in such a way that they were willing, half-seriously and half in fun, to go along with him. At any rate, he commanded their attention; they ceased their work, and breakfast went on for a long time. Although he was sitting at one of the classroom benches and K. was up at the teacher's desk with Frieda on a chair beside him, it seemed that Hans was the teacher, as if he were weighing and judging their answers; a faint smile about his soft mouth seemed to indicate that he knew very well it was all a game, but otherwise he treated the matter with great seriousness – perhaps it was not a smile at all, but the happiness of childhood that played about his lips. He was surprisingly slow to admit that he already knew K. from the time he had called at Lasemann's house. K. was pleased to hear this. 'You were playing at the woman's feet, weren't you?' he asked. 'Yes,' said Hans, 'that was my mother.' Then he was asked to talk about his mother, but he would only do this hesitantly after persistent prompting; and here it became clear that he was a small boy. While at times, especially in the questions he put – perhaps it was a foreshadowing of future maturity, or perhaps again it was merely an illusion on the part of his tense and uneasy audience – it was almost as if a man of keen intelligence and far-sighted vision were speaking, the next minute he suddenly became a schoolboy again who could not understand some questions and misunderstood others; with a child's lack of consideration he spoke too softly although he was asked to speak up several times, and finally, as if in defiance, he lapsed into complete silence when faced with certain urgent questions, but without the slightest embarrassment, which an adult could never have done. Altogether it was as if he thought he was the only one permitted to put questions, as if by putting questions to him the others were breaking some rule and wasting time. Then he was capable of saying nothing for long periods, sitting up straight with his head bowed, pouting his lower lip. This appealed to Frieda so much that she put frequent questions to him, hoping to make him adopt this silent posture. Sometimes she succeeded, but it annoyed K.

On the whole they learned only a little. His mother was unwell, but what her illness was remained unclear; the child that Brunswick's wife had been holding on her lap was Hans's sister Frieda (Hans did not take kindly to the fact that the woman pestering him with questions had the same name). They all lived in the village, but not at Lasemann's, they had only gone there for a bath because Lasemann had the great tub in which it was a special treat for the little children – though Hans was not one of these – to bathe and splash about. Hans spoke of his father with respect or apprehension, but never while he was talking about his mother; obviously his father meant little to him compared with his mother. Any further questions about his family life, however much he was pressed, went unanswered. They learned that his father was a shoemaker by trade, the biggest in the village, there was none like him, as he often repeated in reply to quite different questions; he even gave out work to other shoemakers, for example to Barnabas' father, in this case presumably only as a particular favour – at least, this was suggested by a proud toss of Hans's head, at which Frieda jumped down and gave him a kiss. When asked whether he had ever been inside the Castle, he replied, only when the question had been repeated many times, that he had not; when asked the same question about his mother, he gave no answer.

Finally K. grew tired of asking questions, which he realised was futile; the boy was quite right not to answer. Moreover, there was something shameful about using an innocent child to discover family secrets, indeed it was all the more so because they had learned nothing by this means. And when K. asked the boy in conclusion what sort of help he had to offer, he was no longer surprised to hear that Hans only wanted to help them with their work in order to stop the teacher and the schoolmistress scolding K. so much. K. explained to Hans that he did not need any help of that kind; scolding no doubt came naturally to a teacher, and even the most painstaking work could scarcely avoid it. The work itself, he said, was not hard, and it was only by chance that he was behind with it today. Besides, these reprimands did not affect K. as they would a pupil, he shrugged them off, he hardly noticed them, and in any case he hoped he would soon be rid of the teacher altogether. So as Hans had only offered his help to deal with the teacher,

K. thanked him very much and told him he could go back to his class; he hoped he would not be punished for his brief absence.

Although K. had not emphasised it, and had merely suggested involuntarily that it was only in dealing with the teacher that he did not need help, leaving open the question of help in other matters, Hans inferred this quite clearly and asked whether K. might need some other kind of help; he would be very glad to help him, he said, and if he were unable to himself he would ask his mother, who would certainly be able to. Even his father asked his mother for help when he had problems. And his mother had already asked about K.; she scarcely left the house, it was an exception that she had been at Lasemann's that time, but he, Hans, often went to play with Lasemann's children, and his mother had once asked him whether the surveyor had been there again. But, he went on, because his mother was so weak and tired she shouldn't be bothered with unnecessary questions, so he had just replied that he hadn't seen the surveyor there, and no more was said about the matter; but now he had found him here at the school, he had had to speak to him so that he could tell his mother about it. For his mother preferred him to carry out her wishes without having to be specially told to.

K. thought for a moment, then told Hans he did not need any help, he had everything he needed, but it was very kind of Hans to want to help him; he thanked him for his willingness, saying that it was quite possible he might need something later, in which case he would turn to him – he knew where he lived. However, perhaps he, K., could be of some help just now. He was sorry that Hans's mother was ill and that it was clear no one here could understand what she was suffering from; cases like that, in themselves quite mild, could deteriorate into a serious condition if they were neglected. Well, K. had some medical knowledge and, what was even more valuable, some experience in treating the sick; he had succeeded in several cases where the doctors had failed. At home they used to call him 'the bitter herb' because of his powers of healing. At any rate, he would be pleased to look at Hans's mother and have a word with her. Perhaps he could give her some good advice, he would be glad to do it for Hans's sake. At first Hans's eyes lit up at this offer, which led K. to become more insistent, but the outcome disappointed him because in reply to further questions Hans said, without displaying any great sadness, that his mother could not receive any visits from strangers because she had to be treated with great care; even though K. had scarcely spoken to her the last time, he said, she had taken to her bed for several days afterwards, as she often did. His father had been very angry with K., and would certainly never allow him near his mother, in fact he had wanted to confront K. at the time to punish him for his behaviour, but his mother had stopped him. As a general rule his mother herself had no wish to speak to anyone, and when she asked about K. this was no exception to the rule; on the contrary, when he had been mentioned she could have expressed a wish to see him there and then, but she had not done so, thus making her wishes quite clear. She only wanted to hear about K., not to speak to him. Besides, she didn't suffer from any particular illness; she knew very well the reason for her condition – it was no doubt because the air here didn't suit her, but then again she didn't want to leave the village for the sake of his father and the children. Also, the air was better than it used to be.

This was more or less what K. was told. Hans's arguments clearly became more persuasive as he sought to protect his mother from K., whom he had ostensibly been trying to help; in fact, in his best efforts to keep K. away from his mother he even frequently contradicted his own earlier statements, for instance about her illness. In spite of this, K. realised that even now Hans was still well disposed towards him, it was just that his concern for his mother made him oblivious to everything else. Compared with his mother, everyone was in the wrong; this time it was K., but it could just as easily have been his father, for example. Wishing to test this assumption, K. said it was surely very sensible of Hans's father to protect his mother from any upset and if he, K., had had any inkling of it on that occasion he would certainly not have dared to speak to his mother, and he asked Hans to give his belated apologies to them at home. On the other hand, he still could not quite understand why, if the cause of her suffering was as clear as Hans had said it was, his father held his mother back from recovering in another climate. It had to be said that he was holding her back, because she only refused to go for his sake and the children's; but she could take the children with her, after all she did not need to go very far or for very long – even up on the Castle Hill the air was quite different. Hans's father did not have to worry about the cost of such a trip; he was the biggest shoemaker in the village, and surely he or she had relatives or knew someone in the Castle who would be glad to take them. Why didn't he let her go? He ought not to underestimate the seriousness of such a condition; K. had only seen Hans's mother briefly, but it had been her striking pallor and weakness that had prompted him to speak to her, and even at the time he had been surprised that his father had allowed his ailing wife to stay in the unhealthy atmosphere of the communal bath and laundry, and had not exercised any restraint with his loud talk either. His father was probably not aware of the true state of affairs, her condition might also have improved recently, a condition like that has its ups and downs, but in the end if it is not treated, it returns more virulently and then nothing can be done for it. Even if he could not speak to his mother, K. told Hans, it might do some good if he could talk to his father and point all this out to him.

Hans had listened intently; he had understood most of what had been said, and had vividly sensed the threat behind what he had not understood. But he still told K. he could not speak to his father because his father had taken a dislike to him and would probably treat him as the schoolteacher had done. He said this with a shy smile when speaking of K., but sadly and with a scowl whenever he mentioned his father. However, he added that K. could perhaps speak to his mother, but only without his father's knowledge; he thought for a while with a fixed look, just like a woman who wants to do something forbidden and is trying to find a way of doing it with impunity. Then he said it might be possible the day after tomorrow, when his father went to the Herrenhof in the evening to talk to people. He, Hans, would come and take K. to his mother, provided of course that she agreed, which was by no means certain, especially since she did nothing against his father's will; she deferred to him in everything, even in things that he, Hans, clearly recognised as unreasonable. Now Hans was actually seeking K.'s help against his father; it was as if he had deceived himself in thinking that he wanted to help K., whereas in fact he had wanted to find out, since no one from his previous circle had been able to help him deal with his father, whether this stranger who had suddenly appeared in their midst and whom his mother had even mentioned, might perhaps be in a position to do so. Hitherto the boy's words and behaviour had hardly suggested anything of the sort, he had seemed so reticent, almost devious without being aware of it; only later had it become evident from the grudging admissions extracted from him by accident or design. And now, in the course of his long exchanges with K., he was debating the difficulties that stood in their way, which for all Hans's good will were well-nigh insurmountable; engrossed in thought, but still pleading for help, he kept his eyes fixed on K., blinking nervously. He could not say anything to his mother until his father had left, or his father would find out and that would ruin everything, so he could only mention it later; but even then, out of consideration for his mother, he could not tell her suddenly and all at once – he would have to bide his time and wait for the right moment, then he would have to get his mother's agreement before he could summon K. But would it not be too late by then, was there not a risk that his father might return? Yes – it was impossible after all.

K., however, explained to him that it was possible. There was no need to fear that time might run out; a brief meeting, a short conversation would be sufficient, and Hans would not have to come and fetch K. He would hide and wait somewhere near the house and come as soon as Hans gave the signal. No, said Hans, K. could not wait near the house – again, he was prompted by consideration for his mother; K. must not set out without his mother's knowledge, Hans could not make any such arrangement with K. without telling his mother, he would have to fetch K. from the school, and then not until his mother knew about it and gave her consent. Well, said K., in that case it really was dangerous; it was possible that Hans's father might catch him in the house, and even if that did not happen, his mother would be so afraid it might that she would not let K. come at all – so all their plans would fail because of his father. Then Hans objected to this, and so they argued back and forth.

K. had long since called Hans from his school bench up to the rostrum; he had placed him between his knees, and now and again gave him a comforting hug. In spite of Hans's occasional resistance, being so close had helped to form a bond between them. Finally they reached an agreement: Hans would first tell his mother the whole truth, but in order to make it easier for her to consent he would add that K. also wished to speak to Brunswick himself – not about Hans's mother, but about his own affairs. Moreover, this was correct; it had occurred to K. in the course of the conversation that Brunswick, though he might in other respects be a dangerous and malicious man, could not really be his enemy because he had, at least according to what the mayor had said, been the leader of those who had supported the appointment of a surveyor, even if it had been for political reasons. So Brunswick must have welcomed K.'s arrival in the village. In that case, however, his surly greeting on K.'s first day and his dislike of K. that Hans had mentioned were almost incomprehensible; but perhaps Brunswick had been offended because K. had not turned to him first for help, or perhaps there was some other misunderstanding that could be cleared up in a few words. If that were so, then K. could very well win Brunswick's support against the schoolteacher, even against the mayor, and the whole official bluff – what else could it be? – that the mayor and the schoolteacher had used to stop him reaching the Castle authorities and to force him into the job of school caretaker could be exposed. If Brunswick's quarrel with the mayor over K. restarted, Brunswick would have to enlist K. on his side, K. would be invited as a guest in Brunswick's house, Brunswick's weapons would be put at his disposal to defy the mayor; who could say what progress he might make in that way, and at all events he would frequently be in the company of Brunswick's wife – thus K. toyed with his dreams as they toyed with him, while Hans, thinking only of his mother, watched K.'s silent musings apprehensively, as one watches a doctor who is deep in thought seeking a remedy for a serious case. K.'s suggestion that he should talk to Brunswick about his appointment as surveyor met with Hans's approval, if only because it would protect his mother from his father and because it was in any case only to be used as an emergency measure which they hoped would not be needed. His only further question was how K. would explain to his father why he was calling at such a late hour, and in the end he accepted, though he looked a little downcast at the idea, the suggestion that K. should tell his father that his intolerable position as caretaker and his humiliating treatment by the schoolmaster had led him in sudden desperation to throw caution to the winds.

Now that everything had been thought out as far as they could anticipate and there seemed to be at least a chance of success, Hans, freed from the burden of thought, cheered up and chatted on for a while in his childish way, first with K. and then with Frieda, who had been sitting there for a long time as if engrossed in quite different thoughts, and only now began to join in the conversation again. Among other things, she asked him what he wanted to be when he was older, and without having to think very long he replied he wanted to be a man like K. But when they asked him why, he had no answer, and to the question whether he perhaps wanted to be a school caretaker he replied firmly in the negative. It was only after further questioning that they learned how he had arrived at this wish. K.'s present situation was not at all enviable, on the contrary it was sad and contemptible; Hans saw this quite clearly and did not need to look at other people to realise it – in fact, as far as he was concerned he would have preferred to spare his mother from ever having to see or speak to K. In spite of this he had come to K. and asked him for help, and had been happy when K. agreed; he thought he had noticed a similar reaction from other people too, and above all, his mother had actually mentioned K. herself. From this contradiction he had come to the conclusion that although K. was at present in a wretched and unenviable position, at some time in the admittedly almost unimaginably distant future he would outdo everyone. And it was this absurdly distant future and the noble path that would lead to it that attracted Hans; for this he was willing to accept K. even in his present state. The peculiarly childish and yet precocious nature of this ambition was evident in the way Hans looked down on K. as on a younger person whose future extended further than his own future as a young lad. Prompted over and over again by Frieda's questions, he spoke of these things with a sort of gloomy earnestness. He only perked up when K. said he knew what made Hans envy him – it was his fine gnarled walking-stick which lay on the desk, and with which Hans had been playing absent-mindedly during their conversation. Well, K. told him, he knew how to make sticks like that, and when their plan succeeded he would make Hans an even better one. Hans was so delighted by K.'s promise that it was not clear whether he had actually been thinking about the stick; he left them in high spirits after shaking K. firmly by the hand with the words: 'The day after tomorrow, then.'

14
Frieda's Rebuke

Hans went none too soon, for shortly afterwards the schoolteacher flung open the door. When he saw K. and Frieda sitting quietly at table, he shouted: 'I am sorry to disturb you! But will you tell me when you are going to finish clearing up in here? Next door we have to sit packed together and cannot teach properly, while you lounge about here in the big gym hall. You have even sent the assistants away to give yourselves more room. Now would you please at least get up and do some work!' To K. he said: 'Go and fetch my lunch now from the Brückenhof.' All this he shouted furiously, but his words were relatively restrained, even in the way he spoke down to K. The latter was quite willing to do as he was told, but just to see how the teacher would react he said: 'But I have been dismissed.' 'Dismissed or not, fetch me my lunch,' said the teacher. 'That's just what I want to know,' said K. 'Am I dismissed or not?' 'What are you talking about?' said the teacher, 'you didn't accept your dismissal.' 'Is that enough to reverse it?' asked K. 'Not for me, you can be sure,' said the teacher, 'but it is for the mayor; why, I fail to understand. Now get on with it, or I'll really throw you out.' K. was satisfied – so the teacher had spoken to the mayor in the meantime; or perhaps he had not spoken to him at all, but had simply worked out the mayor's probable opinion, which was in K.'s favour. He was about to hurry off to fetch the meal when the teacher called him back from the corridor. It was unclear whether this was to test K.'s obedience with this further command so that he would know how far he could go another time, or whether he found he liked giving orders and enjoyed making K. rush off and then calling him back again like a waiter. For his part, K. knew that if he gave in too readily he would become the teacher's slave or whipping-boy; but for the moment he was willing to indulge the teacher's whims up to a point because although the teacher, as had been shown, had no authority to dismiss him, he could certainly make his position intolerably uncomfortable. And this job meant more to K. now than it had before. His conversation with Hans had held out new hopes for him, which were admittedly improbable, indeed wholly unfounded, but which he could not now abandon; they almost drove even Barnabas from his mind. If he was going to pursue them – and he had no alternative – he had to devote all his energies to it and care about nothing else, not about food, lodging, the village authorities, not even Frieda, and in the end it was all about Frieda, everything else concerned him only in relation to her. That was why he must try to keep this job which gave Frieda some security, and bearing that in mind he should not resent having to put up with more from the teacher than he might otherwise have been willing to take. None of this was particularly painful, it was all part of the constant flow of life's petty troubles, it was nothing in comparison to what K. was seeking, and he had not come here to lead a quiet and respectable existence.

This is why, just as he was about to run across to the inn, he was also willing to return at once in response to the new command to tidy up the room first so that the schoolmistress could move back in with her class. But he had to clear up very quickly, for then he had to fetch the meal, and the teacher was already very hungry and thirsty. K. assured him that all would be done as he wished; for a while the teacher watched as K. soon cleared away their sleeping area, pushed the gym apparatus back into place and swept the floor in a trice while Frieda washed and scrubbed the rostrum. Their efforts seemed to satisfy him; he told them there was a pile of wood outside the door for the stove – no doubt he was unwilling to let K. have access to the woodshed – then, with a warning that he would be back before long, he went next door to see to the children.

Frieda had been working in silence for a while when she asked K. why he was so obedient to the teacher. No doubt she put the question out of sympathy and concern, but K., thinking how unsuccessful Frieda had been, in the light of her original promise, in protecting him from the teacher's orders and abuse, only replied curtly that since he was the school caretaker he just had to do his job. Then there was silence until K., prompted by this brief exchange, remembered that Frieda had seemed to be lost in anxious thought all this time, especially during the whole conversation with Hans, and now, just as he was carrying in the wood, asked her openly what was on her mind. Looking up at him slowly, she replied that it was nothing in particular; she was simply thinking about the landlady and the truth of much of what she had said. After demurring several times, it was only when K. pressed her that she replied in more detail while she went on with her work – not because she wanted to get on with it, for it was making no progress, but only so that she did not have to look at K. Then she told him how at first she had listened calmly to his conversation with Hans, and then, alarmed by something K. had said, had begun to follow more clearly what he meant; from that moment she had not been able to help hearing what he said as confirmation of a warning the landlady had given her, but which she had never been able to accept as justified. K., annoyed by these vague expressions and more irritated than touched by Frieda's plaintive and tearful voice – irritated above all because the landlady was once again intruding on his life, even if only in Frieda's recollections, for until now she had had little success in person – threw the wood he was carrying onto the floor, sat down on it and in a stern voice demanded a clear explanation.

'Many times now,' Frieda began, 'right from the start, the landlady has tried to make me doubt you. She didn't claim you were lying, far from it, she said you were as candid as a child, but you were so different from us by nature that even when you speak the truth we have to make a great effort to believe you, and unless a good friend warns us in time we must suffer bitterly before we can get used to believing you. She has such a keen eye for people, and even she almost believed you. But after her last conversation with you at the Brückenhof, she said – I'm only repeating the bad things she said about you – she had seen through you, you couldn't fool her any more, even though you did your utmost to hide your intentions. "But he doesn't hide anything," she kept saying, and then she went on: "Make an effort some time to listen to him properly, not just superficially, I mean really listen to what he says." That was exactly what she had done, she said, and as a result she had gathered something like this about your intentions towards me: you had made a pass at me – that was the common expression she used – only because I happened to come along, because you didn't find me unattractive and because you thought, quite wrongly, that a barmaid was supposed to be available to every customer who held his hand out to her. What's more, as the landlady was told by the landlord of the Herrenhof, for some reason or another you wanted to spend the night at the Herrenhof, and there was no way you could do that without me. That would have been reason enough for you to become my lover for the night, but there was more to it than that, which was Klamm. The landlady doesn't claim to know what you wanted from Klamm, she only claims that you were just as desperate to reach Klamm before you got to know me as you were afterwards. The only difference was that you had no hope before, but now you thought I was a reliable way of getting you into an even better position to see Klamm properly and quickly. I was alarmed – but only for a moment, there was no deeper reason – when you told me today that before you met me you had lost your way here. Those could be the landlady's own words; she said too that it was only since you met me that you have known where you were going. That, she said, was because you thought that in me you had conquered a mistress of Klamm's, and so you held a valuable card that you would only give up for a very high price. All you wanted was to bargain with Klamm for this card. Since the card meant everything to you and I meant nothing, she said, as far as I was concerned you were prepared to make any concession, but you were inflexible about the price. That's why you didn't care that I lost my job at the Herrenhof, you didn't care either that I had to leave the Brückenhof, didn't care that I would have to do all the hard work at the school, you have no tenderness, you don't even have time for me any more, you abandon me to the assistants and feel no jealousy, you only value me because I was Klamm's mistress, in your ignorance you do your utmost not to let me forget Klamm, so that when the crucial moment finally arrives I won't put up very much resistance, and yet you also fall out with the landlady, who you believe is the one person who could take me away from you, that's why you quarrel with her so violently that you have to leave the Brückenhof with me; you don't doubt for a moment that as far as I have any say in the matter, I belong to you whatever happens. You see your interview with Klamm as a business deal, a cash transaction. You allow for every possibility; provided you get your price, you are prepared to do anything. If Klamm wants me you'll give me to him, if he wants you to keep me you'll keep me, if he wants you to abandon me you'll abandon me, but if you see any advantage in it you're prepared to put on an act, you'll pretend you love me, you'll try to combat his indifference by emphasising your own insignificance and shame him by reminding him that you took his place, or by telling him the lovers' secrets I've shared with you about him, which I actually did, and asking him to take me back, at your price, of course; and if all else fails, then you will simply beg for the sake of K. and his wife. But then, the landlady finally said, when you realise that you have deluded yourself completely, that your assumptions and hopes, your ideas about Klamm and his relationship with me were mistaken, that's when my life will become hell, because then I really shall be the only thing you possess, the thing you depend on – but at the same time that possession will have proved to be worthless, and you will treat it accordingly because your only feeling for me is that of ownership.'

K. had been listening intently and tight-lipped, the wood he was sitting on had shifted and he had almost slid onto the floor, but he had ignored it; it was only now that he stood up, sat down on the rostrum, took Frieda's hand, which she feebly attempted to withdraw, and said: 'In what you have been saying, I couldn't always tell which were your opinions and which were the landlady's.' 'They were only hers,' said Frieda. 'I listened to everything she said because I admire her, but it was the first time in my life that I totally refused to agree with her. Everything she said seemed so shameful, such a misunderstanding of how things were between the two of us. It all seemed to me the opposite of the truth. I thought of that dismal morning after our first night together, how you knelt beside me with a look as if you thought everything was lost, and how it turned out that however hard I tried I was holding you back rather than helping you. Because of me you made an enemy of the landlady, a powerful enemy you still underestimate; you had me to look after, and for my sake you had to fight for your job, you were at odds with the mayor, you had to kowtow to the schoolteacher, you had to put up with the assistants, but what was worst of all, because of me you had perhaps fallen foul of Klamm. Your persistent efforts to reach Klamm were only a futile attempt to placate him in some way. And I told myself that the landlady, who certainly knows far more about everything than I do, with all her advice was only trying to save me from blaming myself too badly. Her efforts were well-meant, but quite unnecessary. My love for you would have helped me to survive it all, she would have helped you, too, in the end, if not here in the village, then somewhere else; she had already shown what she could do by protecting you from Barnabas' family.'

'So that is what you thought at the time,' said K., 'and how has it changed since then?' 'I don't know,' said Frieda, looking at K.'s hand, which was holding hers. 'Perhaps nothing has changed; when you are so close to me and ask so calmly, then I think nothing has changed. But in fact . . .' She withdrew her hand, sat upright in front of him and wept without hiding her face. She looked straight at him, the tears streaming down her cheeks, as if she had nothing to hide because she was not weeping for herself, but over K.'s betrayal, and it was right that he should share the misery of her plight – 'in fact everything has changed since I heard what you said to Hans. You began so innocently, asking him about his family, about this and that, it reminded me of when you came into the bar, so friendly and forthcoming and so eager to catch my eye, like a child. It was no different from then, and I only wished the landlady had been there to hear you and see if she would still stick to her opinion. But then all at once, I don't know how it happened, I realised why you were talking to the boy so sympathetically; you were winning his trust, which was not easy to do, so that you could get what you were aiming for, and I gradually realised that it was his mother. You talked as if you were concerned about her, and it was perfectly clear that you were only interested in your own affairs. You deceived that woman even before you won her over. What you said not only brought back my past, it also showed me my future, it was as if the landlady were sitting next to me and explaining everything, as if I were doing my utmost to resist her, but realising quite clearly how futile my efforts were; and yet I was not actually the one being deceived any more, in fact I hadn't been deceived at all – it was the woman you hadn't met. And then, when I pulled myself together and asked Hans what he wanted to be when he grew up and he said he wanted to be like you, which meant he was so completely on your side, I thought: was there so much difference between him, this poor lad you were now taking advantage of and me, then, in the bar?'

'Everything you say,' said K., who had recovered his composure as he came to terms with Frieda's accusations, 'is correct in a certain sense; it is not untrue, it's simply a hostile point of view. These are the landlady's thoughts, the thoughts of my enemy even if you think they are your own, and I draw comfort from that. But they are instructive; one can still learn a lot from the landlady. She had not told me this herself, though otherwise she has not spared my feelings; obviously she has put this weapon in your hands, hoping that you would use it at a particularly difficult or critical time for me. If I am taking advantage of you, then so is she. But Frieda, think of this: even if everything were as the landlady says it is, it would only be really bad in the event that you didn't love me. In that case – well, in that case it would be true that I won you with calculated cunning so that I could profit from it. Perhaps it even was part of my plan to engage your sympathy when I appeared arm in arm with Olga, and the landlady simply forgot to add that to the list of all my faults. But if things are not as bad as that and if you weren't snatched away by a scheming predator, if you were attracted to me just as I was attracted to you, and we came together spontaneously, then, tell me, Frieda, what then? In that case I am acting for myself as well as for you, there is no difference here, and only a hostile woman can separate us. That holds for everything, even with regard to Hans. Besides, you show far too much goodness of heart in your view of the conversation with Hans, for even if my plans are not identical to his, the differences are not so great that they actually conflict, and what's more, our disagreement did not escape him; if you believe it did, you would be seriously underrating that canny young man, and even if it did all pass over his head, no one will suffer for it, I hope.'

'It's so difficult to know what to think, K.,' said Frieda, sighing. 'I certainly don't doubt you, and if anything of the sort has rubbed off on me from the landlady, I shall be only too glad to rid myself of it and beg your forgiveness on my knees as I actually do all the time, even though I say such wicked things. But it's still true that you keep a lot secret from me; you come and go, I don't know where you've been or where you're going. When Hans knocked on the door, you called out Barnabas' name. If you had only spoken to me as lovingly as you did, I don't know why, when you called out that name I detest. If you don't trust me, how can I help not trusting you – and then I have to depend entirely on the landlady, and you behaviour seems to prove her right. Not in everything; I'm not trying to claim it proves she's right in everything – after all, it was for my sake you got rid of the assistants, wasn't it? Oh, if only you knew how I long to find some trace of kindness towards me in everything you do and say, however much it tortures me.'

'First of all, Frieda,' said K., 'I don't conceal the least thing from you. Look how the landlady hates me and how hard she tries to tear you away from me and what despicable means she uses – and how you give in to her, Frieda, how you give in to her! Tell me, how do I conceal anything from you? You know I want to reach Klamm, you also know you can't help me to reach him, so I have to do it on my own initiative, and you can see that so far I haven't succeeded. Am I now supposed to recite all the useless attempts I've made, which I've already found quite humiliating enough as it is, and humiliate myself all over again? Am I to boast, perhaps, that I waited a whole afternoon in the freezing cold by the door of Klamm's sleigh? Then I come hurrying back to you, glad not to have to think about these things any more, only to have you reproach me about it like this. What of Barnabas? It's quite true I'm expecting him. He is Klamm's messenger; I didn't appoint him.' 'Barnabas again,' cried Frieda, 'I can't believe he will bring good news.' 'You may be right,' said K., 'but he is the only messenger they send me.' 'So much the worse,' said Frieda. 'All the more reason why you should beware of him.' 'Unfortunately he hasn't given me any cause for that so far,' said K. with a smile. 'He only comes rarely and what he brings is of no significance; it's only because it comes directly from Klamm that it has any value.' 'But you see,' said Frieda, 'you're not even looking for Klamm any more, perhaps that's what worries me most; it was bad enough that you were always trying to use me to reach Klamm, but it's even worse now that you seem to have stopped trying to. That is something even the landlady couldn't foresee. According to her, my happiness, my precarious but very real happiness, would end the day you finally saw that your hopes about Klamm were futile. Now you're not even waiting that long, a little boy suddenly arrives and you start fighting with him over his mother as if you were fighting for your life.' 'You have understood my conversation with Hans quite correctly,' said K., 'that's how it really was. But have you blotted out your previous life so completely (except for the landlady, of course, there was no way you could blot her out) that you have forgotten that you have to fight to get on, especially when you start at the bottom? That you have to seize every chance that holds out any hope? And this woman is from the Castle, she told me so herself when I strayed into Lasemann's house that first day. What could be more obvious than to ask her for advice, or even for help? The landlady knows all about every obstacle preventing me from reaching Klamm, while this woman probably knows the way to reach him, after all she came down that way herself.'

'The way to Klamm?' asked Frieda. 'Yes, of course, to Klamm, where else?' replied K. Then he jumped up, saying: 'Now it's high time to fetch the teacher's lunch.' Urgently, far more so than the situation warranted, Frieda pleaded with him to stay, as if staying with her were the only way to confirm all the reassurances he had given her. But K. reminded her of the teacher, pointing to the door as if it might burst open at any moment with a thunderous crash, and promised to return at once, telling her she need not even light the stove, he would see to it himself. In the end Frieda assented without a word. As K. trudged through the snow outside – the path should have been cleared by now, it was strange how slowly work was progressing – he saw one of the assistants clinging to the railings, exhausted. Only one of them, though – where was the other? Had K. weakened the stamina of one of them, at least? The remaining one was certainly making every effort to hold out, he could tell that when, revitalised at the sight of K., he immediately began to reach out and roll his eyes pleadingly. 'His perseverance is remarkable,' K. said to himself, and could not help adding 'he'll freeze to the railings.' But the only outward sign K. had for the assistant was to threaten him with a shake of his fist, which ruled out any reconciliation, in fact the assistant fearfully retreated some way away. Just then Frieda opened a window as K. had instructed to air the room before lighting the stove. At once the assistant turned away from K. and, as if drawn irresistibly, crept towards the window. Frieda, her face expressing a conflict between kindness to the assistant and a helpless plea to K., waved her hand feebly out of the window; it was not even clear whether it was meant as a rebuff or a greeting, and it did not deter the assistant from approaching. At this, Frieda hurriedly shut the outer window, but remained standing behind it, her hand on the latch and her head on one side, with wide eyes and a fixed smile. Was she aware that this attracted the assistant more than it deterred him? But K. did not look back again; he preferred to get on as quickly as possible and be back soon.

15

At Amalia's

At last – it was already dark, late in the afternoon – K. had cleared the garden path, piling the snow high on either side and packing it down, and now his work was finished for the day. He stood at the garden gate, the only person for a long way round. He had chased off the assistant hours ago, running after him for some time, then the assistant had hidden himself somewhere among the gardens and cottages and was not to be found, nor had he reappeared since. Frieda was at the school, either doing the laundry or perhaps still washing Gisa's cat. It had been a sign of great trust on Gisa's part to allow Frieda to do this; to be sure, it was unsavoury work, beyond the call of duty, which K. would not have agreed to if it had not been highly advisable after their various lapses to take every opportunity to oblige the schoolmistress. She had looked on approvingly as K. brought the small baby bath down from the attic, then as they heated the water and finally lowered the cat carefully into the bath. Then Gisa had even handed the cat entirely over to Frieda's care, because Schwarzer, K.'s acquaintance from the first evening, had arrived. He had greeted K. with a mixture of reserve arising from their encounter that evening and the utter contempt due to a school caretaker, and had then followed Gisa into the classroom. The two of them were still in there.

K. had been told at the Brückenhof that Schwarzer, although he was in fact the son of one of the castle wardens, had been living in the village for some time because he was in love with Gisa. Through his contacts he had managed to get himself appointed by the council as an auxiliary teacher; but he performed his duties mainly by scarcely ever missing one of Gisa's classes, sitting either at a school bench among the children or, preferably, on the rostrum at Gisa's feet. This no longer bothered anyone – the children had long since got used to him, and perhaps it made things easier that Schwarzer neither liked nor had any understanding of children; he hardly ever spoke to them, had only taken the gym classes over from Gisa and otherwise was content to be close to her, to breathe the same air and feel her warmth. His greatest pleasure was to sit beside her and correct exercise books with her, and that is what they were doing today. Schwarzer had brought a great pile of exercise books – the teacher always gave him his books too – and while it was still light K. had seen the two of them working at a table by the window, heads together, motionless; now all that could be seen there was two flickering candles. It was a solemn, silent love that bound them, but it was Gisa who set the tone. Though her awkward temperament led her occasionally to lose control and behave unreasonably, she would never have tolerated such excesses from anyone else, and so the restless Schwarzer also had to conform, had to walk slowly, speak slowly, say little; but he was amply rewarded for all this, it was clear, simply by Gisa's silent presence.

For all that, perhaps Gisa did not love him at all, at least her round grey eyes, which never once blinked, their pupils seeming instead to revolve, gave no hint of it. All she showed was that she put up with Schwarzer without protest, and certainly showed no appreciation of the honour of being loved by a son of one of the Castle wardens; she carried her ample and voluptuous figure with unvarying poise whether Schwarzer's eyes were on her or not. He, however, paid her the tribute of staying permanently in the village; any messengers from his father, who often came to fetch him, were dismissed with such indignation as if even the brief recollection they aroused in him of the Castle and of his filial duty were an unpleasant and irreparable disruption of his happiness. Yet he had plenty of free time, for Gisa generally only let him see her during lessons and while they corrected exercise books; she did this not in a calculated way but because she liked most to relax on her own, and was probably happiest when she could stretch out on the sofa at home in complete freedom with her cat beside her, who could not disturb her because he could scarcely move any more. And so Schwarzer spent most of the day kicking his heels, but even this suited him because he could always go to the Löwengasse where Gisa lived, as he often did, climb up to her little room in the attic and listen at her door, which was always locked, though he then had to go away again once he had made sure that, as always, complete and mysterious silence reigned. But even he sometimes reacted to the effects of this way of life, though never in the presence of Gisa, with absurd momentary outbursts of reawakened official arrogance, in spite of the fact that it was quite inappropriate to his current position; such outbursts, however, usually had unfortunate consequences, as K. had of course seen.

The astonishing thing was that, at least at the Brückenhof, people still spoke of Schwarzer with a degree of respect, even when his behaviour was so absurd as not to merit it, and Gisa, too, was included in this respect. But it was still not right that as an auxiliary teacher Schwarzer believed he was so vastly superior to K. Such superiority was unwarranted, for a school caretaker is a very important person for the teaching staff, especially for a teacher like Schwarzer, and should be respected as such; even if a sense of status inevitably involved a certain hauteur, this must at least be balanced accordingly if it is not to become intolerable. K. intended to bear this in mind; moreover, Schwarzer was still at fault vis-à-vis K. from that first evening, and his fault had not been diminished when the events of the following days had only borne out the reception Schwarzer had given him, for it should not be forgotten that this reception might well have set the course for all that followed. Thanks to Schwarzer the full attention of the authorities had been quite unreasonably drawn to K. from the very start, at a time when he was a complete stranger in the village, when he knew no one, had nowhere to stay, was exhausted from his journey, quite helpless as he lay there on his straw mattress, vulnerable to any kind of action from the authorities. Just one night later everything might have turned out differently, quietly, scarcely noticed. At any rate, no one would have known anything about him, no one would have been suspicious of him, at least they would not have hesitated to take him on for a day as a travelling journeyman, they would have seen how useful and reliable he was, word would have spread through the neighbourhood, he would no doubt soon have found a place somewhere as a hired hand. Of course, he would not have escaped the notice of the authorities. But there was all the difference in the world on the one hand between the head office, or whoever had been at the end of the telephone, being roused on his account in the middle of the night and asked for an immediate decision, with apparent deference but with tiresome persistence, moreover by Schwarzer, who was no doubt disliked up there, and on the other hand K.'s calling on the mayor during office hours and introducing himself in the proper way as a visiting journeyman who had already found somewhere to stay in the village and who would probably be moving on the next day unless, as seemed very unlikely, he found some work here – though of course it would only be for a few days, as he had no intention of staying very long.

That, or something like it, is what would have happened but for Schwarzer. The authorities would have dealt with the matter further, but discreetly and through official channels without being pestered by an impatient client, which was probably what they disliked most. Of course K. was not to blame for all this, it was Schwarzer's fault; but Schwarzer was the son of a Castle warden and to all appearances had acted correctly, so they could only blame K. And what was the absurd cause of all this? Perhaps Gisa had been in a bad mood that day, so that Schwarzer had spent a sleepless night roaming about and had then made K. pay for his ordeal. However, it could also be argued that K. owed a great deal to Schwarzer's behaviour; it was only as a result of it that K. had achieved what he could never have achieved, would never have dared to achieve, on his own, something that the authorities for their part would scarcely ever have allowed – that is, he had from the very beginning, without any subterfuge, confronted the authorities, as far as it was at all possible, face to face. But that was a dubious advantage; although it saved K. a great deal of evasion and secretiveness, it also rendered him almost defenceless, at all events it put him at a disadvantage in his struggle, and might have driven him to despair of it had he not been forced to remind himself that the discrepancy between the power of the authorities and his own was so vast that all the deception and wiles he might be capable of could not have substantially reduced it in his favour; far from it, they would make no noticeable difference in relative terms.

But this was just a notion with which K. consoled himself. Schwarzer still owed him something; if he had done him a bad turn then, perhaps he could help him now. K. was going to need help at the simplest level with his very first moves; and Barnabas seemed to have let him down again. For Frieda's sake K. had put off going to make enquiries at Barnabas' house; to avoid having to receive him in Frieda's presence K. had worked outside, and even when he had finished his work he had stayed out here waiting for Barnabas, but Barnabas did not come. Now he had no alternative but to go and see Barnabas' sisters, just for a few moments; he only wanted to go to the door and ask, he would soon be back. So he stuck the shovel into the snow and ran.

He arrived at the house out of breath, knocked briefly, flung the door open, and without looking to see who was inside, asked: 'Is Barnabas not back yet?' It was only then that he noticed Olga was not there. The old couple were once again sitting dozing at the far table; they had not yet realised what was going on at the door and only slowly turned their heads to see. Then K. saw that Amalia was lying covered in blankets on the bench by the stove; she had sat up in alarm at K.'s appearance and was rubbing her forehead to regain her composure. If Olga had been there, she would have replied at once and K. could have gone away again, but as it was he was obliged at least to take a few steps towards Amalia and offer her his hand, which she pressed in silence, and ask her to stop her startled parents wandering about, which she did with a few words. K. was told that Olga was chopping wood in the yard; Amalia herself – she did not explain why – was exhausted and had had to lie down a short while before; Barnabas was not there yet, but he should be back very soon, for he never spent the night at the Castle.

K. thanked her for the information; he could go now, but Amalia asked if he was going to wait for Olga, to which he replied that unfortunately he did not have time. Then Amalia asked him whether he had already spoken to Olga that day; surprised, K. said that he had not, and asked whether there was anything in particular Olga wanted to tell him. Amalia grimaced as if she were mildly annoyed, nodded to K. without a word, clearly by way of saying goodbye, and lay down again. From there she scrutinised him as if surprised he was still there. The look she gave him was cool, clear, as steady as ever, not directed straight at him, but – this was what unsettled him – slightly, almost imperceptibly but quite definitely to one side; this seemed due not to weakness or embarrassment or a lack of frankness, but to a permanent overwhelming desire to be alone, which she herself perhaps only became aware of in this way. K. seemed to remember that this look had caught his attention that very first evening, indeed that the whole hostile impression this family had made on him from the start probably went back to that look, which was not in itself hostile, but proud and honest in its reticence. 'You are always so sad, Amalia,' said K. 'Is something troubling you? Can you not say what it is? I've never met a country girl like you before. It only really occurred to me today, just now. Do you come from the village? Were you born here?' Amalia answered yes, as if K. had only asked her the last question, then she said: 'So you are going to wait for Olga, are you?' 'I don't know why you always ask the same thing,' said K. 'I can't stay any longer, because my fiancée is waiting for me at home.' Amalia sat up, leaning on her elbow; she knew nothing of any fiancée. K. mentioned Frieda's name, but Amalia did not know her. She asked whether Olga knew of his engagement; K. thought so, after all Olga had seen him with Frieda, and news like that spread through the village quickly. But Amalia assured him that Olga did not know and that it would make her very unhappy, because she seemed to be in love with K. She had not spoken about it openly, for she was very reserved, but then love betrayed itself involuntarily. K. said he was convinced Amalia was mistaken. Amalia smiled, and her smile, sad as it was, lit up her sullen, scowling face, made her silence eloquent, her remoteness confiding; it was the revelation of a secret, the surrender of a hitherto guarded possession which, though it might be reclaimed, could never be retrieved entirely. Amalia said she certainly was not mistaken, indeed she knew even more; she knew that K. was also fond of Olga, and that while the pretext for his visits was some kind of message for Barnabas, he really came to see Olga. But now that she knew all about it, Amalia continued, he need not stand on ceremony any more and could come more often.

K. shook his head and reminded her that he was engaged. Amalia seemed to pay little attention to this fact, what influenced her was her immediate impression of K., who was standing there in front of her alone; she only asked when he had got to know this girl, after all he had only been in the village a few days. K. told her about the evening at the Herrenhof, to which Amalia only replied briefly that she had been very much against the idea of taking him there. She called on Olga, who had just come in with an armful of wood, to bear her out; Olga looked fresh, her face smarting from the cold air, lively and robust, seemingly transformed by her exertions from the girl who had stood stolidly in the room on the previous occasion. She threw down the wood, greeted K. without reserve and immediately asked after Frieda. K. gave Amalia a meaningful look, but she did not seem to think she had been contradicted. Somewhat irritated by this, K. told them about Frieda in more detail than he would otherwise have done; he described the difficult conditions under which she struggled to keep house somehow at the school, and in his haste – he was keen to get back soon – so far forgot himself that by way of saying goodbye he invited the two sisters to pay him a visit. But then he stopped in alarm, whereupon Amalia, not giving him time to say another word, at once declared that she accepted the invitation, which Olga was then also obliged to do. But K., still urgently aware of the need to leave at once and feeling uneasy under Amalia's gaze, hastened to admit quite candidly that he had issued the invitation without thinking and prompted only by his own feelings, but that he was afraid he could not honour it because of the great animosity, which was quite incomprehensible to him, between Frieda and Barnabas' family. 'There is no animosity,' said Amalia, getting up from the bench and throwing off her blanket. 'It's nothing very much, it's just passing on what most people think. Off you go now, back to your fiancée, I can see you're in a hurry. Don't be afraid that we will come, I meant it as a joke from the start, just out of mischief. But you can come to see us often, there's nothing to prevent you, you can always use Barnabas' messages as an excuse. I'll make it even easier for you by saying that even if he has brought a message for you from the Castle, Barnabas can't go all the way to the school to give it to you. The poor boy can't run about so much, the job is wearing him out; you'll have to come here and get the message yourself.'

K. had never heard Amalia put together so many words before; her speech had changed, too, it had a certain dignity that was felt not only by K., but clearly also by Olga, even though she was quite used to hearing her sister. Olga stood a little to one side, her hands folded together in her lap, having resumed her usual posture, slightly stooping with her legs apart; she kept her eyes on Amalia, while Amalia kept hers on K. 'You are mistaken,' said K., 'you are quite mistaken if you think I am not serious about waiting for Barnabas; what I want most of all, in fact the only thing I want, is to sort out my affairs with the authorities. And Barnabas is going to help me.

I have great hopes of him. It is true that he let me down once, but that was more my fault than his, it happened in the confusion of my first few hours here, I thought at the time I could get everything settled in the course of a short evening stroll, and I blamed him when it turned out that I could not achieve the impossible. It even influenced me in my judgement of your family and of you. That is in the past; I think I understand you better now. You are even' – K. searched for the right word, but failed to find it and settled for a less adequate one – 'you are perhaps more kind-hearted than anyone else in the village I have got to know so far. But now, Amalia, you are confusing me again, if not by belittling your brother's services, then certainly by trivialising the importance they have for me. Perhaps you are not privy to Barnabas' affairs, well and good, in that case I won't labour the point; but if you are – and I rather have that impression – then it's not well and good, because it would mean your brother is deceiving me.' 'Calm yourself,' said Amalia. 'I know nothing about his affairs, nothing could induce me to get involved in them, nothing, not even my concern for you, and I would do a lot for you because, as you say, we are kind-hearted. But my brother's affairs are his own business, I know nothing about them other than what I hear by chance now and again without wanting to. Olga, though, can tell you all about them because he confides in her.' And Amalia turned away, whispered something to her parents, then went into the kitchen; she had not said goodbye to K., as if she knew he would be there for a long time and no goodbye was needed.

16

K. stood there astonished. Olga laughed at the expression on his face and drew him onto the bench by the stove; she seemed genuinely happy that she could now sit here alone with him, but it was a calm happiness quite untroubled by jealousy. And it was just this absence of jealousy and therefore of any kind of strain that did K. good; he was glad to gaze into those blue eyes that were not seductive or dominating, but had a modestly calm and steady look. It was as if the warnings of Frieda and the landlady had made him not more susceptible to everything in this house, but more attentive and more aware. He laughed with Olga when she expressed surprise that he had called Amalia, of all people, kindhearted; Amalia, she said, had many qualities, but she was not actually kind-hearted. K. explained that the compliment had of course been meant for Olga, but Amalia was so dominating that she not only took everything that was said in her presence to apply to her, but also that one willingly let her do so. 'That is true,' said Olga, becoming more serious, 'truer than you think. Amalia is younger than I am, younger than Barnabas, too, but she's the one who makes decisions in the family, for better or for worse.'

K. thought she was exaggerating; hadn't Amalia just said, for example, that she didn't bother about her brother's affairs, whereas Olga knew all about them? 'How shall I explain?' said Olga. 'Amalia doesn't bother about either Barnabas or me, she doesn't actually concern herself with anyone except our parents. She looks after them day and night, she's just asked them again what they would like to eat and gone to the kitchen to cook for them, she's forced herself to get up for their sake, because she has been unwell since midday and has been lying here on the bench. But although she doesn't bother about us we depend on her as if she were the oldest, and if she were to give us advice about our affairs we would certainly follow it, but she doesn't, we're strangers to her. You've learned a lot about people, you come from other parts – don't you find her exceptionally clever too?' 'She strikes me as exceptionally unhappy,' said K., 'but if you both respect her so much, then why does Barnabas run these errands as a messenger, for instance, when Amalia disapproves of it, perhaps even despises him for it?' 'If he knew what else to do he would give up carrying messages straight away, he gets no satisfaction from it.' 'Hasn't he trained as a shoemaker?' asked K. 'Of course,' said Olga, 'he does casual work for Brunswick, he could work all day and all night if he wanted to, and earn good money.' 'Well then,' said K., 'he could do that instead of working as a messenger.' 'Instead of it?' asked Olga, astonished. 'Do you think he took it on for the money, then?' 'Perhaps,' said K., 'but you told me he wasn't happy with it.' 'He isn't happy with it, for several reasons,' said Olga, 'but it's a job at the Castle, well, it is in a sort of way, at least that's what we are led to believe.' 'What?' said K., 'even you have your doubts about that?' 'Well, not really,' said Olga. 'Barnabas goes to the offices, he mixes with the Castle servants as if he were one of them, he even sees individual officials from a distance, he gets to deliver relatively important letters and is even entrusted with messages by word of mouth; that's really a great deal, and we can be proud how much he's achieved at such a young age.' 'Does he have his own uniform as well?' asked K. 'You mean his jacket?' said Olga. 'No, Amalia made that for him before he became a messenger. But you've touched on a sore point. Long before now he should have been given, well, not a uniform, they don't have those at the Castle, but an official suit; he's been promised one, but at the Castle they're very slow about things like that, and the worst of it is you never know what the delay means. It might mean that the matter is being dealt with officially, but it can also mean they haven't even begun to deal with it, that they have put Barnabas on probation, for example; but it can turn out to mean that they have already dealt with the matter, that they have withdrawn the promise for some reason or another and Barnabas will never get the suit. You can't find out what's going on, or only long afterwards. There's a saying round here, perhaps you've heard it: official decisions are as shy as young girls.'

'That's well put,' said K., who took it even more seriously than Olga, 'very well put. Their decisions may also have other things in common with young girls.' 'Perhaps,' said Olga, 'though of course I don't quite know what you mean. Perhaps you mean it as a compliment. As for the official suit, that's one of Barnabas' problems, and since we share our problems, it's mine too. Why hasn't he been given an official suit? we ask ourselves in vain. But then the whole thing is far from simple. For instance, the officials seem to have no kind of official dress; as far as we know down here, and from what Barnabas tells us, the officials go round in ordinary clothes, very fine clothes, too. You've seen Klamm for yourself. Now of course, Barnabas is not an official, not even a low-ranking official, and has no ambition to be one. But according to Barnabas even the higher servants, whom we certainly never get to see here in the village, do not have official suits. At first you might think that is reassuring, but it's misleading, for is Barnabas one of the higher servants? No, however fond of him we may be, we can't say he is; the very fact that he comes to the village, and even lives here, proves he isn't. The higher servants are even more aloof than the officials, perhaps rightly so, perhaps they are even higher than some of the officials; there's some evidence for this – they work less, and according to Barnabas it's a wonderful sight to see these specially selected tall, well-built men walking slowly along the corridors. Barnabas always keeps his distance from them. There's no question about it, Barnabas is not one of the higher servants. So he might be a low-ranking servant; but they do have official suits, at least whenever they come down to the village. It's not actually a uniform, they vary a great deal, but they're still immediately recognisable as Castle servants by their clothes – you saw some of them at the Herrenhof. The most striking thing about their clothes is that they are usually close-fitting – a peasant or a tradesman couldn't wear clothes like that. Well, Barnabas doesn't have clothes like that, which is not just embarrassing or humiliating, we could put up with that; but especially when we're in low spirits – and we are sometimes, Barnabas and I, though not very often – it gives us doubts about everything. Is it really Castle work that he is doing, we ask; he goes to the offices, certainly, but are the offices actually part of the Castle? And even if there are offices that are part of the Castle, are those the offices he is allowed into? He's admitted into some offices, but only some of them, then there are barriers, and behind these are more offices. He's not actually forbidden to go any further, but he can't go any further once he's seen his superiors and they have dealt with him and sent him away. What's more, you're watched all the time up there, at least that's what we believe. And even if he did go further on, what good would it do him if he had no official business there; he would just be an intruder. And you mustn't imagine these barriers as a hard and fast divide, Barnabas is always reminding me of that. There are also barriers in the offices he visits, so there are some barriers he goes through, and they look no different from the ones he has not yet gone through, and so it can't be assumed that the offices behind these barriers are any different from the ones Barnabas has been in. But when we're feeling low, that's what we think. And then we start to have more doubts, we can't help it. Barnabas talks to officials, and he is given messages. But what sort of officials, and what messages? At the moment, he says, he is assigned to Klamm and gets his instructions from him personally. Well, that would mean a lot, even higher servants don't get as far as that, it would be almost too much, that's the worrying thing. Just imagine – being directly assigned to Klamm, speaking to him face to face. But is it really true? Well, yes, it is; but then why does Barnabas doubt that the official who is referred to up there as Klamm really is Klamm?'

'Olga,' said K., 'surely you're joking; how can there be any doubt about what Klamm looks like? It's well known what he looks like, I've seen him myself.' 'Not at all, K.,' said Olga, 'I'm not joking, I'm very seriously concerned. And I'm not telling you this, either, to relieve my feelings and depress you, but because you asked about Barnabas, because Amalia told me to tell you, and because I think it will help if you know more about it. I'm doing it for Barnabas, too, so that you don't expect too much of him, so that he doesn't disappoint you and then suffer himself because you're disappointed. He's very sensitive, for instance he didn't sleep last night because you weren't pleased with him, it seems you said it was your misfortune that you "only had a servant" like him. He couldn't sleep after you said that. I don't suppose you noticed how upset he was – Castle messengers have to keep themselves well under control. But it's not easy for him, not even with you. I'm sure from your point of view you don't ask too much of him; you came with certain ideas about a messenger's job and based your demands on them. But at the Castle they have other ideas about it which are not compatible with yours, even if Barnabas were to sacrifice himself completely to his work, which I'm afraid he sometimes seems ready to do. We would have to accept that, we couldn't object; but if only we knew whether it really is a messenger's job he's doing. Of course, he's not allowed to express any doubts to you on the subject, for him that would undermine his own existence and be a gross violation of laws he still thinks apply to him; he doesn't even speak freely to me, I have to kiss him and wheedle his doubts out of him, and even he can't bring himself to admit his doubts are real. He has something of Amalia in him. And I'm sure he doesn't tell me everything, even though I'm the only one he confides in. But sometimes we talk about Klamm. I've never seen Klamm, Frieda doesn't like me very much, as you know, and she would never have let me have a look at him; but of course they know very well what he looks like in the village, some people have seen him, they've all heard of him, and from these glimpses and rumours, as well as some deliberately misleading reports, a picture of Klamm has emerged that is probably generally accurate. But only generally; otherwise it varies, and perhaps it doesn't even vary as much as Klamm's actual appearance. He is supposed to look quite different when he arrives in the village and when he leaves, different before and after he's been drinking beer, different when he's awake and when he's asleep, different when he's alone and when he's talking to someone – and then, as you can imagine, almost completely different up at the Castle. And even when he's in the village there are reports of quite substantial differences, differences in his height, his shape, his weight, his beard. Fortunately, there's one thing the descriptions agree about, his clothes – he's always dressed the same: in a black frock coat with long tails. Of course, all these differences are due to magic, they are quite understandable because they depend on the present mood, the level of excitement, the countless degrees of hope or despair on the part of the observer, who is in any case only able to catch a momentary glimpse of Klamm. I'm telling you all this just as Barnabas has often explained it to me, and on the whole it's reassuring as long as one's not directly or personally involved. It doesn't affect me, but for Barnabas it's a matter of vital importance whether it's really Klamm he is talking to or not.'

'It's just as important for me too,' said K., and they moved even closer to each other on the bench. Though disturbed by all this discouraging information from Olga, he derived some comfort from it, mainly from the fact that here were people who, so it appeared at least, were in much the same situation as he was, so that he could ally himself with them and see eye to eye with them in many things, not just in some as he could with Frieda. It was true that he was gradually losing any hope of success with Barnabas' message, but the worse things went for Barnabas up there, the closer he felt to him down here; K. would never have expected to encounter in the village itself such frustrated hopes as those of Barnabas and his sister. Of course there was much more to find out, and things could still turn out to be quite the reverse in the end; he should not just let himself be beguiled by Olga's undoubted innocence and jump to the conclusion that Barnabas was sincere too.

'Barnabas,' continued Olga, 'knows all about the reports of Klamm's appearance; he has collected and compared a lot of them, perhaps too many. Once he himself saw Klamm, or thought he did, through a carriage window in the village, so he was well enough prepared to recognise him, and yet – how can you explain this? – when he went into an office in the Castle and one of several officials was pointed out to him and he was told it was Klamm, he didn't recognise him, and for a long time couldn't get used to the idea that it was Klamm. But if you ask Barnabas how that man differed from the usual picture we have of Klamm, he can't answer you, or rather he does answer and describes the official he saw at the Castle – but this description fits exactly with the description of Klamm we are familiar with. "Well then, Barnabas," I tell him, "why do you torture yourself with these doubts?" Then he gets visibly upset and starts listing the distinctive details of the official in the Castle, but he seems to be inventing them rather than describing him, and besides they are such minor details – a certain way of nodding his head, for instance, or even his unbuttoned waistcoat – that you can't possibly take them seriously.

'Far more important, it seems to me, is the way Klamm treats Barnabas. He has often described it to me, even drawn it. Usually he is admitted into a large room, but it's not Klamm's office, it's nobody's office in particular. This room is divided in two by a counter running from wall to wall; one section is so narrow that two people can only just get past one another, that's the space for the officials, and the other section is wider, which is for clients, spectators, servants and messengers. There are large books lying open on the counter one beside the other, and at most of them officials are standing reading. But they don't always stay at the same book, they change places, and what surprises Barnabas is that they have to squeeze past one another when they change places because the space is so narrow. Right in front of the counter there are low tables where the clerks sit and take dictation from the officials as required. Barnabas is always amazed how this is done. No actual command is given by the official and he doesn't dictate out loud, you hardly notice that he's dictating; he seems to be reading as he was before, except that now he whispers while he reads and the clerk listens. Often the official dictates so quietly that the clerk can't hear from where he's sitting, so he has to keep jumping up to catch the words, sit down quickly and write it down, then jump up again, and so on. Isn't that extraordinary! It's difficult to believe. Of course Barnabas has plenty of time to observe all this, because he has to stand there for hours, for days sometimes, before Klamm takes any notice of him. And even when Klamm looks at him and Barnabas jumps to attention, nothing has been decided, because Klamm might turn back to his book and forget all about him, that often happens. What sort of messenger service is that, if it's so unimportant? I get depressed when Barnabas tells me in the morning that he's going to the Castle. It's probably a quite futile journey, probably a whole day wasted, hopes raised for nothing. What's the point of it all? And here there's a pile of shoes to be mended, no one does it and Brunswick is getting impatient.'

'Yes, well,' said K., 'Barnabas has to wait a long time before he's given a message. That's understandable because there seems to be a surplus of staff, not all of them can be given something to do every day; you can't complain about that, it probably affects everyone. But in the end, surely, Barnabas is given messages; he's already brought me two letters.' 'It may be,' said Olga, 'that it's not right to complain, especially for me, because I only hear about all this, and being a girl I don't understand it as well as Barnabas, and there's also a lot he doesn't tell me. But let me tell you about these letters, the ones to you, for instance. Barnabas doesn't get these letters directly from Klamm, but from the clerk. Some day or other, at some time or other – that's why his job is so very tiring, however easy it may seem, because Barnabas has to pay attention all the time – the clerk remembers him and beckons him over. Klamm doesn't seem to have told him to, he just goes on quietly reading his book. Sometimes, though, when Barnabas comes over he is polishing his glasses, but he often does that anyway – he might look at Barnabas, that is, if he can see him at all without his glasses, Barnabas doesn't think he can – and when he does this his eyes are almost shut, he seems to be asleep and polishing his glasses in a dream. Meanwhile the clerk looks out a letter to you among all the files and correspondence he's got under the table, so it's not a letter he's just written, from the state of the envelope it looks more like a very old letter that's been lying there for a long time. But if it's an old letter, why did they make Barnabas wait so long? And you as well, I suppose? And then the letter too, because it's probably out of date by now. And that gives Barnabas a bad reputation as a slow messenger. It's all right for the clerk, he just gives Barnabas the letter and says: "For K. from Klamm," and Barnabas is dismissed. Sometimes he comes home out of breath with the letter he's finally got out of them tucked under his shirt next to his skin, and then we sit down on this bench as we are now, and he tells me about it, and we go over everything in detail and weigh up what he has achieved, and in the end we decide it was very little and even that is not worth very much, so Barnabas puts the letter away and doesn't feel like delivering it; but he doesn't feel like going to bed either, so he gets out the shoes and spends all night working at the cobbler's bench. That's how it is, K., those are my secrets, and now I don't suppose you're surprised that Amalia doesn't want to know about them.'

'And what about the letter?' asked K. 'The letter?' said Olga. 'Well, after a while, when I've pestered Barnabas enough, it might be days or even weeks later, he does take the letter and delivers it. In these practical matters he is very dependent on me, you see, because I've got over the initial impression of his story, I can pull myself together, which he isn't capable of doing, probably because he knows more than I do. So I can keep asking him things like: "What do you really want then, Barnabas? What sort of career, what sort of goal in life do you dream about? Do you want to get so far, perhaps, that you have to go away and leave us, leave me, altogether? Is that what you want? Isn't that what I have to believe, because it's the only explanation why you're so dreadfully dissatisfied with what you've achieved so far? Look around and see whether any of the neighbours have got so far. Of course, they're not in the same position as we are, and they have no reason to try to rise above their situation, but even without making comparisons it's clear that you are doing very well. There are obstacles, there are problems and disappointments, but that only goes to show what we already know, that nothing is handed to you on a plate, that you have to fight for every smallest thing yourself, which is another reason to be proud of what you've achieved and not get depressed. Besides, aren't you fighting for us too? Doesn't that mean anything to you? Doesn't it give you fresh strength? The fact that I'm happy, almost bursting with pride, to have a brother like that – doesn't that give you confidence? Quite honestly, what disappoints me is not what you have achieved at the Castle, but what I've achieved with you. You are allowed into the Castle, you visit the offices the whole time, you spend whole days in the same room as Klamm, you're an officially recognised messenger, you have a right to official clothes, you're given important correspondence to deliver, you're all these things and you're allowed to do all these things, and you come back down here and when we should be hugging each other and weeping with joy, you seem to lose all your courage at the sight of me, you have doubts about everything, all you want to do is mend shoes and you leave the letter, which is the guarantee of our future, lying around somewhere." That's how I talk to him, and when I've said it over and over again for days he sighs, picks up the letter, and goes. But I don't suppose that's because of what I've said at all; he just has the urge to go back to the Castle, and he wouldn't dare to go until he had delivered the letter.'

'But everything you tell him is absolutely right,' said K. 'You have summed it up admirably. It's amazing how clearly you think!' 'No,' said Olga, 'you're deceiving yourself, and perhaps I'm deceiving him too. What has he achieved, then? He is allowed into an office, but it doesn't even seem to be an office, more like an anteroom to the offices, perhaps not even that, perhaps it's a room where everyone who is not allowed into the real offices is made to wait. He talks to Klamm, but is it Klamm? A secretary, perhaps, at most, who is a bit like Klamm and does his best to look even more like Klamm and then tries to look important by imitating Klamm's sleepy and dreamy manner. That part of Klamm is easiest to imitate, a lot of people do it, but they're wise enough not to imitate any more of him than that. And a man like Klamm who is so much sought after and so rarely reached can easily take on different guises in people's imagination. For example, Klamm has a village secretary here called Momus. So you know him? Well, he is also very elusive, but I've seen him a few times. A young, well-built gentleman, isn't he? So he probably doesn't look at all like Klamm. And yet you can find people in the village who will swear that Momus is none other than Klamm. That's how people create confusion for themselves. And is it necessarily any different at the Castle? Someone told Barnabas that official was Klamm, and there is in fact a resemblance, but it's a resemblance Barnabas has always doubted. And everything supports his doubt. Do you suppose Klamm has to squash into that public room along with other officials, with a pencil behind his ear? That is highly improbable. Barnabas sometimes says in his naïve way – but this shows he is in a confiding mood – "That official looks very much like Klamm; if he were sitting at his own desk in his own office with his name on the door, I wouldn't have any doubts then." That is naïve, but it's sensible, too. Of course, it would be much more sensible if Barnabas, when he was up there, were to ask some of the people there and then what the truth of the matter was; after all, according to him there are quite enough people standing around in the room. And even if their answers were not much more reliable than the man who pointed Klamm out to him without being asked, then at least some indication, some points of comparison, would emerge from that number of people. That's not my idea, it's Barnabas', but he won't dare to try it; he doesn't dare to speak to anyone for fear he might lose his job by somehow violating some obscure rule without knowing it. He feels so insecure, and this insecurity, which is really so pathetic, tells me more about his job than any of his accounts. How suspicious and threatening it must all seem to him up there if he doesn't even dare to open his mouth and ask an innocent question. When I think about it, I blame myself for letting Barnabas, who is more foolhardy than cowardly, go into those unfamiliar places on his own, which probably make him shake with fear when he is there.'

'There I think you have touched on the crucial point,' said K. 'That's it – from everything you've told me, I think I see it clearly now. Barnabas is too young for this work. Nothing he says can be taken seriously. Because he is scared to death up there he can't take in what he sees, and if you still make him tell you about it down here, he makes up a confused account. It doesn't surprise me. Awe of the authorities is innate in you here, it's dinned into you all your life in all sorts of ways from all sides, and you yourselves do your best to keep it going. Still, I'm not saying anything against that in principle; if an authority is good, why shouldn't we respect it? It's just that you can't suddenly send an inexperienced young man like Barnabas, who has never been further than the outskirts of the village, to the Castle and then expect him to give a truthful account, interpret every word he says as a revelation and let your own life's happiness depend on your interpretation. Nothing could be more misguided. I admit I was misled by him just like you, I placed my hopes in him and was disappointed, simply on the basis of what he said, in other words on no basis at all.'

Olga said nothing. 'I don't find it easy,' K. continued, 'to have to undermine your confidence in your brother; after all, I can see how much you love him and what high hopes you have of him. But it has to be done, not least for the sake of your love and your hopes. You see, there's always something – I don't know what it is – that prevents you fully realising, not so much what Barnabas has achieved, but what he has been given.

He is allowed into the offices, or if you like, into an anteroom; well, it may only be an anteroom, but there are doors that lead further, barriers you can pass through if you know how. To me, for instance, this anteroom is completely inaccessible. I don't know who Barnabas speaks to when he's there, perhaps that clerk is the lowest of the servants, but even if he is the lowest he can take you to the one just above him, and if he can't take you to him he can at least tell you his name, and if he can't tell you his name then he can still refer you to someone who can. The man who is supposed to be Klamm may not have anything remotely in common with the real Klamm, the similarity may only exist in Barnabas' eyes, who is too agitated to see clearly, he may be the lowest of the officials, he may not even be an official, but he has some job to do at that counter, he's reading something in his great book, he whispers something to the clerk, he thinks of something when he finally catches sight of Barnabas after all that time, and even if none of this is true and if he and everything he does mean nothing at all, someone must have put him there, and put him there for some purpose. What I mean by all this is that something is there, Barnabas is being offered something, at least something, and it's his own fault if all he can get out of it is doubt, fear and hopelessness. And this is still assuming the least favourable situation, which is itself highly improbable, because you see, we have the letters in our hands, and though I don't have much faith in them, I have much more than I have in what Barnabas says. And though they may be worthless ancient letters that were pulled out of a pile of equally worthless letters, at random and with no more intelligence than a canary at a fair when it picks someone or other's fortune out of a pile with its beak – even if that is the case, these letters do at least have some bearing on my work, they are clearly meant for me; even though they may not be meant to be of any use to me, they are, as the mayor and his wife confirmed, in Klamm's own hand, and though, again according to the mayor, their meaning is private and not entirely clear, they are still of great importance.'

'Is that what the mayor said?' asked Olga. 'Yes, that's what he said,' K. replied. 'I will tell Barnabas that,' said Olga quickly, 'it will give him a lot of encouragement.' 'It's not encouragement he needs,' said K., 'encouraging him is the same as telling him he's right, that he only has to carry on as he was doing before, but if he does that he will never achieve anything. You can encourage someone who is blindfolded to peer through the blindfold as much as you like, but he'll never see anything; only when you remove it will he be able to see. Barnabas needs help, not encouragement. Just think: up there is the Castle in all its vast unfathomable complexity – I imagined I had some idea of it before I came here, how naïve I was – there are the authorities, and along comes Barnabas, no one else, just him, pitifully alone; it would be enough reward for him not to have to spend the rest of his life crouching forgotten in some obscure corner of the offices.' 'Don't imagine, K.,' said Olga, 'that we underestimate the difficulty of the job Barnabas has taken on. As you said yourself, we're not lacking in reverence for the authorities.' 'But it's misguided reverence,' said K., 'it's misplaced reverence, that sort of reverence demeans its object. Can you still call it reverence when Barnabas abuses the privilege of being admitted to that room, when he spends his time there doing nothing, or when he comes back down here and suspects or disparages those people who have just been making him shake with fear, or when out of despair or exhaustion he puts off delivering letters and messages that have been entrusted to him? I don't think you can call that reverence. But he's not the only one to blame; I hold you responsible too, Olga, because although you think you respect the authorities you sent Barnabas, young and defenceless as he is, all alone to the Castle, or at least you did not hold him back.'

'You blame me for that,' said Olga, 'but I have always blamed myself, too. But you can't blame me for sending Barnabas to the Castle; I didn't send him there, he went of his own accord, but I dare say I ought to have done everything I could, I should have used persuasion, cunning, or force to hold him back. I should have stopped him, but if that crucial day came round again now, if I felt the distress of Barnabas, the distress of our family as I did then and still do, and if Barnabas with his gentle smile, in full awareness of all the responsibilities and dangers involved, were to say goodbye to me and go, I wouldn't hold him back today either, in spite of all I've learned in the meantime, and I don't believe you could have done anything different in my place. You don't know what distress we are in, that's why you do us all an injustice, but especially Barnabas. We had more hope than we do today, but even then we didn't have much, but we were in great distress, and we still are. Has Frieda not told you anything about us?' 'Only hints,' said K., 'nothing definite, but she gets upset when she just hears your name.' 'Didn't the landlady tell you anything either?' 'No, nothing.' 'And no one else?' 'No one.' 'Of course, how could anyone tell you anything! Everyone knows something about us, either the truth as far as they know it, or at least some rumour they've heard or more often made up, and everyone thinks about us more than necessary, but no one will tell you straight, they can't bring themselves to talk about such things. And they're right not to. It's hard to come out with it, even to you, K., and isn't it possible that you too, when you've heard it, could go away and not want to have any more to do with us, however little it affects you. Then we shall have lost you, just now when, I have to admit it, you mean almost more to me than Barnabas' work at the Castle has up to now. And yet – this dilemma has been tormenting me all this evening – you must be told, otherwise you won't fully understand our situation, you'll go on doing Barnabas an injustice, which would pain me most of all, we would lose the solidarity we need, and you could neither help us nor accept our unofficial help. But there's still another question you must answer: do you want to know about us at all?' 'Why do you ask me that?' said K. 'If I need to know it, I want to know it – but why do you ask?' 'Superstition,' said Olga, 'you'll be drawn into our affairs, and you are innocent, almost as innocent as Barnabas.' 'Tell me, quickly,' said K., 'I'm not afraid. With your woman's fearfulness you're making it worse than it is.'

17
Amalia's Secret

'Judge for yourself,' said Olga; 'although it sounds quite simple, you can't understand at first just how important it is. There is an official at the Castle called Sortini.' 'I've heard of him,' said K., 'he was involved in my appointment.' 'I don't think so,' said Olga, 'Sortini hardly ever appears in public. Are you confusing him with Sordini, spelt with a d?' 'You're right,' said K., 'it was Sordini.' 'I thought so,' said Olga, 'Sordini is well-known, he's one of the most hard-working officials, and he's often mentioned, but Sortini is very retiring and most people have never heard of him. I saw him for the first and last time more than three years ago. It was on the 3rd of July at a fire brigade festival, the Castle was also involved and had paid for a new fire-engine. Sortini, who is supposed to have something to do with the fire service, though perhaps he was only deputising for someone else – the officials stand in for each other, so it's difficult to tell which of them is responsible for what – Sortini took part in the handing-over of the fire-engine; of course there were others there from the Castle as well, officials and servants, and Sortini, as he does, kept himself very much in the background. He is a small, frail, thoughtful-looking gentleman, and what struck everyone who happened to notice him was the way he wrinkled his forehead. All the creases –

and there are a lot of them, though he can't be more than forty – fan out from the bridge of his nose all over his forehead. I've never seen anything like it.

'Well, it was at that festival. Amalia and I had been looking forward to it for weeks, some of our Sunday clothes had been smartened up for the occasion, Amalia in particular was beautifully dressed, her white blouse was gathered at the neck, one row of lace above the other, our mother had lent all her lace for it, I was jealous at the time and cried for half the night before. It was only next morning when the landlady from the Brückenhof came to look us over . . .' 'The landlady from the Brückenhof?' asked K. 'Yes,' said Olga, 'she was a very close friend. Well, she arrived and had to admit that Amalia had done better than me, so to console me she lent me her own necklace of Bohemian garnets. But as we were ready to go out, and Amalia was standing there and we were all admiring her, our father said: "Mark my words, Amalia will find a husband today." Then, I don't know why, I took off that necklace, my pride and joy, and put it round Amalia's neck. I wasn't at all jealous any more; I was just bowing to her triumph, and thought everyone ought to. Perhaps we were surprised that she looked different from usual, because she wasn't really beautiful, but her sullen look, which she has worn ever since, just didn't seem to matter and in spite of ourselves we very nearly did in fact bow down to her. Everyone noticed her, even Lasemann and his wife who came to fetch us.' 'Lasemann?' asked K. 'Yes, Lasemann,' said Olga, 'we were well thought of, you see, and the festival could hardly have started without us, our father was third officer of the fire brigade.' 'Was your father still in such good health?' asked K. 'Our father?' asked Olga, as if she did not quite understand him. 'Three years ago he was still a relatively young man, for instance when there was a fire at the Herrenhof he ran out of the building carrying a heavily-built official, Galater, on his back. I was there myself, there was no danger of fire, it was just some dry wood by a stove that had started to smoulder, but Galater panicked and shouted out of the window for help, the fire brigade arrived, and our father had to carry him out even though the fire was out. Well, Galater can only move very slowly and has to be careful in situations like that. I'm only telling you this because of my father, it was not much more than three years ago, and now look at him sitting there.'

It was only now that K. noticed that Amalia had returned to the room, but she was some way away at her parents' table, feeding her mother who could not move her arthritic arms, while she urged her father to be patient for a little longer, she would come and feed him before long. But this had no effect, for her father was impatient for his soup; he overcame his weakness and attempted to sip it from the spoon, then to drink it straight from the bowl, and grumbled angrily when he managed to do neither. The spoon was empty long before he got it to his mouth, and his mouth never reached the bowl, he kept dipping his drooping moustache into the soup and sprayed it everywhere except into his mouth. 'Have three years done that to him?' asked K., but he felt no compassion for the old couple, and for that whole corner of the table, only revulsion. 'Three years,' said Olga slowly, 'or more accurately, a few hours at a festival. It was held in a field outside the village by a stream, there was a large crowd there when we arrived, a lot of people had come from the neighbouring villages, and we were confused by all the noise. First of all, of course, our father took us to the fire-engine; he laughed with joy when he saw it, a new machine always made him feel happy. He began to touch it and explain it to us, he insisted that everyone should show an interest, if there was anything to inspect underneath the machine we all had to bend down and almost crawl under it, and Barnabas was beaten because he refused to.

'Amalia was the only one who took no notice of it, she stood there upright in her beautiful dress, and no one dared to say anything to her, once or twice I ran over and took her by the arm, but she said nothing. I still can't explain even today why we spent so long looking at the fire-engine, and only noticed Sortini once our father tore himself away; he had obviously been standing behind the machine, leaning on a pump handle. It's true there was a terrible noise at the time, not just like it usually is at a festival; the Castle had also presented the fire brigade with some trumpets, special instruments that only needed the slightest effort to produce the most deafening sound, a child could do it. When you heard it, it was as if the Turkish army had arrived, and you couldn't get used to it, every blast made you jump. And because the trumpets were new, everyone wanted to have a go, and because the festival had been put on for the people they were all allowed to. Some of these trumpeters were round us, perhaps they had noticed Amalia; the noise drove everything out of your head, so if we were supposed to be paying attention to the fireengine as our father insisted, that was all we were capable of doing, and that is why we didn't notice Sortini, whom we had never seen before, for such a very long time. "There's Sortini," Lasemann eventually whispered to our father – I was standing nearby; our father gave a deep bow and made frantic signals to us to do the same. Although he didn't know him, father had always revered Sortini as an expert in everything to do with the fire service, and he had often talked about him at home, so it was a great surprise and a very important moment for us to see him standing there. But Sortini ignored us – there was nothing unusual in that, because most officials keep their distance in public and he was tired, it was only his official duty that kept him down here; it's not the worst officials who find official appearances like that especially irksome. Other officials and servants, now that they were there, were mingling with the crowd, but Sortini stayed by the fire-engine, and anyone who tried to approach him with some request or compliment was rebuffed by his silence. That's why he failed to notice us even after we had noticed him. It was only when we bowed respectfully and when our father had tried to apologise for us that he glanced over and looked at us each in turn, wearily; he seemed to be sighing, because when he'd looked at one of us there was always another one to see until he stopped in front of Amalia – he had to look up at her because she was taller than he was. He started, and jumped over the shaft to get closer to her; we misunderstood this at first, and we all made to approach him, led by our father, but Sortini held up his hand to stop us and waved us away. That was all. We teased Amalia about it a lot, telling her she really had found a husband now, and in our ignorance we were very cheerful all afternoon; but Amalia was quieter than ever. "She must have fallen head over heels in love with Sortini," said Brunswick, who is always rather coarse and has no understanding of people like Amalia, but this time we thought he might be right, we were altogether a bit silly that day, and when we got home after midnight all of us, except Amalia, seemed befuddled by the sweet wine from the Castle.'

'What about Sortini?' asked K. 'Oh, yes, Sortini,' said Olga. 'I caught glimpses of him several times during the festival, he sat on the shaft of the fire-engine with his arms folded until the coach from the Castle came to pick him up. He didn't even go to the fire-drills where father outperformed all the other men of his age in the hope that Sortini was watching.' 'And did you hear from him again?' asked K. 'You certainly seem to have great respect for him.' 'Ah, yes, respect,' said Olga, 'and yes, we did hear from him again. Next morning we were roused from our stupor by a scream from Amalia; the others went straight back to sleep, but I was wide awake and rushed over to her, she was standing at the window holding a letter which a man had just handed her through the window. The man was waiting for an answer. Amalia had already read the letter – it wasn't very long – and was holding it in her hand, which was hanging limply; I always loved her so much when she was tired. I knelt down beside her and read the letter. I had hardly finished it when Amalia glanced at me briefly, took it back, but couldn't bring herself to read it again; she tore it up, threw the pieces in the face of the man outside, and shut the window. That was the fateful morning. I call it fateful, but that moment the previous afternoon was just as fateful.' 'And what was in the letter?' asked K. 'Yes, I haven't told you that,' said Olga.

'The letter was from Sortini, it was addressed to the girl with the garnet necklace. I can't repeat the contents; it was a summons to come to him at the Herrenhof, and she was to come at once because Sortini had to leave in half an hour. The letter was written in the most vulgar terms such as I had never heard before, and I could only half guess at what they meant from the whole tone of the letter. Anyone who read that letter without knowing Amalia would have been forced to the conclusion that a girl to whom anyone dared to write like that must be depraved, even if no one had ever laid a finger on her. And it wasn't a love-letter, either; there were no compliments in it, far from it, Sortini was obviously angry that he had been so taken by the sight of Amalia and distracted from his business. We worked out later that he had probably intended to go straight back to the Castle that evening, that he had only stayed in the village because of Amalia, and the next morning had been so annoyed he had not been able to forget about her even during the night that he had written her the letter. Even the most cool-headed woman would have been infuriated by that letter when she first read it, but then anyone other than Amalia would probably have been more alarmed at its nasty threatening tone; but she was just furious, she wasn't afraid, not for herself or for anyone else. And while I crawled back into bed, repeating to myself the unfinished last sentence: "Come right away, or else . . ." Amalia stayed sitting on the window-seat looking out as if she expected more messengers and was prepared to treat them all exactly as she had treated the first one.'

'So that's how the officials are,' said K. slowly. 'Some of them are creatures like that. What did your father do? I hope he put in a strong complaint about Sortini to the proper place, unless he preferred to take more direct and effective action by going to the Herrenhof himself. The most unpleasant aspect of this whole episode is not the insult to Amalia – that could easily have been made up for, I don't know why you're making so much of that, far too much. Why should Sortini have disgraced Amalia for ever with a letter like that, as your account seems to suggest? That simply cannot be; it would have been easy to make amends to Amalia, and the whole thing would have been forgotten in a few days. Sortini didn't disgrace Amalia, he disgraced himself. What I find outrageous is Sortini, the idea that such abuse of power is possible. In this case it failed because it was done quite brazenly and transparently, and because Sortini met more than his match in Amalia; but in a thousand other instances, in only slightly less fortunate circumstances, it could succeed and escape everyone's notice, even that of the injured party.' 'Hush,' said Olga, 'Amalia's looking at us.' Amalia had finished feeding her parents and was undressing her mother; she had just unfastened her skirt, put her mother's arms about her neck to lift her a little, slipped off her skirt and gently set her down again. Her father, who was never happy that the mother was attended to first, which obviously only happened because she was even more helpless than he was, attempted to undress himself, perhaps as a rebuke to his daughter because he thought she was being too slow; but although he started with the easiest and least important things, like the oversized slippers which fitted his feet only loosely, he could not manage to get them off, and before long, wheezing hoarsely, he had to give up and sank stiffly back into his chair.

'There's something important you don't realise,' said Olga. 'You may be perfectly right, but the crucial thing was that Amalia didn't go to the Herrenhof. The way she had treated the messenger might not have mattered, it could have been kept quiet; but when she didn't go there, the curse came on our family, and then her treatment of the messenger also became inexcusable, in fact it was the main issue as far as most people were concerned.' 'What!' cried K., quickly lowering his voice when Olga held up her hands beseechingly, 'you, her sister, you're surely not saying Amalia should have run off to the Herrenhof after Sortini?' 'No,' said Olga, 'I hope no one will ever think that of me, how could you believe such a thing? I don't know anyone who is so unwaveringly right in everything she does as Amalia. Certainly, if she had gone to the Herrenhof, I would have agreed with what she did; but it was heroic of her not to go. For myself, I'll admit quite frankly that if I had had a letter like that, I would have gone. I couldn't have coped with the fear of what might happen otherwise, only Amalia could do that. Of course, there are ways to get out of it, another girl might, for instance, have made herself up nicely and taken her time over it, then she would have gone to the Herrenhof and found that Sortini had already left, perhaps he had left straight after sending the messenger, which is more than likely because the moods of these gentlemen change so quickly. But Amalia didn't do that, she did nothing like that; she was too deeply insulted and gave a straight answer. If she had only somehow pretended to obey, if she'd just delayed getting to the Herrenhof, the disaster might have been averted; we have very clever advocates here who know how to make anything you like out of nothing, but in this case there wasn't even any negative evidence in our favour, far from it, there was the disrespectful treatment of Sortini's letter and the insult to his messenger as well.' 'But what sort of a disaster was it?' said K., 'and what sort of advocates are these? Surely Amalia couldn't be charged, let alone punished, because of Sortini's criminal behaviour?' 'Oh yes she could,' said Olga, 'not legally in court, of course, and she couldn't be directly punished, but she could be punished in a different way, she and our whole family; and I dare say you're beginning to realise by now how severe that punishment is. To you it seems monstrously unjust, but no one else in the village takes that view. Yours is a generous view, and it ought to be of some comfort to us, and it would be if it weren't obviously based on misunderstandings. I can easily prove that to you, you must forgive me if I mention Frieda here, but something very similar to what happened between Amalia and Sortini also happened between Frieda and Klamm, except that it turned out differently in the end; and though you may have been shocked at first, you find it quite acceptable now. And it's not a question of getting used to it, a simple matter of judgement can't be glossed over just by getting used to a situation; it's a question of removing misunderstandings.'

'But Olga,' said K., 'I don't know why you drag Frieda into this, that was a completely different case. Don't confuse such fundamentally different matters, and go on with your story.' 'Please don't take it amiss,' said Olga, 'if I insist on the comparison; there are still some things you don't understand about Frieda's case if you think you have to defend her when I compare the two of them. Frieda doesn't need to be defended at all, she deserves to be praised. When I compare the two cases, I'm not saying they are identical, they are like black and white, and the white is Frieda. At worst we can laugh at Frieda, as I did so rudely in the bar, and I regretted it very much afterwards. Anyone who laughs at her is certainly being malicious or jealous, but they can still laugh; but Amalia can only be treated with contempt, except by her closest relatives. That is why, although their cases are fundamentally different as you say, they are still similar, too.' 'They are not even similar,' said K., shaking his head disapprovingly. 'Leave Frieda out of it; Frieda never received such a charming letter as the one Sortini wrote to Amalia, and Frieda really loved Klamm, anyone who doubts it can ask her, she still loves him even now.' 'But does that make such a difference?' asked Olga. 'Don't you believe Klamm could have written just like that to Frieda? When these gentlemen get up from behind their desks, they're like that; they can't adjust to the world, so in their confusion they say the coarsest things, not all of them, but many do. The letter to Amalia might have been what Sortini was thinking, scribbled down without regard for what was actually being written. What do we know about these gentlemen's thoughts! Haven't you heard for yourself, or been told about the tone in which Klamm spoke to Frieda? It's well known that Klamm is very coarse, apparently he says nothing for hours on end, and then he comes out with something so gross that it makes you shudder. Sortini is not known to do that, but then very little is known about Sortini altogether. In fact, all that is known about him is that his name is similar to Sordini's; if it weren't for the fact that their names are similar, probably no one would have heard of him. He's probably also confused with Sordini as an expert on the fire service. Sordini could be the real expert, who takes advantage of the similarity of their names to offload his public duties onto Sortini so that he can get on with his work undisturbed. Now, when a man with as little experience of the world as Sortini suddenly falls for a girl from the village, of course things are done quite differently from when the joiner's apprentice next door falls in love. And you also have to take account of the great gulf between an official and a cobbler's daughter that has to be bridged somehow; that's the way Sortini tried to do it, someone else might do it another way. Of course, we're all told we belong to the Castle, that there is no gulf between us that needs to be bridged, and that may be true in the usual course of events; but unfortunately we've had occasion to see that just when it comes to something that matters, it's not true.

'Anyway, after all this you will find Sortini's behaviour more understandable, less monstrous, and indeed compared with Klamm's it is much more understandable and, even when you are quite closely involved, much more tolerable. When Klamm writes a love letter, it's more embarrassing than the coarsest letter from Sortini. Don't misunderstand me, I'm not criticising Klamm, I wouldn't dare to, I'm only comparing them because you won't accept any comparison. Klamm lords it over women, he orders one and then another to come to him, doesn't put up with any of them for long, and then sends them away just as he told them to come. Good heavens, Klamm wouldn't even take the trouble to write a letter first. And compared with that, is it then still so monstrous that Sortini, who lives such a sheltered life and whose relations with women are to say the least obscure, should one day sit down and write an admittedly appalling letter in his own elegant official hand? And if Klamm is no better than Sortini, indeed rather the reverse, is Frieda's love for him supposed to make a difference? Women's relations with officials, believe me, are very difficult, or rather always very easy, to judge. There's never any lack of love; there's no such thing as unhappy love for an official. In that sense it's no credit to a girl to say – and I'm not just talking about Frieda, by any means – that she only gave herself to an official because she loved him. She loved him and gave herself to him, that's how it was, but it's no credit to her. But, you may object, Amalia didn't love Sortini. Well, all right, she didn't love him; but perhaps she actually did, who can tell? Even she doesn't know. How can she think she loved him when she rejected him so violently, no doubt more violently than any official has been rejected before? Barnabas says she still shudders sometimes, even now, with the same passion with which she slammed the window shut three years ago. That's true, too, and that's why we can't ask her. She turned Sortini down, that's all she knows; she doesn't know whether she loved him or not. But we know that women can't help loving officials when they approach them, in fact they love the officials before that, however much they want to deny it, and after all Sortini didn't just approach Amalia, he leapt over the shaft when he saw her, with his legs so stiff from sitting behind a desk, he leapt over the shaft. But Amalia is an exception, you'll say. Yes, she is, she proved it when she refused to go to Sortini, that's exception enough; but the idea that she didn't love Sortini either, that would be almost too much of an exception, that would be beyond understanding. I'm sure we were struck with blindness that afternoon, but the fact that we seemed to sense dimly that Amalia was in love shows some kind of awareness. But when you take all that into account, how much difference is there between Frieda and Amalia? Simply that Frieda did what Amalia refused to do.'

'That may be so,' said K., 'but for me the main difference is that Frieda is my fiancée, while basically my only interest in Amalia is that she is the sister of Barnabas, who is a Castle messenger, and her future is perhaps bound up with Barnabas' duties. If an official had done her such a crying injustice as your account initially led me to believe, it would have been a matter of great concern to me, though far more as a public matter than as Amalia's personal misfortune. But now, after what you have told me, the picture has changed in a way I don't fully understand, but since I heard it from you I find it plausible enough, and I'll be very glad to forget it altogether – I'm not a fireman, so what's Sortini to me? But I am interested in Frieda, and so I find it strange that you, someone I've trusted completely and shall always be happy to trust, constantly seek to use Amalia to disparage Frieda and put me off her. I'm not assuming you do this intentionally or even maliciously, otherwise I would have had to leave long ago; you don't do it intentionally, it's circumstances that lead you to do it, your love for Amalia makes you want to glorify her above all other women, and because you cannot find enough admirable qualities in Amalia herself to do this, you resort to denigrating other women. What Amalia did is remarkable, but the more you talk about it the harder it is to decide whether it was noble or ignoble, clever or foolish, heroic or cowardly; Amalia's motives are hidden in her heart, no one will force her to reveal them. Frieda, on the other hand, has not done anything remarkable, she has only followed her own heart, that is clear to anyone of good will, anyone can confirm that, there's no scope for gossip. However, I'm not trying to disparage Amalia, nor to defend Frieda; I'm simply trying to explain to you how I feel about Frieda and how any attack on her is also an attack on myself. I came here of my own accord, and I made myself at home here of my own free will; but everything that has happened to me since, and above all my future prospects – however dim they may be, they still exist – I owe all that to Frieda, that is unarguable. Although I was appointed here as a surveyor, that was just a ruse, they were playing with me; they drove me out of my house, they are still playing with me now, but it's got so much more complicated, I have become a person of some substance, and that means something too. However insignificant all that may be, I do have a home, a position with a real job, I have a fiancée who takes over my professional work when I have other business, I shall marry her and become a member of the community, and apart from my official relationship with Klamm I also have a personal relationship with him, though it's one I haven't been able to take advantage of so far. That is surely quite a lot, isn't it? And when I visit you, who is it you welcome? Who is it you confide your family history to? Who is it you hope will give you the chance, if only the faintest, unlikeliest chance of some kind of help? Surely not me, the surveyor, the man whom just a week ago, for example, Lasemann and Brunswick threw out of their house?

No, it's the man who already has a degree of power, and it's Frieda I have to thank for that, Frieda who is so modest that if you were to question her about any of this, she would certainly tell you she knew nothing whatever about it. And yet it still seems from all this that Frieda in her innocence has achieved more than all Amalia's pride, because you see I have the impression that it's help for Amalia that you're looking for. And from whom? In fact, from none other than Frieda.'

'Did I really say such horrid things about Frieda?' said Olga. 'I certainly didn't mean to and didn't think I had, but it's possible; our situation is so bad that we've fallen out with everyone, and if we start to complain we get carried away and don't know what we're doing. You're right, too, there is a great difference now between us and Frieda, and it needs to be pointed out for once. Three years ago we were respectable girls, and Frieda was an orphan, a maid at the Brückenhof, we didn't even look at her in the street, we were certainly too proud, but that's how we were brought up. But that evening at the Herrenhof you could have seen how things stand today: Frieda holding a whip while I was among a crowd of peasants. But it's far worse than that; Frieda may despise us, her position allows her to, circumstances force her to. But is there anyone who doesn't despise us? Those who choose to despise us find themselves in the best company. Do you know Frieda's successor? She's called Pepi. I only got to know her two evenings ago, before that she was a chambermaid. I'm sure she despises me even more than Frieda does. She saw me out of the window when I went to fetch some beer; she ran to the door and locked it, and I had to plead with her a long time and promise to give her the ribbon in my hair before she let me in. But then when I gave it to her she threw it in the corner. Well, let her despise me, I'm partly dependent on her good will, and she's the barmaid at the Herrenhof; she's only temporary, though, and certainly isn't fit to be employed there permanently. You only have to hear how the landlord speaks to Pepi and compare it to the way he used to speak to Frieda. But that doesn't stop Pepi despising Amalia as well, when just one look from Amalia would be enough to chase little Pepi with all her plaits and ribbons out of the room faster than she would ever manage on her fat little legs. What a lot of infuriating gossip I had to listen to from her again yesterday about Amalia, until the customers finally came to my rescue, even though it was in the way you've already seen.'

'How tense you are,' said K. 'I only wanted to be fair to Frieda, not to denigrate you all as you seem to think. There is something special about your family, I feel that too, I've never made a secret of it; but I don't understand how being special could ever give cause for contempt.' 'Oh, K.,' said Olga, 'you will come to understand it too, I'm afraid. Can you not understand how Amalia's behaviour towards Sortini was the original cause for this contempt?' 'But that would be most peculiar,' said K. 'Amalia could be admired or condemned for it, but why despised? And even if Amalia really is despised, for reasons I don't understand, why is this contempt extended to all of you, to the whole innocent family? It's outrageous that Pepi, for example, should despise you, and when I next visit the Herrenhof I'll make her pay for it.'

'K.,' said Olga, 'if you wanted to change the minds of everyone who despises us you would have a difficult job, because it all stems from the Castle. I still remember everything that happened later that morning. Brunswick, who worked for us at the time, had arrived as he did every day, my father had given him some work and sent him home, then we sat down to breakfast. Everyone except Amalia and myself were in high spirits, our father kept talking about the festival, he had several plans for the fire brigade – you see, the Castle has its own fire service, and they had sent a delegation to the festival to discuss various things with our people. The gentlemen from the Castle who were there had seen our fire brigade perform and had compared it favourably with the performance of the Castle service, they talked of the need to reorganise the Castle service, for which instructors from the village would be needed, and though quite a few people were eligible, our father hoped he would be chosen. That's what he talked about, and in that nice way he had of really spreading himself out at table, he sat there taking up half the table with his arms and looked up at the sky through the open window, and he looked so young and happy and full of hope. I was never going to see him like that again. Then Amalia said, with an air of authority we had never seen in her before, that we should not trust what these gentlemen said; on such occasions they liked to say something agreeable, but it meant very little or nothing at all, they'd scarcely said it than they forgot all about it, though of course everyone fell for it again the next time. Our mother told her not to talk like that, our father just laughed at her precocity and worldly wisdom, but then he stopped and seemed to be looking for something he had only just noticed was missing, but there was nothing missing; then he said Brunswick had told him something about a messenger and a letter that had been torn up, and asked us if we knew anything about it, who was involved and what it was all about. We said nothing; Barnabas, who was young then, like a little lamb, said something particularly silly or cheeky, we began to talk about other things and the whole thing was forgotten.'

18

Amalia's Punishment

'But shortly afterwards we were overwhelmed with questions from all sides about the story of the letter. Friends and enemies came, people we knew and complete strangers, but none of them stayed for long; our best friends were in the greatest hurry to leave. Lasemann, who was usually so unhurried and dignified, came in as if he just wanted to measure up the room, one look around and that was all; it was like some dreadful children's game when he rushed off and our father broke away from the others and ran after him to the front door, then gave up. Brunswick came and told father straight out that he intended to set up on his own, he was a shrewd fellow who knew how to take advantage of the situation. Customers came and searched the storeroom for the boots they had left to be repaired; at first father tried to persuade them to change their mind, and we all did our best to support him, then he gave up and without a word helped them to find their boots; one entry after another in the order-book was crossed out, the leather that people had left with us was handed back, accounts were settled, it was all done without the slightest argument, they were happy to break off all contact with us quickly and completely, even if they made a loss, it didn't matter to them. And finally, as might have been expected, Seemann appeared, the Captain of the fire brigade; I can picture it now – Seemann, tall and well-built, but slightly stooped with a lung condition, he's always serious and incapable of laughing, standing in front of our father, whom he used to admire, he had told him in confidence that he could expect to be made deputy chief of the fire brigade – Seemann now had to tell him that he was dismissed from the service and would have to hand in his diploma. The people who were there left off their business and crowded round the two men.

Seemann can't speak, he just keeps tapping our father on the shoulder as if he were trying to tap the words out of him that he is supposed to utter but can't. He's laughing all the while, presumably trying to reassure himself and everyone else, but since he's incapable of laughing and no one has ever heard him laugh, it doesn't occur to anyone to think he is laughing. Our father is too tired and too bewildered by the day's events to be able to help Seemann, in fact he seems too tired even to think about what is happening. Of course, we were all equally bewildered, but we were young and couldn't grasp that we had been so utterly ruined, we kept thinking someone in all this stream of visitors would finally call a halt and put everything back to rights. In our ignorance, we thought Seemann was just the person to do this; we waited on tenterhooks for him to stop laughing and finally make himself clear. What was there to laugh about just then, other than the stupid injustice being done to us? Oh, Captain, Captain, we thought, please tell everyone; we crowded round him, but that only made him spin round in a strange way. But then at last he did begin to speak, though not to meet our secret wishes, but in response to the shouts of the people there, who were becoming angry or impatient.

We were still hopeful. He began by praising our father handsomely; he called him a credit to the service, an inimitable model for younger colleagues, an indispensable member the service could not afford to lose. That was all very well, if only he had finished there, but he went on. If the service, he said, had nevertheless decided, if only provisionally, to ask our father to step down, we would all realise what serious reasons compelled the service to do this. But for father's outstanding performance at the festival the day before, things might not have come to this; but his performance had attracted the particular attention of the authorities, the fire service was now in the public eye and had to be even more conscious of its reputation than before. And now that the messenger had been insulted the service was left with no option, and he, Seemann, had taken on himself the difficult duty of conveying the decision; he hoped father would not make it even more difficult for him. Seemann was so glad to have got this out that he abandoned his exaggerated show of tact, pointed to the diploma hanging on the wall, and beckoned with his finger. Our father nodded and went over to get it, but his hands were trembling and he couldn't get it off the hook, so I climbed onto a stool and helped him. And from that moment it was all over for him; he didn't even bother to remove the diploma from its frame, and handed it over to Seemann as it was. Then he went to sit in a corner, didn't move and didn't speak to anyone, and we had to deal with people ourselves as best we could.'

'And where do you see the influence of the Castle in all this?' asked K. 'So far it seems not to have intervened. What you have told me so far was only people's mindless anxiety, pleasure in a neighbour's misfortune, unreliable friendships, things you find everywhere, plus, it has to be said, or so it seems to me at least, a degree of timidity on your father's part. For what was that diploma? A testimonial to his abilities, which he still retained; if they made him indispensable, so much the better, and he would have made things really difficult for the captain just by throwing the diploma at his feet before he'd said two words. But what seems particularly significant to me is that you haven't once mentioned Amalia; after all, she was to blame for everything, and I suppose she stood quietly in the background watching the disaster unfold.' 'No, no,' said Olga, 'no one can be blamed, no one could act any differently, it was all the influence of the Castle.'

'The influence of the Castle,' repeated Amalia, who had come in from the yard unnoticed; her parents had long since gone to bed. 'Are you telling tales from the Castle? Are you still sitting here together? You had intended to leave at once, K., and now it's nearly ten. Are you really interested in these stories? There are people here who feed off such stories, they sit down together just like you two and entertain each other, but I didn't think you were one of them.' 'Oh yes,' said K., 'I am one of them, while people who don't take an interest in such stories and just leave them to others don't impress me greatly.' 'Well, yes,' said Amalia, 'but people are interested in very different things. I once heard of a young man who thought about the Castle day and night, he neglected everything else and people feared for his sanity because his whole mind was on the Castle up there; but in the end it turned out that it wasn't actually the Castle he was thinking about, but the daughter of a woman from the Castle kitchens, and he got her, so he was all right again.' 'I think I'd like that young man,' said K. 'I doubt whether you'd like him,' said Amalia, 'but you might like his wife. Now don't let me disturb you, but I'm going to sleep and I'll have to put the light out because of my parents; although they fall fast asleep straight away, they don't sleep properly for more than an hour, and then the slightest sign of light disturbs them. Good night.'

And indeed the room darkened at once; Amalia must have settled down on the floor somewhere near her parents' bed. 'So who is this young man she mentioned?' asked K. 'I don't know,' said Olga, 'perhaps it was Brunswick, although it doesn't quite fit him, perhaps it was someone else. It's not easy to understand her properly because you often don't know whether she's speaking seriously or ironically, she usually means it seriously, but it sounds ironic.' 'Never mind these subtleties!' said K. 'How did you come to be so dependent on her? Was it like that before the great disaster, or only afterwards? And do you never wish you could be independent of her? And does this dependence have any rational basis? She is the youngest, so she ought to be obedient. Innocently or otherwise, she has brought misery on the family. And instead of begging each one of you for forgiveness with every day that comes, she holds her head higher than anyone, cares about nothing except perhaps by condescending to look after your parents; she doesn't want to become involved in anything, as she puts it, and if she does finally speak to you for once, then she "usually means it seriously, but it sounds ironic". Or does she perhaps dominate you because she is so beautiful, as you keep saying? Well, you are all three very similar, but what distinguishes her from the other two is by no means in her favour; the very first time I saw her I was repelled by her sullen, hostile expression. Then again, she may be the youngest, but you can't tell that from her appearance, she looks ageless, like women who scarcely seem to get older but who also hardly ever seem to have been really young. You see her every day, so you don't see what a hard face she has. That's why I can't even take Sortini's liking for her very seriously when I think about it; perhaps he only sent that letter to punish her, not to send for her.'

'I don't want to talk about Sortini,' said Olga. 'With these gentlemen from the Castle anything is possible, whether it's the prettiest girl or the ugliest. But for the rest you're completely wrong about Amalia. Look, I have no particular reason to get you to like Amalia, and if I still try to I'm only doing it for your sake. In a way she was the cause of our misery, certainly, but even our father, who suffered more than anyone from the disaster and was never really able to control his tongue, especially at home, even he didn't have a single word to say against Amalia, even when things were at their worst. And that wasn't because he approved of Amalia's behaviour; how could he, an admirer of Sortini, have approved of it, he couldn't remotely understand it, he would have been glad to sacrifice himself and everything he possessed for Sortini, though not in the way it actually happened, presumably as a result of Sortini's fury. I say presumably, because we heard no more of

Sortini; he had been retiring before, but from then on it was as if he no longer existed. And you should have seen Amalia at that time. We all knew there would be no specific punishment; people just avoided us, people from the village as well as from the Castle. But while of course we noticed that the people from the village avoided us, there was no sign from the Castle. But then we hadn't seen any sign of help from the Castle before, so how could we have noticed any change of attitude now? This silence was the worst, far worse than the people here avoiding us; they hadn't done it out of conviction, perhaps they didn't have anything against us at all, there was none of the contempt they have today, they had only acted out of fear, and now they were waiting to see how things would develop. And we had no fear of being destitute, all our debtors had paid us, things had been settled to our advantage, if we were short of food, relatives helped us out secretly, it was easy for us, it was harvest time too, though we had no land and no one would give us any work, for the first time in our lives we were forced to be almost idle. And we sat there together with the windows closed in the heat of July and August. Nothing happened, no news, no visitors, nothing.'

'Well,' said K., 'if nothing happened and you didn't expect any specific punishment, what were you afraid of? What sort of people are you?' 'How can I explain?' said Olga. 'We weren't afraid of what was going to happen, we were already suffering, we were in the process of being punished. The people in the village were only waiting for us to come to them, for our father to open his workshop again, for Amalia, who could make the most beautiful clothes, though only for the grandest people, you understand, to start taking orders again. They were all sorry for what they had done – when a family respected in the village is suddenly completely ostracised like that, everyone loses out in the same way; they had only thought they were doing their duty by avoiding us, we would have done just the same in their place. And they hadn't even known exactly what it was all about, just that the messenger had gone to the Herrenhof clutching a few scraps of paper, Frieda had seen him leave and then return, she had exchanged a few words with him and passed on what he told her straight away; but again, it wasn't out of hostility towards us at all, it was simply out of duty, just as it would have been anyone else's in the same situation.

'At that point, as I said, a happy outcome to the whole affair is what people would have welcomed most. If we had suddenly come along with the news that everything had now been settled, for instance that it had just been a misunderstanding that had been cleared up, or that we had indeed done something wrong but had made up for it, or that we had managed to get the matter dropped through our contacts with the Castle – and people would have been satisfied with that – then I'm sure they would have welcomed us with open arms, hugs and kisses, there would have been celebrations, I've seen that happen a few times with other people. But not even some news like that would have been necessary; if we had only come along openly and offered our services, if we had picked up our old contacts without saying a single word about the affair with the letter, that would have been enough, everyone would have been delighted to drop the whole thing, because apart from the fear, and above all the embarrassment, caused by the affair, the only reason they had avoided us was simply because they didn't want to have to hear about it, talk about it, think about it or be affected by it in any way. Although Frieda gave the game away, she didn't do it just for her own amusement, but to protect herself and everyone else from the affair, to warn the village that something had happened that they should take care to keep well away from. It wasn't about us as a family, just about the affair, it was about us only because we had been involved in it. So if we had only come out again and let the matter rest, if we had behaved as if we had got over the whole thing, never mind how, and if people had been convinced by this that the affair, whatever it might have been, would not be mentioned any more, then everything would have been all right too, everyone would have been ready to help as they had before, and even if we hadn't been able to forget the affair completely, they would have understood and helped us to forget all about it.

'But instead of doing that we stayed at home. I don't know what we were waiting for, maybe for a decision by Amalia, she had taken over the lead in the family that morning and held on to it, without any special arrangement, without giving orders, without asking, just by saying nothing, almost. Certainly, the rest of us had plenty to talk about, we never stopped whispering all day; at times our father would call for me in a fit of anxiety and I'd spend the night at his bedside. Or sometimes we crouched together, Barnabas and I; he understood very little about the whole thing and kept pestering us for explanations, always the same questions, perhaps he knew that the carefree years that other lads of his age could look forward to had vanished for him. We sat there together rather like we two are sitting now, K., and we'd forget that night had fallen and morning had come again. Our mother was the weakest of all, I dare say because she wasn't just sharing the family's troubles but she felt the suffering of each one of us too, and so to our horror we could see changes in her which, we sensed, awaited all of us. Her favourite place was in the corner of a sofa, it's gone long since, it's in Brunswick's living room now; she would sit there, and either dozed or perhaps, as the constant movement of her lips seemed to suggest, held long conversations with herself – we could never tell which.

'Of course, it was perfectly natural that we should talk about the letter over and over again, going back and forth over all the known details and all the unknown possibilities, that we should continually compete with each other to think up ways of resolving the matter; it was natural and inevitable, but not good, because it only dragged us deeper and deeper into what we wanted to escape from. And what use were all these ideas, however brilliant? None of them could be acted on without Amalia, it was all meaningless talk because none of our conclusions ever reached Amalia, and if they had they would only have met with silence. Well, fortunately I understand Amalia better now than I did then. She bore a greater burden than any of us, it's inconceivable how she bore it and is still alive today. Our mother may have borne the suffering of the whole family, she bore it because it overwhelmed her, and she didn't bear it for long; you can't say she still bears it today – even then her mind was becoming confused. But Amalia not only had to bear our suffering, she also had the intelligence to understand it clearly; we saw only the consequences, she saw the causes, we hoped for some small means of relief, she knew that everything had been decided, we could only whisper among ourselves, she could only remain silent, she confronted the truth and lived with it and had to endure that life, then and now. For all our distress, how much better off we were than she was!

'Of course, we had to leave our house, Brunswick took it over, we were given this cottage and brought our belongings here in a handcart. It took us several journeys; Barnabas and I pulled, Amalia and father pushed, and we found our mother, whom we had brought here straight away, sitting on a chest and whimpering softly all the time. But I remember even during those laborious journeys – which were also very humiliating, for we frequently met carts from the harvest, and the workers fell silent at the sight of us and turned away – how even during those journeys Barnabas and I couldn't stop talking about our troubles and our plans, and sometimes we stopped in the middle of our discussions and it needed a shout from our father to remind us of what we were doing. But all our discussions after the removal made no difference to our lives, except that we gradually became aware of our poverty. The contributions from relatives stopped, we were almost penniless, and it was just then that people's contempt for us, which you have seen for yourself, began to grow. They noticed that we didn't have the strength to work our own way out of the scandal, and they held that against us; they didn't underestimate the extent of our misfortune even though they weren't fully aware of it; if we had recovered from it they would have respected us all the more, but since we hadn't been able to they finally did once and for all what they had so far done only for the time being, and no one would have anything to do with us. They knew that they probably wouldn't themselves have managed any better than we had, but that made it all the more necessary to cut us off completely. They didn't talk about us as human beings any more, they didn't even mention our name; if they had to talk about us they referred to us as the Barnabas family after Barnabas, who was the most innocent of us. Even our cottage got a bad reputation, and if you're honest with yourself you'll admit that when you first came in here, you thought what you saw justified their contempt. Later, when people started coming to see us again occasionally, they turned their noses up at quite trivial things, for instance that the little oil lamp was hanging over the table there. Where else are we supposed to hang it, if not over the table? – but still they found it intolerable. But if we hung the lamp somewhere else it made no difference, they were still disgusted. Everything we were and everything we possessed met with the same contempt.'

19

Petitions

'And what did we do meanwhile? The worst thing we could have done, something that deserved contempt far more than the actual scandal: we betrayed Amalia, we freed ourselves from her unspoken command, we couldn't go on like that, we couldn't go on living without any hope whatever, and we each began in our own way to plead with the Castle or bombard it with requests for a pardon. Of course we knew we weren't in a position to make amends, we knew, too, that the only promising contact we had with the Castle, namely Sortini, the official who was well-disposed towards our father, was now unapproachable because of what had occurred, but we set to work all the same. Our father began by taking futile petitions to the mayor, the secretaries, the advocates, the clerks; mostly he wasn't admitted, and if he ever was, by chance or by cunning – and didn't we rejoice and rub our hands at the news – he was very quickly shown the door and never admitted again. It was all too easy to deal with him, it's always easy for the Castle. What did he want, then? What had happened to him? What did he want a pardon for? When had anyone in the Castle ever so much as raised a finger against him, and who was it? Certainly, he was poverty-stricken, he had lost his customers, and so forth; but that was part of everyday life to do with trade and commerce, was the Castle supposed to be involved in everything? Of course, the Castle was indeed involved in everything, but it could not crassly interfere with the course of events simply and solely in the interests of one person. Was the Castle perhaps supposed to send out its officials to chase after his customers and force them to go back to him? But, our father would protest – we discussed all these things carefully at home before and after his visits, huddled in a corner away from Amalia, who noticed everything but let us get on with it – but, he protested, he wasn't complaining about his poverty, he could easily make up for everything he had lost; none of that would matter if only he were pardoned. But what were they to pardon him for, they answered; no charge had been brought, at least none had been entered in the records, at any rate not in the records available to the public lawyers; consequently, as far as could be established, no charge had been brought against him, nor was there one pending. Could he perhaps identify any official deposition that had been issued against him? Our father could not. Or had there been a submission by an official body? He did not know of any. Well, if he knew nothing and nothing had happened, what did he want? What was there to be pardoned for? At most for pestering the authorities unnecessarily, but that was itself unpardonable.

'Our father persisted, in those days he was still vigorous, and his enforced idleness gave him plenty of free time. "I shall restore Amalia's reputation, it won't take much longer," he would tell Barnabas and me several times a day, but very softly, for Amalia must not hear; and yet he only said it for her benefit, because in fact he wasn't thinking about restoring her reputation at all, only about being pardoned. But before he could be granted a pardon he had to establish guilt, and that is what the authorities denied him. He got hold of the idea – and this showed his mind was already going – that his guilt was being concealed from him because he wasn't paying enough; until then he had paid only the standard taxes, which were quite high enough, for our circumstances at least. But now he thought he ought to pay more, which was certainly not correct, for although our officials do accept bribes to make things easier and avoid unnecessary wrangling, it achieves nothing. But if our father had set his hopes on it we weren't going to interfere. We sold off what we still possessed – mostly only bare necessities – to provide father with funds for his investigations, and for some time every morning we had the satisfaction of knowing that when he set out he always had a few coins to jingle in his pocket. Of course, we went hungry all day, while the only effect our contributions had was to keep his hopes up to some extent. But that was hardly an advantage; he wore himself out with all his calls, which without the money would very soon have quite properly come to an end, but as it was they went on and on. Since nothing in particular could actually be achieved by these extra payments, one of the clerks would sometimes at least make a show of doing something, he would promise to make enquiries, hint that some leads had been found which he would follow up – not as part of his official duties, but purely as a favour; and instead of making our father more sceptical, this made him more and more credulous. He would come home with some such obviously worthless promise as if he were restoring the family's fortunes, and it was painful to see him trying to signal to us by twisting his mouth into a smile and opening his eyes wide, always behind Amalia's back, that her rehabilitation, which would surprise her more than anyone, was just round the corner thanks to his efforts – but it was all still a secret that we had to guard closely.

'Things would certainly have gone on like this for a very long time if we hadn't in the end been totally unable to give him any more money. It's true that in the meantime Barnabas, after much pleading, had been taken on by Brunswick as a messenger-boy, though only to collect orders in the evening after dark and then deliver them, also after dark – admittedly Brunswick was to some extent risking his business for our sake, but then he paid Barnabas very little, and Barnabas' work is impeccable – but his wages were barely enough to keep us from starvation. Very gently, and after much beating about the bush we told our father that we could not contribute any more money; but he took it very calmly. He was no longer capable of understanding how futile his efforts were, but then he was worn out by the constant disappointments. He did say – he no longer spoke as clearly as he used to, in fact he had spoken almost too clearly before – that he would only have needed a little more money, that he would have been told everything tomorrow or even today, that it was all pointless now, that he had only failed because the money had run out, and so on; but his tone of voice showed that he didn't believe any of it. In any case, just that moment, out of the blue, he had thought up another plan. Since he had been unable to establish any guilt and so could achieve nothing further through official channels, he would have to rely entirely on appeals and approach the officials personally. There must be some of them who were kind-hearted and sympathetic, and although they couldn't follow these instincts in an official capacity, they could surely do so in private if they were approached at the right moment.'

At this point K., who had been listening intently to what Olga had to say, interrupted her account and asked: 'And don't you agree with that?' He knew he would get the answer eventually, but he wanted to know immediately.

'No,' said Olga. 'Sympathy, or anything of the sort, is out of the question. We may have been young and inexperienced, but we knew that; of course our father knew it too, but he had forgotten, just as he had forgotten most things. He had dreamt up the idea that he would station himself on the main road by the Castle where the officials' carriages went by, and whenever he could he would submit his request for a pardon. Quite honestly, it was a completely senseless plan even if the impossible had happened and his request had actually come to an official's notice. How can a single official issue a pardon? At best that could only be done by the authorities as a whole, but even they probably can't issue a pardon, only come to a decision. But could any official, even if he were to get out of his carriage and take up the matter, form any idea of the case from what our father, a poor, tired old man, mumbles to him about it? The officials are highly educated, but they are blinkered; in his own field it only needs a word for an official to grasp a whole train of thought, but you can explain something from another area for hours and he may nod politely, but he won't understand a word. That all goes without saying; if you just try to understand the petty official matters that affect you, trivial matters that an official can settle with a shrug of his shoulders – if you try to reach a thorough understanding of such matters, you could spend your whole life at it and never get to the bottom of it. But even if our father had come across a competent official, that official can't deal with anything without a preliminary investigation, especially not at the roadside; he can't possibly issue a pardon, he can only deal with the matter officially, and to do that he can only refer you back to the official channels, and our father had already completely failed to achieve anything that way. What a state he must have been in to think he could get anywhere with this new plan of his! If there were any remote possibility of that, the road up there would be swarming with people submitting petitions, but since we're talking here about an impossibility that even the most rudimentary education will impress on anyone, the road up there is completely deserted. Perhaps even that fed our father's hopes; he found food for them anywhere and everywhere. And he had to in this case; anyone of sound mind wouldn't need to get involved in these complicated arguments, the impossibility ought to be clear to anyone at a glance. When the officials drive to the village or back to the Castle, they're not just going for a ride, they have work waiting for them in the village and at the Castle, that's why they drive at such high speed. It doesn't occur to them either to glance out of the window and look for petitioners; quite the reverse, the carriages are stuffed with files that the officials are studying.'

'But,' said K., 'I have seen inside an official's sleigh, and there were no files in it.' Olga's story was revealing such a vast, almost unbelievable world to him that he could not resist intruding on it with his own little adventure, in order to convince himself of the existence of her world as well as that of his own experience.

'That may be,' said Olga, 'but then that's even worse, because it means the official is dealing with such important matters that the files are too precious or too bulky to be taken with him, and in that situation officials have themselves driven at a gallop. At any rate, none of them has any time to spare for our father. What's more, there are several roads leading to the Castle. Sometimes they prefer one, and most of them use that road, at other times they all rush to use another. No one has worked out what governs their choice. At eight o'clock one morning they all drive along one road, half an hour later they'll all use another one, ten minutes later a third one, another half hour and they might be back on the first, and then they'll use that one for the rest of the day, though it might change at any moment. Certainly, all these roads join up near the village, but the carriages are all going at top speed by then, whereas closer to the Castle they slow down a little. But just as their use of the exit roads is unpredictable, so is the number of carriages. Often there are days when there isn't a carriage to be seen, but then other days there will be lots of them. And just imagine our father in all this. In his best suit, which will soon be his only one, he leaves the house every morning with our best wishes. He takes with him a small fireman's badge which he shouldn't actually have kept, and pins it on his jacket when he's clear of the village; he dare not wear it in the village, even though it's so small you can hardly see it from two yards away, but according to him it's just the thing to attract the attention of a passing official.

'Not far from the entrance to the Castle there's a market garden belonging to a man called Bertuch, who delivers vegetables to the Castle; that's where our father chose to wait, on the narrow stone base of the garden fence. Bertuch let him sit there because he had been father's friend, and one of his most loyal customers too; he has a slightly deformed foot and believed father was the only one who could make a boot to fit him. So there our father sat day after day, it was a dreary, wet autumn, but he was completely indifferent to the weather; every morning at the same time he stood with his hand on the latch and waved us goodbye, in the evening he came back soaked to the skin, looking more bent every day, and threw himself into a corner. At first he would tell us about little incidents, for instance that Bertuch, out of sympathy and for the sake of their old friendship, had thrown him a blanket over the fence, or that he thought he had recognised this or that official as a carriage drove past, or that now and again a coachman would recognise him and playfully give him a little flick with his whip. Then later he stopped talking about these things, it was clear he no longer hoped to achieve anything whatever there, he just thought it was his duty, his dreary job, to go and spend the whole day there. That's when his rheumatic pains started; winter was coming, it comes early here, there was an early fall of snow, and there he sat, one day in the rain on the wet stone, the next day in the snow again. At night he groaned with pain, in the morning sometimes he wasn't sure whether to go out, but then he'd make an effort and leave. Our mother clung to him and wouldn't let him go, so he let her go with him – he had probably started to get nervous because of his unsteady legs – and then she contracted rheumatism too. We used to go out to them and take them food, or just to see them and try to persuade them to come home; so many times we found them there, slumped together on their narrow seat, huddled in a thin blanket that barely covered them, nothing all around but grey mist and snow, not a single person or a carriage to be seen anywhere for days on end, what a sight, K., what a sight!

'And then one morning our father's legs were so stiff he couldn't get out of bed; he was inconsolable, he had a touch of fever and imagined he saw a carriage stop by Bertuch's place just then, an official got out, looked for him up and down the fence, then got back into the carriage looking very annoyed and shaking his head. Father kept shouting out, as if he wanted to attract that official's attention from all the way down here and explain that he couldn't be blamed for his absence. And he was absent for a long time; he had to stay in bed for weeks and never went back up there. Amalia took over everything, feeding him, nursing him, treating him, in fact except for a few breaks she's done it to this day. She knows about herbs to soothe pain, she hardly needs any sleep and never panics, she's afraid of nothing, she never gets impatient, and does everything for our parents; while we dithered around and couldn't help, she always kept cool and calm. But then when the worst was over and father could struggle out of bed again, very carefully, with one of us supporting him on either side, Amalia immediately withdrew and left him to us.'

20

Olga's Plans

'Now we had to find some kind of occupation for our father, something he was still capable of doing, something that would at least make him think he was helping to relieve the family's guilt. It wasn't difficult to find something, because basically anything would suit that purpose as much as sitting up at Bertuch's garden; but I thought of something that gave even me some hope. Whenever there had been any talk of our guilt among officials or clerks or anyone else, it was always only the insult to Sortini's messenger that had been mentioned, no one dared to go beyond that. Well, I said to myself, if the general public just knew about the insult, even if that was only how it appeared, then everything could be put right – again, if only for the sake of appearances – if we could make amends to the messenger. After all, no charge had been brought, we were told, so no office had taken the matter up yet, which meant that the messenger, as far as he himself was concerned – and that was all that mattered – was free to forgive us. None of this would really mean anything, it was all for the sake of appearances and that was all that could come of it, but it would please our father all the same and give him the satisfaction of outwitting all the authorities he had consulted and who had tormented him so much with their replies. First, though, we had to find the messenger.

'When I told father about my plan, at first he was very angry. You see, he had become extremely stubborn, he half believed – this idea had taken root while he was ill – that we had always prevented his final triumph, first by stopping our financial contributions, then by keeping him in bed; and to some extent he was quite incapable of taking in new ideas any more. I hadn't finished telling him about it before my plan was rejected; he believed he had to go on waiting at Bertuch's garden, and as he certainly wouldn't be able to go up there every day, we would have to take him in a handcart. But I persisted, and he gradually accepted the idea; the only thing that disturbed him was that in this matter he was entirely dependent on me, for I had seen the messenger on that occasion and he had not. Of course, one messenger looks very much like another, and I wasn't entirely sure I would recognise him either. Then we started going to the Herrenhof to look for him among the servants there. It's true he had been one of Sortini's servants, and Sortini no longer came to the village; but these gentlemen often change their servants, and we might well find him among someone else's servants, and if we couldn't find him in person we might be able to learn something about him from the other servants.

'In order to do this, though, we had to be in the Herrenhof every evening, and we weren't welcome anywhere, especially not in a place like that; and we couldn't go in as customers. But it turned out that we could still make ourselves useful; you know very well what trouble Frieda had with the servants, at heart they're mostly quiet people, they're pampered and sluggish because their work is so easy – "may you live like a servant" the officials say to wish someone well, and in fact as far as good living goes, the servants are said to be the real masters in the Castle. They know their place, too, and up at the Castle, where they're bound by the rules, they're quiet and dignified. I've often been told that; even down here you can still see traces of it among them – only traces, mind – but otherwise, because the Castle rules don't fully apply to them when they're in the village, they seem to be transformed. They're a wild, unruly bunch, not governed by the rules but by their own insatiable urges. There are no limits to their shamelessness; it's fortunate for the village that they are only allowed outside the Herrenhof under official orders, but inside you just have to put up with them. Well, Frieda found that very difficult, so she was very glad to have me there to keep the servants quiet; for more than two years now at least twice a week I've spent the night with them in the stables. Earlier, when our father could still come with us to the Herrenhof, he used to sleep in the bar and wait for me to bring him news in the morning. It wasn't much; to this day we still haven't found the servant we were looking for, they say he's still with Sortini, who thinks very highly of him and apparently took him with him when he moved to an office further away. Most of the servants haven't seen him since we did, and when one of them claims to have seen him in the meantime, I dare say he's mistaken.

'So it looked as if my plan had failed; but it wasn't a complete failure. Certainly, we didn't find the messenger; I'm afraid all those visits to the Herrenhof and having to spend the night there, perhaps even pity for me, as far as he was still capable of feeling pity, were too much for our father, and for nearly two years now he's been in the state you've seen – and even then he's perhaps better off than our mother, whose end we expect every day, it's only thanks to Amalia's superhuman efforts that she keeps going. But what I did achieve at the Herrenhof was a degree of contact with the Castle; you mustn't think ill of me if I say I don't regret doing what I did. What sort of grand contact with the Castle would that be, you might think, and you would be right, it's not much of a contact. I know a lot of the servants by now, the servants of all the gentlemen who have come down to the village in the last few years, and if I ever get into the Castle I shan't be a stranger there. Of course they're only servants in the village, at the Castle they're quite different, and up there they probably wouldn't recognise anyone, especially not someone they knew from the village, even though in the stables they had sworn a hundred times they'd be pleased to see me again at the Castle. Besides, I've already learnt how little these promises are worth, but that's not the most important thing. I have contact with the Castle not jut through the servants themselves, but also perhaps in the sense, I hope, that anyone up there who is watching me and what I'm doing – and managing the huge staff of servants is of course an extremely important and exacting part of the authorities' work – that anyone who is watching me might judge me more leniently than others, he might recognise that I am, however pitifully, fighting for our family and continuing our father's efforts. If that person looks at it that way, perhaps I'll also be forgiven for accepting money from the servants and using it for the family.

'There's something else I've achieved, too, though I'm sure you will disapprove of it. I found out quite a lot from the servants about how to get taken on at the Castle by getting round the public recruitment process, which is difficult and takes years; of course, if you do that you're not an official employee, only someone who's taken on informally and off the record, you have no rights and no duties, and having no duties is the worst. But you do have one thing – you are not far from what's going on, you can keep your eyes open and take advantage of any opportunities, you are not an employee, but you do have a chance to pick up some kind of work; perhaps an employee is unavailable, a call comes, you run to answer it, and you've become something you weren't a moment ago, an employee. But when do you get an opportunity like that? Sometimes straight away – you've hardly arrived, hardly had time to look around, and there's your chance, not every newcomer has the presence of mind to take it; but another time it will take years, longer even than the public recruitment procedure, and anyone admitted semi-officially like that can never become a proper official employee. So there are quite enough drawbacks involved, but they are nothing compared with the public procedure, where candidates are very carefully selected, and anyone from a remotely dubious family is rejected from the start; someone like that might for instance apply for this procedure and spend years waiting for the result in fear and trembling; from the very first day everyone asks him in astonishment how he dares to attempt anything as hopeless as that, but he still goes on hoping – how could he live otherwise? – but after many years, perhaps when he's an old man, he learns that he has been rejected, learns that everything is lost and his life was in vain. Even here, though, there are exceptions, that's why people are so easily tempted. It can happen that even dubious candidates are accepted in the end, there are officials who in spite of themselves can actually scent such mavericks; during the entrance examinations they sniff the air, smack their lips, and roll their eyes. A man like that seems somehow to stimulate their appetite enormously, and they have to stick close to their rulebooks to control themselves. But then sometimes that doesn't help the candidate to be accepted, it only prolongs the appointment process endlessly, which is never concluded and is only terminated by the man's death. So both the official procedure and the alternative are full of known and unknown difficulties, and before going in for anything like that it's very advisable to weigh everything up carefully.

'Well, we certainly did that, Barnabas and I. When I came back from the Herrenhof, we always sat down together and I told him what I had found out, we talked it over day after day, and Barnabas often neglected his work more than he should have done. And here you may think I was to blame. I knew that what the servants told me was not very reliable, I knew they never liked talking to me about the Castle, they always tried to change the subject and I had to coax every word out of them; but then once they got started they let themselves go, talking all sorts of nonsense, bragging, trying to outdo each other by exaggerating and making things up, so it was obvious that in all their endless shouting matches in that dark stable only a few meagre scraps of truth might emerge at best. But I told Barnabas everything just as I had heard it, and since he was still incapable of distinguishing truth from falsehood and because of the family situation was desperate to know all about these things, he drank it all in and burned with impatience for more. And indeed, my new plan depended on Barnabas. There was nothing more to be gained from the servants; Sortini's messenger couldn't be found and was never going to be, Sortini seemed to recede further and further into the background and his messenger with him, often no one could remember their names or what they looked like, and I frequently had to spend a long time describing them, with no result except that someone might, if they tried, just remember them, but apart from that they couldn't tell me any more about them. As for my doings with the servants, of course I had no say in how that was viewed, I could only hope people would see why I did it, and that a little of our family's guilt might be lifted as a result, but I saw no visible sign of that. However, I still went on with it, because I could see no other way of achieving anything for us at the Castle.

'I did see a chance for Barnabas, though. From what the servants told me I was able to gather, if I so wished – and that was very much what I wished – that anyone who was accepted into the service of the Castle could achieve a great deal for his family. But how much truth was there in this? That was impossible to say, but it was clear that there was very little. Because whenever one of the servants, for instance, whom I would never see again or would hardly recognise if I were to see him, solemnly promised to help my brother find a job at the Castle, or at least, should Barnabas get into the Castle some other way, to support him, perhaps by encouraging him, for according to the servants candidates for jobs sometimes have to wait so long that they get weak or confused, and then they are lost if their friends don't look after them – whenever they told me this and many other things, they were probably quite rightly warning me, but the promises they made were completely empty. But not for Barnabas; of course I warned him not to believe them, but just telling him about them was enough to win him over to my plan. The reasons I put to him had less effect, what persuaded him most was what the servants said. And so I had to rely entirely on myself, no one except Amalia could get through to our parents, the more I carried out father's old plans in my own way the more she cut herself off from me – she will speak to me in front of you or others, but won't ever talk to me alone; for the servants at the Herrenhof I was a plaything that they tried to smash in their drunken fury, in those two years I never had a kind word from one of them, only deceit and lies and nonsense, I was just left with Barnabas, and he was still very young.

'When I was telling him all this and saw the eager gleam in his eyes, which has stayed with him ever since, I felt afraid, but I didn't give up, what was at stake seemed too important. Certainly, I didn't have any of our father's grandiose but futile plans, I didn't have the determination that men have; I only wanted to make amends for the insult to the messenger, and even wanted to be given credit for this modest aim. But what I had failed to achieve on my own I wanted to achieve more surely and in a different way through Barnabas. We had insulted a messenger and driven him away from the nearest offices; what more could we do than to offer them another messenger in the person of Barnabas, get Barnabas to do the work of the offended messenger and let him stay quietly in the background as long as he wanted to, for as long as he needed to forget the insult. Of course I realised that there was an element of presumption in this plan, modest as it was, that it could give the impression that we wanted to dictate to the authorities how they should deal with their staff, or that we doubted whether they were capable of arranging things themselves for the best, that we couldn't believe they had already made arrangements long before it had occurred to us that anything could be done in the matter; but then again, I thought it was impossible that the authorities could misunderstand me so much, or if they did, that they would do so deliberately – in other words, that everything I did was rejected out of hand from the start. So I persisted, and Barnabas' ambition did the rest. During this time, while we were making our plans, he became so conceited that he found shoemaking too dirty for a future office worker, and even dared to contradict Amalia quite flatly on the rare occasions she spoke to him. I was glad to let him have this brief satisfaction, for the first day he went to the Castle, as could easily have been foreseen, all his joy and conceit vanished at once.

'Now the pretence of service that I told you about began. It was astonishing how little difficulty Barnabas had getting into the Castle on the first occasion, or more accurately into the office that has, as it were, become his workplace. This success nearly drove me mad with joy at the time; when Barnabas came home that evening and whispered it to me I ran over to Amalia, got hold of her, pushed her into a corner, and kissed her and bit her so hard that she wept with pain and fright. I was so excited I could say nothing, and in fact we hadn't spoken to each other for such a long time, so I put it off for a few days. But then over the next few days there was nothing to tell her; after the first sudden success, nothing happened. For two years Barnabas led this monotonous, demoralising existence. The servants let us down completely, and I gave Barnabas a little note to take with him in which I commended him to the servants and reminded them of their promises, and whenever Barnabas met one of them he took out the note and showed it to them. Even if he might have come across servants who didn't know me, and even if the ones who did know me were irritated by his way of showing them the note without saying a word, it was still disgraceful that none of them helped him, and it was a great relief, which we could admittedly have contrived for ourselves long before that, when one of the servants, who had probably had the note pressed on him several times already, screwed it up and threw it into a wastepaper basket. As he did this, it occurred to me, he might almost have said: "That's what you do with your letters, too."

'But however unproductive this period was in other ways, it had a positive effect on Barnabas, if you can call it positive, because he grew up prematurely, he became a man before his time, indeed in some ways he became serious and sensible well beyond his years. It often makes me sad to look at him and compare him to the lad he still was just two years ago. At the same time, I have none of the support or comfort he could give me as a man. Without me he would hardly have got into the Castle, but since he did he has been independent of me. I am the only one he confides in, but I'm sure he only tells me a fraction of what's on his mind. He tells me a lot about the Castle, but from what he says, from the few details he gives me, it's impossible to understand how it could have changed him so much. In particular, I can't understand how the courage he had as a boy, which very nearly made us all despair, should have deserted him so completely up there now that he's a man. Of course all this pointless waiting and standing around day after day, always the same thing all over again with no prospect of anything different, it wears you down and makes you unsure of yourself, and in the end it makes you unfit for anything other than that desperate standing around. But why didn't he put up any resistance before then? Especially as he soon realised that I was right and there was no kind of promotion to be had there, though there might well have been something he could have done to improve our family's situation. Up there everything is on a very modest scale, except for the whims of the servants; anyone who is ambitious finds fulfilment in work, and because work then becomes all-important, there's no scope for naïve dreams. But as Barnabas told me, he thought he could see quite clearly how much power and knowledge was held even by those extremely dubious officials whose rooms he was allowed into; how they dictated so fast, their eyes half-shut, with curt gestures, how without a word, just by raising a forefinger, they dealt with the surly servants, who at such moments sighed deeply and beamed happily, or how, when they found an important passage in their books, they would thump the page, and the others would rush to crowd round as well as they could in the confined space, and crane their necks to get a look at it.

'These scenes, and others like them, gave Barnabas great ideas about these men, and he had the impression that if he ever managed to attract their attention and exchange a few words with them, not as a stranger but as an office colleague, even if a very junior one, then incalculable benefits might be gained for our family. But the fact is he hasn't managed to do that so far, and Barnabas doesn't dare to do anything that might enable him to, although he knows perfectly well that in spite of his youth, because of our unfortunate circumstances, he has been put in a position of great responsibility within the family, in fact he is the head of the family.

'And now there's one last thing I must confess. You arrived here a week ago; I heard someone in the Herrenhof mention it, but took no notice – a surveyor had arrived, I didn't even know what a surveyor was. But the next evening Barnabas comes home earlier than usual – I normally went part of the way to meet him at a particular time – and sees Amalia in the living room, so he drags me out into the street, buries his face on my shoulder and weeps for some minutes. He's the little boy he used to be. Something has happened that he can't handle. It's as if a whole new world has opened up before him, as if he can't bear the happiness and the cares of all this novelty. And yet all that's happened to him is that he's been given a letter to deliver to you. But then, it's the first letter, the first duty he's ever been given.'

Olga paused. There was silence except for the heavy, at times laboured breathing of her parents. K. said casually, as if to supplement Olga's account: 'You weren't being honest with me. Barnabas delivered the letter as if he were a very busy experienced messenger, and you and Amalia, who must have agreed with the two of you on this occasion, both acted as if the messenger work and the letters were of no great importance.' 'You must distinguish between us,' said Olga. 'The two letters made Barnabas feel like a happy little boy again, in spite of all the doubts he has about what he is doing. He only has these doubts between ourselves, but he takes pride in acting like a real messenger to you, according to his notion of how real messengers behave. For instance, although he holds increasing hopes of an official uniform at present, I had two hours to alter his trousers to fit closely and at least look something like the trousers of an official suit so that he can face you in them, and of course at this stage you could easily be taken in. That's Barnabas for you; but Amalia really despises his work as a messenger, and now, when he seems to have had some success, as she can easily tell from the way we huddle together and whisper to each other, she despises him even more than before. So she's telling the truth, don't ever let yourself be deceived about that. But if I have occasionally disparaged messenger work, K., it was not with the intention of deceiving you, but because I was afraid. These two letters that have gone through Barnabas' hands so far are the first sign of forgiveness, dubious enough as it is, that our family has been given in three years. This change, if it is a change and not an illusion – illusions are more frequent than changes – is connected with your arrival here, our fate has in some way come to depend on you, perhaps these two letters are just a beginning and Barnabas' work might develop beyond delivering letters to you – let's hope so while we can – but for the time being everything centres on you. Up there we have to settle for what they give us, but down here we might still be able to do something for ourselves, that is to make sure of your good will or at least not to make you turn against us or, most important of all, to do our utmost and use all our experience to protect you so that your contact with the Castle – which might help us to survive – is not lost. And how can we best achieve all that? By ensuring that you don't harbour any suspicion towards us when we approach you, for you are a stranger here and so you're sure to be suspicious of everything, and rightly so.

'What's more, we are despised, and you are influenced by public opinion, especially through your fiancée; how could we get in touch with you without setting ourselves against her, even if that wasn't at all what we intended, and thus offending you? And the messages, which I read carefully before you got them – Barnabas didn't read them, as a messenger he refused to – didn't seem very important at first sight; they were out of date, and by referring you to the mayor they lost any importance they might have had. So how were we to approach you with these messages? If we insisted how important they were, we could be open to suspicion for overrating something so obviously unimportant and claiming credit in your eyes for delivering the information, for serving our own interests rather than yours, indeed by doing that we might lead you to disregard the information itself and thus we would, very much against our will, be deceiving you. But if we didn't attach very much value to the letters, we would be laying ourselves open to suspicion just as much, because in that case why were we taking such trouble to deliver these unimportant letters, why were our actions inconsistent with our words, why were we deceiving not only you to whom the letters were addressed, but also the person who employed us to deliver them, because he certainly didn't give them to us so that we could explain to you how worthless they were. It's also impossible to steer a course between these two extremes, in other words to judge the letters correctly, because their value is constantly shifting, the responses they provoke are endless, so which one you choose, and therefore your reaction, is a matter of pure chance. And when our anxiety for you affects the situation, everything gets confused, and you mustn't judge what I say too harshly. If, for instance, as happened once, Barnabas comes back and tells me you find his work as a messenger unsatisfactory, if his first reaction is to be so upset and if his pride in his work has been offended to the extent that he proposes to give it up, then I am perfectly capable of resorting to lies, deceit, cheating, to any kind of wickedness, just as long as it helps to put things right. But then I'm doing it, at least as I see it, for your sake just as much as for ours.'

There was a knock at the door. Olga ran to the door and unlocked it. A shaft of light from a storm lantern shone into the dark room. The late visitor whispered a few questions and was answered in a whisper, but was not satisfied and tried to push his way into the room. Olga found herself unable to hold him back, so she called Amalia, evidently hoping that she would do her utmost to get rid of the visitor in order to avoid disturbing their parents. And indeed Amalia soon came hurrying over, pushed Olga aside, and went out into the street, shutting the door behind her. A moment later she was back, such was the speed with which she had done what Olga could not.

Olga then told K. that the call had been for him; it was one of the assistants, sent by Frieda to look for him. Olga had wanted to protect K. from his assistant; if K. wished to tell Frieda the truth about his visit here later, she said, he should, but he should not be found out by the assistant. K. approved of this, but he declined Olga's offer that he should stay the night and wait for Barnabas; under other circumstances he might have accepted, for it was well into the night and it seemed to him that whether he wanted it or not, he was now so closely involved with this family that although for other reasons it might cause embarrassment, this house was the most natural place in the whole village for him to spend the night. All the same, he declined Olga's offer; the assistant's visit had alarmed him, he could not understand why Frieda, who after all knew his wishes, and the assistants, who had learnt to fear him, had joined forces again to the extent that Frieda had not hesitated to send one of them for him – just the one, moreover, while the other had presumably stayed with her. He asked Olga if she had a whip; she did not, but she did have a good willow switch, which he took. Then he asked her whether there was another way out of the house; there was one through the yard, she said, but then you had to climb over the neighbour's garden fence and then go through the garden to reach the street. K. decided to do that. As Olga led him through the yard to the fence, K. tried to calm her fears, telling her he was not at all angry with her for the little subterfuges she had told him about, on the contrary he quite understood, and he thanked her for the trust she had shown by telling him her story; he also asked her to send Barnabas over to the school as soon as he got back, even if it was the middle of the night. For sure, Barnabas' messages were not the only hope he had, things would be bad for him if they were, but he certainly had no wish to forgo them, he intended to continue with them; nor would he forget Olga, for she was perhaps more important to him than the messages, as were her courage, her understanding, her resourcefulness, the sacrifices she made for her family. If he had to choose between Olga and Amalia, he told her, he would not have to think for long. And he pressed her hand warmly as he swung himself over the fence of the neighbouring garden.

When he reached the street he saw further up, as far as he could make out in the darkness, the figure of his assistant still walking up and down in front of Barnabas' house; now and again he stopped and tried to shine his lantern through the curtained window into the living room. K. called him; without any sign of alarm he stopped peering into the house and came towards K. 'Who are you looking for?' asked K., testing the suppleness of the willow switch against his thigh. 'You,' said the assistant, coming closer. 'Who are you, then?' K. said abruptly, for it did not look like his assistant – the man seemed older, wearier, more wrinkled, but fuller in the face, and his gait was quite different from the assistants' usual nimble movements which gave the impression their limbs were galvanised; he walked slowly with a slight limp, like a genteel invalid. 'Don't you recognise me?' he asked. 'I'm Jeremias, your old assistant.' 'Are you?' said K., letting him catch sight of the willow switch he had held hidden behind his back. 'But you look quite different.' 'That's because I'm on my own,' said Jeremias. 'When I'm alone, I lose my youthful high spirits.' 'So where is Artur?' asked K. 'Artur?' said Jeremias, 'the dear little boy? He has left. You were rather too hard on us, you see. The gentle soul couldn't stand it. He's gone back to the Castle to lodge a complaint against you.' 'What about you?' asked K. 'I could stay here,' said Jeremias, 'Artur is making a complaint on my behalf too.' 'What are you complaining about?' asked K. 'That you can't take a joke,' said Jeremias. 'Whatever have we done? Fooled about a bit, laughed a bit, teased your fiancée a bit. Besides, it was all part of our orders. When Galater sent us to you . . .' 'Galater?' asked K. 'Yes, Galater,' said Jeremias, 'he was deputising for Klamm at the time. When he sent us to you, as I say – I took careful note of it, that's our job, after all – he told us: You're going to assist the surveyor. We said: But we don't know anything about that kind of work. He replied: That's unimportant; if he needs to, he'll teach you. The most important thing is to cheer him up. I'm told he takes everything very seriously. He has just arrived in the village and right away he thinks it's a big deal, but in fact it's nothing at all. That's what you have to convey to him.'

'Well,' said K., 'was Galater right, and have you carried out your instructions?' 'I don't know,' said Jeremias. 'I don't think it was possible in such a short time. I only knew you were very hard on us, and that's what we're complaining about. I don't understand how you can't see that a job like that is hard work and that it's quite wrong to make it even harder for us as you did, deliberately and wilfully, like a child; after all you're only an employee, and not even a Castle employee. Your callousness in letting us freeze on the railings, or the way you treated Artur, who can be upset for days if he's spoken to harshly, nearly killing him by punching him when he was on the mattress, or the way you chased me up and down in the snow all afternoon so that it took me an hour to recover. I'm not as young as I was, you know!' 'My dear Jeremias,' said K., 'you're right about all that, but you ought to tell Galater about it. He sent you of his own accord, I didn't ask him to send you. And since I didn't ask for you, I was entitled to send you back again; I'd rather have done it peaceably than by force, but you obviously wouldn't have it any other way. Besides, why didn't you speak as frankly as this as soon as you met me?' 'Because I was in service,' said Jeremias, 'that's obvious.' 'And now you're not in service any more?' asked K. 'Not any more,' said Jeremias. 'Artur has given in his notice at the Castle, or at least the proceedings are under way to release us once and for all.' 'But you still come looking for me as if you were in service,' said K. 'No,' said Jeremias, 'I'm only looking for you to reassure Frieda. You see, when you left her for Barnabas' sisters she was very upset, not so much at losing you but because you betrayed her; mind you, she'd seen it coming for a long time and that was already making her very unhappy. I just looked in at the schoolhouse window to see whether you might have come to your senses, but you weren't there, only Frieda, sitting on a school bench crying. So I went in and we came to an agreement. It's all arranged; I'm on room service at the Herrenhof, at least until my business at the Castle is settled, and Frieda is back in the bar. That suits her better, there was no sense in her getting married to you. Besides, you didn't appreciate the sacrifice she was prepared to make for you. But the kind-hearted girl still has occasional misgivings about whether you've been treated fairly, whether you might not have been with Barnabas' sisters after all. Although of course there could be no doubt about where you were, I still went to make quite sure, because after all her upsets Frieda deserves to get a good night's sleep at last, and so do I. So off I went, and I didn't just find you, I also found that those girls follow you as if they were on a lead. The dark one especially, a real wildcat – she's really taken with you. Well, everyone to his own taste. In any case, there was no need for you to go round through the neighbour's garden, I know the way.'

21

So now it had happened; it was predictable, but inevitable. Frieda had left him. It didn't have to be final, it wasn't as bad as that; he could win her back, she was easily influenced by others, even by these assistants, who thought Frieda's situation was similar to theirs, and now that they had given their notice had persuaded her to do the same. But K. only had to confront her and remind her of all the advantages of being with him, and she would be full of remorse and be his again, especially if he could justify his visit to Barnabas' sisters by telling her what he had achieved thanks to them. But in spite of the thoughts with which he sought to reassure himself about Frieda, he was still uneasy. Just a short while ago he had praised Frieda to Olga, calling her his only support; well, that support was not very reliable – it didn't take anyone very powerful to rob him of her, it had only needed this unsavoury assistant, this piece of flesh that sometimes gave the impression of not being fully alive.

Jeremias had already set off when K. called him back. 'Jeremias,' he said, 'I'll be quite frank with you, and I want you to give me an honest answer. After all, we're not in a master-servant relationship any more, and I'm as pleased about that as you are, so we have no reason to lie to one another. Here in front of your eyes I'm breaking this stick that was meant for you; you see, I chose to come through the garden not because

I was afraid to meet you, but to take you by surprise and use it on you a few times. Now don't hold that against me, it's all done with; if you hadn't been a servant foisted on me by the authorities, if you'd simply been an acquaintance, I'm sure we would have got on splendidly, even if I find your appearance rather irritating at times, and we could now make up for what we have missed on that account.' 'Do you think so?' said the assistant, yawning and rubbing his weary eyes. 'I could explain it all to you in more detail,' he continued, 'but I haven't the time, I have to go to Frieda, the poor child is waiting for me, she hasn't started work yet. I persuaded the landlord to give her a while to recover – she wanted to throw herself back into her work right away, probably to help her to forget – and we wanted to spend that time together, at least. As for your suggestion, I certainly have no reason to lie to you, but I have just as little reason to confide in you. You see, I'm not in the same position as you. As long as I was in your service, you were of course a very important person to me, not because of any qualities of your own but because of my conditions of employment, and I would have done anything you wanted me to, but now you mean nothing to me. Even though you broke the stick, it makes no difference; it only reminds me what a brutal master I had, it does nothing to gain my favour.'

'You are talking to me,' said K., 'as if it were quite certain that you will never have anything to fear from me again. But that is not in fact the case. You're probably not free of me yet, things aren't settled here as quickly as that . . .' 'Sometimes even more quickly,' Jeremias interjected. 'Sometimes,' said K., 'but there is nothing to suggest that has happened this time, at least neither of us has any written evidence of a settlement. So the process is only just under way, and I have not yet used my contacts to intervene, but I shall. If the matter is not decided in your favour, you have done very little to endear yourself to your master, and I might not even have needed to destroy my willow switch. And though you have lured Frieda away from me, which has given you the idea that you're cock of the walk, for all the respect I have for you, even if you no longer have any for me, I know that just a few words from me to Frieda will be enough to demolish the lies you've used to trap her. And only lies could have turned Frieda against me.'

'These threats don't frighten me,' said Jeremias. 'You don't want me as your assistant, you're afraid to have me as your assistant, you're just afraid of having any assistants, it was only fear that made you punch poor little Artur.' 'Maybe,' said K. 'Did that make it hurt any the less? Perhaps I shall still have plenty of chances to show how afraid I am in the same way. If I see that being an assistant makes you so unhappy, for my part I shall take the greatest pleasure in forcing you to do it, fear or no fear. What's more, next time I shall make sure that it will be just you, without Artur, so that I can give you my full attention.' 'Do you think,' said Jeremias, 'I am in the slightest afraid of all that?' 'Yes, I do,' said K. 'You are certainly a bit afraid, and if you've any sense you would be very frightened. If you aren't afraid, why haven't you gone back to Frieda by now? Tell me, are you in love with her?' 'In love with her?' said Jeremias. 'She's a good, sensible girl, she was Klamm's mistress, so she's perfectly respectable. And if she keeps pleading with me to get her away from you, why shouldn't I help her, especially since I wouldn't be doing you any harm, seeing how you consoled yourself with those damned Barnabas girls.' 'Now I can see you're afraid,' said K., 'quite pathetically afraid. You're trying to catch me out with lies. Frieda only wanted one thing – to be rid of those wild, lecherous hounds, those assistants; unfortunately I didn't have time to carry out her wishes fully, and now I see the results of my failure.'

'Herr K.! Herr K.!' someone was calling from down the street. It was Barnabas. He arrived out of breath, but did not forget to bow to K. 'I've done it!' he said. 'What have you done?' asked K. 'Have you submitted my request to Klamm?' 'No, I couldn't,' said Barnabas, 'I did my best, but it was impossible. I pushed to the front, and without being summoned I stood so close to the counter all day that one of the clerks even had to push me aside because I was in his light, and whenever Klamm looked up I let him know I was there by raising my hand, which is forbidden. I stayed in the office longer than anyone else, I was the only one left apart from the servants, I was delighted when I saw Klamm come back again, but it wasn't to see me, he just wanted to check something quickly in a book and left again straight away, in the end because I was still there one of the servants almost had to sweep me out of the door with a broom. I'm telling you all this so that you won't say you're not pleased with me again.'

'What use to me is all your hard work, Barnabas,' said K., 'if it doesn't get you anywhere?' 'But I did get somewhere,' said Barnabas. 'As I left my office – I call it my office – I saw a gentleman some way away coming slowly towards me along one of the corridors; apart from him there was no one about, it was very late by now. I decided to wait for him, it was a good excuse to stay there, I would have preferred to stay in any case so I wouldn't have to bring you bad news. But apart from that, it was worth waiting for the gentleman, because it was Erlanger. You don't know him? He's one of Klamm's chief clerks, a small frail man with a slight limp. He recognised me at once, he's famous for his memory and for knowing people; he just frowns, and he can recognise anybody, often people he's never even seen, people he's only heard of or read about – he can hardly ever have seen me, for instance. But although he recognises everyone immediately, at first he asks them as if he's uncertain. "You're Barnabas, aren't you?" he said to me. And then he asked: "You know the surveyor, don't you?" And then he said: "That's most fortunate. I am going to the Herrenhof just now. Tell the surveyor to come and see me there. I am in room fifteen. But he should come straight away. I only have a few meetings there, and I am coming back here at five in the morning. Tell him I am very keen to speak to him." '

Suddenly Jeremias set off. Barnabas, who in his excitement had scarcely noticed him before, asked: 'What's Jeremias doing?' 'He wants to get to Erlanger before I do,' said K. He ran after Jeremias, caught up with him, held him by the arm and said: 'Are you overcome by a sudden longing to see Frieda? I feel like that, too, so we'll go along together.'

Outside the darkened Herrenhof stood a small group of men, two or three of them were holding lanterns, so several faces could be made out. K. saw only one he knew, Gerstäcker the coachman. Gerstäcker greeted him with the question: 'You're still in the village, are you?' 'Yes,' replied K., 'I'm here to stay.' 'Well, it's none of my business,' said Gerstäcker. He coughed loudly and turned to the others.

It turned out that they were all waiting to see Erlanger. He had already arrived, but was discussing business with Momus before receiving his clients. The conversation revolved mostly around why they were not allowed to wait in the inn, instead of having to stand around out here in the snow. Though it was not very cold, it was most inconsiderate to make them wait outside, perhaps for hours, in the middle of the night. Of course, it wasn't Erlanger's fault, because he was most obliging, he probably didn't know about it and would certainly have been very annoyed if he had been told. The landlady of the Herrenhof was to blame, her desperate ambition to be refined meant that she could not put up with a lot of clients in the inn at the same time. 'If it has to be, and if they must come in here,' she used to say, 'then in heaven's name let them come in one at a time.' And she had got her way, so the clients, who at first had simply waited in the corridor, then later on the stairs, then in the hall, and then in the bar, were finally pushed out into the street. And she was not even satisfied with that. She found it intolerable, as she put it, to be constantly 'under siege' in her own house. She could not understand what all these clients' visits were for in the first place. 'To make your front steps dirty,' an official had once answered, probably in exasperation, but she found this explanation very persuasive and was fond of quoting it. Her wish – which was quite in line with the clients' wishes – was that a building should be put up opposite the Herrenhof in which the clients could wait. But most of all she would have preferred the consultations and interviews to take place outside the Herrenhof altogether, but the officials were against this, and when they put up serious opposition, of course she did not get her way, though on less important matters, thanks to her tireless yet gentle woman's persistence, she exercised a sort of petty tyranny. But it looked as if she would have to put up with the meetings at the Herrenhof, for the gentlemen from the Castle refused to conduct their official business anywhere other than at the inn. They were always in a hurry, they only visited the village reluctantly, they did not have the slightest wish to stay there any longer than absolutely necessary, so they could not be expected to waste time by moving temporarily into another building across the street with all their papers, just for the sake of domestic peace and quiet at the Herrenhof. For the officials preferred to conduct their business in the bar or in their rooms, if possible during meals or from their beds before going to sleep or in the morning when they were too tired to get up and wished to lie in a little longer. Nevertheless, the question of constructing a building for clients to wait in seemed to be moving towards a favourable conclusion – though it was a bitter blow for the landlady, and caused some amusement, because the matter required numerous meetings, and the corridors of the inn were scarcely ever empty.

All these things were being discussed in low voices by the people waiting outside. It struck K. that although there was widespread discontent, no one objected to the fact that Erlanger sent for his clients in the middle of the night. He asked about this, and was told that they should actually be most grateful to Erlanger that he did so. It was only his good will and the pride he took in his official duties that induced him to come to the village at all, because if he wanted to – and this might even be more in line with the rules – he could send some junior clerk to take down statements. But mostly he refused to do this, he wanted to see and hear everything for himself, but then he had to devote his nights to the work, for his official schedule did not allow any time for visits to the village. K. demurred, saying that Klamm himself came to the village during the day, and even stayed for several days; so was Erlanger, who was after all only a secretary, more indispensable up there than Klamm? Some people laughed good-naturedly, others kept an awkward silence; the latter prevailed, and K. received hardly any reply. Only one of them said hesitantly that of course Klamm was indispensable, whether at the Castle or in the village.

Then the front door opened and Momus appeared, flanked by two servants carrying lamps. 'Herr Erlanger will see Gerstäcker and K. first,' he said. 'Are they both here?' They came forward, but Jeremias slipped in first, muttering 'I work here in room-service', and was let into the inn by Momus with a smile and a friendly pat on the shoulder. 'I shall have to keep a closer eye on Jeremias,' K. said to himself, though he still realised that Jeremias was probably much less of a threat than Artur, who was working against him at the Castle. It might even be wiser to let them pester him as his assistants than to have them roaming about the place beyond his control, free to indulge in the intrigues for which they seemed to have a particular aptitude.

It was only as K. passed him that Momus affected to recognise him. 'Ah, the surveyor!' he said, 'who so dislikes being questioned, is now in a hurry to be interviewed. It would have been simpler to let me interview you the last time. Ah well, it's difficult to chose the right interview.' When K. made to pause at this, Momus said: 'In you go, in you go! I could have done with your answers then, not now.' Nevertheless, stung by Momus's behaviour, K. replied: 'You think only of yourselves. I don't answer questions just because they are put to me by officials, then or now.' Momus replied: 'Whose questions will you answer, then? Who else is here? In you go!'

In the hall they were met by a servant, who led them along the route already familiar to K., across the yard then through the archway into the low corridor that sloped gently downwards. The rooms of the senior officials were obviously on the upper floors, while those of the secretaries were on this corridor, even Erlanger's, although he was one of the most senior secretaries. The servant extinguished his lantern, for the corridor was brightly lit by electric light. Here everything was small but elegantly constructed, and space was used to the best advantage. The corridor was just high enough for them to walk upright. Along the sides was a series of doors almost next to each other. The side walls did not reach right up to the ceiling, no doubt to provide ventilation, for the tiny rooms along this deep cellar-like corridor probably had no windows. The disadvantage of these walls that were open at the top was that the noise in the corridor must have been heard in the rooms too. Many of the rooms seemed to be occupied, in most of them people were still awake, voices, hammering and the clink of glasses could be heard, and yet the impression was not of any special jollity. The voices were muffled, only now and then could a word be made out, there seemed to be no conversation, probably someone was only dictating something or reading out loud; in particular, from the rooms in which there was the sound of glasses and plates not a word could be heard, and the hammering reminded K. that someone had once told him that many officials occupied themselves from time to time with carpentry, precision engineering work and suchlike in order to relax from their constant mental exertions.

The corridor itself was empty except for a tall, pale, slim gentleman in a fur coat under which his nightclothes were showing, who was sitting outside one of the doors; presumably it had got too stuffy for him in his room, so he had come to sit outside. He was reading a newspaper, but not with any great attention, for he frequently stopped reading and yawned, leaning forward and looking down the corridor, perhaps expecting a client who was late for an appointment. As they passed him, the servant said to Gerstäcker, referring to the gentleman: 'That was Pinzgauer!' Gerstäcker nodded. 'He hasn't been down here for a long time,' he said. 'No, not for a very long time,' the servant agreed.

Finally they came to a door that looked no different from the others, but which, the servant told them, was Erlanger's. The servant climbed onto K.'s shoulders and looked over the gap above the wall into the room. 'He's lying on his bed,' the servant told them as he climbed down; 'he's in his clothes, but I think he's asleep. Sometimes the change of routine down here in the village tires him out. We'll have to wait. He'll ring when he wakes up; though it has happened before that he slept through the whole of his stay in the village and had to go straight back to the Castle when he woke up. It's voluntary work that he does here.' 'I just hope he sleeps right through this time,' said Gerstäcker, 'because when he wakes up and finds he hasn't very much time left for work, he's very annoyed that he's been asleep and tries to get everything done as quickly as he can, so you don't have time to say what you want to.' 'Are you here about the haulage contract for the building?' asked the servant. Gerstäcker nodded, but the servant scarcely noticed; he looked over Gerstäcker's head – he stood head and shoulders above him – and smoothed his hair slowly and solemnly.

22

At that moment K, who was gazing aimlessly around him, saw Frieda some way off at a turning in the corridor. She acted as if she did not recognise him, and only stared; she was holding a tray with some empty plates. He told the servant, who ignored him – the more they spoke to the servant, the more vacant he seemed – that he would be back directly, and ran up to Frieda. When he reached her, he took her by the shoulders as if reclaiming possession of her and asked a few trivial questions, all the time looking her closely in the eye. But she scarcely relaxed her rigid attitude, absent-mindedly rearranged the plates on the tray, and said: 'What do you want from me? Go back to the – well, you know who, you've just come from there, I can tell from the look of you.' K. quickly changed the subject; he had not wanted their conversation to start so abruptly on the worst possible topic, one that showed him in the least creditable light. 'I thought you were in the bar,' he said. Frieda looked at him in astonishment, then gently passed her free hand over his cheeks and forehead. It was as if she had forgotten what he looked like and as if the gesture would help to remind her; her eyes, too, had the distant look of someone making a great effort to remember.

'I was taken on again to work in the bar,' she then said slowly, as if the words she spoke scarcely mattered, and what mattered more was that she was talking to K. again. 'This work is not for me, anyone can do it, anyone who can make beds and put on a friendly smile and doesn't mind being pestered by the guests or even encourages it – anyone like that can be a chambermaid. But it's different in the bar. I was taken on straight way for that job, though I hadn't left it in a very honourable way last time, of course this time I had someone to look after me. But the landlord was pleased that I did, because it made it easy for him to take me on again. I even had to be persuaded to accept the job; if you think of the memories I have of working there, you'll understand why. In the end I accepted, and I'm only helping out down here. Pepi begged to be spared the embarrassment of having to leave the bar right away, so because she had worked so hard and looked after everything to the best of her abilities, we let her stay on for another twenty-four hours.'

'That's all very convenient,' said K., 'except that first of all you left your job in the bar for my sake, and now you're going back to it just before our wedding?' 'There's not going to be any wedding,' said Frieda. 'Because I was unfaithful?' asked K. Frieda nodded. 'Now look, Frieda,' said K., 'we've already talked about this alleged infidelity often enough, and every time you've had to admit in the end that your suspicions were groundless. On my side, nothing has changed since then, everything is still as innocent as it always was, and it always will be. So something must have changed on your side as a result of other people's insinuations or something like that. At any rate you're being unfair to me, because look: what is my position with those two girls? The one, the dark one – I'm almost ashamed to go into such detail to defend myself, but you give me no choice – the dark one I find as awkward as you probably do. Whenever I can keep my distance from her, I do, and she makes it easy for me too, no one could be more reserved than she is.' 'Oh yes,' Frieda burst out, it seemed spontaneously – K. was glad to hear her speak so unguardedly, she was not reacting as she intended, 'you might think she's reserved, you call the most brazen one of all reserved, and unbelievable as it is, you mean it honestly, you're not hiding anything, I know. That's what the landlady at the Brückenhof says about you: I can't stand him, she says, but I can't leave him to his own devices either, if you see an infant who can't walk properly yet running too far ahead, you can't help trying to save it.'

'You should take her advice for once,' said K. with a smile, 'but we can ignore that girl; reserved or brazen, I don't want to talk about her.' 'But why do you call her reserved?' asked Frieda insistently – K. took her interest as a hopeful sign – 'Have you tried to approach her, or are you trying to cast aspersions on someone else?' 'Neither,' said K. 'I call her that out of gratitude, because she makes it easy for me to ignore her and because if she did speak to me very much, I would feel unable to go back there, which would be a great loss for me; as you know, I have to go there for the sake of our future together, yours and mine. And that's why I have to talk to the other girl; I may admire her because she is so capable, sensible and selfless, but no one could call her seductive.' 'The servants think differently,' said Frieda. 'In this and no doubt in many other things,' said K. 'Are you going to conclude that I am unfaithful because the servants are so lecherous?' Frieda did not reply, and let K. take the tray from her and place it on the floor; he put his arm under hers and began to walk up and down with her in the narrow corridor. 'You don't know what it means to be faithful,' she said, trying not to let him get too close. 'It doesn't matter how you behave with those girls; the fact that you go to see that family at all and come back with the smell of their living-room on your clothes is a disgrace I can't put up with. And you rush out of the school without a word, and then you spend half the night with them. And then when someone is sent to ask where you are, you have those girls say they haven't seen you, especially the one who is so extremely reserved. And you sneak out of their house secretly, perhaps to protect the reputation of those girls – of those girls! No, let's not talk about it any more!'

'Not about that,' said K., 'but let's talk about something else, Frieda. There's nothing to say about that anyway. You know why I have to go there. I don't find it easy, but I have to. You shouldn't make it any harder for me than it is. Today I thought of going there just for a moment to ask whether Barnabas, who should have brought me an important message long before, had finally arrived. He hadn't, but they assured me that he would be back before long, and I believed them. I didn't want to have him follow me to the school, to spare you being bothered by his presence. Hours went by, but unfortunately he didn't come. Someone else did come, though, someone I detest. I had no wish to let him spy on me, so I left through the neighbour's garden; but I didn't want to hide from him either, far from it, so I approached him quite openly on the street – I admit, with a very supple willow switch. That's all, so there's no more to be said about it, but there's plenty to be said on another subject. What about the assistants, then? I find the very mention of them as repulsive as you find my mentioning that family. Just compare your attitude to them with my attitude to Barnabas' family. I can understand your revulsion for his family; I can even share it. I only go there for my own ends, sometimes I think I'm treating them shabbily and exploiting them. But what about you and the assistants? You've never denied that they pester you, and you've even admitted you find them attractive. I didn't resent that, I realised that there are forces at work here that you can't cope with, I was pleased enough that you resisted them, I helped you to look after yourself, and just because I took my eye off them for a few hours, trusting your loyalty, though I also trusted that the schoolhouse was securely locked and that I'd finally got rid of the assistants – I'm sorry to say I still underestimate them – just because I took my eye off them and that wretch Jeremias, who when you look at him closely is an elderly, sickly creature, just because of that I have to lose you, Frieda, and you welcome me with the words "There's not going to be any wedding." Surely I'm the one who's entitled to take exception, but I don't; I still don't.'

Once again K. thought he ought to divert Frieda's attention for a while, so he asked her to bring him something to eat, because he had not had anything since lunch. Frieda, clearly relieved at this request, nodded and hurried off, not down the corridor where K. supposed the kitchens were, but down a few steps to one side. She soon brought a plate with some slices of sausage and a bottle of wine, but it looked more like the remains of a meal; the slices had been rearranged on the plate to make it look more presentable, but there were even some sausage skins left on it, and the bottle was three-quarters empty. But K. made no comment and set to with a good appetite. 'Did you go to the kitchens?' he asked. 'No, I went to my room,' she replied. 'I have a room down there.' 'I wish you had taken me with you,' said K., 'I'll go down there so I can sit down to eat.' 'I'll bring you a chair,' said Frieda, who was already on her way down. 'No thank you,' said K., pulling her back, 'I'm not going down there, and I don't need a chair now either.' Looking sulky, Frieda let him grip her arm, hung her head and bit her lips. 'Yes, all right, he's down there,' she said, 'what else did you expect? He's lying down on my bed, he caught a chill outside, he's shivering, he's hardly eaten. It's all your fault, really; if you hadn't chased the assistants away and gone running after those people, we could be sitting quietly in the school now. You alone destroyed our happiness. Do you imagine Jeremias would have dared to abduct me while he was in service? If so, you have no idea how things are here. He wanted to be with me, he tortured himself, he lay in wait for me, but it was only a game, like a hungry dog who will leap around but still won't dare to jump up onto the table. And it was the same with me. I liked him, he's a childhood playmate – we used to play together up on the Castle Hill, those were happy times, you've never asked me about my past – but none of that mattered as long as Jeremias was in service, because I knew my duty as your future wife. But then you got rid of the assistants, and you're still boasting about it as if you had done something for me, which is true in a certain sense. You got your way with Artur, if only for the time being; he's delicate, he hasn't got Jeremias' devil-may-care spirit, and you very nearly did for him when you punched him that night – that blow was also aimed at our happiness – so he fled to the Castle to complain, and even if he comes back soon, he's gone for now. But Jeremias stayed. When he's on duty, he's afraid if his master so much as raises an eyebrow, but when he's off duty he's afraid of nothing. He came and took me away; I'd been abandoned by you, and I was dominated by him, my old friend, I couldn't resist. I didn't open the schoolhouse door, so he smashed the window and pulled me out. We fled here, the landlord thinks highly of him, and the guests like nothing better than a room-waiter like him, so we were both taken on; he's not living with me, but we share a room.'

'In spite of everything,' said K., 'I don't regret having dismissed the assistants. If the situation was as you describe it, and if your fidelity only depended on their sense of duty, then it's just as well it's all over. It wouldn't have been a very happy marriage in the company of those two wild animals who could only be controlled by the whip. In that case, I'm grateful to the family that unintentionally helped to separate us.' In silence they walked up and down together again; it was impossible to say which had made the first move. Frieda kept close to K., and seemed annoyed that he had not taken her arm again. 'So everything seems to be settled,' K. continued, 'and we can say goodbye, you can go to your Jeremias, who is probably still suffering from the chill he caught in the school garden, in which case you have already left him on his own far too long, and I'll go back to the school alone or, since I have nothing to do there without you, I'll go somewhere else where they'll take me in. I only hesitate because I still have good reason to have doubts about what you've told me. I have quite the opposite impression of Jeremias. While he was in our service he was after you the whole time, and I don't think his sense of duty would have held him back for very long from assaulting you seriously. But now that he regards himself as no longer in service, things are different. Forgive me if I explain it this way: since you are no longer his master's fiancée, you don't represent such a temptation to him as you did before. You may be a childhood friend of his, but though I only know him from a brief conversation we had last night I don't think he sets much store by feelings like that. I don't know why you find him such a passionate person; he strikes me as a particularly cool thinker. Galater has told him to enter my service for reasons that are probably not to my advantage, and he threw himself into it with great enthusiasm, I admit – this is not uncommon here – and part of his work was to destroy our relationship; he has tried to do this in various ways, one of which was trying to seduce you with his lewd behaviour, another – and the landlady backed him up in this – was inventing stories about my infidelity. His scheme succeeded – some recollection he had of Klamm's methods might have helped; it's true he lost his job, but perhaps that was just when he no longer needed it, and he was rewarded for his efforts by pulling you out of the schoolhouse window. But now his job is done, his enthusiasm has waned, and he's tired of it; he'd rather be in Artur's place, who is not lodging any complaint, far from it, he's earning credit and getting himself other jobs. But someone has to stay behind and see how things develop. He finds it tiresome keeping an eye on you. There's no trace of love for you, he told me that quite frankly. Because you're Klamm's former mistress, of course he finds you perfectly respectable, and I'm sure it makes him feel good worming his way into your room and feeling like a little Klamm for once, but that's all; you mean nothing to him now, bringing you here to the Herrenhof is just something he's doing on top of his main job, he's only stayed on here to keep you calm, but he won't be here for long, only until he gets new instructions from the Castle or until you've cured him of his cold.'

'Oh, you're telling lies about him!' said Frieda, beating her little fists together. 'Telling lies? No, I'm not telling lies. I might be doing him an injustice, that's quite possible; I know what I've said about him isn't immediately obvious, and there could be other explanations. But lies? The only point about telling lies about him would be to undermine your love for him. If that were necessary and if it were appropriate, I wouldn't hesitate to tell lies. No one could blame me for that; the people who give him his orders put him at such an advantage over me that I have to rely on my own resources, and I might be allowed to resort to lies. It would be a relatively innocent way of defending myself, but in the end it would be pointless. So put your fists down.'

K. took Frieda's hand in his; she tried to pull it away, but with a smile and without trying very hard. 'But I don't need to tell lies about him,' he said, 'because you don't love him at all, you only think you do and you'll be grateful to me for saving you from deceiving yourself. Look, if anyone wanted to take you away from me without using force, but in the most carefully calculated way possible, it would have to be done by using the two assistants, apparently nice, simple, cheerful, couldn't-careless lads who've blown in from up there, from the Castle, with a few childhood memories – that's all very agreeable, isn't it, especially when I'm just the opposite of all that, forever chasing after things you don't understand, things that annoy you, that bring me into contact with people you detest and who, for all my innocence, make me feel rather as you do towards them. It's all just a malicious but very clever scheme to exploit the flaws in our relationship. Every relationship has its flaws, ours too; after all, we came together, each of us from quite different worlds, and since we met both our lives have taken a different direction, we still feel unsure because it's all far too new. I'm not talking about myself, that's not so important, because basically I've been blessed ever since you set eyes on me, and it's not too difficult to get used to that state. But you, on top of everything else, were torn away from Klamm; I can't judge quite what that means, but I've gradually got some sense of it, the feeling of losing your balance and not being able to steady yourself, and even if I was always ready to support you, I wasn't always there, and even when I was there, sometimes you were under the spell of your daydreams, or something more tangible like the landlady, for instance – in other words there were times when you looked away from me, when you were lost in some vague nostalgia, poor child, and at times like those it only needed the right people to be put in front of you for you to be taken in by them and fall for the illusion that what were really only fleeting impressions, ghosts, old memories, what was in fact a former life which was receding further and further into the past – that this was still your real existence. It was an error, Frieda, nothing but the final and, seen in its true light, contemptible difficulty facing our eventual union. Wake up, pull yourself together; even if you thought the assistants were sent by Klamm – which is quite untrue, it was Galater who sent them – and even if they were able to use this illusion to cast such a spell on you that you imagined you could see traces of Klamm in their dirty tricks and their lechery, like someone who thinks he sees a jewel in a dungheap, whereas in fact he could never find it even if it were really there – they are still just rascals, no better than the stable-lads, except that they're sickly, a breath of fresh air makes them feel ill and sends them to bed, which is a place they know how to find best with their low cunning.'

Frieda had leant her head on K.'s shoulder, and they walked to and fro arm in arm in silence. 'If only,' said Frieda slowly, calmly, almost contentedly, as if she knew she only had a little more time to rest on K.'s shoulder and wished to enjoy it to the full, 'if only we had left here at once, that night, we could be safe now, always together, your hand would always be close enough for me to hold it. How much I need you near me, how desolate I feel without you since we met; to be close to you, believe me, is all I dream about, nothing else.'

Then someone called from the side passage – it was Jeremias; there he stood on the bottom step, dressed in nothing but a shirt, though he had wrapped himself in one of Frieda's shawls. He stood there with a pleading and reproachful expression, his hair was dishevelled, his straggling beard looked wet through, he could only keep his eyes open with an effort, his sunken cheeks were flushed and yet sagged limply, his bare legs shivered with cold, making the long fringes of the shawl quiver too; he looked like an invalid who had escaped from hospital, at the sight of whom one's only thought would be to get him back into bed again. That was Frieda's reaction, too; she pulled herself away from K. and was beside him in a flash. Her presence, the care with which she pulled the shawl closer round him, and the haste with which she tried to coax him back into the room seemed to give him renewed strength, it was as if he only now recognised K. 'Ah, the surveyor,' he said, stroking Frieda's cheek to appease her, for she was unwilling to allow any further conversation, 'please excuse the interruption. But I am not at all well, that is excuse enough. I think I have a fever, I must drink tea to sweat it out. Those damned railings in the school garden, I shan't forget them for a long time, and then, when I was already frozen, I had to run around in the dark. Without realising what we're doing, we sacrifice our health for things that really aren't worth it. But you mustn't let me disturb you, sir, come into our room and visit the patient, then you can finish telling Frieda what you have to say. When two people who have got used to each other separate, naturally they have so much to say to each other in their last moments together that a third person, especially when he's lying in bed waiting for the tea he's been promised, can't possibly understand. But just come in, I'll be very quiet.'

'That's enough,' said Frieda, taking his arm and pulling him away. 'He's feverish and doesn't know what he's talking about. But K., I beg you, don't go in there. It's our room, mine and Jeremias', or rather it's mine, and I forbid you to go in. You're pursuing me, oh, K., why are you pursuing me? I'll never ever come back to you, the very thought of it makes me shudder. So go back to your girls, they sit next to you by the stove in nothing but their shifts, I'm told, and if someone comes to fetch you they spit at him. If you find that place so attractive, that's where you belong. I've always tried to keep you away from there, without much success, but at least I tried, that's all over now, you're free. A nice life you've got to look forward to, you might have a bit of a fight with the servants for one of them, but no one in heaven or earth will begrudge you the other one. The union is blessed from the start. Don't deny it; I know you can disprove anything, but in the end it's still true. Just think, Jeremias, he's disproved everything!' They nodded and smiled in mutual understanding. 'But still,' continued Frieda, 'even if you did disprove everything, what good would that do, what do I care? What goes on in that house is entirely his business and theirs, not mine. Mine is to look after you until you're as well as you were before K. tormented you on account of me.' 'So you really aren't coming with us, Herr K.?' asked Jeremias, but then he was pulled away once and for all by Frieda, who kept her back turned to K. At the foot of the steps a small door could be seen, even lower than the doors along the corridor; not only Jeremias, but Frieda too had to bend down to go through it. Inside it looked bright and warm, K. heard some whispering, no doubt fond words to persuade Jeremias into bed, then the door was shut.

23

It was only now that K. noticed how quiet it had become in the corridor, not just in this section where he had been talking to Frieda, which seemed to be part of the domestic quarters, but also in the long passageway where earlier the rooms had been so busy. The gentlemen had finally gone to sleep, then. K., too, was very weary; perhaps that was why he had not stood up to Jeremias as he ought to have done. He might have been wiser to act like Jeremias, who was clearly exaggerating the severity of his cold – his wretched state was not the result of a chill, it was innate and would not be improved by any herbal infusion – to behave just like him and demonstrate just how exhausted he was by collapsing here in the corridor, which would have allowed him to get some sleep and be looked after for a while. But it would not have worked out as well for him as for Jeremias, who would certainly, and no doubt rightly, have won this competition for sympathy, just as he would clearly have won any other contest. K. was so tired that he considered trying to get into one of these rooms, some of which were surely empty, and enjoy a good sleep in a comfortable bed. That, he thought, would make up for a great deal. He even had a nightcap available; on the tray that Frieda had left on the floor was a small flask of rum. Unconcerned about the effort of making his way back, K. emptied the flask.

Now at last he felt strong enough to face Erlanger. He looked for Erlanger's door, but because the servant and Gerstäcker were not to be seen, and because all the doors were identical, he could not find it. However, he thought he remembered in what part of the corridor it had been, and decided to open the door that seemed the most likely one. It would not be too risky to try; if the room was Erlanger's, he would surely welcome him, if it were someone else's it would still be possible to apologise and leave, and if the occupant were asleep, which was most likely, K.'s visit would go unnoticed; things could only go wrong if the room were empty, because in that case K. would scarcely be able to resist the temptation of lying down on the bed and sleeping for ages.

Once again he looked up and down the corridor to see if there was anyone who could tell him where to go and save him taking a risk, but it was silent and deserted. Then he listened at the door; there was no sound in there either. He knocked so softly that he would not wake anyone who was sleeping there, and when even then nothing happened, he opened the door with the greatest caution. He was greeted by a faint cry. The room was small, and more than half of it was taken up by a wide bed; on the bedside table an electric lamp was on, and beside it lay a small grip. In the bed, but quite hidden under the quilt, someone stirred and whispered from among the bedclothes: 'Who is it?' Now K. could not just leave; with annoyance he looked at the inviting but unfortunately occupied bed, then remembered the question and gave his name. This seemed to have some effect, for the man in the bed pulled the quilt away from his face, though not very far and rather timidly, ready to cover himself up again at once if there should be something not quite right out there. But then he threw back the covers without further thought and sat upright. It was certainly not Erlanger. He was a small, healthy-looking gentleman whose face displayed a certain contradiction in that he had the chubby cheeks and the laughing eyes of a child, while his domed forehead, his pointed nose, his narrow mouth with lips that scarcely met, and his receding chin were not at all those of a child, but indicated a superior intellect. It was no doubt his satisfaction with this, his satisfaction with himself, that had preserved distinct traces of childish health in his features.

'Do you know Friedrich?' he asked. K. said he did not. 'But he knows you,' said the man with a smile. K. nodded; there was no lack of people who knew him, indeed that was one of the many obstacles in his path. 'I am his secretary,' said the man, 'my name is Bürgel.' 'Please excuse me,' said K., reaching for the door-handle, 'I'm afraid I mistook your door for someone else's. You see, I have to see Herr Erlanger.' 'What a pity!' said Bürgel, 'not that you have to see someone else, but that you came to the wrong door. Because once I am woken up I can never get back to sleep again. Well, you mustn't let that upset you, it's my own misfortune. And why can't the doors be locked, you may ask. There's a reason for it, of course; it's because of an old adage that the secretaries' doors should always be open. But then they didn't have to take that so literally.' Bürgel looked inquiringly and cheerfully at K.; notwith-standing his complaint, he looked very well rested – Bürgel had probably never felt as tired as K. did just then.

'What are you going to do now?' asked Bürgel. 'It's four o'clock. Anyone you want to see now, you'll have to wake him up, not everyone is as used to being disturbed as I am, and not everyone will put up with it as patiently as I do. The secretaries are a nervous lot. So stay here for a while; they start to get up around five o'clock here, that will be the best time to keep your appointment. So please let go of the door-handle and find somewhere to sit down, there's not much room in here, so you'd better sit on the edge of the bed. Are you surprised I don't have a table or a chair here? Well, you see, I was given the choice of having either a fully furnished room with a narrow hotel bed, or this large bed and nothing but a washstand. I chose the large bed, after all the bed is the main thing in a bedroom. Yes, this bed must be perfect for someone who can stretch out and have a really good sleep. I'm always tired because I never sleep very well, but it's good for me too; I spend most of the day in it, I deal with all my correspondence and take down clients' statements here. It works very well. It's true that there's nowhere for the clients to sit down, but they put up with that, and in any case it's more pleasant for them if they stand and the secretary is relaxed than to be sitting comfortably and be shouted at. So the only place I can offer you is on the edge of the bed here, but it's not an official place, it's only for night-time discussions. But you are so quiet, Herr K.'

'I'm very tired,' said K.; no sooner had he been invited than he sat down, without any display of manners, on the bed and leaned against the bedpost. 'Of course,' said Bürgel, laughing, 'everyone is tired here. For instance, I got through a whole lot of work yesterday, and again today. It's out of the question that

I shall fall asleep now, but if the utterly improbable should happen and I should fall asleep while you are here, please keep quiet and don't open the door either. But don't worry; I shall certainly not fall asleep, or at most only for a few minutes. The fact is, you see, probably because I am so used to dealing with clients, I fall asleep most easily when I have company.' 'Please do go to sleep, Herr Bürgel,' said K., delighted to hear this. 'Then, with your permission, I shall sleep a while too.' 'No, no,' laughed Bürgel again, 'I'm afraid I can't fall asleep just because I'm asked to, the opportunity only arises in the course of a discussion; a discussion is the most likely thing to send me to sleep. Yes, our nerves suffer in this business. I, for example, am secretary for communications. You don't know what that is? Well, I represent the main communication' – at this he rubbed his hands together vigorously in involuntary delight – 'between Friedrich and the village, I mediate between his secretaries at the Castle and those in the village; I spend most, but not all, of my time in the village, but at any moment I must be ready to drive up to the Castle, you can see my travelling grip. It's a restless life, it doesn't suit everyone; on the other hand, it's true that I couldn't do without this sort of work any longer, any other kind of work would pall for me. What is it like being a surveyor?'

'I am not doing any such work, I am not in employment as a surveyor,' said K. He could hardly keep his mind on the subject, he was actually longing for Bürgel to fall asleep, but even that was only to keep up his hopes, in his heart he felt that the moment when Bürgel would fall asleep was still unimaginably far off. 'That is astonishing,' said Bürgel, shaking his head vigorously. 'He took a notepad from under the bedclothes and wrote something down. 'You are a surveyor, and have no surveying to do.' K. nodded mechanically. He had stretched his left arm along the top of the bedstead and rested his head on it; he had already tried several ways of making himself comfortable, but this position was the most comfortable of all, and now he could concentrate a little better on what Bürgel was saying.

'I am prepared,' said Bürgel, 'to go further into this matter. It is most certainly not the way we do things here, to allow a qualified person to stand idle. It must be disagreeable for you too; do you not find it distressing?' 'Yes, I do,' said K. slowly, smiling to himself, for just at that moment it did not distress him in the least. Moreover, Bürgel's offer did not impress him very much, it could not be taken seriously. Without knowing anything of the circumstances of K.'s appointment, of the problems it had caused in the village and at the Castle, of the complications that had already arisen or were about to arise since K. had arrived here – without any knowledge of all that, indeed without any indication that he had even the slightest inkling of it, which one would assume a secretary ought to have as a matter of course, he was offering to settle the whole problem effortlessly with the help of his little notepad. But then Bürgel said: 'You seem to have suffered a number of setbacks already,' once again revealing a shrewd judgement of people that had already on occasion alerted K. not to underestimate Bürgel; but in his present state he found it difficult to form a proper judgement of anything other than his own weariness.

'No,' said Bürgel, as if he were answering K.'s unspoken thoughts and were considerately sparing him the trouble of voicing them, 'you must not let these setbacks deter you. Many things here seem designed to put you off, and when one is new here the obstacles seem quite insuperable. I have no wish to investigate exactly what the situation is, perhaps the appearance does in fact correspond with the reality, in my position I lack the proper perspective to judge that; but then again, mark my words, there are occasions that almost run counter to the overall situation, occasions when a word, a glance, a gesture of trust can achieve more than a lifetime of strenuous effort. That is indeed so. Then again, of course, these occasions can correspond to the overall situation insofar as they are never taken advantage of. But why are they not taken advantage of, I always ask.'

K. had no answer; although he realised that what Bürgel was saying probably concerned him closely, for the moment he felt a great aversion to anything that might concern him. He shifted his head slightly to one side, as if to let Bürgel's questions pass him by and leave him undisturbed. 'It is,' Bürgel continued, stretching himself and yawning, actions that were bafflingly at odds with the gravity of his words, 'it is a constant complaint of the secretaries that they are obliged to conduct most of their interviews in the village at night. Why do they complain about that? Because it tires them? Because they would rather sleep at night? No, that's certainly not why they complain. Of course there are secretaries who work hard and those who work less hard, as everywhere, but none of them complain of being overworked, certainly not in public. That's simply not our way. In this respect we make no distinction between normal time and working time. Such distinctions are foreign to us. So what do the secretaries have against night-time interviews, then? Is it perhaps consideration for the clients? No, no – it's not that either. The secretaries have no more consideration for their clients than they do for themselves, no more and no less. Indeed this lack of consideration, this rigid adherence by the secretaries to their duties, shows the greatest consideration their clients could ever wish for. And in actual fact – though a superficial observer will not realise it – this is fully recognised in that it is the night-time interviews that the clients prefer, no complaints are made about them in principle. Why then do the secretaries still complain about them?'

K. had no answer to this either; he was so bemused he could not even tell whether Bürgel seriously expected a reply or not. 'If you would just let me lie down on your bed,' he thought to himself, 'then tomorrow at midday, or better still tomorrow evening, I'll answer any questions you like.' But Bürgel seemed to be paying no attention to him, he was much too preoccupied with the question he had asked himself: 'As far as I know from my own experience, the secretaries' objection to night-time interviews is something like this: the night is less suitable for discussions with their clients because at night it is difficult, if not impossible, to keep the interviews on an entirely official footing. That does not apply to external procedures; if necessary the formalities can of course still be observed at night just as strictly as by day. So it's not that; it's more because one's official judgement can be affected at night. One is inadvertently inclined to judge things from a more personal perspective at night, the clients' submissions are given more weight than they should, quite irrelevant factors to do with the clients' private circumstances interfere with one's decisions – their worries and their problems; the necessary barrier between clients and officials, while outwardly it may be scrupulously observed, is relaxed, and instead of a straightforward exchange of questions and answers, which is the correct procedure, a strange, entirely inappropriate exchange of personalities seems to take place. At least that is what the secretaries say, and they are after all people endowed with a quite exceptional sensitivity towards such things. But even they – we have often discussed this among ourselves – detect very few of those undesirable effects during night-time interviews, on the contrary, from the start they make every effort to resist them, and in the end they believe they have managed particularly well. But when one reads through their reports later, one is often amazed at their manifest shortcomings; and these are errors which time and again concede advantages to the clients to which they are not fully entitled, and which, at least by our rules, cannot be quickly corrected through the usual procedures. They will quite certainly be corrected at some point by a bureau of control, but purely on legal grounds, it cannot disadvantage the client at that stage. Under these circumstances, are the secretaries' complaints not entirely justified?'

K. had already been half-asleep for a while, now he came to again. 'What is all this for? What is it for?' he wondered, looking at Bürgel through half-shut eyes, seeing him not as an official who was discussing difficult questions with him, but simply as a barrier to sleep, the further significance of which escaped him. Bürgel, however, fully absorbed in his train of thought, smiled, as if he had just managed to mislead K.

slightly. But he was ready to put him back on the right track immediately. 'Well,' he said, 'then again, one cannot simply say these complaints are wholly justified. Although night-time interviews are nowhere actually prescribed, so one is not breaking any rules by trying to avoid them, nevertheless circumstances, the excessive burden of work, the way officials are employed at the Castle, their inaccessibility, the rule that clients should not be interviewed until all other investigations are fully completed but should then be interviewed immediately – all this and much besides has made night-time interviews unavoidable. But if they have become unavoidable – this is what I say – then that is also, at least indirectly, a consequence of the rules, and to object to night-time interviews as such would almost – I exaggerate a little, of course, that is why I can say this – would almost amount to objecting to the rules themselves. On the other hand we must allow the secretaries to protect themselves as far as they can, and within the rules, against night-time interviews and their drawbacks, which may be more apparent than real. And indeed they do this, and go to great lengths to do it; they only accept cases for discussion which are least likely to involve such interviews, they check everything carefully prior to negotiations, and if the results bear them out they will cancel all hearings, even at the last minute, they often steel themselves by summoning a client ten times before they actually see him, they prefer to get colleagues to deputise for them who are not competent to deal with a particular case and so can deal with it more easily, they arrange interviews for late at night or early morning, avoiding the middle of the night – there are many more ruses like that.

They're not so easy to deal with, the secretaries, they are almost as tough as they are vulnerable.'

K. was asleep, though not properly asleep; he heard Bürgel's words perhaps better than he had before when he was awake but dog-tired, one word after another rang in his ears, but his wearisome state of consciousness had gone, he felt free, Bürgel held him no longer, he only sensed Bürgel's presence from time to time, he was not yet profoundly asleep, but he was immersed in sleep, no one was going to deprive him of sleep now. And it was as if he had won a great victory in this way, as if people were already there to celebrate it, and he or someone else was raising a glass of champagne to honour his triumph. And so that everyone should know what it was all about, the battle and the victory were being repeated all over again, or perhaps they were not being repeated, perhaps they were only now taking place and had already been celebrated earlier, and the celebrations had continued because, fortunately, the outcome was certain. A secretary, naked, very like a statue of a Greek god, was being bested in combat by K. It was very funny, and K. smiled gently in his sleep at how the secretary's proud bearing gave way to panic at K.'s thrusts, how he was forced into a hasty use of an outstretched arm or a clenched fist to defend himself, but was too slow every time. The fight did not last long; K. advanced stride by stride, and they were huge strides. Was it a contest at all? There was no serious resistance, only now and again a squeal from the secretary. This Greek god squealed like a girl being tickled. Finally he was gone, and K. was alone in a large room; he turned round ready to fight, looking for his opponent, but there was no one there, the crowd of people had gone, only the champagne glass lay smashed on the floor. K. ground it to pieces underfoot, but the splinters of glass stabbed him, with a start he woke up again, he felt sick, like a small child when it is wakened, but even so at the sight of Bürgel's bare chest the thought flashed into his mind from his dream: 'There's your Greek god! Just throw him out of bed!'

'There is, however,' said Bürgel, looking thoughtfully up at the ceiling as if searching his memory for examples but unable to find any, 'there is, however, despite all the precautions taken, a way in which the clients might have the opportunity to turn this night-time weakness of the secretaries, if it is indeed a weakness, to their own advantage. Of course, it is a very rare opportunity, or rather one that almost never occurs. It is when the client arrives unannounced in the middle of the night. It might surprise you that, although it seems so obvious, it scarcely ever happens. Well, that's because you are unfamiliar with the circumstances here. But even you must have noticed how tightly organised our official system is. This means that any client who has a request of some sort, or who needs to be interviewed about something for other reasons, must receive a summons immediately, without delay, indeed usually before he has had time to think about it, or even before he knows about it. He will not be interviewed this time, or not normally, because the matter is usually still in the early stages, but he has been summoned, which means he cannot then arrive unannounced, that is, entirely unexpectedly, at most he can arrive at the wrong time, in which case he is simply reminded of the date and time of his appointment, and if he then comes back at the right time, as a rule he is sent away, so there is no longer any difficulty; the summons in the client's hand and the entry in the files – these are the secretaries' weapons of defence, which may not always be adequate, but they are still powerful. This, however, only applies to the secretary directly responsible for the matter; it would still be open to anyone to approach the others unexpectedly during the night. But hardly anyone will do that, it makes very little sense. First of all, it would mean alienating the secretary responsible; although we secretaries are not jealous of each other where our work is concerned, each of us has far too heavy a workload lavishly piled onto our shoulders for that, but where clients are concerned we do not tolerate any interference with our sphere of responsibility. Several clients have lost their case because when they thought they were not making any progress through the proper channels they tried to slip through by applying elsewhere. Besides, such attempts must fail because a secretary who is not responsible for the case, even if he is caught unawares at night and is willing to help, cannot, simply because he is not dealing with that case, intervene any more effectively than some lawyer or other, indeed far less so, because even though he may be able to help in other respects – knowing as he does the secret byways of the law better than any of those legal fellows – he simply has no time to devote to matters he is not responsible for, he cannot spend a single moment on them.

'With such prospects, who then would spend his nights going around secretaries who were not dealing with his case? And the clients are fully occupied too, if on top of their other work they are going to answer the summons and directives of those who are dealing with them – "fully occupied", that is, as it applies to the clients, which of course is nothing like the sense that "fully occupied" means for the secretaries.' K. nodded and smiled; now he thought he understood everything, not because it concerned him but because he was now convinced that he was going to fall deeply asleep any minute, this time without any dreams or interruptions. Between the secretaries who were responsible for cases on the one hand and those who were not on the other, and faced with the hordes of fully occupied clients, he would sink into a deep sleep and so escape them all. He was by now so used to Bürgel's soft, complacent voice that it would help him to drift off rather than disturb him, while it was clearly not going to succeed in putting Bürgel himself to sleep. 'Rattle on, old mill, rattle on,' he thought, 'you're rattling just for me.'

'What then,' said Bürgel, stroking his lower lip with two fingers, with wide open eyes and outstretched neck, rather as if he were approaching a splendid viewpoint after an arduous walk, 'what then of that rare occasion I mentioned that almost never arises? The secret lies in the rules governing responsibility. You see, it is not the case, and never can be the case in a large and busy organisation, that only one particular secretary is responsible for each case. It is just that one is chiefly responsible, but many others have responsibility for certain aspects, though to a lesser extent. Who, even if he were the most industrious secretary, could single-handedly grasp all the complexities of even the most trivial case on his desk? Even what I said about one being chiefly responsible is overstating the case. Is not the whole responsibility also contained in the least? Is not the most important thing here the zeal with which the matter is handled? And is that not always constant, always of the greatest intensity? Overall there may be differences between the secretaries, and there are countless such differences, but not in their zeal, not one of them can restrain himself if he is called on to deal with a case for which he has only the slightest responsibility. Publicly, of course, a properly planned procedure has to be devised, and so for each client a particular secretary emerges, who must be approached officially. But this doesn't always have to be the one who is chiefly responsible for the case; that is determined by the organisation and its particular requirements at the time. That is the position.

'And now, sir, consider the possibility that a client for one reason or another, in spite of the obstacles I have already described and which are generally quite sufficient, nevertheless surprises a secretary who has a degree of responsibility for the case in question in the middle of the night. I suppose such a possibility never occurred to you, did it? I can well believe it. Indeed, there is no need to take it into account, because it never happens. What a strange and quite uniquely shaped, clever little grain of sand a client like that would have to be in order to slip through that incomparable sieve! You think it could never happen? You are right, it cannot happen. But one night – who can be certain of everything? – it does happen. It is true it has not happened to anyone I know; but that proves very little, my circle of acquaintances is very limited compared to the numbers involved here, and besides it is by no means certain that a secretary to whom something like that has happened is willing to admit it; it is after all a very personal affair that touches closely on an official's sensibilities. However, my own experience perhaps shows that this is such a rare occurrence, based only on unsubstantiated rumour, that it is scarcely worth worrying about. Even if it should actually happen, one would think it could be rendered harmless simply by demonstrating that there is no provision for such a case in this world, which is very easy to do. At any rate, it is morbid to be so afraid of it that one hides under the bedclothes and doesn't dare to look out. And even if the utterly improbable should suddenly materialise, is everything then lost? On the contrary; that everything should be lost is the least probable of all improbabilities. To be sure, if the client is in one's room, then the situation is serious. It lowers the spirits. "How long can you resist?" you ask yourself. But you will not resist, you know that. Just try to imagine the situation: there he is, sitting in front of you, this client you have never seen but always expected, always yearned to meet, who, you had always sensibly assumed, was out of reach. Simply by his silent presence he invites you to investigate his miserable life, to explore it as if it were your own and to sympathise with his futile demands. Such an invitation in the stillness of the night holds you spellbound; you respond to it, and now you have actually ceased to be an official. You are in a position where it will be difficult to turn down a request. Strictly speaking you are in a desperate position, but in actual fact you are very happy. Your position is desperate because you are sitting there quite defenceless, waiting for the client to make his request and knowing that once it is uttered you have to grant it, even if, as far as you are aware of the overall situation, it just tears the official system to shreds – that is without a doubt the worst thing that can happen to you in your professional career, quite especially, apart from anything else, because you are for the moment blatantly assuming an unimaginable superiority of rank. Our status simply does not authorise us to grant such requests, but in the presence of this client in the middle of the night it is as if greater official powers accrue to us, we commit ourselves to things beyond our remit, indeed, we will even implement them. Like a bandit in the woods, the client wrings concessions from us in the night that we would never grant in other circumstances – well, that's how it is at the time, while the client is still there, encouraging us, cajoling us and egging us on, while we are only half-aware of what is happening; but what it will be like afterwards when it's all over and the client has left, happy and satisfied, and we stand there alone, defenceless in the face of our misuse of power – that is unimaginable. But we are still happy. How suicidal happiness can be. Of course, we could take pains to conceal the true situation from the client, who will hardly notice anything of his own accord. Exhausted, disappointed, apathetic and indifferent as he is from exhaustion and disappointment, he probably thinks he has somehow, for whatever reasons, found his way by accident into a different room from the one he wanted, he sits there unawares, thinking, if he is thinking at all, about his mistake and his weariness. Couldn't you just leave him like that? No, you cannot. You are so happy you cannot hold your tongue, and you have to explain everything to him. Without any consideration for yourself, you have to show him in detail what has happened and why it has happened, what an exceptionally rare and uniquely great opportunity this is, you must explain to the client that although he has stumbled upon this opportunity as unwittingly as only a client could have done, he is now in a position, should he wish to, Herr K., to dictate his terms simply by submitting his request in one form or another, and that it is waiting to be granted, indeed it is already being offered to him – you must explain all this. It is an official's worst moment. But once that has been done, Herr K., the most essential part is over, then you must be content to wait.'

K. was no longer listening, he was asleep, oblivious to everything. His head, which at first had been resting on his left arm with which he was grasping the bedpost, had slipped down while he was asleep and now hung free, slowly sliding down as his raised arm no longer supported it; involuntarily he reached out his right hand towards the bed to support himself, but in doing so accidentally seized Bürgel's foot, which happened to be sticking up under the quilt. Bürgel looked down and, however uncomfortable it may have been, surrendered his foot to K.

Then there were several hefty knocks on the wall; K. started and looked in that direction. 'Is the surveyor in there?' someone asked. 'Yes,' said Bürgel; he freed his foot from K.'s grasp and suddenly started stretching violently and boisterously like a small boy. 'Then it's high time he came over here,' came the reply, without any regard for Bürgel or whether he might still need K. 'It's Erlanger,' whispered Bürgel; he seemed unsurprised that Erlanger was in the next room. 'Go and see him immediately, he's getting annoyed, try to calm him down. He sleeps soundly, but we have been talking too loud, you can't control yourself and keep your voice down when you are discussing certain things. Well, go on, you don't seem able to wake up. Go on, what are you still doing here? No, you needn't apologise for being so sleepy, why should you? The body only has a limited amount of energy, who can help it if that limit is reached occasionally? No one can. That's how the world adjusts itself and keeps its equilibrium. It's an excellent device, a forever inconceivably excellent device, even though it may be dismal in other respects. Now go, I don't know why you are looking at me like that. If you stay here any longer Erlanger will be after me, and that's something I'd much rather avoid. Go on, who knows what's in store for you over there, there are opportunities galore everywhere here. It's just that some opportunities are so to speak too great to be seized, there are some things that come to grief simply by themselves. Yes, it's amazing. Besides, I hope I can get some sleep now after all. Of course, it's already five o'clock and the noise will start soon. I just wish you would go!'

Dazed by suddenly waking from a deep sleep, still unimaginably sleepy, his whole body aching from his uncomfortable position, for a long time K. could not bring himself to get up, he held his forehead in his hands and looked down into his lap. Even Bürgel's persistent urgings could not have made him leave, only a sense of the complete futility of staying in this room slowly drove him to it. The room seemed indescribably desolate; whether it had become so, or whether it had always been like that, he did not know. He would not even manage to go back to sleep in here, indeed this conviction was the deciding factor. Smiling faintly at this, he stood up, and supporting himself wherever he could, on the bed, against the wall, against the door, he left without a word of farewell to Bürgel, as if he had long since taken his leave of him.

24

He would probably have walked past Erlanger's room in the same absent way, if Erlanger had not been standing at the open door, beckoning to him with a single brief twitch of his forefinger. Erlanger was all ready to leave, wearing a black fur coat with a close-fitting collar buttoned up tight. A servant was just handing him his gloves and holding a fur hat. 'You should have been here long ago,' said Erlanger. K. was about to apologise, but Erlanger closed his eyes wearily, indicating that he did not wish to hear. 'The point at issue,' he said, 'is that a certain Frieda was previously employed in the bar. I do not know her personally, only by name, she is no concern of mine. This Frieda used to bring Klamm his beer. Now another girl seems to be there. Of course, this change is of no importance to anyone, least of all to Klamm. But the more demanding one's work is, and Klamm's is undoubtedly the most demanding of all, the less energy one has to protect oneself against the world outside, and as a result any trivial change in the most trivial matter can cause serious upset. The slightest alteration on one's desk, the removal of a stain that has always been there, all this can be disturbing, and so can a new waitress. Of course, while this would disturb anyone else doing any kind of work, none of it can disturb Klamm, that is out of the question. Nevertheless, we are obliged to pay every attention to Klamm's comfort by removing even things that do not disturb him –

and for him there probably are no such things – if it strikes us that they might disturb him. We do not remove them for his sake or because of his work, but for our own sake, for the sake of our conscience and our peace of mind. That is why Frieda must return to the bar immediately. It may be that she will cause some upset simply by returning; in that case we shall send her away again, but for the present she must return. You live with her, I have been told, so make sure she returns at once. It goes without saying that no allowance can be made for personal feelings, so I shall not enter into any further discussion of the matter whatever. I am already going further than I have to when I point out that if we can rely on you in this small matter, it might on some occasion help to further your case. That is all I have to say to you.' He dismissed K. with a nod, put on the fur hat his servant handed him and, followed by the servant, walked quickly, though with a slight limp, down the corridor.

Sometimes orders were given here that were very simple to carry out, but this fact gave K. no pleasure, not only because the order concerned Frieda – and it was meant as an order, though it sounded more like a sneer to K. – but above all because to him it indicated the futility of his efforts. Orders were issued over his head, to his advantage or disadvantage, and even those that were to his advantage probably held some hidden snag; at all events they were issued over his head, and he was in far too lowly a position to be able to intervene, let alone silence them and make his own voice heard. If Erlanger dismisses you, what can you do, and even if he didn't dismiss you, what could you say to him? Certainly, K. realised that today his weariness had done him more harm than any adverse circumstances; but why could he, who had thought he could rely on his body, and would never have set out along this path unless he had, why could he not tolerate a few bad nights and one without any sleep, why did he get so uncontrollably tired here of all places, where no one got tired, or rather where everyone was permanently tired without it affecting their work at all, indeed it seemed to help them to do it? The only conclusion was that theirs was a quite different kind of tiredness from K.'s. Theirs was no doubt a tiredness resulting from work done gladly, something that from the outside looked like tiredness, but was in fact an indestructible peace and calm. When one feels a little fatigued in the middle of the day, that is part of the normal happy course of the day. For these gentlemen, thought K., it's always the middle of the day.

And this thought was clearly confirmed by the lively bustle that broke out now, at five o'clock, all along the corridor. There was something extremely cheerful about the babble of voices in the rooms. At times it sounded like the happy cries of children preparing for an outing, at others like daybreak in a hen-coop, like the joy of being in complete harmony with the dawning day – somewhere one of the gentlemen was even imitating a cock crowing. The corridor itself was still empty, but the doors were already going, now and again one would be opened a little and quickly closed again, the corridor was in commotion with people opening and shutting their doors, here and there K. could see, above the gap where the walls did not reach the ceiling, tousled early morning heads appearing and then immediately disappearing. From the far end appeared a small trolley carrying files, which a servant was pushing slowly along. Another servant walked beside the trolley with a list in his hand, evidently checking the numbers on the files against those on the doors. The trolley stopped outside most of the doors, then the door usually opened and the appropriate file was handed into the room; sometimes it was only a single sheet of paper, in which case there was a brief exchange of words between room and corridor, presumably the servant was being upbraided. If the door remained shut, the files were carefully piled in front of it. In such cases it seemed to K. that the opening and shutting of doors in the vicinity did not lessen, but increased, although files had already been delivered there too. Perhaps the others were eagerly eyeing the files that had unaccountably been left lying outside the door, perhaps they could not understand how anyone who only had to open his door to get hold of his files still did not do so; it might even be that files that remained unclaimed were later distributed among the others, and that they were already making frequent checks to see whether the files were still lying there, and whether there was a chance they might be given them. Moreover, most of the files left lying outside were particularly large bundles, and K. assumed a certain degree of showing off or malice, or even of justified pride to encourage colleagues, had been the reason for leaving them there for the time being. What confirmed this assumption was that sometimes, always at a moment when he was not looking, once the bundle had been left on display for long enough it was suddenly and very quickly pulled inside the room, whereupon the door remained firmly shut as before and the other doors in the vicinity settled down too, whether through disappointment or relief that this object of constant provocation had finally been removed; but then they gradually came to life again.

K. observed all this with a sense of involvement as well as curiosity. He almost felt at ease among this bustle; he looked up and down, following the servants and watching them as they delivered their files – at a discreet distance, to be sure, for several times they had turned and glared at him with heads bent and pursed lips. The further their work progressed, the less smoothly it went; either the lists were not quite in order, or the servants could not always tell which files were which, or the gentlemen raised objections for some other reason, at any rate some files had to be redistributed, in which case the trolley was wheeled back and negotiations for the return of the files were conducted through the half-closed door. The negotiations caused enough trouble in themselves, but it frequently happened that when files had to be returned, the doors that had earlier been most active now stayed obstinately shut as if they wanted nothing more to do with the matter. Then the real problems began. The gentleman who believed he was entitled to the files became extremely impatient, he made a great fuss in his room, clapping his hands, stamping his feet, and continually shouting a certain file number through his door into the corridor. The trolley was then often left unattended; one servant was busy calming the impatient gentleman, the other was standing in front of a closed door, battling for the return of the file. Both had a hard time of it. The attempts to calm the impatient one often only made him more impatient, he refused to listen to the servant's empty words, he did not want reassurances, he wanted his files; one of them poured a whole washbasin over the servant through the gap above the door. But the other servant, who was clearly the more senior, was having an even harder time. If the gentleman concerned was prepared to negotiate at all, there were earnest discussions during which the servant referred to his list, while the gentleman referred to his notes and to the files he was supposed to return; but for the time being he held on to them firmly so that hardly anything of them was visible to the servant's searching eyes. So then the servant had to rush back for fresh evidence to the trolley, which by now had rolled a little further down the gently sloping corridor on its own, or he had to go back to the gentleman who was claiming the files and report to him the objections of the gentleman in possession, only to be given further objections in return.

These negotiations were very protracted; occasionally agreement was reached and one of the gentlemen might hand over some of the files or would be given another file in compensation as there had only been a mistake in the distribution, but it also happened that someone simply had to abandon his claim to any files, either because his claims were refuted by the servant or because he grew tired of the long-drawn-out wrangling – in which case he did not hand the files back to the servant, but with a sudden gesture threw them far out into the corridor so that the ribbons came undone, the papers were scattered, and the servants had to go to considerable trouble to put everything straight again. But this was all rather easier than when the servant received no answer at all when he requested the return of the files; then he would stand outside the closed door, pleading, imploring, quoting from his list, referring to regulations, all in vain – no sound came from the room, and the servant clearly had no right to enter without permission. Then even this exemplary servant would lose his self-control, go to his trolley, sit on the files, wipe the sweat from his brow and for a while do nothing but swing his legs helplessly to and fro. This caused great interest all round, whispers could be heard everywhere, hardly a door was still, and from the gaps above the walls faces, which were strangely swathed almost completely in scarves and were never in the same place for more than an instant, followed everything that went on. In the midst of this commotion it struck K. that Bürgel's door stayed shut the whole time, and although the servants had already been past that part of the corridor, no files had been allocated to him. Perhaps he was still asleep, which amidst all this uproar certainly suggested he was a very sound sleeper; but why had he been given no files? Only very few rooms, which were probably unoccupied anyway, had been passed over like this. On the other hand, there was a new and particularly restless occupant in Erlanger's room, who must actually have driven Erlanger out during the night; this rather belied Erlanger's cool, urbane manner, but was suggested by the fact that he had been obliged to wait for K. outside the door.

But K.'s attention was always quickly diverted from these abstruse thoughts to the servant. Certainly, what he had been told about the servants generally – about their idleness, their easy lives, their arrogance – did not apply at all to this one; no doubt there were exceptions among the servants or, more probably, they fell into different groups, for there were, as K. had noted, many gradations here of which he had seen scarcely any sign before. In particular, he was delighted by the perseverance of this servant. In his struggle with these obstinate little rooms – to K. it often looked like a struggle with the rooms, since he scarcely ever caught a glimpse of the occupants – the servant did not give up. He may have weakened – who would not have done? – but he soon recovered, slid down from his trolley, set his jaw, put back his shoulders and strode back to the door that was to be stormed. And indeed he was repelled two or three times, and very simply, just by that damned silence, but still he was not defeated by any means. When he saw that nothing was to be gained by direct assault, he tried a different tactic – namely, as far as K. could see, cunning. He would appear to give up on that door, as if he were letting it exhaust the resources of its own silence, and turn to other doors; but after a while he would return and shout to the other servant – all this was done loudly and demonstratively – and would begin to pile up files outside the closed door as if he had changed his mind and decided that the gentleman, far from having files withheld from him, was entitled to them. Then he went on, but kept his eye on the door, and then when, as usually happened, the gentleman before long cautiously opened the door to take the files inside, in two bounds the servant was there, jammed his foot in the door and thus forced the gentleman at least to negotiate with him face to face, which then usually ended in a more or less satisfactory outcome. And if that did not work, or if he thought it was not the right method for a particular door, he would try a different approach. For instance, he would turn his attention to the gentleman who was claiming his files; he would shove the other servant aside – he was a quite useless helper who just went on working mechanically – and begin to persuade the gentleman, whispering confidentially to him, poking his head well into the room, no doubt making promises and assuring him that with the next delivery the other gentleman would be appropriately penalised, at least he would frequently point to his rival's door and, as far as his weariness permitted, laugh. Then again there were one or two occasions when he would give up any attempt, though here too K. believed he was only pretending to give up, or at least pretending he had good reason to do so; he would then walk on calmly without looking round, ignoring the fuss the deprived gentleman was making, the only sign that it affected him being that he shut his eyes once or twice. But then the gentleman would slowly calm down too; just as the continual crying of a child gradually turns into sporadic sobbing, so it was with his shouting, though even after he had gone quiet there was still an occasional single shout or a brief opening and shutting of his door. At all events, it turned out that here too the servant had undoubtedly acted in just the right way, because in the end there was only one gentleman who would not calm down; for some time he was quiet, but only in order to recover his voice, then he started up again as loud as ever. It was not entirely clear why he shouted and complained like this, perhaps it had nothing at all to do with the distribution of the files.

Meanwhile the servant had completed his work, and only one file, in fact no more than a small sheet of paper, a page from a notepad, was left on the trolley through the negligence of his assistant, and now they did not know who should have it. 'That could very well be my file,' thought K. to himself. The mayor had after all kept referring to his case as one of the most trivial of all. And however arbitrary and absurd K. himself found his assumption in reality, he attempted to approach the servant, who was thoughtfully examining the piece of paper. This was not so easy, for K.'s liking for the servant was poorly rewarded; even at his busiest he had found time to glare impatiently at K., jerking his head irritably. Only now that he had finished his work did he appear almost to have forgotten about K., indeed he had become altogether less conscientious, which was understandable given his great weariness. He did not take much trouble with the piece of paper, perhaps he did not even read it through and only pretended to, and although he would no doubt have delighted any one of the gentlemen along this corridor by handing it to him, he decided not to; he was tired of delivering things, and putting a forefinger to his lips as a signal to his colleague to say nothing, he tore the sheet – K. was nowhere near him at this point – into shreds and put them in his pocket. It was probably the first irregularity that K. had seen in this administration, though of course it was possible that he had not understood it properly. And even if it was an irregularity, it was excusable; under the conditions that prevailed here the servant could not do his work impeccably, his pent-up frustration and annoyance had to break out some time, and if it found expression simply by tearing up a little piece of paper, it was innocent enough.

The voice of the gentleman who refused to calm down still rang through the corridor, and his colleagues, who in other respects did not behave very amicably to one another, seemed to be entirely of one mind as far as the noise was concerned; it gradually began to look as if he had taken it on himself to make enough noise for all of them, and they just encouraged him to keep at it by calling to him and nodding their heads. But the servant was now not in the least bothered, he had finished his work; he pointed to the handle of the trolley to indicate that his colleague should take it, and they left as they had come, only much more cheerfully and so quickly that the trolley bounced along in front of them. Only once did they start and look back. The gentleman who had not stopped yelling – K. was now loitering outside his door because he was curious to know what the man wanted – realising that his shouting was getting him nowhere, had evidently located the button of an electric bell, and no doubt delighted with the relief it offered, stopped yelling and began to ring the bell continuously. At this a loud murmur arose from the other rooms, which seemed to indicate general approval; the gentleman was apparently doing something they would all have liked to do long since, and had only desisted for some unknown reason. Could it be the domestic staff, perhaps Frieda, he was ringing for? In that case he would have to ring for a long time, for Frieda was busy wrapping Jeremias in wet towels, and even if he had recovered she would have no time, because then she would be lying in his arms.

But the ringing did have an immediate effect. Already in the distance the landlord of the Herrenhof himself came hurrying along the corridor, dressed in black with his jacket buttoned up as always, but it was as if he had forgotten his dignity, he was in such a hurry. He had half raised his arms as if he had been summoned to some great disaster and was coming to seize it and quickly smother it against his chest; at every brief pause in the ringing he seemed to give a little jump and increase his pace. Then his wife appeared too, a good way behind him; she was also running with her arms stretched out, but she ran with short tripping steps; K. thought she was going to arrive too late and the landlord would in the meantime have done all that was needed. In order to make room for the landlord to run past, K. stood close against the wall, but the landlord stopped next to him as if that were his objective; soon afterwards the landlady also arrived, and both upbraided him in terms which, with the speed and surprise of it all, he could not understand, especially since the ringing of the gentleman's bell interrupted them, and other bells, too, started to go off – though they were no longer being rung as a sign of emergency, but simply for fun and as an expression of joy.

Because it was important to K. to understand exactly what he had done wrong, he readily allowed the landlord to take him by the arm and lead him out of this noise, which was getting louder all the time, for behind them – K. made no attempt to look back, because the landlord on one side, and the landlady even more on his other side, went on scolding him – all the doors were now flung open, the corridor came alive, and a flow of people seemed to emerge as into a busy street; the doors in front of them were obviously waiting impatiently for K. to go past so that they could at last let out their occupants, and in the midst of all this the bells were being rung over and over again as if to celebrate some great victory.

Then at last – they were now once again in the silent white courtyard where some sleighs were waiting – K. gradually learned what it was all about. Neither the landlord nor the landlady could understand how he could have dared do such a thing. But what had he done, in fact? K. asked again and again, but for some time got no answer because his guilt was so very self-evident to both of them that they did not remotely believe his questions were serious. Only very slowly did K. realise everything. He had no right to be in the corridor, in principle he was allowed at most into the bar, and even that was a favour that could be withdrawn. If he was summoned by one of the gentlemen, of course he had to appear at the appointed place, but he should always remember – surely he had at least the normal amount of common sense? – that he was in a place where he did not really belong, a place to which he had only been summoned by one of the gentlemen with the greatest reluctance because official business required and justified it. And so it was up to him to appear without delay, submit himself for interview, and be gone, if possible with even less delay. Had he not felt, when he was in the corridor, that he had no right whatever to be there? But if he had, how could he have wandered about like an animal in a field? Had he not been summoned to a night-time interview, and did he not know why night-time interviews had been introduced? Their sole purpose – and here K. was given another explanation for them – was to interview clients the gentlemen could not stand the sight of by day, to see them quickly, at night, by artificial light, and to give them the chance to forget the unpleasantness of it all by sleeping immediately after the interview.

But K.'s behaviour had made a mockery of all these precautions. Even ghosts vanished towards dawn, they said, but K. had stayed on, his hands in his pockets, as if he had expected that because he didn't go away, the whole corridor, doors, gentlemen and all, would go away. And this would most certainly have happened, too, he could be sure of that, if it had only somehow been possible, for the gentlemen's sensitivity was boundless. Not one of them would do anything like drive him away, or even tell him what in any case went without saying – that he should just leave; not one of them would do that, even though they were probably trembling with agitation at K.'s presence and it was ruining the morning for them, which was their favourite time. Instead of taking action against K. they would rather suffer, while of course hoping that K. would finally be forced to accept the blindingly obvious, would realise what pain he was causing them, and would himself find it unbearably painful to stand there in the corridor in the morning, visible to all, in such a dreadfully unsuitable way. A vain hope; they did not know, or in their graciousness and goodness did not wish to know, that there are people with such hard unfeeling hearts that no reverence or respect can soften them. Does not even the humble moth seek out a quiet corner when day comes and flatten itself, unhappy that it cannot vanish altogether?

But K. – he put himself just where he was most highly visible, and if he could have stopped the day dawning by doing so, he would have. He could not stop it, but unfortunately he could delay it or obstruct it. Had he not witnessed the distribution of the files? Something no one was permitted to watch except those immediately involved, something neither the landlord nor his wife had ever been allowed to see in their own house, something they had only known about from oblique hints, as they had today for instance from the servant. Had he not noticed the difficulties involved in distributing the files, something that was in itself incomprehensible because each of the gentlemen served only the common good, never sought his personal advantage and therefore had to devote all his energies to ensuring that the vital and fundamental work of distribution proceeded swiftly, smoothly and faultlessly? And had it really not even remotely dawned on him that the greatest difficulty of all was that this distribution had to be carried out almost behind closed doors, with no possibility of direct communication between the gentlemen, who would of course be able to agree among themselves in an instant, whereas distribution by the servants almost inevitably took hours, could never be done without complaints, was a lasting torment for gentlemen as well as servants, and would probably have damaging consequences for their subsequent work? And why were the gentlemen not able to communicate with each other?

Well, did K. still not understand? The landlady declared – and her husband agreed for his part – that she had never heard the like before, and they had certainly had to deal with some awkward customers, too. They had to spell out to K. things that they would not normally have dared to utter out loud, otherwise he could not grasp the most crucial matters. Well, then it had to be said: it was because of him, simply and solely because of him, that the gentlemen had not been able to emerge from their rooms, because just after waking up in the morning they were too shy, too vulnerable, to expose themselves to a stranger's eyes, although they might be fully dressed, they felt quite frankly too naked to show themselves. It was difficult to say why they felt ashamed; perhaps these tireless workers were ashamed simply because they had slept. But perhaps they were even more reluctant to see strangers than to let strangers see them; having safely survived, thanks to the night-time interviews, the sight of the clients they found so hard to bear, they had no desire to let these clients intrude on them again suddenly, early in the morning, unannounced and just as nature made them, they simply weren't up to it. What sort of person could fail to respect that? Well, it would have to be someone like K., someone who in his dull-witted torpor and disregard set himself above everything, above the law and common human courtesy, who thought nothing of making the distribution of the files almost impossible and bringing the place into disrepute, who had contrived to do what had never been done before, forcing the desperate gentlemen, after they had exercised superhuman self-restraint, to defend themselves by reaching for the bell and summoning help in order to get rid of this person who could not be dislodged by any other means. Just think – these gentlemen had to call for help! Wouldn't they all, the landlord, the landlady and their entire staff, have come running long before that if they had only dared to appear in front of the gentlemen in the early morning without being summoned, even if it had only been to bring help and then disappear immediately. Shaking with indignation at K.'s behaviour and dismayed by their own helplessness, they had waited there at the end of the corridor, and the bell, which they had never expected to hear, had been a blessed relief for them. Well, the worst was over now! If only they could catch a glimpse of the joyful celebrations of the gentlemen who were now rid of K. at last! For him, though, it was not over; he would surely have to answer for the trouble he had caused.

In the meantime they had reached the bar. It was not quite clear why the landlord, furious as he was, had brought K. here; perhaps he had realised that K. was so tired he could not possibly leave the inn for the time being. Without waiting to be invited to sit down, K. simply collapsed onto one of the barrels. He felt comfortable there in the dark; the only light in the large room came from a feeble electric light over the beer taps. Outside it was still pitch dark too, and there seemed to be flurries of snow. Sitting here in the warmth was something to be thankful for, and he ought to take care he was not made to leave. The landlord and his wife remained standing in front of him, as if he still represented a certain danger, as if with someone so totally unpredictable they could not rule out the possibility that he might suddenly get up and try to get back to the corridor again. They too were tired from the night's disturbances and from having to get up so early, especially the landlady, who was wearing a full-skirted brown dress that rustled like silk and was rather untidily gathered and fastened – where had she got it from in her haste? She was resting her head awkwardly on her husband's shoulder, dabbing at her eyes with a dainty handkerchief and glancing at K. with childishly malevolent eyes.

In order to calm the couple down, K. said that everything they had just told him was quite new to him, but that in spite of his ignorance of these things he would not have stayed so long in the corridor, where he really had no reason to be, and had certainly not intended to cause anyone distress; it had all happened simply because he was exhausted. He thanked them for putting a stop to the embarrassing scene. If he should be called to account, he would welcome that, because it was the only way to prevent his behaviour being wildly misconstrued. Exhaustion, sheer exhaustion, had been to blame; but that exhaustion arose from the fact that he was not yet accustomed to the strain of the interviews. After all, he had not been here very long. Once he had some experience of things, something like that would never happen again. Perhaps he took the interviews too seriously, but that was in itself no drawback, surely; he had had to get through two interviews in a short time, one with Bürgel and one with Erlanger. The first one in particular had exhausted him, though the second had not lasted very long; Erlanger had merely asked him a favour, but two interviews in succession were more than he could cope with at one time – something like that might also be too much for anyone, perhaps even, he suggested respectfully, for the landlord. In fact he had only been able to stagger away from the second interview. It was almost as if he had been drunk; after all, it was the first time he had seen or heard the two gentlemen, and he had still had to answer their questions. As far as he could tell everything had gone very well, but then that disaster had occurred, for which he could hardly be blamed given what had happened earlier. Unfortunately, only Erlanger and Bürgel had realised the state he was in, and they would surely have looked after him and prevented everything that had followed, but Erlanger had had to leave immediately after the interview, presumably to drive back to the Castle, and Bürgel, probably exhausted from the same interview – so how was K. supposed to get through it unaffected? – had fallen asleep, and had even slept through the whole distribution of the files. If K. had had a similar opportunity he would have been delighted to take it and would have gladly have missed seeing anything forbidden, all the more so as he had in fact been incapable of taking in anything at all, so even the most sensitive gentleman could have appeared in front of him without embarrassment.

The mention of the two interviews, especially the one with Erlanger, and the deference with which K. spoke about the gentlemen, met with the landlord's approval. He seemed about to consent to K.'s request to let him place a board on top of the barrels and sleep there, at least until dawn, but the landlady was clearly against it; only now noticing the disordered state of her dress, she tugged at it here and there ineffectually, shaking her head repeatedly – an evidently long-standing quarrel about the proper running of the inn was on the point of breaking out again. In K.'s exhausted state the couple's conversation assumed exaggerated importance for him. To be thrown out of here again seemed to him a misfortune greater than any he had suffered before; it must not happen, even if the landlord and landlady should join forces against him. Slumped on the barrel, he watched them both furtively. Then the landlady who, as K. had long since realised, was in a more than usually irascible mood, suddenly stepped aside – she had no doubt been discussing other matters with her husband –

and shouted: 'Look how he's watching me! Send him away, won't you!' K., however, seizing his opportunity and now wholly resolved to stay, almost to the point where he no longer cared, said: 'I'm not looking at you, I'm just looking at your dress.' 'Why my dress?' asked the landlady in agitation. K. shrugged his shoulders. 'Come along,' said the landlady to her husband, 'he's drunk, the lout. Let him sleep it off here.' And she told Pepi, who at her call emerged from the darkness sleepy, dishevelled, and limply clutching a broom, to throw K. a cushion of some kind.

25

When K. woke up his first impression was that he had hardly slept; the room was unchanged, empty and warm, the walls were all in darkness, the single light glowed above the beer-taps, and it was dark outside the windows. But as soon as he stretched himself, pushing the cushion onto the floor and making the board and the barrels creak, Pepi appeared and told him it was already evening and he had slept well over twelve hours. The landlady had asked about him several times during the day, and Gerstäcker, who had been waiting here in the dark with a glass of beer that morning while K. was talking to the landlady but had then not dared to disturb him, had also called in once to see him, and finally Frieda had come too, so Pepi told him, and had stood by him; however, she had hardly come to see him, but because she had various things to get ready in here, as she was going to take up her old job that evening. 'I suppose she doesn't care for you any more?' asked Pepi, bringing some coffee and cakes. But she did not ask maliciously as she had before, but sadly, as if in the meantime she had got to know the cruelty of the world, beside which all personal malice pales into insignificance. She spoke to K. as if to a companion in suffering, and when he tasted the coffee and she seemed to think it was not sweet enough for him, she ran and fetched him the whole sugar-bowl.

Nevertheless, her sadness had not stopped her dressing up, perhaps more so today than the last time; she had lots of bows and ribbons tied in her hair, which had been carefully curled over her forehead and at her temples, and round her neck she wore a light chain that hung down into the deep décolleté of her blouse. When K. in his satisfaction at having slept soundly at last and having been able to drink a good cup of coffee, stole his hand towards one of the bows and tried to untie it, she said wearily: 'Leave me alone,' and sat down on a barrel beside him. K. did not need to ask her what the matter was; she immediately began to tell him herself, her eyes fixed on K.'s coffee-pot as if she needed some distraction even as she told her story, as if even when preoccupied with her own sorrow she could not completely surrender to it, for that would be more than she could cope with.

Firstly, K. learned that he was actually responsible for Pepi's misfortune, though she did not hold it against him; and she nodded energetically as she talked to stop K. raising any kind of objection. He had taken Frieda away from the bar in the first place, thus making Pepi's promotion possible. Nothing else could conceivably have made Frieda give up her job, she sat there in the bar like a spider in its web, she had threads everywhere, which only she knew about; it would have been quite impossible to dislodge her against her will, only love for someone inferior, that is something incompatible with her status, could drive her from her job. And what about Pepi? Had she ever thought of taking over the job herself? She was a chambermaid, in a lowly job with few prospects; like every girl she dreamed of a great future, you can't help dreaming, but she had no serious thoughts of promotion, she had come to terms with what she had achieved. And then Frieda suddenly disappeared from the inn, it had happened so quickly that the landlord didn't have a suitable replacement available, he looked around and his eye fell on Pepi, who had admittedly put herself in a position to be noticed.

At that time she loved K. as she had never loved anyone before; for months she had been sitting below stairs in her tiny dark room, she was prepared to spend years, or at the very worst her whole life there unnoticed; then all at once K. had appeared, a hero, a knight errant who had cleared the way for her to rise to higher things. Of course, he had known nothing about her, he had not done it for her sake, but that did not diminish her gratitude in any way; during the night before her appointment – which was then not yet certain, but already very likely – she had spent hours talking to him, whispering her thanks into his ear. And what made his deed even nobler in her eyes was that it was Frieda of all people he had saddled himself with; there was something unimaginably selfless in the way he had become Frieda's lover to help Pepi – Frieda, a plain, ageing, skinny girl with short, thin hair, what's more a shifty sort of girl who always had some secret or other, which surely goes with her appearance, her face and her figure are so awful that she must have secrets no one can check, for instance her alleged affair with Klamm. And at the time Pepi had even had thoughts like these: is it possible that K. really loves Frieda, is he not deceiving himself, or is he perhaps only deceiving Frieda, and might the sole outcome of all this be just Pepi's promotion, and will K. then realise his mistake or not want to conceal it any longer and then not see Frieda any more, only Pepi, which was not necessarily a crazy idea of Pepi's at all, for side-by-side with Frieda she was more than a match for her, no one could deny that, and it had been Frieda's position more than anything else and the glamour Frieda had managed to give it that had dazzled K. momentarily. And then Pepi had dreamed that once she had the job, K. would come pleading to her and she would then have the choice of either giving in to him and losing her job, or rejecting him and climbing further. And she had worked out that she would give up everything and condescend to him and teach him true love, which he could never find with Frieda and which is above all the most coveted jobs in the world. But then it didn't turn out like that. And who was to blame for that? K. most of all, and then of course Frieda with her cunning. K. most of all, because what does he want, what sort of a strange person is he? What is he looking for, what are all these important matters that make him forget everything that is dearest and best and most beautiful? Pepi is the victim, and it's all stupid and pointless and whoever had the power to set fire to the Herrenhof and burn it to the ground, really burn it to ashes like a piece of paper in the stove so that nothing was left – he would be the one Pepi would choose then.

Well, so Pepi went to work in the bar, four days ago, just before the midday meal. The work here isn't easy, it nearly kills you, but you can achieve quite a lot. Even before, Pepi hadn't just lived from day to day, and even though she had never dared to dream of claiming this job for herself, she had kept her eyes open, she knew what the job involved so she hadn't taken it over unprepared. You can't do that, or else you'll only last a few hours. Especially if you tried to behave like a chambermaid here! As a chambermaid you feel quite lost and forgotten after a time, it's like working in a mine, at least it's like that in the secretaries' corridor – for days on end, apart from a few daytime clients who scurry along and don't dare to look up, you see no one except the other two or three chambermaids, who are just as discontented. In the morning you're not allowed to leave your room because then the secretaries want to be together on their own, the waiters bring their meals from the kitchen, the chambermaids normally have nothing to do with that, and even during mealtimes you mustn't be seen on the corridor. The chambermaids can only tidy up when the gentlemen are working, not of course in the rooms that are occupied, only in the empty ones, and this has to be done very quietly so as not to disturb the gentlemen's work. But how can you tidy up quietly when the gentlemen live in their rooms for several days on end, and then the waiters, that filthy lot, mess about in them, and when the chambermaid is finally allowed into the rooms they're in such a state that even the Great Flood couldn't wash them clean. These are really important gentlemen, but you have to make a great effort to get over your disgust when you have to clean up after them.

The chambermaids don't have an enormous amount of work, but it's hard. And you never hear a kind word, only complaints, especially the most upsetting one of all, which is the most frequent – that files have gone missing while the rooms were being cleaned. In fact nothing gets lost, every last scrap of paper is handed over to the landlord. Of course, files do get lost, but it's not the maids who lose them. And then they have investigations and the maids have to leave their room and the investigators ransack their beds; the maids don't have any possessions, the few things they have will fit into a rucksack, but the investigators still search for hours. Of course they don't find anything – how are files supposed to get there? What do the maids want with files? But the result is always the same, abuse and threats from the disappointed investigators, passed on by the landlord. And there's never any peace, day or night. Noise for half the night and noise from first thing in the morning. If only you didn't have to live there, but you've got to, because it's the chambermaids' job to fetch small orders from the kitchen between times, especially at night. Time after time there's a sudden banging on the door of the maids' room, the order is dictated, you run down to the kitchen, shake the kitchen lads awake, put the tray with the orders outside the maids' room for the waiters to fetch it – it's all so dreary.

But that's not the worst. The worst is when there are no orders, and then in the middle of the night when everyone should be asleep, and most of them finally are asleep, there's the sound of someone creeping around outside the maids' room. Then the maids get out of their beds – the beds are one on top of the other, there's altogether very little space in there, the whole room is actually no more than a big cupboard with three shelves; they listen at the door, kneel down and cling to each other in terror. And all the time they hear this shuffling outside the door. They'd all be glad if someone finally came in, but nothing happens, nobody appears. And then they have to tell themselves that it's not necessarily anything to be alarmed about, perhaps it's just somebody walking up and down outside the door who is wondering whether to place an order and can't make up his mind. Perhaps that's all it is, but perhaps it's something quite different. They don't actually know the gentlemen at all, in fact they've hardly ever seen them. Anyway, the maids inside are frightened to death, and when the shuffling finally stops they lean back against the wall and don't have the strength to climb back into their beds.

This was the life in store for Pepi again, she was to move back into the maids' room that very evening. And why? Because of K. and Frieda. Back to the life she had only just escaped, admittedly with K.'s help, but also thanks to huge efforts on her part. And in that job the maids neglect their appearance, even those who normally look after themselves. Who should they dress up for? Nobody sees them, or at best the kitchen staff do, and any girl who fancies them should go ahead and dress up. But otherwise they are always in their tiny room or in the gentlemen's offices, and just to set foot in those in clean clothes is a stupid waste. And always by artificial light in a stuffy atmosphere – the heating is on the whole time – and always, always tired. The best way to spend your one free afternoon a week is to have a quiet undisturbed sleep in some cupboard in the kitchen. So why dress up? It's hardly worth getting dressed at all.

And then Pepi was suddenly transferred to the bar, where, if you wanted to make your mark, just the opposite was required; here people's eyes were on you the whole time, and some of them were very observant and choosy gentlemen, so you always had to look as smart and attractive as possible.

Well, that was a change. And Pepi could say she made the most of it. She wasn't worried about how things might turn out later. She knew she had the abilities needed in the job, she was quite sure of that, she was still convinced she did and no one could take that away from her, not even today, the day of her defeat. The only problem had been how she would manage at first, because she was only a poor chambermaid with no proper clothes and no jewellery, and the customers didn't have the patience to wait until she had got used to the job; they want a proper barmaid right away there and then, otherwise they'll go somewhere else. You might think they weren't too fussy if they put up with Frieda; but that's not how it was.

Pepi had often thought about this; she had spent quite a lot of time with Frieda, and for a while they had shared a room. It's not easy to make Frieda out, and if you're not very careful – and which of the gentlemen is so careful? – you can soon be misled. Nobody knows better than Frieda herself how awful she looks; the first time you see her let down her hair, for instance, you clasp your hands in pity. By rights, a girl like that shouldn't even be a chambermaid; she knows that too, and she spent many nights weeping about it, clinging to Pepi and draping Pepi's hair round her own head. But when she's working all her doubts have vanished, she thinks she's the most beautiful of all, and she knows how to get everyone to believe it. She knows all about people, that's her real trick. She lies easily and soon fools people so that they don't get a close look at her. Of course, that doesn't work for long, people have eyes and would soon see the truth. But as soon as she sees any risk of that, she has another trick up her sleeve, most recently, for instance, her affair with Klamm. What, her affair with Klamm? If you don't believe it, you can check it for yourself, go to Klamm and ask him. How very clever. You might not dare to go to Klamm with such a question, you might not be allowed to see him even if you have far more important questions for him, Klamm might even be completely inaccessible for you – just you and your sort, that is, because Frieda pops in to see him whenever she likes – in that case you can still check the truth of the matter, you only have to wait. Klamm won't tolerate such a false rumour for long, he's certain to keep a very close track of what's being said about him in the bar and the guest-rooms, all this is of the greatest importance to him, and if it's untrue he'll put it right at once. But he doesn't put it right; well then, there was nothing to put right – it's the plain truth. Of course, what you see is that Frieda takes Klamm's beer into his room and comes back out with the money, but what you don't see you have to be told by Frieda, and you have to believe her. But she doesn't tell you anything, she's not going to spill secrets like that, oh no; the secrets spill out all round her by themselves, and once they're out, then of course she's not afraid of talking about them herself any more – but she does it modestly, without boasting, she just hints at what everybody knows already.

Not everything, though – for instance, she doesn't mention that since she's been barmaid Klamm drinks less beer than before, not much less, but still noticeably less. Now, this could be for various reasons – perhaps it was just a time when Klamm didn't like his beer so much, or Frieda might even have made him forget about beer. Either way, however astonishing it may be, Frieda is Klamm's mistress; and how could the others fail to admire someone who is good enough for Klamm, so before anyone realises, Frieda has turned into a great beauty, just the sort of girl they need in the bar, almost too beautiful, even, too powerful, almost too good to be a barmaid. And indeed people find it amazing that she's still just a barmaid. Being a barmaid is quite something, it makes her affair with Klamm seem very plausible; but if the barmaid is Klamm's mistress, why does he let her stay in the bar, and for so long too? Why doesn't he see to it that she gets a better job? You can tell people a thousand times over that there's no contradiction in this, that Klamm has good reasons for acting as he does, or that suddenly, perhaps very soon, Frieda will be promoted; but that has no great effect, people have fixed ideas and no amount of clever argument will shake them in the end.

No one doubted any longer that Frieda was Klamm's mistress; even those who obviously knew better were tired of questioning it by now. 'What the hell, be Klamm's lover then,' they thought, 'but if you are, we'll know it when you get promoted.' But it didn't happen and Frieda stayed on in the bar, and secretly she was very glad to. But she went down in people's opinion, which didn't of course escape her notice, she usually notices things before they happen. A really pretty and attractive girl, once she's established herself in the bar, doesn't need to put on airs; as long as she's pretty she'll be kept on as barmaid unless something particularly unfortunate occurs. But a girl like Frieda always has to be careful to keep her job; of course she's clever enough not to show it, far from it, she's more likely to complain about it and curse it. But in secret she's always keeping an eye on the mood. So she noticed how people were getting indifferent, they didn't even think it was worth looking up when she appeared, even the labourers didn't bother about her any more, understandably enough they kept to Olga and girls like her. She also noticed from the landlord's attitude that she was becoming less and less indispensable, and she couldn't go on inventing more and more stories about Klamm, there's a limit to everything – and so dear Frieda decided to try something new. Who could possibly have seen through it right away? Pepi suspected something, but unfortunately she didn't see through it.

So Frieda decided to cause a scandal. She – Klamm's mistress – would throw herself at someone, anyone, preferably someone beyond the pale. That will cause a stir, that will give them plenty to talk about, and that will remind them at long last what it means to be Klamm's mistress and what it means to throw away this honour in the ecstasy of a new love affair. The only problem was finding a suitable man to play this clever game with. It couldn't be somebody Frieda knew, or one of the labourers; he would probably just have gaped at her and gone on his way, above all he wouldn't have taken the affair seriously enough, and for all her ability to tell tales it would have been impossible to spread the story that he had waylaid her, that she had been unable to defend herself, and without thinking had surrendered to him. And if it was to be someone beyond the pale, he would have to be plausible enough to pass as someone who in spite of his graceless and clumsy behaviour still longed for no one but Frieda and whose sole desire was – dear God! – to marry her. But even if it had to be someone common, perhaps someone lower than a labourer, much lower even, it still had to be a man who would not make every other girl laugh at her, a man any discerning girl might even find quite attractive.

But where do you find a man like that? Another girl would probably have spent her whole life looking for him in vain; but Frieda's luck brings the surveyor into the bar, perhaps on the very evening her plan first occurs to her. The surveyor! Well, whatever is K. thinking of? What exactly is going on in his mind? Is there anything in particular he wants to achieve? A good job, some kind of distinction? Does he want something like that? Then he should have set about it differently right from the start. He is nobody, nobody at all, it's pitiful to see the position he's in. He's a surveyor, that might mean something, it means he's had an education, but if he can't use it in some way it's no good to him. And he thinks a lot of himself, too; without having the slightest support he makes demands, not outright, but you can see he's making demands, which is outrageous. Doesn't he realise that even a chambermaid is demeaning herself if she speaks to him for very long? And with all these great expectations he falls straight into the most obvious trap on his first evening. Isn't he ashamed of himself? What is it about Frieda that he's so smitten by her? Surely he could admit it now. Did she really appeal to him so much, that skinny, sallow creature? No, he hardly looked at her, she only had to tell him she was Klamm's mistress, this piece of news impressed him and he was lost.

But then she had to leave, of course, there was no room for her at the Herrenhof any longer. Pepi saw her the morning before she left, all the staff gathered to watch, they were all curious to see it. And her influence was still so powerful that they all felt sorry for her, even her enemies. So that was how things had worked out for her – no one could understand why she had thrown herself away on a man like that, it was a blow of fate, the little scullery maids, who of course look up to any barmaid, were inconsolable. Even Pepi was moved by it all, even she couldn't help herself, although her mind was actually on something else. It struck her that Frieda was not really so very sad; it was a truly dreadful misfortune that had overtaken her, and she did act as though she were very unhappy, but this act didn't fool Pepi. What kept her going? Was it perhaps the happiness of new love? No, that didn't come into it. But what else was it? Where did she get the strength to be as calm and friendly as ever, even to Pepi, who was already seen as her successor?

Pepi did not have enough time to think about it just then, she was too busy getting ready for her new job. She probably had to start in a couple of hours, and she had still not done up her hair, she had no smart dress, no fine linen, no proper shoes. This all had to be seen to in an hour or two; if she couldn't make herself presentable, it would be better to give up the job there and then, because she would be sure to lose it in the first half hour. Well, she managed to some extent. She had a special gift for hairdressing, once even the landlady called her in to do her hair because she had a particularly light touch; of course, with hair that grows as well as Pepi's you can do anything. She got help with the dress, too; the other two chambermaids stood by her – it's quite an honour for them, too, when one of those girls becomes a barmaid, and besides when Pepi took over she would be able to do them some favours later on. One of the maids had had some expensive material stored away for a long time, it was her treasure-hoard, she had often let the others admire it; she might have dreamed of using it herself one day for a special occasion, and now that Pepi needed it – it was a wonderful gesture on her part – she offered it to her. And they were both keen to help with the sewing, they couldn't have been more willing if they'd been doing it for themselves. It was rewarding work, and they did it happily. Each sat on her own bed, one above the other, they sewed and sang and handed the completed sections and the accessories up and down to each other. When Pepi thinks about it, she feels all the worse because it was all for nothing and she had to return to her friends empty-handed. What a disaster, the result of such frivolity, especially on K.'s part!

How pleased they all were with the dress. It seemed to promise success, and when it was finished and they found room for another ribbon, all their doubts vanished. And it really is a beautiful dress, isn't it? It's got creased now and a bit stained, Pepi just didn't have another one, she had to wear this one day and night, but you can still see how lovely it is, even that damned Barnabas girl couldn't make a better one. And look how you can take it out and let it in again as you like, above and below, it may only be a dress, but it's so adaptable, which is a real advantage, it was actually her invention. Of course, it's not difficult to sew a new dress for her, Pepi's not boasting about it, but everything fits a young girl with a good figure. It was much more difficult to find linen and boots, that's where things started to go wrong. Her friends helped her out here too as much as they could, but they couldn't do very much. They only managed to find some coarse linen and mend it, and instead of high-heeled boots she had to make do with slippers of the sort she would rather hide than show off. They consoled Pepi, telling her that Frieda was not so very smartly dressed either, sometimes she went round looking so slovenly that the customers preferred to be waited on by the potboys rather than her. That was true, but Frieda could get away with it, she was in favour and they respected her; if a fine lady turns up for once in a soiled and sloppy dress it makes her all the more attractive, but not a new girl like Pepi. Besides, Frieda has no dress sense, she's got no taste at all; when a girl has a sallow skin like hers, of course she can't do anything about it, but she doesn't have to be like Frieda and wear a low-cut cream blouse too, so that all that yellow makes your eyes hurt. And even if she hadn't been that colour, she was too mean to dress well, she saved everything she earned, nobody knew what for. She didn't need any money at work, she got by with lies and tricks, Pepi couldn't be like that and didn't want to, she was quite entitled to dress up and make the most of herself, especially at the start. If only she'd been more determined she would have won, for all Frieda's cunning, for all K.'s foolishness.

She got off to a good start, too. There were a few tricks of the trade and things she needed to know, and she had learned these well in advance. As soon as she was in the bar, she knew the ropes. No one missed Frieda – it wasn't until the second day that any of the guests asked where she was. Pepi made no mistakes, and the landlord was satisfied; on the first day he had been so anxious he had stayed in the bar the whole time, later he only looked in occasionally, and in the end, as the till was in order – the average takings were rather higher than in Frieda's time – he left everything to Pepi. She introduced some changes. Frieda had served the labourers as well, at least sometimes, especially when anyone was looking; she did this not because she was hard-working, but because she was jealous, she wanted to keep control, she wouldn't give up any of her privileges to anyone else. But Pepi handed this work over to the potboys, who can do it better anyway. That gave her more time for the guest-rooms, so the gentlemen were served more quickly, and she could still have a few words with each of them, unlike Frieda, who was supposed to have kept herself entirely for Klamm and treated every word, every approach from anyone else as an insult to Klamm. That was clever of her, too, of course, because if she ever allowed anyone near her it was an unheard-of favour.

But Pepi hated tricks like that, and in any case they don't work at first. Pepi was friendly to everyone, and they were all friendly to her. They were obviously pleased at the change; when the overworked gentlemen are at last able to sit down for a while with a beer they can be quite transformed by a kind word, a glance, or a tilt of the shoulders. They were all so keen to run their hands through Pepi's curls that she must have had to redo her hair ten times a day, no one can resist these curls and bows, not even K., who is usually so inattentive. So the days flew by, it was hard work, but exciting and rewarding. If only they hadn't gone so quickly, if only there had been more of them! Four days aren't enough, even when you're working yourself into the ground, perhaps a fifth day would have been enough, but four days weren't. It's true, Pepi had won friends and admirers in those four days, if all the looks she got were anything to go by – why, when she came along with the mugs of beer she floated on a sea of affection. A clerk called Bratmeier was mad about her, he gave her this locket and chain and put his picture in the locket, which of course was very cheeky of him – all sorts of things had happened, but then it was only for four days; if Pepi made a real effort they might almost forget Frieda, though perhaps not completely, and they would have forgotten her even sooner perhaps if Frieda hadn't made sure she would still be talked about because of the great scandal she caused. It had put her back in the news, they would have liked to see her again just out of curiosity; they had grown sick and tired of her, and now they were interested in her again thanks to K., who was of no significance apart from that. Of course, for all that they wouldn't have given up Pepi as long as she was there with them making her presence felt; but they're mostly elderly gentlemen and set in their ways, and it takes them a few days to get used to a new barmaid however welcome the change may be; in spite of themselves it takes them a few days, maybe only five days, but four aren't enough, in spite of everything they still only regarded Pepi as a temporary barmaid.

And then there was the worst thing of all: in those four days Klamm didn't once come down to the guest-room, although he was in the village for the first two days. If he had done, that would have been the acid test for Pepi, which she was not in the least afraid of, on the contrary she was looking forward to it. She would never – of course these things are better left unsaid – have become Klamm's mistress, and she wouldn't have lied that she was, either, but she could have put his glass of beer on the table just as nicely as Frieda had, she could have greeted him and said goodbye to him just as sweetly as Frieda had, but without being as forward as Frieda, and if Klamm ever does look for anything in a girls' eyes, he could have found more than enough in Pepi's. But why didn't he come? Was it just by accident? Pepi had thought so at the time. For those two days she had expected him at any minute, she waited for him at night too. 'Klamm will come now,' she kept thinking, and she rushed about restlessly just because she was impatient and eager to be the first person to see him when he arrived. The constant disappointment tired her out, perhaps that's why she didn't get as much done as she might have. When she had time she would slip up to the corridor, which is strictly out of bounds to the domestic staff, and squeeze herself into a corner to wait for him. 'If only Klamm would come now,' she thought, 'if only I could take him in my arms and carry him out of his room down to the guest-room. I would never collapse under a burden like that, however heavy he was.' But he didn't come.

It's so quiet in those corridors up there, you can't imagine what it's like if you've never been there. It's so quiet you can't stand it for long, the silence drives you away. Pepi climbed up there again and again, ten times she was driven away, ten times she went back. It was just pointless. If Klamm wanted to come, he would come, but if he didn't want to, Pepi wasn't going to lure him out, even if her heart pounded fit to burst in her corner of the corridor. It was pointless, but then if he didn't come, almost everything was pointless. And he didn't come.

Pepi knows now why Klamm didn't come. Frieda would have been most amused if she could have seen Pepi in her corner up in the corridor, clutching at her heart with both hands. Klamm didn't come down because Frieda was stopping him. She hadn't done it by pleading with him, her pleas had no effect on Klamm. But that little spider has contacts no one knows about. When Pepi says something to a customer she says it out loud, the people at the next table can hear it too; Frieda says nothing, she puts the beer on the table and goes away, all you hear is the swishing of her silk petticoat, which is the only thing she spends money on. But when she does say anything, she doesn't say it out loud, she bends down and whispers to the customer, so that the people at the next table prick up their ears. What she says is probably quite trivial, not always though, she has contacts, she plays one off against the other, and if most of them fail – who would bother with Frieda the whole time? – one of them will pay off now and again.

So now she started to exploit these contacts. K. gave her the opportunity; instead of staying with her and keeping an eye on her, he's hardly there, he roams around having meetings all over the place, he pays attention to everything except Frieda, and in the end he moves out of the Brückenhof into the empty schoolhouse to give her even more freedom. What a fine start to a honeymoon! Well, Pepi is certainly the last person to blame K. for not being able to put up with Frieda, nobody can put up with her. But why didn't he leave her then for good, why did he keep coming back to her, why did he give the impression that all his roaming about was for her sake? It looked as if it was only when he met Frieda that he had realised what a nonentity he was, as if he wanted to prove himself worthy of her and pull himself up somehow, that was why he went without her company for the time being so that he could make up for what he had missed in peace and quiet afterwards. Meanwhile Frieda loses no time, she sits there at the school, where she probably schemed to install K., and keeps an eye on him as well as on the Herrenhof. She's got an excellent pair of messengers, namely K.'s assistants; it beggars belief, even when you know K. it still beggars belief, but he leaves them entirely to her. She sends them to her old friends, reminds them about herself, complains that she's being kept prisoner by a man like K., casts slurs on Pepi, announces her imminent return, asks for help, implores them not to reveal anything to Klamm, acts as though Klamm needs to be protected and so should on no account be allowed down into the bar. To one person she claims this is to protect Klamm, while to the landlord she makes the most of it by reminding him what a success she was, pointing out that Klamm doesn't come down any more – how could he when someone like Pepi is serving downstairs? Of course, she says, the landlord's not to blame; this Pepi was still the best replacement he could find, but she wasn't good enough, even for a few days.

K. knows nothing about all this activity on Frieda's part; when he isn't roaming about, he's lying at her feet quite unsuspecting while she counts the hours before she returns to the bar. But the assistants aren't just running messages for her; they're also there to make K. jealous, to keep him interested. Frieda has known them since childhood, they certainly don't have any secrets from each other; but to provoke K. they start longing for each other, and in K.'s eyes this risks turning into a big love affair. And K. does everything Frieda wants, even the most contradictory things; he lets himself get jealous of the assistants, but puts up with the three of them staying together while he goes roaming about on his own. It's almost as if he's Frieda's third assistant. Then when she sees how things have developed, Frieda finally puts her master plan into action – she decides to go back. And it really is high time; you have to admire her cunning, the way she realises this and makes the most of it. Her powers of observation and her ability to act decisively are like no one else's; if Pepi was as clever, how different her life would be. If Frieda stays at the school another day or two, Pepi can't be removed, she's barmaid for good, loved and wanted by everyone, she's earned enough money to add spectacularly to her meagre wardrobe, just another day or two and no amount of scheming will stop Klamm coming down to the guest-room, he'll arrive, have a drink, feel comfortable, and if he notices Frieda's absence at all, he'll be perfectly happy with the change, another day or two and Frieda with all her gossip, her contacts, the assistants and all that will be completely forgotten, she'll never be mentioned again.

Perhaps then she might hold on to K all the more tightly, she might, if she's capable of it, really get to love him? No, not that either. Because even K. doesn't need more than a day to get tired of her, to realise how disgracefully she's deceiving him in every way, her supposed beauty, her supposed loyalty and most of all her supposed affair with Klamm; just one more day, and no more, is all he needs to chase her and the whole squalid domestic set-up with the assistants out of the house, just imagine – even K. doesn't need longer than that. And then, caught between these two dangers, with the grave actually beginning to close over her, K. in his naivety keeps one last narrow escape route open for her, and she bolts through it. Suddenly – hardly anyone was expecting it, it's just not natural – suddenly she's the one who throws K. out, the man who still loves her and is still pursuing her, and she's the one who appears to the landlord as a saviour with the support of her friends and helpers, and now she's so much more alluring than before because of her scandal, she's obviously wanted by the lowest and the highest; she had only succumbed to the lowest for a moment and soon rejected him, now she is quite properly beyond his reach and everyone else's, as she was before – except that before people might have had their doubts about that, perhaps with good reason, but now they were quite convinced.

So she comes back. The landlord, with half an eye on Pepi, hesitates – should he get rid of her when she has done so well? – but he's soon persuaded, Frieda has too much going for her, and most of all she'll bring Klamm back to the guest-room. They're closing for the night now anyway. Pepi isn't going to wait for Frieda to come back and let her make her return into a triumph. She's already handed over the takings to the landlady, she can go. The bunk bed downstairs in the maids' room is ready for her, she will arrive to be greeted with tears by her friends, rip off her clothes and her ribbons and stuff everything into a corner, where it will be well out of sight and won't remind her needlessly of times that were best forgotten. Then she will pick up the big bucket and the broom, grit her teeth and get on with her work. But first she had to tell K. all this so that he can see quite clearly once and for all how badly he has treated Pepi and how unhappy he has made her, because even now he would not have realised it unless he was told. Admittedly, he has also been treated badly in all this.

Pepi had finished. She sighed, dried her eyes and wiped the tears from her cheeks, then she looked at K. and nodded, as if to say that in the end her happiness did not matter, she could put up with that and needed no one's help or sympathy, least of all K.'s; she may be young but she knew what life was like, and her unhappiness only confirmed what she knew. It was for K.'s benefit, she had wanted to show him what sort of a person he was, even after the collapse of all her hopes she had thought she had to do that.

'What a wild imagination you have, Pepi,' said K. 'It's quite untrue you've only just discovered these things, they're nothing but dreams from your dark, narrow maids' room downstairs, which are all very well down there, but sound very strange here in the public bar. You couldn't get away with ideas like that in here, that's quite obvious. Even the dress and hairdo you're so proud of are fantasies arising from that darkness and those beds in your room; I'm sure they seem very fine down there, but up here everyone laughs at them, openly or in secret. And what else have you told me? That I've been badly treated and deceived? No, my dear Pepi, I've been no more badly treated and deceived than you have. It's true that Frieda has left me for the moment, or as you put it, she's run off with one of the assistants. You see a glimmer of the truth, and in fact it's very unlikely that she will ever be my wife, but it's entirely untrue that I got tired of her, let alone that I threw her out the next day, or that she betrayed me as any other woman might betray a man. You chambermaids are used to spying through the keyhole, and you get into the habit of drawing general conclusions, which are as exaggerated as they are false, from the trivial details you actually see. That is why I know far less than you do about this situation, for instance; I can't explain why Frieda left me anything like as exactly as you can. The most likely explanation, it seems to me, is the one you touched on but didn't elaborate on – that I neglected her. I'm sorry to say that is true, I did neglect her, but I had particular reasons for doing so which are not relevant here; I would be glad if she came back to me, but I would immediately start to neglect her again. That's how it is. When she was with me I was always roaming about in the way you have made fun of; now that she's gone I have almost nothing to do, I'm tired, I long to have less and less to do. Don't you have any advice for me, Pepi?' 'Oh yes,' said Pepi, suddenly perking up and taking hold of K.'s shoulders, 'we've both been betrayed, let's stick together, come downstairs with me to the girls.'

'As long as you complain about being betrayed,' said K., 'I can't see eye to eye with you. You always think you've been betrayed because you think it's flattering and moving. But the truth is you're not suited to this job. That must be quite obvious when even I realise it – the person you think knows less than anyone else. You're a good girl, Pepi, but it's not too easy to see that; for instance, at first I thought you were cruel and conceited, but you're not, it's only this job that makes you insecure because you're not suited to it. I don't mean the job is too grand for you, after all it's not such a marvellous job. When you look at it, it may be a little more prestigious than your previous job, but on the whole there's very little difference, they are so similar they're almost indistinguishable, in fact you could almost say being a chambermaid is preferable to working in the bar, because down there you're always among the secretaries, whereas here, although you're allowed to wait on the secretaries' superiors in the guestrooms, you also have to associate with quite common people like me, for instance. I'm not allowed to go anywhere except here in the bar; is it such an extraordinary honour to be able to associate with me? Well, you think it is, and perhaps you have reason to believe it is. But that's exactly what makes you unsuitable for the job. It's just a job like any other job, but for you it's heaven on earth, and so you throw yourself into it with excessive enthusiasm, you dress up the way you think the angels dress (in fact they're quite different); you're terrified of losing the job, you feel constantly persecuted, you try to win over everyone you think might be able to help you by being over-friendly to them, but that only annoys them and puts them off, because they come to the inn to have some peace and don't want to hear about the barmaid's worries on top of their own.

'It's possible that after Frieda left, none of the important guests actually noticed what had happened, but now they know about it and really miss Frieda because she probably did manage everything quite differently. Whatever she may be like otherwise and whatever she may have thought of the job, she was very experienced in the work, calm and collected – you stress that yourself, but you don't learn anything from her example. Have you ever noticed the look in her eye? It was nothing like the look a barmaid gives you, it was more like the look of a landlady. She saw everything, but at the same time she saw every single person, and the look she reserved for each of them was enough to keep them in order. What did it matter that she was rather thin, that she was getting on a bit, that she could have had more hair, these things are trivial compared with what she actually had, and anyone who is worried by these defects is simply showing he has no feeling for better things. You certainly can't accuse Klamm of that, and it's only the false perception of a young and inexperienced girl that won't allow you to believe in Klamm's love for Frieda. Klamm seems – and quite rightly – out of reach for you, and so you think he must be out of reach for Frieda as well. I would trust Frieda's word alone on this even if I didn't have certain proof of it. However incredible it may seem to you, and however hard it may be to make it tally with your notions of the world and officialdom and social status and the power of female beauty, it is still true that just as we are sitting here together and I am holding your hand in mine, Klamm and Frieda probably also sat together as if it were the most natural thing in the world, and he came down of his own free will, in fact he even rushed down; no one was waiting around in the corridor for him neglecting other work, Klamm had to make the effort of coming down here himself, and Frieda's bad dress sense, which horrified you so much, didn't disturb him in the least. You just won't believe her; you don't know how that gives you away and shows how inexperienced you are. Even someone who knew nothing of Frieda's affair with Klamm ought to have realised from her nature that it had transformed her into someone who was far above you and me and all the people in the village, that their conversations went far beyond the usual pleasantries exchanged between customers and waitresses that you seem to regard as your aim in life.

'But I'm doing you an injustice. After all, you're well aware of Frieda's qualities yourself, her perceptiveness, her decisiveness, her ability to influence people, but then you misinterpret everything and imagine she's using them selfishly or maliciously for her own advantage, or even as weapons against you. No, Pepi, even if she had weapons like that, she couldn't fire them at such close range. You think she's self-seeking? You might rather say that by sacrificing what she had and what she could have expected, she gave both of us a chance to prove ourselves in better positions, but that we both failed her and are actually forcing her to return here. I don't know if that is the case, and I'm not at all sure how far I'm to blame, but when I compare myself with you, that's how it seems to me; it's as if we had both tried too hard, that we'd made too much fuss, as if we'd been too childish, too naïve, demanding something that could have been achieved easily and without attracting attention if we'd gone about it in Frieda's calm and matter-of-fact way, instead of crying, scratching and tugging at it like a child pulling at a tablecloth who just drags the whole wonderful spread onto the floor and puts it out of its reach for ever. I don't know if that is the case, but I'm convinced it's more likely than your version.'

'Well of course,' said Pepi, 'you're in love with Frieda because she's left you, it's not difficult to love her when she's not there.

But whatever the truth may be, and even if you are right about everything, even in the way you make fun of me – what are you going to do now? Frieda has left you, whether you accept my version or yours, there's no hope of her coming back to you, and even if she were to you've got to have somewhere to go in the meantime, it's cold and you have no work and nowhere to sleep, so come in with us, you'll like my friends, we'll make you comfortable. You can help us with our work, it really is too hard for girls on their own, we won't have to look after ourselves and we won't be afraid in the night any more. Come in with us! My friends know Frieda too, we'll tell you stories about her until you don't want to hear any more. Come on! We have pictures of Frieda, too, we'll show them to you. In those days she was even plainer than she is now, you'll hardly recognise her except perhaps by her eyes, which had a sneaky look even then. Well, are you coming?'

'But am I allowed to? There was a great fuss yesterday when I was caught on your corridor.' 'Yes, because you were caught; but if you're in with us you won't get caught. Nobody will know about you, just the three of us. Oh, it'll be fun. Life down there already seems much more bearable than it did just a while ago. Perhaps I'm not losing so much after all by having to leave here. I tell you, even when there were just three of us we didn't get bored, you've got to make the most of life and have a taste of honey, they make it bitter enough for us when we're young to stop us getting spoilt, so the three of us stick together and live as good a life as we can down there; you'll like Henriette especially, Emilie too, though. I've already told them about you, they listen to such stories as though they can't believe anything like that happens beyond our room, it's warm and snug down there and we squeeze up together, and although there's just the three of us we haven't got tired of each other, far from it, when I think about my friends I almost feel I want to go back to them, why should I do better than they have? That's what kept us together, that we were all in the same boat and had no future, and then I escaped and we were separated. Of course, I didn't forget them, and my first thought was how I could do something for them; my own job was still not secure – I had no idea just how insecure it was – and I was already talking to the landlord about Henriette and Emilie. He was quite open to persuasion as far as Henriette was concerned, but for Emilie, who's much older than us, she's about Frieda's age, he didn't promise anything. But just imagine – they don't want to leave at all; they know what a miserable life they lead down there, but the poor dears have accepted it. I do believe they cried before I left mainly because they were sad that I had to leave the room we shared and go out into the cold – down there we think everywhere outside our room is cold – and would have to cope with a lot of strangers in big strange places just to scrape a living, which I'd been able to do anyway until then with the three of us together. They probably won't be at all surprised when they see me back, and just to please me they'll have a little cry and commiserate about my bad luck. But then they'll see you and realise what a good thing it was that I left. They'll be glad to have a man to help them and look after them, and they'll be absolutely delighted that it's all got to be kept secret, and this secret will bring us even closer together than we were before. Come on, oh please, come in with us! You won't be under any obligation, you won't be bound to our room for ever like us. When spring comes, if you find somewhere else to stay and if you don't like it with us any more, you can go – though of course you'd still have to keep our secret and not give us away, or it would be goodbye to the Herrenhof for us. And of course you'll have to be careful in other ways while you're with us, you mustn't let yourself be seen anywhere we don't think is safe, and always take our advice. That's the only restriction, and it'll be just as important for you as it is for us, but apart from that you'll be absolutely free, the work we give you won't be too hard, you needn't worry about that. Are you coming, then?' 'How long will it be till spring?' asked K. 'Till spring?' repeated Pepi. 'We have long winters here, the winter is very long and dreary. But we don't complain down there, we're protected from the winter. Yes, spring does come, and summer too, they come round eventually, I suppose; but looking back now, spring and summer seem so short, as if they didn't last much more than two days, and even on those days, even on the most beautiful days, snow still falls sometimes.'

Then the door opened. Pepi started violently; in her thoughts she had strayed too far away from the bar, but it was not Frieda, it was the landlady. She affected to be amazed at finding K. still there, and he excused himself by saying that he had been waiting for her, and thanked her for allowing him to spend the night there. The landlady could not understand why K. had waited for her. He said that he had been under the impression that she still wanted to speak to him, he was sorry if he had been mistaken, but now he really had to go, he had neglected the school, where he was caretaker, for far too long, yesterday's summons was to blame for everything; he still had too little experience in these things, he said, and he would certainly not inconvenience the landlady again as he had done the evening before. He bowed and made to leave. The landlady stared at him as if in a dream, and the look she gave him held him back for longer than he had intended. Then she also gave a faint smile, and only K.'s look of astonishment seemed to waken her; it was as if she had expected an answer to her smile, and only now that none was given did she rouse herself.

'I believe you had the impertinence to make a remark about my dress yesterday,' she said to him. K. could not remember. 'You don't remember? Then we can add cowardice to your impertinence.' K. excused himself by referring to his weariness of the previous evening; it was quite possible, he admitted, that he had said something foolish yesterday, at any rate he couldn't remember now. Whatever could he have had to say about madam's clothes? That they were the finest he had ever seen? Certainly, he had never seen a landlady on duty dressed like that before. 'That's enough of your comments,' the landlady interrupted. 'I don't want to hear another word from you about my clothes. My clothes are no concern of yours. I forbid you to mention them once and for all.' K. bowed once again and moved towards the door. 'What is that supposed to mean?' the landlady shouted after him, 'that you've never seen a landlady on duty dressed like that? Why do you make such senseless remarks? What do you mean? It just makes no sense at all.' K. turned round and begged her not to upset herself. Of course it was a senseless remark; after all, he knew nothing whatever about clothes. As far as he was concerned any dress that was clean and hadn't been mended looked expensive; he had just been astonished to see her appear there in the corridor, at night, among all those half-undressed men in such a fine evening gown, that was all. 'Aha!' said the landlady, 'it seems you have finally remembered what you said last night after all. And you cap it with more nonsense. It's quite right that you know nothing about clothes. But in that case, I earnestly beg of you to refrain from passing judgement on what you think are fine clothes or unsuitable evening gowns and suchlike. In fact' – and here it was as if a cold shudder went through her – 'you should have nothing whatever to say about my clothes, do you hear?' And as K. once again made to turn away without a word, she asked: 'Where do you get your knowledge of clothes from, then?' K. shrugged; he had none, he told her. 'You have none,' said the landlady. 'Then you shouldn't pretend you have. Come over to the office, I'll show you something that I hope will put a stop to your impertinence for good.' She led the way out of the door; Pepi sprang to K.'s side, pretending that he was paying his bill, they quickly came to an arrangement. It was quite simple, as K. knew the courtyard and the gate leading into the side street; next to the gate was a small door, in about an hour Pepi would be standing behind it and would open it after three knocks.

The private office was opposite the bar. K. only had to cross the hallway; the landlady was already standing in the lighted office, looking out impatiently for him. But there was a further interruption; Gerstäcker had been waiting in the hall and wanted to speak to K. It was not easy to shake him off; the landlady joined in too, and scolded Gerstäcker for intruding. 'Where shall I go then? Where?' Gerstäcker could still be heard shouting after the door was shut, his words horribly interspersed with wheezing and coughing.

It was a small, overheated room. Against the end walls stood a tall desk and an iron safe, against the side walls a wardrobe and an ottoman. The wardrobe took up more space than anything else – it took up not only the whole length of the side wall, it was so deep it also made the room very narrow; to open it fully, three sliding doors were needed. The landlady motioned K. to sit on the ottoman, while she sat on the revolving chair at the desk. 'Have you never learned dressmaking?' she asked. 'No, never,' said K. 'So what are you actually?' 'A surveyor.' 'And what is that?' K. explained; his explanation made her yawn. 'You're not telling the truth. Why don't you speak the truth?' 'You don't speak it either.' 'I don't? I suppose this is more of your impudence. And if I wasn't telling the truth, am I answerable to you for that? And what is it I'm not telling the truth about?' 'You are not just a landlady as you pretend to be.' 'Well now, you're full of discoveries. What else am I then? Your impudence is really getting out of hand.' 'I don't know what else you might be. I see only that you are a landlady, apart from that you wear clothes unlike those anyone else wears here in the village, as far as I know, which are quite unsuitable for a landlady.' 'Now we're getting to the point. You just can't keep things quiet, perhaps you're not impudent at all, perhaps you're like a child that knows some piece of nonsense and can't possibly keep it to itself. Tell me then, what's so special about these clothes?' 'You'll be angry if I tell you.' 'No, I shall laugh, because it will just be childish babble. So what about my clothes?' 'If you want to know, well, they're made of good material, very expensive, but they're old-fashioned, they're ornate, they've been mended a lot, and they're unsuitable for your age, your figure and your position. I was struck by them as soon as I saw you for the first time, it was about a week ago, here in the hall.' 'So that's it, is it? They're old-fashioned, ornate, and what else? And where do you get all this expert knowledge?' 'I can tell. I don't need any expertise for that.' 'You can just tell. You don't need to ask, you can tell right away what fashion requires. I shan't be able to do without you, because I do have a weakness for fine clothes. And what do you have to say if I tell you this wardrobe is full of clothes?' She pulled the sliding doors apart to reveal dresses tightly packed together, filling the length and breadth of the wardrobe; most of them were dark grey, brown or black gowns, all carefully hung up and arranged. 'These are my dresses, all of them old-fashioned and ornate, as you put it. But these are only the ones I have no space for upstairs in my room; I've got two more wardrobes full up there, two more, each almost as big as this one. Aren't you amazed?' 'No, I expected something of the sort. I said, didn't I, that you weren't just a landlady, that your mind was set on something else.' 'My mind is set on being welldressed, nothing else, and you are either a fool or a child or a very wicked, dangerous person. Now get out, will you!' K. was already out in the hall, and Gerstäcker was tugging at his sleeve again, when the landlady called after him: 'I'm getting a new dress tomorrow, perhaps I'll send for you.'

Gerstäcker flapped his hand angrily as if to silence the tiresome landlady from a distance, and told K. to come with him. At first he would not give K. any further explanation, and paid little attention to his objection that he had to go to the school now. Only when K. resisted as he tried to drag him away did Gerstäcker tell him not to worry; K. would have everything he needed at his house, he said, he could give up the school caretaking job, he should just come along with him. He had been waiting for him all day, and his mother had no idea where he was. K. gradually gave in, and asked Gerstäcker why he wanted to give him board and lodging. Gerstäcker replied briefly that he needed K.'s help with the horses; he had other things to do at the moment, but for now would K. just not make him drag him along like this and not make any unnecessary difficulties. If he wanted to be paid, he would pay him too. But then K. stopped in spite of Gerstäcker's efforts. He knew nothing at all about horses. That wasn't necessary either, said Gerstäcker impatiently, clenching his fists in annoyance to make K. go with him. 'I know why you want me to go with you,' said K. finally. Gerstäcker couldn't care less what K. knew. 'It's because you think I can get Erlanger to do something for you.' 'Of course,' said Gerstäcker, 'why else should I bother with you?' K. laughed, took Gerstacker's arm and let him lead him through the darkness.

The parlour in Gerstäcker's cottage was only dimly lit by a fire in the hearth and the stump of a candle, by the light of which someone sat reading a book in an alcove formed by the steeply sloping roof beams. It was Gerstäcker's mother. She held out a trembling hand to K. and made him sit down beside her; she spoke with difficulty, and it was difficult to understand her, but what she said

METAMORPHOSIS
and other stories

METAMORPHOSIS

The Transformation of Gregor Samsa

I

One morning Gregor Samsa woke in his bed from uneasy dreams and found he had turned into a huge verminous insect. He lay on his hard shell-like back, and when he raised his head slightly he saw his rounded brown underbelly, divided into a series of curved ridges, on which the bedding could scarcely stay in place and was about to slip off completely. His numerous legs, which were pitifully thin relative to the rest of his body, wriggled helplessly in front of his eyes.

'What has happened to me?' he thought. It was not a dream. His room, quite adequate for one person though rather too small, was there as usual with its familiar four walls. Spread out on the table was a collection of samples of material he had unpacked – Samsa was a travelling salesman – and above it hung the picture he had recently cut out of an illustrated magazine and set in a handsome gilt frame. It showed a lady with a fur hat and wrap sitting upright and holding out towards the viewer a heavy fur muff which covered the whole of her forearm.

Then Gregor turned his eyes towards the window, and the dreary weather – he could hear the rain dripping onto the metal window-ledge – made him feel quite depressed. 'Why don't I just sleep on a little longer and forget all this nonsense,' he thought, but that was quite impossible; he was used to sleeping on his right side, and in his present situation he could not get into that position. However hard he tried to throw himself to the right, he always rolled onto his back again. He must have tried a hundred times; he closed his eyes so he did not have to see his wriggling legs, and only gave up when he began to feel a slight dull ache in his side that he had never felt before.

'Oh God,' he thought, 'what a strenuous job I've chosen! On the move day in, day out. The stresses of this work are much greater than in the office at home, and on top of that I'm plagued with all this travelling, have to worry about catching trains, put up with irregular bad meals and constantly meeting different people for a short time without ever getting to know them more closely. To hell with it!' He felt a slight itch on his belly and squirmed slowly on his back towards the bedpost so that he could raise his head more easily. He found the place that was itching; it was covered with small white spots that he could not account for. He tried to feel the place with one of his legs, but withdrew it immediately because he felt a cold shiver whenever he touched it.

He slid back to his previous position. 'All this getting up early,' he thought, 'numbs the mind. One has to have one's sleep. Other travellers live like women in a harem. For instance, if I go back to my lodgings during the morning to dispatch the orders I've taken, these gentlemen are just having their breakfast. I should try that with my boss – he'd sack me on the spot. Still, who knows, that might suit me very well. If it weren't for the sake of my parents I'd have given notice long ago, I would have gone up to the boss and told him what I thought from the bottom of my heart. He would have fallen off his desk! It's a strange way he has, too, of sitting up there on his desk and talking down to his employees, and what's more, you have to go right up to him because he's hard of hearing. Well, I haven't given up all hope yet; once I've saved enough money to pay off what my parents owe him – it can't be more than another five or six years – I'll do it for sure. Then that will be the end of it. Still, for the moment I must get up; my train goes at five.'

He looked at the alarm clock that was ticking on the chest of drawers. 'Dear God in heaven!' he thought. It was half past six, and the hands were moving steadily on, it was even gone half past, getting on for quarter to. Had the alarm not gone off? He could see from his bed that it had been set correctly for four o'clock; it must have rung. Yes – but was it possible to sleep peacefully through that din that shook the furniture? Well, he had not slept peacefully, though probably all the more deeply. But what was he to do now? The next train went at seven; to catch it he would have to make a mad dash, the samples hadn't been packed yet, and he didn't feel particularly fresh and lively himself either. And even if he did catch the train he wouldn't avoid a thunderous rebuke from his boss, because the message boy from the firm would have been waiting for the five o'clock train and would have reported his absence long since; he was the boss's creature, spineless and stupid. What if he were to call in sick? But that would be extremely embarrassing and suspicious, for Gregor had never once been sick in five years' service. His boss would surely come along with the doctor from the insurance company, he would complain to his parents about their lazy son and dismiss any excuses by referring to the doctor, who regarded everyone as perfectly healthy but sometimes workshy. Besides, would he be so very wrong in this case? Gregor did in fact feel quite well, apart from feeling drowsy, which was really quite unwarranted after such a long sleep; indeed, he even felt extremely hungry.

While he was thinking all this over in a great hurry without being able to bring himself to get out of bed – just then the alarm clock struck a quarter to seven – there was a cautious knock on the door behind his head. It was his mother. 'Gregor,' she called, 'it's quarter to seven. Weren't you going away?' That gentle voice! Gregor was alarmed when he heard himself answer. It was unmistakably his own voice, but it was mixed with a painful piping sound from inside him that he could not suppress; the words could be understood clearly only the moment they were uttered, but then the sounds became so distorted that one could not tell whether one had heard them properly. Gregor had wanted to give a full answer and explain everything, but in the circumstances he merely replied: 'Yes, yes, thank you, mother; I'm getting up now.' His mother must not have noticed the change in Gregor's voice through the wooden door, for she was reassured by this explanation and shuffled off. But this brief exchange had alerted the other members of the family to the fact that Gregor was unexpectedly still at home, and now his father was banging feebly, but with his fist, on one of the doors. 'Gregor, Gregor,' he called, 'what's going on?' And after a short pause he spoke more urgently in a deeper voice: 'Gregor! Gregor!' At the other door, though, his sister asked softly and plaintively: 'Gregor? Are you unwell? Is there anything you need?' Gregor replied to both of them: 'I'm coming now,' making a great effort to speak as normally as possible by pronouncing his words with the utmost care and taking long pauses between each of them. His father went back to his breakfast, but his sister whispered: 'Gregor, open the door, I beseech you.' But Gregor had no intention of letting her in; on the contrary, he congratulated himself on the cautious habit he had acquired while travelling of locking all doors at night, even when he was at home.

First he intended to get up quietly and without interruption, to get dressed and above all have breakfast; then he would think about how to proceed – for he realised perfectly well that nothing sensible would be achieved by lying in bed thinking. He recalled that he had often felt some slight discomfort, perhaps brought on by lying awkwardly in bed, which on getting up had turned out to be purely imaginary, and he was curious to know how what he had imagined this morning would gradually fade away. He had not the slightest doubt that the change in his voice was nothing more than the symptom of a severe cold – an occupational illness of travelling salesmen.

It was a simple matter to remove the bedcover; he only needed to expand a little and it just slid off. But then things became more difficult, especially because he was so unusually broad. He would have needed hands and arms to get himself upright; but instead he only had all these little legs which continually waved about in different directions, and in any case he was unable to control them. When he tried to bend one of them the first thing it did was to straighten itself out; and if he finally managed to get this leg to do what he wanted, all the others in the meantime would wriggle about in an intense state of excitement, as if they had been liberated. 'You can't just stay in bed doing nothing,' Gregor said to himself.

The first thing he tried to do was to get the lower part of his body out of bed, but this part, which in any case he had not yet seen and could not properly imagine to himself, proved very difficult to move. It took so long that when, becoming almost frantic, he finally summoned all his strength and shoved himself forwards regardless, he chose the wrong direction and collided violently with the far bedpost; the sharp pain he felt taught him that this lower part of his body was for the moment perhaps the most sensitive.

So then he tried to get his upper body out of bed first, and cautiously turned his head towards the edge of the bed. He managed this easily, and finally, in spite of its width and its weight, the whole of his body slowly followed the turn of his head. But when his head was at last out of the bed, hanging in mid air, he was afraid to make any further progress this way, because if he were to fall it would really need a miracle to save him from injuring his head. And at all costs he must not lose consciousness just now; he had better stay in bed.

But when, after a similar struggle, he lay there panting, still in the same place, once again watching his tiny legs fighting each other, if anything even more wildly than before, and finding it impossible to calm or control their wayward behaviour, he again told himself that he could not possibly stay in bed, and that the most sensible thing would be to risk anything that might give him even the slightest hope of getting him out of bed. Meanwhile he took care to remind himself from time to time that thinking in the most calm and collected way was far better than taking desperate measures. At such moments he focused his gaze as sharply as he could on the window, but unfortunately there was little to encourage him or cheer him up in the sight of the morning fog that even obscured the other side of the narrow street. 'Seven o'clock already,' he said to himself as the alarm clock struck again, 'seven o'clock and there's still such a fog.' And for a while he lay there quietly, breathing gently as if he expected that in the total stillness things might return to normal.

But then he said to himself: 'I absolutely have to get all of myself out of bed before it strikes quarter past seven. In any case, by then someone from the office will have come to ask about me because the office opens before seven.' And then he set about getting the whole length of his body out of bed by rocking steadily to and fro. If he managed to fall out of bed in this way his head, which he would lift quickly as he fell, would probably not be injured. His back seemed to be hard; surely nothing would happen to it if he fell onto the carpet. What concerned him most was the loud crash that would inevitably result, and which would surely cause anxiety, if not alarm, to those on the other side of the doors. But that was a risk he had to take.

By the time Gregor was hanging halfway out of the bed – this new method was more like a game than a struggle, he only needed to keep rocking to and fro – it occurred to him how simple it would all be if someone came to help him. Two strong people – he thought of his father and the maid – would have been quite enough; they would only have to put their arms underneath his rounded back, scoop him out of bed, bend down with their load, and then just carefully help him to roll over onto the floor, where he hoped he would find out what his tiny legs could do. But quite apart from the fact that the doors were locked, ought he really to call for help? For all his distress, he could not help smiling at the thought.

By rocking more vigorously he had reached the point where he could scarcely keep his balance, and very soon he would have to make a final decision, for in five minutes it would be quarter past seven. Then there was a ring at the door of the apartment. 'That's someone from the office,' he said to himself and almost froze, while his legs just went on waving about all the faster. For a moment there was silence. 'They're not opening the door,' Gregor said to himself, clinging to some absurd hope. But then of course the maid as usual went with firm steps to the door and opened it. Gregor only needed to hear the first word the visitor uttered to know who it was – the head clerk himself. Why ever did Gregor have the misfortune to be employed by a firm where the slightest delay immediately aroused the greatest suspicion? Were all its employees idlers, every one of them, was there not one loyal and devoted person among them who, if he failed to put in just a few hours of the morning in the firm's service, suffered such pangs of conscience that he lost his head and was incapable of getting out of bed? Wouldn't it be quite enough to send a junior trainee to enquire – if such enquiries were necessary at all? Did the head clerk himself have to come, and did Gregor's whole blameless family have to be shown in this way that the investigation of such a suspicious matter could only be entrusted to the competence of the head clerk? And it was more because of the state of agitation these thoughts induced in Gregor than of any actual decision on his part that he swung himself with all his strength out of bed. There was a loud thud, but it was not really a crash. His fall was slightly muffled by the carpet, and his back was more flexible than Gregor had thought, so the dull thud he made was not so noticeable at all. But he had banged his head because he had not held it up carefully enough; he shook it and rubbed it on the floor in fury and pain.

'Something fell over in there,' said the head clerk in the next room to the left. Gregor tried to imagine whether something similar could ever happen to the head clerk as had happened to him today; such a possibility had to be allowed after all. But as if in brusque answer to this question, the clerk's lacquered boots squeaked as he took a few firm steps in the next room. From the side-room to the right his sister informed him in a whisper: 'Gregor, the head clerk is here.' 'I know,' said Gregor to himself; but he did not dare to raise his voice enough for her to hear.

'Gregor,' his father then said from the room on the left, 'the head clerk has come to enquire why you didn't leave on the early train. We don't know what to tell him. Besides, he wishes to speak to you personally. So please open the door. I'm sure he will be good enough to excuse the mess in your room.' 'Good morning, Herr Samsa,' the head clerk intervened in a friendly voice. 'He is not well,' said Gregor's mother to the head clerk, while his father was still talking at the door. 'Believe me, sir, he's not well. Otherwise how would Gregor ever miss a train! The boy thinks of nothing but his work. I almost get annoyed that he never goes out in the evening; he's been here for eight days now, but he's stayed in every evening. He sits quietly at home with us at the table and reads the paper or studies timetables. His only distraction is to get on with his fretwork. For instance, he spent two or three evenings making a small picture-frame; you'll be amazed how pretty it is, it's hanging in his room, you'll see it as soon as he opens the door. And I'm so happy that you're here, sir; we would never have got Gregor to open the door on our own, he's so stubborn, and I'm sure he's not well, although he insisted he was this morning.' 'I'm coming right away,' said Gregor slowly and cautiously, not stirring so that he did not miss a single word of the exchange. 'It is the only explanation I can think of, madam,' said the head clerk. 'I hope it is nothing serious. Though I must also say that we businessmen very often – fortunately or unfortunately, depending on how you look at it – simply have to overcome a slight indisposition for the sake of our work.' 'So are you going to let the head clerk in now?' Gregor's father asked impatiently. 'No,' said Gregor. There was an awkward silence from the room on the left; in the room on the right his sister began to sob.

Why didn't his sister join the others? She must have only just got out of bed and hadn't even begun to get dressed. And why was she crying? Was it because he wouldn't get up and let the head clerk in, because he was in danger of losing his job, and because his employer would then pursue his parents with his old demands? But for the moment these worries were surely unnecessary. Gregor was still there and had not the slightest intention of forsaking his family. Certainly, just now he was lying there on the carpet, and no one who knew the state he was in could seriously have expected him to admit the head clerk into his room; but he could not very well be dismissed on the spot for this trivial lack of courtesy, for which he would later find a suitable excuse. It seemed to Gregor that it would be much more sensible to leave him in peace just now instead of bothering him with tears and entreaties. But it was their lack of awareness that upset them and excused their behaviour.

'Herr Samsa,' the head clerk then called in a louder voice, 'what is the matter? You barricade yourself in your room, answer only yes or no, give your parents quite unnecessary cause for serious concern, and – I mention this only by the way – neglect your duties to the firm quite outrageously. I am speaking on behalf of your parents and your employer, and in all seriousness I am asking for an immediate and clear explanation. I am astonished, quite astonished. I thought of you as a calm and sensible person, and now you suddenly seem to have started playing the fool and indulging in strange whims. The chief actually suggested to me this morning a possible explanation for your absence – it was about the funds you were recently entrusted with; but I very nearly gave him my solemn word of honour that this explanation could not be correct. But now in view of your inexplicable obstinacy I no longer have the slightest desire to speak up for you. And your position is not at all secure, by any means. I had originally intended to say all this to you between ourselves, but since you are making me waste my time here to no purpose, I do not see why your parents should not know it too. It is that your performance has recently been most unsatisfactory; it may not be the most productive time of year to do business, we recognise that; but there is not and cannot be a time of year when no business is done, Herr Samsa.'

'But sir,' cried Gregor, beside himself, forgetting everything else in his agitation, 'I will open the door at once, this moment. A slight indisposition, an attack of vertigo, prevented me from getting up. I am still in bed. But now I feel perfectly well again. I am just getting out of bed. Only be patient for a moment, please! It's not as easy as I thought. But I'm quite well now. It's odd how these things can suddenly affect you! Yesterday evening I was still quite well, my parents will tell you, or rather, yesterday evening I already felt something. They must have noticed it. Why didn't I report it to the office! But then one always thinks one can get over an illness without having to stay at home. Please consider my parents, sir! All the charges you have just brought against me are groundless; no one has said a single word to me about them. Perhaps you have not read the latest orders I sent in. Besides, I am going to leave on the eight o'clock train, these few hours rest have given me my strength back. Don't let me take up your time, sir; I'll be in the office myself right away, please be good enough to tell them that and give my respects to the chief!'

While Gregor was stammering all this out, scarcely knowing in his haste what he was saying, he had managed without difficulty – no doubt thanks to the exercises he had already practised in bed – to get close to the chest of drawers, and was now trying to use it to pull himself upright. He really wanted to open the door, wanted to show himself and have a word with the head clerk; he was curious to find out what the others, who were just now so eager to see him, would say at the sight of him. If they were alarmed, then Gregor had no further obligation and could keep calm. If they accepted it all calmly, then he had no reason to get worked up and could indeed, if he hurried, be at the station for eight o'clock. At first, however, he slid down the smooth chest of drawers a few times; but then he gave one final heave and stood there upright. He no longer paid any attention to the pain in his abdomen, however much it stung. Then he let himself fall against the back of a nearby chair and held on tight to its edges with his tiny legs. In this way he also regained his self-control and was silent, for now he could listen to what the head clerk was saying.

'Did you understand a single word?' the head clerk asked his parents. 'Surely he isn't trying to make fools of us?' 'In heaven's name,' cried his mother, beginning to weep, 'perhaps he's very ill, and we're tormenting him. Grete! Grete!' she then shouted. 'Mother?' his sister called from the other side. They were communicating through Gregor's room. 'You must fetch the doctor at once. Gregor is ill. Quick, fetch the doctor. Did you hear Gregor speak just now?' 'That was the voice of an animal,' said the head clerk, remarkably quietly in contrast to the shouts of Gregor's mother. 'Anna! Anna!' his father called through the hall into the kitchen, 'fetch a locksmith at once!' And now the two girls were running through the hallway, their skirts rustling – how had his sister got dressed so quickly? – and wrenched the doors of the apartment open. He did not hear them close the doors; he assumed they had left them open, as was usual in an apartment when a great calamity had happened.

Gregor, however, had become much calmer. They may not understand what he was saying, in spite of the fact that his words had seemed to him clear enough, clearer than before, perhaps because his ears had got used to them; but at least they now understood that all was not quite right with him and were prepared to help him. The confident and assured way the initial arrangements had been made did him good. He felt a part of human society again, and hoped for great and extraordinary things of the doctor and the locksmith, though without really distinguishing between them very clearly. In order to make his voice as clear as possible for the crucial discussions to come, he cleared his throat gently, being careful to do this very discreetly, since it was possible that even this could sound quite different from a human cough, something he was no longer confident that he could judge for himself. Meanwhile not a sound was heard from the next room. Perhaps his parents were sitting at the table with the head clerk, whispering; perhaps they were all crouched by the door, listening.

Gregor slowly pushed himself towards the door with the help of the chair, then let it go and threw himself against the door, held himself upright against it – the round pads on his legs had some sticky substance on them – and stayed there for a moment to recover from his exertions. Then he began to turn the key in the lock with his mouth. Unfortunately, it seemed that he had no teeth, so what was he going to grasp the key with? On the other hand, he did have very strong jaws, and with these he actually managed to move the key, paying no heed to the damage he was clearly doing to himself, for a brown liquid oozed out of his mouth, ran over the key and dripped onto the floor. 'Listen,' said the head clerk in the next room, 'he's turning the key.' This encouraged Gregor greatly; but they should all have called out to him, his father and mother too: 'Go on, Gregor,' they should have shouted, 'keep at it, keep going at the lock!' And imagining that they were all following his efforts in suspense, he frantically clamped his jaws onto the key with all his strength. As the key turned in the lock he too turned with it; now he was only holding himself upright with his jaws, alternately hanging onto the key or forcing it down again with the whole weight of his body. The click of the lock as it finally snapped open brought Gregor abruptly to his senses. With a deep breath he said to himself: 'So I didn't need the locksmith after all,' and pressed his head down on the handle to open the door.

Because he had to open the door in this way it was in fact already wide open, and he himself was still nowhere to be seen. First he had to edge his way slowly round the door, very carefully of course, to prevent himself falling flat on his back before he got into the next room. He was still concentrating on this difficult manoeuvre, having no time to pay attention to anything else, when he heard the head clerk gasp out loud: 'Oh!' – it sounded like the wind sighing – and then, since he was nearest to the door, Gregor caught sight of him, holding his hand over his wide open mouth and slowly retreating as if driven back by the steady pressure of an unseen force. His mother – in spite of the presence of the head clerk, she was standing there with dishevelled hair, still tousled from her night's sleep – first clasped her hands together and looked at his father, then took two steps towards Gregor and collapsed amid her spreading petticoats, her face sunk out of sight against her breast. His father raised his clenched fist menacingly, as if he intended to shove Gregor back into his room, then looked helplessly around the living room, covered his eyes with his hands and wept, his sobs shaking his powerful chest.

Gregor now made no move to enter the room; instead he leaned from the inside against the firmly bolted wing of the double door so that the others could see only half of his body, and above it his head, tilted to one side, peering at them. Meanwhile it had become much lighter outside; on the other side of the street, part of the endless grey-black building – it was a hospital – stood out clearly with its evenly-spaced windows harshly intruding into the façade; the rain was still falling, but only in huge single drops that could be seen as they fell heavily one by one to the ground below. The breakfast dishes were piled up on the table, for breakfast was for his father the most important meal of the day, which was protracted for hours while he read various newspapers. On the wall directly opposite hung a photograph of Gregor from his military service, showing him as a lieutenant, his hand on his sword, smiling and relaxed, his posture and his uniform commanding respect. The door to the hallway was open, and since the main door of the apartment was also open, through it could be seen the landing and the top of the staircase leading down.

'Well,' said Gregor, fully aware that he was the only one who had remained calm, 'I shall get dressed right away, pack my samples and leave. You will let me leave, won't you? You see, sir, I'm not obstinate, and I enjoy my work; travelling is tiresome, but I couldn't live without travelling. Where are you going, sir?

To the office? You are? Will you report everything truthfully? One can be temporarily unfit for work, but that's just the right time to remember one's past achievements and to remind oneself that later, once the problem has been resolved, one will work all the harder and more carefully. I am so indebted to the chief, as you very well know. On the other hand I have to care for my parents and my sister. I'm in a quandary, but I shall work my way out of it. Don't make it more difficult for me than it already is. Put in a good word for me at the office! They don't like the travelling salesmen, I know. They think we earn big money and lead a grand life, too. They have no particular reason to correct this prejudice. But you, sir, in your position, you have a better view of things than the rest of the staff, indeed I'd say, strictly in confidence, you have a better view than the chief himself, who as a businessman can easily be misled into judging an employee unfairly. You also know very well that a salesman who is away from the office almost the whole year round can so easily become a victim of gossip, chance, and unfounded complaints he can't possibly defend himself against because he doesn't usually hear about any of it, and if he does, it's when he comes home exhausted from travelling and only then experiences for himself the awful consequences without being able to make out what caused it all. Please don't leave, sir, without a word to show that you agree with me, at least in part!'

But the head clerk had turned away at Gregor's first words, and only looked back at him over his shuddering shoulder with his mouth agape. And while Gregor was speaking he could not stand still for a moment; without once taking his eyes off him he backed towards the door, but very gradually, as if there were some secret prohibition against leaving the room. He had already reached the hall, and finally withdrew his foot from the living room with a sudden movement that gave the impression that he had just stepped on hot coals. But in the hallway he stretched out his right hand towards the staircase, as if some truly unearthly redemption awaited him there.

Gregor realised that he could not possibly let the head clerk leave in this frame of mind without putting his position in the firm at the utmost risk. His parents did not fully understand all this; over many years they had become convinced that Gregor had a secure position for life in the business, and in any case they were so preoccupied with their present worries that they had become incapable of looking ahead. But Gregor could look ahead; the head clerk had to be detained, reassured, persuaded and finally won over – after all, Gregor's future and that of his family depended on it! If only his sister were here! She was clever; she had wept while Gregor was still calmly lying on his back. And the head clerk, that ladies' man, would surely have listened to her; she would have closed the front door and in the hall she would have talked him out of his fright. But his sister was not there, so Gregor himself had to act. It did not occur to him that at present he still had no idea of his ability to move about, nor did it occur to him that his speech had possibly, indeed probably not been understood; he let go of the wing of the door and pushed himself through the opening, he wanted to go across to the head clerk, who was gripping the hallway banister tightly with both hands in a ridiculous manner, but Gregor, trying to find a hold, immediately slid and fell onto his many tiny legs with a faint cry. He had scarcely done so than he felt, for the first time that morning, physically comfortable; his legs were on firm ground, he realised to his delight that they did their best to carry him where he wished to go, and now he believed that very soon he would finally be cured of all his ills. But just as he lay there, shaking with intense relief, not far across the room from his mother, who had seemed so completely absorbed in herself, she suddenly jumped up, her arms outstretched and her fingers spread out wide, and cried out: 'Help, in God's name help!' She bent down as if to look at Gregor more closely, but instead she recoiled instinctively, forgetting that behind her stood the laden table; as she reached it she hurriedly perched herself on it, and in her distraction seemed not to notice when she upset the large coffee pot beside her, sending a great stream of coffee pouring onto the carpet.

'Mother, mother,' said Gregor softly, looking up at her. He had completely forgotten about the head clerk for the moment; but at the sight of the stream of coffee he could not resist champing his empty jaws several times. At this his mother shrieked again, fled from the table, and fell into his father's arms as he rushed towards her. But now Gregor had no time for his parents; the head clerk was already on the stairs, and with his chin against the banister took one last look back. Gregor started off in an attempt to catch him, but the head clerk must have suspected something, for he leapt down several steps and disappeared with a shout of 'Aah!' that echoed through the whole stairwell. Unfortunately his father, who had so far kept relatively calm, seemed completely unnerved by the head clerk's flight, for instead of running after the head clerk himself, or at least letting Gregor run after him, he seized in his right hand the stick the clerk had left on a chair together with his hat and his overcoat, with his left hand took a large newspaper from the table, and began to drive Gregor back into his room by waving the stick and the newspaper at him and stamping his feet. No pleading from Gregor helped, and no one understood him; however meekly he turned his head, his father only stamped his feet the harder. Across the room his mother had thrown open a window in spite of the cool weather, and leaning far outside she buried her face in her hands. Between the street and the stairwell a violent draught blew up, the curtains flew about, the newspapers on the table rustled, and single sheets blew across the floor. Implacably his father advanced, hissing like a savage. But so far Gregor had had no practice at all in going backwards, and so moved very slowly. If only he had been able to turn round he would have reached his room at once, but he was afraid this timeconsuming exercise would try his father's patience, and at any moment he faced the threat of a deadly blow on his back or his head from the stick in his father's hand. But in the end Gregor had no alternative, for he realised to his horror that while going backwards he could not even keep his direction; and so, casting constant sideways glances at his father, he began to turn round as fast as he possibly could, though it actually happened very slowly. Perhaps his father noticed his good intentions, for he did not interrupt him in this process, and even directed Gregor's movements from a distance with the end of his stick. If only his father would not make that intolerable hissing noise! It made Gregor lose his head completely. He had almost turned right round, with that hissing still in his ears, when he made a mistake and even turned back a little. But when at last he managed to get his head as far as the door, it turned out that his body was too wide to get through the opening. Of course, it did not remotely occur to his father, in his present state of mind, to open the other wing of the door for instance, to give Gregor enough space to pass through. His only thought was that Gregor had to get back into his room as soon as possible; and he would never have permitted the elaborate preparations Gregor needed to haul himself upright and perhaps get through the door that way. Instead he drove Gregor on with more noise than ever, as if there were no obstacle; at Gregor's back it no longer sounded like the voice of a single father, it really was no laughing matter any more, and Gregor squeezed himself, come what may, against the door. He lifted one side of his body until he was lying askew in the door opening; his one side was rubbed quite raw and left ugly blotches on the white door. Soon he was stuck tight and could no longer move without help, his legs on one side were wriggling in the air, those on his other side were painfully pressed against the floor – when his father gave him a truly liberating violent shove from behind and he shot, bleeding heavily, right across his room. The door was slammed shut with the stick, and at last it was quiet.

2

Dusk was falling when Gregor woke from his deep, almost comatose sleep. He would surely have woken up not long afterwards even if he had not been disturbed, for he felt he had slept long enough and was sufficiently rested; but it seemed to him that he had been wakened by the sound of light footsteps and the cautious shutting of the door leading to the hall. The light from the electric street lamps shone faintly here and there on the ceiling and on the upper parts of the furniture, but down where Gregor was it was dark. Moving slowly and awkwardly with the help of his feelers, which he was only now beginning to appreciate, he pushed himself towards the door to see what was going on out there. His left side felt like one long unpleasantly tight scar, and he was forced to hobble on his two rows of legs. Moreover, one of his legs had been injured during the events of that morning – it was almost miraculous that only one had been hurt – and trailed lifelessly behind him.

Only when he reached the door did he realise what had really enticed him there; it had been the smell of food. For there stood a bowl full of sweetened milk with small slices of white bread soaked in it. He could have laughed with delight, for he was even hungrier than he had been earlier that morning, and he immediately dipped his head almost up to his eyes into the milk. But he quickly drew it out again in disappointment; not simply because the soreness on his left side made eating difficult for him – and he could only eat if his whole body made a strenuous effort to cooperate – but also because this milk, normally his favourite food, which was certainly why his sister had placed it there, was not at all to his taste; in fact he turned away from the bowl almost in disgust and crawled back into the middle of the room.

In the living room, as Gregor could see through the gap in the door, the gas was lit, but whereas at this time of day his father usually read aloud from the afternoon paper to his mother, and sometimes to his sister too, no sound could be heard now. Perhaps these readings, which his sister had always spoken and written to him about, had recently been suspended anyway; but there was silence all round, although the apartment was certainly not empty. 'What a very quiet life the family leads,' said Gregor to himself as he stared out into the darkness with a feeling of great pride that he had been able to provide such a life in such a fine apartment for his family and his sister. But what if all this peace, all this prosperity and all this happiness should now end horribly? Rather than dwell on such thoughts, Gregor preferred to move about, and crawled up and down in his room.

Once during that long evening one of the side doors and then the other was opened just a small crack and quickly closed again; someone evidently wanted to come in, but then had second thoughts. So Gregor stopped right next to the door to the living room, determined to tempt the reluctant visitor in somehow, or at least to find out who it was; but this time the door was not opened again and he waited in vain. Earlier, when the doors were locked, they had all wanted to come in to his room; now that he had unlocked one door and the others had been opened in the course of the day, no one came, and moreover the keys were in the other side of the door.

It was late into the night before the light in the living room was turned out, and now it was easy to tell that his parents and his sister had stayed up till then, because he clearly heard all three of them leaving on tiptoe. Now it was certain that no one would come into Gregor's room until morning, so he had plenty of time without being disturbed to think about how he was now going to reorganise his life. But the high spacious room in which he was forced to lie flat on the floor intimidated him, though he could not think why – after all he had lived in it for five years – and turning half-instinctively and feeling a little sheepish, he scuttled under the sofa where, although his back was rather squashed and he could not raise his head, he immediately felt comfortable, his only regret being that his body was too wide to fit right underneath.

There he remained the whole night, which he spent partly half-asleep, constantly being jerked awake by pangs of hunger, but partly in a state of anxiety and vague hopes, which all led to the conclusion that he must for the time being remain calm and exercise the greatest patience and consideration to allow his family to cope with the inconvenience he was forced to inflict on them in his present condition.

Early the next morning – it was still quite dark – Gregor soon had occasion to put these resolutions to the test, for his sister, almost fully dressed, opened the door from the hallway and looked in nervously. She did not see him at first, but when she noticed him under the sofa – good heavens, he had to be somewhere, he couldn't have flown away – she was so startled that she could not control herself and slammed the door shut from the other side. But then, as if regretting her behaviour, she immediately opened the door again and came in on tiptoe as if she were visiting someone who was seriously ill, or even a stranger. Gregor had pushed his head out to the very edge of the sofa and watched her. Would she notice that he had left the milk, though certainly not because he wasn't hungry, and would she bring in some other food more suitable for him? If she didn't do it of her own accord, he would rather starve than draw her attention to it, even though he actually felt an overwhelming urge to dash out from under the sofa, throw himself at his sister's feet and beg her for something decent to eat. But his sister, wondering, immediately noticed that the bowl of milk was still full and that only a little milk had been spilt round about; she quickly picked it up, though with a rag rather than in her bare hands, and took it out. Gregor was most curious to know what she would bring instead, and he imagined all kinds of different possibilities. But he could never have guessed what his sister in her kindness actually did. In order to test his appetite, she brought him a wide selection, all spread out on an old newspaper. There were old half-rotting vegetables, bones from last night's supper in some congealed white sauce, a few raisins and almonds, a cheese that two days before Gregor had pronounced inedible, a slice of dry bread, a slice of buttered bread and a slice of bread with butter and salt. In addition to all this she also put down the bowl that was probably now intended once and for all for Gregor's use, which she had filled with water. Tactfully – for she knew he would not eat in front of her – she left quickly and even locked the door, just for him to know that he could make himself as comfortable as he wished. Gregor's little legs wriggled as he came out to eat. Moreover, his injuries must have healed completely by now, he no longer felt restricted; this amazed him as he remembered how more than a month ago he had cut his finger slightly with a knife, and how this wound had still hurt badly enough just the day before yesterday. 'Could it be that I'm less sensitive now?' he thought, already nibbling greedily at the cheese, which of all the food had instantly appealed to him the most. One after the other, his eyes watering with satisfaction, he quickly devoured the cheese, the vegetables and the sauce; but he disliked the fresh food, he simply could not bear the smell of it, and even dragged the things he wanted to eat a little further away. He had long since eaten his fill, and was now lying lazily in the same place when his sister slowly turned the key in the lock as a sign that he should move back. This startled him, although he was almost asleep, and he scurried back under the sofa. But even for the short time his sister was in the room it cost him a great effort to stay under the sofa, because he had eaten so much that his body had become rather swollen, and he could hardly breathe in the confined space there. Between brief bouts of suffocation he watched with protruding eyes as his unsuspecting sister swept up with a broom both the remnants of his meal and the food he had not touched, as if this too was no longer of any use, threw everything hurriedly into a pail which she covered with a wooden lid, and took it all outside. Scarcely had she turned to go than Gregor pulled himself out from under the sofa, stretching himself and taking deep breaths.

In this way Gregor was now fed every day, once in the morning while his parents and the maid were still asleep, and again after everyone had finished lunch, when his parents again slept for a while and his sister sent the maid out on some errand. For sure, they did not want Gregor to starve either, but perhaps they could not have put up with knowing any more about his meals than his sister told them, or perhaps she wanted to spare them even the slightest degree of grief, for indeed they were already suffering enough.

What excuses they had used to get rid of the doctor and the locksmith on that first morning Gregor could never find out, for since they could not understand him, no one, not even his sister, imagined that he could understand them, and so whenever his sister was in his room he had to be content just with listening to her occasional sighs and appeals to the saints. Only later, when she had begun to get used to everything – there was of course no question of her becoming fully accustomed to the situation – Gregor sometimes overheard a well-meant remark, or one that could be understood as such. 'Well, he enjoyed his food today,' she would say whenever he had laid into it with gusto, while if the opposite happened, which gradually became more frequent, she would say almost sadly: 'Now he's left it all again.'

Although Gregor was not able to hear any news directly, he learnt some things from the neighbouring rooms, and whenever he heard voices he would run straight over to that door and press his whole body up against it. For the first few days especially, there was no conversation that was not about him in one way or another, if only in private. For two days at every mealtime the family discussed how they should deal with the situation; but even between meals they talked about the same thing, for there were always at least two of them at home, no doubt because no one wanted to be there alone, and on no account did they want to leave the apartment empty. Moreover, on the very first day the housemaid – it was not entirely clear what and how much she knew about what had happened – had begged Gregor's mother on her knees to let her give her notice immediately, and when she left a quarter of an hour later, she wept as she thanked them for letting her go as if it had been the kindest thing they had done for her, and though no one had asked her to, solemnly swore that she would not divulge the slightest thing to anyone.

So now his sister had to help his mother with the cooking too; but this did not give her much trouble, for they ate almost nothing. Again and again Gregor heard one of them vainly urging the others to eat, but the only answer was: 'No thank you, I've had enough' or something of the sort. Perhaps they didn't have anything to drink either. His sister frequently asked her father if he would like some beer, saying she would gladly fetch it herself, and when he did not reply, to overcome his reluctance she would say she could send the caretaker's wife for it; but then her father would finally give her an emphatic 'No' and that was the end of it.

On the first day Gregor's father had already explained the family's whole financial situation and their prospects to his wife and daughter. Now and again he stood up from the table and took some certificate or account book from the little strongbox that he had kept when his own business collapsed five years earlier. He could be heard opening the complicated lock and closing it again after taking out the document he was looking for. These explanations of his father's were in some way the first cheering news Gregor had heard since his confinement. He had believed that his father had been left with nothing at all from his business, at least he had told him nothing to the contrary, but then Gregor had not asked him about it either. Gregor's sole concern at the time had been to do everything he could to enable his family to get over the collapse of the business, which had reduced them all to a state of complete despair, as quickly as possible. So he had then begun to work with a particular zeal, and almost overnight had advanced from junior clerk to travelling salesman, which of course gave him much more scope to earn money; his successes in this work in terms of commission were instantly converted into cash, which could be laid out on the table at home in front of his surprised and delighted family. Those had been good times, and they had never returned, at least not as splendidly as then, though Gregor had later earned so much money that he was in a position to meet all the family's expenses, which he did. They had simply got used to it, both he and the family; they took the money gratefully, he provided it gladly, but that special warmth was missing. Only his sister had remained close to Gregor, and because unlike him she loved music and could play the violin with great feeling, he had a secret plan to send her to the Conservatoire the following year, regardless of the great expense it would inevitably involve, which he was confident could be met by other means. During Gregor's brief stays at home, the Conservatoire would often be mentioned in his conversations with his sister, but always only as a beautiful dream they could not hope to realise, and his parents were unwilling to listen even to these innocent remarks; but Gregor had very definite ideas about it, and intended to announce it with great ceremony on Christmas Eve.

Such thoughts, quite pointless in his present condition, went through Gregor's head as he stood upright clinging to the door and listened. Sometimes he was so overcome with exhaustion that he could no longer listen and inadvertently let his head bump against the door but then immediately held it still, for even the slightest noise he made would be heard next door and they would all fall silent. 'Whatever is he up to now?' his father would say after a while, obviously turning towards the door, and then the interrupted conversation would gradually be resumed.

Since his father tended to repeat himself frequently while he set out the family's financial situation, partly because it was a long time since he had gone into it himself, and partly because his mother did not always understand everything at first – Gregor now learned clearly enough that in spite of all their misfortune there were still some funds, though not a great deal, left from the old days, and that they had grown a little in the meantime with the interest which had not been touched. Moreover, the money Gregor had brought home every month – he had only kept a modest amount for himself – had not all been used up and had accumulated into a small lump sum. Behind his door Gregor nodded eagerly, delighted with this unexpected foresight and thrift. In fact, he could have used this surplus to pay off his father's debt to his employer, and the day he could quit this job would have been much closer; but now he was sure it was better the way his father had arranged things.

However, there was not nearly enough money for the family to live on the interest; there was perhaps enough for them to live on for a year, or two years at the most, but no more. So it was just a sum that could not actually be touched and had to be kept for an emergency; money to live on would have to be earned. Now though his father was in good health, he was an old man who had not worked for five years, and in any case he could not be expected to take on very much; over those five years, which had been the first holidays of his hard-working yet unsuccessful life, he had put on a lot of fat, which had made him very ungainly. As for his old mother, who suffered from asthma, for whom it was an effort just to walk around the apartment, who spent every other day lying on the sofa at the open window gasping for breath – was she supposed to go out and earn money? And was his sister supposed to earn a living, when at seventeen she was still a child and had so far led a life no one could begrudge her, dressing nicely, sleeping late, helping in the home, enjoying a few modest pleasures, and above all playing the violin? Whenever their discussions turned to the need to earn money, the first thing Gregor did was to leave the door and throw himself onto the cool leather sofa beside it, burning with shame and grief.

Often he lay there sleepless through the long nights, just scrabbling at the leather for hours. Or he would make a huge effort to push an armchair up to the window and crawl up to the window-sill, prop himself up on the chair and lean against the window looking out, evidently somehow recalling the feeling of liberation this had once given him. For in fact his sight was deteriorating by the day; even things no great distance away he could see less and less distinctly, and the hospital opposite he had looked at all too often and cursed the sight of it – that he could not see at all now. If he had not known for certain that he lived in the Charlottenstrasse, which though quiet was right in the middle of the city, he could have believed that from his window he looked out onto a wasteland in which the grey sky and the grey earth merged together indistinguishably. His observant sister only needed to notice twice that the armchair was next to the window; after that she would carefully push it back to the window every time after clearing up the room, and from now on she even left the inner windows open.

If only Gregor had been able to speak to his sister and thank her for everything she had to do for him, he would have found it easier to accept her help; as it was, however, it pained him. Of course, his sister did everything she could to dispel the embarrassment of it all, and indeed the more time went by the more she was able to; but in time Gregor too noticed things more closely. He even dreaded the moment she entered the room. Scarcely had she come in than she would dash straight to the window without even taking time to close the door, however careful she was at other times to spare everyone the sight of Gregor's room, hurriedly fling it open as if she were almost suffocating, and stand there for a time, however cold it was, taking deep breaths. She alarmed Gregor twice a day with all this hurry and bustle; he spent the whole time trembling under the sofa, although he knew very well that she would certainly have been glad to spare him all the upset if only she could have brought herself to stay in the same room as Gregor with the window closed.

Once, it must have been a month since Gregor's transformation, when she surely no longer had any reason to be surprised by his appearance, his sister arrived a little earlier than usual and found Gregor motionless, propped upright and looking out of the window – a sight to frighten anyone. It would not have surprised Gregor if she had not come in, since being where he was he prevented her from opening the window right away, but not only did she not come in – she recoiled and shut the door; a stranger might well have thought Gregor had been lying in wait and was going to bite her. Of course he immediately hid himself under the sofa, but he had to wait until midday before she came back, and she seemed much more agitated than usual. This made him realise that she still could not bear the sight of him, that she would continue to be unable to, and that she no doubt had to make a great effort not to turn and flee when she saw even the small part of his body that stuck out from under the sofa. One day, in order to spare her that too, he dragged the linen cloth on his back from the table onto the sofa – this all took him four hours – and arranged it so that he was completely covered and so that his sister could not see him even if she bent down. If she thought this covering was unnecessary, then she could have removed it, for it was clear enough that Gregor did not derive any pleasure from totally isolating himself like this; but she left the cloth where it was, and Gregor once thought he even glimpsed a look of gratitude when he cautiously lifted the cloth a little way with his head to see what his sister thought of the new arrangement.

Over the first two weeks his parents could not bring themselves to come into his room, and he often heard them say how much they appreciated the work his sister was doing, whereas before they had frequently got annoyed with her because they regarded her as a rather useless girl. But now they both often waited outside Gregor's room while his sister was tidying it up, and she had scarcely emerged when she had to tell them exactly how the room looked, what Gregor had eaten, how he had behaved this time, and whether she might have noticed any slight improvement in his condition. His mother had even wanted to go and see him quite early on, but his father and sister dissuaded her with reasonable arguments which Gregor listened to very carefully and fully approved of. But later she had to be held back by force, crying: 'Let me go and see Gregor, won't you, after all he's my poor son! Can't you understand that I must see him?' On these occasions Gregor thought it might be a good thing if his mother did come into his room, not every day of course, but perhaps once a week; after all, she understood things much better than his sister, who for all her pluck was only a child, and as a matter of fact had perhaps only taken on such a difficult task on a childish impulse.

Gregor's wish to see his mother was soon granted. If only out of consideration for his parents, he was reluctant to show himself at the window during the daytime, but he could not crawl very far across the few square yards of floor space. Even during the night he had trouble lying there quietly; he soon lost his appetite and no longer took the slightest pleasure in eating, and so by way of diversion he took to crawling to and fro over the walls and the ceiling. He especially enjoyed hanging from the ceiling. It was quite different from lying on the ground; he could breath more easily, he felt a gentle swaying sensation through his body, and in the almost blissful state of distraction he experienced up there he would occasionally, to his own surprise, let go and crash to the floor. But by now of course he had more control over his body than before, and did not injure himself even by falling from such a height. His sister at once noticed this new form of amusement Gregor had devised for himself – in fact, in crawling about he left traces of his sticky substance here and there – so she hit on the idea of giving him more space to crawl about by removing the furniture that was in his way, especially the chest of drawers and the writing table. But she was not able to do this on her own; she did not dare to ask her father for help, and the housemaid would certainly not have helped her. Although this girl of about sixteen had bravely stayed on after the previous cook had left, she had asked as a special favour that she might be allowed to keep the kitchen door permanently locked and have to open it only when specifically required to; so his sister had no choice but to call on her mother while her father was out. Her mother came along with cries of delight and excitement, but fell silent when she reached the door to Gregor's room. His sister of course first checked to see that everything in the room was in order, and only then let her mother in. With the greatest haste, Gregor had pulled the cloth even lower and made more folds in it; now it really did look just like a cloth that had been thrown casually over the sofa. This time Gregor also refrained from peeping out from under the cloth; he forfeited the chance of seeing his mother on this occasion, and was simply glad that she had come at last. 'Come in, he's nowhere to be seen,' said his sister, evidently leading her mother by the hand. Then Gregor heard the two women struggling to shift the old chest of drawers, which was heavy enough, while all the time his sister took on most of the work without listening to her mother's warnings not to strain herself. It took them a very long time. They must have been at it for a quarter of an hour when his mother said they had better leave the chest where it was, firstly because it was too heavy for them to be finished before her husband arrived, and if they left it in the middle of the room it would block Gregor's way completely; and secondly it was not at all certain that they were doing him a favour by taking the furniture out. She seemed rather to think the opposite; her heart sank when she saw the bare wall, and why shouldn't Gregor feel that way too, after all he had got used to the furniture in his room long since and would feel desolate if it were empty. 'And anyway,' his mother concluded in a hushed voice – not knowing exactly where Gregor was hiding, she generally spoke almost in a whisper, as if she did not even want him to hear the sound of her voice, for she was convinced he could not understand what they said – 'if we took the furniture away, wouldn't it look as if we had given up all hope of recovery and were cruelly abandoning him? I think it would be best if we tried to leave the room exactly as it was before, so that when Gregor comes back to us he'll find everything unchanged and it will be all the easier for him to forget what has happened in the meantime.'

When Gregor heard his mother's words he realised that the absence of all direct human contact in the course of these two months, combined with his monotonous life at home, must have confused his mind, for there was no other way he could explain to himself how he could seriously have wanted his room cleared. Had he really wished to have his warm cosy room with its comfortable family furniture turned into a cave in which he would be able to crawl around wherever he wanted, but at the cost of very soon completely forgetting his previous existence as a human being? Indeed, was he even now so close to forgetting it that only his mother's voice, which he had not heard for so long, had jolted him out of the idea? No, nothing must be removed. Everything must stay; he could not do without the comforting presence of the furniture, and if it stopped his senseless crawling about, then so much the better.

Unfortunately, though, his sister thought otherwise. In the discussions about Gregor with her parents she had become accustomed, not without some justification it must be said, to act as the expert in the matter, so on this occasion too her mother's advice was sufficient to make her insist on clearing out not only the chest of drawers and the desk, which was all she had intended at first, but also all the other furniture with the exception of the indispensable sofa. To be sure, it was not just childish defiance and the hard won self-confidence she had recently acquired so unexpectedly that prompted her to insist on this; she had also noticed that Gregor did in fact need a lot of room to crawl around, while as far as she could see he did not use the furniture at all. But perhaps it was also the over-eager imagination of girls of her age, which seizes every opportunity to indulge itself, that now tempted Grete to see Gregor's situation in yet more lurid terms, so that she could do even more for him than she had hitherto. For surely no one else would ever venture to set foot in a room where Gregor, and Gregor alone, had the freedom of the empty walls.

And so she refused to be persuaded otherwise by her mother, who in any case seemed agitated and unsure of herself in this room; she soon fell silent and gave her daughter what help she could to move the chest of drawers out of there. Well, Gregor could do without the chest of drawers at a pinch; but then the desk had to stay. And scarcely had the two women got the chest of drawers out of the room, groaning as they heaved at it, than Gregor poked his head out from under the sofa to see how he could intervene as discreetly and considerately as possible. But unfortunately it happened to be his mother who came in first while Grete was in the next room holding the sofa with both arms, rocking it to and fro on her own without of course managing to move it an inch. But his mother was not used to the sight of Gregor, it might have made her ill, so he hurriedly retreated to the other end of the sofa; but he could not prevent the front of the cloth moving slightly, which was enough to catch his mother's eye. She stopped, stood still for a moment, and then went back to Grete.

Although Gregor kept telling himself that nothing out of the ordinary was happening, it was just a few pieces of furniture being moved around, all the same he soon had to admit to himself that all this coming and going by the women, the brief instructions they addressed to each other, and the scraping of the furniture across the floor, caused a great commotion all round him, and however tightly he drew in his head and legs and pressed his body against the floor he was forced to conclude that he could not stand it all for very long. They were clearing out his room, taking away everything he cherished; they had already taken the chest of drawers containing his fretsaw and other tools, now they were heaving at the desk that seemed to have grown into the floor, the desk at which he had written his assignments when he was at business school, at secondary school, even at his primary school – now he simply had no more time to weigh up the good intentions of the two women, besides he had almost forgotten about them, for in their exhaustion they were now working in silence and all that could be heard was the weary tread of their feet.

So he emerged from his hiding-place – the women were leaning against the desk in the next room to recover their breath – and ran this way and that, changing direction four times, for he really had no idea what to save first. Then the picture of the lady swathed in furs hanging on the otherwise empty wall caught his attention; he quickly crawled up to it and pressed himself against the glass, which held him firmly and soothed his burning underbelly. His body covered the whole picture – at least no one would remove the picture now, for sure. He swivelled his head towards the living room door in order to watch the women as they returned.

They had not allowed themselves much of a rest, and were coming back already; Grete had put her arm around her mother and was almost carrying her. 'What shall we take now, then?' said Grete, looking round. Then her eyes met Gregor's on the wall. It was probably only because her mother was there that she kept her composure; she bent her face down close to her mother's to prevent her from looking round, and without thinking said in a tremulous voice: 'Come on, let's go back into the living room for a moment, shall we?' Her intention was quite clear to Gregor; she wanted to get her mother safely out of the way and then shoo him down off the wall. Well, just let her try! He was sitting on his picture and wasn't giving it up. He would rather jump out at Grete's face.

But Grete's words had only unsettled her mother, who stepped away, caught sight of the huge brown blob on the flowered wallpaper and, before she actually realised that it was Gregor she was looking at, cried 'Oh God! Oh God!' in a loud hoarse scream, fell onto the sofa with outstretched arms, as if giving up completely, and lay there motionless. 'Gregor, you . . .' cried his sister, glaring at him and raising her fist. These were the first words she had addressed to him directly since his transformation. She ran into the next room to fetch some smelling salts to rouse her mother from her swoon. Gregor wanted to help, too – there was still time to save the picture – but he was stuck fast to the glass and had to use force to free himself; then he too ran into the next room, as if he could give his sister some advice as he had done in the past. But then he had to stand helplessly behind her while she rummaged about among various small bottles, and then gave her a fright when she turned round. One of the bottles fell and smashed to bits; a splinter of glass hurt Gregor in the face and some kind of caustic medicine spilled all over him. Then Grete hurriedly seized as many bottles as she could carry and ran in to her mother with them, slamming the door shut with her foot. Now Gregor was shut off from his mother, who through his fault was perhaps close to death; he could not open the door for fear of driving away his sister, who had to stay with her mother – there was nothing he could do now but wait. Overwhelmed by remorse and anxiety, he began to crawl about. He crawled over everything, the walls, the furniture, the ceiling, and finally in his desperation as the whole room began to spin around him, he fell onto the middle of the big table.

For a while Gregor lay there exhausted. It was quiet everywhere; perhaps that was a good sign. Then the doorbell rang. The maid had of course locked herself in the kitchen, so Grete had to open the door. His father was back. 'What has happened?' were his first words; Grete's face must have told him everything. She answered in a muffled voice – her face was evidently buried in her father's chest – 'Mother has fainted, but she's better now. Gregor has got out.' 'I knew it,' said her father, 'I always said so, but you women wouldn't listen.' It was clear to Gregor that his father had misinterpreted Grete's all too brief explanation and had assumed that he had committed some act of violence. So Gregor now had to try to pacify his father, for he had neither the time nor the ability to explain the situation to him. He fled to the door of his room and pressed himself against it, so that as soon as his father came in from the hall he would see that Gregor had every intention of returning to his room at once and that there was no need to chase him back in there, he only had to open the door and Gregor would disappear immediately.

But his father was in no mood to appreciate such niceties; 'Aha!' he shouted the moment he came in, as if he were furious and pleased at the same time. Gregor withdrew his head from the door and lifted it towards his father. He really had never imagined his father as he was standing there now; to be sure, he had recently been so absorbed in his new ways of crawling around that he had not bothered to follow what was going on in the rest of the apartment as he had done before, and he really ought to have been prepared to find that things had changed. Even so, even so – was this still his father? The same man who before had lain exhausted, buried in his bed when Gregor had set out on a business trip, who had greeted him from an armchair in his dressing-gown on the evenings he returned; who had not been properly able to get up, but simply raised his arms to express his delight, who during the rare walks they had taken together on a few Sundays and on the main holidays of the year, had always struggled along between Gregor and his mother, who themselves walked slowly enough, but even more slowly than they did, bundled up in his old overcoat, always cautiously feeling his way with his walking-stick – who, whenever he wanted to say something, almost always stopped and gathered his companions around him? But now he held himself quite upright, dressed in a close-fitting blue uniform with gold buttons, as worn by messengers in a bank; his strong double chin protruded above the high stiff collar of his jacket, his dark eyes gazed out keenly and alertly from under his bushy eyebrows, and his white hair, unkempt before, now glistened, combed into a meticulously neat parting. He threw his cap with its gold monogram, probably that of a bank, in an arc right across the room onto the sofa, and thrusting his hands in his trouser pockets and tucking the tails of his long uniform jacket behind him, he advanced on Gregor with a fierce expression on his face. Perhaps he did not know what he intended to do; at any rate he lifted his feet extraordinarily high, and Gregor wondered at the huge size of the soles of his boots. But he did not stop to look, for he had known from the very start of his new life that his father believed he had to treat Gregor only with the utmost severity. And so he ran ahead of his father, stopped whenever his father paused, and hurried on again the moment his father moved. They circled the room several times like this without anything decisive happening, indeed it all took place so slowly that it did not look as if Gregor were being pursued; so for the time being he stayed on the floor, especially as he feared his father might regard it as particularly bad behaviour if he sought to escape by crawling up the walls or onto the ceiling. All the same, Gregor had to admit that he could not even keep up this form of progress for long, for while his father took one step he had to make countless movements. He soon noticed he was short of breath – indeed even in his earlier days his lungs had not been very robust. As he staggered along, gathering all his strength in order to run, he could hardly keep his eyes open; in his sluggish state he could think of no other way of escape than to run – he had almost forgotten by now that he could take to the walls, even though they were cluttered with carefully carved pieces of furniture full of sharp points and spikes – then something, thrown with no great force, narrowly missed him and rolled away in front of him. It was an apple, quickly followed by another. Gregor stopped in terror; there was no point in running – his father had decided to bombard him. He had filled his pockets from the fruit bowl on the sideboard, and without taking careful aim for the moment, was throwing one apple after another. The small red apples rolled about on the floor as if they were charged with electricity, bumping into one another. One, thrown feebly, grazed Gregor's back but glanced off harmlessly. But another followed immediately and actually embedded itself in his back; Gregor tried to drag himself onwards, as if the unexpected, unbelievable pain might pass with a change of location, but he felt as if he were nailed to the spot and lay stretched out, his senses reeling. The last thing he saw was the door of his room being flung open and his mother rushing out in her shift, followed by his sister who was screaming – she had undressed her mother so that she could breathe more freely after she fainted; then his mother rushed over to his father, her unfastened petticoats slipping to the floor one after the other, and stumbling over her underskirts she threw herself at him and embraced him, wholly united with him – Gregor's sight was already failing now – and clasping his father's head in her hands begged him to spare Gregor's life.

3

The serious injury Gregor had sustained, from which he suffered for more than a month – because no one dared to remove it, the apple stuck in his back as a visible reminder – seemed to have made even his father realise that Gregor, in spite of his present sorry and repulsive shape, was a member of the family who should not be treated with hostility, and that family duty obliged them to swallow their revulsion and tolerate him – but no more than that.

Although Gregor's wound meant that he had lost his mobility, probably for ever, and that for the time being he took many long minutes, like an ancient invalid, to cross his room – crawling up the walls was out of the question – yet this worsening of his condition was compensated, in his view quite adequately, by the fact that towards evening the door to the living room, which he took to watching closely an hour or two beforehand, was opened, so that from where he lay in the darkness of his room he could, without being seen, observe the whole family around the well-lit table and listen to their conversation, as it were with their general approval – a quite different situation from before.

To be sure, these were no longer the lively exchanges of earlier times such as Gregor had always recalled with a certain longing when he had thrown himself wearily between the damp bedclothes in the tiny room of some hotel. Things were mostly very quiet now. His father went to sleep in his chair soon after supper; his mother and sister urged each other to silence; bending down low under the light, his mother sewed fine linen for a fashion shop; his sister, who had taken a job as a shop assistant, was learning shorthand and French in the evening in the hope she might get a better job later on. Sometimes his father would wake up and, as if unaware that he had been asleep, say to his wife: 'What a long time you've spent sewing again today!' and drop off to sleep again at once while mother and sister smiled wearily at each other.

With a certain stubbornness his father also refused to take off his messenger's uniform at home, and while his dressing-gown hung unused on a hook would doze fully dressed in his chair, as if always ready for duty and waiting, even here, for his boss's voice. As a result his uniform, which had not been new even at the start, became soiled in spite of the care his mother and sister took with it, and Gregor often spent whole evenings gazing at this heavily stained coat, with its gold buttons kept shiny by constant polishing, in which the old man slept so very uncomfortably and yet peacefully.

As soon as the clock struck ten, Gregor's mother would try to wake his father in a quiet voice and then persuade him to go to bed, because he couldn't sleep properly here, and he needed his sleep because he had to start work at six. But with the obstinacy that he had developed since he became a messenger, he always insisted on staying at table even longer, although he fell asleep regularly and could then only with the greatest difficulty be persuaded to leave his armchair and go to bed. However much his wife and daughter tried to induce him with gentle hints, he would slowly shake his head for a quarter of an hour, keep his eyes shut and stay put. His wife would tug at his sleeve and whisper encouragingly into his ear, his daughter would leave her work to help her mother, but nothing could move him. He only sank deeper into his chair. Only when the two women seized him under the arms would he open his eyes, look at each of them in turn and say: 'What a life. So this is the peace and quiet of my old age.' And supported by the two women, he would struggle to his feet as if he were a great burden to himself, let the women lead him to the door, where he would wave them away and continue on his own, while his wife would quickly drop her sewing and his daughter her pen in order to run after him and help him along.

Who, in this exhausted and overtaxed family, had time to look after Gregor any more than was absolutely necessary? The household was reduced even further; now the maid was finally dismissed, and a huge, bony cleaner with tousled white hair came in mornings and evenings to do the heaviest work. Gregor's mother looked after everything else along with all her sewing. Even various pieces of family jewellery, which his mother and his sister had previously worn with great delight at social occasions and celebrations, were sold, as Gregor learned when they discussed among themselves the prices they had fetched. But what they complained about most was that they could not leave this apartment, which was far too large for their present circumstances, because they could not think of how they were to move Gregor. But Gregor realised that it was not only consideration for him that stood in the way of a move, for he could easily have been transported in a suitable box with a few holes for air; the main thing holding the family back from moving to another apartment was more their complete hopelessness, and the thought that they had suffered a misfortune such as no one else had in the whole circle of their family or acquaintances. To the very limits of their abilities they did what the world demands of impoverished people; his father fetched breakfast for minor bank officials, his mother devoted herself to washing other people's linen, his sister rushed to and fro behind the counter at the customers' bidding, but that was as far as the family's energies stretched. And Gregor would feel the pain from the wound in his back all over again when his mother and his sister returned after putting his father to bed, put aside their work and huddled together cheek to cheek, and when his mother then pointed to his room, saying: 'Shut that door, Grete,' and he was left there in the darkness while next door the women wept together or simply stared at the table, dry-eyed.

Gregor spent his nights and days almost entirely without sleeping. Sometimes he imagined that the next time the door opened he would take over the family's affairs again just as he had done before. In his thoughts his boss and the chief clerk would reappear after a long absence, as well as the under-clerks and the trainees, the slow-witted janitor, two or three friends from other firms, a chambermaid from a hotel in the country (a sweet and fleeting memory), a cashier in a milliner's shop whom he had courted in earnest, but not urgently enough – these all appeared, together with strangers or people he had forgotten; but instead of helping him and his family, they were all unapproachable, and he was glad when they vanished. But then at other times he was in no mood to worry about his family, he was only filled with rage at how badly they treated him; and though he could think of nothing he might wish to eat, he would plan ways of getting into the larder and take what he was still entitled to, even if he was not hungry. His sister now no longer gave any thought to giving Gregor something he might really enjoy; before she dashed off to work in the morning and after lunch, she hurriedly pushed some kind of food into his room with her foot, and then in the evening, unconcerned as to whether he had even tasted it or – as was more usually the case – had not touched it at all, she would clear it out with a swish of her broom. As for cleaning his room, which she now always did in the evenings, this could not have been done more hurriedly; dirty streaks ran along the walls, and here and there lay heaps of dust and filth. Initially, Gregor would position himself in some particularly dirty corner of the room when she arrived, by way of indicating his disapproval to her. But he could well have stayed there for weeks before she did anything about it; she saw the filth just as clearly as he did, and had simply made up her mind to leave it there. At the same time she saw to it, with a touchiness that was quite new in her, and which had indeed spread to the whole family, that tidying

Gregor's room was left entirely to her. His mother had once given Gregor's room a thorough cleaning, which she had managed to do only after using several buckets of water – moreover, the excessive dampness upset him, and he lay stretched out on the sofa, resentful and immobile – but his mother did not get away with it. As soon as she noticed the change in his room, his sister, deeply offended, rushed into the living room, and though her mother raised her hands imploringly, burst into a fit of tears at which her parents – her startled father had of course jumped up from his armchair – at first looked on in helpless astonishment until they too began to stir; his father upbraided his mother to his right for not leaving the cleaning of Gregor's room to his sister, while to his left he shouted at his sister that she would never again be allowed to clean the room, while his mother tried to drag his father, who was beside himself in his agitation, into the bedroom. His sister, shaken by sobs, hammered on the table with her little fists, while Gregor hissed out loud, furious that it occurred to none of them to shut the door and spare him this spectacle and this uproar.

But even if his sister, exhausted from her work, had tired of looking after Gregor as she had before, there was still no need whatever for his mother to do it instead, and there was no reason why he should be neglected, for they now had a cleaner. This old widow, whose powerful frame must have helped her to survive the worst that had happened to her during her long life, was not in fact repelled by Gregor. Without being particularly curious, she had once happened to open the door to his room and at the sight of him had stood there astonished, her hands folded in front of her, as Gregor, taken completely by surprise, began to scurry to and fro, even though no one was after him. Since that occasion she never failed to open the door a little for a short while every morning and evening and look in on him. At first she would even call him over to her with words which were no doubt meant to be friendly, such as: 'Come over here, you dirty old beetle!' or 'Just look at that filthy old beetle!' Gregor made no response to these approaches; he remained motionless where he was as if the door had not been opened. If only this cleaner had been told to clean his room every day, instead of letting her disturb him for no reason whenever the mood took her! Once, early in the morning – a heavy shower, perhaps an early sign of approaching spring, was spattering the window-panes – Gregor was so exasperated when the cleaner started on her usual patter that he turned on her, albeit slowly and feebly, as if to attack her. But instead of being afraid, she simply took a chair from near the door and lifted it above her head; standing there with her mouth wide open, it was quite clear that she only intended to close it again once she had brought the chair crashing down on Gregor's back. 'That's quite close enough now,' she said as Gregor turned away, and calmly replaced the chair in the corner.

Now Gregor was eating scarcely anything. Only if he happened to come upon the food that had been made for him he would try a mouthful just for something to do, keep it there for hours and then usually spit it out again. At first he thought it was his depression at the state of his room that stopped him eating, but in fact he very soon came to terms with the changes to his room. The family had taken to putting things they could not keep anywhere else into his room, and now there were a lot of these things, because they had let one room of the apartment to three lodgers. These dignified gentlemen – all three wore full beards, as Gregor once observed through a crack in the door – were punctilious about tidiness, not only in their own room but also, now that they were renting a room here, in the whole household, particularly in the kitchen. They could not tolerate useless junk, especially if it was dirty. Besides, they had brought most of their own furniture with them; so a lot of things that could not be sold, but which the family did not want to throw out, had become superfluous. All these things found their way into Gregor's room, including the ash box and the rubbish bin from the kitchen. The cleaner, who was always in a great hurry, simply flung anything that was not immediately needed into his room; fortunately all Gregor usually saw was the object in question and the hand that held it. The cleaner might have intended to take these things out again when time or opportunity allowed, or to throw it all out at once; but as it was they just lay where they had been thrown, except when Gregor wriggled his way through the junk and shifted it about. At first he was forced to do this because he had no space to crawl around, but later he did it with increasing pleasure, although after these exertions he felt tired to death and depressed, and would lie motionless for hours.

Because the lodgers also occasionally took their evening meal in the family living room, on many evenings the door to this room remained closed; but Gregor could quite easily do without having the door open – after all, on several evenings when the door was open he had not taken advantage of it, but had kept to the darkest corner of his room without the family noticing. But on one occasion the cleaner had left the door to the living room ajar, and it stayed like that even when the lodgers came in that evening and the lights were turned on. They seated themselves at the head of the table, where in earlier times Gregor, his father and his mother had sat, unfolded their serviettes and picked up their knives and forks. At once Gregor's mother appeared in the doorway with a dish of meat, followed closely by his sister with a bowl piled high with potatoes. Clouds of steam rose from the food. The lodgers bent over the dishes put in front of them as if to test the food before they ate it, and the one sitting in the middle, to whom the other two seemed to defer as being in authority, actually cut a piece of meat while it was still in the dish, obviously to establish whether it was tender enough or whether it ought perhaps to be sent back to the kitchen. He was satisfied, and Gregor's mother and sister, who had been watching in suspense, sighed with relief and began to smile.

The family itself ate in the kitchen. Even so, before he went into the kitchen, Gregor's father came into the living room, bowed once, and with his cap in his hand walked round the table. The three lodgers rose and murmured something into their beards. Then, when they were alone, they ate in almost complete silence. Gregor found it strange that among all the various sounds of eating he could always hear them chewing, as if to show him that teeth were needed in order to eat, and that even the finest jaws were no use without teeth. 'I feel hungry too,' said Gregor to himself sadly, 'but not for these things. Look at those lodgers tucking in, and I'm starving!'

It was that same evening – Gregor could not remember having heard it all this time – that the sound of a violin came from the kitchen. The lodgers had finished their meal; the one in the middle had produced a newspaper and given each of the others a page, and they were leaning back in their chairs, reading and smoking. When the violin began to play, they listened attentively, got up and tiptoed to the door of the hallway, and stood there huddled together. They must have been heard from the kitchen, for Gregor's father called: 'Perhaps the gentlemen don't like the music? I can have it stopped at once.' 'On the contrary,' said the middle one, 'would the young lady not like to come in here and play? It's much more convenient and comfortable here.' 'With pleasure,' said the father's voice, as if he were the musician. The gentlemen went back into the living room and waited. Soon Gregor's father came in with the music stand, his mother with the music and his sister with the violin. His sister calmly arranged everything for playing; her parents, who had never let rooms before, and so behaved over-politely towards their lodgers, did not dare to sit in their own chairs. The father leaned against the door, his right hand tucked between two of the buttons that fastened his uniform jacket; but his wife took a chair offered by one of the gentlemen, and because she left the chair just where he had happened to place it, sat there in a far corner of the room.

Gregor's sister started to play; her father and mother on either side followed the movements of her hands attentively. Gregor, drawn by her playing, had ventured to move forward a little, and his head was already in the living room. He did not find it particularly strange that he had recently shown so little consideration for the others, though earlier he had taken pride in doing so. And yet just now he had all the more reason to hide away, for because of the dust that lay everywhere in his room and flew around at his slightest movement, he himself was also covered with dust. On his back and his flanks he dragged around fluff, hairs and left-over bits of food, and he cared far too little about anything to have rolled onto his back, as he had previously done several times a day, and rub himself clean on the carpet. So in spite of the state he was in, he was not afraid to crawl a little way out onto the spotless floor of the living room.

Besides, no one took any notice of him. The family were wholly absorbed in the sound of the violin; the lodgers, however, who had initially been standing with their hands in their pockets far too close behind his sister's music stand so that they could all read the notes, which must surely have disturbed her, soon withdrew to the window, bending their heads and conversing in low voices, and there they remained. Gregor's father watched them anxiously. It now really seemed all too clear that that they had been disappointed in their anticipation of hearing some beautiful or entertaining music on the violin, that they had had enough of the whole recital and were only allowing their peace to be interrupted out of politeness. In particular, the way they blew cigar smoke up into the air out of their mouths and noses suggested their great irritation. And yet Gregor's sister played so beautifully. She held her head on one side, and her eyes followed the rows of notes intently and sadly. Gregor crawled a little further forward and held his head close to the floor, trying to catch her glance. Was he a beast, when he was so moved by music? It was as if he were being shown the way to the unknown nourishment he craved. He was determined to go right up to his sister and tug at her dress to persuade her to bring her violin into his room, for no one here appreciated her playing as he would. He would not let her out of his room, at least not while he was still alive; for the first time his repugnant appearance would be of some use to him; he would appear at all the doors of his room at once and hiss defiance at intruders; but his sister would not be forced to stay with him, she would do so voluntarily; she would sit beside him on the sofa, bend down to listen to him, and he would then confide in her that he had firmly resolved to send her to the Conservatoire, and that if this misfortune had not prevented him, he would have told everyone about it last Christmas – surely Christmas was past by now? – and would have ignored any objections. After this explanation, his sister would be moved to tears, and Gregor would lift himself up to her shoulder and kiss her throat, which she had left exposed, without a ribbon or a collar, since she had been going out to work.

'Herr Samsa!' cried the middle lodger, and without another word pointed to Gregor, who was advancing slowly. The violin fell silent; the middle lodger smiled briefly, shaking his head, then looked at Gregor again. Although the lodgers were not at all put out, in fact they seemed to find Gregor more entertaining than the violin, his father evidently thought it more important to reassure them rather than to chase Gregor away. He rushed over to them with his arms stretched out wide and tried to usher them back into their room, at the same time attempting to block their view of him with his own body. Now they really did become quite annoyed, though it was unclear whether this was because of the father's behaviour or because they only now began to realise that they had been living with a neighbour like Gregor without knowing it. They demanded an explanation from him, raised their own arms, fiddled with their beards, and only slowly retreated towards their own room. Meanwhile Gregor's sister had emerged from the daze into which she had fallen after the sudden interruption of her playing; for a while she had continued to hold the violin and the bow in her limp hands, gazing at the sheet of music as if she were still playing, but now she suddenly pulled herself together, laid the instrument in her mother's lap – she was still sitting on her chair, fighting for breath with heaving lungs – and ran into the next room, which the lodgers, urged by her father, were now rapidly approaching. Her practised hands could be seen throwing blankets and pillows around and arranging them on the beds. Before the gentlemen reached their room she had finished her work and slipped back out. Her father again seemed so unable to control his own obstinacy that he forgot all the respect he still owed his tenants. He pushed them back again and again as far as the door, where the middle gentleman stamped his foot thunderously on the floor and brought him to a standstill. 'I hereby declare,' he said, raising his hand and also addressing Gregor's mother and sister, 'that in view of the disgusting conditions prevailing in this apartment' – at this point he paused to spit emphatically on the floor – 'I am giving my notice immediately. I shall not, of course, pay a penny for the time I have lived here either, indeed I shall consider whether or not to proceed against you with certain claims which, believe me, can very easily be substantiated.' He stopped and looked straight in front of him, as if expecting something further, and indeed his two friends immediately added: 'We are also giving immediate notice.' Then he seized the handle and slammed the door shut with a crash.

Gregor's father groped his way unsteadily to his armchair and collapsed into it. It looked as if he were stretching out for his usual evening nap; but from the violent way his head rolled about as if unsupported, it was clear that he was anything but asleep. All this time Gregor had lain motionless just where the lodgers had caught sight of him. Disappointment at the failure of his plan, but perhaps also his weakness after being deprived of food for so long, made it impossible for him to move. Dreading that at any moment a wholesale calamity was almost certain to descend on his head, he waited. He was not even startled when the violin on his mother's lap slipped from her trembling fingers and fell with a reverberating sound.

'Dear parents,' said his sister, bringing her hand down on the table for attention, 'this cannot go on. If you can't see that, then I can. I won't utter my brother's name in front of this dreadful creature, so I'll just say this – we must try to get rid of it. We have done everything humanly possible to look after it and put up with it, and I don't think anyone can blame us in the slightest.'

'She's absolutely right,' Gregor's father said to himself. His mother, who was still struggling for breath, held her hand over her mouth to stifle a coughing fit, with a wild look in her eyes.

His sister ran over to her and held her forehead. Her words seemed to have prompted her father to marshal his thoughts; he had taken his place at the table and sat there upright, fiddling with his official's cap among the plates which were still lying there from the lodgers' meal, and glanced from time to time at the motionless Gregor.

'We must try to get rid of it,' said his sister, addressing herself solely to her father, as her mother could hear nothing for coughing, 'it will be the end of both of you, I can see it coming. If we all have to work as hard as we do, we can't put up with this endless torment at home as well. I can't stand it any more myself.' And she burst out crying so violently that her tears ran down over her mother's face, which her mother wiped away with mechanical movements of her hands.

'But my child,' said her father with compassion and remarkable understanding, 'what are we to do?'

His daughter could only shrug her shoulders as a sign of the helplessness that, in contrast to her earlier self-assurance, had overwhelmed her while she was weeping.

'If only he could understand us . . .' said her father half questioningly; but she shook her head violently in the midst of her tears to indicate that there was no question of that.

'If he could understand us,' her father repeated, and by closing his eyes he accepted her conviction that such a thing was not possible, 'then we might come to some arrangement with him. But as it is . . .'

'It's got to go,' cried Gregor's sister, 'that's the only way, Father. You just have to get rid of the idea that it's Gregor. Our real problem is that we've believed it for so long. But how can it be Gregor? If it was Gregor, he would have realised long ago that it's impossible for human beings to live with a creature like that and he would have gone of his own accord. Then we wouldn't have a brother any more, but we would be able to carry on with our lives and honour his memory. But as it is this creature plagues us, drives our lodgers away, it clearly wants to take over the whole apartment and make us sleep in the street. 'Look, father!' she gave a sudden shriek, 'he's off again!' And in a panic that was totally incomprehensible to Gregor his sister even abandoned her mother and quite simply fled from the chair where she sat, as if she would rather sacrifice her mother than be anywhere near him. She dashed behind her father's chair; alarmed by her behaviour, he also stood up and half-raised his arms in front of her as if to protect her.

But Gregor had not the slightest wish to frighten anyone, least of all his sister. He had merely begun to turn round in order to get back to his room; however, his efforts attracted their attention because in his weakened condition he could only turn round laboriously, and had to use his head to help him by raising it several times and banging it on the floor. He stopped and looked round. The family had apparently understood his good intentions; it had only been a momentary panic. Now they all looked at him sadly in silence. His mother was lying in her chair, her legs stretched out and pressed tightly together, her eyelids drooping wearily; his sister was sitting next to her father with her hand around his neck.

'Now perhaps I'll be able to start turning round again,' thought Gregor, resuming his efforts. He could not help gasping with the exertion, and had to stop and rest now and then. In any case, no one was harassing him, it was all left to him. Once he had turned himself round, he immediately started to crawl straight back. He was amazed at the distance between him and his room, and could not understand how only a short time before he had covered the same distance in his weakened state almost without noticing. All the time he was so intent on making rapid progress that he scarcely noticed that no word or cry from his family had distracted him. Only when he had reached the door did he turn his head round, not completely, for he felt his neck stiffening; but he could still see that behind him nothing had changed, except that his sister had stood up. His last glance took in his mother, who was now fast asleep.

He was scarcely inside his room when the door was quickly shut, locked and bolted. Gregor was so alarmed at the sudden noise behind him that his tiny legs gave way. It was his sister who had been in such a hurry. She had been standing there ready and waiting, then she had leapt across the room so lightly that Gregor had not heard her coming. 'At last!' she called to her parents as she turned the key in the lock.

'What now?' Gregor wondered, looking around in the dark. He soon discovered that he could no longer move at all. He was not surprised at this, instead it struck him as not normal that he had actually been able to move around at all on such thin little legs. Otherwise he felt relatively comfortable. Although his whole body hurt, it seemed to him that the pain was gradually getting less severe and would finally go away entirely. Now he could hardly feel the rotten apple in his back and the inflammation around the wound, which was completely covered with a layer of soft dust. He recalled his family with tenderness and love. His conviction that he had to go was if anything even firmer than his sister's. He remained in this state of vacant and peaceful reflection until the clock in the bell tower struck three a.m. He still survived to see the light breaking everywhere outside the window. Then his head drooped involuntarily to the floor and from his nostrils flowed his last weak breath.

When the cleaner came early that morning – with her energy and bustle, however many times she had been asked not to, she slammed every door shut so loudly that it was impossible to sleep peacefully anywhere in the apartment after her arrival – at first she found nothing out of the ordinary on her usual brief visit to Gregor's room. She thought he was deliberately lying there motionless and pretending to be offended; she gave him credit for understanding virtually everything. She happened to be holding her long broom, so she tried to tickle Gregor with it from the doorway. When even that had no effect, she got annoyed and poked him gently; it was only when she pushed him a little way without any resistance on his part that she looked more closely. When the truth dawned on her, she opened her eyes wide and whistled to herself, but she did not wait around; she flung open the bedroom door and shouted into the darkness: 'Come and have a look, it's croaked; it's lying there dead as a doornail!'

The Samsas sat bolt upright in the marriage bed, and it took a while before they got over the fright the cleaner had given them and grasped what she was telling them. But then they hurriedly got out of bed, one each side, Herr Samsa threw the blanket over his shoulders, his wife got up wearing only her nightdress, and in this state they went into Gregor's room. Meanwhile the door of the living room was opened too; Grete had been sleeping there since the lodgers had moved in. She was fully dressed as if she had not slept at all, as her pallor seemed to confirm. 'Dead?' asked Frau Samsa, looking enquiringly up at the cleaner, although she was quite capable of going to see for herself, and could even see without looking closely. 'I should say so,' said the cleaner, and to prove it she shoved Gregor's corpse a good distance sideways with her broom. Frau Samsa made a gesture as if to hold back the broom, but refrained. 'Well,' said Herr Samsa, 'now we can give thanks to God.' He crossed himself, and the three women followed his example. Grete, who had not taken her eyes off the corpse, said: 'Look how thin he was. He hasn't eaten anything for so long. His food came out just as it was put in.' And indeed Gregor's body was quite flat and dried out, as they only realised now that his little legs no longer supported him and there was nothing else to distract their attention.

'Come in with us for a while, Grete,' said Frau Samsa with a mournful smile, and Grete, after a backward glance at the corpse, followed her parents into the bedroom. The cleaner shut the door and threw the windows wide open. Although it was still early in the morning, there was already a hint of mildness in the cool air, for by now it was late March.

The three lodgers emerged from their room and looked round in astonishment for their breakfast; they had been forgotten. 'Where is our breakfast?' the middle one asked the cleaner crossly. But she put her finger to her lips and without a word beckoned them to come quickly into Gregor's room, which they did, and stood, their hands in the pockets of their rather shabby jackets, around Gregor's corpse in the room which was now in full daylight.

Then the door of the bedroom opened, and Herr Samsa appeared in his uniform with his wife on one arm and his daughter on the other. They were all rather tearful; now and then Grete buried her face in her father's sleeve.

'Leave my house at once!' said Herr Samsa, and pointed to the door without leaving hold of the women. 'What do you mean?' said the middle lodger in some dismay. He smiled ingratiatingly; the other two held their hands behind their backs, rubbing them together all the while as if in anticipation of a great quarrel that could only end in their favour. 'I mean exactly what I say,' replied Herr Samsa, advancing on him with his two companions on either side. At first the lodger stood there looking at the floor, as if he were putting things into a new order in his mind. 'Then we shall go,' he said, looking up at Herr Samsa, as if in a sudden access of humility he even needed permission for this decision too. Herr Samsa simply glared at him and nodded curtly several times, at which the gentleman did in fact stride out into the hall; his two friends, who all this while had stopped rubbing their hands and had been listening closely, now skipped after him as if they feared Herr Samsa might reach the hallway before them and cut them off from their leader. In the hall the three of them took their hats from the coat-rack, picked up their canes from the umbrella stand, bowed silently and left the apartment. With a feeling of mistrust that proved to be quite groundless, Herr Samsa stepped out onto the landing with the two women; leaning over the banister, they watched as the three gentlemen slowly but steadily descended the long staircase, disappearing at a bend in the stairs on each floor and reappearing a few seconds later. The further down they got, the less interest the Samsa family took in them, and as a butcher's delivery boy with a tray on his head swaggered up the stairs towards them and then climbed far above them, Herr Samsa and the women soon came away from the banister and returned, seemingly relieved, to their apartment.

They decided to spend that day resting and taking a walk; not only had they earned this respite from work, they absolutely needed it. And so they sat down at the table and wrote three letters of apology, Herr Samsa to his manager, Frau Samsa to her client, and Grete to her employer. While they were writing the cleaner came in to say she was going, because she had done her work for the morning. At first the three of them simply nodded without looking up; only when the cleaner made no move to go did they look up in annoyance. 'Well?' asked Herr Samsa. The cleaner stood in the doorway, smiling, as if she had some very good news to announce to the family, but would only tell them if they quizzed her about it. The little ostrich feather she wore almost upright in her hat, which had irritated Herr Samsa ever since she started work in the house, swayed gently this way and that. 'What is it then?' asked Frau Samsa, to whom the cleaner still showed most respect. 'Well,' replied the cleaner, laughing good-naturedly and unable to answer for a moment, 'well, you needn't worry about getting rid of that thing next door. It's all been done.' Frau Samsa and Grete bent over their letters again as if to go on writing; Herr Samsa, who realised that the cleaner was about to describe everything in detail, held his hand out firmly to silence her. Thus prevented from telling her story, she remembered she was in a great hurry and, clearly offended, called out 'Goodbye all, then,' turned round angrily and left the apartment, furiously banging doors behind her.

'She'll be dismissed this evening,' said Herr Samsa, but neither his wife nor his daughter answered; the cleaner seemed to have shattered their barely restored peace of mind. They rose and went to the window, where they stayed hugging each other closely. Herr Samsa turned in his armchair and watched them in silence for a while. Then he called: 'Come over here, then. It's time to let those old things be. And have some consideration for me, too.' The women immediately obeyed; they hurried over to him, caressed him, and quickly finished off their letters.

Then all three left the apartment together, something they had not done for months, and took the tram into the country outside the town. The carriage, which they had to themselves, was flooded with warm sunshine. Sitting back comfortably in their seats, they discussed their future prospects, which turned out on closer inspection to be not so bad at all; for the jobs all three of them had – they had never actually asked each other about them before – were very good ones, and especially promising with regard to the future. For the moment, the greatest improvement in their situation, of course, had to be a change of apartment; they would take one that was smaller and cheaper, but better situated and altogether more convenient than the present one, which Gregor had found for them. While they were talking about these things, it occurred to the Samsas almost simultaneously, watching their increasingly lively daughter, that in spite of all the worry that had given her such pale cheeks, she had recently blossomed into a good-looking and full-bodied girl. Falling into silence and almost unconsciously understanding each other's glances, they thought how it would soon be time to find a good husband for her. And it was as if to confirm their new-found dreams and their good intentions that when they reached their destination their daughter got up before they did and stretched her young body.

IN THE PENAL COLONY

'It is a remarkable machine,' said the officer to the visiting traveller, surveying the apparatus with a certain admiration, although he must have been very familiar with it. It was apparently only out of politeness that the visitor had accepted the governor's invitation to attend the execution of a soldier who had been condemned for insubordination and insulting a superior officer. There seemed to be no great interest in the penal colony for this execution; here, at least, in this deep, sandy little valley surrounded by bare slopes, the only people present apart from the officer and the visitor were the condemned man, a dim-witted fellow with a slack mouth, dishevelled hair and a wild look, and a soldier who held a heavy chain to which were attached the lighter chains that bound the prisoner's wrists and ankles as well as his neck, and which were themselves held together by connecting chains. Moreover, the prisoner had a look of such dog-like submission that it seemed he could have been left free to roam about the slopes, and only a whistle would be needed to summon him when the execution was due to begin.

The visitor had little interest in the machine, and walked to and fro behind the prisoner with a marked display of indifference while the officer made the final preparations, first crawling underneath the machine, which was built deep into the ground, then climbing a ladder to inspect the upper sections. These were tasks that could actually have been left to a mechanic, but the officer carried them out with great zeal, either because he had a particular attachment to this machine, or because for some reason no one else could be entrusted with the work. 'It's all ready now!' he announced finally, climbing down the ladder. He was quite exhausted; he was panting, his mouth was wide open, and he had stuffed two delicate ladies' handkerchiefs into the collar of his uniform. 'These uniforms are surely too heavy for the tropics,' said the visitor, rather than asking about the machine as the officer had expected. 'Indeed,' said the officer, washing oil and grease from his soiled hands in a nearby bucket of water, 'but they stand for home; we don't want to lose touch with home. – But now look at this machine,' he added quickly, drying his hands on a cloth and pointing to the contraption. 'I've had to do things manually so far, but from now on it will work on its own.' The visitor nodded and followed the officer who, seeking to cover himself against all eventualities, added: 'Of course things can go wrong; I hope that won't happen today, but one must allow for it. You see, the machine should run continuously for twelve hours. But if anything goes wrong, it won't be serious and can soon be put right.'

'Won't you sit down?' he asked finally, pulling a cane chair from a pile and offering it to the visitor, who was unable to refuse it. Now he was sitting at the edge of a trench, into which he glanced briefly. It was not very deep. On one side of the trench the earth had been piled up to form a rampart, on the other side stood the machine. 'I don't know,' said the officer, 'whether the governor has already explained the machine to you.' The visitor made an uncertain gesture; that was all the officer wanted, for now he could explain the machine himself. 'This machine,' he said, taking hold of a crankshaft and supporting himself on it, 'was invented by our former governor. I was involved in the very first trials, and worked on every stage up to its completion. Of course, all the credit for its invention is due to him. Have you heard about our old governor? No? Well, I'm not exaggerating when I say that the establishment of the whole penal colony was his work. We, his friends, already knew by the time he died that the colony was so tightly organised that his successor, even if he had a thousand new plans in mind, would not be able to alter anything in it, at least not for many years. And it was as we had predicted – the new governor had to accept it. What a pity you did not know the old governor! – But,' the officer broke off, 'I'm chattering on, and his machine is here in front of us. As you can see, it consists of three parts. In the course of time each part has acquired what you might call a popular name. The lower part is called the bed, the upper part is the scribe, and this part hanging down in between is called the harrow.' 'The harrow?' asked the visitor. He had not been listening very attentively; the valley, devoid of shade, formed a suntrap, and it was difficult to gather one's thoughts. He found it all the more admirable that the officer, in his close-fitting parade-ground uniform, heavy with epaulettes and hung with braid, explained his business with such enthusiasm – and even as he spoke he made various adjustments here and there with the help of a screwdriver. The soldier seemed to be in the same state as the visitor; he had wrapped the prisoner's chain around both his wrists, leaned on his rifle with one hand, let his head hang down and paid no attention. This caused the visitor no surprise, for the officer spoke in French, which it was certain neither the soldier nor the prisoner could understand. It was all the more surprising, then, that the prisoner still made an effort to follow the officer's explanations. With a sort of sleepy persistence he turned to look at whatever the officer was pointing to, and when the visitor interrupted him with a question, he too looked at the visitor just as the officer did.

'Yes, the harrow,' said the officer. 'The term fits. The needles are arranged like the tines on a harrow, and the whole thing operates like a harrow, though only in the one place and in a much more refined way. Anyway, you will soon understand how. The condemned man is laid here on the bed. – Now, I shall first explain the machine and then show you how it works, so you will be able to follow it better. One of the cogs in the scribing mechanism is badly worn; it screeches when it's in motion, and you can hardly make yourself understood. Spare parts are hard to come by here. – Now, as I said, this is the bed. It is completely covered with a layer of cotton wool; you will learn why later on. On this padded surface the condemned man is laid, naked of course, on his stomach; these straps are to secure his hands, these are for his feet, and these for his neck. Here at the head of the bed, where as I said the man initially lies face-down, is this small stump of wadding that can easily be adjusted so that it fits into the man's mouth. Its purpose is to prevent him from screaming and biting off his tongue. Of course he has to take this gag into his mouth, otherwise his neck will be broken by the strap.' 'That is cotton wool?' asked the visitor, leaning forward. 'Yes, indeed,' said the officer with a smile, 'feel it for yourself.' He took the visitor's hand and ran it over the bed. 'It is a special sort of cotton wool, that's why it looks so different; I'll come to the purpose of it later.' By now the visitor was becoming quite interested in the machine; shading his eyes from the sun with his hand, he looked up at it. It was a large construction. The bed and the scribing mechanism were the same size and looked like two dark boxes. The scribing mechanism was positioned about two metres above the bed; both were connected at the corners by four brass rods that flashed in the sunlight. Between the two boxes the harrow was suspended on a steel band.

The officer had scarcely noticed the visitor's earlier indifference; but he must have sensed that his interest was now growing, because he broke off his explanations in order to give the visitor time to inspect the machine undisturbed. The condemned man copied the actions of the visitor; since he could not shield his eyes with his hand, he squinted up at the machine.

'So now the man is lying there,' said the visitor, leaning back in his chair and crossing his legs.

'Yes,' said the officer. He pushed his cap back slightly and wiped his warm face with his hand. 'Now listen carefully! The bed and the scribing mechanism each have their own electric battery; the bed needs one for its own operation, and the scriber needs one to operate the harrow. As soon as the man is strapped in, the bed is set moving. It vibrates with minute, very rapid movements simultaneously from side to side and up and down. You will have seen similar pieces of equipment in clinics, but with our bed all the movements are precisely calculated; you see, they must be coordinated with those of the harrow with the utmost accuracy. But it is the harrow that actually carries out the sentence.'

'And what exactly is the sentence?' asked the visitor. 'Do you not know that either?' said the officer in astonishment and bit his lips. 'Forgive me if my explanations are not very systematic; I am very sorry. Previously, you see, the governor would explain things, but the new governor no longer honours this obligation; but not even to inform such a distinguished visitor' – the visitor raised both hands to resist the compliment, but the officer insisted on the expression – 'not even to inform such a distinguished visitor about our sentence is a further innovation that –' he was about to utter an oath, but controlled himself and simply said: 'I was not told, I am not to blame. In any case, I am certainly the person best able to explain the sort of sentences we impose, for I carry with me in here' – he patted his breast pocket – 'the relevant designs drawn by the previous governor himself.'

'Sketches made by the governor himself?' asked the visitor. 'So did he possess all these talents? Was he soldier, judge, engineer, chemist and designer all in one?'

'Yes indeed,' said the officer, nodding his head with a fixed and thoughtful stare. Then he examined his hands closely; they did not seem to him clean enough to handle the designs, so he went over to the bucket and washed them once more. Then he took out a small leather folder and said: 'This sentence does not sound harsh. The order that the condemned man has disobeyed is inscribed by the harrow onto his body. For example, this man' – the officer pointed to the prisoner – 'will have "Honour your Superior Officer!" written on his body.'

The visitor glanced over to the man; when the officer pointed to him he put his head forward and seemed to be making every effort to listen and glean some information. But the movements of his thick lips as he pressed them together clearly showed that he understood nothing. There were various questions the visitor would have put, but since the man was watching him he only asked: 'Does he know his sentence?' 'No,' said the officer, about to resume his explanations there and then, but the visitor interrupted him: 'He doesn't know his own sentence?' 'No,' repeated the officer; he hesitated for a moment, as if waiting for the visitor to explain the reason for his question, then he said: 'It would be pointless to inform him. He will feel it on his own body.' The visitor was going to say no more, but he sensed the prisoner's gaze on him; he seemed to be asking whether the visitor approved of the procedure just outlined. So the visitor, who had by now leaned back in his chair, leaned forward and asked again: 'But surely he knows that he has been condemned?' 'He doesn't know that either,' said the officer, smiling at him as if anticipating further strange queries from him. 'He does not?' said the visitor, passing his hand over his brow. 'So the man doesn't know, even now, how his defence was received?' 'He has had no opportunity to defend himself,' said the officer, looking away as if he were talking to himself and did not wish to embarrass the visitor by explaining such obvious things to him. 'But he must have had an opportunity to defend himself,' said the visitor, rising from his chair.

The officer realised that his explanation of the machine was in danger of being held up for a long time; so he went over to the visitor, took him by the arm, and pointed to the condemned man, who, now that he was so clearly the object of their attention, stood up straight – the soldier also gave the chain a tug – and said: 'This is the situation. I have been appointed as judge here in the penal colony. In spite of my youth. For I assisted the previous governor in all matters relating to punishments, and I also know the machine better than anyone. The principle on which I base my decision is that guilt is always beyond doubt. Other tribunals cannot follow this principle, because there are many people involved, and there are higher courts set above them. That is not the case here, or at least it was not under the previous governor. Although the new one has shown signs of wishing to interfere in my tribunal, so far I have succeeded in preventing this, and I shall continue to do so. – You wished me to explain this case; it is as simple as all the others. This morning a captain reported that this man, who was assigned to him as his servant and sleeps outside his door, fell asleep while on duty. His duty is to wake up on the stroke of every hour and salute outside the captain's door. Not a difficult task, certainly, and a necessary one, because he is supposed to remain alert on guard and ready to serve his master. Last night the captain wished to see whether he was doing his duty. On the stroke of two o'clock he opened the door and found him curled up asleep. He fetched his riding crop and struck him across the face. And instead of getting up and apologising, the man seized his master by the legs, shook him and shouted: "Throw that whip away, or I'll eat you!" – Those are the facts of the case. The captain came to me an hour ago, I took down his statement and immediately afterwards wrote out the sentence. Then I had the man put in chains. It was all very simple. If I had first had to summon the man and question him, it would only have caused confusion. He would have lied, and if I had been able to refute his lies, he would have made up more lies, and so on. But as it is I've got him and I'm not going to let him go. – Is that all clear? But time is getting on, the execution ought to have started by now and I still haven't finished explaining the machine.' He urged the visitor to his chair, approached the machine again and began: 'As you can see, the harrow is made to fit the shape of a man's body; this section is for the torso, these are for the legs. This small spike is meant just for the head. Do you follow?' He bent over the visitor with a smile, prepared to explain things in every detail.

The visitor looked at the harrow with a puzzled frown. The officer's account of the judicial process had not satisfied him. Certainly, he had to tell himself that this was a penal colony, that special measures were necessary here and that military procedures had to be scrupulously observed. Moreover, he had some hopes of the new governor, who evidently intended to introduce a new procedure, albeit gradually, which the limited mind of this officer could not grasp. Following this train of thought, he asked the officer: 'Will the governor attend the execution?' 'That is not certain,' the officer replied; embarrassed by this direct question, his amiable expression gave way to a scowl. 'For that very reason we must get on. I'm sorry to say I shall even have to curtail my explanation. But tomorrow, when the machine has been cleaned up – its only fault is that it gets so very soiled – I could fill in the details for you. So for now I shall explain only the essentials. – Once the man is lying on the bed and it has started to vibrate, the harrow is lowered onto the body. It adjusts itself automatically so that the needles just come into contact with the body; as soon as this is done, this steel band becomes rigid and functions as a rod. And now the performance begins. From the outside the inexpert eye will detect no difference in the punishments. The harrow appears to operate uniformly. As it vibrates, the needles pierce the body, which is also vibrating from the movement of the bed. Now, so that everyone could see that the sentence was being carried out, the harrow was made of glass. Fixing the needles into it caused some technical problems, but after a series of trials these were solved. We spared no effort, you see. And now everyone can see through the glass how the sentence is inscribed on the body. Would you like to come closer and look at the needles?'

The visitor got up slowly, went over and bent over the harrow. 'You can see,' said the officer, 'two kinds of needle arranged in various ways. Next to every long one is a shorter one. You see, the long ones write the script, and the short ones spray water to wash away the blood so that the script is always clear. The water sluices the blood into these small channels and then into this main trough, which drains into the trench.' With his finger the officer indicated the exact course the mixture of blood and water had to take. When, in order to demonstrate this as clearly as possible, he actually cupped his hands at the outflow as if to catch it, the visitor lifted his head from the trench and, feeling his way behind him with one hand, made to return to his chair. But then he saw to his horror that the prisoner had also followed the officer's invitation to inspect the mechanism of the harrow close to. He had dragged the sleepy soldier by the chain and was also leaning over the glass. He could be seen searching uncertainly for what the two men had just been examining, but it was clear that he did not follow, for it had not been explained to him. He bent this way and that, running his eyes again and again over the glass. The visitor wanted to pull him back, for what he was doing was probably punishable. But the officer held the visitor firmly with one hand, while with the other he took a lump of earth from the rampart and threw it at the soldier, who looked up with a start, saw what the prisoner had dared to do, then dropped his rifle, dug his heels into the ground, jerked him back, pulling him over, and looked down at him as he writhed about and rattled his chain. 'Get him up!' shouted the officer, who realised that the visitor was being distracted far too much by the condemned man. And indeed the visitor was looking beyond the harrow, paying no attention to it, wishing only to see what was happening to the prisoner. 'Handle him carefully!' shouted the officer again. He ran round the machine, seized the prisoner under the arms with his own hands and, although the man's feet kept sliding underneath him, with the soldier's help he managed to pull him to his feet.

'Now I know everything,' said the visitor, when the officer returned. 'Except for the most important thing,' he replied, taking the visitor by the arm and pointing upwards: 'Up there in the scribing mechanism is the machinery that controls the movement of the harrow, and this machinery is set to the design that corresponds to the sentence. I am still using the designs made by the previous governor. Here they are,' – he took some sheets from his leather folder – 'but I'm afraid I cannot let you handle them; they are my most treasured possessions. If you sit down I will show them to you from here, and you will be able to see them quite clearly.' He showed the first sheet to the visitor, who would have liked to express some interest; but all he could see was a sort of maze of criss-cross lines that covered the paper so thickly that it was difficult to see any white space between them. 'Read it,' said the officer. 'I can't,' said the visitor. 'But it's quite clear,' said the officer. 'It's very well designed,' said the visitor, equivocating, 'but I can't decipher it.' 'Yes,' said the officer with a laugh, returning the folder to his breast pocket, 'it is not a script for schoolchildren to copy. It takes a long time to read it. I'm sure you would able to make it out in the end. Of course, it's not supposed to be a simple script; it's not meant to kill immediately, but only after an average time of twelve hours; the turning-point is reckoned to be the sixth hour. So the actual script must be very elaborately decorated. The script itself is only printed in a narrow band around the body; the rest of the torso is for the decorations. Now can you appreciate the workings of the harrow and the whole machine? – Just watch!' He leapt onto the ladder, turned a wheel, and called down: 'Look out, move aside.' The whole thing began to work; if the wheel had not screeched, it would have been most impressive. As if the noisy wheel had taken him by surprise, the officer shook his fist at it, then gestured apologetically towards the visitor and hurriedly climbed down to observe the operation of the machine from beneath. Something was still not in order, something that only he noticed; he clambered up again, reached into the interior of the scribing mechanism with both hands, then, in order to get down more quickly, instead of using the ladder slid down on one of the rods, and to make himself understood above the noise shouted with intense enthusiasm into the visitor's ear: 'Do you understand the process? The harrow begins to write; once it has inscribed the first outline of the text on the man's back, the layer of padding turns and rolls the body slowly onto its side to give the harrow a new surface. As a result the lacerated areas come into contact with the specially treated padding, which immediately stops the bleeding and prepares the flesh for the text to be inscribed more deeply. As the body is rotated further, these teeth at the edge of the harrow strip the padding from the lacerations, drop them into the trench, and the harrow sets to work again. In this way it inscribes more and more deeply over the twelve hours. For the first six hours the condemned man is alive almost as before, except that he feels pain. After two hours the gag is removed, for the man has no strength left to scream. This electrically heated bowl at the end of the bed here contains warm rice gruel; if he wishes, the man can lap up as much as he is able to with his tongue. Not one misses the chance; I don't know of one who has, and I have a lot of experience. Only around the sixth hour does the man lose his appetite. At this stage I usually kneel down here and observe the phenomenon. He rarely swallows his last portion, he only swills it round his mouth and spits it into the trench. Then I have to duck, or else it hits me in the face. But how quiet the man goes after six hours! Even the most stupid begin to understand. It starts with the eyes. Then it spreads further.

It's a sight that almost tempts you to join him under the harrow. Nothing else happens, the man just begins to decipher the text, he purses his lips as if he were listening. As you have seen, it's not easy to decipher the text with your eyes; but our man deciphers it through his wounds. This is certainly hard work; he takes six hours to do it. But then the harrow stabs him through and tips him into the trench, where he flops down among the blood and water and padding. Then the sentence is complete and we, the soldier and I, cover him over.'

The visitor had bent over to listen to the officer, and with his hands in his pockets watched the machine as it worked. The prisoner was also watching, but without understanding it. He was leaning over slightly, following the vibrating needles, when at a signal from the officer the soldier took a knife and slashed the back of his shirt and trousers so that they fell off him; he tried to catch them as they fell to cover his nakedness, but the soldier lifted him up and shook off the rest of his rags. The officer switched off the machine, and in the ensuing silence the prisoner was put underneath the harrow. The chains were removed and the straps fastened instead; at first this seemed to come as a relief to the man. And now the harrow was lowered a little, for the man was thin. As the needles touched him a shudder ran through his body; while the soldier was busy tightening the strap on his right hand, he stretched out his left hand without knowing where – but it was towards where the visitor was standing. The officer continued to watch the visitor from the side, as if trying to read from his face the impression made on him by the method of punishment that he had, however superficially, explained to him.

The strap holding the man's wrist snapped; the soldier had probably over-tightened it. The soldier needed the officer's help, and showed him the broken strap. The officer went over to him, and turning to face the visitor, said: 'The machine is made up of many parts, now and then something is bound to tear or break; but one should not let that affect one's general impression. We can replace the strap right away; I shall use a chain instead. Of course, that will upset the precision of the inscriptions on the right arm.' While he was attaching the chain, he added: 'We have only very limited resources available to maintain the machine. Under the previous governor I had free access to funds earmarked for this purpose. There was a store in which all manner of spare parts were kept. I admit I was almost extravagant with them – I mean earlier, not now – or so the new governor maintains; he uses any pretext just to combat the old ways. Now he administers the funds for the machine himself, and if I ask for a new strap, the damaged one is required as proof; the new one arrives ten days later, and then it's of inferior quality and is not much use. But how I'm supposed to operate the machine meanwhile without straps – no one cares about that.'

The visitor reflected that it is always unwise to intervene decisively in other people's affairs. He did not belong to the penal colony, nor was he a citizen of the country that governed it. If he were to condemn this type of punishment or even try to obstruct it, he might be told: You are a foreigner, you have no say here. He would have no answer to this, and could only have added that he did not understand his own reaction in this case, for he was travelling simply as an observer and had not the slightest intention of changing the legal institutions of a foreign country. In this case, however, he was strongly tempted to intervene. The injustice of the procedure and the inhumanity of the method of punishment were beyond doubt. No one could assume any kind of self-interest on his part, for the condemned man was a stranger to him, he was not a fellow-countryman and certainly not the sort of person to arouse his sympathy. The visitor himself had letters of recommendation from people in high office; he had been received here with great courtesy, and the very fact that he had been invited to this execution seemed to suggest that his opinion on this case was being sought. And this seemed all the more probable since the governor, as had been made all too clear to him, was not a supporter of this procedure and was on almost hostile terms with the officer.

At this point he heard a shout of rage from the officer; he had just managed, not without difficulty, to force the stump of wadding into the prisoner's mouth when the man closed his eyes in an uncontrollable fit of nausea and vomited. The officer quickly pulled him up away from the gag and tried to turn his head towards the trench, but too late; the vomit was already dripping down onto the machine. 'It's all the governor's fault!' cried the officer, shaking the brass rods in a blind fury. 'My machine is as filthy as a cowshed.' His hands shook as he showed the visitor what had happened. 'Haven't I spent hours trying to make it clear to the governor that no food should be given to the prisoner for a day before the execution. But this new soft regime thinks otherwise. The governor's ladies stuff the man full of cakes before he's taken away. All his life he's lived off stinking fish, and then he has to eat confectionery! I wouldn't necessarily object to that – but why can't they supply a new gag, as I've been asking them to for three months? How can anyone put this gag in his mouth without feeling sick, when more than a hundred men have sucked on it and bitten it as they were dying?'

The prisoner had lowered his head and looked calm, while the soldier was busy cleaning the machine with the man's shirt. The officer went over to the visitor, who instinctively took a step back, but the officer grasped his hand and led him to one side. 'I would like a few words with you in confidence,' he said. 'May I?' 'Of course,' said the visitor, and listened, lowering his eyes.

'There is at present no open support in our colony for the procedure and the means of execution that you are now being given the opportunity to admire. I am its only supporter, as I am the only one who upholds the legacy of the old governor. I can no longer think of devising any further refinements in the procedure, I have to put all my energy into preserving what is left. When the old governor was alive, the colony was full of his supporters; I possess some of his gift of persuasion, but I have none of his power. As a result his supporters have melted away; there are still plenty of them, but not one will admit to it. On an execution day like today, if you go to the tea-house and keep your ears open, you might only hear some non-committal opinions. These are all supporters, but under the present governor and his current views they are no help to me whatever. And now I ask you: is a life's work like this' – he pointed to the machine – 'to be destroyed because of this governor and the women who influence him? Can one allow that to happen? Even as a foreigner who is only visiting our island for a few days? But there is no time to lose, moves are being made to undermine my judicial authority; discussions are being held in the governor's office to which I was not invited. Even your visit today seems to me to sum up the whole situation; they are cowards, and they send you here, you, a foreigner. – How different it used to be! The day before an execution the whole valley was already full of people, everyone came to watch; early in the morning the governor arrived with his ladies; fanfares woke the entire camp; I made the announcement that everything was ready; the whole company – all the senior officials had to attend – took their places around the machine; this wretched pile of cane chairs is all that is left from those days. The machine had been newly cleaned, and it gleamed; for almost every execution I used new spare parts. In front of a hundred eyes – all the spectators stood on tiptoe right to the top of the hill – the governor himself placed the condemned man underneath the harrow. What a common soldier is allowed to do today was then my honourable duty as president of the tribunal. And then the execution began! No grating sounds disturbed the smooth working of the machine. Some did not even watch any more, they closed their eyes and lay in the sand, but everyone knew: justice is now being done. In the silence only the groans of the condemned man, muffled by the gag, could be heard. Today the machine is not capable of forcing a groan out of the victim so loud that the gag can't stifle it; but in those days as they wrote, the needles exuded a corrosive liquid that we are forbidden to use today. And then the sixth hour arrived! It was impossible to meet the wishes of all those who wanted to have a close view. The governor, enlightened as he was, arranged that the children should be given special preference; of course, thanks to my position I was always allowed to stand close by; I often crouched there with a child in each arm. How we all felt the transfiguration of the martyred victim's face, and how our cheeks glowed in the reflection of this justice that had at last been achieved and was so soon over! What times those were, comrade!' The officer had clearly forgotten who was in front of him; he had thrown his arms around the visitor and laid his head on his shoulder. The visitor was deeply embarrassed and brusquely turned his head away from the officer. The soldier had finished cleaning the machine and was now pouring rice gruel out of a tin into the bowl. No sooner had the prisoner, who seemed to have recovered fully in the meantime, noticed this than he began to lunge towards the gruel with his tongue out. The soldier kept pushing him away, for the gruel was in fact meant for later; even so, it was not right that the soldier should dip his filthy hands into it and eat some of it in front of the ravenous prisoner.

The officer quickly controlled himself. 'I did not mean to arouse your feelings,' he said, 'I know it is impossible today to convey a sense of those times. Besides, the machine still works and runs itself. It runs itself even when it stands there alone in this valley. And at the end the corpse still drops into the trench, falling unbelievably gently, even if there are no longer hundreds of people gathered around like flies as there once were. In those days we had to put up a strong fence round the trench, but it was torn down long ago.'

The visitor tried to turn away from the officer, and looked about aimlessly. The officer thought he was taking in the deserted valley, so he seized his hands, moved round to catch his eye and asked: 'You see how shameful it is?'

But the visitor said nothing. The officer left him to himself for a moment and stood looking at the ground with his legs apart and his hands on his hips. Then he smiled encouragingly at the visitor and said: 'I was standing close to you yesterday when the governor invited you. I heard the invitation. I know the governor. I understood at once what he was aiming at with his invitation. Although he is powerful enough to take action against me, he doesn't dare to yet, but he does want to expose me to the judgement of a respected foreigner like yourself. He has worked it out carefully; you have been on the island for two days, you didn't know the old governor and his way of thinking, you are caught up in European attitudes, perhaps you are opposed in principle to the death penalty in general and to a mechanical means of execution like this in particular. Moreover, you can see how the execution is carried out in such a dismal way, without public support, and on a machine that no longer works perfectly. Now, taking all this into account, is it not quite possible (so the governor thinks) that you will think my way of doing things is not right? And if you think it is not right, perhaps (I'm still putting myself in the governor's place) you will not keep this to yourself, for you will surely trust your own well-founded convictions. Of course, you have seen the peculiar customs of many peoples and learned to respect them, so you will probably not express your disapproval of the procedure as vigorously as you might in your own country. But the governor doesn't need that; a casual word, just an unguarded comment will do. It need not express your convictions at all, just as long as it seems to meet his wishes. He will use all his cunning to question you, of that I'm sure. And his ladies will sit around in a circle and prick up their ears. You might say: "Our criminal procedures are different", or "In my country the accused is questioned before sentence is passed", or "In my country the condemned man is informed of his sentence", or "We have other punishments than the death penalty", or "We only used torture in the Middle Ages". These are all comments that seem so right to you that you take them for granted, innocent comments that do not challenge my methods. But how will the governor receive them? I can see him, our good governor, hastily pushing his chair back and hurrying onto the balcony, I can see his ladies pouring out after him, I can hear his voice – the ladies call it his voice of thunder – saying: "A distinguished Western scholar, appointed to make a study of criminal procedures in every country, has just said that our traditional procedure is inhumane. After hearing this opinion from such a distinguished person, I find it of course impossible to sanction such a procedure. I therefore decree that as from today – etc." You try to intervene: you didn't say what he is announcing, you didn't call my methods inhumane, on the contrary, your deep insight has persuaded you that it is the most humane procedure that respects human dignity, and you also admire this apparatus – but it is too late; you are unable to get onto the balcony, which is packed out with ladies, you try to catch their attention, you want to shout out loud, but a lady's hand is held over your mouth – and I, and the work of the old governor, are both lost.'

The visitor had to suppress a smile; so it was as easy as that, this task he had thought would be so difficult. He equivocated, saying: 'You overestimate my influence; the governor has read my letter of introduction and knows that I am no expert on criminal procedures. If I were to express an opinion, it would be that of a private individual, no more meaningful than the opinion of any other person, and in any case it would carry far less weight than the opinion of the governor who, as I understand it, has very extensive powers in this penal colony. If his views are as decided as you believe them to be, then I fear the end has come for this procedure without my modest help.'

Did the officer understand this? No, he still did not. He shook his head vigorously, glancing towards the prisoner and the soldier, who both flinched and stopped eating the gruel. He stepped quite close to the visitor, not looking him in the face, but at some part of his coat and said, more quietly than before: 'You don't know the governor; your view of him and of us all, forgive me for saying so, is somewhat naïve; believe me, your influence cannot be overestimated. I was delighted when I heard that you, and you alone, were to attend the execution. This order of the governor's was aimed at me, but now I am turning it to my own advantage. Undeterred by false insinuations and contemptuous looks, which could not have been avoided if a great many people had attended the execution, you have listened to my explanations, you have seen the machine, and now you are about to witness the execution. I am sure your mind is firmly made up already; should any minor doubts persist, they will disappear once you have witnessed it. And now I appeal to you: help me against the governor!'

The visitor interrupted him. 'How could I do that?' he cried, 'It's quite impossible. I cannot help you any more than I can harm you.'

'Yes, you can,' said the officer. To his alarm the visitor noticed that the officer had clenched his fists. 'You can,' the officer repeated even more urgently. 'I have a plan that is certain to succeed. You think you do not have enough influence. I know that you do. But even if you are right, is it not vital to try everything, even what might seem inadequate, to preserve this procedure? Then listen to my plan. Above all you must be as reticent as you possibly can in the colony today in expressing your opinion about the procedure. Unless you are asked directly, you must not say anything at all. Your comments must be brief and non-committal, people should be led to believe that you find it difficult to talk about it, that you are outraged, that if you had to speak about it you would only be able to express yourself in the most violent language. I am not asking you to lie, not in the least, only that you should answer briefly, for example "Yes, I have seen the execution", or "Yes, I have had everything explained to me". Just that, no more. People should be made aware of the outrage you feel – there's cause enough for it, after all – but not in the sense the governor understands it. Of course he will misinterpret it completely and see it from his own point of view. That is the basis of my plan. Tomorrow in the governor's residence he is going to chair an important meeting of all the senior officials. Of course, the governor has managed to make these meetings into a great occasion. A gallery has been built which is always packed with spectators. I am obliged to attend these meetings, very much against my will; they horrify me. Now, you will most certainly be invited to the meeting, and if you act according to my plan today, the invitation will take the form of an urgent request. However, if for some inconceivable reason you should not be invited after all, then of course you would have to demand an invitation, which you would doubtless receive. So there you are tomorrow, sitting with the ladies in the governor's gallery. He will look up frequently to make sure you are there. After various trivial and absurd items of business solely for the benefit of the spectators – mostly to do with harbour construction yet again – the question of legal procedure will come up. If the governor does not bring it up, or if it does not come up soon enough, I will make sure it does. I'll stand up and report today's execution. Quite briefly, simply report it. Although this is not usually done at these meetings, I shall do it. The governor will thank me, as he always does, with a friendly smile, and then – he won't be able to resist – he seizes his opportunity. He will say something like this: "We have just heard the report of the execution. I would like to add that on this particular occasion the execution was attended by the distinguished expert who, as you all know, has paid us the great honour of visiting our colony. His presence at our meeting today also enhances the importance of the occasion. Should we not now ask our distinguished visitor his views on this traditional execution, and on the procedures that led up to it?" Everyone applauds, general agreement, I am the loudest of all. The governor bows to you and says: "Then I put the question to you in the name of all of us." Now you step forward to the balustrade. Place your hands on it for everyone to see, otherwise the ladies will take hold of them and play with your fingers – then at last you have your say. I don't know how I shall bear the tension of all the hours between now and then. You must not hold back in your speech, you must speak the truth out loud, lean over the balustrade and bellow, yes, bellow out your opinion, your unshakeable opinion, to the governor. But perhaps you would rather not do that, perhaps it is not in your character, perhaps in your country things are done differently in such situations; that is quite acceptable, that will do perfectly well, don't stand up at all, just say a few words, whisper them so that the officials below you can just about hear them, that's enough, you don't even have to mention the lack of attendance at the execution, the screeching of the wheel, the broken strap, the disgusting gag – no, I'll see to everything else, and believe me, if my speech doesn't drive him out of the place, it will force him to his knees so that he will have to confess: I accede to you, old governor. – That is my plan; will you help me to carry it out? But of course you will, no, more than that – you must!' And the officer took the visitor by both arms and, breathing heavily, stared him in the face. He had shouted his last words so loudly that the soldier and the prisoner looked up; although they could not understand anything, they stopped eating and looked across at the visitor, still chewing.

From the start the visitor was in no doubt about what his answer was to be. He had experienced too much in his life to waver now; he was fundamentally honest and had no fear. Yet even so, he hesitated for a brief moment under the gaze of the soldier and the prisoner. But finally he said, as he must: 'No.'

The officer blinked several times, but did not take his eyes off him. 'Do you want an explanation?' asked the visitor. The officer nodded silently. 'I am opposed to this procedure,' the visitor went on. 'Even before you took me into your confidence – and of course I shall not betray this confidence under any circumstances – I was already debating whether I would be justified in taking steps against it and whether any action on my part could have the slightest chance of success. It was clear to me who it was I should first turn to in the matter – the governor, of course. You have made this even clearer to me, though you have not influenced my decision either way, far from it; I have some sympathy for your honest convictions, even though they can do nothing to deter me.'

The officer said nothing. He turned to the machine, grasped one of the brass rods and then, leaning backwards a little, looked up at the scribing mechanism as if checking that all was in order. The soldier and the prisoner seemed to have become friends; the prisoner was making signs to the soldier, difficult though this was when he was strapped in so tightly. The soldier bent down towards him, the prisoner whispered something and the soldier nodded.

The visitor went over to the officer and said: 'You don't yet know what I intend to do. I shall indeed tell the governor what I think of the procedure, but in private, not at a public meeting. I shall not be staying here long enough to be called to any such meeting; I am leaving early tomorrow morning, or at least boarding my ship then.'

The officer seemed not to have been listening. 'So the procedure has not convinced you,' he said to himself and smiled, as a grown-up smiles at a child's foolish prattle and conceals his true thoughts behind the smile.

'Then the time has come,' he said at last, suddenly turning to the visitor with bright eyes that seemed to hold some challenge, some call to participate.

'For what?' the visitor asked uneasily, but received no reply.

'You are free,' the officer said to the condemned man in his own language. At first the man did not believe him. 'You're free, do you hear?' For the first time the prisoner's face showed some animation. Was it true? Was it just a passing whim on the part of the officer? Had the foreign visitor obtained a reprieve for him? What was it? His face seemed to be asking all this, but not for long. Whatever the case, he certainly wanted to be free if he could, and he began to roll around as far as the harrow allowed.

'You'll break those straps,' shouted the officer. 'Keep still! We're going to undo them.' He gave a sign to the soldier, and they both got to work. The prisoner laughed to himself, softly and wordlessly, turning his face now this way towards the officer, now that way towards the soldier, and even towards the visitor.

'Pull him out,' the officer ordered the soldier. Because of the harrow this had to be done with some care. As a result of his impatience the prisoner already had some lacerations on his back.

But now the officer scarcely bothered about him any more. He went over to the visitor, took out the small leather folder once again, leafed through it until he finally found the sheet he was looking for, and showed it to the visitor. 'Read it,' he said. 'I can't,' said the visitor, 'I told you before, I can't read these sheets.' 'Look at it closely, though,' said the officer, standing beside the visitor to read it with him. But that did not help either, so he held his little finger some way above the paper, as if it should on no account be touched, and moved it across the sheet to help the visitor to read it. The visitor made an effort to oblige the officer in this respect at least, but he found it impossible to decipher. So the officer began to spell out the script, and then read the whole text back to him again. 'It says: "Be just!" Surely you can read it now,' he said. The visitor bent his head so close to the paper that the officer, fearing he might touch it, moved it further away; but though the visitor said nothing, it was clear that he still had not been able to read it. 'It says: "Be just!" ' the officer repeated. 'Perhaps,' said the visitor. 'I believe that is what it says.' 'Good,' said the officer, half-satisfied at least, and climbed the ladder with the sheet in his hand. He inserted the sheet with great care into the scribing mechanism and appeared to recalibrate the machinery completely. It was a very laborious exercise which must have involved some tiny cogs; at times he had to examine it so closely that his head disappeared into the mechanism.

The visitor continued to watch this operation from below; his neck grew stiff and his eyes smarted from the brightly sunlit sky. The soldier and the prisoner were concerned only with each other. The prisoner's shirt and trousers were already lying in the trench; the soldier hooked them out with the point of his bayonet. The shirt was dreadfully soiled, and the prisoner washed it in the bucket. Then, when the prisoner pulled on his shirt and trousers, they both had to laugh, for the clothes had of course been slit at the back. The prisoner seemed to feel he had to amuse the soldier; he danced round and round in front of him in his tattered clothes, while the soldier squatted on the ground, laughing and slapping his knees. But they still exercised some restraint in the presence of the two gentlemen.

When the officer had finally finished working on the mechanism above, he smiled as he checked over every part of the machine one last time, then he closed the lid of the scribing mechanism that had been open all this time, climbed down, looked into the trench and then at the prisoner, noted with satisfaction that he had retrieved his clothes, and went over to the bucket of water to wash his hands. Too late he noticed how disgustingly filthy it was, and unhappy that he was unable to wash his hands, finally plunged them – an unsatisfactory alternative, but he had no choice – into the sand, then he stood up and began to unbutton his uniform. He had scarcely undone the first buttons when the two ladies' handkerchiefs that he had stuffed under his collar fell into his hands. 'Here are your handkerchiefs,' he said, throwing them to the prisoner. 'Presents from the ladies,' he explained to the visitor.

For all the obvious haste with which he took off his tunic and then undressed completely, he still handled every article of clothing with great care; he even stroked the silver braid with his fingers and shook one of the tassels straight. It seemed incongruous that he should take such pains, for no sooner had he finished folding each item of clothing than he flung it abruptly into the trench. The last item was his sword-belt with its short sword. He drew the sword from its scabbard, broke it in two, then gathered everything together – the pieces of the sword, the scabbard and the belt – and flung them away so violently that they clattered into the bottom of the trench.

Now he stood there naked. The visitor bit his lip and said nothing. Although he knew what was going to happen, he had no right to intervene in anything the officer did. If the punishment the officer was so attached to was about to be abolished – possibly as a result of the representations the visitor, for his part, felt he had to make – then the officer was acting perfectly correctly; in his position the visitor himself would not have done otherwise.

The soldier and the prisoner did not immediately understand; at first they did not even look. The prisoner was delighted to have the handkerchiefs back; but he was not allowed to enjoy them for long, for the soldier snatched them from him with a sudden unexpected movement. Then the prisoner tried to pull them out from the belt into which the soldier had tucked them, but the soldier was on his guard. So they struggled, half in play. Only when the officer was completely naked did they pay attention. The prisoner in particular seemed struck by a sense that some great reversal had taken place. What had happened to him was now happening to the officer. Perhaps it would continue like this to the very end. The foreign visitor had probably given the order. So this was revenge. Although he himself had not suffered the full punishment, he was still being fully avenged. A wide, silent smile spread across his face and did not leave it.

Meanwhile the officer had turned to the machine. If it had been clear before that he understood the machine very well, it was now almost astonishing to see how he handled it and how it responded. He only had to stretch his hand out to the harrow, and it raised and lowered itself several times until it had reached the right position to take him; as soon as he touched the edge of the bed, it began to vibrate; the felt gag approached his mouth, and one could see that he did not really want to take it, but he only hesitated for a moment, then he quickly gave in and accepted it. Everything was ready, except that the straps were still hanging down at the sides; but they were clearly unnecessary – the officer did not need to be strapped in. But then the prisoner noticed the loose straps; he did not consider the execution complete unless the straps were fastened, so he eagerly beckoned the soldier over to him and they hurried to strap the officer in. The officer had already stretched out a foot to kick the starting-handle that would set the scribing mechanism in motion when he noticed that the two of them had approached, so he withdrew his foot and let them strap him in. But now he could not reach the handle; neither the soldier nor the prisoner would know where it was, and the visitor was determined not to help. It was not necessary; the straps had scarcely been fastened when the machine began to work. The bed vibrated, the needles danced over his skin, and the harrow moved up and down. The visitor had been watching for some time before he remembered that one of the wheels in the scribing mechanism should have screeched; but everything was silent, not even the slightest hum could be heard.

So quietly was the machine running that the visitor simply did not notice it. He looked across at the soldier and the prisoner. The prisoner was the livelier of the two; everything about the machine interested him, one moment he was bending down, the next he was stretching up, all the time using his index finger to point something out to the soldier. The visitor found it all disagreeable. He was determined to stay there to the end, but he could not have put up with the sight of these two for long. 'Go home,' he said. The soldier might have been prepared to obey, but to the prisoner the command amounted to a form of punishment. He clasped his hands and begged to be allowed to stay, and when the visitor shook his head and refused to give in, he even fell to his knees. The visitor saw that his commands were futile, so he went over, intending to chase the two men off. But then he heard a noise up in the scribing mechanism. He looked up. So was one of the cogwheels malfunctioning after all? But it was something else. Slowly the lid of the mechanism began to lift and then opened completely. The teeth of a cogwheel appeared and rose until the whole wheel was visible; it was as if some great force were pressing on the mechanism so that there was no longer room for this wheel. The wheel lurched to the edge of the mechanism, fell to the ground, rolled upright for a while in the sand and then toppled over. But by now another one appeared up there, followed by more, large ones and small ones, some roughly the same size, and the same thing happened with all of them until it seemed there could be none left in the mechanism; then a whole lot more appeared, dropped off, rolled in the sand and fell over. All this made the prisoner forget the visitor's command, he was so delighted by the cogwheels; he kept trying to catch one, urging the soldier to help him, but had to withdraw his hand in fright, for another wheel would follow it immediately, scaring him as it started to roll towards him.

The visitor, however, was most disturbed. The machine was obviously disintegrating, its smooth running was an illusion; since the officer was no longer able to help himself, he now felt he ought to intervene. But his attention had been entirely focused on the falling cogwheels, and he had failed to keep his eye on the rest of the machine, so now, after the last cogwheel had fallen out of the scribing mechanism, he leaned over the harrow and was given another even more unpleasant surprise. The harrow was not writing, but was just stabbing, and the bed was not turning the body, it was just shaking it and lifting it towards the needles. The visitor wanted to intervene, to stop the whole thing if possible; this was not the sort of torture the officer intended, this was outright murder. He stretched out his hands. But the harrow was already rising and moving sideways with the skewered body, as it would normally do only after twelve hours. Blood flowed undiluted in a hundred streams, for this time the water supply had also failed. Then the last stage failed as well, the body did not slide off the long needles, it streamed with blood, but hung above the trench and did not drop. The harrow made to return to its original position, but as if it sensed that it had still not shed its load, it remained suspended over the trench. 'Help me!' the visitor screamed at the soldier and the prisoner as he seized the officer's feet. He meant to push at the feet while the other two took hold of the head and lifted the body slowly off the needles. But the two of them could not be persuaded to come; the prisoner actually turned his back, and the visitor had to go over to them and force them towards the officer's head. As he was doing this he could not avoid seeing the dead man's face.

It was as it had been in life; it bore no trace of the promised redemption; what all others had found in the machine, the officer had not; the lips were firmly shut, the eyes were open, they wore the expression they had in life, a look of calm conviction; the brow was pierced by the point of the great iron spike.

* * *

When the visitor, followed by the soldier and the prisoner, reached the first houses of the colony, the soldier pointed to one of them and said: 'That is the tea-house.'

On the ground floor of one house was a deep, low, cavernous room. Its walls and ceiling were blackened with smoke. In front it was entirely open to the street. The tea-house differed very little from the other houses in the colony, which with the exception of the governor's palatial residence were all very dilapidated; and yet to the visitor it conveyed a sense of history, and he felt the powerful influence of earlier times. He went closer and, followed by his companions, made his way between the empty tables set out on the street in front of the tea-house and breathed in the cool, stale air that came from inside. 'The old man is buried here,' said the soldier. 'The priest refused him a place in the graveyard. For a time they couldn't decide where to bury him, and in the end they buried him here. I'm sure the officer didn't tell you anything about it, because of course that's what he was most ashamed of. He even made a few attempts to dig the old man up at night, but he was chased off every time.' 'Where is the grave?' asked the visitor, who could not believe what the soldier was telling him. At once the soldier and the prisoner ran on ahead and pointed to where the grave was supposed to be. They led him towards the back wall, where some customers were sitting at tables, powerfully built men with short shiny black beards, probably workers from the docks. None of them wore jackets, and their shirts were ragged, they were poor, deprived people. As the visitor approached some of them got up and stood with their backs to the wall, watching him. 'He's a foreigner,' the visitor heard them whisper, 'he wants to look at the grave.' They pushed one of the tables aside, and there was indeed a gravestone underneath. It was a simple stone, low enough to be hidden under a table. It bore an inscription in very small letters; the visitor had to kneel down to read it. It said: 'Here lies the old governor. His followers, whose names may not be mentioned today, dug this grave and placed this stone for him. There is a prophecy that after a certain number of years the governor will rise again and lead his followers from this house to reconquer the colony. Have faith, and wait!' When the visitor had read this he stood up and saw that the men were standing around him smiling, as if they had read the inscription with him, had found it ridiculous and were expecting him to share their opinion. The visitor pretended not to notice, distributed a few coins, waited until the table had been pushed back over the grave, then left the tea-house and went down to the harbour.

The soldier and the prisoner had been held up in the tea-house by some people they knew. But they must soon have torn themselves away from them, for the visitor was only halfway down the long flight of steps leading to the boats when they came running after him. They probably wanted to make the visitor take them with him at the last minute. While the visitor was negotiating with a boatman to take him out to the steamer, the two of them were racing down the steps, silently, because they did not dare to shout. But as they reached the foot of the steps the visitor was already in the boat, and the boatman was just pushing off from the quay. They might still have been able to leap into the boat; but the visitor picked up a heavy knotted rope, threatened them with it and prevented them jumping aboard.

THE JUDGEMENT

A Story

For F

It was a Sunday morning on a beautiful spring day. Georg Bendemann, a young businessman, was sitting in his room on the first floor of one of the mean, flimsily constructed houses, virtually indistinguishable except in height and colour, that ran in a long row beside the river. He had just finished a letter to a friend from his youth who was now living abroad; he sealed it with playful deliberation, then propped his elbows on the desk and gazed out of the window at the river, the bridge and the pale green of the slopes on the far bank.

He reflected how this friend, dissatisfied with his progress at home, had quite simply fled to Russia years ago. Now he ran a business in St Petersburg which had done very well at first, but for some time now seemed to have been failing, as his friend lamented on his increasingly infrequent visits home. And so he wore himself out fruitlessly working abroad, his foreign-looking beard ineffectually concealing the face familiar to Georg since their childhood, which with its yellowish colour seemed to suggest some impending illness. As he told Georg, he had no real connections with the colony of his fellow-countrymen out there, but neither did he have very much social contact with local families, and so he was settling for a life as a confirmed bachelor.

What could he write to a man like that who had obviously lost his way, for whom he could feel sorry, but could not help? Should he perhaps advise him to return home, to take up his life here again, to resume all his old friendships – there was nothing at all to prevent this – and to rely on his friends to help in other ways? But that would just amount to telling him (and the more tactfully this was done, the more hurtful it would be) that his previous attempts had failed, that he should finally give up, come home and have to put up with being the focus of attention as someone who had returned for good, to telling him that only his friends understood how to manage things, that he was a grown-up child who simply had to do what his more successful friends who had stayed at home told him to. And was it certain, even then, that there would be any point in putting him through all that anguish? Perhaps he might not even be persuaded to come home at all – hadn't he said himself that he didn't understand things back home any more? – in which case he would stay out there after all, further alienated from his friends and embittered by all their advice. But if he did follow their advice and was then made to feel unhappy here – not, of course, deliberately, but by force of circumstances – if he was unable to get on with his friends or get on without them, if he felt ashamed, if he really didn't feel at home here and thought he had no friends any more, would it not be much better for him to stay abroad, just as he was? In these circumstances was it possible to think he would really get on here?

For these reasons Georg could not, if he wanted to keep up any kind of correspondence with him, give him the sort of real news that one would candidly pass on even to the most remote acquaintance. It was now more than three years since his friend had been home, and he had explained this very unconvincingly by referring to the uncertain political situation in Russia, which by his account did not allow a small businessman even the briefest period of absence, while a hundred thousand Russians were perfectly able to travel all over the world. For George, though, much had changed during these three years. His mother had died some two years ago, since when he had lived together with his ageing father; his friend had been told of this, and had written to express his sympathy in an impersonal tone that could only be explained by the fact that the grief of such an occasion was quite unimaginable from abroad. Since then, however, Georg had applied himself to his business, as he had to everything else, with greater determination. Perhaps his father had hindered Georg's real involvement in the business during his mother's lifetime by insisting on doing things his own way. Perhaps his father had become more withdrawn since his mother's death, although he still worked in the business, or even more probably, perhaps good fortune had been a far more important factor – at any rate the business had prospered quite unexpectedly in these two years. They had had to double the number of staff, turnover had increased by five hundred per cent, and further progress seemed assured.

But his friend knew nothing of these changes. Earlier (the last time had perhaps been in that letter of condolence), he had tried to persuade Georg to emigrate to Russia and had said much about the prospects in St Petersburg for Georg's line of business in particular. The figures he quoted were minute compared with the present scale of Georg's business. But Georg had had no wish to write to his friend about his successes, and to recall them now really would seem most inappropriate.

And so Georg confined himself to writing only about insignificant events to his friend as they occurred to him at random on a quiet Sunday morning. All he wished was to leave undisturbed the image his friend had doubtless created for himself of his home town, and had come to terms with, in the long intervening years. Thus it happened that Georg announced to his friend in three letters written at quite long intervals the engagement of some person of no consequence to a girl who was also of no interest to them, until his friend, quite contrary to Georg's intentions, actually began to take an interest in this episode.

But Georg preferred to write about such things than to admit that he himself, a month ago, had become engaged to a Fräulein Frieda Brandenfeld, a young woman from a well-to-do family. He often spoke to his fiancée about this friend and the particular relationship he had with him through their correspondence. 'So he certainly won't be able to come to our wedding,' she said. 'But I'm still entitled to get to know all your friends.' 'I don't want to bother him,' Georg replied. 'You see, he would probably come, at least I believe he would, but he would feel obliged to come and feel hurt, perhaps he would envy me; certainly he would feel unhappy and never be able to get over this unhappiness, so he would go back to Russia alone.

Alone – do you know what that means?' 'Well then, can't he be told about our marriage some other way?' 'Of course, I can't prevent that, but with his way of life it's unlikely.' 'If you have friends like that, Georg, you should never have got engaged.' 'Yes, we're both to blame; but even as it is I wouldn't have it otherwise.' And when, breathless from his kisses, she retorted: 'But it still hurts me, really,' he thought it could do no harm to write to his friend and tell him everything. 'That's how I am and that's how he has to take me,' he said to himself. 'I can't turn myself into someone who might be a better friend to him than I am.'

So he did in fact tell his friend, in the long letter he wrote on that Sunday morning, about his engagement in the following words: 'I have saved the best news for last. I'm engaged to a Fräulein Frieda Brandenfeld, a girl from a well-to-do family that moved here a long time after you left, so you probably won't know them. I'll have plenty of opportunity to tell you more about my fiancée, for now let me just say that I'm very happy, and that the only difference in our relationship is that instead of just having a friend, you will now have a happy friend. What's more, in my fiancée, who sends you her warmest regards and will write to you herself very soon, you will gain a sincere friend, which is of some significance for a bachelor. I know there are many things that prevent you from visiting us. But wouldn't my wedding be the very opportunity to remove all these obstacles for once? However that may be, you must do as you see fit without regard to us.'

Georg had sat at his desk for a long time holding this letter in his hand, looking out of the window. An acquaintance had greeted him from the street as he walked by; Georg, smiling absently, had hardly answered him.

At last he put the letter in his pocket, left his room, and crossed a small corridor into his father's room, where he had not been for months. He normally had no reason to, for he was constantly in touch with his father in the business. They took their midday meal together in a restaurant, though in the evening each provided for himself; however, they would then sit for a while, each usually with his own newspaper, in the living room they shared, unless Georg, as was most often the case, was out with his friends or, nowadays, was visiting his fiancée.

Georg was amazed at how dark his father's room was, even on this sunny morning; that high wall on the other side of the narrow courtyard cast such a deep shadow. His father was sitting by the window in a corner surrounded by various mementoes of his late mother, reading a newspaper which he was holding at an angle close to his eyes in order to compensate for his poor vision. On the table were the remains of his breakfast, of which he seemed to have eaten very little.

'Ah, Georg!' said his father, standing up at once and coming towards him. His heavy dressing-gown fell open as he moved, the ends flapping around him. 'My father is still a giant of a man,' thought Georg to himself.

Then he said: 'It's intolerably dark in here.'

'Yes indeed, it is dark,' replied his father.

'Have you shut the window too?'

'I prefer it that way.'

'But it's quite warm outside,' said Georg, as if to follow up his previous observation, and sat down.

His father cleared the breakfast things away and put them on a chest.

'Actually, I only wanted to say,' Georg continued, absently following the old man's movements, 'that I have just sent the news of my engagement to St Petersburg after all.' He pulled the letter part way out of his pocket, then put it back again.

'To St Petersburg?' his father asked.

'Yes, to my friend,' said Georg, trying to catch his father's eye. 'He's not like this at all at work,' he thought, 'the way he sits back here in his chair with his arms folded across his chest.'

'Ah yes, your friend,' said his father with heavy emphasis.

'As you know, Father, at first I didn't want to tell him about my engagement. Out of consideration, for no other reason. You know yourself what a difficult person he is. I told myself that he might well hear about my engagement from someone else, even though that's scarcely likely given his way of life – I can't prevent that – but he was not going to hear about it from me, anyway.'

'And now you have changed your mind?' asked his father, putting his newspaper down on the window ledge, and his spectacles on the paper, covering them with his hand.

'Yes, I've thought it over again. If he is a good friend to me, I told myself, then my happiness at becoming engaged ought to make him happy too. So I had no further hesitation in telling him. But still, I wanted to tell you before I posted the letter.'

'Georg,' said his father, opening his toothless mouth wide, 'listen to me! You have brought this matter to me to ask my advice. That certainly does you credit. But it means nothing, it's worse than nothing, unless you now tell me the whole truth. I don't want to stir things up unnecessarily. Since the death of our dear mother certain unpleasant things have occurred. Perhaps the time will come for them too, and sooner than we think, perhaps. At work there is much that escapes my notice, perhaps it is not being withheld from me – I certainly don't wish to assume that is the case – I don't have the energy any more, my memory is failing. I can't keep my eye on everything. Firstly, that is the natural course of things, and secondly the death of our dear mother affected me far more heavily than you. – But since we are on the subject of this letter just now, I beg of you, Georg, do not deceive me. It is a trivial matter, it's not worth wasting breath on it, so do not deceive me. Do you really have this friend in St Petersburg?'

Georg stood up, nonplussed. 'Let my friends be. A thousand friends could not replace my father. Do you know what I think? You don't look after yourself enough. But age demands its due. You are indispensable to me in the business, you know that very well; but if the business threatened to affect your health I would close it down tomorrow for ever. It's not right. We must think of a new way of life, a radically new way of life for you. You sit here in the dark, and in the living room you would have lots of light, it would be lovely. You peck at your breakfast, instead of keeping your strength up properly. You sit at a closed window, and fresh air would do you so much good. No, father! I will fetch the doctor, and we'll follow his instructions. We'll change rooms, you'll move into the front room and I'll move in here. It won't be any great change for you, everything will be moved over there with you. But there's time for all that, just lie down in bed now for a while, you really need to rest. Come along, I'll help you to undress, you'll see I can do it. Or would you rather go into the font room straight away, then you can lie down in my bed for the time being. That would be the most sensible thing to do.'

Georg was standing right beside his father, who had let his head with its unkempt white hair sink onto his chest.

'Georg,' said his father softly, without moving.

At once Georg knelt beside his father; he saw the abnormally wide pupils in his father's tired face fixed on him from the corners of his eyes.

'You have no friend in St Petersburg. You always were a joker, and you have not spared me your jokes either. Why should you have a friend there, of all places! I don't believe a word of it.'

'But Father, do try to remember,' said Georg, lifting his father out of his chair and taking off his dressing-gown as he stood there so feebly. 'It will soon be three years since my friend visited us here. I can still remember that you didn't like him very much. At least twice I had to pretend he wasn't there, although he was sitting in my room at the time. Of course, I could understand your dislike of him perfectly well, my friend has his peculiarities. But then later you got on with him quite well. I was so proud then when you listened to him, nodded and asked him questions. If you think about it, you must remember. It was when he told us unbelievable stories about the revolution in Russia, for example how there was a riot when he had been on a business trip to Kiev, and he saw a priest on a balcony who carved a big cross in blood into the palm of his hand, then held up his hand and addressed the mob. You've repeated that story yourself on several occasions.'

Meanwhile Georg had managed to get his father to sit down again, carefully removed the woollen trousers he wore over his linen underpants, and then took off his socks. At the sight of his father's not particularly clean underwear, Georg reproached himself for having neglected him. It was surely also his responsibility to see that his father's underwear was changed. He had not yet actually discussed arrangements for his father's future with his fiancée, but they had tacitly assumed that he would stay in the old flat on his own. However, there and then he made the firm decision that he would take his father with him into their future household. On closer inspection it looked as if the care his father would receive there might almost come too late.

He picked his father up in his arms and put him to bed. As he carried him the few steps towards his bed, he had a terrible shock when he saw that his father was playing with the watchchain on his chest, grasping it so tightly that for a moment Georg was unable to put him down on the bed.

But once he was in bed everything seemed well. He covered himself up and then pulled the bedcover right over his shoulder. He looked up at Georg in a not unfriendly way.

'You do remember him though, don't you?' asked Georg with a nod of encouragement.

'Am I covered up?' asked his father, as if he could not see whether his feet were fully covered.

'It's nice being in bed, isn't it?' said Georg, arranging the bedclothes for him.

'Am I covered up?' his father asked again; he seemed particularly intent on an answer.

'Don't worry, you are well covered.'

'No!' cried his father before Georg could finish. He threw back the bedcover with such force that it flew off, and stood upright in his bed, with just one hand held lightly against the ceiling. 'I know – you wanted to cover me up, you young puppy, but I'm not buried yet. And even if this is all the strength I have left, it's enough for you, too much for you! I know all about your friend. He would be a son after my own heart. And that's why you've been deceiving him all these years. Why else should you do that? D'you think I haven't wept for him? That's why you shut yourself in your office – no one must disturb you, the boss is busy – just so that you can write your bogus letters to Russia. Fortunately, though, no one needs to teach a father how to see through his son. And now, just when you thought you'd brought him down so that you could sit on him and keep him quiet, that's when this son of mine decides to get married!'

Georg looked up at the terrifying vision of his father. He felt for his friend in St Petersburg, whom his father suddenly knew so well, as he never had before. He pictured him lost in far-off Russia. He saw him at the door of his empty, looted business. He was still standing there among the ruined shelves, the ransacked wares, the hanging gas brackets. Why did he have to move so far away!

'Look at me, though!' shouted his father, and Georg, almost distracted, ran to the bed to take it all in, but stopped halfway.

'Because she lifted her skirts,' his father went on in a piping voice, 'because she lifted her skirts like this, the disgusting trollop,' and to make himself quite clear he lifted his nightshirt so high that the scar from the war wound on his thigh was exposed. 'Because she lifted her skirts like that, and that, and that, you made up to her, and to satisfy your lust with her undisturbed you dishonoured the memory of our mother, betrayed your friend and put your father to bed so that he can't move. But can he, or can't he?'

He stood there quite unsupported, kicking out with his legs. His face shone with triumphant insight.

Georg stood in a corner, as far away from his father as he could get. A long time before he had firmly resolved to observe everything with the closest attention, so that he could not be caught unawares by some hidden move from above or from behind. Now he recalled his long-forgotten resolve, then forgot it, as if pulling a short thread through the eye of a needle.

'But your friend was not betrayed, you see!' cried his father, wagging his forefinger to and fro emphatically. 'I was his representative here.'

'So it was an act!' Georg blurted out; he realised at once the mistake he had made, stared in horror, and bit his tongue so hard that he winced with pain – but too late.

'Yes, of course it was an act! An act! Well said! What other comfort was there for an old widowed father? Tell me – and for the time it takes you to answer, you will continue to be my living son – what else could I do, in my back room, plagued by disloyal staff, racked by old age? And my son paraded around the place, concluding deals that I had prepared, jumping for joy and putting on a straight face in front of his father, pretending to be an honourable man! Do you imagine I didn't love you, my own flesh and blood?'

'Now he'll lean forward,' thought Georg. 'Perhaps he'll fall over and smash himself to bits!' The words hissed through his head.

His father leaned forward, but did not fall over. Since Georg did not come any closer, as he had expected, he straightened up again.

'Stay where you are, I don't need you! You think you still have the strength to come over here, and you're only holding back because you choose to. But don't fool yourself! I'm still far stronger than you. On my own I might have had to give in to you, but as it is your mother left me her strength, I've formed a splendid alliance with your friend, and your customers are all here in my pocket!'

'He's even got pockets in his nightshirt!' Georg said to himself, believing that with this observation he could make his father a laughing-stock in the eyes of the world. But this thought only occurred to him for a moment, for he kept forgetting everything.

'Just try coming here arm in arm with your fiancée! I'll brush her away from you, you'll see!'

Georg pulled a face as if to express his disbelief. His father merely nodded towards Georg in the corner of the room to emphasise the truth of his words.

'You don't know how amused I was today when you came and asked me whether you should write to tell your friend about your engagement. You see, he knows everything, you stupid boy, he knows everything! I wrote to him, you see, because you forgot to take my writing materials away from me. That's why he hasn't been here for years, because he knows everything a hundred times better than you do. He crumples up your letters with his left hand without reading them, while he holds mine in his right hand and reads them!'

He waved his arm above his head in his excitement. 'He knows everything a thousand times better!' he cried.

'Oh yes, ten thousand times better!' said Georg, mocking his father, but even as he said it his words sounded deadly serious.

'For years I've been waiting for you to come along with this question! Do you imagine there's anything else I think about? Do you imagine I'm reading the papers? Here!' – and he threw a newspaper at Georg which had somehow found its way into bed with him. It was an old newspaper with a title Georg had never heard of.

'What a long time you took to grow up! Your mother had to die, she didn't live to see the happy day, your friend is coming to grief in Russia, three years ago he was already so yellow he was good for nothing, and as for me, you can see the state I'm in, you've eyes enough for that!'

'So you've been waiting to pounce on me!' cried Georg.

With sympathy his father replied in an undertone: 'I dare say you wanted to say that before. But it's far too late now.'

Then he added, louder: 'So now you know what was going on outside your own world; until now you only knew about yourself! Oh yes, you were an innocent child – but in actual fact you were the very devil! – Know this, then: I now sentence you to death by drowning!'

Georg felt himself driven from the room; behind him he heard the crash as his father fell back onto the bed. He fled down the stairs as if sliding down a steep slope, and startled his cleaner as she was on her way up to tidy his rooms for the day. 'Jesus!' she cried, covering her face with her apron, but he had already gone. He leapt through the gate, driven across the road towards the river. Now he was gripping the railing like a starving man holding on to his food. He vaulted over the barrier like the excellent gymnast he had been, to his parents' pride, in his early youth. While he still held on with a weakening grip, through the railing he caught sight of an omnibus which would easily drown out the sound of his fall. He called softly: 'But I always loved you, dear parents,' and let himself drop.

At that moment a quite endless stream of traffic passed over the bridge.

LETTER TO MY FATHER

Dearest Father,

You asked me once recently why I claim to be afraid of you. As usual, I could not give you an answer, partly because of my fear of you, and partly because in order to convey the reasons for this fear through the spoken word I would have to go into such detail that I would be unable to give anything like a full account. And if I now attempt to give you a written answer, it will still only be a very incomplete one, because even as I write it my fear, and the consequences of this fear, inhibit me, and because the whole scope of the subject far exceeds the reach of my memory and my mind.

To you the matter has always seemed very simple, at least as far as you have spoken about it to me and, indiscriminately, to others. To you it looked something like this: you have worked hard all your life and sacrificed everything for your children, for me above all, while I have lived 'high on the hog', have had complete freedom to study what I wanted to, had no reason to worry about providing for myself, in short I have had no worries at all. You asked for no gratitude for this – you know what 'children's gratitude' means – but you expected at least something in return, some sign of affection; instead of this, I have always slunk away from you – to my room, to my books, to my crazy friends, to my overwrought ideas; I have never talked openly to you, never come near you in the Synagogue, never visited you in Franzensbad or had any sense of family duty in other ways, I have never taken any interest in the business or your other affairs, I lumbered you with the factory and then left you in the lurch, I supported Ottla in her willfulness, and while I don't lift a finger for you (I don't even give you a ticket for the theatre), I'll do anything for strangers. If you were to sum up your opinion of me, it would be that while you don't exactly accuse me of anything improper or wicked (except perhaps my recent engagement), you do find me cold, aloof and ungrateful. What's more, you accuse me of this as if it were my fault, as if with a touch on the wheel I could have arranged everything differently, while you are not to blame in the slightest, except perhaps in that you have been too good to me.

This is your usual explanation, which I consider to be correct only in so far as I also believe that you are in no way to blame for our estrangement. But I, too, am entirely blameless. If I could get you to acknowledge that, then it might be possible, not to start a new life – we are both much too old for that – but at least to establish a kind of truce, not to put a stop to your incessant reproaches, but at least to moderate them.

Strangely enough, you have some idea of what I am trying to say. For example, you told me recently: 'I have always been fond of you, even though I have not appeared to treat you as other fathers do, simply because I cannot hide my feelings as they do.' Well, Father, on the whole I have never doubted your fondness for me; but I do not believe this remark to be true. You cannot hide your feelings, that is correct; but to try to claim therefore that other fathers are hiding their feelings is either just being opinionated, in which case there is no point in further discussion, or else – and this is what I really believe – it is a veiled admission that there is something not quite right between us, for which you are in part responsible, but blameless. If that is what you really mean, then we are in agreement.

Of course I am not saying that I have become what I am solely through your doing. That would be greatly exaggerated (and I do in fact tend to such exaggeration). It is perfectly possible that even if I had grown up quite free of your influence, I could still never have become someone after your own heart. I would probably still have become a sickly, anxious, timid, nervous person, not a Robert Kafka or a Karl Hermann, but still quite different from what I actually am, and we could have got on together splendidly. I would have been glad to have you as a friend, a boss, an uncle, a grandfather, indeed even (though more doubtfully) as a father-in-law. But it was as a father that you were too strong for me, especially since my brothers died young and my sisters came much later, so that I had to suffer the first assault quite alone, which I was far too weak to do.

Compare the two of us: I, to put it very summarily, a Löwy on a Kafka base, as it were, though not someone driven by the Kafka will for life, trade, and domination, but rather by the Löwy impulse, which works more mysteriously, more timidly, and often gives up altogether. You, on the other hand, a true Kafka in your physique, health, appetite, your powerful voice, your loquacity, self-confidence, authority, stamina, presence of mind, knowledge of the world, a degree of generosity, and of course allied to these qualities all the faults and weaknesses to which your temperament and at times your fits of rage impel you. Perhaps you are not wholly a Kafka in your general outlook, as far as I can judge if I compare you with Uncle Philipp, Uncle Ludwig or Uncle Heinrich. That is odd, and I am not very sure about it; you see, they were all more cheerful, more lively, more relaxed, more carefree, less strict than you. (Moreover, in this respect I have inherited a great deal from you and have lived up to my inheritance far too well, though it is true I lack the necessary correctives in my nature that you possess.) And yet on the other hand, you too have had different experiences at times, you were perhaps happier before your children, myself especially, disappointed you and saddened you when you were at home with the family (for whenever strangers visited, you were of course quite different); and perhaps you have become happier again now that your grandchildren and son-in-law are giving you some of the warmth that your children, except for Valli perhaps, could not give you. At any rate, we were so different, and being so different we were such a danger to each other that if one had tried to work out how I, the slowly developing child, and you, the grown man, would behave towards each other in the future, one might have assumed that you would simply stamp on me until there was nothing left of me. But that didn't happen, life is incalculable; but perhaps something worse happened – though again I beg you not to forget that I have never remotely believed that you are to blame. You treated me as you had to treat me; but you must stop seeing it as due to some particular malice on my part that I became the victim of that treatment.

I was an anxious child; even so, I was certainly stubborn, as children are. My mother surely spoiled me too, but I cannot believe that I was especially uncontrollable, I cannot believe that a kind word, a fond look, or being taken gently by the hand, would not have got me to do anything you wanted. I know you are at heart a kind and tender person (what I have to say will not contradict that, you see I am only talking about how you appeared to the child, and the effect on him); but not every child has the tenacity and the pluck to search long enough to find the kindness. You are only able to treat a child in your own way, with force, shouting and rage, and besides in this case that seemed to you all the more appropriate because you wished to bring me up as a robust and fearless lad.

Of course, today I cannot describe directly how you brought me up in my very first years, but I can imagine roughly how it was by extrapolating from my later years and from the way you deal with Felix. This is thrown into sharper relief by the fact that you were younger in those days, and therefore more energetic, more impulsive, more down-to-earth, even more outspoken than today, and on top of that you were totally bound up with the business, you scarcely had time to see me once in the day and so the impression you made on me was all the more vivid and was hardly ever something I just got used to.

I only remember one incident directly from those first years; perhaps you remember it too. Once I went on whining for water in the night, certainly not because I was thirsty, more probably partly to annoy and partly to amuse myself. When a few dire threats had failed to work, you took me out of bed, carried me out onto the balcony and left me to stand there for a short while alone outside the locked door in my nightshirt. I don't wish to say this was wrong, perhaps at the time it was the only way you could get some peace; I only want to give it as an example of the way you brought me up and its effect on me. Afterwards, I dare say, I was more obedient, but it damaged me inwardly. Being the child I was, I could never grasp the true connection between the senseless begging for water, which for me was the most natural thing in the world, and the extraordinary terror of being put outside. Years later I was still tortured by the notion that this huge man, my father, the ultimate authority, could come along in the night for almost no reason, take me out of bed and out onto the balcony, which showed that to him I was simply a nobody.

At the time this was only a minor early incident; but this overpowering sense I often have of being a nobody (which can, however, in other respects be a noble and creative feeling) stems largely from your influence. It would have helped to have some encouragement, some kindness, some clearing of the way for me, but instead you put obstacles in my way, albeit with the good intention of making me take a different one. But I was not up to it. For example, you encouraged me when I marched and saluted properly, but I was never going to make a soldier; or you encouraged me when I ate heartily, or even drank beer with my meal, or when I sang songs I couldn't understand or learned to repeat your favourite turns of phrase – but none of this was part of my future. And it is significant that even today you only really encourage me in matters that affect you personally, when I offend your own feelings (by my marriage plans, for example) or when they are offended on my account (when Pepa tells me off, for example). Then you buck me up, then you try to restore my self-respect, you point out the partners I would be entitled to choose, and you dismiss Pepa out of hand. But quite apart from the fact that at my present age I am almost beyond encouragement, whatever good would it do me if it is only offered when it is not about me in the first instance?

It was at the time, and in every way at that time, that I needed encouragement. I was intimidated enough by your sheer physicality. I remember, for example, how we often used to undress together in a bathing hut. I was lean, weak, and thin; you were strong, tall, and broad. Even in the hut I felt pitiable, and not just in front of you, but in front of the whole world, for you were the measure of all things for me. But then, when we went outside the hut where everyone could see us, as I held onto your hand, a little skeleton, unsure, barefoot on the boards, frightened of the water, incapable of imitating the swimming motions you kept showing me, with the best intentions but actually to my deep embarrassment – then I felt quite desperate, and at such moments all my painful experiences in every kind of situation merged into one great dread. I would feel most at ease whenever you undressed first, and I could stay back in the hut alone and put off the shame of appearing in public until in the end you came to see what I was up to and chased me out of the hut. I was grateful to you for not seeming to notice how upset I was, and I was proud of my father's body, too. And even today there is still a similar kind of difference between us.

In a similar way you dominated me intellectually. You had worked your way so far up the ladder solely through your own efforts that as a result you had boundless confidence in your own opinion. When I was a child, this did not overwhelm me as it did later when I was growing up. You ruled the world in your armchair. Your opinion was correct, everyone else's was crazy, overwrought, *meschugge*,* abnormal. Not just that, you were so self-confident that even when you contradicted yourself, you were still right. It could even be that in some matter you had no opinion at all, therefore every opinion it was possible to express on that matter had to be wrong, without exception. For example, you could upbraid the Czechs, then the Germans, then the Jews, not just in some particular respect but in general, and in the end there was no one left but you. For me you acquired the baffling nature of all tyrants, who are right because of who they are, not because of what they think. At least that is how it seemed to me.

And indeed, in matters concerning me you actually were right surprisingly often; in conversation of course – not that we had any conversation to speak of – but also in fact. But that was understandable enough; all my

---

* *meschugge* (Yiddish): deranged*

thinking was heavily influenced by you, even when I did not share your ideas – especially then. Any thoughts I had that seemed independent of you were from the start blighted by your dismissive opinion, which made it almost impossible for me to pursue a thought to its conclusion and to sustain it. I'm not talking about any lofty ideas here, but about all those little projects of my childhood. I only had to be pleased about something, to be full of it and come home and tell you all about it, and your response would be a disparaging sigh, you would shake your head or tap your fingers on the table. 'I've seen better things than that,' you would say, or 'Is that all you're worried about?' or 'I'm not in the mood,' or 'Go and buy yourself something,' or 'Well I never!' Of course, I couldn't expect you to be thrilled by every little childish whim when you had your own cares and worries. That was not the point, either. It was more that you were always inevitably going to disappoint the child like this because of your completely different nature; moreover, this difference became more and more marked the more instances of it occurred, so that in the end it became a matter of habit even when you shared my opinion for once, and ultimately these disappointments suffered by the child were not just the disappointments of everyday life – because you were the source of authority in all matters, they marked him profoundly. His morale, his determination, his confidence, his pleasure in this or that could not be sustained if you disapproved, or even if your disapproval could be assumed – and it could be assumed in almost everything I did.

This applied to people as well as to opinions. It was enough for me to show some interest in a person – which, being what I am, I did not do very often – for you to intervene without any regard for my feelings or respect for my judgement with abuse, slander and denigration. Innocent, childlike people like the Yiddish actor Löwy, for example, fell foul of this. Without even knowing him you compared him, in a dreadful way that I've now forgotten, to vermin, and as you so often did with people I was fond of, you automatically came out with the proverb: 'If you go to bed with a dog, you get up with fleas.' I particularly recall the actor here because at the time I wrote down a remark about your opinions of him: 'This is what my father says about my friend (whom he has never met) only because he is my friend. I shall always be able to put that to him whenever he accuses me of lacking in filial love and gratitude.' I could never understand your complete lack of sensitivity towards the suffering and shame you could inflict on me with your words and your opinions; it was as if you had no idea of the power you had. Certainly, I have also hurt you by what I have said; but I always knew I had, and it upset me, but I could not control myself, I could not hold the words back, I regretted them as soon as I spoke them. But you just lashed out when you spoke, you felt sorry for no one, not at the time, not afterwards; I was utterly defenceless against you.

But your whole way of bringing up children was like that. I believe you have a talent for instruction; someone like you could certainly have benefited from your methods, he would have seen the sense of what you said, would not have worried any further about it and just done as he was told. But for me as a child your every word was a command from heaven; I never forgot what you told me, it was always the most important means I had of understanding the world, above all of understanding you – and in this you failed utterly. Because it was mostly at mealtimes that I was with you when I was a child, your instruction consisted largely in teaching me table manners. Whatever was put on the table had to be eaten, I was not allowed to say how the food tasted – but you often found it inedible, called it 'fodder' and said 'that cow' (the cook) had ruined it. Because you had a hearty appetite and much preferred to eat everything quickly in great mouthfuls while it was hot, the child had to hurry his food; there was a gloomy silence at table, interrupted by commands to 'eat first, talk afterwards', or 'come on, faster, faster', or 'look, I finished long ago'. I was not allowed to gnaw at the bones, but you could. I was not allowed to suck at the vinegar, but you did. The main thing was to cut the bread straight; but when you did it with a knife dripping with sauce, it didn't matter. I had to be careful not to drop any food on the floor, but then you left more than anyone else under your chair. At table I had to eat, and nothing else, but you would cut and file your fingernails, sharpen pencils, or clean out your ears with a toothpick. Please understand, Father; in themselves these would have been quite insignificant details, they only irked me because you, who were so hugely important as the standard by which I measured myself, did not observe the rules you imposed on me. As a result the world for me was divided into three parts – one that I, the slave, inhabited, under laws which were devised only for me, laws moreover which, for reasons I did not understand, I could never fully comply with; then a second world that was infinitely removed from mine, the world in which you lived, ruled, issued orders and were angry when they were not followed; and finally a third world in which other people lived happily, free from the giving and obeying of orders. I was constantly in disgrace; either I obeyed your orders, which was shameful because they only applied to me, or I defied you, which was shameful too, for how could I dare to defy you; or else I was unable to obey because I did not have your strength, for example, your appetite, or your competence, although you demanded all this of me as a matter of course – and that was the greatest shame of all. These are the lines along which the child's feelings ran – not his thoughts, but his feelings.

My position at the time might be made clearer if I compare it with that of Felix. You treat him in a similar way too, indeed with him you even use a particularly terrible method of instruction; whenever he eats in what you think is a slovenly way, you are not content to say, as you used to say to me: 'you're a proper pig', but you then add: 'a real Hermann', or: 'just like your father'. Now perhaps – one cannot say more than 'perhaps' – that doesn't really do Felix any fundamental harm, for to him you are just a grandfather, a particularly important one, it is true, but still not everything as you were for me. Besides, Felix is a calm person, in a sense already grown up, who might be disturbed by a thunderous voice, but won't be permanently affected by it. But most of all, it's only relatively rarely that he is with you, and of course he is exposed to other influences; to him you are more of a funny old thing he's quite fond of, and he can take you or leave you as he wishes. To me you weren't at all funny. I had no choice – I had to take it all.

What's more, I had to take it and couldn't object, because you are inherently incapable of discussing calmly anything you don't agree with or anything that isn't your idea; your overbearing temperament won't let you. In recent years you have attributed this to your nervous heart condition; but I can't recall that you were ever essentially different, or at best your heart condition has been a pretext to assert your dominance all the more strictly, since the very thought of it is bound to stifle any form of contradiction. This is of course not a reproach, only a statement of fact. Take what you often say about Ottla, for example: 'You can't say anything to her before she snaps at you.' But in fact she doesn't snap at you at all at first; you're confusing the topic at issue with the person – it's the topic that snaps at you, you make up your mind without listening to the person, and any subsequent argument can only irritate you further and never convince you. Then all you can say is: 'Do what you want; as far as I'm concerned, you can please yourself; you're grown up; I've no advice to give you' – and all this is said with that awful harsh undertone of fury and utter condemnation, which makes me tremble less today than when I was a child only because the child's overwhelming sense of guilt has to some extent been replaced by the insight into the helplessness of both of us.

The impossibility of any calm exchanges between us had a further effect, and a perfectly natural one: I was unable to talk. I dare say I would not have been a great speaker anyway, but I'm sure I would have mastered normal fluent human speech. However, at an early stage you forbade me to speak; your threat: 'Not a word of contradiction!' and the raised hand that went with it have been with me ever since. In front of you – you are, as long as you are talking about your own interests, an excellent speaker – I adopted a hesitant, stuttering way of speaking, and even that was too much for you; in the end I fell silent, at first perhaps out of defiance, then because I could not think or speak in front of you. And because you were my real tutor, it affected my whole life. It is altogether a strange mistake on your part to believe I never obeyed you. 'Always contrary' was honestly not my guiding principle towards you, which is what you believe and accuse me of. Far from it; if I had been less amenable, you would surely have been more pleased with me. It's rather that all your instruction achieved its objective exactly, I soaked up everything; what I am, I am (apart from my basic nature, of course, and what my experience of life has given me) as a result of your instruction and my obedience. That the end result nevertheless causes you distress, that you even subconsciously refuse to accept that it is the result of your instruction, is because your methods and my nature were so incompatible. 'Not a word of contradiction!' you said, in an attempt to stifle any resistance on my part, which you found intolerable; but the effect this had on me was too powerful, I was too obedient, I held my tongue, crept away, and did not dare to make a move until I was beyond the immediate reach of your authority. But you still stood in the way, and everything I did seemed 'contrary' to you, whereas it was simply the natural consequence of your strength and my weakness.

The extremely effective rhetorical methods you constantly used, at least for my instruction, were curses, threats, sarcasm, mocking laughter and – curiously enough – self-pity.

I cannot recall that you ever cursed me directly in specific terms; but you did not need to. You had so many other ways, and in any case in conversations at home, and especially in the shop, there were so many curses flying all round me directed at other people that as a small boy I was sometimes almost stunned by them and had no reason to believe they were directed at me, for the people you were shouting at were certainly no worse than I was, and you were certainly no more dissatisfied with them than you were with me. And this was another example of your puzzling artlessness and imperviousness; you cursed without a thought, and yet you deplored it in others, indeed you forbade it.

These curses you backed up with threats – and these really did apply to me. 'I'll tear you apart like a fish!' for example, is one that terrified me, although I knew that nothing worse would happen (as a small child, however, I did not know that); but it fitted my impression of your strength that you would be able to do that too. It also terrified me when you ran shouting round the table to get hold of me; you obviously didn't mean to catch me, but pretended you did, so that in the end Mother had to rescue me, it seemed. Once again, so it seemed to the child, you had mercifully spared my life, and my survival was an undeserved gift from you. The same was true of your threats about the consequences of disobedience. Whenever I started something you did not approve of, you would warn me it would fail, and such was my respect for your opinion that it was, though perhaps only much later, doomed to failure. I lost the confidence to do anything myself. I was hesitant, uncertain. The older I became, the more evidence you could produce to show how useless I was, and as it turned out you were proved right in a sense. Again, I have no wish to claim that it was only you that made me like this; you just reinforced what was there, but you reinforced it all the more because you had such power over me, and you used all the power you had.

You relied especially on sarcasm in your instruction, which was best suited to your superiority over me. Your reprimand usually went something like this: 'Can't you do such and such? I suppose that's too much for you? Of course, you haven't got time for it, have you?' And each of these questions would be accompanied by a nasty laugh and a cruel look. In a way, I was already punished before I knew I had done anything wrong. It was also upsetting to be reprimanded in the third person, when you didn't even think it was worth telling me off directly, when you pretended to be speaking to my mother, but were in fact addressing me as I sat there, for example: 'Of course, we can't expect that of the young man,' and suchlike. This tactic was then reversed when I didn't dare to ask you anything directly (and later it became a habit, if Mother was there, never to do so). It was far less dangerous for the child to address his mother as she sat next to you and ask: 'How is Father?' – thus avoiding any surprise attacks. Of course there were also occasions when I was quite in favour of the heaviest sarcasm, that is, when it was directed at someone else, Elli for example, with whom I was on bad terms for years. For me it was a feast of malicious glee when you told her at almost every mealtime: 'The girl's so fat she has to sit ten yards away from the table.' Then you would sit there glowering on your chair, and in a bitterly hostile manner without the slightest trace of kindness or humour, you would put on an exaggerated imitation to convey to her how repulsive you found the way she sat at table. How often this and similar antics were repeated, and how little they actually achieved! The reason for this was, I believe, that the offence and the degree of rage and malice you brought to it seemed to be out of proportion; one did not feel that your rage was caused by this trivial issue of sitting too far away from the table, but that it was there from the start in all its violence, and only needed this chance incident as an excuse to erupt. Since we were convinced that some pretext or other would occur in any case, we did not pay too much heed, and our response was blunted by the everpresent threat; gradually we felt almost certain that we weren't going to be beaten, and the child became surly, inattentive, disobedient, always intent on escape, mostly by withdrawing into itself. So you suffered, and so we suffered. From your point of view you were quite right when, with the clenched teeth and the hoarse laugh that gave the child its first inkling of hell, you would say (as you did only recently about a letter from Constantinople): 'What a dreadful bunch!'

It seemed quite at variance with your attitude towards your children when you felt sorry for yourself, which you often did quite openly. I admit that as a child I had no feeling at all for this (though I did later), and could not understand how you could expect to find any sympathy whatever. You were such a giant in every respect – how could you need our sympathy, let alone our help? Surely you would treat that with the same contempt as you treated us. So I didn't believe your complaining, and tried to detect some hidden reason for it. Only later did I understand that you really suffered on account of your children; but then, when under different circumstances your laments might have found a response in an open, candid, childlike mind that was eager to help in any way it could, for me they could only be yet another blatant example of your humiliating methods of instruction – in itself not a particularly telling one, but one that had the damaging consequence that the child got into the habit of not taking seriously the very things he should have done.

Fortunately, however, there were exceptions to this, mostly when you suffered in silence and the full force of love and kindness overcame all resistance and flowed freely. This happened rarely, to be sure, but when it did it was wonderful. Like those times on a warm summer day when I would see you asleep in the shop after the midday meal with your elbows resting on the desk, or the Sundays when you were worn out and came to join us in the fresh summer air; or when Mother was seriously ill, and you would hold on to the bookcase, shaking with tears; or during my most recent illness when you came quietly into Ottla's room to see me, then stopped and peered round the door to see me in bed, and in order not to disturb me just waved a hand in greeting. At such times I would lie down and weep with joy, and I weep again now as I write about it.

You also have a particularly nice way of smiling, which is not often seen – a quiet, satisfied, approving smile that can make the person it is meant for very happy. I cannot recall that it was ever directed specifically at me; but I dare say it might have been, for why should you have withheld it from me then, when I still seemed innocent to you and was your great hope? However, even such benevolent impressions in the end only increased my sense of guilt and made the world yet more incomprehensible for me.

I preferred to hold on to the concrete and the familiar. In order to stand up to you a little, and partly also as a form of revenge, I soon began to observe some little absurdities you had, to collect and exaggerate them – for example, how easily you were dazzled by people who were apparently – but only apparently – of higher status than yourself, how you would go on and on about them, about some Imperial Councillor or suchlike (on the other hand, I also found this sort of thing distressing, that you, my father, thought you needed such worthless ways of bolstering your self-esteem, and that you showed off about them). Or I noted your predilection for indecent remarks, which you would utter as loudly as possible, and laugh at them as if you had said something particularly grand, whereas it was no more than a banal little indecency (at the same time, however, it was yet another expression of your virility that put me to shame). There were of course plenty of observations like these; I was pleased with them, they were funny and made me snigger; sometimes you noticed and it annoyed you, you thought it malicious and cheeky – but believe me, it was for me simply a means of self-preservation, a quite ineffectual one, moreover. It was the way one laughs at a god or a king, the sort of laughter that is not only consistent with the deepest respect, but is even part of it.

What's more, you also attempted a sort of counter-attack that reflected your similar attitude towards me. You would point out how exceptionally well off I was and how well I had actually been treated. That is correct, but I do not believe that it did me any real good in the prevailing circumstances.

It is true that Mother was boundlessly good to me; but as far as I was concerned that was all part of my relationship with you, which was not a good one. Without knowing it, Mother played the part of a beater in a hunt. While your way of bringing me up might, in some improbable instance, have helped me to stand on my own two feet by provoking defiance, dislike or even hatred in me, Mother would counteract this by showing kindness, by talking sensibly (in the confusions of childhood she was the very model of common sense), by pleading for me, and I was driven back into your sphere of control, from which I might otherwise have escaped – to your benefit and mine. Or it so happened that no real reconciliation took place, and Mother simply protected me from you by stealth, gave me something or let me do something behind your back – and then I was once again the creature that shunned the light, the deceiver, full of guilt, the nobody who could only obtain by underhand means what he felt was his by right. Naturally I then got used to using those means to obtain what even I thought I had no right to; and that again only added to my sense of guilt.

It is also true that you scarcely ever actually beat me. But your bawling, when your face was red with rage, the way you quickly took off your braces and put them ready on the back of the chair was for me almost worse. It's like when someone is going to be hanged; if he really is hanged, then he's dead and it's all over. But if he has to go through all the preparations for being hanged, and then only hears he is to be pardoned when the noose is dangling in front of his face, he can suffer from it for the rest of his life. Moreover, those many occasions when you made it clear that you thought I deserved to be beaten, and that I had only narrowly escaped it thanks to your forgiveness, again only contributed to a huge sense of guilt. In all ways I came to feel indebted to you.

You have always held it against me (in private or in front of others; you had no sense of how humiliating that was – matters concerning your children were always aired in public) that thanks to your hard work I wanted for nothing and lived in peace, comfort and prosperity. I am thinking here of remarks that must really have become etched into my mind, like: 'When I was only seven I had to push the cart round the villages'; 'We all had to sleep in one room'; 'We were lucky if we had any potatoes'; 'For years I had open sores on my legs because I had no proper clothes for winter'; 'When I was a little boy I had to go and work in the shop in Pisek'; 'I got nothing at all from home, not even when I was in the army, I sent money home myself'; 'But even so, even so – my father was always my father. Who understands that today! What do children know about it! Nobody has had to struggle like that! Can a child understand that today?' Under other circumstances such stories might have been an excellent way of teaching a child, they might have encouraged it and given it the strength to survive the same troubles and hardships its father had put up with. But that was not your intention at all, the situation had changed as a result of your own efforts, and there was no opportunity for the child to achieve what you had done. Such an opportunity could only have been created by violent upheaval, by breaking away from home (provided one had the determination and strength to do that, and if Mother had not somehow been able to prevent it). But of course you didn't want anything like that, you described it as ingratitude, perversity, disobedience, betrayal, madness. So while on the one hand you encouraged your children to follow your example by telling them all about yourself and shaming them, on the other hand you forbade them to most strictly. Otherwise, for example, if it hadn't been for the particular circumstances, you ought to have been delighted with Ottla's Zürau adventure. She wanted to return to the land, where you had your roots; she wanted to work and know hardship, as you had done; she did not wish to enjoy the results of your labours, just as you too were independent of your father. Were these such terrible plans? Were they so far from your example and your teachings? Yes – Ottla's project didn't work out in the end, perhaps it was rather absurd and perhaps she made too much fuss about it and didn't think about her parents enough. But was that entirely her fault, was it not because of the circumstances too, and above all because you were so hostile towards her?

Was she really (as you tried to convince yourself afterwards) any closer to you in the shop than she was later in Zürau? And would it not surely have been in your power (if only you could have brought yourself to do it) to make this adventure into something very positive by giving her encouragement, advice, and supervision, or perhaps even just by tolerating it?

As a result of such experiences you used to say as a bitter joke that we were too well off. But in a certain sense this was no joke. What you had to struggle for, you gave us with your own hands; but the struggle for existence, which you embarked on from the start and which we of course were not spared either – that is something we have had to cope with much later, with the strength of children, in our adult life. I am not saying that our situation is therefore necessarily less fortunate than yours was – it is probably very similar (though this takes no account of our fundamentally different natures); it is just that we have the disadvantage that we cannot pride ourselves on our hardships and cannot humiliate anyone with them as you have done with yours. Nor do I deny that I might have been able to enjoy the fruits of your hard and successful labour to the full, put them to good use and earned your approval by building on them; but our estrangement prevented this. I was able to enjoy what you gave me, but only with a sense of shame, lethargy, weakness, and guilt. That is why I could only show my gratitude to you for everything as a beggar does, rather than through anything I did.

The most immediate outward result of this whole upbringing was that I shunned everything that reminded me even remotely of you. First it was the business. In itself I ought to have liked it a lot, especially when I was a child, when it was just a shop on the street; it was so lively, lit up at night, there was a lot to see and hear, I could help here and there, make myself noticed, but above all I could admire your great gifts as a salesman, the way you sold things, handled people, made jokes, never tired, immediately had the answer to any problem, and so on. Even watching you wrap things up or open a box was worthwhile, and all things considered it was certainly not the worst schooling for a child. But as you gradually began to frighten me in so many ways and as you and business merged into one for me, I no longer felt comfortable in the shop either. Things that had at first seemed to me quite normal tormented me and embarrassed me, especially the way you treated the staff. I don't know – perhaps it was the same in most businesses (in my time in the Assicurazioni Generali, for example, it really was like that; I told the manager there, not entirely truthfully, but not quite untruthfully either, that I was giving my notice because I could not put up with the cursing – although it had not directly affected me at all; I was already too painfully sensitive to it from home). When I was a child I wasn't bothered about other businesses; but I did hear and see you shouting and cursing and raging in the shop in a manner, as I then thought, to be found nowhere else in the whole world. And not just cursing – other forms of tyranny too; for example, the way you would sweep goods you didn't want mixed up with others off the counter onto the floor – only your blind rage could serve as some excuse – for the assistant to pick them up. Or what you were always saying about an assistant who had lung disease: 'Let him croak, the decrepit hound!' You called your staff 'paid enemies', and so they were; but before that's what they turned into, it seemed to me that you were their 'paying enemy'. It was there that I was taught to see that you could be unjust – left to myself, I wouldn't have noticed this so soon, the sense of guilt I had acquired was so great that I believed right was on your side; but these people were, in my childish view – a view that was of course later slightly, though not radically corrected – after all strangers who worked for us and for that reason had to live in constant fear of you. Of course this was an exaggeration on my part, because I assumed that the effect you had on these people was just as terrifying as the effect you had on me. If that had been the case, they simply would not have survived; but since they were grown-up people and most of them had excellent nerves, they easily shook off your insults, which in the end did you more harm than them. But for me it meant the shop was unbearable – it reminded me far too much of my relationship with you. Quite apart from your interest in the business and your need to dominate people, you were, simply as a businessman, so much more capable than anyone who had been apprenticed to you that nothing they achieved could satisfy you, just as you were never going to be satisfied with me. That's why I had to be on the side of the staff – and not just that, but also because I was so timid I could not understand how anyone could treat strangers so badly, and so I was anxious, if only for my own safety, to do what I could to improve relations between the staff, who, so I thought, were bitterly hostile, and you and our family. For this it was not enough for me to treat the staff with common decency, or even to behave in a more unassuming way, no, I had to treat them with respect, not only to wish them good day before they greeted me, but also, if possible, to spare them having to return my greeting. And even if I, a person of no importance, had licked their feet, it would still not have made up for the way you, as their master, attacked them from above. The sort of relationship to others I established here extended beyond the business and into the future (there is something similar, though not as dangerous or as deep-seated as in my case, for instance, in Ottla's preference for the company of poor people, for sitting together with the maidservants – the sort of thing that annoys you so much). In the end I became almost afraid of the business, at any rate I was no longer involved in it well before I went to secondary school, where I grew even further away from it. And if, as you said, it exhausted even your abilities, it seemed to me that it was far beyond mine. Then you tried to make my aversion to the business and all you had achieved (which I know you found very hurtful) a little more palatable for yourself by claiming that I had no business sense, that I had my mind on higher things, and so on – something that today I find touching, and which makes me blush. Mother of course was pleased with this explanation that you forced out of yourself, and even I was vain and desperate enough to be impressed by it. But if it had in fact been only, or even mainly, these 'higher things' that put me off the business (which I now, but only now, sincerely and really do hate), they ought to have manifested themselves differently, rather than letting me drift gently and timidly through school and my law studies until I finally ended up behind an office desk.

If I wanted to escape from you, I would also have to escape from the family, even from Mother. Certainly, I could always count on her to protect me, but even then I still couldn't get away from you. She loved you too much and was too loyally devoted to you for her to provide permanent or independent emotional support for the child in its struggle. And the child's instinct was correct, for Mother became more and more closely tied to you as time went by; while she always retained her own independence, within strict limits, tactfully and tenderly and without ever really hurting your feelings, as the years went by she did blindly adopt, emotionally rather than rationally, your judgements and criticisms of the children more and more completely, especially in the admittedly difficult case of Ottla. Of course, one should always remember how agonising and how very stressful Mother's position in the family was. She wore herself out in the shop and at home, and suffered all the family illnesses twice over; but worst of all was what she had to put up with, caught as she was between you and us. You were always loving and considerate towards her; but in this respect you spared her just as little as we did. Thoughtlessly we battered away at her, you from your side, we from ours. It was a diversion, it was not malicious; our only thought was the struggle between you and us, and Mother bore the brunt of it. Nor was it a good contribution to a child's upbringing that you – I do not blame you for this, of course – would make her suffer because of us. That even seemed to justify our otherwise inexcusable behaviour towards her. How much she had to put up with from us because of you, and from you because of us – quite apart from those occasions when you were right – because she spoiled us, even if 'spoiling' us was sometimes perhaps only her quiet unconscious way of rebelling against your system. Of course, Mother could not have put up with all that if her love for all of us, and the happiness she found in that love, had not given her the strength to cope with it.

My sisters were not entirely on my side. Valli got on with you best of all; she was the closest to Mother, and like her she complied with you without much trouble. But you also accepted her more kindly because she reminded you of Mother, although she had little enough of the Kafka in her. But perhaps that was just what suited you; where there was no trace of a Kafka, even you could not demand that there should be, nor did you feel with her, as you did with us, that something was being lost that would have to be recovered by force. Besides, you probably never had any great liking for Kafka family characteristics when women displayed them. You might have got on even better with Valli if the rest of us had not upset things between you.

Elli is the only example of someone who managed to escape from your sphere of influence with almost complete success. It was what I would have least expected of her when she was a child. She was such an awkward, listless, timid, surly, shifty, submissive, malicious, lazy, greedy, selfish child that I could hardly bear to look at her, and certainly couldn't talk to her, she reminded me so much of myself; we were both victims of the same upbringing. I particularly detested her selfishness, because I was possibly even worse in this respect. Selfishness is one of the surest signs of profound unhappiness; I was so unsure of everything that I only really possessed what I was actually holding in my hands or in my mouth, or at least what was on its way there – and that is just what she, being in a similar situation, most enjoyed taking off me. But that all changed when, while she was still young – that is the most important thing – she left home, married, and had children; she became happy, carefree, plucky, generous, unselfish, hopeful. It is almost beyond belief that you haven't actually noticed this change in her at all, at any rate you haven't given her the credit she deserves, because you are so blinded by the grudge you have always had, and still have, against Elli; nothing has changed, except that this grudge is no longer to the fore because Elli no longer lives with us, and besides, your love for Felix and your liking for Karl have pushed it into the background. Only Gerti still has to suffer from it sometimes.

I hardly dare to write about Ottla, because if I do I know I might ruin the whole effect I am hoping this letter will have. Under normal circumstances, that is, unless she is in some kind of actual distress or danger, you feel nothing but hatred for her; indeed, you have admitted to me yourself that you think she deliberately hurts you and annoys you time and again, and it satisfies and pleases her when you suffer on her account – in other words, she is some sort of devil. What a monstrous estrangement, even greater than ours, must have grown up between you and her to create such a monstrous misunderstanding! She is so remote from you that you can hardly see her any more, so you see a spectre instead. You did, I admit, have particular problems with her. I can't quite work out this very complicated situation, but at any rate in her you had a sort of Löwy armed with the best Kafka weapons. You and I were not engaged in a proper fight – I was soon done for, and all that was left was flight, bitterness, grief and inner conflict. But you two were constantly at each others' throats, always eager and full of fight. A splendid sight, but a depressing one. Initially, you were certainly very close, for still today, of the four of us Ottla is perhaps the one whose situation corresponds most closely to the marriage between you and Mother and the forces that came together in it. I do not know what deprived you of a happy and harmonious relationship between father and child; I am inclined to believe that it took a similar course to mine – on your part a tyrannical nature, on her part the defiance, sensitivity, self-righteousness and restlessness of a Löwy, all this bolstered by her sense of Kafka strength. I dare say I had some influence too, though scarcely of my own initiative, but through the very fact of my existence. Besides, she was the last to arrive into pre-existing power struggles, and she was able to form her own judgement from the large body of evidence available. I can even imagine that for a time she was unsure in herself as to whether she should embrace you or your opponents; you evidently missed an opportunity at that point and rejected her, but had it only been possible, you two would have got on wonderfully together. Although I would have lost an ally, the sight of you both would have more than made up for it, and the boundless happiness of finding complete satisfaction in at least one of your children would have transformed you, greatly to my advantage. Of course, today that is all just a dream. Ottla has no contact with her father, she must find her way alone, like me, and since she is so much more confident, self-assured, healthy and nonchalant than I am, she is all the more wicked and treacherous in your eyes. I can understand that; from your point of view she cannot be otherwise. In fact, she is capable of looking at herself through your eyes, of empathising with your suffering, and while it does not drive her to despair – despair is what I feel – it does make her feel very sad. Certainly, it may seem to contradict this when you see us often whispering and laughing together, and when you hear us mention you. A pair of shameless conspirators, you think. Peculiar conspirators! To be sure, you are one of the main topics of our conversations, just as you have always been central to our thoughts, but it is honestly not in order to conspire against you that we sit together; we are making every effort, whether jokingly or in all seriousness, whether with love, defiance, anger, antagonism, devotion or with a sense of guilt, with all the resources of mind and feeling, between the two of us to talk through in every detail, at every opportunity, from near and far, this terrible trial being held between us and you, this trial in which you always claim to be the judge, whereas you are, for the most part at least (here I admit the possibility of all the misunderstandings I may of course be guilty of), just as feeble and partial a defendant as we are.

An instructive example of the effects of your training, and one which has a bearing on the whole situation, was that of Irma. On the one hand she was a stranger, she joined your business as an adult and had to deal with you mainly as her employer, so she was exposed to your influence only in part and at an age when she could resist it; on the other hand, though, she was also a blood relation, she revered you as her father's brother, and so you had far more power over her than simply that of an employer. Yet in spite of this, Irma, who for all her frail health was so competent, clever, hard-working, modest, reliable, unselfish and loyal, who loved you as her uncle and admired you as her boss, who proved herself in other jobs before and after this – for you, Irma was not a very good office worker. Her relationship to you was almost that of a child – of course, we encouraged this too – and such was the force of your personality that you were still able to shape her development, with the result that she became (only towards you, though, and without, one hopes, experiencing the deeper suffering of a child) forgetful and careless, and developed a sort of gallows humour and perhaps even, as far as she was capable of it, some defiance (quite apart from the fact that she was in poor health, was not very happy in other respects and had a miserable family life). Your complex relationship to her was summed up for me in a remark that became a byword for us, an almost blasphemous remark, but one that showed just how insensitive you were in your treatment of others: 'The dear departed left me a dreadful mess to clear up.'

I could describe further areas of your influence and the struggle against it; but here I would be dealing with uncertainties and would have to speculate; in any case the further you are from your business and your family, the more friendly, accommodating, polite, considerate, sympathetic (I mean outwardly, too) you always become – just as a despot, for example, once he is beyond the borders of his own country, no longer has any reason to be tyrannical and can rub shoulders with the most humble people. And indeed in the group photographs from Franzensbad, you were always standing there so grand and genial, like a monarch on his travels. Your children might have benefited from this too, of course; but we would need to have been capable of realising it even as children, which we could not possibly do. If we had, I for one would not have been made to live forever in the innermost, harshest, most suffocating circle of your influence, as I in fact had to do.

Because of this I did not just lose any family feeling, as you call it; on the contrary, I still had a sense of the family, though it was above all a negative sense of my emotional release from your influence – which was of course never to happen. But my relations with people outside the family suffered perhaps even more from your influence. You are entirely mistaken in believing that I will do anything for other people out of affection and loyalty, whereas coldness and disloyalty allow me to do nothing for you and the family. I repeat for the tenth time: I would probably have become a shy and timid person in any case, but it is a long and dark way from there to where I actually am.

So far in this letter there is relatively little I have deliberately left unsaid; but now and later I shall have to hold back some things that are still too difficult for me to admit – to you or to myself. I say this so that if the whole picture should at times become rather unclear, you will not think it is because of a lack of evidence; it is more because the evidence that there is would make the picture unbearably bleak. It is not easy to strike the right balance here. Anyway, for now it is enough to recall what I said earlier: in my dealings with you I had lost my self-confidence, which had been replaced by a limitless sense of guilt. (Remembering this limitless guilt, I once wrote rightly of someone: 'He fears the shame might outlive him.') I could not suddenly transform myself when I came in contact with other people; instead I felt even more guilty towards them, because as I have already said, I had to make up for what you had inflicted on them in the shop, and for that I shared the responsibility. What's more, you always had some objection, overtly or covertly, to everyone I knew, and I had to make up for that too. The mistrust you contrived to inspire in me, whether in the shop or at home, towards most people (name me one person who meant anything at all to me in my childhood whom you didn't thoroughly belittle on at least one occasion), which remarkably didn't seem to trouble you very much at all (you were simply robust enough to cope with it, and besides it was in fact perhaps just a sign of your dominance) – this mistrust, which as a child I never found justified in my own experience, since all round me I saw nothing but perfectly admirable people, turned into a mistrust of myself and a lasting fear of everyone else. So in that direction as a rule I could certainly not escape from you. Perhaps it was because you actually knew nothing at all about the people I frequented that you were so wrong about them, because you assumed, suspicious and jealous as you were (do I deny that you are fond of me?), that I must be trying to compensate elsewhere for what I failed to find in family life, since it was surely impossible that I could live like that outside the family. Moreover, it was in my childhood that I found some consolation for all this in my lack of confidence in my own judgement; I would say to myself: 'No, you're exaggerating, like all young people you are too ready to think trivialities are great exceptions.' But in time, as I have come to know the world better, I have almost lost this consolation.

Nor was there any more escaping from you in Judaism. One might have thought it possible to find some refuge here – or rather, one might have thought that we could have found each other in Judaism, even that we might have found a common cause in it. But what kind of Judaism did I get from you! Over the years I have adopted three different attitudes towards it.

As a child I followed your lead and blamed myself because I did not visit the synagogue frequently enough, didn't observe fast days, and so on; in this I did not believe I was offending against myself, but against you, and I was filled with a sense of guilt, which I was always prone to.

Later, in my youth, I did not understand how you, with your empty faith in Judaism, could criticise me for not making an effort (just out of piety, as you put it) to display a similarly empty form of faith. It was, as far as I could see, just empty, a joke, not even a joke. You went to the synagogue four times a year, and you were much closer to the ones to whom it meant nothing than to those who took it seriously, you meekly recited the prayers as a matter of form, sometimes you amazed me by being able to turn to the passage in the prayer-book that was just being recited; otherwise, as long as I was there in the synagogue (that was the main thing), I was allowed to do as I liked. So I yawned and nodded my way through all the time there (later, I think, the only time I was so bored was in dancing-lessons), and tried to find what amusement I could in the few small diversions there were, such as when the Ark of the Covenant was opened, which always reminded me of the shooting-galleries, where if you scored a bull's-eye a door to a box would also open – except that there something interesting always came out, while here it was only ever the same old dolls with no heads. What's more, I was also very apprehensive in the synagogue, not just of course because of all that crowd of people, but also because you once casually mentioned that I might also be called on to read from the Torah. For years I trembled at the thought. But apart from that, my boredom was not seriously interrupted, or at most only by my bar mitzvah, which only required some absurd learning by heart and then taking an absurd examination; or by some quite insignificant incidents in which you were involved, for example when you were called on to read from the Torah, and you performed well in what I felt was a purely social obligation, or when you stayed behind in the synagogue for the Service for the Dead and I was sent away; for a long time, obviously because I was sent out and because I was ignorant of these mysteries, this aroused a vague feeling that something indecent was going on here. – That's what it was like in the synagogue; at home it was even more perfunctory and went no further than the first evening of Seder, which increasingly turned into a game with fits of giggles – admittedly thanks to the prompting of the children as they got older. (Why did you feel you had to join in their hilarity? Because you encouraged it yourself.) So that was the religious instruction I received, supplemented at best by your pointing out to me 'the sons of Fuchs the millionaire' who came to the synagogue with their father for the most important festivals. I could not think of any better way of dealing with this exposure to religion than to rid myself of it as soon as possible – and that seemed to me the most pious course of all.

But then later I came to see it differently, and understood how you might believe that I was maliciously letting you down in this respect too. You actually had brought some degree of Jewishness with you from your little ghetto-like village community; it was not very much, and you lost some of it in the city and the army, but the impressions and memories of your youth were still just enough to maintain a sort of Jewish existence, especially since you didn't need too much help of that kind – you came from a robust family, and would hardly let yourself be deterred by religious scruples as long as they were not too closely bound up with social considerations. Basically, the faith that governed your existence was your belief in the absolute validity of the opinions of a certain Jewish social class, and because these opinions were an intrinsic part of your nature, this in fact amounted to a belief in yourself. Enough Jewishness remained, even in this, but it was too little to be passed on to the child; it all seeped away as you passed it on, partly because it consisted of youthful experiences that you could not pass on, and partly because of your intimidating nature. It was also impossible for a child, who out of sheer anxiety observed things too intently, to understand how the few trivial matters you observed, with an indifference appropriate to their triviality, in the name of Judaism, could have any higher meaning. For you they held some meaning as reminders of earlier times, and so you wanted to pass them on to me; but because they no longer meant anything to you, you could only do this by persuasion or threat. Not only could this never work; it also meant that because you were quite unaware of the weakness of your position, it was sure to make you angry with me because of my apparent obstinacy.

All this is not an isolated phenomenon, either. Many among this transitional generation of Jews who emigrated from the still relatively devout countryside to the towns were in a similar situation; it had to happen, but it only added a further painful element to our relationship, which was already prickly enough. On the other hand, while you must believe, as I do, that you are not to blame in this matter, you should attribute that to your own nature and to the conditions of the time we live in, not simply to external circumstances – and not say, for example, that you had too much else to do or too many other worries to be able to concern yourself with such things. You are undoubtedly blameless; but this is how you turn your blamelessness into unjust accusation of others. This is very easy to refute, in general and in this particular case. It is not a question of some kind of instruction you should have given your children, but of setting an example; if your Judaism had been stronger, your example would have been more effective; that goes without saying – again, this is not to censure you at all, merely to ward off your accusations. Recently you have been reading Franklin's recollections of his youth; in fact, I gave them to you intentionally, not, as you remarked sarcastically, because of a short passage on vegetarianism, but because of the account it gives of the relationship between the author and his father, and of the relationship between the author and his son as it emerges in these recollections that he wrote for his son. I won't go into any details here.

My understanding of your Judaism was retrospectively confirmed, in a certain sense, by your attitude in recent years, when it seemed to you that I was involving myself more closely in Jewish affairs. And just as you have always disapproved of anything I did, quite particularly of the sort of things I became interested in, so too you disapproved of this. But apart from that, it might have been expected that you would make some small allowance in this case, since it was after all your kind of Jewishness that was making itself felt here, and with it the possibility of establishing a new relationship between us. I don't deny that if you had shown any interest in these matters, then that in itself would have made me wary of them; I wouldn't think of asserting that I am any better in this respect than you. But that was never put to the test. Through me, Jewishness repelled you, you found Jewish texts unreadable, they 'made you sick'. This might be taken to mean you were convinced that the Jewishness you had demonstrated to me in my childhood was the only true sort, and beyond that there was nothing. But it was hardly thinkable that you should believe that. So your 'disgust' (apart from the fact that it was not primarily directed at Jewishness, but at me) could only mean that you unconsciously recognised the weakness of your own Jewishness and of my Jewish upbringing, that you did not wish to be reminded of it in any way, and responded with frank hatred to any reminder of it. Moreover, your negative attitude towards my new sense of Jewishness was very exaggerated; for one thing it carried your curse with it, and for another my relationship with other people was essential to its development – so in my case it was doomed.

You were nearer the mark with your disapproval of my writing and what it meant to me (of which you knew nothing). Through it I actually did manage to get away from you and gain some independence, even if it was rather like a worm that had been trodden on its tail, but had torn its front end free and squirmed away. I had found some sort of safety, I could breathe; of course, you immediately disapproved of my writing too, but for once I welcomed it. Certainly, my vanity, my ambition suffered from your reception of my books, which became a byword for us: 'Put it on my bedside table!' (you were usually playing cards when a book arrived); but in fact I welcomed this, not just out of defiant malice, not just because I was pleased to have further confirmation of my view of our relationship, but in the depths of my being – because to me that form of words meant something like: 'Now you are free!' Of course, it was an illusion; I was not free, or at the very best I was not yet free. My writing was about you, indeed I was only confiding my troubles to a book because I could not confide in you. It was a deliberately extended farewell to you; but although you impelled me to write, my writing took the course I set for it. But of what little consequence it all was! In fact, it is only worth mentioning because it was part of my life – in any other context it would scarcely be noticed – and further, because it dominated my life, in my childhood as an intuition, later as a hope, and then later still often as despair, and because it dictated – though again, as it were, in your guise – my few minor decisions.

For example, my choice of career. It is true that you gave me, in your generous and even patient way, complete freedom in this – though here too you treated me in the way the Jewish middle classes generally treat their sons, or at least you followed their values, for these were your values too. But then one of your misconceptions about me also played a part here. That is, out of paternal pride, out of ignorance of what I actually am, and because of my weak health, you have always regarded me as particularly hard-working. As a child, you believed, I was forever studying, and later I was forever writing. But that is not remotely the case. With much less exaggeration it can be said that I studied very little and learned nothing; that something sank in during all those years, thanks to a moderate memory and a certain intelligence, is not so very remarkable, but at all events the end result in terms of knowledge, and especially of intellectual discipline, is quite lamentable, especially compared with almost all other people I know, given the expenditure of time and money and the outwardly carefree and peaceful life I led. It is lamentable, but to me comprehensible. Ever since I can remember I have had such deep fears about my existential security that I was indifferent to everything else. In our society, Jewish schoolboys can be rather odd, there are all sorts of strange types; but nowhere else have I come across such cold, scarcely concealed, ineradicable, helplessly childlike, almost ridiculous, inhumanly complacent detachment, such a self-contained but coldly imaginative child as I was – though to be sure, this was the only protection I had against a nervous breakdown from anxiety and guilt. I was preoccupied only with my own worries, but these took many forms. Worries about my health, for example; they started innocuously, now and again there was some small anxiety about my digestion, hair loss, curvature of the spine, etc., which gradually increased through countless stages until it finally ended in a real illness. What did it all mean? Not actually a physical illness; but since I was not sure of anything, and at every moment needed renewed confirmation of my existence, since I had nothing that was really my own, undoubted, sole possession I could call mine and mine alone, since I was truly a disinherited son, I naturally enough became unsure about what was nearest to me – my own body. I shot up in height, but this put too great a strain on my back, I became round-shouldered; I scarcely dared to move, let alone do exercises, I remained weak; I was amazed at anything that was still in order, and regarded my good digestion, for example, as a miracle – but that was enough for it to go wrong, and that opened the door to every form of hypochondria, until finally the superhuman stress of wanting to get married (I shall speak about that later) brought on bleeding in the lungs. I dare say the apartment in the Schönborn Palace had something to do with that – I only needed it because I thought I could use it for my writing, which makes it relevant to this topic. So all that was not a result of overwork, as you always imagine. There were years when I was in the best of health, and spent more time lazing on the sofa than you have spent in your whole life, including all your illnesses. When I rushed off pretending I had so much to do, it was usually to go and lie down in my room. The total amount of work I do in the office (where it's true slacking doesn't get noticed much, and in any case my anxiety didn't let it get out of hand) and at home is tiny – if you had any idea of it, you would be horrified. By nature, I am probably not at all lazy, but there was nothing for me to do. At home I was rejected, put down, oppressed, and though I made every effort to escape, that was not work – it was an impossibility, something that was, with some minor exceptions, beyond my powers.

So this was the situation in which I was given the freedom to choose my career. But was I at all capable of actually using this freedom? Did I even have the confidence to go for a proper career? My belief in my own abilities was far more dependent on you than anything else – than any kind of outward success, for example. That gave me some brief encouragement, no more than that – but against this your weight was always greater, dragging me down. I would never get through the first year of primary school, I thought – but I did, and even won a prize; I certainly wouldn't pass the entrance exam to secondary school – but I did; now I'll surely fail the first year at the school – but no, I didn't, and I got further and further. But none of this gave me any confidence, far from it; I was always convinced – and your dismissive look was the living proof of it – that the more success I had, the worse it was sure to turn out in the end. I often imagined I could see the awful assembly of schoolmasters (school is only the most striking single example, but it was much the same for me everywhere) as they met after I had got through the first year into the second year, and after I had got through the second year into the third year, and so on – to examine this unique and outrageous case of how I, the most incapable and at any rate most ignorant pupil, had managed to worm my way up as far as this class, which would, now that everyone's attention had been drawn to me, of course spit me out at once, to the joy of all right-thinking people from whom this nightmare had been lifted. It is not easy for a child to live with such ideas. Under these circumstances, why should I care about lessons? Who was capable of striking a spark of interest from me? The lessons interested me – and not only the lessons, but everything that was going on around me at this crucial age – much as a fraudulent bank clerk, who is still in post and fearful of being exposed, is interested in the little everyday jobs he has to do as an employee of the bank. Everything was so trivial, so remote compared with the main issue. Things then went on until the school-leaving exam, some of which I passed only by cheating, and then it all came to an end and I was free. Despite the pressures of school, I had only ever been concerned with myself, and now I was free I could indulge myself to the full. So I had no real freedom in the choice of a career; I knew that compared with the main issue, everything would be as unimportant to me as all the lessons at school had been, and so it was a question of finding a profession that would allow me to maintain this indifference without hurting my vanity too much. So law was the most obvious choice. Some small attempts at other subjects, prompted by vanity or hope, such as two weeks of chemistry, or six months of German, only confirmed my conviction. So I studied law. That meant shredding my nerves for a few months before exams by simply feeding my mind on sawdust that had in any case already been chewed over by thousands of jaws before. But in a certain sense that was just to my taste, as it had been in a certain sense at school earlier, and as it was to be later in my office job – it all fitted my situation perfectly. Moreover, I showed amazing foresight in this respect; even as a small child I was clear enough in my mind as to my future studies and career. I expected no rescue from this direction; I had long since given up on that.

But I showed no foresight at all about the significance and the possibility of getting married; this, the greatest terror of my life so far, overtook me almost completely without warning. As a child I had developed so slowly that such things were outwardly far too remote; now and then I needed to think about them, but I was not to know that a permanent, decisive, indeed the most desperate ordeal was lying in wait for me. In fact, though, my attempts at marriage were my most spectacular and hopeful attempts to escape from you – and then, of course, their failure was all the more spectacular too.

Because none of my attempts to get married succeeded, I fear I shall not succeed in explaining them to you either. And yet the success of this whole letter depends on it, because on the one hand all the positive energies I could summon up were invested in these attempts, and on the other hand all the negative forces I have described as your contribution to my upbringing – my weakness, my lack of self-confidence, my sense of guilt – converged in a fearful combination to throw up a barrier between me and marriage. This will be all the more difficult to explain because I have thought it all through and brooded on it for so many days and nights that I have myself become confused about how to do it. The one thing that makes it easier for me is that I believe you misunderstand the matter so completely; it should not be too difficult to clear up such a total misunderstanding.

In the first place, you include the failure of my attempts at marriage among my other failures. In principle, I would have no objection to this, provided you accept the explanation I have already given for those failures; it is indeed one with those other failures, but you underestimate its importance, so much so that when we talk to each other about it we are actually talking about quite different things. I would venture to say that nothing that has happened to you in your whole life has been as important to you as my attempts at marriage have been to me. By this I don't mean that you have never experienced anything as important; on the contrary, your life has been much richer and fuller, more full of cares than mine – but for that very reason nothing like this has ever happened to you. It is as if someone has five low steps to climb, while someone else has only one step, but that step is as high as the other five together; the first person will not just manage those five steps, but hundreds and thousands of others, he will have lived a successful and very strenuous life, but none of the steps he has climbed will be as important to him as that single first huge step is to the second person, who in spite of all his efforts finds it impossible to climb, will never climb it, and will of course never get any further.

To marry, to establish a family, to take on all the children that might come along, to look after them and perhaps even guide them is, I am convinced, the highest thing anyone can ever achieve. That so many appear to achieve it easily is not evidence to the contrary, for in the first place not many really achieve it, and secondly these few often don't 'do' it – it just happens to them. This may not be the 'highest thing' I mentioned, but it is still something great and most honourable (especially since there is no very clear distinction between 'doing something' and 'something happening to you'). And finally, it's not a matter of actually achieving this 'highest thing' at all, but only of aiming at some distant but decent approximation to it; we don't have to fly straight into the sun, but we do need to creep into some tidy little place on earth where the sun sometimes shines and where we can find a little warmth for ourselves.

And how well was I prepared for this? As badly as possible. That follows from what I have already said. But insofar as there is any way of directly preparing an individual person, or of directly laying the general foundations for it, outwardly you made little effort to intervene. It could not be helped; these matters are determined by the prevailing sexual conventions of the day and age, and of one's social and ethnic origins. Nevertheless, you did intervene here too, though not to any great effect, for a condition of such intervention has to be a strong mutual bond of trust – and this had long been lacking between us at the crucial stage. Your intervention was doomed to fail, because our needs were quite different; my enthusiasms cannot interest you, and vice versa, what for you is innocence can be guilt for me, and vice versa, what is of no consequence to you can be a nail in my coffin.

I remember going for a walk one evening with you and Mother – it was in the Josefsplatz, near what is today the Länderbank – and I started to talk to you about the things that interested me. I spoke in a stupid, boastful, superior, arrogant way, I spoke coolly (that was put on), coldly (that was genuine), and I stuttered, as I usually did when I spoke to you; I accused you of keeping me in ignorance, I said that my classmates had had to teach me everything, that I had very nearly been in great danger (here I was lying shamelessly, as I often did, to show how bold I was, for thanks to my timidity I had no clearer notion of what this 'great danger' was, other than the usual sins that city children commit in bed); but in the end I hinted that fortunately I knew everything now, I needed no more advice, and everything was all right. I raised these matters mainly because I enjoyed talking about them, certainly, but also out of curiosity, and finally in some way to pay you both back for something or other. You took it straightforwardly, as was your nature, you just said something to the effect that you could give me some advice about how I might be able to do this sort of thing without any great danger. Perhaps that was just the sort of answer I had wanted to get out of you – it was after all an appropriate answer for a libidinous child overfed on meat and all sorts of good things, physically inactive and constantly preoccupied with himself; and yet my affected modesty was so offended by it, or I believed it ought to be so offended, that in spite of myself I was unable to talk to you about it any further, and with high-handed insolence broke off the conversation.

I do not find it easy to assess the answer you gave me on that occasion. On the one hand there is something disconcertingly frank, in a sense primitive, about it; on the other hand, the thinking behind it is certainly modern and uninhibited. I do not know how old I was then, certainly not much more than sixteen; but for a boy of that age it really was a very odd answer, and it indicated the gap between the two of us in that it was actually the first direct lesson about life that I had from you. But its real meaning, which even then impressed itself on my mind, though I became half-aware of it only much later, was this: what you were advising me to do was in your view – and certainly in my view at the time – the very filthiest thing there could be. It wasn't just that you wanted to ensure that I didn't physically bring home any of this filth; that was only to protect yourself and your house. The main thing was rather that your own advice did not apply to you, a married man who was above such things; I probably felt this all the more acutely at the time because even marriage seemed impure to me, so it was impossible for me to apply what I had heard generally about marriage to my own parents. This made you even purer and raised you even higher. The idea that you might have given yourself similar advice before you married was quite unthinkable to me. So you bore scarcely a trace of earthly filth; and yet it was you who, with a few candid words, plunged me into this filth as if I were destined for it. So if you and I should be the only people in the world – an idea that was never far from my mind – then the purity of the world ended with you, and thanks to your advice its filth began with me. On the face of it, it seemed incomprehensible that you should condemn me in this way; only habitual guilt on my part and the deepest contempt on yours could explain it. And so once again I was shaken to the core of my being, and very severely.

Perhaps this shows most clearly that neither of us can be blamed. A. gives B. a candid piece of advice consistent with his own outlook on life, which is not very elegant, but still perfectly normal in today's urban environment, and which might prevent injury to B.'s health. This advice does not bolster B.'s morale – but there is no reason why he should not in time be able to rectify any damage done; besides, he is not at all obliged to follow the advice, and at any rate there is nothing in the advice itself to blight B.'s whole future life. And yet something like this does happen, just because you are A. and I am B.

I am in a particularly good position to see that neither of us is to blame because of a similar conflict that arose between us under quite different circumstances some twenty years later; it was a horrid business, though in itself far less damaging – for at the age of thirty-six there was little enough that could damage me further. It was a little speech you made on one of the frantic days after I announced my recent engagement. You said something like this: 'I dare say she was wearing some choice blouse – the Jewish girls in Prague know all about that sort of thing – and so of course you decided to marry her, as soon as possible, too: next week, tomorrow, today. I don't understand you; you're a grown man about town, and you can think of nothing better than to marry some girl or other right away. Are there no other possibilities? If you're scared, I'll go along with you myself.' You went on to say more, and made yourself quite clear, but I don't remember the details – perhaps my eyes had glazed over. I was more interested in Mother; she agreed with you entirely, but even so she picked up something from the table and took it out of the room.

I don't think your words ever humiliated me more deeply or showed your contempt for me more clearly. When you talked to me like that twenty years before, it might even have been possible to detect in you some respect for the precocious city lad you thought could find his way in life without following too many false trails. Looking back today, making any such allowance could only increase your contempt, for the lad who was then just setting out in life is still the same, and seems to you not to have gained anything by experience, only to be twenty years more pitiable. My choice of girl meant nothing whatever to you. You had always (unconsciously) disparaged my ability to make decisions, and now you thought (unconsciously) you knew how feeble it was. You knew nothing of my other attempts to escape, therefore you could know nothing of the thought processes that had led to this attempt at marriage; you had to try to guess at them, and in accordance with your general opinion of me you drew the most disgusting, crass and absurd conclusions – and you didn't hesitate for a moment to express yourself in exactly the same terms. To you, the ignominy you heaped on me in this way was as nothing compared to the disgrace you believed my marriage would bring on your name.

Now, you have plenty to tell me about my attempts at marriage, and you have said it too: that you couldn't have much respect for my decision when I twice broke off the engagement to F. and twice took it up again, when I dragged you and Mother pointlessly to Berlin for the engagement, and so on. That is all true; but how did it come to that?

The basic idea behind both my engagements was perfectly respectable: to set up house and become independent. It's an idea that appeals to you, except that in reality it turns out like the children's game, where one child takes the other's hand and even holds on to it, shouting: 'Go on, then, go – why don't you go?' However, in our case the situation is complicated by the fact that when you said 'go', you meant it seriously, while at the same time, without realising it, simply by the force of your personality, you have always held me back – or, more accurately, you have held me down.

Both girls were, albeit by chance, extraordinarily good choices. It is another sign of your complete misunderstanding that you can think someone as timid, hesitant, and wary as I am could decide to get married on an impulse – that I could fall for a blouse, for example. More likely, both marriages would have been sensible matches, in the sense that I devoted my whole mind, day and night, to planning them – the first time for years, the second time for months.

Neither girl let me down – it was just that I let them both down. My opinion of them today is exactly the same as it was then, when I wanted to marry them.

Nor is it the case that with the second engagement I disregarded the lessons of the first – that is, that I was acting frivolously. The two cases were simply quite different, and it was those earlier experiences that could give me hope for the second one, where the prospects were altogether much more favourable. But I don't want to go into details here.

So why did I not marry? There were some obstacles, as there always are; but life consists in getting over such obstacles. The fundamental obstacle, however, which sadly has nothing to do with particular cases, is that I am clearly mentally unfit for marriage. This is clear from the fact that from the moment I decide to marry, I am unable to sleep, my head feels feverish day and night, I stumble about in desperation; it is no way to live. This is not a result of worrying; although it is part of my melancholy and pedantic personality that I worry endlessly, these worries are not the crucial factor – like worms with a corpse, they only complete the process of decay. The decisive factor is something different: it is the whole weight of anxiety, of weakness and self-contempt.

I will try to explain this in more detail. In my attempts to get married, two seemingly opposing aspects of my relationship with you clash more violently than ever. Marriage is surely the clearest guarantee of liberation and independence of the self. I would have a family, in my view the highest thing one can achieve – and the highest thing that you have achieved, too. It would make me your equal; all the old and constantly renewed disgrace and tyranny would just be history. That would indeed be a fairy-tale; but that is just what makes it dubious. It is too much – so much that it is beyond achieving. It is like someone who is in prison, and intends not only to escape, which he might be able to do, but at the same time to convert the prison into a pleasure dome for himself. But if he escapes, he cannot build his pleasure dome, and if he builds it, he cannot escape. If, in this unhappy relationship I find myself in with you, I wish to become independent, I must do something that distances me from you as far as possible; but though marriage is the greatest state, and one that bestows the most honourable form of independence, it is also something that brings me closest to you. To escape from this situation, therefore, is a form of madness, and every attempt to do so is punished with something akin to madness.

But then, it is this close connection that in part attracts me to marriage too. The thought that we would then be on an equal footing, something you would be able to appreciate more than anything else, appeals to me so much because I could then be a free, grateful, blameless, true son of yours, and you could be an untroubled, forbearing, sympathetic, contented father. But in order to achieve that, everything that has happened would have to be wiped out – in other words, we ourselves would have to be obliterated.

As we are, however, marriage is closed to me precisely because it is your territory. Sometimes I imagine a map of the world laid out with you stretched out right across it. Then it seems to me that the only areas I could live in would be either those you weren't lying on, or those you couldn't reach. And because I imagine you as so vast, the areas that are left are very few and most unpromising – and marriage, quite particularly, is not one of them.

This metaphor is evidence enough that I am in no way suggesting that your example deterred me from marriage, as it did, for instance, from the business – far from it, in spite of all the broad similarities. Your marriage held up to me an exemplary model in many ways – in fidelity, mutual support, the number of children; and even when the children grew up and increasingly disrupted the peace of the marriage, it remained unaffected. It was also perhaps this very example that formed my lofty concept of marriage; the reasons for my failure to marry lay elsewhere, namely in your relationship to your children, and that is the whole theme of this letter.

There is a belief that fear of getting married is based on the fear that your children might later pay you back for the sins you committed against your own parents. I do not think that has any great significance in my case, because my sense of guilt actually stems from you and is too deeply rooted in our specific circumstances – indeed, this feeling that it is unique to us is what makes it so distressing; it is impossible to imagine it could be replicated. Even so, I have to say that I would find such a taciturn, unresponsive, reticent, withdrawn son intolerable; if there were no other alternative, I would no doubt wish to escape from him or emigrate, as you said you did when you heard I wanted to marry. So that too might have contributed to my inability to get married.

But far more important in this is fear for myself. What I mean, as I have already suggested, is that through my writing and associated activities I was making small efforts to be independent, to escape – with minimal success; there is plenty of evidence that they will hardly achieve anything. Even so, it is my duty, or rather it is my life's task, to safeguard them and to ward off any danger that threatens them – even the possibility of such a danger. Marriage is such a possible danger – though of course it also holds the possibility of furthering them greatly; but for me it is enough that it is a possible danger. What would I do if it were in fact a danger! How could I continue to live in a marriage while I sensed this danger, which perhaps could not be proved, but could certainly not be refuted! Although I might equivocate when faced with this dilemma, the final outcome is certain – I must give it up. The saying about the bird in hand and the two in the bush is only remotely apposite in this case. I have nothing in hand, in the bush there is everything; but even so, the struggle for existence and the demands of life dictate that I must opt for nothing. For similar reasons I also had to choose the career I did.

The greatest obstacle to marriage, however, is my by now ineradicable conviction that to support and quite especially to control a family requires everything I have recognised in you – and all at the same time, good and bad, as they are naturally combined in you; that is, strength combined with contempt for others, health with a measure of excess, volubility with aloofness, self-confidence with disapproval of everyone else, a sense of superiority with tyranny, a knowledge of people with mistrust of most others – and in addition entirely positive qualities like diligence, stamina, presence of mind, fearlessness. Compared with you, I possessed practically nothing, or very little, of all this – how then could I intend to risk marrying, when I could see how even you had to struggle so hard at it, and even you had failed where your children were concerned? Of course, I did not put this question to myself, nor did I answer it, in so many words, or else common sense would have intervened and shown me other men who are unlike you (to name one who is close, but very different to you: Uncle Richard), who have got married all the same and at least have not come to grief on it – which is still an achievement, and would have been quite enough for me. But I did not put this question to myself; I had lived it since childhood. I did not measure myself against marriage, but rather against every little detail; in every little detail you convinced me by your example and by the way you brought me up, as I have tried to make clear, of my inadequacy – and what was true of every little detail and bore you out, was naturally bound to be overwhelmingly true of the greatest thing of all, marriage. Until my attempts to get married, I had grown up something like a businessman who takes each day as it comes and, in spite of all his worries and foreboding, fails to keep his accounts in order. He makes some small profits, which are so infrequent that he always cherishes them and exaggerates them in his imagination; but otherwise he makes only losses. Everything is entered, but his books are never balanced. Then comes the day of reckoning, that is, the attempt to get married; and with the huge sums that have to be reckoned with here, it is as if there had never been even the slightest profit, nothing but one single huge debt. And now marry without going mad!

This is how my life with you thus far ends, and these are the prospects it holds for the future.

If you consider my explanation of my fear of you, you might answer as follows: 'You claim I am making it easy for myself when I explain my relationship to you simply by putting the blame on you; but I believe that for all your obvious efforts, you are at the very least not making it any more difficult for yourself, in fact you are turning it to your advantage. First of all, you refuse to accept any blame or responsibility on your part; in that respect our procedure is the same. But whereas I quite candidly, as I see it, put all the blame on you, you set out to be "over-subtle" and "over-considerate" by exempting me from blame too. Of course, this is only a pretext (and that is your whole intention, after all), and reading between the lines it turns out that for all your rhetoric about nature and personality and contrariness and helplessness, I have been the real aggressor, while all you did was simply defend yourself. So now you think you have achieved enough by your mendacity, for you have proved three things – firstly, that you are blameless, secondly, that I am to blame, and thirdly that out of sheer generosity you are prepared not only to forgive me, but also something that is both more and less than that; you are even prepared to prove – and are willing to believe it yourself, though it flies in the face of the truth – that I too am blameless. That ought to be enough for you; but you are still not satisfied, because you have got it into your head that you want to live off me utterly and completely. I admit that we fight each other, but there are two ways to fight. There is chivalrous combat, in which two independent opponents pit their strength against each other, where each one stands for himself, wins for himself and loses for himself; and then there is the battle waged by a verminous insect, which doesn't just bite, but also sucks blood to sustain itself. That is how a mercenary fights, and that is how you fight. You are unfit for life; but so that you can come to terms with this and settle down without care or self-reproach, you prove that I have taken all your fitness for life from you and put it in my pockets. Why should it worry you that you are unfit for life when I am to blame? You just stretch out and let me tow you through life, physically and mentally. As an example: when you wanted to get married recently, at the same time – as you admit in this letter – you didn't want to get married; but in order to save yourself the effort, you wanted me to help you not to get married by forbidding the match on account of the "disgrace" it would bring on my name. But that didn't occur to me at all. Firstly, I never, on this occasion or any other, wanted to "stand in the way of your happiness", and secondly, I never want to hear one of my children accuse me of anything like that. But did it help when in spite of myself I did not oppose the marriage? Not in the slightest. My opposition to the marriage would not have prevented it; on the contrary, it would of itself only have encouraged you all the more to marry the girl, for that would have made your "attempt to escape", as you call it, complete. And my consent to the marriage didn't stop your accusations, because you have shown that I am to blame for your not marrying in any case. But basically, as far as I am concerned all you have proved, in this and in everything else, is that all my charges were justified – and that I have missed out other particularly justified charges, namely those of mendacity, humbug and sponging. If I am not greatly mistaken, you are still sponging on me with this very letter.'

My answer to this in the first instance is that this whole interjection, which can in part also be directed against you, is not yours, but mine. Not even your mistrust of others is as great as the mistrust you have taught me to have of myself. I do not deny that this interjection, which does contribute something new towards characterising our relationship, is to some degree justified. Of course, in reality things cannot fit together as easily as the arguments in my letter suggest; life is more than just a jigsaw puzzle. But with the counter-arguments in this interjection – arguments that I neither can nor wish to pursue in detail – I believe something has been achieved, something that approximates so nearly to the truth that it can give us both some peace of mind, and can make living and dying easier.

FRANZ

A HYBRID

I have a strange animal, half-kitten, half-lamb. It was inherited from my father, but has only developed in my lifetime; earlier it was more lamb than kitten, but now it has more or less equal parts of both. It has the head and claws of a cat, it is the size and shape of a lamb; from both it gets its eyes, for they flash and are mild, its fur, which is soft and close-growing, and its movements, for it both skips and slinks; it curls up on the window-sill in the sunshine and purrs, in the fields it runs about madly and can hardly be caught. It runs away from cats and tries to pounce on lambs, on moonlit nights it likes best to walk along the roofgutters, it cannot miaow and loathes rats. It can lurk for hours beside the hen-coop, but so far it has never made an attempt to kill. I feed it with sweetened milk, which it loves; it sucks it in through its predator's fangs. Of course it is a great sight for children. Sunday morning is visiting time – I hold the little creature on my lap and the children from the whole neighbourhood gather round me. They ask the strangest questions, to which there is no answer; I don't bother to answer them either, but I'm happy to show them what I have without further explanation. Sometimes the children bring cats with them, and once even brought two lambs along, but against all their hopes, no recognition scenes took place; the animals looked calmly at each other with their animal eyes and each obviously accepted the other's existence as a god-given fact.

On my lap the creature has no fear, nor does it feel the urge to hunt. It feels happiest when it snuggles up to me. Its loyalty is to the family that has brought it up. I dare say this is not any exceptional kind of loyalty, but just the true instinct of an animal that has countless fellow-creatures on earth, but perhaps not one close blood relative, and so the protection it has found with us is sacred to it. Sometimes I have to laugh when it prowls round me, walks between my legs and will not be parted from me. Not content that it is a cat and a lamb, it almost wants to be a dog as well. I seriously believe something of the sort; it has the restlessness of both creatures in itself, that of the cat and that of the lamb, however different they are. But that is why it is uncomfortable in its own skin. Perhaps the butcher's knife would be a release for the creature; but since it is part of my inheritance I must deny it that.

A MESSAGE FROM THE EMPEROR
[from *The Great Wall of China*]

The Emperor, so they say, has sent a message from his deathbed to you – to you personally, his miserable subject, a tiny shadow at the remotest distance from the imperial sun. He made the messenger kneel by his bed and whispered the message into his ear; it meant so much to him that he bade the messenger repeat it back to him. He nodded his head to confirm the accuracy of the words. And before all those assembled to witness his death – all intervening walls have been torn down, and on the wide, lofty curving flights of steps the great lords of the Empire stand around him – before all these he dispatched the messenger. The messenger set out at once, a powerful, tireless man; reaching out first one hand, then the other, he forges a path through the crowd; if he is held up, he points to the emblem of the sun on his chest, and makes progress as no other could. But the throng is so great, there is no end to their habitations. How he would fly once he reached the open countryside, and soon you would surely hear the glorious beating of his fists on your door. But instead – how vainly he struggles; he is still squeezing his way through the apartments of the inner palace; he will never get through them; and even if he did, nothing would be gained; he would have to fight his way down the flights of stairs; and if he did this, nothing would be gained; he would have to cross the courtyards, and after that the outer palace enclosing them; then more stairs and courtyards; and another palace; and so on through millennia; and if he were at last to burst through the outermost gate – but it can never, never happen – the city still lies before him, the centre of the world, piled high with its detritus. No one gets through here, even with a dead man's message. – But you sit at your window when evening comes, and dream it to yourself.

ON METAPHORS

Many have complained that the words of wise men are only ever metaphors that do not apply to everyday life, which is all we have. When a wise man says: 'Cross over', he does not mean that we should cross to the other side of the street, which we could still manage if it were worth our while; he means some mythical Other Side, something we do not know, something he cannot describe any more closely either, and therefore cannot be of any help at all to us here. All these metaphors really only mean that what is incomprehensible is incomprehensible, and we knew that. But what we actually have to put up with every day is something else.

Then someone said: Why resist? If you abided by the metaphors, you would become metaphors yourselves, and then you would soon be free from everyday troubles.

Someone else said: I bet that's a metaphor, too.

The first person said: You have won.

The second said: But only metaphorically, alas.

The first said: No, in reality; metaphorically you have lost.

A COMMENTARY

It was very early in the morning, the streets were clean and empty. I was going to the station. When I saw a clock on a tower and compared it with my watch, I saw that it was much later than I had thought and that I had to hurry. The shock of this discovery made me unsure of the way, for I was not yet very familiar with this town; fortunately, there was a policeman nearby, so I ran up to him and breathlessly asked him the way. He smiled and said: 'You want me to tell you the way?' 'Yes,' I said, 'because I can't find it myself.' 'Give it up, give it up,' he said, and abruptly turned his back, as people do when they want to be alone with their laughter.

A LITTLE FABLE

'Oh,' said the mouse, 'the world gets narrower every day. At first it was so wide that I was afraid, I went on and was glad when at last in the distance I saw walls to left and right, but these long walls converge so quickly that I am already in the last room, and there in the corner stands the trap I am running into.' 'You only have to run in a different direction,' said the cat, and ate up the mouse.

COLLECTOR'S EDITIONS

List of Titles

Louisa May Alcott	*Little Women*
Hans Christian Andersen	*Hans Christian Andersen Fairy Tales*
Jane Austen	*Emma*
Jane Austen	*Mansfield Park*
Jane Austen	*Northanger Abbey*
Jane Austen	*Persuasion*
Jane Austen	*Pride and Prejudice*
Jane Austen	*Sense and Sensibility*
J.M. Barrie	*Peter Pan*
L. Frank Baum	*Wizard of Oz*
Charlotte Brontë	*Jane Eyre*
Emily Brontë	*Wuthering Heights*
Frances Hodgson Burnett	*The Secret Garden*
Lewis Carroll	*Alice in Wonderland*
Lewis Carroll	*Alice Through The Looking Glass*
Daniel Defoe	*Robinson Crusoe*
Charles Dickens	*A Christmas Carol*
Charles Dickens	*Great Expectations*
Charles Dickens	*Oliver Twist*
Fyodor Dostoevsky	*Crime and Punishment*
Arthur Conan Doyle	*A Study Scarlet & Sign Four*

COLLECTOR'S EDITIONS

Arthur Conan Doyle	*Adventures of Sherlock Holmes*
Arthur Conan Doyle	*Casebook Sherlock Holmes & Last Bow*
Arthur Conan Doyle	*Hound Baskervilles & Valley Fear*
Arthur Conan Doyle	*Memoirs of Sherlock Holmes*
Arthur Conan Doyle	*The Return of Sherlock Holmes*
Alexandre Dumas	*Count of Monte Cristo*
George Eliot	*Middlemarch*
F. Scott Fitzgerald	*The Great Gatsby*
Kenneth Grahame	*The Wind in the Willows*
Jacob Grimm	*Grimms Fairy Tales*
Thomas Hardy	*Far from the Madding Crowd*
Thomas Hardy	*Tess of the d'Urbervilles*
James Joyce	*Dubliners*
James Joyce	*Ulysses*
Franz Kafka	*Best of Kafka*
Rudyard Kipling	*The Jungle Book*
D.H. Lawrence	*Lady Chatterley's Lover*
Gaston Leroux	*Phantom of the Opera*
Herman Melville	*Moby Dick*
L.M. Montgomery	*Anne of Avonlea*
L.M. Montgomery	*Anne of Green Gables*
Edith Nesbit	*The Railway Children*
George Orwell	*Animal Farm*
George Orwell	*Nineteen Eighty-Four*
A. de Saint-Exupery	*The Little Prince*
Anna Sewell	*Black Beauty*
William Shakespeare	*Othello*
William Shakespeare	*A Midsummer Night's Dream*

COLLECTOR'S EDITIONS

William Shakespeare	*Hamlet*
William Shakespeare	*Macbeth*
William Shakespeare	*Romeo and Juliet*
Mary Shelley	*Frankenstein*
Robert Louis Stevenson	*Treasure Island*
Robert Louis Stevenson	*Dr. Jekyll and Mr. Hyde*
Bram Stoker	*Dracula*
Oscar Wilde	*Picture of Dorian Gray*
Virginia Woolf	*Mrs Dalloway*